Jim —

Good Luck with your Book —
And Hope you enjoy This one!
Keep 'Em laughing!

TAKEN IDENTITY

by

Chuck Igo

authorHOUSE®

AuthorHouse™
1663 Liberty Drive, Suite 200
Bloomington, IN 47403
www.authorhouse.com
Phone: 1-800-839-8640

First published by AuthorHouse 8/16/2007

ISBN: 978-1-4343-1905-0 (sc)
ISBN: 978-1-4343-1906-7 (hc)

Library of Congress Control Number: 2007905016

Printed in the United States of America
Bloomington, Indiana

This book is printed on acid-free paper.

Dedication

To Debbie, Erin, Emily & Connor –
For being there when a person needs love, affection, encouragement
and family.

Foreword

This novel is a labor of love, born of a realization that a radio production director writes, and re-writes, almost fifty pages of commercial copy in a week. In fewer than three months' time, that would create enough material for a good sized book. And at the onset of this adventure in 1996, political events and a fist-shaking quiet rage helped to drive the plot. In college, an English professor, Ed Rudd, encouraged us not just to write, but to write what we know. That said, personal experiences and friendships have found themselves woven into the following pages. Names, in many cases, haven't been changed, their usage in homage to the lasting friendships that have spanned decades. The inference to any actual person, living or dead, is not intentional, with the exception of Bill & Laurie Williamson, a writer and a teacher, respectively, and dear friends collectively, whose inclusion in this work, with the passage of time, now comes with only the deepest of sadness in their passing. This was done with their blessing and encouragement during the formative stages of this work.

This story was pecked out a few words at a time during lunch hours and stolen moments between daddy-duties at home in South Portland, Maine, and continued with help from a two-hour, one-way commute to work for an overnight shift in Boston. The long

ride was made that much shorter with thoughts of character &
plot development, all of which would be hastily noted once off the
highway. After a morning's return to Maine, the transcribed notes
would become more of the story while hunched over a keyboard
in the sun on the family home's screened porch or while sitting in
the waiting room at dance school. The stateside travels in "Taken
Identity" mirror those with which I am familiar. The overseas settings
come through imagination, although I discovered upon my first trip
to Europe a few years back that I wasn't all that far off the mark on
some of the settings.

To my helpful eyes, Jan Spear & Bill Therriault, thank you so much
for your careful readings and notes. To my manuscript readers, your
honest evaluations of the book have helped to keep me inspired to
see this through, and your honest evaluations have likewise driven
me to keep it real (although we will differ on the brief suspensions
of belief for the sake of a fictional story line, okay?).

My wish is that you find in this story a touch of hope and a belief
that good things can, and do, happen to good people.

one

New York State, January 18, 1976

Marvin Moore, now deceased, was a political junkie of the highest order. His work as an independent advertising guru had enhanced his somewhat enigmatic reputation. The mystery aspect of Marvin Moore surrounded the lack of solid roots. He'd roll into a campaign's headquarters, work his magic and before the final votes had been counted, he'd be out of the picture, never there to share in the glory of victory. Yet his reputation did indeed precede him at each stop and by last count, the legend was up to twelve and oh. All in the past six years.

From what Michail's contacts could ascertain from their extremely thorough research, Moore was born in California in 1948. He went to schools in San Diego and then graduated from San Diego State in 1970 with a degree in Political Science. From there, he immediately went to work on an Oregon state senate campaign and thus the legend was born.

His parents had both died in an auto accident just prior to his graduation and he had no siblings. A check on extended family had turned up only his maternal grandmother in Los Angeles county, as well as his father's sister in Phoenix. Neither, when asked, had heard from him in some time, other than both having received Christmas cards with Des Moines, Iowa postmarks. Neither had seen him in at least four years and only the grandmother had actually spoken with him, by phone, in the past year.

The KGB operatives poked around the Des Moines campaign scene, as both Iowa and New Hampshire were gearing up for their Presidential primary caucus and election respectively. The Iowa postmark had given thought to the possibility that Moore might have been in a much more visible position working on one of the Presidential campaigns. Michail had gotten this news back in January which was a cause for some concern. Fortunately, that level of concern lasted only a few days. When word arrived to him at the Berlin station that Moore was not involved with a Presidential race, the hunt was then on to find the man and proceed to pick his brain.

The operation was simple in its design, ruthless in its execution. The advance team found Moore in New York state, up near Albany. He'd been working as a part-time substitute teacher for only a month, so there was not much chance of his presence being noted nor memorable. The two men picked for this project were both specialists and expert at what they did. Mr. Dayle was well-versed in getting answers. Especially answers that did not want be offered voluntarily. To those who knew him well, Mr. Bello was known as "Lungboy."

Dayle and Bello met Marvin at a small restaurant one evening. There they bought several rounds for each other while engaging in lengthy discussions on politics and the best way to solve the problems facing those attempting to gain elected office. This led to names of people with whom Moore had worked and his opinions of them. Dayle and Bello took mental notes, deciding which were names to be remembered, such as the member of the Oregon Congressional delegation elected with the help of Moore two years ago and which names could be tossed aside, among them the former Governor of Arkansas who was forced to resign in order to begin a rather lengthy prison sentence for land fraud. The higher Marvin's opinion of the individual, the more likely that this would be a possible future contact in the world that would become Marvin Moore's, but not *this* Marvin Moore.

The next day, Dayle and Bello met with Moore once again. This time, it was suggested that they spend this beautiful winter afternoon skiing at Lake Placid. Moore noted that he did not have a teaching assignment that day and figured why not. On the way to the mountain, Dayle and Bello turned off onto a remote farm road and stopped at the deserted farmhouse under the guise of checking on Dayle's elder mother. The road had been plowed and the chimney was offering up a gentle plume of white smoke consistent with a wood stove or fireplace in use. The three exited the car and never made it to Lake Placid.

Mr. Dayle and Mr. Bello had an array of recording equipment set up in the larger room of the house, what might be considered the living room in most cases, but it was definitely an oxymoron in this particular situation. There wouldn't be much living in store for Marvin Moore once his visit was completed. Along with video and audio recording machines, there was an assortment of medical equipment. Syringes, scalpels, dental drills and pliers, plus a variety of injection vials.

The rest of the house was sparsely furnished, save for light-blocking draperies on every window. There was a table, two chairs, stove and refrigerator in the kitchen, two fold out cots in what might have served as a den or family room and a couple of towels hanging in the bathroom. The upstairs was empty of any furniture whatsoever. The only items in the upper level of this drafty old farmhouse was a single, bare lightbulb in an overhead fixture at the top of the stairs and a folding stepladder for access to the overhead attic crawlspace.

Moore was immediately taken aback when they entered the front door and took in that which was visible in the larger room. As he turned to Mr. Dayle to ask just what was going on, his face was met with a white rag and that was the last thing he recalled prior to waking up, secured in an old wooden armchair.

Marvin had no idea how long he'd been unconscious. He did have quite the headache working, however and asked if he could have a glass of water and maybe an aspirin or two. The headache felt more like a hangover, to which Moore was no stranger. Post-

3

election celebrations, all of them in his case of the victory variety, tended to be beer and booze filled occasions. The morning after left the bittersweet combination of joy and misery in aftertaste form in his mouth. Dayle had water and a couple of small white tablets at the ready, which Moore took as best he could. His arms were restrained from just above the elbow. His body was strapped just below his ribcage. His legs were secured at both the thigh and ankle. He was able to hold the white tablets in one hand and bend himself forward enough to slip them onto his tongue. Then he attempted to hold the glass of water, but without much success. His hands were shaking and he wasn't able to raise the glass to a comfortable position to his lips in order to sip. Sipping is not what he wanted at that point. He wanted to knock it all back in one, drenching gulp. Bello reached over from his right side and slowly loosened the strap holding Marvin's left arm. This allowed him to drink the water freely. Slowly, thought Marvin, slowly. Too fast and it'll all come right up. As he drained the glass, he turned to Dayle, who had been passively sitting by, observing the fairly normal occurrence of a man drinking a glass of water.

"Could I possibly have a little more to drink, please?" ask Moore.

Dayle nodded his head in the affirmative and produced a pitcher of water, rattling with the sound of ice cubes. He took the glass from Marvin and slowly filled it up, letting Moore take it all in. Then, the glass once again filled, it was returned to Marvin's left hand, the arm restraint still relaxed to allow the glass to reach his lips.

As Marvin took several small sips, Dayle broke the silence.

"Marvin. You've no doubt realized that we are not just political junkies, like yourself. We are, however, interested in the contents of your vast mind. You are sharp. You are cunning. You are smart and savvy. You also, in all likelihood, possess a remarkable level of recall. Mr. Bello and I are also enabled with recall abilities far beyond the abilities of most. Almost photographic memories, according to the experts who trained and tested us both. With your acumen in the field of politics, the simple act of remembering names and faces instantaneously is a hallmark. No delay in snapping to recognition of Jimmy Jones or Sally Smith as your candidate worked the crowds.

That's what you are rightfully most proud of being able to do, as you so artfully recounted to us last night over dinner and drinks.

"Our meeting you last night was not by chance. You have been personally chosen by some very, very powerful people to be a part of something really big. The level of "really big" is beyond mine and Mr. Bello's need to know. We're here to finish off the chapters that have been compiled on just who Marvin Moore is. Now you can help us by remembering, freely, any and all of the details of which we might inquire. We'll ask you for names, dates, places. You'll provide us with answers and then we'll check your answers for accuracy. Any answer that may sound to us as if it's untrue, or perhaps slightly different than the truth, will be double-checked for accuracy on the spot. As you've no doubt noticed, we have a variety of accuracy-verification tools right here at our disposal."

Dayle made a sweeping gesture towards the tray of medical apparatus.

Moore slowly sipped his water and wondered just what the hell this was all about. Was this some Watergate-type scheme for one party or person to gain inside information in an attempt to gain an upper hand? Or was this retaliation from a vanquished candidate who might not have appreciated the level of defeat suffered? Whichever situation was the impetus, Marvin knew that he was pretty much in as deep a pile of shit as he'd ever seen. Having come up with a few pre-election trump cards in his time, he'd seen some people in some pretty deep piles of the stuff, having helped in their placement into the aforementioned situations.

"Mr. Dayle?" inquired Marvin. "Just who did I piss off to...."

"No one, Marvin. No one. In fact, we're all here because of your ability to impress, leave a mark, but very little memory. You, Mr. Moore, are at the top of your game, but no one has your face associated with you. You are a legend, yet an enigma at the same time. Let me see if I can come with an appropriate comparison...."

Dayle thought for a moment, then continued.

"The Jackal. The international terrorist of whom everyone has heard and perhaps even been touched by, yet no one knows who he is or what he looks like. You, Marvin, are the American political equivalent of Carlos the Jackal. Many have heard of you and your work and fear going up against any candidate being handled by you, yet if they were to trip over you at the next convention, wouldn't know you from some drunken delegate laying in the aisle of the convention floor. This, I would guess, is a result of your innate desire to be a private person. It's admirable to be humble, especially here in the country where prestige is power and power is everything. You have the prestige and the feeling of many is that you, Marvin, could probably rise through the political ranks faster than any of the pretenders to the throne who will eventually be pushed to the pinnacle by the mysterious 'boys in the backroom'."

Dayle stopped and took out a pack of cigarettes and offered one to Marvin. Moore had given up the habit a few years back during a California campaign where the habit was no longer considered de rigueur, but given his present situation, he readily accepted. Bello removed the slackened arm restraint from Marvin's left arm, which allowed him to wipe his brow which was dripping wet from perspiration. Marvin held the cigarette to his lips as Dayle produced a silver Zippo lighter with what appeared to be a monogram on it. Marvin recognized it as his own lighter. Although he'd no longer smoked, he kept the lighter ready for just the right situation whenever needed. He'd left the lighter back at the small rental unit in Albany. They must've found an opportunity to sneak back and get that. They'd probably gathered up all of his belongings at this point, he thought. The flick of the wheel against the flint produced an orange and blue flame, backed by the distinct odor of lighter fluid. This odor made Marvin swoon a bit as his head had not recovered from whatever it was that was on the white rag prior to his losing consciousness and his stomach was still somewhat unsettled from the after-effects. Once the room stopped spinning, he took a soft drag from the cigarette. The familiar dizziness of a first smoke overtook him and he almost passed out, dropping the butt to the floor. Dayle leaned over, picked it up and passed it back to Moore.

"Oh, that's right, you quit smoking a few years ago. Let's see, California, wasn't it? Smoking in public had lost its sex appeal early out there. Those wacky Los Angelinos. Always ahead of their time, so long as it's the cause of the week." Dayle was smiling and shaking his head at the absurdity of the right-thinking denizens of America's trend base. "It almost seems hypocritical, don't you think? There they are, all driving solo in their own smog-producing automobiles, turning what should be clean, crisp Pacific air a sandy-brown color that can be seen and smelled and felt the minute you step within the LA city limits. Yet, try and light up a smoke in a public place and you'd think that you were not only Satan incarnate, but you were singularly responsible for the bubonic plague and syphilis."

Marvin had gotten his first couple of lungs-full of smoke and remembered why he smoked in the first place, but also remembered why he quit as well. The health hazards were becoming more well known each day and the benefits to those who quit were noticeable within the first two weeks of cessation. He savored this cigarette, though. By now, he'd figured out that any health benefit he might enjoy by not smoking would never be apparent. In all likelihood, he'd never have to worry about being short of breath after climbing a flight of stairs or jogging from the parking lot to get out of the rain. He'd probably never have to worry about getting wet in the rain again, either. Marvin took another drag and was now possessed of the full realization that the extracting or obtaining of information could have been handled with a sizable deposit into his checking account. He was, if anything, a reasonable, rational man who could be bought. Easily bought, especially in cases involving deserted farmhouses in upstate New York where no one either knew who he was nor cared. And very easily bought when said farmhouses were occupied by two very genteel yet cold individuals with needles and scalpels and pliers and chairs with heavy leather restraints. Yes, thought Marvin, so much for the humble aspect of being damn good at what you do. Next time, he thought, next time, take the money and the glory. Yeah, that's what we'll do next time.

Marvin chuckled softly, which brought Dayle to inquire, "Something funny, Marvin?"

"No, Mr. Dayle, not really. I was just thinking that if I weren't so satisfied with just doing a good job, I wouldn't be here. And that if there is a next time, you can bet the farm that I'll be up there with the newly-elected governmental minion with hands held high. But we both, excuse me, Mr. Bello, but we three know that THAT just isn't going to happen."

Dayle took out a notebook and a pen and offered Marvin another cigarette, which was accepted readily. Another flick of the Zippo, another lung-filling inhale and another exhale that put yet another layer of smoke into the air of the farmhouse, which was beginning to cool. Marvin shivered a bit and all it took was a nod from Dayle to Bello. Mr. Bello quietly stood to turn towards the wood pile next to the once-blazing woodstove. Once another few logs were tossed into the fire, Bello returned and took his seat behind Marvin.

"Is there anything else we can do to make this as easy as possible for you, Marvin?" asked Dayle. "How's your head?"

"Feeling better, thank you," Marvin responded. "You wouldn't have any beer, would you? I could use a cold one right about now."

"Well, Marvin, we'd prefer to stick to the ice water for now. Perhaps, if things go smoothly, then we should be able to accommodate you. I could have Mr. Bello put on some water for coffee?"

"Sure, Mr. Dayle, coffee would be great, too." Marvin shook his head in the affirmative as he spoke and took a quick look around to re-gather his bearings in the room.

"Uh-uh, Marvin. Please don't even think about it. Yes, Mr. Bello can put on some water on the kitchen stove for coffee. But, no, you won't even consider trying to get out of the chair and take me on while we're alone. You may have a few inches and a few pounds on me, but let me assure you that it would be one of the last mistakes you might ever make. Your choice." Dayle's steel-blue eyes seemed to burn a hole right through Marvin's forehead.

"I guess I'd like mine with sugar and, if you have any, milk or cream?"

"Fine choice, Mr. Moore, fine choice indeed." Dayle stood and stretched his legs a bit and bent over to loosen the straps on Marvin's legs. "Feel free to get up for a bit, Marvin. I think that we all understand each other so far. If I feel it's needed, then we'll go back to using the un-comfy chair."

At that, they both laughed at the reference to a very funny skit about the Spanish Inquisition featured on the British television series "Monty Python's Flying Circus" which aired regularly on public television in the States. It was unusual, thought Marvin, that here he was enjoying a light, social moment with the men who would in all probability be his executioners.

Bello returned with their drinks in a few moments and they sat in silence, enjoying their coffee, yet prolonging the final minutes of Marvin Moore's notable true existence.

After they finished, Bello prepared several syringes. Then, he quietly powered up the video and audio equipment. He did a few cursory tests of the two microphones and stepped behind the bulky camera to make sure the video image was clear. He nodded to Dayle, who turned to Moore.

"We're going to have to start now, Marvin. It's going to be a fairly painless procedure, that is, if the versions of what we know to be true are accurately recounted by you. The infliction of pain in this process is dependent solely on you. Do you understand me so far?"

Moore nodded his head in the affirmative. His mouth, even after the cup of coffee, was suddenly as dry as the high desert of Nevada. His thoughts began to run together as he frantically tried to find the one thing he might mention that could make this nightmare end. There had to be a name. A place. Was it an election? Did he really piss off some loser of a candidate? It couldn't be a woman. He'd never had much luck with women at all. Oh please, God, he thought. Please let me think of the right thing to say to make this all go away.

Dayle reached across to the tray that held the now-filled needles. Grasping one, he pointed the syringe upwards and pressed on the plunger. A small stream of liquid spurt forth.

"Just getting any extra air bubbles out, Marvin," Dayle said. "This is just a little sodium pentathol. It's an anesthetic that will help you relax. It will also help you to easily speak the truth. Some call this 'truth serum.' It's not guaranteed to produce accurate results, though. That's why we have this collection of tools here. I need to remind you again that we do have information about you going as far back as your childhood. We'll be asking some simple questions. Mostly names of people you know and when you might have known them. We'll give you time to collect your thoughts and give us accurate answers. If we suspect, though, too lengthy of a delay, that's when things will get nasty. If we receive from you an item we know to be untrue, the benefits of the pentathol will not spare you from serious discomfort."

Dayle lit another cigarette and offered one to Moore, which Marvin eagerly accepted.

"We'll let you finish this smoke. And if we can get through the first series of questions without incident, then we'll take a break for coffee and another smoke. I'll also make sure we give you a few aspirin to take off the effects of the drug. It'll feel somewhat like a hangover. And please be sure to tell us if at any time you feel sick to your stomach. Bello here has a weak constitution when it comes to that kind of thing." Dayle laughed and even Bello managed a smile.

Marvin was taking his time with the cigarette. He was in no hurry to see what serious discomfort awaited him should they not like his response. And, he correctly figured that his time in this life was growing way too short.

"Okay, Marvin," Dayle spoke. "Let's roll up that sleeve and let me get started. It'll take a few minutes for the narcotic to take effect, so you can finish that butt while it kicks in. Let's see if we've got a good vein here."

Marvin rolled up his left sleeve and offered his forearm for inspection.

"This is the side I usually give blood from," offered Marvin. "They found the vein no problem about two weeks ago."

Dayle took a small length of rubber tubing and tied it off in a half-knot on Moore's upper arm. Then, taking a couple of fingers, he tapped solidly on the bared forearm. The syringe was not overly large, thankfully and Mr. Dayle expertly inserted the needle gently so that Marvin hardly noticed it.

"I suspect you'll have to finish that smoke up pretty quickly here, Marvin."

Dayle extended the ash tray and Marvin took one last deep drag.

"Thanks, Mr. Dayle," said Marvin. "I had quit a few years ago, but you never really lose the desire for a cigarette."

Moore snubbed out the butt and that's when the room began to spin. It was the last thing Marvin Moore, the original, would remember.

two

Kennebunkport, Maine   Friday, April 3, 1998   3:03 am (local)

Another mundane morning to start yet another non-extraordinary day. Don Hough dragged himself through the fresh, six inch snowfall. It wasn't all that uncommon in Maine in April. Sure beat the dust storms of March in Riyadh and at least this white blanket would be gone in a week or so, leaving a fresh layer of mud with which to contend.

He'd gotten up at his usual 2:45 am to the sound of the clock radio's beeping alarm and the smell of the coffee brewing. Thank God for the timer function on his trusty old coffee maker, he thought. He stepped into the bathroom and turned on the hot water, full. He hadn't looked outside to see the white blanket that now hid the rocks along the edge of Turbat's Creek, his backyard. The Atlantic Ocean had more than a few good qualities, he'd noted on more than one occasion. Its finest was that one didn't need to cut it, at least if the ocean was one's backyard. As he opened the bathroom window a crack, he felt the cold rush of the wind off the water, but felt it somewhat amplified. He raised the shade covering the now open window and confirmed his suspicion that it was cold wind over fresh snow. With a forty-five minute drive to South Portland ahead of him, he calculated that he'd have less time to prepare this morning, so he plunged into the shower and resigned himself to the five minute version. At least with snow, he had an excuse to dress down. Jeans, a sweater and a pair of Bean's finest boots made the morning's wardrobe selection complete and quick. He filled his insulated travel coffee mug with his own version of coffee. Some of his guests would equate the texture and thickness to a combination of sludge and jet fuel. Don simply used it to get him going each morning. He grabbed his ski coat and dependable Navy issue watchcap and put them on while checking for his gloves. He hadn't needed them in the past two weeks, so, naturally, they'd somehow migrated to a place less convenient. Once he'd found them, he grabbed his briefcase, coffee mug and keys and stepped out onto the snow covered porch just past three am.

Figuring he could leave the shoveling for later, he trudged through the half-foot of snow to his car and pulled open the driver's door. He placed his mug on the dashboard, set the briefcase on the passenger seat and started the car. Reaching into the backseat, he pulled out the window brush and pushed the heavy accumulation off of the roof first, then cleared the windows, followed by the front and rear lights. That done, the car was showing its first signs of warmth. He slid into the car, buckled his seat belt and put the car in reverse. A combination of yesterday's mud and this morning's snow gave the tires a reason to spin instead of grab. He let off the gas and with the spinning wheels slowed to idle speed, the tires caught and he backed out of his driveway. The path to the road was really that, a common, shared path that connected his house and that of the Williamson's, to the rest of the world, by way of the hotel's parking lot. Both families had owned their homes and land long before the developers came up with the brilliant idea of putting a luxury hotel on the rocks in Kennebunkport.

As he slowly made his way through the tall pine trees that sheltered his house from the rest of the world, he saw a light on the Williamson's front porch and Bill himself out pushing the snow off the steps with a broom, the family pets, Greta and Garbo, dashing about in the new-fallen snow.

Don rolled down the window and said "Geesh, Bill. Why don't you go back to bed and just let the sun melt this? You know it'll be gone by tomorrow."

"Couldn't sleep, Don. Just one of those things. You want a nice, hot muffin? Just made them and they're right out of the oven."

"Sure, Bill. Maybe this meeting can be a column? You know? Neighbors sharing a kind word and a hot muffin at five past three in the morning? You are a strange one, indeed."

"A column, eh? That it might, Don. Hold on one sec. I'll be right out."

Bill Williamson and his wife, Laurie, had lived here for years, Bill for his whole life. They'd raised three kids who were now off and raising families of their own. Laurie taught school. Bill was a good man who did the right thing in his chosen field of social work. He'd worked for years for the state's child services division, having retired from the full-time occupation a few years back and was now running self-help groups a couple of times a week. Plus, he wrote columns for a few of the state's newspapers under his nom du guerre "The Different Drummer." Bill emerged from the house moments later, a muffin with visible steam rising from it, wrapped in a paper towel.

"You want some butter on this, Don?"

"Naw, Drummer. This is just great, thanks. I saw the snow and lost my breakfast time. Go back in and get some sleep, will you?"

"I will, Don. Drive safe. You know how the 'pike can be this time of year, especially when they've already put the blades away for the season."

"Thanks again, Bill. We'll see you later."

Forty-five minutes later, just about four am, Don arrived at work. The ride up from Kennebunkport had been slow. The plows had probably all been stripped of their blades and returned to the dump truck fleet. The Maine Turnpike was a slow crawl through one pair of tire tracks in each direction. There were times when the big trucks would actually slow down enough to exercise caution and this morning had been one of those occasions. When the trucks went slower, the traffic was better able to play follow-the-leader. The off-ramps and the secondary roads would be a mess until the public works directors from all of the area towns were able to roust enough crews to get rolling. South Portland's D.P.W. had, at least, been up and out before the last flakes fell. With luck, Don thought, the rest of the city's streets would get more than a quick-pass from the plows before the morning commute. Otherwise, driving in the Portland area would be comparable to playing Russian roulette. Far too many people were done with winter. Bring on the spring! Don included himself in that grouping. Just when they thought they were out of the woods and ready for warmer weather, Mother Nature rears her fickle head and decides on one more for the road. At least the ski areas would benefit. The mountains had gotten almost a foot of "freshies."

The South Portland snowplows had done a good job of getting the roads cleared. Unfortunately, the contractor responsible for taking care of this parking lot had not yet gotten around to this neighborhood. Don took a look at the white blanket that surrounded the building and covered the sidewalk. The dark green boughs of the pine trees along the right side of the radio station's property were heavy and drooping, each holding more than its fair share of the heavy snow. A small set of animal tracks came from the drainage culvert near the roadway and ended at the Dumpster. Probably a rat, Don thought as he walked quickly back to his car. He took the snowbrush out of the back seat, required equipment for automobiles up this way until at least Mother's Day. Setting his briefcase down on the front seat, he made his way over to the three satellite dishes and cleared the accumulated snow from them. This way, what he needed to hear and read would be clear. Once he'd removed what he could reach, he gave each of the large dishes a good whack on the edges. That helped free the snow from the top, unreachable section. He stepped back with each vibrating blow. On the third dish, he was not quick enough as a small avalanche came down faster than expected. Brushing the snow from his coat and pants, he trekked back to the car, replaced the brush, grabbed his briefcase and went for the building.

Don took his key and opened the back door to the radio station. Four in the morning, a god-awful time to start any work day, but other than Elton John's request for someone to listen to him good, it was as good a point as any to get going. Erik, the all-night jock, stuck his head in the newsroom door as Don was hanging up his coat.

"G'morning, Don!"

"Hey, Erik, how ya holding up?"

"Not bad. Had a good shift, so far. Here's a list of no-school announcements we've gotten."

Don took the sheaf of papers from Erik. Only four-oh-five and already most of the Cumberland and York County schools had cancelled. Kids'll love this one, for sure. But the moms and dads who've got to come up with a game plan to keep their charges out of trouble for the day won't be too thrilled.

While checking over the list of cancellations, he walked out towards the kitchenette. He had smelled the fresh coffee as soon as he opened the station's back door. And for that, he was more than ready. He poured a hot cup into his mug and started back to the newsroom.

He settled into his chair and opened up the computer file for the latest news from the Associated Press. After a perusal of the headlines, which included some late breaking news from a violation of the no-fly zone in Iraq, the rotating of troops on duty in Bosnia, preparations being made by the President Griffen camp for the upcoming trial, quotes from a speech given by O'Reilly from the Federal Reserve Board regarding market impact from lower interest rates, he went onto the Internet and pulled up the home page for his old stomping grounds, The Biddeford Journal Tribune. The Trib published in York County to the south, so that gave him access to some of the other stories of interest for the southern Maine WCBR audience. It also afforded the opportunity to see what kind of mischief his friend and neighbor, Bill Williamson, was getting into this week. The columns from "The Different Drummer" were always a hoot. Of course, being able to spend two hours talking politics and boats with a guy like Bill was a laugh riot in itself. Bill never tipped his hand, though, as to the content of his weekly bringing of clarity and focus to the events that shape and direct our lives.

Don smiled as he noted the Drummer was right on the money. An almost precognitive column on, of all things, the Maine Turnpike.

Don finished his on-line information gathering with a stop at the Portland Press Herald's web page, then grabbed the phone and punched in his voice-mail code. Listening to the voice-mail envelope, he selected the new messages and made some hasty notes about a noon time press conference at Portland City Hall with the chief of police, Mike Chitwood and a 3 o'clock meeting with the press flack from Maine Medical Center about the progress of the new children's wing going up.

As soon as he hung up, the phone rang. Assuming it would be another superintendent of schools calling in to cancel classes for the day, he grabbed his no-school checklist. Instead of a sleepy-sounding voice, however, he was somewhat shocked. He made sure the phone-activated digital recorder had indeed been recording the incoming call. The voice was not sleepy, nor was it really "human." And the message it conveyed was one that had definitely rocked his world. Four oh nine in the morning and he gets a call from someone who says he's got the goods on the Speaker of the House. The U.S. Speaker of the House. The ultra-conservative, god-fearing man who has, to now, been able to bring the wheels of government to a screeching halt whenever it suited his agenda.

Now, if all of the facts contained in this one minute phone call could be verified, it was certainly not going to be just another mundane, snowy day for Don Hough. It was, if anything, the beginning of a trek he felt he might regret starting. But it had to be done. There was too much unsolicited information, some of which he knew to be true and that which was not known as fact, if verified, would put the Speaker of the House of Representatives in prison for a very, very long time. For treason, sedition, espionage and for murder. And that's just for starters.

three

"Mr. President, it's time to start a little prevent defense."

"Well, Bud, what did you have in mind?"

"Let's get rolling on containing some of these ancillary assets and see where it takes us. Maybe we can get some verifiable proof to help our case. The way it stands now, Attorney General Vernon is going to proceed with what she's got. She has to. The opening of the trial is next week. The only way we'll be able to defend against any of this is to present something more than plausible in our defense."

"Listen, Bud. It's *my* defense, not yours. I appreciate your team spirit. And I really appreciate that you believe me. You are about the only one left. So what do you suggest. I'm willing to try *anything* at this point. You have to admit, the girl was good. Very, very good. And very convincing, as evidenced by the first mug shots ever of a sitting American president."

"Be thankful they didn't do the de-lousing thing."

"Or the body cavity search, Bud. Let's not forget that."

"What we know is that there are two assets in place. They've been there for far too long. God only knows what would have

17

happened if you hadn't been approached and offered what we now know. Damn them. But, giving credit where it's due, they've got balls. Exceptionally large ones."

Bud paused a moment and then added "Let's not forget about their patience, either, Mr. President."

"It'll be a great abject lesson for the American people to learn from, Bud. We've come to expect way too much, way too quickly."

"Let's start with him," said Bud, showing the president a small list of names. "He'll be ripe for the picking tonight. We'll need to make this black, though. Accountability to you and you alone. And here's my idea for a cover story to help explain some of it away. Maybe all of it, if we're wrong about this."

"I don't like it, Bud. It makes me look like I'm grasping at straws to keep my butt out of a sling. And I won't let any cover story hold up as the gospel. I am not the bastard everyone thinks me to be and I won't start being one now by lying."

"Until we can get the written proof we need and until we can get one verifying source, it's all we've got. You are keeping a personal log on all of this?"

"Yes, Bud. As much as it pains me to do so, I am. But I am, if anything, not a bottom-dwelling leech. Or letch, for that matter. I'd like to present this written record to the Congressional Oversight committees that are sure to evolve from this mess. I've already written a letter to the joint bodies suggesting, at the very least, censure for me. I will take the heat for crossing the lines on the current matter at hand. I will not, though, take the blame for that which I did not do. Stupid, stupid me. I should have known better than to let her close the door."

"That much is done, Mr. President. Remember, I believe you. And I believe *in* you. What now makes sense is that we wouldn't be dealing with one without the other."

"You honestly think they have something to do with this?"

"Abso-freakin'-lutely, Mr. President. I'd bet my career on this."

"You already have, Bud. You already have." President Griffen stretched his lanky, six foot, five inch frame out in his high backed chair. The gray in his hair had spread to eliminate any trace of its original sandy color. The job of being president exacts a hellacious physical toll on the occupant of the Oval Office. Griffen was no longer an exception.

"Did you get a chance to send off a photo to the British? You know, so that they might be able to check around quietly for any kind of a match on our new friend? It would be a solid rung in the ladder of accountability we'll be climbing."

"Yes, Jay. I sent it off yesterday afternoon. I also asked them to run a data base search on a few others as well."

"What others, Bud? I hope you didn't go too far in asking for specifics. Or very well known subjects."

"I'm guessing then that, yes, I did go too far. I sent photos of our two principals and mixed in a few other staffers. Kind of as a litmus test for the results they might bring in from their data bases."

"Your thinking was along what lines, Bud?" The president appeared to be irritated.

"That if we ask to see what, if any, match results come up from the British intelligence photo data bases, they may be as surprised as we that there was a match on, say, for instance, the Speaker of the House."

"Then should it be found out that we submitted the speaker's picture for a data base search....?"

"We just say that we put that photo, as well as mine, yours and the Senate Majority leader, into the batch for a sort of baseline test of the system. You know, like a polygraph test. Simple, known-truth type questions to establish the pattern, then we see what the results are on the remainder."

"You submitted our photos, too?"

"Yes sir, that I did. We're also running a data base search at Langley, too. Sir Stephen Jennings at MI-6 told Terrio that he thinks we should have some results a little later on this morning. Terrio thought it was good idea, too. Getting results on what we do know, or think we know, will help lend credence to any match results we get. Back to my initial suggestion, sir? Let's at least get something set up to start taking these sons of bitches down."

"Remind me to get some warrants. Custody and general search for starters. Make the call. And for God's sake, tell them to take it slow and by the book."

"You're right here if they need any additional verification? I am only a lowly civil servant, you remember."

"Civil you are, Bud. Servant? Not in this lifetime. I briefed General Edwards and he's with us on this first step. He gave me the okay, so let's make the call."

Bud picked up a secure phone on the corner of the president's desk and dialed the numbers. He listened to the slight echo of the connection being made through a satellite and waited for the ringing to stop.

"Yes, the president calling for Colonel Menneally, please. Yes, President Griffen."

Bud looked at the president and gave him a nod. The situation was pretty lousy right now. But it would get better. Jay took the phone from Bud.

"Colonel Menneally?" The president inquired. "This is President Griffen. We're secure and you are on speaker phone. My communications director is present with me. Under authority of the National Security Acts, I'm tasking you with the following mission. I will, however, offer you the following caveat. If you feel that I am requesting that you do something illegal and consider what I'm suggesting falls into the category of an "unlawful order," then please feel free to tell me to go to hell. I hope I've made myself clear and that you might understand exactly what I'm trying to say."

"Mr. President, sir," Menneally responded. "With all due respect, sir, I can't follow any option you present until you tell me what you need."

"Colonel. May I call you Bob? Or is it Rob?"

"Bob. Bobby. Rob. Robby. Just don't..."

"Call you late for dinner? No, Bob. I won't. And from here on out, I am Jay. Is that clear?"

"With all due respect, sir, I'd prefer the more formal forms of address. Kind of hard to break this many years of military tradition and protocol."

"Understood, Bob. Call me what you will, but for the record, I am either the genius who gave you a direct set of orders. Or I am the stupid son-of-a-bitch who tried to pull one over on the American people and along the way tried to pull down a bunch of really good people with me. You will, I assure you, suffer no direct consequence because of this action. I am, as we speak, drafting a notice to the Joint Chiefs of Staff, requesting their presence here at the White House at eleven hundred, local. I will then inform them that, based on what we know, ordering you and Go Team One into action was the only course we could take. And that it could not wait for a consensus ruling. Follow me so far, Bob?"

"Loud and clear, Mister Presid, er, Jay. Permission to speak candidly?"

"Get to it, Bob."

"I'd like to hear it from you, right now. Yes or no?"

President Griffen paused, looked at Bud and nodded his agreement that it was a fair enough question. He'd been asked by literally hundreds of people in the past month and he'd not dignified any of the inquiries with a response.

"No. That's why I'm calling you now, Bob. It's an unequivocal *no*. And I need the help of a few good people who not only believe me, but believe *in* me. The Secretary of Defense and the Joint Chiefs are included and have given us permission to proceed with this conversation. Next question?"

"Tell me what you need me to do, sir. I'm all ears. And I'm all yours."

President Griffen walked through the details of what they knew to be going on.

"That, Bob, is what we've got. And trust me when I say there are no hard feelings if you think it's just a bit too far out there to fathom as the truth."

"What's that they say on the *X Files*, sir? *"The truth is out there?"* Well, sir, what you've just told me is indeed, *out there*. So I'm willing to fall in under the truth column."

"Thank you, Bob. It means the world to hear that from the mouth of a human being other than my communications director. By the way, if I may, Bob? Say hi to Bud. Bud? Bob."

The two exchange hello's and the president continued.

"I'm going to let Bud walk you through what we need from you. And then you can tell him if you think we can do it. I want you to know that my personal assets are available to you for use in this mission. I will personally be funding your expenses. Please let Bud know approximately how much you will need to get rolling. We will keep track of all expenditures at this end and upon conclusion of this thing, compare the list to yours. You have a blank check. I'm good for any amount up to about eight figures. That's a lot of gas. And bullets."

Menneally whistled down the line. He'd been the commanding officer of Go Team One for little more than six months. Other than the occasional support mission for the area NATO commanders working around Bosnia, or the quick hops to help out the Allied commanders near the no-fly zones of Iraq, Go Team One really hadn't been tested.

"Well, sir. I am all for spending someone else's money. But I will make sure I run any large figures by you or Bud personally, just out of respect, if I may."

"Bob, I appreciate that. Don't worry about me. If this thing turns out to be the truth, the government will be picking up the tab. I will, though, need some of my cash in that event, to defend against the various charges that will no doubt be brought, just as a reminder of how this country is supposed to work. That *checks and balances* thing. Now, I'm going to turn this call over to Bud, who, by the way, as of right now, is the only individual in this building who believes in my innocence and has the most direct knowledge of what is really a problem of no small standing for the United States.

"Let me also go ahead an authorize phase one for you and your team. It's something that has to be done tonight. We'll be faxing you some warrants, just to keep this legal and above board. And again, you heard me say it's quite alright."

"Will do, Mr. President. And good luck. To us all."

"Amen, Bob. Amen."

President Griffen put the speaker phone on hold and Bud grabbed the handset. He started to give the colonel the background and then spelled out that evening's mission.

"That, Bob, is what we know. And for now, it's what we need from you. Any questions?"

"None that I can think of, Bud. You got a cellular number where you can be reached twenty-four/seven? I'd rather not leave anything to chance."

"Here's the number, Bob." Bud recited the cellphone number. "Program it in your phone. And use it. No matter the question, call. Also, here's the direct, secure line to the Oval office." Bud gave him that number as well.

"Will do, Bud. I hope to call you late tonight and confirm we've got the package."

"I look forward to hearing those words from you lips, Bob. Thanks again."

Bud hung up the phone and looked at the president.

"Looks like step one is rolling, Mr. President."

"Let's hope that it is successful. It'll make getting the next steps officially approved that much easier. Do you think delivery will be a problem?"

"No sir. Not for these guys. They are the absolute best we've got. If they can't get it done, then we'd be pretty much screwed before we got going."

"So what do we need to do next?"

"I made some notes, Jay. Here's what I've come up with."

Bud leaned in over the president's shoulder and opened up a file on his pocket-sized, personal p.c.. The president looked over the notes and nodded his agreement.

The intercom buzzed and Jay picked up the phone.

"Thanks, Joannie. Send her in."

Bud looked at the president, somewhat puzzled.

Jay completed the thought to answer Bud's quizical look. "The attorney general's here. We need to tell her what we're doing, Bud. I told you, no secrets on this. Plus, it'd be good to have her in the loop on this."

"How do you figure? We've just gone ahead and issued direct orders that break several international treaties, not to mention our own laws."

"You'll see what I'm getting at in a minute. Just give me a chance, okay?"

The door opened and Attorney General Gayle Vernon came into the Oval Office.

"Good morning, Gayle. Always nice to see you."

"Good morning, Mister President," she replied, coolly.

"Please, have a seat. Can I offer you a cup of coffee?"

"That would be great, thanks."

Bud stood and walked towards the little pantry where the coffee maker was finishing a brewing cycle. As he poured a cup, he leaned back into the office and asked Gayle how she liked her coffee.

"Just a touch of cream, please, Bud. And a sweet 'n' low."

Bud finished fixing the cup and brought it to the coffee table in front of the office's sofa.

"Here you go, Ms. Vernon."

"Thanks, Bud. No need to be so formal. You know it's Gayle."

President Griffen smiled at the exchange. At least Bud was able to break the ice a bit. Jay looked at the attorney general and began.

"Gayle. This allegation of which I stand charged notwithstanding, we have a new problem. I need you to hear me out. This is not a smokescreen. This is not a diversion. I am ready to have my say in a court of law, the way our system is designed. I would, however, ask that you put that to the side right now. I need your undivided, objective mind on this. You are this country's chief law enforcement officer. Your record speaks volumes. Harvard Law. Ten years with the Massachusetts A.G.'s office, four of them as attorney general. Then, six years with the U.S. Attorney and now, here we are in your fifth year as the U.S. Attorney General. You've been fair and dauntless in your search for the truth and relentless in the pursuit of justice. You may view what we are about to tell you as a crock. If so, then you will have to pursue what we are about to tell you in a manner that befits your position."

She took a sip of her coffee and maintained her unemotional gaze. She was listening. And, at least right now, she was not ready to buy into anything that was being said.

"Gayle. Unless I know I'm getting a fair shake here, then all I am going to do by disclosing that which I must is flap my gums and waste your time. I need to know that you'll be able to weigh this current matter separate from the incident."

"Mister President, I'm listening. It's what you asked me to do. So, talk."

"Damn it, Gayle. I did not touch that woman. Do you think I'd risk all that we've worked so hard to get for, what, a quick feel?"

"That's not this issue, is it? If it is, then you know that we are not able to talk about this without the benefit of your counsel being present."

"No, that is not the issue. It is, though, what's keeping you from being what I need right now. I need America's lawyer, here and now. We have a big problem. We have, right now, serving as the Speaker of the House of Representatives, an agent of the now defunct KGB. This man, who is not the person born as M. Bradford Hewes, is a pawn being controlled by the former president of the USSR. Romanov sent agents here in the seventies and those agents, acting on direct orders, committed murder here in the United States with the express intent of sedition and control of the United States Government. That's as simple as I can put it to you, right here, right now."

Gayle's eyes had widened as Jay went on and she was now looking at President Griffen with an intense expression; a mix of disbelief and shock.

"Mister President, the story you've laid out is quite the tale. You want America's lawyer? Then here I am. What do we have for proof? Evidence? Witnesses?"

"Witnesses we've got, Gayle. Allow me to turn this over to Bud. He's the one who was contacted and brought this directly to me. Bud?"

Gayle finished her coffee and took out a yellow legal pad, scribbling her notes furiously as Nelson walked through the scenario. When Bud finished the outline, she looked at the president.

"Now what, Jay? Where does it go from here?"

"I need a warrant. Maybe a couple."

As Jay outlined his plan, Gayle nodded in agreement while she wrote. Finishing her notes, she said. "You realize that this is separate from the other event, correct?"

"Perfectly, Gayle. I expected no less. I just needed you to be able to put that issue to one side while we talked this thing through. I know that on this matter I am violating several laws, but time is against us. I've had to start things without clearance from the proper channels in Congress. I'd rather go down in flames for something of which I know I'm guilty."

"Mister President, let's see if we can keep those flames to a minimum. I'll get the proper paperwork done up and we'll take it from there. You will keep me apprised from this point on, correct? These are serious accusations and if they are not verifiable then you are right, you will be very much in a world of trouble. Before I go," she said, as she stood, gathering up her paperwork and briefcase. "Is there anything else?"

"Such as?"

"Oh, I don't know? Any other plans to pick up perpetrators, conspirators or seditionists that you've not yet told me? Any other acts that might be considered illegal search and seizure? Things that would help these people walk away laughing at you if we didn't take the correct steps? I'm not trying to anger you, here, boss. Just trying to make sure we do the country's business properly."

"No, Gayle. But if anything comes up, I will call you. Promise."

"When do you need these warrants?"

"Before close of business today."

"I'll have them back here for you by lunchtime."

"Thanks, Gayle. I appreciate it."

They shook hands and President Griffen walked Attorney General Vernon to the door, then escorted her down to the West Wing entrance where her car and driver were waiting.

"Remember, chief. Nothing else without me first. I can't promise to back you up on this if you take any other steps on your own."

"I promise, Gayle."

Jay walked back to the Oval Office where a stunned Bud Nelson sat.

"Hey, Jay? Next time you sandbag me like that, how about a little warning?"

"I've told you before, Bud. I don't like pulling punches. With anyone. Even you. It keeps us all honest if we don't have time to spin this shit. Now, help me work the rest of this stuff out, will you?"

Bud pulled his chair closer to the president and realized that he was indeed working for a good man. A very good man.

four

Cheltenham, England Friday, April 3, 1998 1:32pm (local)

Menneally hung up the phone in his office, still somewhat dumbfounded. The President of the United States tasks him with a mission, complete with the ultimate safety net. All he had to say was "no thanks" and that would have been it. But with more than eighteen years in the Army as an officer and a pilot, trained to exercise snap judgments, his gut instinct was to believe the man and help. In any way he could.

"Morris! Come in here a sec, will ya?"

"Yes, colonel?"

"Are we ready to roll? We'll need to be ready to move out later today. Maybe this evening. We'll be getting a call and it's going to be a fast-move once the call comes. Who's left we can grab?"

"Already counting you and me? We've got Zallonis and Murphy."

"Is Z feeling better? He was kind of off the other day. He had a flu or an allergy attack or something."

"He's ready to swoop into action, sir. At least he was when I saw him heading for lunch."

"Damn leave policy leaving us shorthanded. I'm kidding, Hank, just kidding. I wish I could have taken a few weeks off after that last cluster-fuck in Iraq. If we have to work with the French again, it'll be much too soon."

"That French commander wasn't that bad, sir. He was just following that stupid United Nations dictum. Nothing like sticking us in a hot-zone and then the organization controlling us suddenly gelds us, themselves and everyone else but the bad guys."

"Still. What's our equipment status, without raising eyebrows? If we go out tonight, it's a training hop. Out, over some water and back in a few hours. But we'll need some small arms, ammunition and fuel."

"The bird is ready to roll right now. She's topped off and somewhat stripped down, so that will get us a few extra reserve miles if needed. You want the crew to put the external tanks back on? It won't take long to put 'em on and top them off, too. The ground crew did a full scheduled maintenance and they replaced the overhead manifold.

"The armory has already received a visit from the gunny. We're ready to lock and load, if necessary."

"Very well, Morris. Round up Z and Murphy, tell them to grab a little snooze and then be ready go around twenty-two hundred or so."

"Aye, aye, sir."

"Cut that Navy crap out, will you? Just because you're a SEAL by training, doesn't mean you can try and convert me."

"Yes, sir! I will try and make myself appropriate for use by any and all armed services, sir!"

"Cut the shit, Hank. And get out of here, will you?"

Both men laughed as Go Team One's executive officer, Lieutenant Commander Henry Morris, saluted and left the office. Morris was as ominous a specimen of a man as anyone would ever hate to meet in a dark, secluded alley. Standing six two, he packed a solid two-hundred-twenty-five pounds on his tapered frame. Morris had thrived, physically and mentally, since joining this special operations group seven years ago.

Prior to that, he was a lieutenant j.g. on board a fast-attack submarine. His SEAL training came prior to his submarine duty.

This had made him a valuable asset to both the sub fleet and any SEAL detachments assigned to the boat, allowing him to act as a liaison and an integral SEAL team member whenever the need arose to deploy special ops personnel from the sub. Occasionally, the men in the field might not want to stick to a hard and fast timetable while executing a mission. The role Morris was able to play was that of devil's advocate. Yes, the objective being successfully reached was of import. But being able to stop a sub on a dime, or having it do a quick cut and run within a mile of a foreign coast was not a maneuver which the average nuclear submarine was equipped to do should the away team feel that just another ten minutes would complete the task. Hank had the authority of rank as well as the respect afforded to one with his level of training and experience to abort a mission so as to not put the crew of the submarine in jeopardy.

He'd had to call for an abort once. That was during a beach incursion in Kuwait. They'd come out of the water only to take fire from some Iraqi troops that had escaped the big eyes of their intel snoops. Hank had helped one of the younger SEAL team members who had taken a hit in the shoulder back into the water and then carried him through some high waves back to their extraction point. The following night, the team's second attempt at the mission clicked.

When the dust from Desert Storm settled, the stories of the atrocities visited upon the women and children of Kuwait by Saddam's Republican Guard forces surfaced. Morris felt responsible. The self-imposed burden was no lighter, even in the wake of honors quietly bestowed upon him and the SEAL team he accompanied into Kuwait. The Kuwaiti president had privately assured Morris that the damage had been done prior to the team's first attempt; that even if they had been able to secure the beachhead on the first try, the animals of the Iraqi army had done their worst. The lingering doubt, however, led Hank to pursue a different assignment. Helicopter flight training along with a stop at the language school in Coronado helped to make him a man of many military talents. He came out of his additional training with a set of wings to go with his SEAL trident and submariner dolphin. He was fueled and ready for a new challenge, Go Team One, assigned to the United States Joint Armed Forces Command for Europe.

Menneally smiled at the thought of going into the field again with Hank. They worked together every day - they had for the past five years since Bob came in as the unit's new executive officer. Theirs was an almost brother-like relationship which made for interesting exchanges in the field, but kept them on a very even keel, to borrow a Navy term. When they went into action, the two of them were able to act as one. The other team members were attuned to the closeness of their two senior officers and knew that when the two were in consensus on a particular point, there was no need to question the logic.

Bob picked up the phone to call flight operations for a weather forecast and to file a training flight plan. They'd be going out late and returning around daybreak. He'd also have to arrange for fuel at the other end. No need to raise any red flags by asking for mid-flight refueling should they be close to fumes on the return leg. He hung up the phone, having been told he'd have VFR conditions both ways and got an okay for his flight plan.

He then took out his little black book and called a buddy of his from college, now working as an agent-in-residence for Interpol. He listened as the connection gave a third ring.

"Hello?" The sleepy voice on the other end answered.

"Greg? Did I wake you? It's Bob."

"Oh, hey Bob. Yeah. You woke me, but that's all right. What time is it?"

"Pushing thirteen hundred, my friend. Late night?"

"You could say that. Got a bunch of work yet to do with all the mucky-mucks coming in for the big economic summit. What's up?"

"I'm going to need some ground transportation late tonight. Maybe a mini-van? Something plain. And very, very quiet."

"You're coming to my town? And you want it quiet? What's going on, Bob?"

"I need you to trust me on this one, Greg. It's almost against the law. Hell, it probably is against the law, the way they keep rewriting things back home. It's just one of those things that will get done, one way or the other. And I'd prefer you be the one way."

"How many you bringing? And are there going to be dead people when you leave?"

"Fair enough question, buddy. It's going to be me and three. Leaving, hopefully, with one more. Nobody's going to die. That's a guarantee."

"How are you coming in? Is it cleared and stuff? You know, so that if something really bad happens we don't have to treat your arrival like an invasion?"

"It's as cleared as cleared gets, Greg. When things fall into place, I'll get permission to bring you in, for information and maybe some of the glory. And plenty of cold beers. How's the life of my favorite expatriate?"

"It's alright. I miss being home sometimes. But for the most part, who's left at home? You're over here. And Christ, it's not like we can just go out and pound a few brews with Jimmy."

"That's true. If only the people knew what a lowlife degenerate one of the sitting Supreme Court Justices was. Of course, he's cleaned up his act since college"

"As have we all, Bob."

"Speak for yourself, Greg. I'm still a rock and roll devotee, not at all above getting fall-down-in-the-gutter-swimming-in-my-own-puke drunk. I just can't do it in uniform."

"Even so, I'm doing okay over here. Plus, it's nice to know you're not that far away when it comes to some serious male-bonding. I'm doing just fine on the female-bonding thing."

"Ah, yes. The life of a secret agent. The name is Wood. Greg Year Wood. Secret agent double-oh-for-four."

"Will you ever let me live that damn game down?"

"What? The time you went oh-for-four, including the last at-bat when you left the bases loaded for the final out in the game that those idiots from Sigma Pi beat us for the St. A's all-fraternity softball championship? It hasn't crossed my mind in almost twenty years."

"You are an asshole. I love you. But you're still an asshole."

"Hence the big bucks and the big shiny bird on my U.S.Army issue collar."

Bob stopped for a moment to think.

"Hey, M?" asked Yearwood. "You still there?"

"Yeah, I'm here Greg. Just thinking about something you said about female-bonding. I'm wondering if that's an idea we can put into play tonight."

"Now you've got to tell me what's going on. You want to come over here, do something clandestine that might involve women and you can't clue me in? Uh-uh. Give."

"Without specifics. Got to grab someone up and put this person on ice for a few days. It's got to be done quietly. And maybe leaving us an option to offer an explanation. That's all I can give you, Greg. If you've ever had reason to trust in me blindly and without question, this is time."

"Since when did the U.S.Army get into the business of kidnapping, Bob? I'm serious. It's not something normally associated with the word "defense," correct?"

"Correct. I promise you I will have permission to bring you into the loop when and if we arrive. As of now, we are go for this. But there will be a final confirmation. Without that call, we'll be playing darts and having a pint or two down the road at the Special Forces Club."

"Call me and let me know if you're coming or not. I'll take care of doing what I can for you."

"Thanks, Greg. I will explain it all when I see you."

Menneally hung up the phone wondering how the hell they'd be able to pull this off with a minimum of containment. Getting in and out of a remote village in Bellarus was one thing. Trying to sneak into Paris for a snatch-and-grab was quite another. Terrorists did it all the time. Go Team One did not have the much needed luxury of time for planning and executing this project. Finesse and help were called for to avoid attracting too much unwanted attention.

Having justified the reasoning for bringing in Greg Yearwood from Interpol, Colonel Bob Menneally stood up behind his desk. He'd have to go to Operations and pick up his flight plans. And the receipt for the fuel. That would be a first, Bob thought. Asking for a receipt. He'd have to remember to ask them if they checked the air in the tires, too.

five

"Yevgeny, listen to me. This whole thing is playing out better than we could have expected! They thought that they could make the entire episode disappear with a wave of a hand and a balanced budget."

Dimitri was just working his usual magic. Calming the fears of the insecure Yevgeny who had, since the breakup of the body politic back home, been wondering what would become of them. This morning was like many others: a somewhat distraught Yevgeny losing a little of the confidence that had gotten them this far. But this little plan had been in motion long before Glasnost. Long before the Berlin Wall came crashing down. Yes, this little baby hatched shortly after Chairman Nikita threw his little Disneyland temper tantrum. Can you believe that? All because Kruschev couldn't get to ride on The Pirates of the Caribbean, the entire government of the great United States of America was about to come tumbling down. Too bad, thought Dimitri, that the Chairman and his minions were not around to see it happen.

"But Dimitri," protested Yevgeny. "I don't see how we are as close to fulfilling this dream as you think. I'm just not sure how much longer our luck will hold out."

"Yoshi, listen to me. Take a deep breath and just 'chill out'," Dimitri responded. "You are, right now, the second most powerful man in America. We won't count the vice president in the power line. For over twenty years we've had this plan in motion, not to mention the years of planning that went into it. Chairman Krushchev died in '71 and he never even saw this thing get off the ground. Now, we are right on the edge of doing that which we've pledged our lives to completing. The President is going down, so to speak and we are on the express lift to the very top."

"All right, Dimitri, we'll keep a cool head for now. I just wish you'd been the one to be in my position."

"Yevgeny, I was not blessed with the looks of a politician, you were. But I look passable for an assistant Secretary of State. Now you go have a great day as M. Bradford Hewes, Speaker of the House of Representatives, elected to Congress by the good people of South Carolina in 1976. And now, twenty-two years later, you stand poised to simply catch the job of President of the United States as it tumbles by your window. You have health care to push through for a vote today, remember?"

Dimitri disconnected the call on his cellular phone in his private study and went to the mirror to finish the windsor knot on his four-in-hand. Looking pretty good, he thought to himself. Now for another day as Marvin Moore, assistant Secretary of State.

Yes, he thought to himself, Yevgeny had the looks. As a matter of fact, it didn't take much physical altering at all to come up with the exact facial match needed to get the wheels rolling on this project in 1976.

Yevgeny and the real M. Bradford Hewes were exactly the same height. They had the same coloring, the same build. They even had the same webbing between the second and third toes of each foot. The colonel in charge of the KGB special operative unit, Michail Rostokovich, really had everything clicking for him on this particular operation. Although Yevgeny and Dimitri had no idea what the road ahead held for them. Once the entire operation was spelled out, the entire plan made sense for the good of the State; for the good of the Party; for the good of Mother Russia. And now twenty-two years later, it was still hard for Dimitri to believe that fate had brought them this far, safely, without any hint of compromise. The documentation on this project was minimal. Only four people currently living had known about its existence from the start. Yevgeny, Dimitri, Col. Rostokovich and the former Chairman of The Party, Aleksandr Romanov - famous last name but no relation, currently living the good life as advisor to the new governmental regime in Moscow.

Now, seven years after the dissolution of the Union of Soviet Socialists Republics, the foundation to rebuild the Motherland to a position of total world dominance had been laid. As a matter of fact, the house had been framed, the roof put on and all that was left of this little political allegory was to install the fixtures.

The current President of the United States was John Francis Griffen, the former governor of New Hampshire. Not only had he trusted Marvin Moore to help him rise to a position of prominence in the national spotlight, he'd trusted Marvin with everything.

Marvin's political reputation had preceded him from several elections around the country, including that of M.Bradford Hewes to Congress in '76. John ("call me Jay") Griffen had spirited Marvin to the Granite State to spearhead the 1984 and 1990 gubernatorial campaigns.

In late 1991, when Jay thought that the White House would make a nice place to finish raising his family, he once again enlisted Marvin for his expertise. The 1992 election was won, handily. And when it came time to reward hard work with some cushy appointments, Marvin stood up and graciously accepted his appointment to the Department of State as an assistant. That would, unfortunately, be the undoing of John Francis Griffen, 45th President of the United States of America and soon to be her latest figurative martyr in the cause of liberty.

Dimitri, in his role as Marvin, had grown to like Griffen. Not like a brother but as a pal. Not the best of pals, though, Dimitri realized. They'd not had the close, intimate contact of the campaign since his posting to the State department. Otherwise, he might be tempted to slow this process down until that idiot of a vice president was ready to slide into the job. That would put this operation into another two years of hoping that nothing went wrong. No, Dimitri surmised. We had waited long enough. We had probably used up our allotment of luck. Now was the time to make something happen. Of course the irony of this train of thought struck Dimitri as funny. He glanced at his watch, grabbed his travel bag and headed for the front door. The cab had arrived and he had a nine-thirty flight to catch. The last thing he wanted to do this morning was spend a five hour flight to Paris being chewed out by Secretary of State Paparelli for being late.

six

South Portland, Maine Friday, April 3, 1998 9:07am (local)

"Fred, we've got to talk." Don had just finished his final morning-drive newscast when Fred Singletary, owner and general manager of WCBR, came into the newsroom.

"And a good morning to you, lieutenant," Fred replied. "Nice job on the storm stuff this morning. Sure makes for a better day than another one filled with Old Port drunkenness stories, doesn't it?"

"Yeah, it does. But do me a favor. Close the door. I've got something you've got to hear."

Fred closed the door to the newsroom as Don turned down the police scanners and shut off the TV.

"I know that we've got our share of wackos around these parts," Don began. "But this is what came in this morning just after I got my coat off."

Don pressed play on the digital recorder and watched for any sign of reaction from Fred. Fred simply listened and a small smile crept across his face.

"Hey, that's pretty good, Donny. When did you finally learn to use the harmonizer?"

"I didn't learn to use the harmo... that's it! Geesh, you'd think I was a complete techno-idiot! It's a harmonizer. I was thinking it was a computer generated voice... you know, like you can do with a home p.c."

A harmonizer is an electronic device that is used on a daily basis in just about every audio and video production studio. It takes the original sound and electronically alters the sound to change it. If the creators of the Chipmunks had possessed one of these, their little niche of creative vocal animation would have been more easily filled. The harmonizer is capable of changing the pitch of a spoken voice to sound faster, slower, fuzzier or even more ethereal. It's used in public situations where an individual wishes to retain a level of anonymity, such as official inquiries into corruption, organized crime and the like.

Fred began to look puzzled. "You mean you didn't do that?"

"No," Don replied. "I didn't. And considering what this 'voice' had to convey, I think we've got to give it a little more consideration than a cursory dismissal."

Fred thought for a moment and then said. "Let's bring the whole unit over to Chucker's place. He's got some really nice, new digital toys that might be able to bring this 'funky voice' back to reality and then maybe we can make a few calls from there."

Don powered down the digital recording unit and removed the plugs from the back.

The whole device is about the size of a laptop, designed for easy moving.

Fred hung up the phone. "Chuck says to get on over now. He's got a noontime studio appointment booked, but he says if we need more time, he can reschedule."

The drive to Scarborough was slushy but uneventful. As they pulled off Route One into the driveway of Michaud Media, Don gave a gentle pat to the digital unit in his lap. This was one piece of new technology he was glad to have.

"Gentlemen! To what do I owe this unique pleasure? It's way too early for beer and cigars. So, grab a cup of joe and one these highly illegal Cubans." Chuck Michaud was always ready to gab and play with his favorite cigar clipper, a bright chrome one with his initials. It had been a gift from Fred for Christmas not too long ago. Business was his mistress. Storytelling was his love. "Besides, I hate snow. I hate snowblowers. And I hate snowblowing the snow out of my driveway in April. It's just not natural. I should be on my Harley, going for a ride!"

"Hey Chucker, glad you could squeeze us in," said Don as he and Fred shook the freshly-fallen, soon-to-be melted snow from their shoes.

Chuck shot Don and Fred a quizzical look. "You guys look way too serious for this hour of the day. What's up?"

"We've got to get you to run something through the harmonizer for us so it'll sound normal." At that, Don presented Chuck with the laptop sized digital recorder. "The file's in there. I took it off a phone call this morning at the station, so you might have to do some tweaking to compensate for any phone line noise."

"Seriously Chucker, we really need to get this figured out quickly. You've got Bud's phone number here, right?" asked Fred.

"Speed dial number 3. Right after my lovely bride Susan on 1 and Mother on 2." Chuck replied. "Let's meander our way up to the studio and see what we can come up with for you."

Michaud Media was in a converted Cape Cod-style, single-family house. Chuck had picked it up for a song when it was time to grow the business beyond a spare room in his family's primary residence. The recording studios were situated up stairs with the downstairs relegated for office space, a kitchen and bath area, as well as an oversized living room which housed the official Michaud Media Harley-Davidson during the winter months. Fred took a look at the combination conversation-piece / long-summer-days-riding machine.

"What, no new chrome this week?"

"I've chromed everything but the seat, Fred," chortled Chuck. "There's nothing left to chrome. So why is this matter of extreme importance of concern for our buddy, Bud?"

Don started up the small stairway and turned back towards Chuck. "You'll find out in about three minutes."

After plugging in the unit and grabbing a couple of audio connectors, Chuck turned on the power switch to his audio console, then brought up the master volume for his auxiliary input. Flipping a few switches and depressing a few buttons, he hit play on the digital recorder, sat back and listened.

The machine produced a fuzzy, sped-up voice, the kind of effect one hears from another who has inhaled a little helium and then started talking.

"Got a deep cover operative as Speaker of the House. Bastards killed the real man. Back in 1976. Charleston, South Carolina. Plan is to find the right time, take down or out the president and vice president and go with the unanimous decree of Congress that our nation's champion of all that is right, Speaker Hewes, is crowned via the line of Constitutional succession. The man's been working for twenty-two years. I think he has enough inside support, so does our source. Probably will wait for you to resign, then they'll kill the Veep."

The recording ended there. There were pauses throughout as if the audio had been edited, deleting questions, perhaps, leaving only the one voice doing the description or providing the answers.

Then Chuck listened again. Only this time he smiled.

"Gentlemen, there's no need for us to call Bud about this one."

"Why not?" exclaimed Don. "You've heard this for yourself. Dates. Places. Names. And events. Plus the stuff that only someone inside would really know! Of course, we know about the inside stuff because of Bud, but the data..." At that point, Fred and Don looked at each other and a knowing smile of recognition crept across their faces.

"That son-of-a-bitch!" Fred commented. "He got you good, Donny boy. Got you really, really good."

"Uh, Fred, that would be *us*," Don replied.

"Yessirree. Harmonized, digitized, simonized. I'd know that voice any way it came through. The illustrious L. Bud Nelson, presidential communications director and our patron saint. All praise Bud!" And at that, Chuck raised his coffee mug in a mock toast to the missing member of this little confab. Then, Chuck made a few adjustments to his harmonizer in order to reverse the fuzzy-affect that had come through on the original phone call and pressed play again. Sure enough, dripping with enough of a drawl to now make it distinguishable was the unmistakable voice of Bud.

"Pass me that phone there, Chucker, would you please? I've got a call to make," said Fred.

Chuck reached over and handed the cordless phone to Fred, then reminded him "Speed dial 3, Freddie. That's his private line."

seven

The office was plush and overly ostentatious, as it should be, thought Yevgeny in his role as M. Bradford Hewes. Yes, things are as they should be. The Speaker of the House of Representatives of the United States of America should be surrounded by nothing but the best. The desk was solid oak and polished to a glossy shine. The desktop was clutter free, the Speaker's idea of efficiency. When something hit his desk, it was handled, or immediately delegated out to one of the many on staff.   And in this office, there was no room for error. There was no Yevgeny Polnichy, operative of the now defunct KGB. There was only M. Bradford Hewes, Brad to all who know him, former teaching assistant at Clemson University and full professor at the College of Charleston. Now, he is simply Brad, or, in strictly formal situations, Mr. Speaker.

His staff was not top heavy with old friends and cronies. There really were none of the former and only those who aspired to curry favor with the Speaker qualified as the latter. He had no room for hangers-on. More to the contrary, this Speaker of the House held extensive interviews to fill all of the assistant-level positions. Those hired to do the business of the United States of America found out quickly that there was little room for slacking off or ineptitude on the job. The Speaker had fired the first two personal secretaries within a week of their hiring shortly after he'd been elected to Congress for the first time. Their firings were not the result of a whim or personality conflicts. The poor unfortunate souls had the temerity to question the Speaker's instructions. Once they'd been informed that the language used in this particular office was English, the Speaker had done his part to lay down the ground rules.

All work done here was well within the boundaries of the law. The persona adopted by Brad was that of a devout Christian and he held those beliefs firmly, wearing them proudly like a suit of armor. His word was law in this office, as he'd explained during the interview process with each prospective candidate. His favorite saying was "that there are two ways to do things here in this office. And the other way is the wrong way."

The original M.Bradford Hewes was a child of the old south. Charleston, South Carolina. Old money and a privileged upbringing helped to pave the way for his rise to the top, with help from military schools as a youngster, a bachelor's degree from Clemson with a brief stint there as an undergraduate teaching assistant. Further studies earned him Masters' and Doctorate degrees in World History from Yale which all helped to bring his abilities into focus for the faculty committee at The College of Charleston. It was they who invited him to join the professorial ranks in 1976.

The early 70's bothered the real Brad, owing to the apparent loss of morality of the people of this country he so loved. Free love, lack of faith in God combined with easy divorce and abortion all set the stage, so he felt, for the demise of his United States of America. That was when he got the idea to run for elected office. He'd decided to use his knowledge and try to turn it into power. Power that could help right the course his country was currently taking. It was also when he'd had the worse case of timing in the history of bad timing.

His initial meeting with Mike Rosty in the early spring of 1976 was at a small tavern in Charleston, South Carolina. Rosty was a political consultant who'd happened upon a lecture Brad was giving at the College of Charleston on the rise of Stalin to power in Russia. Rosty was taken by Brad's charisma and sheer magnetism. These students were locked into what Professor Hewes had to say and they heard it loud and clear. After that lecture, Rosty introduced himself and asked if there were someplace way out of the way for them to meet and talk of the future of America. Intrigued, M.Bradford Hewes suggested that they meet at the Hogpenny in Charleston's college district. Hewes explained that he spent his weekends at his family's estate for the solitude and quiet. So, over a couple of cold beers, Mike Rosty explained his plan to M.Bradford Hewes, a plan that would put Brad in the House of Representatives on behalf the people of South Carolina, of course, if not by the upcoming November election, then by 1978.

Mike Rosty had sold Brad on running for office. Then, Mike Rosty left the Hogpenny, boarded a flight from Charleston to Atlanta which then led to an international flight to London. From there, he caught a connecting flight to Helsinki and one last change of planes. An Aeroflot flight which would return him to Moscow and his other job as Michail Rostokovich, Colonel of the KGB and brother-in-law of Soviet President and Chairman of the Communist Party, Aleksandr Romanov.

eight

"Nelson ! What the hell was that phone call this morning all about?" asked Don. "You've certainly got our interest piqued as well as our undivided attention."

"Bud, don't know quite what it is you're talking about," replied L.Bud Nelson, White House Communications Director. He also called everybody 'Bud.' "Wanna fill me in?"

At that, Michaud spoke up. "Bud, it's Chuck. Listen, man. Hough and Singletary showed up here this morning before Mother even called, getting snow all over my floor, toting their Shortcut Personal Audio Editor in here and played me the following. I'll let you hear it the way I first heard it. Here it comes."

Chuck pressed the "send" button on his audio console to allow Nelson to hear the recording and then pressed play. The three in Scarborough listened intently and waited for a response from their running mate in Washington.

"Gentlemen..." intoned Nelson. "I don't know where you got that but I've got to ask you to make sure it goes no further. You unnerstand what it is I'm sayin' atcha?"

"Bud, did you make that phone call?" asked Hough.

"That, gentlemen, is one of many questions I'm sure you've got for me that will have to wait until I get off the damn company jet at the Portland Jetport in about, oh, two hours. You guys meet me at the General Aviation Terminal? With hot coffee?"

"Er, yeah, L. We'll be there. Make sure you bring your mittens and booties. We had a little snow event up here last night."

"Great! See you then!" And at that, L.Bud Nelson hung up the phone, leaving three very puzzled men sitting in a Scarborough, Maine studio.

"What was that all about?" asked Fred.

"Damned if I know, gentlemen," replied Chuck. "We've known Nelson for too many years now and that is the quickest I've ever seen him make any kind of a decision involving an aircraft with a destination of Maine, on a workday, no less! A snow filled workday at that. Hell, it's Friday and we all know what Friday night means."

Don and Fred recited the ritual like a school child's song. "Bud's in his chair, with Chinese food and a beer."

"It's got to be somewhat serious, boys," Chuck said.

"I'll drive," offered Fred "Let's go grab a quick bite at the eggs'n'stuff place and we'll grab Nelson some hot joe for the ride."

Chuck picked the phone while thumbing through his electronic rolodex. He made a couple of short calls, explaining that something had come up and they'd need to reschedule the studio sessions for another day. When he finished clearing the schedule for the day, the three locked up the digital recorder in Chuck's office safe and piled into Singletary's Lincoln, one of the few luxuries he allowed himself. The car pulled out onto Route One and headed off towards The Portland Jetport and a day that would be a vivid memory in the weeks and years, to come.

nine

"Michail Ivanovich, come in! It is good to see you!" bellowed Chairman Romanov. "Take off your coat and warm yourself. You would like a warm drink, no?"

"Yes, Aleksandr, I would like a warm drink. How old is this coffee?"

"Fresh less than an hour ago! Help yourself, Misha. And come, sit, tell me of your latest adventure!" The former was a polite offering, the latter an order from the Chairman of the Soviet Union as he sat behind his desk in the most coveted office in the Kremlin.

"Yes, my Chairman. But first, how is my sister, your wife? And the little monsters?" queried Michail.

"Your sister, my wife, is fine. Other than her constant complaints of the demands on my time that come with the job, you know, she is well. And the children are fine, also. Misha, your namesake, was asking for you as a matter of fact, over breakfast this morning. He so enjoys your company when you two go for a skate in Gorky Park."

"Please tell Misha that I will be by on Saturday and we can hopefully sneak in a day in the park. Unless, of course, we experience a brief taste of spring?"

The laughter from Chairman Romanov could be heard down the halls.

"Misha, the long range forecast here, unfortunately, will allow you to go skating for the next ten days, at least! I'm afraid you got spoiled on your latest journey to the American south. So tell me. I've read your telex, but that was merely an outline of what you think you've accomplished. Give me all the details."

For the next thirty minutes, the Chairman listened while his brother-in-law spoke. And it seems that the research obtained laid the groundwork, no, more than just the groundwork, but the entire structure of what would become the greatest legacy of Chairman Aleksandr Romanov and the glorious Union of Soviet Socialist Republics.

"This Hewes fellow, Misha. He's 'ordinary looking'? With no immediate family to speak of?" questioned the Chairman.

"None to speak of, Aleksandr. We've talked at length on a couple of occasions and he's made it a point to mention the family's estate that is his and his alone. His fortress of solitude, if you will. And ordinary? Well, ordinary enough that any man of Scandinavian decent could be 'surgically sculpted' to look like him. We've got the linguistics experts to help work out the accents and inflections. He has no immediate family, but he does have a distinct enough presentation of his speech and a wide enough audience through his years at the college to require our strict attention to this detail."

The Chairman nodded his approval at this answer and then asked the toughest question of all. "When do we put this part of the plan into motion?"

"Aleksandr. We've got to proceed one step at a time. First, let's find the "new" M.Bradford Hewes. Then we'll take it from there. We've already taken care of the political consultant. We simply need an agent who can come close. As we discussed about this Moore fellow, he's very good at what he does, er, did. But no one really knows him."

At that, Michail finished his coffee and stood. "With your permission, Comrade Chairman, I would take my leave of you and return home where I can take nice, hot shower and relax for a few minutes?"

"Misha! Go, shower and relax. But would you be up for joining us for dinner this evening? I did promise your sister I'd ask."

"How about breakfast tomorrow morning?" replied Michail. "A good night's sleep will help me shake off this 8 hour jet lag and then I'll be more prepared to whip your children into an unmanageable frenzy, as is my right as the doting uncle."

"Done!" bellowed Chairman Romanov. "We'll see you for breakfast in the morning. But please, at least call her when you get settled later on today, okay?"

"Yes, I will. Anything to keep you out of the dog house!" laughed Michail Rostokovich. "I will!"

At twenty-five past six, Michail stepped off the elevator on the tenth floor of what, by Russian standards, would be a luxury high-rise apartment building. He shook off the cold of the unheated lobby and the even draftier lift. But at least the water supply was useable and the electricity was more than reliable. His apartment, he knew, would be warm. The steam heat that ran through the building was piped via conduits in the walls, into which he'd tapped a good sized vent hole to grab some of the heat destined for the upper levels. The upper levels of this building, he knew, were for a select few in the Politburo who were not married and lived beyond the realm of imagination of any "wild and crazy guys" in 1976 Moscow. To hell with them, thought Michail. They'll grab additional heat from any one of a number of Moscow prostitutes who'd be more than willing to give a 'free one' with a hope of latching onto a man of means. Occasionally, that would happen, making one former woman of the night a woman of standing in a matter of months. Yes, thought Michail, maybe there is hope for the people of Russia after all.

He put his key in the lock of his apartment door only to discover that it was already unlocked. He reached into his overcoat and removed the 9mm baretta he carried. Standing to one side of the door, he gently pushed the door inward, expecting a rush of bodies or bullets - he wasn't sure which it might be but he was not taking any chances. Being as tired as he was, this was definitely the time to take no foolish chances. He entered slowly, sliding in to the right where he could grab cover behind the ratty old recliner he'd had since his days at the university. Quickly checking his bearings, he noticed no lights on, but enough filtered streetlight filled the room to give him an affordable view of the living room, kitchen and dining area. The door to his bedroom was open, as was the bathroom door. The spare room, which served as his study, was closed with a small stream of light creeping out from under. Michail removed his shoes and stepped softly toward the closed door. He checked his breathing, which was understandably rapid and put one of his many learned relaxation techniques to work. Once he was sure of himself, he listened and could hear nothing. Just as he reached for the doorknob, the door swung open and he was suddenly falling toward the floor with his grip on his weapon lost.

"Misha! What the hell are you doing back? You weren't supposed to be here until next week!"

"Stasya?" queried Michail, now completely taken by surprise.

"Yes, my darling Misha, Stasya. Who else could take you down that quickly?"

Stasya was Anastasia Fidoryvich. She was his little sister's best friend, his love from the university days and into the early years with the KGB. They'd trained together and spent the first three years in service on assignments together as husband and wife. Their last pairing had been over five years ago, but they had decided to keep their partnership professional and also, as mutually agreed upon, physical. Michail had told Stasya of his duties that would take him out of the country and yes, he had returned sooner. But Stasya had no idea of what those duties were. Perhaps, he thought, that there will be a way to include her in this operation. They work great together and this assignment had the makings of being a very, very long one.

"No one else on earth, my darling. No one else," gasped Michail. "And yes, I'm back early, but you were in Warsaw, if I remember correctly. Something about a rogue shipyard worker and his grand plans to unionize?"

"Yes, Misha. We did the background work on this Walesa fellow. Seems loud enough to attract attention. We'll have to give this situation some very serious consideration before it escalates. The people of that area also seem to have a religious leader of some consequence, as we discovered quite by accident. It was almost a two-fer. I returned and gave my report to the directorate yesterday and was just checking some of our private files on the Polish leadership. You remember, from one of our first ops together?"

"That I do, Stasya, that I do. Listen. What have they got for you after you do the paperwork on this?"

"Well, there's an assignment for me out of the country and they told me to plan on a bit of a lengthy stay. Unless, of course, all hell breaks loose in Iran or someplace more important, why?"

"We're about to kick off something really, really big. It's actually bigger than any other op that I can recall the directorate taking on. If I can get you cleared, do you want in?"

"How big is this 'big'?" asked Stasya. "My orders were somewhat implicit that what they wanted me to do was not just scut work."

"I can't really say right now. Like I said, it's going to take me a day or two to work on getting you on board. The circle on this one is going to be extremely small, but it is a huge undertaking. It's all I can tell you for now, so I must ask that you trust me on this one. You will want in once you grasp the whole picture."

At that, Michail reached out and pulled Anastasia towards him. It had been a while for both of them. She offered no protest whatsoever and gently allowed his tongue to part her lips. The kiss led to a night full of other learned-and-never-forgotten activities.

The ringing phone at eight the next morning woke Michail from the best sleep he'd had in weeks. He grabbed the phone before it had a second chance to wake Anastasia. She was curled up next to him. "Spooning" was the term they used in America for this position.

"Yes," Michail answered the phone. Listening for a moment, he replied. "Yes, comrade, I'll be right there." He hung up the phone and rolled quietly out of bed. He faced what was going to be another day of long travel, so he figured he'd do it refreshed. Stepping into the shower, he turned on the hot water full blast in the hopes that this "luxury" apartment building would be able to grant him one of life's small pleasures. After about twenty minutes, the hot water turned cool.

"Well," he said to himself. "At least I got that much."

"Oh? I could give you more." It was Anastasia, stepping into the shower. She playfully reached down and began what could be considered another of life's small pleasures. Two of life's small pleasures in a half hour, thought Michail. Not a bad way to start a miserable day at all. About an hour later, the two of them stepped into the shower and miraculously, the hot water had returned. Stepping out and drying off, Michail explained to her that he'd have to leave, no, that he should have left about an hour ago.

With a wry smile on her face, Anastasia said "Misha. You're putting me ahead of duty?"

"Yes, Stasya, this time... and every time!"

They both had a good laugh and finished dressing. As Michail grabbed his coat, he walked over to the table in the kitchen, took another sip of his coffee and gently kissed Anastasia on the cheek.

"I'll be gone for a day or two, Stasya. But I hope to combine this trip with getting you in the loop, okay?"

"It's okay, Misha. I've got to finish finding that information to complete my report. They want it today, but I'll have to try and put them off until tomorrow. It seems I lost some valuable research time last night," she said, smiling. "Are you going to see Elenya? I wish I could come with you, but as you well know, I'm in it up to here."

"I'm planning on seeing her. It's one of the things I *need* to do, as you well know. The other thing I *need* to do. . . let's just say that was done a couple of times, thanks to you, Stasya, my sweet. Of course I'll give your love to my sister."

Michail closed the door behind him as he stepped back out into the hall. It was a little warmer today, he thought while he waited for the elevator to arrive. But it certainly won't be warmer where he was heading. The northwest coast of Russia this time of year, or anytime of year, is chilly. Hence the designation of Arctic Circle. In any language, it's a cold place with few warm spots. At least the locals who are acclimated to the conditions know how to make the best of it, making a trip to any one of the small villages on the outposts of humanity pleasant, from a people perspective. His first stop would be at headquarters. Then, off to catch Aeroflot to Murmansk, followed by a chilly, short train ride to the small but well appointed KGB outpost along the Barents Sea.

The trip to the office contained one small detour. Pulling his car to the gatehouse, he rolled down his window as the morning sentry stepped towards the vehicle.

"Good morning, Andre Vassilyich! And how are you today?" Michail greeted the young soldier.

"Good morning, Comrade Inspector. I'm fine, but will be better when this cold weather finally breaks!" laughed the sentry. He gave the back seat a cursory glance and a shorter one at the identification folder Michail held up in plain view for inspection. "Comrade Chairman has already departed for the Kremlin, but your sister is still home."

"Excellent, Andre! I've already seen my brother-in-law. It's my sister and those little rascals I'm here to see, anyway. Stay well and warm, too!"

Michail returned the salute from the sentry, rolled up the window and pulled slowly through the gate, up the winding driveway and stopped at the front portico. There he was greeted by a pair of sentries, each about two meters tall and solid all the way through. Again, the cursory glance at the i.d.. folder which Michail had readily presented and he also surrendered his weapon to one of the two. Purely for safety reasons, plus, Michail agreed with his sister's edict that there be no weapons inside the house. With half of the Soviet Army only steps away, there was no need for arms inside the home of the Chairman of the Soviet Union. Michail returned the salute from the two and stepped through the front door.

ten

Portions of the Portland International Jetport are physically located in South Portland, but the largest city in the Pine Tree state gets to lay claim to the name. The main approach to the airport is over water, as the planes descend from their flight paths over Casco Bay and then down along the Fore River which separates Portland from South Portland. This approach is to appease those residents of the elevated sections of South Portland, who, at times, feel as if they can deliver the request to return their seat backs and tray tables to the upright position. On a clear day, when VFR is a joy and the westerly winds that whip down out of the White Mountains are at a minimum, this approach is an extremely pretty and pleasant adventure. The final moments of flight prior to touchdown are not unlike most major airports around the country. The last hundred feet are usually over the rushing traffic of the local interstate, which, in this case, is I-295.

Don, Fred and Chuck had made the stop at the quick mart at the end of the runway. There you can get gas and real coffee! They each got a large cup and grabbed an extra for Bud, who likes his coffee the way he fancies himself... light and sweet. From there, it was a quick left and a right onto the main access road.

The three pulled up in front of the general aviation terminal and parked near the smaller of the snowbanks where they could get a view of the approaching aircraft. Right on schedule, the black jet dropped from one thousand feet through five hundred and made the turn for final approach. It settled down gently and rolled the length of the runway.

Don was first out of the car as Bud's jet rolled up to the tarmac at the general aviation terminal. The door from the plane swung up and the staircase lowered automatically. An Air Force colonel was first off the plane, his black flight bag in one hand and his overcoat draped over the other arm. Next out was the president's communications director, L.Bud Nelson. He was dressed for the weather, complete with hand-knitted hat and gloves, probably a holiday present from his dear widowed aunt from Mississippi. The colonel held the door open for Bud and, after a brief exchange, Nelson stepped briskly through the small lobby and out the front door.

"Damn, Don! Don't you all pay the heating bills up here? It's freakin' cold!"

"Good to see you, too, Bud!" laughed Don.

They shook hands and hugged, as is the tradition of really good friends. Then, in the same tradition, Bud turned to the car and flipped Fred and Chuck the one fingered salute.

Don held the car door open for Bud, who climbed in and slid over.

"Here's your coffee, you self important ...."

"Michaud, don't finish that sentence, you communist-goat-lover. Do you have any idea of how quickly I can get three different government agencies to start sifting through your trash? Your humidor?" interrupted Bud.

"Hi, Bud!" piped in Fred. "Nice flight?"

"Just finest-kind, Fred. Thanks for asking. Nice job on the coffee, boys. Just the way I like it! Light..."

"And sweet!" finished the trio on cue. They all enjoyed a good laugh as Fred backed the car out of the parking spot, onto the loop road that would take them around the general parking area and back out the way they came in.

"Say, boys, is that little lobster place out at Two Lights open?" asked Bud.

"Oh, you mean The Lobster Shack?" laughed Don.

"Yeah, that place. I'm starved, so how about we take a swing out that way so I can grab a little Maine lunch on the rocks. And save the sarcasm, Donny boy, or I'll have the IRS on you quicker than you can say "hidden Bahamian assets." Got it?"

"A little on the edge today, Bud?" Inquired Chuck. "You've been right off the chart since we spoke on the phone this morning. Besides, Fred's the one with the hidden Bahamian assets."

"Boys, you three, the President of the United States, the vice president, the directors of the NSA and CIA and one, I repeat, one field operative know what you heard on that recording. That was, indeed, my voice. That was my voice as spoken to the President of the United States two days ago, responding to his questions. Present at that meeting were the boss, the veep, the two spook directors and me. There were no minutes. And there were supposedly no recording devices in operation. Kind of like the 'Cone of Silence' from 'Get Smart'."

"Or the Loren & Wally show. You know, the one in Boston. God, they're funny!" piped in Fred.

"Yeah, Fred. Quit thinking like a broadcaster for a few minutes, will ya?" Bud continued. "I got that information from the one field operative. This thing has been in play for over twenty damn years and until three days ago, nobody on our side knew anything, I mean absolutely nothing, about this op. This is the most conniving, deceptive, well-kept undercover operation I, or anyone at that meeting, had ever heard of. And, giving credit where it's due, a pretty goddamn good one at that. Now here's where I'm going to need some help. From the outside. That would be you three."

"Us? Jeez, Bud, we're just a bunch of broadcast geeks. Well, two geeks and a successful broadcast magnet."

"Thank You!" chimed in Fred and Chuck simultaneously.

"Don, you may be broadcast geeks," Nelson continued. "But, remember, I was one, too. We think outside of the box. We have lots of preconceived notions about how the government and its organizations work. We think we know it all. And you know what's really scary? We really do know which end is up. Then, we take our little analytical brains and work through all of the "what if" kind of scenarios, eliminating the totally absurd. Those little off-the-wall scenarios we come up with to help brighten our image of what would be a normally mundane story out of Washington are right on the freakin' money. There is no such thing as objective, especially in the media. We like to think that we are removed, professionally and that we don't allow ourselves personal opinion. Looking at a blank slate and treating it as a blank slate is not what winds up in the news. Not from you, not from me. Not from anyone, for that matter. Everybody's got an idea about something. Hell, remember that ruckus the I-man raised when, a full year before anything hit the streets, he cracked wise at the press dinner about the Chief and the office gals. The boss was pissed and embarrassed. Here's this nationally-syndicated broadcaster making off-color jokes about the President and some little girl, while the President and his wife are sitting right there. And now, based on the news of the day, it was more prophetic than anyone at 1600 Pennsylvania would like it to have been. The last blank slate for ideas is when we're about five years old. From that point on, there is a starting point that's already been established to everything else we approach.

"Now what I need help with is keeping this goat-fuck contained until it's time to quietly and I mean quietly, bring the whole thing to a close. And I and your President, need help to set these bastards up to within an inch of their goal. We do not want to tip them off in any way that we're on to them, finally. They've been at this for over twenty years. Twenty years! Christ. We were all going through O.C.S. together, doing pushups in the morning and drinking way too much beer at night when this little nightmare was getting started. Hey, Fred? We almost there?"

"Got a few more minutes, Bud. They've put up a few more traffic lights since you were last here. Now, it's like driving downtown DC. Go a block and stop. Go a block and stop. At least they plow the streets up here, unlike our nation's capitol where they wait 'til it melts before driving. We'll be good to go once we get on 77."

"So, tell me, oh great inner-circle sage. How the hell did they get you giving up the goods?" Chuck asked. "That was some pretty heavy quality sound. There's no way they used a parabolic mic, as, if I remember correctly, there's an electronic buzz-field in and around the White House. So it had to be a device either on somebody or in the room."

"And," Don added, "It had to be somebody who knows you very well."

Bud looked puzzled. "How so?"

"They knew that once they had your voice, they had to do something with it," Don continued. "How did they know to call me?"

Bud thought about that and said "We don't know that they called ONLY you. For all we know, whoever did the taping might have had a nationwide distribution list. Hell, it's probably out on the Internet. Damn!"

Nelson took his cellphone out of his pocket and dialed in a number.

"Yo, Billy T. It's Nelson. Are we secure? Good. Yeah, my end's encrypted. Get a check on the Internet servers. See if there were any mass-mailings of file-attached messages this morning or last night. It'd be an audio file if they come up with anything. This is priority stuff. Per the chief, okay? Get on it and call me back at this number. I'll be waiting. And thanks, bud. You're the man!"

Bud folded the phone back up and slipped it back into his topcoat. "Now, where were we?"

Don continued. "So let's suppose they called only me. They did that for a reason."

"Maybe they wanted Bud to know that his tight little circle isn't as tight or little as he thought." Chuck had stoked up one of his fine, highly-illegal Cuban cigars and was about to add to the brain-trust currently moving along route 77 in Cape Elizabeth, Maine. "Let's suppose it's one of the people who were present in that room."

"I don't think the President of the United States is going to call a radio newsroom in Portland, Maine at four in the morning and dime out his own undoing, do you?" asked Fred.

"Whoa!" yelled Bud. "Say that again, Fred?"

"What? The President calls Don and drops the dime on this whole thing? What's he got to gain by this thing going public... Jeeeeezus! Okay, Bud, suppose he did. This takes the focus off the little scandal-cum-impeachment proceeding. Turns a little sympathy his way. Especially along the lines of his off-the-cuff defense that he was set up...."

"Fred. You've just made me a believer that he WAS set-up," Bud interrupted. "IF the recording was made by him and dumped in Dons' lap in the hopes that he'd use it, then send it to the wires, it might work as a bit of a diversion. If so, this is a little problem. Not as big as I thought it was. I hope."

"Yeah, that's my man, L.Bud! Mr. Decisive!" guffawed Chuck as he sent another mushroom cloud of cigar smoke around the inside of Fred's Towncar.

"But why would he try to blow this thing out of the water before we can get all the players nailed down?" Bud thought out loud. "I know that he'd probably sleep easier if he was able to quickly draw the focus off his alleged episode of slap'n'tickle. The timing of this coming so soon after we all just found about it, though, I'm puzzled."

Nelson waited for a little more input from his running mates. Years of friendships and working relationships had allowed them all the luxury of being able to tap into each others' trains of thought and often left one literally finishing the other's sentences.

Don was next, "So, what if he is somehow involved in this little scheme. What if he is also an operative who has made it to the top. What if...."

Nelson cut him off abruptly. "Don, you scare me. You scare me big time! The thought of this little plan of theirs getting this far is nightmarish enough. You want me to even consider that a Soviet sleeper program of this magnitude was mirrored?"

"What if there were more than two?" Fred piped in. "Suppose you were running this kind of an op, Bud. You'd make sure it worked, right? And what better way to make sure than to make it redundant. In this case and with this type of undertaking, you, being the man in charge, keep it compartmentalized. Only need-to-know in each little scenario. You've got need-to-know working in multiple little clusters. Each operating independently of the other. You, being the big cheese, know where all the mice are. The mice all know where the cheese is. They just don't know about the other mice."

"Fred's getting a little lost here, guys." It was Chuck's turn to weigh in. "But Fred's heart is in the right place. And his mind is still as sharp as ever! Let's assume that Nelson's initial contact information is correct. That the current Speaker of the House, second in line for the Oval office by way of the laws of succession as provided for by the Constitution, is actually a deep-cover Soviet KGB operative who was given a mission and told to take his time. Make it happen, smoothly, so as not to raise any more undue attention than would occur in other situations, like in a coup d'etat. And stay away from dangerous pursuits, such as skiing or skydiving. Do your best to stay alive until the time is right. For all we know, our last three presidents could have been from the USSR and we wouldn't know it."

"There is that possibility," mused Bud. "But I think we'd be feeling the effects of a socialist-backed POTUS long by now if that were the case. Last I checked, the economy is doing swell and you're smoking illegal Cuban cigars."

"Hey, wait a sec, there Nelson. If the commies take over, does that mean we'd be friends again with the Cubans? Legal Cohibas! This might not be so bad," Chuck smiled.

Nelson gave Michaud a friendly slap upside his head.

"No," Bud continued, "I think we're dealing with the "first layer" of this thing, but what if it is redundant. And what if the Chief is one of them. He'd now know what the plan is, considering he stepped into it, instead of having to make it work. Jesus! This is absolutely insane. No, the boss is not one of them. But the Speaker, yeah. I'm banking on everything our deep cover guy fed us."

"Just how deep and knowledgeable is your source, L.?" Don was now digging. The newshound in him had been once again roused. "Is this source credible enough to risk yours and your boss's career on?"

"Don, this source is as credible as it gets. Yessirree, he's worth the roll of the dice. Only I know the dice are loaded and they'll be coming up sevens every time. You remember Romanov?"

"The "last" last Czar? You bet we do. He made for great copy about six years ago. Racing for the dacha on the Black Sea while all the statues of Lenin came tumblin' down." Don was on his mark and continued his probe of Bud. "Wasn't he in hiding somewhere in the Urals? With a small detachment of his select guard to keep the press and others at bay?"

"Was. He came out of hiding two years ago and is now quietly working the back room as an assistant to President Yevchenko. Thanks to the new openness, he can actually be a little critical of the new regime. And he's now living the good life on the shores of Lake Onega. A dacha - slash - palace kind of place. Of course, he was completely against the breakup of the Union, but it turns out he was a bit of a visionary, actually. He'd laid some groundwork for a little realignment of idealism and entrance into the free market economies of the world. We actually got a chance to look at some of his files a few months back. Stuff the intel gang had gotten hold of and the boss and I got to do some fun reading. There was just one problem, however."

"Which was?" the three others chorused.

"His wife and two children. A girl and a boy. Young man, eighteen and the girl was just sixteen, actually. The Chairman was at the office when the insurrection started and he booked without the family. They were in the custody, under house arrest, of the new regime. But your basic angry mob busted down the gates and torched the palace. She was dead on the scene. The two kids didn't make it through the Soviet hospital system. Romanov never looked back. Strictly a cover-your-ass situation. He was able to garner a huge amount of sympathy out of the whole damn thing. Plus, he'd still had this sleeper op running over here, so it appears it was in his best interest to just cut his losses and wait for the outcome in the States. He kind of forgot one thing."

"What one thing would that be, Bud?" again, the three chimed in as Fred pulled the car to a stop into the snow-filled parking lot cut out of the rocks of Maine's jagged coastline.

"Comrade Chairman Romanov forgot about his doting brother-in-law, Michail. Ol' Misha did not take kindly to finding out that his sister and the two children were left to fry, literally, while the big man boogied it out of Dodge. Michail, it seems, is no fool and is command and control for the operation that involves our Speaker of the House. And Assistant Secretary of State Marvin Moore."

The silence was deafening. Only the rush of another wave futilely dashing towards the rocks and the slow, collective exhale of the other three could be heard.

"Boys, I don't know about you, but a cup of "chowdah" and a 'lobstah' roll would hit the spot right now. Let's go eat!"

"So, Bud, does dropping a large thermonuclear weapon usually create this type of hunger?" queried Chuck as he flipped the remnants of his cigar into a tide pool.

"No, not always, Mr. Michaud. But I was hungry before we had the little talk that we NEVER had. Got it?'

"Loud and clear, Bud," the other three said on cue.

"Hey, Bud, if we keep this up, you can take us on the road as your trained pony act!" chuckled Fred.

"Naw," came the retort from Nelson. "Then I'd have to clean up after Chuck. The man's an eco-terrorist if ever I saw one. I need the EPA on my ass for his crap like I need another mole in the White House lawn."

eleven

Moscow, April 3, 1976   9:30am (local)

"Elenya! It's great to see you!" Michail rejoiced as he picked his sister up in a bear hug.

"Michail! Aleksandr told me you were home. For how long, this time?"

Michail looked at the floor. "Sorry, sister, but it won't be long enough for a meal. I've got a flight to catch in about two hours. I still need to swing by the office before I fly. Where are the cherubs?"

"They're upstairs playing peacefully, for a change. But they'll be so disappointed." Elenya was noticeably sad.

"Oh, c'mon, kiddo. Cheer up. I'll be back sooner this time. Just your husband has me doing some legwork for him and that's on top of my regular duties. Besides, with the way this winter's hanging on, we'll be skating in Gorky Park until June," Michail chuckled in an attempt to get his sister to brighten a bit.

Unfortunately, Michail was unaware that his sister Elenya was not only unhappy at his not being able to stick around for at least a meal, but she was very unhappy in her marriage to Aleksandr. His quest for power in the Politburo and subsequent rise to the position of Chairman left him little room for love. For his wife and even his children. Aleksandr had become cold and detached. He had become Comrade Chairman, at the loss of his love of life and family.

"I'm here on orders of your husband, I'll have you know. He does care about you and Christina and Michail. He specifically had asked me to be here for dinner last evening. But by the time I woke up from a nap, jetlag had gotten the best of me. That was this morning, by the way, my waking. A little late for dinner, don't you think?"

At that, Elenya laughed. "Yes, late for dinner, but you'd have been on time to do the dishes."

She wanted to ask her brother why he had to leave so quickly, especially when she needed him to be here for her. She would not come out and explain the situation, point blank. It's one she'd like him to figure out, a little bit at a time. He was good at that. Always had been. Perhaps that's why he was in the business of intelligence. Michail was highly intelligent. He'd slid through schools and the university, while she struggled with basic math and spelling. But her Misha was always there for her when she needed him, when she needed someone to help her without asking. This was one of those times, but his comings and goings of late left little time for him to help her sort it all out, without asking.

"Do you really have to leave so soon? You did just get back in town," she asked.

"I'm afraid so. It's something that has to be done now. Orders from the Boss, you know. What is it? You seem troubled."

She sighed as she got her opening. He always knew when to ask.

"It's Aleksandr. He's been, well, more cold and distant than preoccupied. I know that being the leader of our country is a demanding job. But it would not seem such a lonely existence if he could make some time for us. He's here. But he's not. Do you understand what I mean?" Elenya offered her hands in an open gesture of pure puzzlement.

"When you mean cold and distant, do you feel that there might be someone else?" asked Michail.

"No, it's not that. It's just that it seems we, the children and I, have become, a, oh, I don't know. A burden or something. It's frustrating.

I've tried to ask him about it. I've suggested that maybe he needs some time alone. Maybe he needs to grab his hunting gear and go spend some open ended time in the Urals. Just go and get away for a break. He merely laughs it off and tells me I'm imagining things." At that, Elenya began to cry.

The cry turned to sobs in an instant. All Michail could do was to reach out and hold her. The way he'd done when they were smaller and she skinned her knee, or when she'd come home from school, her feelings hurt. He held her the way a big brother holds a younger sibling who needs comfort right at that time.

"Maybe," offered Michail, "I can delay this trip for a day or two. Let me check with control and see if we can't help you through this. I can explain it's a family emergency."

"But won't that point interest directly at Aleksandr?" asked Elenya. "Your family, you may recall, is not exactly anonymous," she said as her sobs turned to a chuckle.

"Well, let me talk with Aleksandr. I'll ask him to make a discreet suggestion that my trip be put off for a day or two. I'll tell him I'm burned out and need to recharge. Nothing that a few hours skating with little Misha wouldn't fix. And maybe we can work in a few games of billiards and a few snifters of brandy to get him to loosen up a bit?"

"No, you will not get my husband drunk!" Now Elenya was smiling. She had gotten this huge weight off her chest and was able to move on through the next event. One day at time, she'd been telling herself of late. Maybe with Michail's help, she'll be able to get through this after all.

"Let me go check in at the directorate and then, if I have to, I'll go to the top banana to make sure I'm here for dinner this evening." At that, Michail gave his sister another hug and a kiss on the cheek, checked his coat pocket for his car keys and went towards the front door. She walked him to the door and gave him another hug for good measure.

"Aleksandr said he should be home here by 6, so please let me know before then if you'll be here with us, okay? I know even if you have to go to him to get permission to hang around another day, he probably won't think of it to tell me. He seldom calls home during the day anymore." Elenya added the last as a bit of reinforcement, not that her brother hadn't received the message loud and clear previously.

"I'll call as soon as I have a definite answer, kiddo. Promise." Michail stepped to his car, climbed in and started it up. "Tell Misha that maybe we can go skating tonight after dinner. No, don't tell him until we're sure I'll be here. I hate to break promises to little Michail."

Elenya waved and watched him pull out of the circular drive and down the lane that would take him back to the main drag. Michail knew he needed to spend some time, today, with his sister. He also knew that this mission and his trip to the Baltic were given the highest priority from the highest level. His brother-in-law. What the hell, Michail thought, he'd lay it out straight for Aleksandr and hope for the best. Certainly Comrade Romanov wasn't that cold hearted.

It was a twenty minute drive to the directorate on the outskirts of Red Square. And with the cold April winds still keeping the comfort levels down, the Square itself was almost deserted. Open, but not very inviting. A good place to land a small plane, laughed Michail to himself. No people and lots of room. Of course, the only aircraft that would ever get clearance to get close to the cobble-stoned clearing would be an official helicopter for only those in the highest levels of the Politburo. Anyone even thinking about bringing an unauthorized aircraft into not just Red Square, but Soviet airspace would be dealt with quickly and severely.

Michail parked his car, pulled his coat up around his neck and stepped briskly towards the building that housed the directorate of the KGB. This was the more welcoming of several buildings that did the business of security and information of the USSR. The others were colder and more desperate, inside and out. Those buildings are where citizens would be brought for questioning. Quick answers often led to quick stays. Those who thought to think it through before responding to inquiries were usually invited to spend the night, or the week. Or longer. He stepped through the outer door and into the entryway, which was locked and would only be opened by the armed guard on duty inside. Michail waved to the young sentry and dutifully presented his official I.D. for inspection as was required for everyone entering. The soldier returned the smile and opened the door.

"Welcome, Colonel Rostokovich. It is nice to see you again," said the guard.

"Yes, it's nice to be seen again, as well!" laughed Michail in response. He took a look around and saw that the main foyer was empty of others. Odd, he thought, for the middle of the day. "It's been quiet around here without me?"

"Yes, Colonel. It's been quiet and cold. Do you think they'll ever fix the heat for this part of the building, sir?" asked the soldier.

"I'll ask the building supervisor when I see him. If that doesn't work, then I'll make sure I mention it to my sister's husband. Maybe he can get something done about this for you. But I'll make sure he's in a good mood when I do. Otherwise, you'll be on your way to Murmansk for extended outdoor sentry duty. It's pretty cold there year round, from what I hear," Michail offered in jest. "Only kidding, soldier. Relax. I'll tell him I think it's too cold here and that we should do something about it."

"Your sister's husband, sir?"

"Yes, my sister, Elenya, is married to Comrade Chairman Romanov. If he can't get some heat in this lobby for us, then all is indeed lost."

The poor soldier did not know how to respond at the mention of The Chairman's name. He actually looked pale. "Breathe, soldier, breathe," grinned Michail. "Don't let the mention of the Chairman make you feel uneasy. He farts, picks his nose and snores like the rest of us. He just has a few more perks than the rest of us." Michail nodded and patted the young sentry on the shoulder and started through the inner doors that would take him up three flights of stairs to his office where he would check for any messages. He also hoped the short list of candidates would be there as well. He asked for photographs and profiles of operatives who might fit this mission. If he had enough material on hand, he could use the inspection of the information as an excuse to delay his trip north.

"Good morning, Comrade Colonel," chimed the directorate's secretary.

"And a good morning to you, too, private." responded Michail. "Is the director in yet?"

"Yes, sir. He arrived about an hour ago, actually."

"Is he, uh, looking for me?"

"He asked once and I, well sir, I must admit that I told a little white lie. I told him had checked in and were getting caught up on some files at home, sir."

"You weren't all that far off the mark, private. But thanks for getting him off my trail for a few minutes. I was actually visiting my sister."

"Oh? And how is she? She and I became kind of acquainted when she would call inquiring if you had yet returned," offered the soldier.

"Well, I received no bad reports from her on your phone demeanor, so I will thank you for being a voice of reason for her. When are you up for promotion? Should be soon, shouldn't it?" asked Michail.

"Well, Comrade Colonel, the next list is due out in May. I think I fared well on the test."

"Let me check with the Director. I believe he thinks very highly of you as well. Your kindness as well as your professional manners have been duly noted by all around here."

With that, Colonel Rostokovich hung up his coat, gave the desk clerk a kind smile and walked over to the Director's door and knocked.

"Come!" boomed the voice. "Michail? Is that you?"

Michail opened the door and answered, "Yes, Comrade Director, it is the prodigal son returned home. How are you today, sir?"

"I am well, Misha. Please, come, sit and dispense with the formalities. Your brother-in-law, our Chairman, has brought me up to speed already on that which you told him upon your return. But I'm sure there is more, yes?"

"Yes, Stephan Illyich. There is much more than I would dare tell The Chairman at this point. It is way too early and much too soon in this operation to, if you'll pardon my bluntness, to trust him with any of the actual particulars. He's been told that I've found a possible candidate. He's aware that we messengered back the photos. And that you have already tasked a select few to go through files and find some possible matches. He was the one who told me of the trip to Murmansk and that a few possible candidates will be at our field office there awaiting orders. I take it you set the matching process in motion and obtained some fairly quick results?"

"That we did, Michail. That we did. Here are the dossiers on the two leading prospects. There is a third who I think will work out well as our liaison."

Michail opened the first folder, as the Director opened his copy.

"This first man is Ivan Stansky. He's been one of our operatives for about three years. Studied at Oxford while his father was posted to the embassy in London. The major drawback is that while he is a good company man, he's still very tight with his family. Father and mother now reside in Luzon, on a full diplomatic pension and he's got two brothers currently attending the university in Moscow."

"Next is Dimitri Brischev. He's the one I think will work best as our point man. Six years in service. The last five in Berlin, worked very nicely as a double for us and the British. He's knows people in Eastern Europe you'd never want to meet in a dark alley and he's well respected by those who know his work. He's been what you might call an enigma. You see him one minute and the next he's blended in without a trace. He's there, but he's gone. Do you understand what I mean by that, Misha?"

Michail nodded. "Yes, Stephan, I do understand. It is a summary of what we have learned of the life of Mr. Moore. I remember working with this man Dimitri while getting some information on the Israelis a year or two ago. And you're right. This photo does not ring a bell. Is it recent?"

"Da. Taken last month when he came in for a debrief. He's very much a loner, too. No family and very few close friends. He's more than willing to cut whatever losses arise at a moments notice. No feelings. No attachments."

"His background?" asked Michail.

"He attended the University of California at Berkley for two years in the late sixties. Then, he returned here. While going through his military screening, his background came up what we might call very colorful. His association with several college radical groups was deemed an asset by the Directorate, so he came directly to us. They even made him an officer instead of grunting it out through the enlisted ranks for a year. It turned out to be a very good move on our part. He understands the Americans and he fits in comfortably wherever he goes."

"Lastly, there is Yevgeny Polnichy. He is my choice, without the benefit of having met or talked with him, to be the one. Visually, there's not even a need for surgery. According to what you've provided us on the American, Professor Hewes, they're exactly the same height, weight, general build and hair color. We'll need to stroke in a little distinguished gray on Yevgeny, but otherwise, he's more than adequate. Hewes is about two years older, but once we get Dimitri over there to work with you on reshaping the image of the professor turned politician, I believe no one will know Yevgeny is not M.Bradford Hewes."

"But Stephan Illyich..." interrupted Michail. "What of the basics?"

"Read on while I fill in some blanks." At that, Michail turned the pages of Yevgeny's dossier.

"Yevgeny was raised in Montreal where his parents both worked for the Ambassador. He was schooled in the English sector, as opposed to the French speaking quarters. He returned with his family before he was a teenager, so any links to anyone in North America were severed before a long-lasting bond would have been formed. After a few years in the university here, he was sent to Auburn University in the States. He just happened to major in History. He even worked on his thesis with research done two years earlier by your Mr. Hewes. What we have here, Misha, is the perfect man to replace, no, to become M.Bradford Hewes, our man in Washington. And with Dimitri to guide him along, getting the input from you, me and the Chairman, this should be a challenge that will bring results none of us could have imagined!"

"Stephan, relax. We've not yet spoken with these men. We really need to sit them down and feel them out before we think about telling them what we have in mind," Michail sighed. "When do you need me in Murmansk to meet with them?"

"Well, Misha, you know that the orders came straight from him that you be there today," Stephan replied. "Why do ask this again?"

"I've not been home in almost three months. That last trip to the States took up a lot of the winter."

Stephan laughed. "Yes, Michail, I know of this winter you spent in South Carolina. Let me see if my memory serves me correctly. Leisurely lunches at the marketplace down by the Customs House, a walk through the old district and along the, uh, Battery, right? Then a drive over the Cooper River Bridge to the sandy beaches of the Isle of Palms. Water temp this time of year about 68, maybe 70, Fahrenheit? Stop me if I'm off the track."

"Not that far off, Stephan, not that far off at all," Michail laughed in response. "But there are some, how can I best put this? Some pressing personal problems that I need to work on. I'd really rather say nothing more than that, with all due respect. I think a week at most would be of great help."

"You take these files and go over them. I'll reschedule your flight for forty-eight hours from now. That gives you two days. The best I can do under these circumstances. But it's more than The Chairman wanted. Being part of his family, however, I am sure we can allay any concerns he has for a couple of days."

"Thank you, Stephan. I'll go over these files. Already, I've got a good feeling about Yevgeny. And I think your instincts on Dimitri are on the money, too," Michail offered. "Let me get to work now and then I can devote some time to my other concern. Thank you, Comrade Director."

Michail stood, offered his hand, which Stephan took and returned the heartfelt handshake. Then, snapping to attention, Michail saluted Stephan, as is the respect deserved of rank and upon its return from General Stephan Janosky, Colonel Rostokovich turned and left the director's office.

He had indeed had good feelings about the two choices, Dimitri and Yevgeny. Dimitri was an operative of the highest order. His previous assignments had produced higher than expected results and he appeared to be meticulous when it came to getting the job done. Yevgeny was eerily alike, if not actually akin, to M. Bradford Hewes. They say everyone has a twin, but this was perhaps too good to be true.

With his mind made up, Michail decided it was time to go home and take another shower. And maybe some more quality time with Stasya. She seemed to be especially playful earlier. No, playful was not the proper word. More like downright horny, as the Americans like to say. With a smile on his face, Michail put on his overcoat, sealed the files in his valise, checked out with the private at the desk and left to take care of some very urgent business. Brother-in-law cum Chairman of The Union or not, someone was about to get a good, verbal ass-whoopin', as they say in the American south.

twelve

"Gentlemen, now that you've successfully finished your training here at O.C.S. Newport, I have the privilege of sending your asses out into the fleet. And heaven help us all!"

With that, the small class of graduating Ensigns laughed and lined up for their certificates of completion and orders. Each accepted his commissioning certificate and gold ensign bars from Admiral Daryl Bullinger, the school's commanding officer. The group had graduated from various institutions of higher learning from around the country and had come from a variety of backgrounds. What led them to the Navy is another question that could go forever without being answered. Most would head their separate ways, maybe crossing paths on a port call someday, or taking class at the War College down the road.

There were, however, four newly commissioned Ensigns who were actually able to continue their little "buddy system" they had started several months back. Ensigns Nelson, Michaud, Hough and Singletary were clumped together in line, as had become the custom anywhere they went. Whether it was a downtown Newport bar, or on the deck of a misappropriated sloop that might have belonged to an Admiral of some standing in the U.S.Navy, or in the brig where they waited to explain how they might have gotten that aforementioned sloop halfway down Long Island Sound before they were discovered by the SAR team the Admiral had personally dispatched to find them, they were pretty tight. Now, somehow, the U.S.Navy had seen it as a plus towards retention if these four were granted their request of proximity duty, if not actually together.

Nelson was bound for the Communications Station at Naval Station Charleston. Michaud had been assigned to the U.S.S. Affray, a minesweeper. Hough and Singletary were both bound for the U.S.S. Sierra, a tender-supply ship, which also served as the flag ship for the Commander, Submarine Group Two. Both ships currently homeported in Charleston.

The south might never be the same with the arrival of Michaud, Singletary and Hough, but the saving grace would be Ensign L.Bud Nelson. Ivy League trained as he was and being so enamored of his three Yankee-bred running mates as he had become, Bud's humble, down-home, Mississippi background would bring a balance to the natural order of things. He might at least be able to explain to the local constabulary the odd affectations of his three friends of Yankee descent, which, in all likelyhood, would inevitably bring undo attention upon them. People from up north will, no matter how hard they try, still be people from up north. Ensign Chuck Michaud looked at this situation as unique. His view was that they had a built-in translator. A man who could, while spitting, look cool. collected and be able to "y'all" their way out of any jam. Ensign Don Hough and Ensign Fred Singletary figured if they were going to do the Navy thing together, there was always safety in numbers. Plus, the four had become fast friends in just the first few weeks of O.C.S.

Now it was time to check out of their quarters and decide whether to head south together early in order to stake out the new territory that would officially be known as South Carolina, but have the added distinction of being their new playground. Or they could head home to their respective native locales for a little family time before dropping anchor on the muddy Cooper River.

As Michaud was the only one with a significant other waiting back in the Worcester, Massachusetts area, he was headed north for a little leave time before reporting to his ship, Nelson, Hough and Singletary chose to head down I-95 and set up house. As they'd done their research, Naval Station Charleston was home to a good number of submarines that set out for regular ninety-day patrols, but also it was homeport to more than a few Naval Reserve Force ships, of which the Sierra and Affray were two. The NRF ships usually only made a once-a-month weekend journey out past Two-Charlie, the furthest buoy at the head of Charleston Harbor, into open waters and out into the Virginia Capes or Jacksonville operational areas. The ships' manning levels would be increased on these weekend excursions by the members of the ships' reserve force, otherwise know as the "weekend warriors." The rest of the time, the NRF ships would be secured to the pier with all the comforts of home, primarily plenty of electricity and hot water. For the regular crews of these ships, they'd found that the Navy was indeed a job and not just an adventure. Sure, once a week they'd have to stay on-board to serve as that day's duty officer, but otherwise, it's basically a nine-to-five job. Actually, it was more like an eight-to-four, from morning quarters to liberty call. Still, that meant they'd be able to use their monthly pay and an allowance for quarters to set up house off-base.

Bud, Don and Fred collected Chuck's share of the deposits they'd need to rent a place and bid him a fond, but temporary, farewell. Chuck loaded his bags into his green '73 Triumph, tooted the horn a few times and zipped out of Naval Station Newport headed for route 24 north towards Massachusetts. Bud, Don and Fred had decided on a convoy that would have them rolling down Interstate 95 with a stopover in Maryland at the B.O.Q. near Annapolis. It's a free night's accommodation, plus they'd be able to grab a meal or two in the mess hall gratis. They were carrying their share of student loans and like any recent college grad, were watching every penny. Following the lead of Mr. Michaud, the three boot ensigns began their trip south towards the land of magnolias, antebellum mansions and cypress trees.

thirteen

"Hewes here," said Brad as he answered his phone, "how can I help you this fine day?" He leaned back in his chair, set his feet on his desk and grabbed a pen and notepad. "Yes, Senator. Yes, Senator. I see what you mean, Jerry. Yes, I think we can get those two swing votes on that later today. Oh, you hadn't heard? We got asked from "the top," if you get my drift, to push this thing through so y'all can get it through committee and out for a vote next week. That's right, Jerry. They want this thing put to bed before the attorney general has any more opportunities to rake The Chief's butt over the coals again. I think you know how I feel about that stuff, anyway." At this point, the Speaker chuckled and added, "That's right, lettin' the little head do the thinkin' for the big one. Yes, Jerry, we'll make sure you've got the package on your desk for morning coffee Monday, okay? Great! My best to Arlene and have a great weekend. Right. Bye, now."

Hewes hung up the phone and marveled at how easily things could get done when you've got the power seat. Or in Seinfeldian terms, when you've "got hand." Gotta have hand in order to get through life. Unfortunately for President Griffen, if he'd only stuck to his own hand, he might not be under the scrutiny of that relentless Attorney General Vernon. But the "master of one's domain" was another issue for another day. Hewes checked his appointment book and saw that he was pretty much free for the rest of the day. But he would have to make sure that they took the call for the vote on HR 1557, the sweeping medical care package, that of which the good Senator Jerry Bonanno from the great state of New York had inquired and Hewes had promised for Monday morning. Not a problem, not when you're the Speaker of the House, soon to be the President. It had taken over twenty years to get this far and things were in as a good a position as any to proceed.

The sitting President was a judge's gavel away from an assault conviction, which would lead to resignation, at which point, the vice president would be unfortunate enough to suffer a fatal m.i. as well as a collapsed lung en route to the White House from whichever primary-election campaign stop he might be visiting at the time of the announcement. Granted, the primary season was still almost two years away, but Vice President Fulton had started early.

Dimitri had managed to take care of ensuring Fulton's impending myocardial infarction two years ago when he'd pulled a few strings and helped to hand-pick the V.P.'s security detail. That was easy enough for Assistant Secretary of State Marvin Moore, who just happened to have an attempt made on his life, only to have it thwarted by one of the agents assigned to protect Secretary of State Paparelli. The agents had been hand picked for this assignment, but not from a recruitment class at Quantico. No, they were actually hand-picked from a training class outside of Moscow many years ago, by a senior KGB officer and then given instructions by Romanov himself, pretty much the same way both Marvin/Dimitri and M.Bradford/Yevgeny had been chosen. And so, the agent who had taken a bullet was rewarded for his heroic action and the secretary of state agreed that these two, fine agents could better serve the country if they were to be closer to the top and were assigned to Vice President Donald Fulton's personal detail.

Hewes was still not sure where things would go from that point. Dimitri had been with him every step of the way since that day in Murmansk when they met with Colonel Rostokovich. They accepted this mission over twenty years ago with the ultimate goal being for Mother Russia to assume the power seat. The Colonel had told them what they needed to know as they needed to know it. The last contact with Michail had been a little less than a month ago, when the President's personal problems had become those of the country. At that point, he had not given the go ahead to the final phase of this operation, much to the dismay of Dimitri. Yevgeny was all but dumbstruck at the possibility of this mission coming to an end. Dimitri reminded him that it was not an end, but merely the beginning of something bigger than either of them would be able to fully comprehend. But, both Yevgeny and Dimitri had been reassured of their roles, not only in the new establishment that would be empowered in the United States, but also of their roles in history.

At that, M.Bradford Hewes picked up his phone and called his assistant to see if the chamber held enough members of Congress for a quorum call. After all, they had several pieces of legislation to work on this afternoon, including HR 1557, the medical care funding bill, which had been promised to the senior Senator from New York. Yes, thought Brad, this power stuff was something to which he had become accustomed and would not soon wish to relinquish.

fourteen

Michail pulled his car into his parking space at the apartment building and let the car run for a moment or two before turning it off. Sometimes, just a minute or two of idling would help keep enough of a charge in the battery and thereby guaranteeing a better chance of the car starting next time out. The cold winds did a number on these little Russian cars as it was. This, hopefully, was a hedge against a dead battery. Michail had another stop to make before he left this particular technological marvel here for what could be a very long time.

Turning off the car, he pocketed the key and stepped back out into the chilly April zephyr that just did not want to stop. He was actually looking forward to an extended period in the American south. April in South Carolina could be like July here in Moscow. Daytime highs in the 70's, with the overnights a comfortable 55 or so. And the ocean temperatures could easily hit 70 on a nice, sunny day. Once again, he bundled up against the wind and made his way to the relative warmth of his building's lobby. He stepped into the elevator and waited for the inevitable clunk that would follow the closing of the door. It wouldn't have surprised him if one day the elevator went into a fifteen foot freefall down into the service pit half a level below the basement. However, he was more pleased that the ancient machine decided to do as it was asked and began its ascent to the tenth floor.

As he stepped off the elevator, his thoughts turned to the lovely Anastasia and the previous evening's homecoming. Yes, he thought, another night like that would be more than welcome. This time, however, the door to his apartment was locked. He fished his keys out of his coat pocket and opened the door.

"Stasya? Hello?" His calls went unanswered as he took his coat off and hung it up in his usual fashion, over the back of the sofa. He walked out into the kitchen and saw the note on the counter. He picked it up, read it and then crumpled it up and tossed it into the trash. She was gone this time. And this time, she explained that she'd be gone for a while. Business. And since they were in the same business, Michail knew that "for a while" could be for a long, long time, as he was about to experience that aspect of this profession firsthand.

He left the kitchen and proceeded to the room that served as his study. He'd made arrangements with his command and control headquarters to come by weekly and check on things in the apartment. Now, he carefully arranged his files in one neat stack in the corner of the room and took out his tape measure. The files he had here were sensitive enough in most respects that it would cause a great deal of difficulty for some people in very high places if the contents of these folders were to become public knowledge. These files were his safety net. His "get out of jail free" card, if you will. He'd committed the most sensitive of his materials, case by case, to memory, as was his training. He took the latest files he'd been given by both Aleksandr and Stephan and added them to the collection.

Now, he'd use some of this afternoon to build his own little "fortress of solitude," lest any of these files fall into the wrong hands while he's away on this next, prolonged assignment. He wrote his measurements down and proceeded to cut what is commonly passed off as a building grade two by four. He figured he'd just build a small enclosure on the inside corner. Cover it up with some wallboard and slap a fresh coat or two of paint on the whole room.

About two hours later, he'd put the first coat of paint on the new enclosure. He'd not bothered taping the seams. The rest of the room had a chipped and unfinished look about it, so the corners not being perfect would help to keep any undo attention from being directed that way. He'd hinged the bottom twelve inch section so it would lift upward from the rug, allowing him to insert materials as he needed. Plus, he'd intended to leave the extra heat-holes he'd poked into the walls exposed. No sense in passing up a little extra free warmth when you could grab it.

He stepped back to admire his work and agreed to himself the rest of the room could use a quick coat of paint to finish the project. He'd need to let the first coat on the new corner enclosure dry first, so he went back to the kitchen and grabbed what passed for a bottle of beer. He then made a quick call to his sister to tell her he'd be by for a visit and some fun time with the kids afterwards. The relief in her voice spoke the remainder of the unspoken volumes that had been implied by their earlier conversation. He asked briefly about their older brother and she mentioned she'd not heard from him in a while. Michail finished the conversation by promising he would see her for dinner. Yeah, Comrade Chairman brother-in-law was going to get a wake up call from a non-Orwellian big brother.

fifteen

In Charleston, South Carolina, it was a glorious summer-like spring day. Blue sky with only a wisp of a cloud here and there and a gentle breeze off the waters of the Atlantic, warmed by the Gulf Stream that made the ocean waters welcoming to swimmers. Don and Fred were used to the uncertainties of New England in April, where one day it could be sunny and 70 degrees, the next, 35 with a bone-chilling breeze along with a "snow event" that could produce up to eighteen wet and heavy inches of the white stuff. Fortunately for the two northerners, they had their own interpreter/guide in the person of L.Bud.

Bud grew up a child of the deep south. Born and raised in the Mississippi Delta, he knew what hot was and knew how to say it in just the right words. His folks still lived in the house in Biloxi, right on the water's edge of the Gulf of Mexico. Mr. and Mrs. Harold Nelson were proud of their little "Bud." They'd made the trip to Clemson to see Larry graduate magna cum laude. Bud was the first of their family to graduate from college, with a degree in Political

82

Science. But he'd done so on an ROTC scholarship, which required him to attend O.C.S. upon completion of his undergraduate studies and then onto a hitch in the U.S.Navy. The Navy seemed a natural choice to Bud. He'd grown up on the water, working when he could with his father's shrimp operation. It was just one boat, but it was the only life that not just Bud's dad, but the others in their little community on the Gulf, knew. They'd be out before the sunrise and would hit the piers of Biloxi to offload around the time the sun went down. There'd be days when he'd rather skip school and go out for the day, but, his father was a strict disciplinarian when it came to education. So, Bud remained attentive to his studies and with his nose firmly in the books, he graduated in the top five of his high school class. The class ranking, along with his family's meager income, helped him grab an almost-full scholarship to Clemson. The ROTC commitment helped cover the rest of the costs, as well as providing some additional income through his active-reserve status in the Navy.

While at Clemson, he didn't really form any lasting friendships, but did cultivate more than a few serious acquaintances. These were his fellow students who came from deep south big money families, the kind that knew where the door to the "back room" was and could easily walk in and set their feet up while adding their ideas to the shaping of political futures. Bud didn't necessarily have high political ambitions, but he was not ready to remove himself from the potential avenues of opportunity associated with that world.

He did recall a young grad student who was a teaching assistant with the history program who managed to get Bud, a true believer in America and all it stood for, to at least consider things from the point of view of the Russians at the time of their revolution and shift to Stalinism. What caught Bud's attention most was this young man's ability to impart not just knowledge, but an objective passion for the knowledge, not necessarily the ideas therein contained. Bud remembered thinking that this was a communicator of the highest order and an intelligent one as well. In America, that could be a great thing! In American politics, that combination could be dynamite. It would be the first time of many that Bud would find he possessed an above average sense of foresight. The idea that crossed Bud's mind at that time was that this young man was going places.

It turns out that the young teaching assistant at Clemson University in the early 70's would indeed be going places. First to Congress in 1976 as an out-of-nowhere candidate who swept the Charleston congressional district in his first ever political contest. And subsequently to the office of the Speaker of the House of Representatives less than twenty years later.

Bud, Don and Fred rolled into Charleston three days after they'd set out from Newport in their little three car caravan, past the magnolias that lined both sides of I-26 and through the accompanying crescendo of the cicadas whose drone seems to coincide with high levels of temperatures and humidity. They took their time on the way south, stopping for a few nights of revelry in Washington, D.C.'s trendy Georgetown section. This day was indeed what many a native of the North would consider a stiflingly hot day, yet to those of the climes south of the Mason-Dixon line, it was simply another day of tall iced teas and easy conversation.

As they pulled off the highway, both Don and Fred had to double-take the strand of trees at the bottom of the ramp. Yes, they figured they'd arrived in the tropics as they gaped at the palm trees springing out of the well-trimmed and manicured lawns of this little section of North Charleston. Fortunately, before they'd be able to publicly make one of many gaffes that would instantly identify them as Yankees, Bud would set them straight on the proper term of palmetto tree.

They pulled into the gas station just off the highway's exit and figured they'd take advantage of some cheap gas and a chance to stretch their legs before they finished the last five miles or so to the base.

"Boys," bellowed Bud, "Welcome to the true south, where the men are gentle, the women are sweet and the cockroaches are palmetto bugs."

"What the hell is a palmetto bug?" inquired Fred.

"A palmetto bug is a roach. Big, ugly, hard to kill but laid back, like most everyone and everything down here," replied Bud. "This is a whole new way of life for you, so start getting used to it. Don, I can see you looking for the man who might be coming out here to pump some gas. Stop looking. He'll be here when he gets here. You won't find much in the way of fast paced motion around these parts, unless of course, you're fixin' to stomp one of those palmetto bugs. Then, my friend, you'll see motion."

At that, the proprietor ambled out to the pumps and nodded an easy hello. The three all requested fill-ups and with that, the man set to taking care of business while Don offered to buy the tonics.

"Don, Don, Don," sighed Bud. "You may buy me a soda if you'd like. Tonic is what you put on your hair down here. You wanna drink tonic? Go back to Maine, you inbred hick."

The subsequent laughter even brought a smile to the gas man's face, who'd no doubt heard similar exchanges in the past. His was the gas station at the exit for the Charleston Naval Shipyard and many a young man and woman from up north came for a fill-up and a drink. And yes, even he had taken it upon himself to act as de facto translator for these fine service people. There are those area natives who have no use whatsoever for the interlopers from the North. Yet, there are many others who recognize the basic face value of U.S. currency and that these sailors got a wallet full of it twice a month. Why not extend the hand of friendship, especially when it involves the regular exchange of money.

"Son, if you'd rather have a tea, there's a pitcher on the desk in there," offered gas man as he looked to Bud.

"I'm much obliged, sir, but the two wayward sons of the north here have infected me with their penchant for carbonated beverages and I'm almost ashamed to admit that I might have to reacquire my taste for real tea," Bud responded sheepishly. He was actually somewhat crimson around the ears, embarrassed to admit that he might have become "Yank-ified."

At that moment, a small red Fiat pulled into the gas station, top down and driven by a very attractive woman. Don and Fred both stared at Bud as he strolled up to the car and started a conversation with the lady. The Fiat had North Carolina plates on it and from the looks of things, Bud had the situation well under control. The woman had an unfolded road map and she and Bud were exchanging ideas, as that was probably the best either could do, although Nelson appeared more fluent in the lay of the land here in the Charleston area than she. A few more nods, a couple of points down the road and what looked like a business card slipped into the ready grasp of Bud, the lady backed away from the pump and back out onto the main road.

"Gentlemen," exuded Bud, "She is also newly moving to this area and I'm proud to say that I'm her first local friend. Yes, this Charleston duty is going to suit me just fine, thank you very much!"

Fred was staring at Bud and inquired "You mean to say you got her name and a phone number just for helping out with directions? How does she know you're not some kind of ax murderer or something?"

"Fred, she doesn't know about the ax murder thing, at least not yet. And besides, I believe the statute of limitations expires tomorrow on that unfounded charge. Really," Bud continued, "Her name, according to this card, is Annie Fidrych, newly appointed marketing manager for First South Bank and Trust here in Charleston. Said she's moving here from up around Raleigh-Durham. From what I could make out, though, she's definitely not a southern gal. More of a northern Michigan, upper peninsula thing working on the accent. My guess is a trace of Slavic in there somewhere."

"Well, Bud, from the looks of things, she's got the nice end of the Slavic looks. And that auburn hair just does so much for me!" added Don. "You sure know how to make yourself at home."

"That, my friends, is what southern hospitality is all about. Yessir, it's good to be back down here where the charms of a well-heeled man are not lost on women of obvious taste."

At that, Fred burst out laughing, "Bud, you are many things, but well is not one of them."

The gas man by now had finished the filling up of the three cars and after a quick rundown of the station's service bay hours, which did include Saturday mornings, the three exchanged handshakes with the proprietor and resumed their convoy to Naval Station Charleston.

sixteen

Washington, DC   Friday, April 3, 1998   2:45pm (local)

President John Griffen sat back in his chair to catch his breath, if only for a moment. Of late, things had been what one might call "downright crappy." The allegations of improper relationships were earth-shaking for him. The fact that somehow, someone had managed to get one of the younger ladies on the White House staff to actually testify at the hastily arranged preliminary hearing, believably, under oath, that the CEO of the United States had indeed acted not only improperly with her, but in ways that some consider overtly beyond the norms of acceptable sexual behavior. Others, especially the late-night talk show hosts, have taken to using the first fifteen minutes of their shows to lambaste him. The past five of seven Top Ten Lists had been about him and his alleged sexcapades. Well, thought Jay, if only it were true, at least there'd be some way for him to rid himself of a little tension. Unfortunately, all of the heart-to-hearts with his wife of twenty-four years, Anne Marie, registered nothing on the marital scale. She, like the rest of the nation, was truly believing the story of record. That the President had sexually attacked a young, attractive White House office assistant on a night when the First

Lady was out of town. Now, the calls for him to resign over this alleged incident had him looking for a lifeline of any sort.

That was when the private line in the Oval Office rang. Only family members and a chosen few of his staff had the number. And of late, the family hadn't been calling. He glanced at the caller i.d. screen and saw that it was one of his best buds, as well as his Communications Director, Bud Nelson.

"Speak to me, Bud," commanded the President.

"Sir, I've been doing a little non-descript brainstorming with my own little cadre of compadres. Nothing that wasn't already common knowledge for them, but it should be of major concern to us," Nelson replied. "Are you going to be at the office this evening? I've got a few things to go over with you and secure or not, this phone and your office is not the place to discuss anything further."

"Bud, are you trying to tell me this place is wired by someone other than us?" asked the President incredulously.

"Mr. President, let me put it this way. Remember our meeting yesterday? I heard a recording of my voice not two hours ago. This recording was made from a phone call to a Maine radio station at about four-thirty this morning. Fortunately for us, as far as we know, this call was the only one made, or at least given more than a sleepy shrug-off. We are also fortunate that the call was made to one of my best friends, Don Hough."

"Your friend from your Navy days, correct?" inquired President Griffen.

"Yes sir, the one and only," responded Bud. "He, Fred Singletary and Chuck Michaud are all privy to what is going on. All three, if you remember that campaign swing through Maine a few years back, are my running mates from the Navy. And to be honest, I'd trust them with state secrets more than I'd trust anyone from State, with all due respect to Ms. Paparelli's crew. But again, I'd rather we discuss this particular situation further when I get back to town. I have a feeling that secure and encrypted ain't what it used to be right now. I think I've probably said more than I should have at this point."

"I concur, Bud. Wrap up what you've got going on there and get back here as fast as you can."

"Uh, sir. Are you still doing the quasi-bachelor thing? If so, I'll grab you a little Downeast feast for a late supper," offered Nelson.

"That would be great, Bud. Thanks. For everything."

The President hung up the phone and called over to Dan Josten, his chief of staff.

"Danny. I need you to get John Realto and an NSA sweep team here. Now. And thanks."

If there was a bug in this office, the team would find it. They knew where all of the recording devices authorized by the President were in this office. All of the devices were supposedly secure, with a direct recording link from each to the master communications relay on this floor, which went directly to the NSA bunker in the White House sub-basement. There, each days' office activity were recorded directly to a digital master disc, complete with a copy guard coding that would reveal any attempts to edit or tamper with the master, as well as preventing any duplication whatsoever. The House and Senate had both signed off on this system as a fail-safe to one side or an other possibly altering whatever events transpired within the Oval Office on any particular day. This system, actually, had been in operation for the past two years, but it was known only to the select NSA communications team, the President's closest circle of advisors and the leaders of the House and Senate. This system, as well, might be the one saving grace the President had in dealing with the impending mess that would undoubtedly be tagged with the suffix "gate." The playback of the time frame in question on the Oval Office video had the young lady just out of camera range and showed President Griffen running to where she was positioned near the door. The thing that Lindsey Dean, Jay's personal attorney, had latched onto was that the screams preceded the running. There was, though, one little hitch in that defense. The sound of the screams followed by Jay's heavy footfalls were for some inexplicable reason not in sync with the motion of the video. They would have a tough time explaining in a court of law how a multi-million dollar surveillance system would pick that one moment to malfunction. The NSA was prepared to testify that the problem may have existed for some time before, as they've not yet had a reason to pull up one of the digital files for review since after the system was installed.

The pundits had all taken their best shots at giving Jay's situation a catchy nick-name, but nothing so far had stuck. President John Francis Griffen was not going to go gently into that good night, nor was he going to maintain his pride in the face of shame. There was nothing of which he should be ashamed. And he was damned sure going to go kicking and screaming if the truth be damned and he were to be ousted by a tale even more frightful, to him at least, than one spun by the master of the macabre, Stephen King.

seventeen

Finishing their shore dinners in the quaint dining room of the Lobster Shack, Michaud, Singletary, Hough and Nelson were sharing a few more light moments before the return trip to Michaud's studios, then to the Portland Jetport for Nelson's return flight to Washington.

Michaud was in the middle of one of his notorious anecdotes, which most people refer to as a soliloquy. With Chuck, it was never brief and often left those within hearing distance in need of an antidote.

"Chucker," interjected Fred, "We've both got businesses to run, so how's about we finish up this tale on the ride back to your shop. Bud needs to get a copy of that call to bring back to work with him and, since the President would like him back at work as soon as possible, we should probably not keep too many important people waiting."

"Fred, I didn't vote for the man and even though he's keeping our mutual friend here gainfully employed, he can wait while I finish this story. And these clams. And Bud's lobster."

"Men, we can let the Chucker finish," said Bud. "The Boss would like me to bring him back a shore dinner, so I've got to go place the order first. And I have to hope they have one of those insulated bags to carry the darn thing in. Nothin' worse than cold lobster and steamers. Especially when you're hand-delivering them to the President."

Bud walked up to the counter to place the order. The three friends began to rehash all they'd been privy to since the early morning.

Don was first to inquire "So, men, what the hell can we determine about all this?"

"I figure it this way," Fred opined, "That the former head of the former Soviet Union came up with a pretty ingenious plan to usurp the power of the political system of the United States, if not in fact actually take over and correct the error of our imperialist, capitalist ways. Now, Bud, the President and a few others, us included, are in on the scheme courtesy of one former KGB operative-slash-very pissed off ex-brother-in-law. But the questions that beg to be answered now are: Who wanted this op to become public knowledge to the point of obtaining high-quality, first generation, actual sound of the briefing Bud gave to the President and his inner-circle types? Or, who wants those present at that meeting to know that the actual making of the knowledge public is only a dime away?"

"Uh, Fred, I know you're a master of finance and all, but phone calls are up to a quarter in most places now."

"Chuck, thank you ever so much for the update. Don't you have a few fries left in that pile of rubble to finish off?"

"As a matter of fact, I do! Better not leave any for the gulls. It's 'gainst the law 'round he-aah to feed any of them gulls, doncha know."

"Man, your Maine accent still sucks!"

"Yessir, that it does. But gory, don't them folks from away love t'he-aah it on they-ah commercials. It's my biggest sell-ah, by gum."

Don was at this point shaking his head. "Chucker, some day, in the great scheme of things, some angel from on high will swoop down upon us all and send you straight to Biddeford."

"Ayuh. Biddeford, Maine. Only place on the planet where you can find college professors and mill workers speaking the same language, some of the time, them, eh?"

"Methinks you've spent too much time at Rapid Rays. It would be in your good luck that it's right across the street from Bud's old summertime crash pad on Factory Island."

"Yes, Don. But remember, Rapid Rays is a Saco establishment. Not like one of those Biddeford emporiums of gluttony. Saco, on the banks of the scenic Saco River. Where all currents lead to Wormwoods by the Sea. Now there is one of the best kept secrets on the east coast!"

Fred had to call an end to this. "Gentlemen, we're off the subject here. Can we focus for a minute? Bud is trying to help an innocent man from being fed to the wolves and here you two sit arguing the merits of one of Maine's much-maligned and under-appreciated twin-cities."

Bud walked back to the table and took a seat, catching the tail end of the exchange. "Another diatribe on Saco on the Saco?"

"You got it, Bud. Good thing these boys weren't drinking or they'd be fixing to engage in fisticuffs."

Maine has several communities built up on the banks of her rivers, the more powerful of the rivers hosting sets of twin-cities who built their commerce on millwork utilizing the strong and swift currents of the rivers. In the northeast, many of the workers who operated these mills migrated southward from the Canadian Maritimes, with a resulting local language that crossed between Acadian French and Downeast Yankee. The Acadian is not all that different from a Louisiana Cajun accent, but mixed with the heavy New England flavor and desire for proper grammar, the Franglais that emerged in these Maine communities oft times resulted with most sentences being concluded with a modifying pronoun. It is this unique language trait that has kept these tightly woven communities considered as objects of derision by those who deem themselves "above" such malapropism. Unbeknownst to these uppity sots, they're missing out on some of the best of what certain areas of Maine have to offer. Although some of those yuppie flatlanders did catch on when they tried to have Biddeford Pool established as their own little town in their failed secession movement.

Bud and Don had a unique fondness for Biddeford and Saco. Bud for its unique New England charm and Don because its proximity to his hometown of Kennebunkport. Chuck didn't necessarily hold the twin cities in disdain; he found reason to deride many things and people, just on principle. If anything, his own French heritage gave him a kinship with the majority ethnic populace. Fred merely wanted to help bring some of this discussion back into focus. Plus, he well knew that Don and Chuck could go for hours and that in itself was enough to send Bud right off the charts. Nelson feels that time is fleeting, so much to the point that if you can't explain something in, oh, twelve seconds, then it didn't need explaining in the first place.

"Okay, Fred. We get it. We get it. Bud's in jam here. From what we've heard, the President's being set up for a big fall and Vice President Fulton is being measured for a coffin, all to help the alleged Speaker of The House move into the White House via the Constitutional line of succession. The problem here is two-fold. One, the President is facing the prospect of resigning in disgrace over the tryst-that-never-was. Bud needs to gather all of the facts as he has them in an attempt to help the President build a defense against those who would love to see him gone from the picture, post-haste. Two, how do they manage to head off the assassination of the VP, while taking down Mr. Comrade Speaker at the same time."

"Chucker," Fred responded, "You've actually been paying attention. I'm really impressed."

"I'm not always talking without listening..."

"Naw. Usually just talking though!" added Don with a laugh. "The President and Bud are definitely on the same team. That leaves who, the NSA? What was his name again?"

Fred refreshed their memories. "NSA is John Realto. He's a holdover from the previous administration. Worked as a White House liaison to several Senate subcommittees and came highly recommended to Griffen during the transition. I don't think he's a problem.

"The CIA director is William Terrio, the guy Bud called on the way out here."

Bud took over from there, nodding to Fred. "He's got family here in Maine, if I'm not mistaken. He's been a company man for years, with a brief stint at State during the Bush administration. He'd apparently done some work with Bush during George's tenure as Director. So, when George became President, Terrio got the nod as an assistant undersecretary. This way, the Oval office had a direct pipeline to State. No spinning or filtering. Then, once the Bush team was finished, they offered Billy a slot back at Langley as the Ops guy.

"During Griffen's transition, the President-elect picked the brains of Bush, Ford and Carter on those they knew who were still in the loop. Apparently, the words were more than kind from Bush, so much so that President Griffen appointed Terrio as the head and that was one of several nominations that breezed through confirmation."

"Then that leaves Vice President Fulton," interjected Chuck.

"Correct! Michaud wins a cigar... oh, never mind, you've already got one," laughed Fred.

Don then offered "Fulton was, what? A civic leader in Charleston when we there in the Navy?"

As Michaud started to answer, Bud got back up, having gotten a wave from the counter that his order-to-go was ready.

"I do believe he was President of First South Bank and Trust, Don." Chuck imparted his own knowledge of the subject. "He was elected Governor of South Carolina within two years of our arrival and was the sitting Governor until President Griffen asked him to be his running mate for the '96 election. Wasn't that sweet young thing Bud was seeing for a while part of his organization? Yeah, it was that stunning Annie whats-her-name."

"Fidrych," Don reminded Chuck. "She was the director of marketing for First South and then became one of Fulton's campaign managers. She was on his staff in Columbia and she's still part of the VP's crew in Washington."

"Does Bud still see her?" asked Fred. "She was, if I remember, quite the fox."

"How '70's of you, Fred. Fox?" commented Chuck

"Chucker, Fox or Babe or Schwing-Magnet or whatever, she was a fine looking lady," Fred responded. "But maybe we've got some kind of connection here. Between Fulton and Hewes?"

"From what I can recall, Fred, Fulton and Hewes are not the best of buddies, even though both hail from the great state of South Carolina." Don then continued, "I believe that, at most, Hewes has had polite words for his fellow South Carolinian, but not much more than that. Both men are good party men, right down the line. Fulton the Democrat and Hewes the Republican. Beyond that, though, from what we've seen, they aren't what you'd call birds-of-a-feather."

"Let's ask Bud about the connection, though. It seems to be the one thread that might pull this thing together," suggested Fred. "That's the cast of characters in this little play to this point. Of course, there are bound to be more. A lot more."

Bud was holding a large, red insulated bag as he stepped from the counter to the edge of the dining area and motioned to the three to follow, indicating it was time to move on. They caught up to Bud at the stairs heading down to the parking area and all piled into Fred's car for the ride back to Michaud's office.

"Bud," Don started, "We've thrown around a few ideas for you to think on for a few minutes and you've heard a few. Fred, you're the rational one here...."

Chuck interrupted "Yeah. And you're the quiet one, Bud's the cute one and I'm the goofy one! Christ, we're just like the Beatles!"

As if on cue, the other three intoned Chuck to "SHUT UP!." Enjoying another much-needed good laugh, Fred summed up what the three of them had been able to piece together. Bud listened and for once, so did Michaud.

eighteen

Murmansk, Russia   April 8, 1976

Rostokovich was cold. He thought it had been cold in Moscow four days ago, but these past 72 hours in this frost-bitten tip of the Earth was about 71 hours more than he cared to endure, ever again if he could help it. His assessment of the operatives for this mission was on the money. Dimitri Brishev was every bit as sharp and bright as the files had indicated. And in person, Yevgeny Polnichy was a spitting-image of Professor Hewes. Michail had to make this trip, though, regardless. The Chairman had insisted.

The Chairman had also taken off his "Boss" hat for a few minutes and was actually receptive to his brother-in-law's concerns over the well being of Elenya and the children. It went smoother than Michail had anticipated, but then again, his brother-in-law was still a politician and that is what really good pols do best. Placate and redirect. Michail hoped, though, that Chairman Aleksandr Romanov would remember how to be the adept role-juggling master he was just a few short years ago: that of loving husband, doting father and head of the largest country in the world, The Union of Soviet Socialist Republics.

As Rostokovich stepped from his car at the airfield, the winds whipped up once again and cut right through the four layers of clothing he'd put on for protection. Not much protection at this point, but the saving grace was that the skies were blue and the sun was shining. That meant that the flight that would whisk them off to Oslo would be leaving on time and without any problems or delays.

Once in Oslo, Yevgeny would have some minor surgery around his eyes and nose to correct the slight differences in appearance between he and Hewes. After that, they'd have precious little time to get the rest of the operation rolling.

The language aspects, though, were less of a problem than any of them had expected. Yevgeny and Dimitri both spoke flawless English and both had the ability to drop in the American regional accents as needed, whether it was the Olde English with a New England flair, or the dripping, easy-going drawl of the south. The latter was what was called for, although in the case of Yevgeny, he'd not have to slap it on as thick. Hewes, after all, had spent enough time in academia around those who did not posses the drawl many thought quaint. It takes work on any level to avoid regional affectations on speech and the southern drawl or the southwestern twang seem to be the easiest for most to pick up. Conversely, it is not all that hard for those looking to avoid this pattern to do so.

Brad Hewes was a clear, easily understood speaker. He was also a powerful, compelling speaker. This was the area on which Yevgeny would have to work. Yevgeny was not an exact vocal match for Hewes, but Michail had a plan for that problem to all but correct itself. It wasn't that Yevgeny lacked confidence. He just did not possess the level that Hewes did.

Dimitri would be perfect as the figurative and literal, campaign manager. Dimitri Bishev was cocksure and steady, much more than his files and fitness reports would lead one to believe. It was indeed fortuitous for both Michail and Dimitri that Dimitri was picked as a candidate for this operation. Otherwise, he'd likely have spent an undistinguished career, performing admirably, but without the recognition and honor he'd be more than capable of bringing to the KGB and the USSR.

Michail, Yevgeny and Dimitri all stepped toward the waiting aircraft. Along with the favorable weather, the other bright side to this whole trek was that they weren't flying Aeroflot. They'd be doing direct to Oslo, but not before their flight plan would take them south by several hundred miles, so that their approach would be more from Moscow than from over the Arctic Circle.

Coming in under a diplomatic cover to Oslo, they'd want to call as little attention to themselves as possible. They would, of course, be watched from the moment they landed in Norway, until they went into the Soviet Embassy there. The United States and other European intelligence organizations would have their operatives keeping track of anyone coming into a country where they have field offices, as would the Soviet Union. It was how the game was played.

The trick would be getting Yevgeny and Dimitri out of the Embassy without being seen once Yevgeny's surgery was completed. The initial phase involved the reconstructive surgery. Again, it would be a minor procedure, but would require Yevgeny to remain in the embassy for several weeks. They'd need time to allow the incisions to heal. Since Yevgeny and Dimitri would be traveling to the States via commercial airlines, that would require trips through customs. The customs inspectors in many of the larger, more organized countries might tend to want a closer look at someone bearing any telltale signs of recent surgery. The thought being that there must be reason why this person has had his or her facial features redesigned; something to hide. Once questions are asked, or additional attention is paid to these individuals, they'd be marked for surveillance for the remainder of their journey. For Dimitri and Yevgeny, that is the last thing Rostokovich desired at this point. There would be enough time in the future for people to pay extra attention to Yevgeny, soon to be M.Bradford Hewes, candidate for United States Congress. As well, they'd no doubt sit up and take notice of the Hewes for Congress campaign manager, Marvin Moore, formerly known as Dimitri.

The current plan was that Michail would see to the remaining details about Yevgeny's surgery and to make sure that all the proper documentation would be handled properly and expertly. Michail already had several passports at his disposal, all of which had safely gotten him in and out of every country he's set foot in, all without the slightest hint of a problem. Dimitri and Yevgeny both had several travel packets that they'd used on various assignments. This time, they needed to start fresh so that their one-time entry might be noted, but then those identities would be gone forever. Dimitri's new identity of Marvin Moore had been already established. The information which Dimitri would study over the next week or so was contained in a very thick file on Marvin Moore. There were also audio and video tapes for review which would help Dimitri further adopt his new nom du guerre, so to speak. Michail had studied the folder's contents once already since the material was made available to him at the end of February, just before his trip to South Carolina. Since they were on a private, military jet and the three were the only passengers on board, Michail thought it would be a good time to review the material for himself and preview it for Dimitri and Yevgeny. The written details of how the necessary information had been obtained in that small house in upstate New York were disturbing. But not nearly as disturbing as hearing and seeing the actual procedure on the videotapes. The methods employed by the two advance operatives were effective, yet brutal. There would be time enough for Dimitri and Yevgeny to watch the tapes in Oslo. For now, some lighter reading would suffice.

Rostokovich closed the file and looked at the two agents. They had taken it in stride, professionally.

"The rest of the session in the farmhouse went fairly well. Mr. D, as he's referred to in the files here is Mr. Dayle. And, as you will see on the videotape when we arrive at the embassy, Mr. D takes a few liberties with Moore's fingers. The information we obtained from Moore is invaluable. He was able to provide us with dirt on some current people of stature. He also told us everything that we needed to know about who might one day walk up to you, Yevgeny, on the street and challenge your identity. That one point is the one on which we needed to be absolutely sure."

"Colonel," Dimitri spoke. "What happened to the real Moore? I mean, I'm sure he was terminated, but just curious as to how."

"Dimitri, you'll see the entire session, through to its conclusion, on the videotape. You'll also see how Mr. Bello, Mr. B in the reports, got his nickname of Lungboy. A pneumothorax is an ugly thing to inflict on a person. Fortunately, Mr. Dayle was satisfied enough with Mr. Moore's responses and the quality of the data, that he gave Moore a knockout dose of the sodium-pentathol before the infliction of the big needle containing nothing but air."

Michail pressed the intercom button for the plane's cockpit.

"Captain, how much longer until we arrive in Oslo?"

"We're still about ninety minutes out, Colonel," came the pilot's reply.

"Thank you, comrade Captain."

Then, turning to Yevgeny and Dimitri, he said, "I suggest we all grab a quick nap. There's lots to be done when we land and Yevgeny, you'll need to get prepped for surgery. Dimitri, you may go over the materials of Marvin Moore as often as you need, but both of you must remember that we're on a fairly tight schedule. Yevgeny, we'll work on feeding you some of your information while you are sleeping. The idea of sleep teaching is not scientifically proven, but when combined with the level of recall you have, it'll make the material seem more familiar each time you scan it. I'll be heading to South Carolina once I see the initial results of your surgery. We should be able to provide you with audio, video and written transcripts of the Hewes interviews within the week. Hopefully by then, you'll be up for spending some quality time with the new materials. And even with the real Mr. Hewes."

"Are Dayle and Bello involved in the Hewes operation?" inquired Dimitri.

"Yes, Dimitri, they are. And I've arranged with the Directorate for them to be permanently assigned to your security staff. They will be good men to have on our side as this operation progresses. Now, please, let's work on grabbing a power nap before we land."

At that, the three men stood up from the small sectional-type sofa at the rear of this cabin and went to the fixed, conventional airline-style seats. Michail pressed the recline button on his chair.

The plane they were in was a converted Soviet Air Force troop transport. It had been outfitted with five rows of comfortable seats, two on each side of the plane, with a small conference area set up behind the last row. It might almost be considered a first-class section, especially compared to what passed for first class on Aeroflot, the Rodney Dangerfield of commercial airlines. Aeroflot truly deserved "gettin' no respect." The rear of this plane was equipped with folding jump seats for up to one hundred enlisted troops. The plane could, if needed, serve as a delivery vehicle for airborne troops.

As he began to doze, Michail thought of Anastasia. They were inseparable when they first teamed together. Their first assignment was shortly after both left the enlisted ranks of the Soviet Army. They had met in language school in Moscow and were put together by a random combination. It was on this first mission that they became friends while working one leg of a multiple part drop in West Berlin, the American sector.

Their initial cover was as lovers, out for an evening stroll that took them by the Brandenberg Gate. It was there, while in a passionate embrace that caught the attention of several passers-by that Michail fell in heavy "like." For Anastasia, however, the embrace and the kiss were just part of the job. At least at first.

They had seen the drop go down at an empty table of a sidewalk cafe just off the square. They strolled over and seated themselves, with Anastasia putting the newspaper-wrapped document pack into her denim shoulder bag. They were only going to order coffee, but Michail was so smitten that he asked for a vintage bottle of wine. Anastasia gently protested, as if to remind Michail that they had a schedule to keep with the next leg of the drop a few blocks away. Michail nodded his agreement with her assessment of the situation, but still, poured the wine when it was delivered to the table. He smiled a knowing smile to the waiter as he handed him a wad of Deutch Marks and returned his undivided attention to the current lust of his life. They only had the one glass of wine each while seated and departed the sidewalk cafe with the bottle and glasses in hand. They talked of simple things. Spring. Flowers. The mountains. The lakes. And did so in perfect German. To any who saw them or heard them, they were a couple in love, enjoying a lovely evening in Berlin. After they made their drop, it was back to their hotel with the separate, but adjoining rooms.

Thinking of their overt cover for that mission always made Michail laugh. Marketing Directors for General Motors. They had easily convinced the somewhat incredulous desk clerk that GM was going to attempt to make inroads in the German automobile market. Germany, after all, was home to the world's finest motorcars, such as Mercedes-Benz, BMW and even Volkswagen. Michail found this assignment's cover story ironic as, were it true, they would both probably be wealthy beyond the dreams of any red-blooded capitalist. And who knows, maybe they'd be married, with a big house and a couple of kids.

Instead, both stayed in the service of Mother Russia and now, five years later, they were often too busy on their own assignments to spend any real time together. It was the time that they could spend together that Michail truly enjoyed, on all levels,. especially the physical.

His airborne dream soon turned to skating with his three year old nephew and namesake Michail, while Elenya and one year old Christina watched from the warming hut. This was always one of Rostokovich's favorite things, in his whole world, to do. But the dream of late had been taking an eerie turn. Michail would skate over to the warming hut to join his mother and sister for a quick hot chocolate break and suddenly the warming hut was engulfed in flames. The propane fueled space heater had apparently exploded. The screams were always real enough in this dream to wake him up. This time was no exception.

He awoke, brow covered in a cold sheen of sweat to hear the plane's engines powering down to begin their descent into Oslo. Michail brought his seatback up and reached over to nudge Yevgeny on the outer seat. Yevgeny in turn woke up Dimitri and both men rubbed the sleep from their eyes as they brought their seatbacks up. In the service of the KGB, or any other organization involved in activities that run twenty-four hours a day, seven days a week, you grab the sleep when and where you can. The comfortable bed was a luxury, as was a hot shower and a cold beer. All three of these things were waiting for them, however, in the embassy of the Soviet Union in Oslo. They'd be landing in a few minutes and with their diplomatic pouches secured, it'd be a quick stroll through customs and into a waiting limousine to take them on their way.

The plane touched down gently at the airport in Oslo, Norway. The flight itself had taken almost five hours. Given the light load of the aircraft, it was able to do it without stopping to refuel. The extra time was due to the evasive course they took.

The flight plan brought them southeast out of the Arctic Circle, down out of the range of air traffic radar in Finland. Then, once they were just north of Moscow and somewhat parallel to Helsinki, they were able to head west northwest towards Oslo.

Had they traveled in a direct line from Murmansk to Oslo, the trip would have taken merely a few hours and actually would have had them arrive just about the time departed, thanks to the two hour time zone difference. That course, however, would have brought them to the attention of more than just the air traffic controllers along the route.

A Soviet aircraft, under diplomatic cover, originating from a remote city such as Murmansk might have sent up one too many red flags. The Directorate and Chairman as well, had insisted on as little attention as possible. So far, so good, at least as far as Michail was concerned on this mission.

The plane taxied up to the international terminal at Oslo Airport. The exit ramp rolled out to meet them and took only a moment for the flight's engineer to open the exit door. The three men stepped out into the brisk, April evening, bundled against the cold with their drab, gray greatcoats and warm, fur-lined gloves. Warmer weather would be slow to arrive here. Michail was pleasantly surprised that it wasn't much colder than Moscow and there was no fresh snowfall here to amplify the chill.

The three men stepped down the stairs and saw an airport ramp attendant waving them towards an open door. The attendant was just inside the door, holding it slightly ajar. Michail nodded to the man and gestured to his two traveling companions to follow him. All three walked through the door, diplomatic passports and valises in hand and were ushered through the concourse towards a customs inspector on the far right hand side of the terminal.

Theirs was the only flight being processed at the moment and the three men exchanged pleasantries, in Norwegian, with the customs man. They merely presented their diplomatic passports for inspection and showed the agent their valises, all of which carried a diplomatic seal. This prevented the agent, under international arrangements, from opening their briefcases for inspection. The agent smiled and asked if they had any other luggage and Michail explained that their personal belongings had arrived at the Soviet Embassy ahead of them. Wishing them all a pleasant stay, the passports were stamped, returned to the three men and the agent sent them on their way.

Stepping out of the airport, they were met by a waiting Mercedes and driver. The driver snapped to attention, but Michail merely gave a cursory nod of acknowledgment and directed his eyes towards the vehicle's rear door. The driver returned the nod and opened the door for the three travelers. They settled into the spacious rear seat and Dimitri noted how much nicer a Mercedes was compared to the Soviet-made and issued claptraps that passed for automobiles. Yevgeny softly chided Dimitri with a clucking of his tongue and a gentle side to side nod of the head.

"Ah, Dimitri. Already you are being swept up in the charms of Western Capitalism. What will do with you when we get to America?"

Dimitri softly replied, "Get me a large house with a TWO car garage?"

"Boys, now let's not get too far ahead of ourselves here," came a directive warning from Michail. The two look at the Colonel, as he gave an almost-imperceptible nod of the head towards the driver. "I think that things of this nature will be better suited for discussion at a future time."

They nodded their agreement and glanced out the windows at the city of Oslo rolling by them. They saw the palace of King Olav, then crossed over a bridge spanning one of the many rivers that fed the very busy harbor of Oslo. They pulled up to the gates of the Soviet Embassy, where a uniformed corporal opened the gate and waved them through with a salute.

The Mercedes pulled up to a side portico, flanked on the side by a thick hedgerow. This prevented any unwelcome views from the side street that bordered the Soviet Embassy compound. The three men climbed out of the driver's side, nearest the entrance and stepped through the door, into the relative calm and safety of the stately building.

Rostokovich took care of the introductions with the night duty officer and a private was instructed to take Dimitri and Yevgeny to their respective rooms. The Colonel was taken to a service elevator off the kitchen area, which took him two levels down below the building's main floor. Once here, he stepped out and faced a steel door with an electronic cipher lock. Entering the six digit code, the door opened and buzzed to alert those on the other side that someone was coming into the communications center.

Once again, Michail made a proper introduction and presented his authentic credentials for cursory inspection. The young Captain on duty acknowledged the younger Colonel with a sharp salute and directed Michail to a secure room which contained an encrypted phone. Michail checked his watch and called his brother-in-law, Comrade Chairman Aleksandr Romanov's private, secure line in the Kremlin. The conversation was brief and Michail was given the go ahead to proceed. Rostokovich exited the secure room, thanked the Captain and proceeded back up to the living area of the dwelling, where he was shown to his room. He wasted no time in taking a quick, hot shower and crawled into bed. His flight schedule over the next week would be understatedly busy. As he tossed the plan around in his head, he thought of Anastasia and drifted contentedly off to sleep.

Outside the embassy, the entire arrival scene was captured on film by a Norwegian national, working under private contract with the Norwegian intelligence service. In turn, the information garnered would be shared with other intelligence agencies who had allied themselves under the umbrella of NATO.

The photographer had shot a dozen quick frames of what he assumed was merely another ordinary arrival of an embassy staff member. Of course, at most embassies, staff members are usually associated with the intelligence organizations of their respective countries. Just who or what would be revealed in the photos would be ascertained by the photo surveillance operations crews who would handle this film. The shots would be enlarged and enhanced to the point where a facial image might be brought out enough to clarify the individual's identity. Information on where and when the photo was taken would be compared with known arrivals from data compiled at train stations, ship embarkation points and airports, as well as highway border checkpoints.

What might be gleaned from this arrival would probably be thought ordinary. The various agencies involved would piece together that the three Soviet citizens who had arrived at Oslo Airport, under diplomatic cover, less than an hour before these photos were taken, were most likely the occupants of this particular vehicle. The arrival and clearance through customs was noted as three Soviet Embassy staff personnel arriving on official embassy business. The names given matched the passports. And a check of known diplomatic personnel assigned to this particular embassy showed the names of all three. The other foreign service intelligence groups investigating this arrival would no doubt be aware that the three names were simply "house names." Identities adopted by any agent who wished his or her arrival to be noted as less than remarkable.

The resolution of the photos, though, would produce three full-facial shots. Two of them obtained with a zoom lens as they alit the car on the way into the building. The third facial image, not quite clear enough for a positive identification due to the heavily tinted automobile glass. All three photos would be checked against photographs of known Soviet intelligence assets. This would not be a setback to the groups trying to put names and faces together, but in hindsight, it would have been a major discovery towards preventing the steps that were about to be taken against America and her government. The first two photographs would be matched with files covering two known KGB agents.

Had the third photograph been matched with a name, that would have been the first and only, to this point, known positive identification of one KGB Colonel Michail Rostokovich. His name was known, yet an accurate description was unavailable to all of the foreign service agencies whose work keeps their particular group in an opposition status.

Thus far in his career as an intelligence operative and now, high ranking officer, Rostokovich had managed to remain enigmatic. He'd been seen, but never matched with his position. He'd been mere feet away from known agents of opposing intelligence groups and given only a polite smile or a nod as he'd walked by, a normal, common occurrence on a busy street or inside a crowded airport terminal. This fact has been to his benefit so far. His comings and goings to various foreign countries, including the United States, had been done openly. With his letter-perfect documentation, he'd been able to adopt whatever persona du jour he needed. And it had also been possible thanks, in no small way, to a goodly amount of luck.

nineteen

The boys had decided to pool their resources and car pool to the base each day, as often as they could. The beach house they'd found out on the Isle of Palms was a bachelor's dream palace. Four bedrooms, kitchen, two full bathrooms, plus a dining area, overly large living room and one extremely spacious two-level deck built off the beach side of the house. The living room on the first level was equipped with sliding doors to allow easy, beach level access to the bottom deck, which one-stepped directly to the sand. The upper level deck offered three access points from the house. One from a center hallway and the other two from different bedrooms. The rental agreement had them in for a year, renewable each April. But it didn't come cheap. The monthly rate was one-thousand dollars and that didn't include utilities. The four had agreed that the amount was workable, considering they'd receive an allowance for quarters and "comrats," or an allowance for food, each month, on top of their salary. Ensigns in the United States Navy weren't necessarily rolling in the dough, but it was more than any of them had made to this point in their young lives.

When they approached the main gate, the Marine sentry on duty glanced at the front bumper of Don's Chevy Malibu, saw the blue decal and promptly snapped to attention, gesturing for them to stop for an I.D.. check. The four, all dressed in their khakis, had their wallets open and their Navy issued identification up for inspection. The corporal leaned down to check the cards of the four young officers and waved them through the gate, while snapping a sharp salute. Don returned the salute and they drove on the base.

Their first stop was the communications center where Bud had been assigned. Shore duty for a boot ensign was a genuine stroke of luck and as usual, Nelson had stepped into it graciously.

Climbing out of the car, Bud leaned in and said, "Boys, you all have a fine day serving my country on those most excellent ocean going vessels, y'hear?"

Michaud flipped Nelson a one fingered salute, which left Don and Fred chortling.

"Oh, I forgot about that flat-bottom thing you're on, Chucker. Wooden decks and tight quarters, right? Hey, boys, what say we meet for lunch over by the O club?"

"Sure, Bud, so long as you're buying," responded Chuck.

"Now, now, Mr. Michaud. We're all on a budget here. If you want me to treat, I'm afraid it'll be at the roach coach or the sauerkraut guy," Bud replied.

"Never mind him, Bud. Just try to stop reminding him that the Affray actually does go out to sea. And that it's got that wooden, flat bottom," offered Fred. "You know how seasick he gets."

"Yeah. Just last night, I got sick seeing Bud come out of the shower," Chuck said.

At that, they all laughed and Bud walked down the path through the well-groomed lawn towards the front entrance of the comm center.

Don pulled the car away from the curb and headed off towards Pier Quebec, mooring point for the Affray. The station's piers were lettered and Q was the last one in line.

The base was actually on the Cooper River, about four miles from Charleston Harbor and close to six miles from open sea. This was a benefit for the Navy, as it kept the ships from being in the direct path of any hurricane that might come in off the Gulf Stream.

The Cooper River was a busy little waterway. Way upriver there were a series of paper and pulp mills, whose hallmark for the boys onboard the ships downriver and downwind was the odor. The pulp making process produced a bad cabbage like smell, which was none too appetizing when one stepped out of doors each morning. The level of odor was amplified by the amount of beer a young sailor might have imbibed the night before.

Also upriver but before the paper mills, was the Naval Weapons Station, where ships would go to load up on shells for the big guns, as well as torpedoes, anti-submarine rockets for the ASROC launchers, tomahawk missiles which were featured on the new Perry-class frigates, plus conventional bullets for the various smaller caliber weapons on board; everything from handguns to computer-guided Gatling-type machine guns. It was also where the submarines stationed here would go to load, or reload, her ICBM tubes.

Don eased the car to a stop at the end of pier Q and said "Okay, Chuck, out you go. Keep us safe for democracy today, willya?"

Chuck grumbled his response and hopped out of the backseat.

Fred asked "Will we see you for lunch? 1130 hours or so?"

"I'll see if the oxymoronically-named 'Old Man' will let me off for lunch. You know how these headstrong lieutenant commanders are," Chuck answered.

"Well, why not bring him along?" asked Don. "The guy's gotta eat, right?"

"Don, unlike the Sierra, the floating, somewhat welded hulk up there on pier Mike, the Affray here does not have a heavy contingent of officers. There's the skipper, the x.o. and the engineer. I'm lower than low on this command, so I suppose that if they say we eat on board, then we eat on board. I'll try to make it. And thanks for the ride."

Chuck gave Don and Fred a quick wave, put on his hat and strolled towards the pier sentry shack. The Affray was the only ship currently tied up here and the boys were hoping that the current engine problems she was having would be enough to keep Chuck here with them for a bit. If the Navy came through with the funding, the little minesweeper would be off to Norfolk for a new engine and then possibly a shift in homeport to Portland, Maine. Chuck was torn over the possibility. Portland, Maine was only a two and a half hour drive from Worcester and Sue. But here was his chance for a little adventure, with the financial support of Uncle Sam. Chuck stepped quickly up the metal gangplank, snapped a sharp salute towards the stern where the colors were posted and a sharp salute to the officer of the deck, in this case a first class machinist mate. He then stepped onto the Affray and into the ship's superstructure for another day as the operations assistant.

Don drove the short distance along the edge of the parking area provided for the sailors who opted to live off-base. Most of the enlisted men here were married, with wives and kids and houses and lawns and car payments. It was peacetime and the availability of base housing made it easier for most of the men to get a head start on life after the Navy, although most had found it a decent way of life and many made the Navy their life. Put in twenty years, retire with pay and benefits, all by the age of 40 for most and you still had time to go out and live.

There was an officer's parking area up by the main entrance to the pier complex and Don wheeled the Malibu into an open spot. He and Fred got out and didn't bother to roll up the windows or lock the doors. It was going to be a nice, hot spring day here in Charleston and neither of them seemed to care. Their work stations onboard the Sierra were air conditioned. Fred had been assigned to the personnel office, while Don was given to operations. Don's area was cooled due to the communications equipment. Fred's was cooled due to the new computer equipment installed to help support ComSubGru2, the Admiral in charge of the submarine group stationed here at Charleston.

Don and Fred put on their hats, walked towards the pier and past the manned-sentry shack. Here, there was a sailor on duty to keep an eye on things, unlike the empty sentry shack down at pier Q. Fred grabbed a quarter from his pocket and grabbed a newspaper from the honor box next to the sentry shack. The front page featured a photo of Georgia governor Jimmy Carter, who was in Charleston for the day on a campaign swing. For whatever reason, this seemingly kind and genteel man wanted to be the President of the United States.

"How are the Sox doing?" asked Don.

"How the hell do you think they're doing, Donny?" was Fred's reply. "It's April and they're three games up on the Yankees. But don't worry, the season's still young and you know how they do after they've been to the World Series. Lousy."

"So what's the big story today?"

"The governor of Georgia is running for President. And plans are being readied for Spoletto, whatever the hell that is."

"It's an arts festival. You know, music, paintings, interpretive dance. Crap like that."

"Yeah, Donny boy, a true patron of the arts you are."

"That's me. When I'm not dropping quarters to the old guy with an accordion at Park Street Under, I'm taking in the latest Peter Max exhibit. I am a top shelf contributor to the arts and a true patron saint of free expression."

"Okay, Mister First Amendment. Think we should get up there and go to work?"

"Careful, Fred. Calling what we do 'work' will give the enlisted men who signed on for adventure the wrong idea."

"Most of them are still stuck in the backup at the main gate. I don't think we'll passing many wrong ideas about adventures here, my friend."

The two started up the forward gangplank, reserved for officers. It was more of a set of stairs that doubled back on itself, as the main deck of the U.S.S. Sierra was probably a good thirty feet up when the ship was tied dockside at even a low tide. The Cooper River is tidal, so the ships would rise and fall with the tides. At high tide, the climb would be an additional five feet or so. At the top of the metal stairway, there would be a gangplank secured to the landing at the top of the stairs and then to the ship to allow for the height differences. The two junior ensigns stopped at the edge of the gangplank, saluted the aft section of the ship where the Stars & Stripes would soon be flying and then saluted the officer of the deck. Unlike the Affray, the officer of the deck on the Sierra was an officer. In this case, one of the other ensigns who had the overnight watch sleepily returned their salute and granted them permission to come aboard. They exchanged brief greetings and Don and Fred went down to the officers wardroom to grab a cup of coffee and, if there were any left, a danish. Then it would be time for morning quarters. In school, you'd call it attendance. Only a note from home in the event of an absence wouldn't be sufficient for excusing.

Once quarters was concluded and the flag was raised on board the ship for the day, the crew would turn to their assigned duties for the day. Thus the business of the U.S.Navy was done.

On board the Sierra, it was always a busy day. It was here that the crewmen of the other ships and boats would come for routine items such as haircuts or dental work. Yes, there were facilities on the base that handled these tasks, but most times a divisional petty officer, or the supervisor, would only be inclined to let you cross the pier for a haircut.

The dental facility on board was kind of a satellite office. Simple procedures such as cleanings or checkups could be handled here, as well as minor invasive applications such as fillings or x-rays.

There was also a doctor on board the Sierra, as opposed to a non-commissioned officer on board the smaller ships who would serve as the "doc." The non-com was trained to a level of a good EMT, but the Sierra offered a bona fide med school graduate who could give you once over and then, if needed, a shot and a lecture on the proper use of protection while enjoying the company of a woman during a night on the beach. The base had a full clinic and Charleston was home to one of the finer Navy hospitals, so good medical care was readily available.

Don and Fred entered the wardroom and were surprised to find only Rear Admiral Gary Dericksen, Comsubgru2, seated at the large table. He was working on a cup of coffee and a big, gooey bear claw.

"Morning, boys."

"Good morning, sir," both said in respectful reply.

"What the hell is wrong with those Red Sox of yours? Coming off that World Series last year, I would've expected them to be six games up on the Yankees."

"Funny you should mention that, Admiral," Don piped in. "I was just bemoaning that very fact with Fred as we perused the sports page."

"Of course, sir, I did remind Ensign Hough here that it's only April and by September, we'll look back at being a mere three games out as having a chance."

"Singletary, are you sure you're not from Chicago? You sound like every Cubs fan I know, myself included."

"Actually, sir, I did spend some years in Waukegan."

The three laughed at their self-inflicted misery. Admiral Dericksen was originally from Washington State, but had adopted the Cubs as his team. He thought of them as his patron saints of lost causes. When things might look bad for him, or the men in his command, he'd remind them that it could be worse. If on a submarine patrol they found themselves caught in a sonobuoy pattern by the Soviets trying to pin down their location for targeting purposes, Dericksen would remark that at least they weren't the Cubbies.

"So, how you boys like this man's Navy so far?"

"Admiral, so far, so good," Fred offered. "Beats digging ditches. We," gesturing to himself and Don, "We got a good college education thanks to Uncle Sam. And now we're getting a little real life experience."

"Ensign Singletary, what do you consider "real life" about being confined in a metal container that could drop into an oceanic abyss several miles down, never to be found?"

"Well, sir, I, er, mean that we're getting some real life experience for, umm, management duties and such," Fred stammered.

"Relax, Singletary. I know what you were talking about. Just bustin' your chops, that's all. Hough, where'd you find this guy?"

"Newport, sir. We tried to lose him a few times, but he kept following us."

"Fred, you should relax and take a cue from Don, here. Don't let all this damn gold they make me wear fool you. I'm just a guy doing my job, too. I just happen to really love it. You may or may not love what you're doing a couple of years from now. Once your initial obligation's up, you'll probably take your degree and three solid years experience as a Naval officer into the private sector and land a nice job in the mid-fifties to start. Then, you'll deal with different types of people in power. Only power is such an ugly word. Those who wield it are not really deserving of it. If you go corporate when you do go your own way, make sure it's for a person who has to get up every morning and go to the bathroom. Not for someone who is so full of themselves that they have someone to go to the bathroom for them. Now grab a donut and a coffee and let me see the sports page, willya?"

Don and Fred each grabbed a pastry and coffee and sat down at the table with Admiral Dericksen. The Admiral grabbed the offered sports section, while Don took the front page section. Fred dug into the business section, which caught the Admiral's eye.

"Dabbling in the market, Fred?"

"Yes sir. I've had some luck with it over the past couple of years. I found a broker downtown the other day. I dropped a few bucks on Digital Equipment. They've got these smaller computers and they're using some software from a small company. Looks pretty promising. They've got a couple of programs out that we're demo'ing for them now. This new company is set up in New Mexico right now and already they're making waves."

"Is that the new computer system we've got set up in your office?"

"Yes sir. It's a smaller version of the old mainframes we've been using, but the operating software is really very easy to use. Sure beats trying to decipher COBAL or FORTRAN."

"Are you, um, offering me a stock tip, Singletary?"

"Only if you consider it unsolicited, sir. Digital is using this new stuff. But I haven't seen any info about an IPO. Microsoft is the name of the software company. I just got a hunch about them. So I gotta keep an eye open."

"Be careful, Admiral," Don said. "He had a hunch about the Ford Pinto, too."

"Thanks for the heads up, Hough. And thanks for the tip, Fred."

"Our pleasure, sir," the two answered simultaneously.

"So Don, where about in Kennebunkport are you from?"

"Sir?"

"You know, Kennebunkport? That little town on the Maine coast you call home? What part of the 'Port?"

"Well, sir, my family's home is right off Route 9. Right on the rocks at Turbat's Creek, as a matter of fact. Are you familiar with the area?"

"Yes, Hough, I am. My wife's family's from Wells. Spend a lot of time up that way whenever I get the chance. Met her while my first command was in the yard there at Kittery. There's a damned confusing situation that only New England could manage. They put the Portsmouth Naval Shipyard in Kittery, Maine. Go figure. But back to Kennebunkport. Nice little town. Love that restaurant right downtown. What's it called? Alisson's?"

"Yes, sir. That'd be the one. Good food and cold beer."

"Hough, we'll have to go out some night and do us some drinking."

"That's one direct order he'll have no problem following, Admiral," Fred said. "Drinking is one of the things he does best."

"Good. I knew I liked that Yankee spirit for a reason," Dericksen said.

At that, the three officers continued their perusal of the daily paper and enjoyed a second cup of coffee.

Later, Don and Fred met at the officer's gangplank to head out for lunch. The Admiral's staff car was waiting at the head of the pier and as if on cue, the Admiral came out of the bulkhead door, saluted the officer of the deck, then the aft section of the ship and was halfway down the stairs before the messenger of the watch could announce the departure of Comsubgru2 over the ship's p.a. system. Don and Fred informed the officer of the deck that they had permission to go ashore, saluted the O.O.D., the colors aft and headed down the gangplank.

When they got down to the bottom of the stairs, the Admiral was climbing into his vehicle and gave them a friendly wave. Flustered, Fred gave a half wave, half salute. Don threw the Admiral a salute and laughed at Fred. The Admiral had witnessed the exchange and, in not quite a yell, directed Hough to keep an eye on his shipmate.

"You know how them people from Chicago can be, ayuh," added the Admiral.

Fred turned a bright crimson from the neck up and Don just shook his head.

"Freddie, you gotta really lighten up. Don't let the extra stripes fool you. He's okay. He just happens to get paid a whole lot more than we do and he's got six submarines at his beck and call. But if we were to pull up to his backyard with a keg of beer, he'd be one of the first to get down and roll in the mud and squeal like a pig if meant having a good time."

"I know, Don, I know. I'm still shell-shocked from the L.T.'s who drilled us at O.C.S. Couple of them up there could use a weekend with the Commodore here."

"That's affirm, shippy, a big roger. Let's go find Michaud and meet up with Nelson at the O club for lunch."

The two ensigns walked sharply down the pier, returning each salute offered by the sailors who were coming down the pier towards their respective ships. It only took a few minutes to reach the Affray down at pier Quebec, where they found Chuck waiting on the quarter-deck, looking at his watch. They waved to him from the empty sentry shack and got his attention. Chuck did the snappy double-salute routine, stepped down the small gangplank to the pier and strolled up to meet his friends.

"What? No car? Don, you mean to tell me we're walking to the O club?" asked Michaud. "You know, boys, some of us actually work for a living. Your day probably started, where, the wardroom? Donuts and coffee? Maybe some polite small talk with who, your skipper? Maybe the Admiral? Then off to your little air conditioned offices. Me, I spent the morning supervising a couple of young seamen working on a broken oil pump. At least the engine room is near the water line. There was some relief. I need a beer."

"Are you done?" asked Don. "If so, let's walk off some of that frustration."

"So how did the Bruins do?" Chuck asked.

"I don't know, Chuck. The Admiral took the sports page before I had a chance to find out," Fred said.

At that, Chuck gave both Don and Fred a playful slap off the back their heads and the three walked down the street towards the Officer's Club where Bud was hopefully awaiting their arrival.

As they walked in the door, Bud gestured to them from a table near the front.

"Boys, how the hell are we?"

"Just fine, Bud. Just fine. Well, maybe not Chuck," Fred replied.

"A little too much time in the bilges, Ensign Michaud?" asked Bud.

"Aw gimme a break, will ya? Just shut up and buy a beer. No, better make that two beers," Chuck said.

From the hallway where the bathrooms were located walked Comsubgru2, Admiral Gary Dericksen.

"Afternoon, men!" smiled the Admiral.

"Sir. How 'bout those Red Sox?" asked Don.

"Don't get me started, Hough. Don't get me started." The Admiral flagged down the waitress. "Say, darling. These fine young men will dine on me this afternoon. Will you see to it that they're well taken care of?"

The waitress nodded her understanding and looked at the table.

"Gentlemen, I'll cover your meal and no more than two beers today. It's my pleasure and kind of a welcome aboard treat," the Admiral offered. "But no more than two beers. Understood?"

"Aye, aye, sir," came the reply in four-part harmony.

"Just remember that next time you see me on the beach, don't be afraid to say hi. And if we're in an establishment that serves any kind of liquid refreshment, order two of whatever you're drinking and send one my way. I've yet to meet a drink I didn't like."

"Thank you, sir," said Don. "I don't believe you've had the pleasure of meeting our roommates, Ensign Chuck Michaud,"

Bud and Chuck both stood and Chuck offered his hand. The Admiral gave him a healthy return handshake.

"And this is Ensign Bud Nelson."

"Pleased to meet you, sir," Bud said. "And may I apologize in advance for any and all transgressions perpetrated upon you and our Navy by our two illustrious sidekicks here. I do hope that incident with Admiral Bullinger's private launch will not be held against them in any decisions you may need to make regarding their respective futures as naval officers of the line."

"Admiral Darrell Bullinger? Up at Newport? What the hell did you do to his boat? He loves that thing."

Bud spoke as Don and Fred did their best to hide in plain sight.

"Well, sir. It was late. It was our last weekend at OCS. And the weather was unusually pleasant for March."

"How far did you get?" asked the Admiral, smiling.

"Not quite down to Groton. We hadn't realized that the current in Long Island Sound would carry an out-of-gas thirty-five footer that far."

"Why didn't you just call the Coasties for gas?"

"Never had the chance to call for help, sir. The Coasties, along with a small detachment of Marines were actually following us just after Newport Harbor. We never saw the mooring-alarm Admiral Bullinger had hooked up. Base security had started things shortly after we motored away from the pier."

"And for penance you had to...?"

"Let's just say that Admiral Bullinger's pride and joy is the most freshly painted thing in Newport Harbor."

"Thanks, Bud. Thanks a lot. Sir, I can assure you that..." Fred offered, but the Admiral shook his head and said,

"No need to worry, Fred. You either, Don. My launch is yours whenever it's available. Do me a favor, though. Ask me. And buy the bait. I know some great spots for fishing just past the Cooper River Bridge. Not all of us lifers are sons of bitches, boys. Even Bullinger is a hot shit, once you get to know him."

"Thanks for the offer, Admiral. And we'll keep it mind for the next duty-free weekend. What's your pleasure so we'll make sure we grab a six for you?" asked Don.

"Don, anything cold and frosty is fine by me. Never been picky. Just buy six more of whatever you all will be having and I'll help finish it. And by the way, thanks for telling me about the boat incident. It'll come in handy to help explain away any questions that come up during your b.i.'s."

"B.I.'s?" asked Fred. "You mean our background investigations for security?"

"Yes, Fred. NIS is working on them as we speak. Any red-flagged info will be forwarded up the chain to see if there is a plausible explanation so that you won't be rejected for proper clearances. And being newly commissioned ensigns, you all will need at least a TS. Bud, where are you assigned?"

"At the comm center, sir."

"And Chuck, what about you?"

"On board the Affray, sir."

"Bud, I'll speak to Commander Mike Griffin on your behalf this afternoon and make sure he knows about it. I'll be over there anyway. Chuck, who's the skipper of the Affray?"

"Lieutenant Commander Milsap, sir."

"Hmmm. Don't know him. What's the ship's extension over there?"

"5724, sir."

The Admiral took out a small notebook from his shirt pocket and wrote the number down.

"You said "Milsap," right?"

"Yes, Admiral. Lieutenant Commander Charles Milsap."

"Got it. Seriously, boys. One little thing like this without the whole story can keep you from getting a proper clearance and can not only keep you from a decent rate of advancement, but it will also seriously affect your duties. Bud, without a Top Secret clearance, at least, you'll be out of that building and supervising the base grounds crew in a flash. And for you three, being on board ship, you'll need to be cleared all the way up. If the old man is ashore and you're the duty officer, then it's imperative for you to know just what is what. Without that clearance, some punk seaman apprentice in the comm shack is going to be forced to wake up your skipper at two in the morning because you aren't cleared to receipt a TS message. And that makes for a very unhappy 'old man'."

"Thanks, sir. For lunch and the helping hand," Fred said.

"My pleasure. Now, I've wasted enough of your time, but just in time, here come the beers. Enjoy and carry on."

"Aye, aye, sir," came the simultaneous reply once again.

The Admiral walked back towards the table where his aide and another flag officer were waiting.

"Nice guy for an admiral," said Chuck. "I wish Commander Milsap could take a few human lessons from that guy."

"I wonder what Commander Griffin will say when the Admiral comes in to give him a heads up on me?" asked Bud. "It's good to have friends in high places. I knew you two would come in handy for something. To the Admiral!"

Bud hoisted his mug of beer in toast and the other three raised theirs also.

"To the Admiral."

Drinking their beer, they enjoyed a relaxing lunch and kept themselves amused with thoughts of Bud running the grounds crew at Naval Station Charleston.

"Boys, I gotta get me a new vehicle. My little '70 Impala just ain't going to make it much longer," Bud said.

"You got any money stashed away?" asked Chuck. "Wheels cost money, Bud."

"Got enough put away for a down payment, but I'm definitely going to have to go the finance route."

Don said, "The base credit union's got some new and used car loan programs. Decent rates. And they're right here."

"No, I may try them later. First, I think I'll try and see what the commercial banks have to offer. There's a First South right downtown."

"First South. Why does that sound familiar?" asked Fred.

"Remember the young red-haired lady with the business card and Bud's undivided attention at that gas station?" Don replied.

"Did I miss something here, guys?" Chuck asked.

Don spoke up "Yes, Chuck. Bud here took all of thirty seconds to score once we were physically stopped within the outer limits of the City of Charleston. There we were getting gas and a few "south lessons" when off the highway comes this very, very, very nice looking... did I mention nice looking... lady in a shiny new car. Bud sidles up and gives her directions and she hands him a card. Annie something or other. Last name doesn't matter much. It'll be Nelson before week's end, eh Bud?"

"No, I'm not looking for a marriage proposal here, boys. Just a car loan. And maybe a date for Friday night. And maybe Saturday night. And maybe Sunday..."

"We get it, Bud. We get it," Chuck cut in. "Go get your car loan and date. Then, find out if she's got any friends for Donny and Fred."

"What about you?   Staying-Mister-True-Blue-to-Sue?" asked Don.

"Well, yeah. I told you we're getting married."

"Eventually you were getting married. Is it now sooner than eventually?" asked Bud.

"Looks like it might be even sooner than we'd planned. We were talking next May, so we'd be able to work out getting our own place down here after the lease is up in April. But the old man said we're definitely heading up towards Norfolk, the Newport News shipyard for a two month engine job and then being reassigned to the Reserve Center in Portland, Maine. Should be in and settled by late August. So we're thinking about a Labor Day Weekend ceremony. You guys up for being there for me? I've asked my brother to be the best man. The family thing, you know."

"Mister Michaud," said Fred, "You firm it up, give us the date and the place and we'll be there."

"Gentlemen, I think this calls for another toast!" Bud said.

"As if we need an excuse?" added Don.

The four friends raised their mugs once again in salute.

"To Chuck and Sue. Bless her soul," said Fred.

"To Chuck and Sue," added the other two.

After their meal, with a second beer, on the admiral, thank you very much, the four left the Officer's Club and walked their way back to their work assignments.

Later that evening, back at the beach house, or as it was aptly nicknamed, The Casa du ChaCha, the four were cleaning up after an on-the-beach cookout. Burgers, dogs and cold beer. Typical bachelor fare. Chuck and Fred were doing dish duty, while Bud and Don were burying the coals from the hibachi.

Once the chores were done, Don, Fred and Chuck settled down to watch "Happy Days," while Bud was still working to settle into his room. He had a few boxes to unpack and brought one out onto the living room floor where he could sort the stuff out while keeping half an eye on the tube.

"What's in the box, Bud-man?" asked Chuck.

"Just some old notebooks from my last year of college. Couple of old cassettes of lectures I thought were worth keeping. Letters from old girlfriends, crap like that."

"Those old letters could be worth money someday," offered Don.

"Naw, bud. They're not worth anything. None of these ladies will ever amount to anything so that their 'early writings' would be of value," Bud said.

"Think you missed his point, Bud. They'll be worth something for you to pay to ensure that they don't fall into the wrong hands at an inopportune moment," laughed Fred.

"So it's the old blackmail game, eh? I might have been born in the dark, but it certainly wasn't last night. I catch on. Eventually."

"Speaking of catching on. How'd you make out down at First South? Get the car loan?" asked Don.

"They took some info from me and told me they'd get back to me."

"Well, Mr. N., did you bump into the marketing fox?" Don asked.

"Uhhm, let me think about whether or not I should answer that in light of our previous verbal exchange. Okay, long enough. Yes, I did. And yes, we are. Going out Friday night. She suggested a little restaurant down by the new marketplace."

"When do we get to meet her?" asked Chuck. "We need to make sure she's good enough for our little L-person."

"You have my total assurance that she's good enough for me. And you will NEVER meet her, if I can help it."

"Did you at least mention you were at the bank for a car loan? A good word from someone who works there and trusts you enough to go out with you on a Friday night after only your second meeting wouldn't hurt," Chuck added.

"Well, when she asks, as she did, "What are you doing here?," you tell her. And when she says she was hoping I'd find a reason to come by or call, as she also did, well, it's just nice to know that my sixth grade education wasn't going to go to waste."

"Speaking of budding relationships, Chuck, any more on the engine overhaul and move?" asked Fred.

"Looks like we'll be puttering or getting towed into Newport News before Memorial Day. They figure about eight weeks in the yard, then it's off to Portland. The skipper figures our first weekend warrior cruise will be the weekend after Labor Day. Talked with Sue and right now, we're planning on the last weekend in August. My C.O., by the way, does have a heart. He's offered to send me T.A.D. to the Reserve Center in Portland while the ship's in the shop. That'll give me time to get a place to live and make the wedding plans."

"What's so tough about your part in this matrimonial expedition?" Fred asked. "You just need to wear, what, a nice set of summer whites and comb your hair. Say 'I Do' or 'Yes Dear' or whatever lines she gives you. Then, when the party's over, go somewhere and have lots of sex."

"Something like that, yeah, Fred. Nice of you to simplify it for me."

"Seriously, when is the ceremony? And when do you need us there? Probably a couple of days ahead? We need to make arrangements at this end to get some time off and book a flight."

"The ceremony is the Saturday the 28th and we're planning the rehearsal for the night before, Friday the 27th. Think you guys could be in Boston sometime Thursday night or Friday morning? I'll pick you up at Logan and we'll take it from there."

"What time is the ceremony on Saturday? Is it early or later?" asked Don. "Gotta know whether we do the bachelor party thing here or up there."

Bud offered, "Let's do it up down here, before they make way for Virginia. She'll never know what went on and he won't be waiting at the end of the aisle in some church in Worcester with a blistering hangover on the morning of his wedding. No sense in ticking off the in-laws right off the bat."

"That's a real good idea. We'll invite the O's from the Affray and maybe the Admiral?" asked Don.

"Sure, why not. If we're gonna get locked up, we may as well have someone with enough gold to get us out of the poky," chuckled Bud.

"Now that that's settled, what time does "Starsky and Hutch" come on?" Chuck asked. "I think Bud needs to buy him a nice Ford, just like the *Striped Tomato*. Really stands out in the crowd."

"Gentlemen, the Ford Motor Company has, this year, in response to the overwhelming success of "Starsky and Hutch," decided to manufacture a limited number of the Grand Torino, outfitted just like the one on the show," Bud said. "Matter of fact, they just started rolling them off the line last month. Very nice machines indeed. A 351 V-8 engine, the paint job, the mirrors, the whole ball of wax. Not, however, very practical. And I am, if anything, practical. Plus, who needs to be driving a car that screams at the top of its lungs to any and all law enforcement officers to 'stop me if you can catch me'?"

"Gee, Bud. It'd would be fun to call you *Zebra 3*. And we're really hoping that you might be able to get one. Then you could give us all a ride. Really, really fast!"

"Chucker, you're the sports car guy here. That little green TR of yours is all the speed the rest of us here need. Heck, you even got out of the carpooling duties because the thing only seats two."

"Just planning ahead, Bud. Always plan ahead."

"So tell me, oh planner-ahead of events, what will you do with your pride and joy once the first little bundle of joy makes its arrival?"

"Well, Mr. Nelson. In this age of enlightenment in which we live, there is birth control, you know."

"We'll see. Just make sure you get a house with a garage. That'll be the compromise. 'You can keep the car for the summer, but we'll need a station wagon for the family.' I can hear it now, in her own voice."

Bud went back to sorting through the college box, putting some items in a trash pile and others to a keep pile. Typical guy. Can't throw it all away at once. Although, in fifteen years, he might have some left; in twenty, who knows what will remain and be of any use, other than the memories.

twenty

Scarborough, Maine   Friday, April 3, 1998   3:44pm (local)

Fred Singletary's Towncar pulled into the driveway at Michaud Media on Route One. Chuck had never really gotten a chance to get all of the snow out of the driveway and as is the norm, the town's snowplows had built up a pretty good wall of slush and snow chunks. Fred's Lincoln made light work of the impediment, confident that the slowly warming temperatures had softened the build up.

The four climbed out of the car and Chuck unlocked the front door.

"Wait here, boys. I'll be right down with the Shortcut. Bud, do you want me to make a copy on the JazzDisc? It'll only take a minute."

"That might not be a bad idea, Chucker. Do that for me? And lock the damn thing up. Use it as a get-me-out-of-jail-free card if we need it. And you know what else? Why don't you email that thing to my home address. Not the work one. Upload it as a .wav file. That way, I don't have to worry about not having the right application to open it up."

Chuck re-plugged in the Shortcut and powered it up. He really was very good at what he did.

He had moved to Maine when his ship, the Affray, was shifted to Portland as her new homeport back in the summer of 1976. His commanding officer had sent him to the Naval Reserve Center on Commercial Street under temporary orders. The temporary assignment allowed him to come north earlier than the rest of the Affray's crew and set up an apartment for him and his soon-to-be wife Sue.

They were married in August in a nice ceremony at St. John's Catholic Church in Worcester, Mass. Both his family and hers were from Worcester, making the location the logical choice.

Bud, Fred and Don had come north for the ceremony, as had the commanding officer of the Affray, Lieutenant Commander Charles Milsap and even Comsubgru2, Admiral Gary Dericksen. The guest list included those who came along for the ride the night of the bachelor outing in Charleston back in May before the Affray sailed north for the engine work in Virginia. And some newer friends Chuck had made in Portland.

The wedding was actually a very impressive sight, with all of the younger officers in their summer whites, with the same bar of ribbons on their left breast. The ribbons were in lieu of the commendation medals that are awarded to service members. A full-military honors type of ceremony would have had them wearing the actual medals.

The Admiral was the most impressive. His ribbons were spread out in five neat rows on his left breast. Plus, he wore the light blue ribbon of the Medal of Honor on his right breast, along with the purple ribbon indicating a Purple Heart.

The males of the wedding party were all in dress whites, save Chuck's brother, Rob, who wore a rented tux for the occasion.

Sue looked fabulous in her wedding gown and her attendants were all dressed in pastel greens. Her sister, Jennifer, was dressed in a pastel pink.

After a wild and fun wedding reception, Chuck and Sue piled into the little green Triumph TR6 and got onto Route 495 north for a week's getaway to Bar Harbor in Maine. They had already set up their apartment in Portland, actually just over the bridge in South

Portland. They figured they'd spend their wedding night in their own place and get a fresh start the next morning for their drive up the Maine coast.

The next couple of years went by quickly for Chuck, as the Affray's at-sea duties were minimal at best. The longest stretch was a two week underway period each summer when the reservists would come on board for their two week commitment.

They'd take a quick cruise out into the Gulf of Maine and run drills with the P-3 Orion sub-chasing aircraft from Brunswick Naval Airstation. Occasionally, the P-3's sonobuoys would catch a Soviet sub just off the Canada coast and the reservists would get a chance to really test their skills. It was a game of chicken. And it was certainly no fun for the crew on board the wooden "target" if the Soviets would go active with their targeting systems. The P-3 would then sweep low, going MAD and painting a pretty magnetic picture of the intruders with the magnetic anomaly detector. The, they'd drop one final sonar buoy, pinging away loud enough to let the visitors know that the home team had the final at-bat.

Chuck spent a lot of time running the Reserve Center's administration office, which helped him make some valuable contacts in the Portland business community. His duties had him acting as more of a de facto liaison and he had impressed a few people of stature with his communication skills. He had made a very close friend in Portland advertising superstar, David Botty. It was this relationship with Botty and Company that helped him eventually launch his audio production house, Michaud Media.

He and "the boys" had kept in regular contact, with them coming up for long weekends when there were flights available from Charleston to Brunswick. Plus, Chuck and Sue made a trek each of their first two springs together to Charleston for some r&r at the beach house on the Isle of Palms.

When Lieutenant (jg) Chuck Michaud finished his active duty commitment, he walked out the front door of the Reserve Center on Portland's Commercial Street and drove cross-town to the little radio station off Allen Avenue for his first post-navy professional gig. He worked there as an on-air announcer and, most importantly, production director. It was his duties in the off-air studios that helped him hone his ability to turn mere words and music into radio advertising magic. His talents were soon in demand by not just the advertising sales people at the radio station, but the ad agencies in town were all vying for his time, too.

That's when the decision was made to cut the string with radio and open up his own production house. With a promise of regular work from several high-profile agencies, including Botty and Company, Chuck left the twenty thousand dollar per year gig.

Within two years, his business was grossing over a hundred thousand dollars a year, with very minimal overhead. His voice was seemingly everywhere. If there was a furniture store somewhere in the country "going out of business ... forever!," it was a very strong possibility that Chuck was the announcer.

Then, in the 1992 Presidential election, Chuck got his best account. Ever. Governor John Francis Griffen of New Hampshire was running for President. Guiding the candidate on matters regarding media was one L.Bud Nelson. The money flowed freely for many, many months. Michaud was the voice of the party to elect Griffen for President. On radio. And on television.

With the profits realized from this one account alone, Chuck was able to invest modestly in a few companies on the cutting edge of digital recording technology. And as a private investor, he befriended the techies who were heading these budding, upstart enterprises. His input became invaluable. He was the "beta" tester for these businesses, passing on his comments and suggestions on how to make the various devices more user-friendly. Not only did he wind up as a major shareholder in the ventures that would eventually go public, but he was able to enter the digital era of audio and video production thanks to equipment provided to him at no cost. The simple act of upgrading his studio from analog tape recorders and turntables to state-of-the-art digital recorders, CD players and ISDN delivery systems would have easily cost him hundreds of thousands of dollars. Instead, his portfolio was worth more than ten times that amount, putting his net worth in 1998 at a comfortable seven figures.

"That should just about do it, Bud," Chuck said as he finished sending the file to Nelson's private email address. "Now, while I'm here, let's see what Jenni is up to!"

"Stop it, you pervert," Don said. "Besides, she's usually at work this time of day."

"Don, you're usually at work this time of day and I'm usually paying you to be at work this time of day. Just how would YOU know what is going on at Jennicam?" Fred asked sheepishly.

"Gentlemen. You may all sort this out later," Bud said. "Fred, can you get me back over to the Jetport? I'll call the pilot and tell him to warm up the G-IV so we can boogie back to Washington. The old man is hungry and that lobster and steamer dinner down in the car is getting cooler by the minute."

"Just swing it through the kitchen and have them steam it up for ten minutes. And make sure they melt up some fresh butter. None of this margarine crap," Chuck offered.

"Roger that, Michaud. You know, for a goat-farmer, you do good work. Now, for the tough question. Anyone come up with any possibilities yet on just how this damn recording was made?" Bud asked.

"I will say that somehow it was filtered. Not really filtered, but when I was transferring the file, I had the headphones on. You know me, half-deaf. It's clear, no mistake about that. Sure as we're sitting here, that recording was made not more than four feet away from your mouth, Bud. But..." Chuck stammered.

"But what, Chuck?"

"But, it sounds like the old put-the-hanky-over-the-mouthpiece thing they used to do in old, bad movies. And we all know how much doing THAT can really disguise a voice. Right?"

"Save me the sarcasm, Michaud. Continue. And please. The short version," Bud added, looking at his watch.

"In a nutshell, Nelson. It's your voice. It's a very clean recording. But the sounds sound somewhat diluted, as if they were made through cloth. My guess is that the actual device was there, probably inside someone's suitcoat pocket. I wouldn't guess a transmitter, only because you've said they have a kind of "buzz field" around the Oval Office to thwart off any unauthorized recording. But, you did say there is an installed audio/video system that goes directly to a secure, digital unit somewhere in the bowels of the White House. And that access to this is controlled solely by NSA, on authorization from the

President and the Senate and House leaders. Do you think that any tech doing maintenance could have got a splitter on the main feed without being noticed?"

"I can check on that, but if I remember correctly, there is an impedance monitor on the system, designed to detect a degradation of signal. But it is definitely worth checking out."

"If I think of anything else, I'll get you on your phone. I don't have an encryption device on my end, though. Do you think we can talk in the clear?"

"Not at this point. Here's what we do. If you have something, call me. Just ask me how the President liked his steamers. I'll get online as soon as possible and will assume you've sent me an email, on my own server, detailing what you might have come up with. I need you to keep on this. All three of you. This is my voice on this recording. It's going to look like I'm behind this crap. And a leak of this information now, before we are ready to move, could be just disastrous. If the bad guys plan is as we were told, the pieces will fall into place by themselves and that'll be the end of many things we, the good guys, have come to enjoy. Like financial security and stock portfolios with multiple commas. Capice, Fred and Chuck?"

"Capice," replied the two.

"Don, I need some digging from some of our old contacts in New York. Who's left at NBS?"

"Awww, frig me, Bud! The only one left is Sandy."

"Don. I wouldn't ask if it were not this important. I thought you two worked it all out?"

"We did. But, man. Making me go back down that road just to save the United States? Wow, you know how to test a guy. I'll call her when I get back. We'll be looking for what exactly?"

"I want file footage of the Speaker. We want to see if there are any common threads in his public appearances, specifically, maybe the same face hanging out in the background? Going back as far the tape morgues can handle. He ran for office in, what? '76?"

"That's what I remember. He came out of nowhere around that first Memorial Day we were in Charleston and by the 4th of July, he was kissing every baby and momma in sight. He certainly wasn't the kind of character I'd vote for, but from what I recall, he had a pretty good thing working for a dark horse candidate."

"Call Sandy. Don't tell her what it's about. If she asks, make something up. But for Christ sakes, Don, make it good, will ya?"

"Aye, aye, Bud."

"Fred, who's left in Charleston we might know who can do some freelance digging on this murdering bastard?"

"With phrasing like that, I can only think of one guy. He's pushing 65 now, but he's still a hot shit. How about Comsubgru2?"

"Hot damn! I know he's plugged in. Do me a favor, Fred. Go down there. Today. Shit, here's what we'll do. Freddie, I need you to come with me. I'll have the G-IV drop me in DC and then have them take you to Charleston. Can do?"

Fred looked at Don and shrugged. "Geez, Bud. I dunno. I mean, I know this is important, but..."

"No f'ing "buts" about it. We need to do this. Today. Now.

"Don, if Sandy can dig up some archive footage, have her FedEx it to you, in care of Michaud here, overnight. Tell her Chuck's helping you put together a retrospective for the senior Congressman from Lewiston. What's his name again?"

"Her name, Bud. Remember? Olivia?"

"Right. So you guys are working on a tape for Olivia and the footage might help you find some material suitable for roasting. Like a tribute thing for the Speaker and you two are getting the good parts ready for the Congresswoman."

"That should work, Bud."

"Gimme a second here, boys. I gotta make another fast call."

Bud took out his cellphone and hit the speed dial.

"Mr. President, it's Bud. Couple of things have come up and I'd like your permission to bring in somebody else on this. We need to do some fast digging out of town and there is an individual whom I feel we can trust, implicitly. However, I think we'll make more ground if we're able to completely clue this person in on just what it is we're attempting to do. I was going to send my buddy, Fred. He's fully aware of what we know and at this point, he has no ulterior motive. He's also very familiar with the area we have to check on, as well as very close to our new research assistant."

There was a noticeable pause and Bud was nodding his head. He snapped his fingers at Chuck and made a writing motion with his hand, pointing at a pen and paper on the desk behind the audio console. Chuck passed him the paper and the uncapped pen. Nelson made some hastily written notes and continued with the nodding.

"Yes, sir. Yes, sir. I absolutely understand, sir. I'm really going to have to ask you to trust me on this one, Mr. President. We're not secure on this line. At least not if you're at your desk. I'll be in the office in about two hours and change, depending on traffic down there."

Another pause, then "Yes, sir. I'll look for Hannity at Andrews. Yes, sir. I guess I'll be there in about two hours. Oh and Mr. President? You might call down to the kitchen and ask them to put on a nice big pot of boiling water. Right, big enough for a two-pounder and a half a peck of steamers. As a matter of fact, they did have some nice corn on the cob. Yep, they'll be able to warm it all up nice for you."

Chuck yelled "And tell them to melt you up some REAL butter!"

"Chuck, your President says to say 'thank you.' Yes, sir. I'll see you in a few."

Nelson hit the "end" button on the cell phone, terminating the call and put the phone back into his coat pocket. He took out his personal electronic organizer and turned it on.

"Wow, Bud. You got a pocket p.c., too! Those things are still pricey. Is that the kind you can write your stuff into?" asked Don.

"Nope, it's got a little keyboard. Does the trick. I've got to transfer this stuff from the Chief into my locked file in this thing. By the way, in case I get run over by a Chinese tank on the way home, the password for this thing is 'goatman.' Cap sensitive. You all think you can remember that?"

"Goatman. Isn't that the name you used to use when you wrote those rogue memos at NBS?" Don asked.

Nelson chuckled at the memory.

"What memos?" asked Chuck.

"Mr. Fred Goatman, director of financial services for the NBS network, used to issue the most ridiculous edicts regarding network expenditures. Things such as 'all employees will please refrain from submitting reimbursement requests relating to adult escort services' and the like. These memos usually appeared mysteriously in all employee mail slots after a hellacious breaking news event had wrapped. The best ones came after Hinkley took his shots at Reagan and after we'd beat the Challenger disaster story into the ground.

"Try as they may, the network powers never found out who the mysterious Mr. Goatman was. Still a legend in the hallways, from what I understand."

Nelson smiled wryly and took a mock bow.

"Bud, if you are that well versed, how about abolishing the income tax when you're done cleaning up this mess?" Chuck asked.

"Consider it done, Michaud. You greedy, capitalistic, Cuban cigar smoking voice-over god."

"That is, course, God with a big "G," right?"

"Don't push your luck. Fred, let's get going. Chucker, thanks for all of your help. We get this clusterfuck cleared up, we do some serious fishing."

"Then when we sober up, we'll play some bad golf?"

"That's the only kind I know, my friend. The only kind I know."

"Will you guys drop me back at the station? Fred does have a business to run, but since he's going where it's warm, someone has to lock up the safe tonight," Don suggested.

"Sure, we can do that. Going right by the place on the way to the Jetport. And use my office for the phone call you need to make. That which I just know you're anticipating with dripping excitement," Fred added sarcastically.

"You and the horse you rode in on, Fred." Bud smiled in response.

"Oh, Bud. What are we looking for on the footage of Hewes, exactly?" Don asked.

"We are going to keep our fingers crossed that our friends at NBS have some nice, stock campaign footage. The kind with all of those "Friends of Brad" gathered around tightly while the candidate pounds the podium for emphasis and everyone cheers wildly. We'll be looking to see if we can put some faces with the other known parts of this puzzle. There are the murderers of the real Hewes we need to pin down and to make sure we can put Assistant Secretary of State Moore with this band of ne'er-do-wells. Don, we'll go over the rest of this in the car. We've really got to get going."

Bud reached out and gave Michaud a bear hug. The two shook hands heartily and Bud walked out of the studio, down the stairs and out to Fred's car.

Chuck walked to the door, gave the three a wave and called out to Don, "I'll call you when your package arrives, Hough. Good luck!"

Fred's Lincoln motored through the snowbank and onto Route One. About ten minutes later, they pulled into the parking lot at Casco Bay Radio, Incorporated.

Fred started to open his door and said "Bud, give me two minutes. I've got to grab my emergency overnight bag and my little pocket phone directory. It's got Deucey's number and I will need that.

"Deucey? Who the hell is Deucey?" Bud asked.

"Dericksen, Bud. I call him Deucey. As in Comsubgru2.

"Don, will you drive us over and then bring my car back here?"

"Sure, Fred. Let me run down the hall and make sure the kid's are all set."

"Bud, we'll be right out," Fred said.

"Make it fast, gents. I'll call over to the G-IV and have them warm it up for us."

Fred and Don entered the radio station while Bud took out his phone and called the pilot. The G-IV was fueled and running as they spoke.

Bud took out his personal pocket-sized p.c. and powered it up again. He cast a cursory glance at the notes he'd made while talking with the President, then powered it down. It was a very handy device. All the conveniences of a personal computer, in a very handy size.

It was a gift. From Annie. He wouldn't tell the boys, yet, that they do "bump into each other" from time to time. He and Annie were both grown ups and had agreed to keep it strictly physical. She offered the gift as just something to be passed along and not that which needed reciprocation.

She said they had received several of these p.c.'s at the office of the vice president from a computer manufacturer who sent them along with a nice campaign contribution. The contribution was one of many that were arriving even before Fulton had officially declared his candidacy. The actual campaigning was still over a year away. The monetary contribution was within acceptable limits and would be documented as to its early arrival. But the personal organizers might have been seen as items with a dollar value that would exceed the group contributor limit.

When Fulton called to pass thanks for the contribution, he did ask for an address where the gadgets could be returned, explaining why.

The manufacturer faxed a letter of instruction regarding the gifts, directing that they be distributed among Fulton's staff for their personal use, as a way of thanking them for their loyal, public service.

Since the items were no longer contributory gifts to the Fulton for President campaign, they were passed out to a few select aides. These would have to be noted as "gifts received" on the annual declaration that all federal employees are required to file.

Annie said she'd already been using her own, so she gave it to Bud. That was a little over a month ago and Nelson had been asking himself how he had ever gotten along without it.

Fred came out of the building with a small suitcase. He tossed the small bag into the backseat and climbed in after it.

"Don should be right out."

"Good. The plane's all warmed up and waiting on us. Pilot figures about two hours flying time down to DC and then I'll have them get you right down to Charleston. Once we're airborne, you call Dericksen and ask him to meet you at the Air Force base, okay? The phone on the plane is secure and at least, unlike mine, not traceable. I really hated calling the Chief on this" as he gestured holding up his own cellphone, "twice today. Damn! I just wish we could find out how they got that meeting recorded."

"Is the President having the office checked out for transmitting or recording devices?"

"Yeah, he's got his Chief of Staff, Dan Josten and a team in there right now. I have a feeling though, that they're not going to find anything. However this leak happened, my hunch is that it was portable."

"Aren't all persons entering the Oval Office checked out beforehand?"

"They are. And there's a metal detector built into the door frame. But, things like my little p.c. here, we hand them to the detail and they pass 'em back to us."

"Hopefully the guys checking out the office will find something. Maybe that theory about there being a tap into the master monitoring system will play out?"

"That would be the best-case scenario. The access point to the main equipment room is electronically monitored. You need a personal, magnetic key card to get in. There's a running log of when the door was opened and just who gained access. And there's a running log of signal strength, designed, as we talked about, to indicate any drop in impedance of the audio and video feed. It will also give us a date and time stamp as to when there might have been a change in signal strength. That, combined with the access log time stamps would give us a solid path to follow."

Don came out of the building and settled into the driver's seat.

"You know, Fred, I really wish you'd buy a new news car that was kinda like this. It would sure beat clunking around that not-so-late model Subaru."

"Outback?" asked Bud.

"No, it's parked right over there, Bud," Don replied.

Bud reached over and slapped Don off the back of the head, smiling.

"Don, let's get moving here and save the good jokes for the beer blast we'll have at the House of White when this mess is cleaned up."

"The Casa Blanco! I can hardly wait. And thank you."

"Thank you for what?"

"That's the first time you ever called one of my jokies 'good'."

This time, Fred slapped Don off the back the head and they all shared another laugh. Sometimes, a little humor will help to make a dire situation that much more manageable. The four friends had shared some laughs, cloaked under the guise of "black humor" that day.

As the sun was getting lower over the White Mountains of New Hampshire to the west, Don pulled the car out of the radio station's parking lot and turned left onto Western Avenue for the short drive to the General Aviation terminal at the Portland International Jetport.

The trip was unusually quiet. Don pulled up to the gate at the General Aviation terminal, where, surprisingly, a uniformed airport agent was waving them through the open gate and out onto the tarmac.

"Don, see what happens when you know people? You can drive through airports. Don't even have to run through them like O.J. used to."

"Thanks, Bud. I'll keep that in mind."

Don pulled up right next to the extended stairway of the G-IV where an Air Force captain stood at the bottom, holding a clipboard. He gave Nelson and Singletary a nod as they climbed out of the car and onto the stairs. Stepping through the door, Bud yelled to Don.

"Good luck with Sandra. And be NICE to her! Y'hear?"

"I hear, Bud. I'll be nice."

Fred waved and stepped through the door, followed by the Air Force captain. The stairwell was folded up and into the plane and the locking handle could be seen turning from outside the plane.

The G-IV's jets wound up to a higher pitch and the aircraft began to move onto the taxiway. Within minutes, the sleek looking Gulfstream was lined up on her departing runway, jet engines sending rising warm waves of exhaust towards the bright yellow blast deflector that abutted the airport's perimeter road. The jet suddenly rolled out, smoothly gaining speed with each passing yard and lifted effortlessly up into the air out over Portland Harbor before turning south towards Washington, DC

Don cranked the wheel of the Lincoln hard and pulled off the tarmac, through the gate and back onto the inner airport roadway. He watched the final glow of the Gulfstream's engines as it climbed up through the late day cloud cover that was encroaching from the southwest.

Good luck, thought Don. Good luck and God help us all.

twenty-one

About the time Nelson's flight was passing over New Jersey en route to Maine, Michail stepped off an Air France flight from Paris to Moscow and walked in line with the rest of the passengers towards customs.

Things had certainly changed from the "good old days," he thought. Back when a flash of his KGB credentials would have not only gotten him past any line without losing a step, but would have also had a car waiting for him.

"Passport, please?" asked the customs inspector.

Michail presented his new, Russian passport. It looked the same. Just didn't open as many doors as the older, official USSR one did.

"Did you have a pleasant trip to..."

"Paris, by way of Monte Carlo. And it was very nice indeed, thank you for asking," responded Michail.

"Do you have anything to declare, Mr. Rostokovich?"

"No, sir. No winnings from Monte Carlo and sadly, no romance from Paris."

The customs inspector actually smiled, gave a cursory look through Michail's carry-on and stamped the passport.

"Have a nice day, Mr. Rostokovich."

"And you, too, inspector."

Michail closed up his bag and slipped his passport back into his overcoat. The pilot had told them on approach that it was a balmy 8 degrees Celsius. The weather had been a whole lot nicer on the French Riviera. More than four times the temperature for starters and the women on the beaches did not feel the need to wear all of the overpriced pieces of cloth that passed for bathing suits. The freedom of an open culture did have its advantages.

He walked up to the Hertz counter and presented his international drivers license. The clerk smiled at him and checked the computer on the counter.

"Yes, Mr. Rostokovich, here you are. We've got a nice 1998 Ford Explorer in slot B-33 for you. You're paying for this on American Express, yes?"

"Yes," said Michail, noting the irony as he presented his Platinum card.

"Just sign here, please. Did you want the optional insurance for nineteen-ninety-five per day?"

"No, just the rental. I have coverage through my company," he said as he presented the automobile insurance card issued by International Exporters of Moscow, Inc.

"Very good, Mr. Rostokovich. There's your paperwork and here is your insurance card."

Michail put the insurance documentation back into his wallet, folded the rental agreement neatly and placed it into his monogrammed leather travel organizer. He slid his American Express card back into one of the many slots provided for in his organizer and slipped the entire package into his L.L.Bean shoulder bag.

The clerk slid the key across the counter and invited Michail to "have a nice day."

Michail returned the pleasantry and began to wonder whether or not he'd be able to get away with his plan.

It's not unusual for an agent to go rogue and double out, but was it really a double situation? The question existed only due to the fact that the organization for whom Michail was actually employed no longer existed. The KGB was broken up with the dissolution of the Union. The assets and duties, however, were farmed out to various state and military departments. Some, though, such as Michail and other deep cover agents, were unofficially kept on in their assignments. In as much as the KGB would disavow any asset exposed in a compromising situation, the asset was still considered a key piece in their ongoing operation. Some deep cover assets were pulled out and brought home. In Michail's case, the two deep cover agents were kept in place as a matter of ego by Aleksandr. And Michail was kept in his role to please the whim of his brother-in-law, too.

The KGB as the world knew it, went out of business almost ten years ago. And now, Michail was out to make the remaining days of his brother-in-law, Aleksandr Romanov, former Chairman of the former USSR, former husband of the late Elenya Romanov, former father of the late Christina and the late Michail, an absolute, living hell. This was not an action against the organization of the union that set up and put the Hewes operation into motion. This was personal. A vendetta against a man who put his job ahead of his family. Many times there have been men who have put work before home, but not usually with the deadly results that befell Elenya, Christina and Michail.

In the past ten years, Aleksandr had gone from despised head of a despised group of old men who were seen to be holding back progress for the people of the Union of Soviet Socialist Republics, to a man for whom many in the new Russia now held in esteem and pity. The poor man had lost his wife and children as the result of an action by an unruly, lawless gang.

Now, Aleksandr Romanov was looked upon as an elder statesman. One to whom subsequent leaders have been able to consult and, more importantly, one to whom subsequent leaders have been able to publicly embrace. A photo with Romanov was worth a lot of votes for someone seeking a seat in the new Russian government.

Romanov had been living comfortably, alone, in a dacha cum castle on the shores of Lake Onega, near Petrozavodsk, north of Moscow, west of St.Petersburg.

St. Petersburg. Now there's an interesting Orwellian take on society, thought Michail. Let's erase the past as seen through the eyes of a Stalin-Leninist society and try again.

Michail had always thought that keeping the name of Leningrad would have been a good reminder to the people of Russia of what it was like to be an almost-perfect communist society. The intent of Stalin and Lenin was noble. A chance for all of the people of the USSR to share in all that is good. And yes, with it would also come the bad.

But the changes towards a more free and capitalist society that Romanov tried to implement moved much too slowly for some and were seen as far too radical for others. That was when those members of Russia's grand old party decided enough was enough and staged an attempted coup. Romanov fled to Lake Onega from his office at the Kremlin, with a select few guards in tow. He had sent a driver for his wife and children. The driver had gotten to with a quarter mile of the Romanov house, when he saw the angry mobs moving in loud protest towards the gates of the house. The driver turned around and never even tried to pick up Elenya and the two children.

Elenya had the two children with her in the house. The soldiers assigned as the family's security detail had suffered a split amongst themselves. Several had felt an unfaltering loyalty to the Romanovs. A few others had fallen under the influence of the forces loyal to the hard-liners. As the mob approached the house, having broached the gates without any resistance, the two factions of security squared off against each other.

Although no shots were fired, they were distracted enough to not see the make-shift torches that were being tossed into open windows on the ground floor. By the time the screams of Elenya and the children were heard and the guards had stopped their stand-off long enough to react, it was too late.

The three were found in the second story bathroom. The window there was small enough to prevent them from climbing out. Perhaps Elenya had thought the smaller window and a locked door were enough protection in case the mob was able to penetrate the trusty guard detail at the front door. The cause of death was smoke inhalation for all three.

They were buried in a highly publicized service. The international news media was even invited to cover the story. The new, self-declared President was on hand to offer condolences to the grieving widower, Aleksandr.

Michail had watched it all on CNN from a hotel room in Virginia. At the time, the reigning Speaker of the House was stepping down and Michail had to ensure the consensus election of M.Bradford Hewes to the seat that would get him even closer to the Oval Office.

Michail had come close to blowing the lid off the entire plan right then and there, but he thought on it a while and decided that waiting until Romanov and his minions could taste it would be much sweeter.

Oh yes, Rostokovich thought, no doubt by now Romanov had brought a few of his newer buddies in on the plan. Aleksandr had a big mouth and would have reason to gloat if this was pulled off.

Michail put his luggage into the back of the new s.u.v. and closed the rear window. He hadn't been in Moscow for almost a year. He'd taken to keeping Romanov updated via courier. Many times, Michail simply used FedEx. It was more efficient and for a couple of bucks, the updates would arrive at Aleksandr's dacha by nine am. By sending his briefs in writing, Michail would not have to worry about betraying the level of hate he felt for the man by showing up in person.

Michail had laid out the entire plan, as it was known, to President Griffen privately first. He was present in Oval Office meeting the president held with Mr. Nelson, the vice president and the two other cabinet members, although Michail never spoke nor was he named. Although Michail would be brought to face charges, including two murders, he had no second thoughts about making sure that Aleksandr Romanov would be swinging at the end of a rope in just a few weeks time as well. He'd rather kill him personally, though. If given the chance, he was pretty sure he would.

It was shortly after 7pm when Michail got into the rented Ford, started it up and backed slowly out of the space in the Hertz lot. It was a warmer April evening than most, but still not as warm as yesterday in Monte Carlo.

He'd left Washington after his Oval Office meeting for an Air France flight bound for Monte Carlo. The connecting flight to Paris was delayed due to equipment failure and he'd been given the option of rail travel to the City of Lights, or he could spend the day and be placed on the next morning's departure.

Since the flight had left Dulles in the afternoon, eastern time and arrived around daybreak in Monte Carlo, Michail decided to have at least one more enjoyable day. Some time on the beach. A few stiff drinks. Maybe the company of a woman. Even if he had to pay for the pleasure, he would.

As it turns out, he did spend time on the beach, watching the firm, young women of the world go by, drinking probably the best damn scotch he could recall having. And he did manage to finesse the intimate company of a woman. France in the springtime. Michail thought he could settle here.

Driving through the streets of Moscow, he thought it darker than it used to be. Not dark as in nightfall, although, the dusk had passed, with just a hint of the lingering sunset in the western sky. No, it was darker in a spiritual sense. Many buildings had fallen into disrepair. They were offset by a number of newer, high rise office buildings and the red and yellow glow of McDonald's Golden Arches every ten blocks or so. There were many people on the streets, busy and bustling. Michail would venture a guess that many were involved in activities that were no doubt against the law, but now a necessity in a society where one either has money, or doesn't. Drugs and prostitution had risen dramatically in the past seven years in Russia. New cars would most likely be stripped within minutes were they left unattended on some public streets.

The black-market for newer things from the West was still strong. It had been tolerated, within limits, in the final few years of the old regime. But now, the black-market provided goods and services, at hefty prices for those who could pay, that the average citizen might have hoped to find in the department stores. The goods destined for the shelves of the local stores were all to often hijacked and made available for sale to only those who could pay. This was easier for the new generation blackmarketeer than for those of the past. The old black-marketeer used to have to pay a high price for a smuggler to bring the goods into the country. Now, the goods are shipped in legally and trucked right onto the city's streets. Certainly makes it that much easier to practice the law of supply and demand. Pull a gun and demand. Then, sell the supply.

Michail pulled into the parking lot of his apartment building. The security lights were still working. Not a bad sign, thought Michail. The rent was paid by a government subsidy on a yearly basis. The subsidy had been set up by Romanov before the coup and had continued through some little stroke of luck. Michail wondered when some bean counter would notice the yearly payment for a luxury apartment for an agent on State business.

He parked the rented Explorer in a spot under his apartment windows. From ten floors up, the vehicle would look small, but the new car shine reflected from the streetlights in the parking area would help keep it visible.

He stepped into the lobby. It smelled of fresh paint and the carpet had been recently cleaned. Not bad, thought Michail. Somebody was actually taking some pride in their product. Maybe there was some hope for a country currently being presided over by a drunk with major health problems.

The elevator doors opened and Michail stepped in, careful not to touch the freshly painted walls. The control panel had also been replaced recently and Michail touched the Braille-enhanced button for the tenth floor.

The elevator gave a familiar creak, but then settled into a smooth yet steady ascent. Michail gave a cursory inspection to the emergency phone. It was new, but where it went was a mystery. There was no full-time concierge in the lobby of this building. Perhaps it was linked to the local police station or fire brigade.

The elevator slowed to a stop and the doors opened onto the tenth floor. Michail stepped off the lift and glanced up and down the hall. The walls were clean and the rug actually looked as if it had been newly placed within the past year or so. It had been a while and Michail put his incredible powers of recall to work. No, he thought. It was not new when he was here for last year's May Day non-celebration.

He approached the door to his flat and noticed a small envelope sticking out from underneath. He picked up the envelope and saw a pre-printed logo indicating a property-management company.

Opening the envelope, he read that the doors in the building had been replaced in January to bring them closer to the most recent fire safety standards that had been put in place by the local public safety administration. But, the letter went on, he should be assured that the original locks were re-installed and his keys would work without problem.

Michail's internal sensor net went into high gear. It was natural for a man in his line of work. The door had been replaced, which means the apartment had been entered. This would require a full check of the unit before he could think about relaxing and putting his guard down.

He undid the deadbolt, then put the key into the doorknob lock. Gently, he turned the key, not yet allowing the door to open.

He bent down, holding the knob and key in position with one hand. Then, starting at floor level, he slid the envelope up the length of the door jamb between the door and the frame. Feeling no sign of resistance which might have come from a telltale or some sort of triggering device, he then opened the door just past the opening of the latch plate. This allowed the door's latching mechanism to rest against the solid portion of the latch plate. He then repeated the resistance check across the bottom and the top of the door frame. And then he checked the hinge-side of the door's opening.

Satisfied that any triggering device was not associated with the door frame, he took a step to the latch side of the door frame. Using his Bean shoulder bag, he swung the soft-sided carryall out into the hall and then into the door.

He half expected to feel the concussion of an explosion, or perhaps to feel the sting of a bullet zipping by his head as the door swung open. Neither of these things occurred.

His next thought was that it was time to get into a new line of work. The joy of traveling anonymously and being able to drop onto a king-size hotel bed, for the most part worry-free and just falling asleep if he so desired was one of his life's little pleasures. Just once, he thought, it would be nice to come "home" without having to make sure that someone or something was not out to get him.

Michail noticed the apartment's main living area and kitchen appeared unremarkable from the last time he was home. This was a good sign. He closed the door behind him and set the deadbolt. Then, for good measure, he used the sliding latches at the top and bottom of the door. If anyone was here, it wouldn't be easy for them to get out, he thought.

He took the shoulder strap off his Bean bag and remarked to himself what a utilitarian piece of luggage this purchase had turned out to be. The strap had a rubber-backed, suede-faced shoulder pad to alleviate any discomfort carrying the bag fully loaded. The rubber backing would serve as an insulator. The strap itself could be used in a variety of ways to disable any aggressor.

Holding the padded section of the strap, he used it to flip on the living area wall-switch. The small lights on the two end tables came on, giving a warm glow to the apartment. He then repeated this ten feet to his right for the kitchen's overhead lights.

He first walked the apartment to look for any sign of a trip wire, or a slight bulge in the carpet. Damned new technology allowed things to be made so much smaller than in the good old days. He turned on the lights in each of the two bedrooms and the bathroom

Back in the kitchen, he grabbed the small broom that stood in the corner near the waste basket and used the handle to gently open each of the cabinets as well as the refrigerator.

He repeated the broom-handle ritual on the bathroom cabinets, then the living area on the small desk and finally on the end-table drawers.

Next, he started along the outer walls searching for any sign of audio or video monitoring equipment. Once again, he cursed the ease with which one could now do that which had been for years the hallmark of a good old fashioned spy.

It had taken him almost an hour to verify that all was as it had been when he left almost a year to the day. He had paid particular attention to his get-out-of-gulag free card; the false corner section which contained the only known written details of this operation. The paint was that which he put on twenty-two years ago. Michail had taken pride in what might be considered sloppy work. The thicker, deliberate brush marks at the top, bottom and along the seam of the edge gave him small comfort that the contents were intact. Even the faceplate of an electrical outlet showed no sign of having been tampered with or removed. There was no opening in the wall, the faceplate had simply been put there to give it a more ordinary appearance.

Michail glanced out the window towards the parking area. The rented Ford was still there and there was no other traffic coming or going. Nor did he notice anyone lurking about on foot.

He went to the bathroom and turned the shower on. Hot water gleefully jumped from the shower head and Michail gave a sigh of slight relief.

Emerging from the shower, he heard the phone ringing from the living room. He walked, dripping water, into the living room. No need for modesty, he was here alone.

"Da," Michail said as he answered the phone.

"Michail!" came the greeting from Romanov. "When did you get back? I was just informed of your arrival."

"Nice to see some things never change, Aleksandr.

Michail had enjoyed being able to call his brother-in-law by his first name and had even taken to calling him by the more familiar Sasha in public meetings.

"I got back about an hour ago and apologize for not calling you. It seems the management company here has taken an interest in this building. So many fresh coats of paint and new doors and carpeting. Can't help but think there's a rent increase on the way."

"Yes, Michail. The rent has been raised, but you've been paying the new rate happily for a couple of months now. So, when will you come see me? I assume we have some things to discuss or you would still be in Virginia."

Red flags went up everywhere. Virginia! How did Romanov know he was in Virginia. Every communiqué sent to the former President was done via FedEx through an elaborate system of relays. The packages were always originated in New York and then sent to either the Russian Embassy in Ottawa or London. From there, they took an untraceable, yet commercial route through Oslo and then to St. Petersburg. In St.Petersburg, the original wrapper would be discarded and the address label would clearly read "For the personal attention of Aleksandr Romanov only."

Michail was very careful when speaking to Aleksandr, specifically using the real names of the players in this operation, as any disclosure of their current identities could have been disastrous.

"Yes, Sasha, I would much prefer to spend the early spring there. Daytime temperatures climbing to around twenty-five degrees, blue skies and the smell of the blooming flowers. But I needed to come back to give you a one-on-one brief. There are a number of movements taking place that need us to be ready to make the next step."

"You'll come tomorrow then?"

"Yes, Sasha. I'll probably hit the road around seven and I should be there at the lake by two or so. What's for lunch?"

"I'll have some fresh lake bass on the grill when you arrive, Misha. Get a good night's sleep and come see me."

"Will do, Sasha. Can I bring anything?"

"No, just yourself. We have much to discuss, I'm sure. Maybe we can do some fishing before nightfall. It's cold, but the big ones are biting. Bring a change of clothes. You'll spend the night here."

"All right, then, Sasha. I'll see you tomorrow."

Michail hung up the phone and walked to the refrigerator. He grabbed a bottle of imported American spring water. He'd tried a year-old beer on his last trip and the contents had undergone some unpleasant changes. He contemplated a trip down to the late-night market, but thought better of it. The water would be fine. And if it needed a little something, he could always add a dash of scotch.

He checked on the vehicle and saw that it was still where he had parked it. Untouched and, no doubt, probably the most secure vehicle in the city of Moscow right now. Romanov still had a long, powerful reach and the watchful eyes would most likely be under orders to ensure the safety of Michail. For now.

How Romanov had come into the Virginia information was the item that now needed Michail's undivided attention. Yes, there were assets of the Russian intelligence community still at work in Washington and elsewhere. The end of the Cold War didn't mean the end to information gathering.

The American people were suddenly in a feeding frenzy for details on the alleged assault by the American President on a young, female employee. Most were calling for his resignation and then trial on the charges. Others clamoring for the gossip concerning the state of the marriage involved. The less-than-whispered inside information that Mrs. Griffen had left the White House were banner headline fodder for the various tabloid newspapers around the globe.

Too bad, thought Michail. Mrs. Griffen had married and spend a great many years with a really, really good man.

Michail now knew that after having sat in the room and talked with the man, one on one. He regretted his part in what he had helped to start. At the time, it was, the right thing to do. He was simply a soldier following orders. But the new World Order had changed those instructions he had pledged to carry out. Which is why the plan of events was about to change. The vendetta against Aleksandr would be brought about on several levels. It was as intricate a trap as the original plan, code named "No Corners." But this time, only Michail knew the "when." The "where" and "how" would fall into place by themselves, given the current course of events.

Obviously, there were assets watching his every move. That would also mean that Romanov might be in possession of the knowledge that Michail had been to the White House. This was of great concern. Michail could not walk into the secluded lakeside dacha of his brother-in-law, especially if he knew of Rostokovich's private audience.

Michail got up from the sofa where he'd been drinking his bottled water and walked into the spare bedroom. He opened the bottom drawer of a dresser and removed a hammer and a cats paw. Admiring his handiwork for the last time, he quickly and quietly set about opening up the sealed vault. He didn't need to tear the whole thing down, just about fourteen inches of one side near the bottom. The condensed file of the particulars of this operation were in one small folder in the bottom storage box. He slid the correct box out, removed the folder and slid the box back in. He folded the creased drywall section back down then slid the dresser into that corner. No need to make this a permanent renovation again.

The other information inside the wall would no doubt be discovered by the investigating teams that would be dispatched to help unravel this fiasco. It would be of little use to anyone, however. Michail had made sure that good men or women in the field would not be exposed to danger. He'd simply made up his own coded version of assets and events. And Michail currently held no illusion that he'd be alive to translate any of the information.

Rostokovich pulled a FedEx overnight document envelope out of his Bean bag and filled out the address box. This package would go to a post office box in Alexandria, Virginia, in care of Mike Rosty. He took the sheaf of documents out of its folder, giving the paperwork a cursory once-over.

Then, inspiration hit him. He went back into his room and opened up the factory sealed box. Aleksandr himself had given this to Michail as a gift a few months back. The latest in technology, Sasha had said. It's a wonder! A marvel! He went to work and when he was able to review what he had done, he walked over to the stereo system. There it was!

If Michail were inclined to believe in a God, then God bless the person who'd given him this cassette. A recording of Tajikistan goatherds at work entitled, quaintly enough, The Songs of Tajiki Goatherds. Michail had gotten this tape several years ago as a gift from a local Tajiki operative. The Tajik held their goats as a measure of wealth and the greatest honor that could be bestowed upon an individual was to have a goat sacrificed in their honor. The short-lived Tajik Air, a brave first attempt at free-market enterprise by this offshoot Soviet Republic, was welcomed, but delayed getting to the gate for its first arrival for the custom of ritual goat sacrifice. The crew of the 747 was mostly American, mostly former employees of the original PanAm airlines. They had been briefed that local leaders might wish to bestow this honor upon them, so they had learned the local protocols on how to best accept this. The pilots and crew had all been honored each with their own copy of this tape and the Tajik operative had been a steward on the crew. Since he was able to enjoy the songs of the goatherds at work whenever he wished by simply opening a window, he'd passed the tape to Michail as a symbol of friendship, but was honest in the way in which he'd come into its possession.

Michail turned on the stereo and took a set of audio connectors out of the laptop section of his Bean carryall. He hooked the input connector to the auxiliary audio port of the laptop and the analog phono-type plugs into the cassette deck's output jacks. He then took out two blank, recordable CD's and inserted the first into the laptop's CD-ROM drive. The advent of recordable compact discs had proven pricey at the inception, but for Michail's purposes now, the technology was invaluable. He set up the laptop's recording mode and started the recording function, while pressing play on the cassette deck. The sounds of the goatherds at work, treating their goats to serenades, filled the apartment. He got up and turned down the volume, then sat back, double checking the documents. When the tape finished, he paused the CD-ROM drive's record function and had one more step to take before he "fixed" the disc. "Fixing" would finalize the recording and leave the disc unable to further record any information. Once the CD was finished, he repeated the process with a second disc.

While working on the recording, he put his other marvel of technology to work, wryly smiling to himself that Aleksandr would probably have need of fresh underwear when he realizes that his gift was responsible in part for the undoing of the master plan.

Once the second disc was finished, he took the generic looking CD packaging and transformed it with a little artwork, then did so with the disc as well. He put one disc in his Bean bag and the other in his coat pocket. It would be a gift for Aleksandr, one which would, ironically, put the Michail version of events to come right in Sasha's hands.

Michail then took out another overnight folder and addressed it to Michaud Media in Scarborough, Maine, USA, for the personal attention of Goatman. This folder would contain instructions for Mr. Nelson, including how to retrieve the other package at the post office box. The instructions would be coded and it would probably take a few days for Nelson to get the translation. That would buy Michail a few days to get settled somewhere warm, sunny and hopefully, beyond the long arm of the United States justice system. Provided, that was, that his visit with Aleksandr went according to Michail's plan.

If the visit to Romanov's dacha turns out to be his last living act, Michail was assured that at least the Romanov-Hewes connection would be brought down. Quickly and without mercy.

Michail got dressed, tucked the two FedEx envelopes into the back waistband of his pants and put his overcoat back on. He didn't want to leave any of this to chance. He'd go down to the business district in Moscow and drop the packages in one of the many FedEx pickup boxes located on just about every corner in this part of the city. There was enough activity down there with those movers and shakers in the financial markets, even at this late hour. Late here in Moscow, but the trading day was beginning in the Asian markets. If you want to make a couple of bucks, you couldn't do it sleeping.

He grabbed his keys and wallet then headed for the door. As he opened the door, he saw a shadow retreating down the hall and watched it recede around the corner.

He closed the door, nonchalantly. He took his time working the keyed deadbolt and turned towards the elevator.

Then, with a wry smile, he called out "I'm going downtown to find some cold beer, my friend. Can I bring you back one?"

There was no answer, just a soft shuffling of feet and the sound of the door to the stairway being opened.

Michail pushed the call button for the elevator and listened for the gentle click of the stairwell door closing. He heard it just as the doors to the lift opened.

Sloppy, sloppy, sloppy, thought Michail. But the next generation of intelligence operative would not be relying much on actual field work. No, in this new era of portable technology, the bulk of intel gathering would be done in the soft glow of a computer monitor. Web cams, real time audio-video and the anonymity of the Internet make it possible for even homebodies to engage in the gathering of data. Hacking into what should be the most secure computer systems in the world was literally the work of children. Surveillance would no longer rely on human assets being on scene. Slip in a few remote cameras, some with lenses smaller than ball-point pens and just hope the link to the Internet server didn't fail.

The elevator opened at the lobby level and Michail casually stepped out. He walked out the front doors and turned into the parking area. He used the remote control that unlocked the vehicle's doors and deactivated the alarm system.

As he reached the vehicle, he once again caught a shadowed figure around the side of the apartment building, near where the stairwell would allow access to the ground level. He just shook his head and climbed into the oversized s.u.v., closed the door and started it up.

As he backed out of the parking spot, he gave a look up and down the length of the lot for any telltale headlights. There were none.

He approached the street and turned right out of the parking area. A glance in the rear view mirror gave no indication of a trailing vehicle.

Taking advantage of having a head start, he quickly took a left into a fairly well developed part of the neighborhood. There were a series of small streets, crossing at odd angles, that allowed him to put enough distance between any trailing car.

He was nearing the campus of Moscow State University, where he'd be able to jump on one of the main roads into the downtown section.

He slowed, intentionally, as he approached a busy intersection. The traffic signals would give him a few more feet of running room. He didn't need a whole lot of space. Just enough to drop the FedEx packages out of the sight of his baby-sitters.

Keeping his eyes on the rear and side mirrors, watching for any sign of a vehicle coming from the side streets he'd used, he continued his deliberate pace. Then, just as the light turned yellow, he hit the gas and made it through the intersection and up onto the highway. A fairly heavy amount of traffic worked its way through the intersection from the opposing direction, thereby ensuring that he had managed to evade any trailing vehicle, even if only temporarily.

As he hit a decent cruising speed, he was pleased to see a large number of newer, larger vehicles on the roadway as well. The American s.u.v. frenzy seemed to have taken hold here, too, thought Michail. This would make his trek through the busy financial center that much easier as he wouldn't be quite so noticeable.

He got off the boulevard as part of a small line of cars all heading into the business district. Even though it was almost nine-thirty, lights were burning in many offices, the new ideal of work hard and make a lot money having firmly taken hold, at least in this part of Russia.

He took his first right, then a quick left through the tightly woven maze of buildings. Some of these, he noticed, looked as if they'd been built in the past few years. Just up ahead, he saw a FedEx van making a pickup at one of the drop boxes. Luck was with him now, he thought.

He pulled up along side as the driver was placing the picked up parcels into the back of the van.

"Excuse me? Do you have room for two more?"

"No problem," said the FedEx man.

"These will get out on the next flight? My boss will be less than pleased with me if I can't tell him that these are on their way."

"Shouldn't be a problem. This pickup run usually gets on the last flights, around one am or so. They'll get to the London distribution point around five am, their time. Where are they bound?" The driver gave the address forms a cursory glance. "Oh, to the U.S. Yeah, these should be in the States in time for the morning runs over there. With the time difference, the package pretty much arrives at about the same time it left. Almost as good as a fax machine."

"Great!" exclaimed Michail. "You've really saved me a dressing down. The boss gets grouchy when he doesn't hear what he wants to hear."

"Aren't they all that way?"

They both laughed and Michail gave a wave as he pulled back into the light flow of traffic. Still no indication of being followed. Good.

The Ford backtracked to the busy main thoroughfare that would take him back towards his apartment complex. He approached the next intersection and saw an open store. He parked the rental and went inside.

"Do you have cold beer?" asked Rostokovich.

"Da. You have any particular favorite?" asked the clerk in response.

"What do you have for imported beer?"

"We have a few American beers, but a better selection of German ones."

"How about Lowenbrau?"

"Yes, we have Lowenbrau. Light or dark?"

"Light, please. Could I have two six packs?"

"Certainly. Give me a moment."

The clerk went through a door into the store's cold storage cooler. He emerged moments later with two six packs.

Michail paid the man and carried the beer out to the car. Out of the corner of his eye, he saw a car parked about a half a block back, with two darkened figures in the front seat.

Took you long enough, Michail thought. At least they saw me come out of the store with two six packs of cold beer, just as I had told them when I left the apartment. Now, I can only hope that they didn't see my little exchange with the FedEx man.

He hopped back into the Explorer and, making the amber light just in time, he zipped through and up the ramp to the busy boulevard. He watched the lurking car in the rear view mirror, saw the headlights come on and then, he watched them pull out directly into the path of a passing car. The collision was not spectacular, but he had seen enough and was thankful that his time in the same service as those poor souls was just about done.

He arrived back at his apartment about ten minutes later, having taken the more direct route home. No need for the evasive tactics through the older neighborhood thanks to the "Less Brothers," Hope and Use.

Michail smiled at that little piece of American humor that just didn't translate well into other languages. The nuances of slang were present in each culture.

He recalled the night in a bar in Boston when a high school French teacher helped him learn the difference between merde and shit, at least in the correct manner of the idiomatic French. The word "merde" means excrement. But to deliver it with the proper punch, there's a circuitous route to take to get there. The wind up involves a French General leading his troops into battle. All of the intelligence he'd been given gave them no pause for concern. It would be a breeze, or so they'd been told. When the troops crested the hill, they saw that they were greatly outnumbered. It was then that the General uttered the single word, "merde." That situation leading to the use of the word "merde" gives the base starting point to the level of "merde" in which you may find yourself mired. Therefore, "merde" alone will occasionally fit the situation. But "really deep merde" involves the invocation of the General's name, in this case, "le mot de Cambronne."

He grabbed the two six packs and exited the vehicle, activating the remote lock and alarm system.

He strolled around to the side of the building and left two cold bottles of beer, figuring his clumsy shadows had earned these. Even though they did their jobs horribly, Michail had to smile with a nod towards "been there, done that." He pulled one of his International Exporters business cards out and jotted a quick "thanks for the floor show" on the back of the card. They'd be pissed, but hopefully, they'd learn from this experience.

He walked back around to the lobby and used the elevator for the return trip to his tenth floor apartment.

Once inside, he put the beer in the refrigerator, taking one for himself. He hung up his overcoat and plopped down on the couch. At least he'd be able to rest easy knowing his rental car was under the watchful eyes of Aleksandr's henchmen, accident prone klutzes that they were.

He flipped on the television to see if there was anything on worth watching. It was just about ten-thirty pm. Not too late to hope for something decent. All of the government run television stations still ran on a sporadic schedule, although you could at least count on the evening news programs to be there. And those had come a long way from the days of not so long ago when it was not really news, but governmental press releases. Now, a freer flow of information was allowed. It was still recommended, however, that a news reporter not be free with anything that might be considered critical. There were still those who held to the old ways.

There was a newscast on. New development since he'd last been sitting still long enough to watch a television in his Moscow apartment.

The lead story was about some troubles involving Kurdish rebels north of Iraq, in the offshoot republic of Tajikistan. There was a brief story about a hospital visit, termed routine, for the current President of Russia. Damned drunk, Michail thought. Maybe he checked himself in to dry out in time for the summit next week in Paris.

As if the news director had read his mind, there was a preview of the economic summit set for less than a week away. There was montage of the world's leaders who were expected to attend, including the prime minister of Great Britain, the Russian president and prime minister and United States President John Griffen.

Michail took another deep sip of beer and listened to the story. There was a voice-over translation of comments being made by the United States Secretary of State, Ms. Julie Paparelli. Not bad looking, thought Michail. No wonder Marvin enjoys his current assignment.

Ms. Paparelli was addressing a news conference in Paris and she was passing along her strongest hopes that the leaders of the new European Economic Union would be able to come to agreement on terms of more equitable trade. And to that end, President Griffen was coming with a promise from American businesses to increase imports from all of the European manufacturing centers. The details of what the United States would be willing to do in this regard would be forthcoming at the summit and hence the attendance of the American President.

From there, the story slid into a positive mode regarding Russian industrial ventures being saved with help from a German investment firm. The footage showed massive ocean-going tanker ships in various stages of construction at a shipyard in St. Petersburg, on the Baltic coast.

Michail used his remote to click the television off and got up, walking back towards the kitchen. He finished off the bottle and opened the refrigerator for another. He opened it and walked back into the living area. The phone rang.

As he waited for the second ring, he suddenly thought of Anastasia.

"Hello."

"Misha?"

"Stasya. You won't believe this. I thought of you just as the phone rang. How are you?"

"I'm fine, Misha. Just fine. And you?"

"Doing that wacky thing we do. I just got in this evening and I've got a lunch date up at the lake tomorrow. What about you? We haven't been in the same room in what, six months now?"

"A little here and a little there, Misha. I'm actually going to be in town on business next week. Right now, I'm on my way to Madrid for a few days. There's a conference at which I have to give a lecture. Will you be there? In Moscow next week?"

"I don't think so. The lunch date is kind of a business meeting with the boss and he might be looking at moving me to a new territory. He wasn't really clear about the details."

"Since I am coming in next week, can I use the apartment? It saves the expense account the hotel charges, plus, it just feels good to have a place I can maybe call home?"

"Yes, Stasya. This is as much your home as mine. And when one travels as much as we do, there is something comforting about have a home to which we can come. The building has actually had some care attention paid to it. You might not recognize it."

"So long as the bed has clean sheets, the shower hot water and something cold to drink in the refrigerator, I'll be happy."

"I hadn't planned on doing laundry, but for you..."

At that, they both laughed. Then, the long pause. Michail hadn't seen Anastasia since they crossed paths at Orly in Paris. He heading one way, she the other. They actually spent a long October weekend at EuroDisney and were thought to be newlyweds by several of the hotel's staff.

He missed her touch. He missed her wit. He missed her. And this has been the nature of their relationship for over twenty years.

Anastasia loved being with Michail. But she did not love him. He was bright. Caring. Attentive. Very good in bed. He was the ideal man, for a woman seeking an ideal man. She was not adverse to spending lengthy periods of time with a man. Just not the same man. If there was a time when she felt the need for companionship on a full-time basis, she was positive it would be with Michail. This much she had repeatedly told him.

"Well, Misha, my darling. Don't worry about doing the wash. But save me something cold to drink?"

"As a matter of fact, there should be at least two cold Lowenbraus for you. I am drinking my second right now."

"What happened to the other two?"

"That's my Stasya. Quick mind and fabulous math skills. I left the other two for the two new superintendents here. They're learning to keep an eye on things around here, but they've been having an especially rough night tonight."

"I suppose you've passed along a thing or two from which they might be able to learn?"

"One can only hope, Stasya. One can only hope."

"Listen, old wise and sage one. I'll let you go. But I'm glad you were there. I needed to hear your voice."

"You know, if we were to enter into a partnership arrangement of some sort, we could enjoy each others company and conversation on a daily basis."

Stasya sighed. "Misha, in time. Just not at this time."

"You can't blame a fellow for trying."

"You'd get a gold star for effort, my darling. I must go and get some sleep before my Madrid flight in the morning. And you, you've got a bit of a drive to make. Say hello to the big guy for me, will you?"

"I'll tell him you say hello and that you think we need to work on a long term project together. Just kidding. Get your rest, I'll get mine and we'll both have great days tomorrow!"

"Goodnight, Misha. Sweet dreams."

"Goodnight, my Stasya. I'll be dreaming of you."

Michail hung up the phone and took another sip of his beer. He found it odd that Anastasia would find him at home. He wondered if she called on a regular basis, hoping to catch him. If so, that would mean he still had a chance.

He walked over to the window that looked down into the parking lot and saw the newly dented sedan parked in a dim corner of the lot, but not completely out of view. Michail raised his bottle in toast to the unseen occupants and took another drink. He hoped they'd found the beer he left for them. At least they could do is enjoy a cold one before they start to explain this one to their superiors.

Anastasia hung up the phone in her hotel room and flopped back on the bed. She was wearing the big, soft, white robe the hotel provided and she pulled it tight around her. The air conditioning unit was on high, as it was a very warm and humid night in Madrid and the very cold air felt refreshing.

President Romanov had briefed her personally on her current assignment, imparting upon her its importance to Russia and her people. He had also asked that she minimize her contact with Michail. Actually, he had ordered her to have no contact with Michail, so as not to distract him from an equally important assignment. She had managed to gain from Romanov the small concession regarding incidental meetings, such as the one they'd enjoyed in Paris in October. This way, if they did bump into each other, then the light was green. But, the former Chairman warned, no permanent arrangements. Yet. He then offered his future blessing and support for the couple should they wish to be married. But he again reiterated his strong request for them to wait.

She did call the apartment in Moscow on a regular basis. She called every evening around ten-forty-five, Moscow time. She could not tell him that. Not right now. She would though. She would tell him very soon.

She loved to hear his voice. His thoughts and hers were all too often one. They were good for each other and he, especially, was good to her. She only wished she could reciprocate. Daily. But she spoke the truth to Michail that she wasn't completely ready to do so and that when she was, there was no doubt in her mind that Michail would be her mate and not just her soul mate.

She could never tell Michail that she did enjoy the company of other men. She was a grown woman, in a line of work where physical release often brought a small sense of mental relief. Nothing emotional. Purely physical. Occasionally, it was part of the assignment. She was also sure that Michail did the same with other women. They both had needs.

The biggest demon with which she had been wrestling of late is that she was truly ready to cancel her commitment to Aleksandr Romanov and sign on with Michail Rostokovich. The reasons were two-fold. And one of them was her love for Michail.

Anastasia was, like Michail, considered an asset too valuable to be reassigned to simple police or investigative work. Anastasia was therefore, also like Michail, in the employ of International Exporters of Moscow. It should, she thought, be easy enough to walk away from the grip of Romanov. Once the current operation was brought to a successful conclusion.

She got up from the bed and opened the well-stocked mini-fridge in the hotel room. She reached in and smiling, pulled out a cold bottle of beer. Flipping the top off the bottle, she raised the Lowenbrau to no one in particular, toasting her love, Michail.

She drank the beer while towel drying her short, blonde hair. The auburn wig she wore for her current op sat on the hotel's dresser. They'd brought up a wig form so she could make sure it didn't lose its shape. She'd gotten used to the hairpiece. Just below the shoulders, with lots and lots of body. It stood out so brilliantly, that many men to whom she spoke had a tough time deciding between talking to her hair or her breasts. She'd even seen agents she'd trained with who did not give her a cognitive glance. They were too busy starting with the hair and working their way down. It sure beat sunglasses and a scarf.

Men, she thought. They really need to start with the face. Good solid eye contact gets a guy to first base faster than any other way she could think of, short of rape. And the one man who had tried the latter route with her got a taste of swift and unmerciful justice. He was found in an alley behind a high rise hotel, an apparent suicide. Fifteen stories and no note, so the story in newspaper had read.

She finished the cold beer, imagining she was sharing it with Michail in a tropical beach house, somewhere far, far away from the seemingly endless cycle that had become her life.

She picked up the phone and asked the hotel's desk for a five-thirty wake up call. There was an early breakfast meeting and things to get done in Madrid during the day.

She turned off the light and fell asleep, dreaming of better days to come with Michail.

Michail finished his beer and tossed the empty into the trash. He double-checked the deadbolts on the door and headed for bed.

Crawling into the fresh sheets, he smiled at the thought of Stasya being in this bed next week. He was sad at the same time, however, with the thought that he might not even be alive.

No! he thought to himself. He would be alive. He'd figure out a way to get out of this and suddenly, the idea he'd been kicking around in his began to formulate. He'd talked about this possibility with Nelson. Looking at the bedside clock, he figured the time difference for Washington and figured he nothing to lose. Would twelve hours be enough? It might be if the wheels could turn at speed.

He got out of bed and grabbed his shoulder bag. He opened the padded compartment and removed the power cord, base and extra antennae for his satellite phone. It was risky, but there was no way he'd call Nelson on his living room phone. The sat phone offered the best chance of getting through undetected. At least for a few days. If the transmission were picked up, it would be garbled and would take the techies time to get it cleaned up and deciphered. He checked the l.e.d. for signal strength. Seven out of ten. Got to go for it, he thought. He dialed Nelson's number and listened to the echoed rings on the line.

twenty-two

Nelson pulled into the beach house driveway in his shiny, new Chevy Malibu. Bright blue, with a tasteful white pinstripe and brilliant chrome wheels. Bud spent the extra bucks on the mags. They just made the car look that much better.

Don, Fred and Chuck all stood in the doorway and applauded. Bud got out of the car and took a modest bow.

"Bud, that is a nice looking car," said Don.

"Thank you, Mr. Hough," replied Bud, tossing the keys to him. "You may have the honor of the first guest ride."

"Sure, Bud always liked him best," Chuck said to Fred. The two of them flipped Nelson the bird and cast an enviable eye on Don as he opened the door and slid in behind the wheel.

"Now Don. I don't think I need to tell you that this thing is so new, it hasn't been manufactured yet, right? And that it's got the temporary dealer plate on it? And that the temporary registration is in the glove box with the bill of sale? And that I would really appreciate it if you didn't beat on it or crash it into anything?"

"That's right, Bud," said Don. "You don't have to tell me any of those things, but if you did, I'm sure you'd tell me about all of them. Fortunately for you, I am a very fast learner."

"Yes, I am fortunate and will remain grateful as well, so long as..."

"No need to finish the sentence, Bud. I'll treat her nice."

Don buckled the lap belt and adjusted the mirrors. Then, gently slipping the car into reverse, he backed out of the driveway, carefully. As he pulled it out onto the street, he gave a toot, a wave and dropped a twenty foot patch of rubber from brand-new squealing tires.

Bud was furiously waving and yelling, but Don was done with his fun. He slowed down and took the car for a careful, leisurely drive around the Isle of Palms.

"See, Bud. That's why I never let Don drive the TR. He's a maniac," offered Chuck.

"Don't be mad, Bud," said Fred. "He's just having a little fun at your expense."

Bud smiled, but was still fuming around the ears. The crimson that had instantly flushed his face was fading.

"Just wait 'til he gets back here. Bastard."

"Now, Bud, you know his parents got married before he was born," Chuck said. "Not everyone from Maine is illegitemi."

"Latin, kind of. Very nice, Michaud, very nice."

"It's good to know how to swear in several languages, Bud. Want to know how to say "shit" in French?"

"I'll pass, Monsieur Michaud, thanks. Do they all drive like that in Maine?"

"I'll be able to give you a full report in about a month, Bud," Chuck offered.

"Maybe we'll have to see if the Affray needs another boot ensign."

"Nope. You're not going to give me any more competition than I've already got, okay Bud?"

"I'm just bustin' your balls, Michaud. But when he gets back here..."

Don was enjoying his little ride in Bud's new car. He shouldn't have "lit 'em up" like he did, but it was too good to resist.

The roads on the Isle of Palms were tight and winding, like the roads in and around Kennebunkport. The only difference was the trees. Substitute pines for palms and he could be working his way by the Clock Farm on the way to Goose Rocks Beach.

Don enjoyed Maine. Growing up in Kennebunkport was like living in a Rockwell painting. The families in town had been there for generations. The quaint buildings that made up the downtown Dock Square; the classic white New England styled churches; the working farms; the bustling lobstermen; the volunteer fire department.

He had a good childhood. His mother and father were both also born and raised in The Port, as it was affectionately called. He had a younger sister still living at home, going to Kennebunk High. Joyce was class vice president and National Honor Society. She'd already been accepted to Bowdoin College on a full scholarship and was the apple of his eye. He loved his little sister more than life itself, much the same as he'd loved his little brother.

Davey had drowned just off Turbat's Creek one summer day while rowing his little skiff in and out of the coves. A wave had swamped him and the boat and he was caught in a vicious undertow. Just like that. At the time, Don was twelve, Davey was ten. Normally, Don would join his brother on an adventure like this, but he had chores to finish before he could go and play. One of the men from down at the Creek, Bill Williamson, had seen it happen and had made every attempt to get to the boy. By the time the first police and fire personnel had arrived, Williamson was hanging onto a submerged rock ledge, with a length of line he had tossed to Davey. The receding current was just too strong and it took four men to safely retrieve Mr. Williamson. Davey's body had been found almost a half mile off shore by a returning lobster boat. The image of Davey in the coffin at the funeral home still haunted Don. It was the one memory he could not shake and he dearly would love to have it bury itself deep down, where it could never again surface. Davey would be going on twenty-one and living and loving life just like Don was.

Don had gotten a part-time job while still in high school. He had landed at the Biddeford Journal-Tribune, the local evening paper. By the time he'd arrive each day, that day's paper was already on the trucks, being delivered to news stands. Don was given the title of "Assistant Sports Editor." The pay was three bucks an hour and it was Don's job to sort out all of the evenings sports scores and stories from the Associated Press and United Press International teletype machines. From there, he was tasked with taking the scores and recaps of the local high school games called in by the coaches. His first byline was a small story about the state Babe Ruth league championship that was held in Saco and won by his own hometown team, Kennebunk. The next day at school, he made it a point to track down his buddies from the team and remind them that they should make sure they read the paper that evening. As the Red Sox were doing poorly at that point of the season, the sports editor was seeking anything to gloss up the section currently the leading favorite for "most likely to be used for lining shelves." Don had taken a couple of photos, one of which showed his best friend Carl Libby crossing the plate with the winning run. That shot had been enlarged to fill most of the front sports page above the fold. And the editor had called Don at school to ask about any other particulars about the game that might have been left out. Not that Don would have missed important facts, but his editor knew that if he told Don to write four columns, then four columns it was. Don gave him a few descriptions of some really good plays and was back in class in minutes. The story was expanded to fill the bottom half of below the fold, with Don's name in bold type. At the urging of his high school guidance counselor and with a few good words from the editor of the Journal-Tribune, Don was accepted into the journalism program at the University of Maine. He received a partial scholarship and applied to ROTC to help make up the difference.

His four years at UMaine Orono passed uneventfully. He had some fun, wrote for the school paper and met Sandra Rose. He and Sandy were just friends working together on the paper and they did some casual dating. She was off to New York for an entry level job at NBS. He graduated cum laude, with a baccalaureate in Journalism and orders to report to the United States Navy's Officer Candidate

School in Newport. It was there that he met up with and became lifelong friends with the other seventy-five percent of "the gang of four."

Don stopped by a store to buy an inexpensive bottle of champagne. He figured he could help finish smoothing Bud's ruffled feathers with a classy toast to his new wheels.

He went into the store and found the champagne, right next to Admiral Gary Dericksen, ComSubGru2.

"Admiral, er, I mean, uh, Gary. Hi."

"Hey Don, how you doing?"

"Just fine. I took Nelson's new car out for a spin and so now it's time for me to bring it back with a bit of a peace offering."

"What did you do to the man's new car, Hough?"

"Just a little breaking in of the rubber parts."

"You laid rubber with a man's new car. How new?"

"He'd driven it off the lot about an hour before."

"Okay, let me help you out here. Try this one. It's a good year and it's not cheap. Plus, take one of these." The Admiral handed him a good sized cigar, encased in its own plastic tube. Unmarked.

"Don, this is a Cohiba. Cuban made. And illegal in this country. It's now in your hands and I have absolutely no knowledge about how it came into your possession. Understood?"

"Aye, aye, sir. Understood. Care to come over and join us in toasting the new Bud-mobile?"

"Let me see," said Dericksen, glancing at his watch. "I've probably got about fifteen minutes before ComComsubgru2 starts wondering..."

"ComComsubgru2?"

"Yeah, my wife, Sue. She being the Commander of the Commander of Submarine Group Two."

"Gotcha. Let me pay for this and I'll meet you outside. Oh and how much do I owe you for the cigar?"

"Cigar? What cigar, Don? I have no idea what you're talking about."

"Right. I'll see you outside?"

"Coming right behind you, Mr. Hough."

Don paid for the champagne. It had better be good for eighteen bucks for a bottle. He thanked the clerk and headed out the door.

He waited on the curb near the entrance for the store and Gary came out within a minute.

Don got into Bud's new Chevy and Gary climbed into his little British Racing green MGB. Michaud will like this, thought Don. The two of them will start talking British autos and it'll be ten o'clock before you know it. The thought of a shore patrol pulling up to the beach house to ensure that Admiral Dericksen, Comsubgru2 was actually all right made Don smile.

They pulled out of the parking lot and it took less than five minutes to make it back to the beach house. Bud was sitting on the front stoop, just waiting.

"Hey, Bud! Here she is, still clean and scratch free. Peace offering for the tires?" Don said as he held out the cigar tube and champagne.

Chuck and Fred had come out front from the beach side.

Fred said "Don. Champagne and cigars? Couldn't find flowers?"

"It's alright. This time," Bud said to Don.

The Admiral had timed his arrival perfectly, pulling up next to Chuck's Triumph. Chuck's face lit up like a child seeing a new toy and bolted to open Dericksen's door.

"Nice wheels, sir. Is this a '73?"

"It's "Gary" on the beach, Chuck, remember? And yes, it's a '73. Spoke wheels, two batteries, two S/U carbs and three wipers. Your TR6 there, right?"

"Yep. My pride and joy, also a '73."

The Admiral and the Ensign strolled over to Chuck's Triumph and instantly formed their own mutual admiration society.

Gary turned towards Bud and said "Oh, Bud? That cigar would best be consumed here. Do not try and bring it on base."

"Cohiba?"

"If it had a label, then yes, that's what it might say," Gary said, with the emphasis on "might" and a wink of an eye.

"Don, you live. For now," Bud said to Hough.

Don just smiled at Bud and walked over to Fred.

"You know what, Fred? That car moves very nicely."

"Like 'Hot Rod Lincoln'?"

"I guess that if she had a set a wings..."

"It'd probably fly," Fred finished.

Fred and Don joined the other three at the impromptu British Auto Show in the driveway.

Fred asked "Gary, can you stay for dinner? Nothing fancy, just burgers and beers."

"Wish I could, men. But Mrs. Gary, otherwise known as Sue, would neuter me without the benefit of anesthesia. She's got supper on the stove and I was supposed to be just grabbing a bottle of wine. Can I have a raincheck, though?"

"Sure. You come by anytime. And if we're not here, that means we've got duty. Of course, being an Admiral and all, you could fix that, right?"

"Sorry, Fred. But nice try. I'd just come back another night when you are here. Hough, remind me to remind myself to check the duty schedule each day, okay?"

"Aye, aye, Gary," Don said.

"I really should be going," Gary said. "Chuck, nice car. Great color, too!"

"Thanks, Gary and allow me to return the kind words."

"Done. And Nelson, that's a beautiful car." Gary walked over, opened the door and tossed a handful of change into the back seat. "It's a little tradition. Don't know who started it, but it's supposed to bring you good luck."

"Thanks, Gary," said Bud. "And it'll come in handy the next time I'm digging for coins to get over the Francis Scott Key bridge in Baltimore."

Gary was easing his lanky frame into the little MG and gave the boys a wave as he back out of the driveway. Then, with a wry smile, he left a little rubber, just about where Don had not too long ago.

The four all gave Gary a wave and Nelson took advantage of the situation and plunked Don off the back of the head.

"What was that for?" asked Don as he gave his head a rub.

"Gary reminded me of what I forgot to do." Nelson smiled as he bit the end off the cigar.

The four walked back towards the deck, where the coals were white hot and ready for cooking. Bud leaned into the hibachi and lit the cigar. Sending a great white puff of smoke upward, he sat down on one of the deck chairs.

"Boys, right now, it doesn't get much better than this."

"I'll drink to that!" said Fred, reaching into a cooler and producing four cold beers.

They all took one, pulled the flip tabs and drank in concession to Bud's proclamation. Another great night on the shores of the Atlantic, nestled between the gangly palm trees on the aptly named Isle of Palms.

twenty-three

"Very good, Mr. Moore. I'll await your call. And please pass my best wishes to Secretary of State Paparelli. Thank you, again. Goodbye."

Brad hung up the phone and used the intercom to buzz his secretary.

"Robin, any calls in the past few minutes?"

"No, Mr. Speaker, none. But we do have a quorum call in ten minutes."

"That's right," he said, checking his watch. "This is the social security vote this afternoon, correct?"

"Yes, sir. Hopefully, you'll get the seats filled and get the vote finished by four-thirty."

"Very good, Robin. And thank you!"

Brad had been extremely pleased with Robin's ability to keep him on track. Sometimes, when he got sidetracked by an issue, such as the phone call he'd just finished with Marvin Moore, she'd be right there to re-align his sights. The fact that she was single helped Brad out as well. There wasn't any call for sick children at school, nor did she have to rush home to get dinner on the table. Not that Robin didn't have a life. As a matter of fact, even though it was against the rules, Brad and Robin had a casual thing working outside of the office. It made it easier for them both when things got tense in the People's house and the work had to be done.

All in all, Yevgeny was fairly pleased of the persona he'd adopted for his role as Speaker of the House, The Honorable M.Bradford Hewes of the great state of South Carolina. Coming up with the right mix had been tough. He didn't want to appear too religious, although some aspect of that had been necessary due to the large percentage of Southern Baptists in the district's voter base. He certainly could not be too liberal so as to offend the Republican Party backing he enjoyed, but he had to keep the options open to pushing for funding for public programs and entitlements. After all, when he ascended to the Oval Office, the gradual shift towards Communism would begin, with an emphasis placed on an equal sharing for all; the basic tenet of communal systems. If he had spent years in Congress as an opponent of social programs and spending, then suddenly pushed for a sharing of the wealth from the White House, far too many people would sit up and take notice of something that drastically changed.

He and Dimitri had received coded words of encouragement from President Romanov over the years. Their progress had been watched proudly from the dacha by the lake. These messages often contained suggestions for both in the direction they both should take on various matters. The directing of events in America had started back in January of 1979 when Yevgeny/Brad took the oath of office as a freshman member of Congress. Prior to that, Yevgeny had several lengthy conversations with the then President. Romanov had detailed how gradually this operation would work. One small step a time, he'd advised. There would be times when a huge opportunity would arise and that Yevgeny would need to jump on it. The American political scene was full of armchair quarterbacks who would not hesitate to point out a blatant missed opportunity and Romanov had asked Dimitri to help out by being a second set of eyes. There would be times when spilt second decision making would be involved and the two had been told that their ability to make the right choice was specifically why they had been selected for this mission, the striking resemblance of Yevgeny and Hewes notwithstanding.

The most unsettling situation Yevgeny found himself in was the one-on-one session with the real M. Bradford Hewes at his family's secluded Charleston plantation back at the start of this adventure, in 1976. The facial resemblance was indeed like looking into a mirror and Yevgeny did not want to be in attendance for the final interrogation of Hewes. A phone call, actually made in the clear, from Romanov was able to settle his nerves enough to be in the room. The President had urged him, strongly, to make it through this part. It was the point where Hewes would be at his most vulnerable and the emotions that would accompany the various stages of coercion being applied would be important for Yevgeny to see, to feel, to adapt as his own. Hewes may have been an only child and might have, for some time, been a loner, but there were still people out there, somewhere, who might pick up on noticeable differences between the real Hewes and Yevgeny's adaptation. The first year would be the most important, the President had told Yevgeny. It would be the time where the people who knew Brad best would be more attuned to deviations from the norm of Hewes' behavior. After that first year, Yevgeny would be free to start changing Hewes to better suit the needs of the USSR and the long-term goals of the operation. These changes would be explained away as a man adapting to the newer challenges of a new position, that as a United States Congressman.

His phone call with Marvin had been in regards to the lining up of support in the House for ensuring his ascension to the White House. Not that they were overtly campaigning for the top spot. They were simply doing some informal polling on Brad's approval rating as Speaker and as an overall Congressman. Marvin had checked in from Paris where he was part of the advance team for the upcoming European Economic Conference. Also, by being in Europe, it was easier for Moore to receive updated orders from Romanov. Marvin had simply used a payphone in the hotel's lobby and called the dacha directly and brought Aleksandr up to speed personally. Both Yevgeny and Dimitri got that warm, fuzzy feeling by dealing directly with Romanov, instead of through the Rostokovich channel. Not that Michail had been remiss in handling their situation. Far from it. But the personal touch and the direct pipeline made them feel somewhat important by being able to deal straight-on with the man in charge.

Romanov had approved the set-up involving the elimination of the vice president. Along with the President's personal, potentially career-ending situation, there was a rumor circulating in the halls of the Senate, where Vice President Fulton served as the President, that there might be a vice presidential cardiac problem. This rumor was started with the help of Moore, with actual origins at Bethesda Naval Hospital, where Fulton had a physical in March. The physical included an EKG. With the aid of a hired employee in the records department, Fulton's actual EKG strip had been replaced with one of a person suffering an irregular heartbeat. The information had been leaked, quietly making the rounds in the halls of the Senate. This in turn had led to a spoken consensus that the Speaker of the House might be called upon to assume the duties of the President in the event of a resignation of President Griffen. It would take some time to straighten out the EKG confusion, but, Yevgeny knew, the correcting of the mistake would never come to pass. For at the effective moment of President Griffen's resignation, Vice President Fulton would suffer a severe myocardial infarction, induced by an apparent embolism. This would lend credence to the EKG strip that had been inserted into Fulton's medical file. The vice president would also be found to have suffered a collapsed lung. And the certainty that it would happen was ensured by the presence of Mr. Dayle and Mr. Bello as part of the Secret Service detail assigned to Vice President Fulton.

The rumor was working and the Fulton staff had not yet gotten wind of it. Marvin's conversation also included a benign exchange about the new Star Wars movie. The fact that the tales of Luke and Leah and Yoda and The Force had transcended international lines and a generation for a well-earned place in contemporary pop culture made it easier to have a coded real-time conversation in the clear. Brad had made his notes while talking with Marvin and then was able to break down the key words into an intelligible set of sentences.

The message was actually a coded directive from Romanov, "The Force Is Strong With This One." It let them both know that the plan was to proceed as outlined. And that the time for the final steps was drawing closer.

Each time they'd talk in terms of the Empire versus the Alliance, they'd insert their own personal likes and dislikes of the movie serial.

And each time, Yevgeny waited in dread for the abort phrase. It never came and it always had him on edge whenever Dimitri would shift their discourse to the tales of the Dark Side.

Brad grabbed his suitcoat, checked his hair and tie in the mirror and left his inner office. He told Robin that he'd be heading into the chamber and hoped that he'd have the vote finished and tallied in time for dinner. Robin smiled and nodded her understanding. A mention of dinner usually meant meeting at the parking lot of a shopping mall just east of Washington, over the line into Maryland. From there, they'd take an early evening ride to any one of a number of small, Chesapeake Bay grottos for a quiet, candle-lit dinner. The clandestine meeting and the somewhat anonymous dinner was needed, Brad felt, to keep the air of impropriety from thickening. The owners of the restaurants were thrilled to have the Speaker of the House in their establishment and the Speaker made sure that their desire for privacy was clear. No media involvement would connect Brad to Robin; employer to employee. This relationship was one that gave Dimitri pause for concern. He felt it was foolish for Brad to take any chances, but on this point, Yevgeny was actually the self-assured one. That Brad and Robin got together, maybe once a month, for a dinner, Yevgeny had explained, could be interpreted any number of ways, including the boss treating for a meal now and again. Dimitri would yield his agreement on this, but felt it wasn't the dinner that would raise eyebrows. It was the rented motel room that followed that would be the undoing of M. Bradford Hewes.

Brad left his office, stopping to greet a few House staffers in the hall and then continued on his way to the chamber, where he would once again conduct the business of the People. This time, to help save the Social Security system from economic collapse. A check of his watch showed he was, as usual, right on time. Just about four in the afternoon. If the quorum call was successful, they'd be able to get the vote down and over with in short order. The debates on the issue had been intense and completed. All that remained was the vote and the bill's plan to keep the system solvent for another few years looked solid, providing the senior circuit in the Senate didn't mess it up with a bunch of hidden provisions and riders.

twenty-four

The Gulfstream touched down just past six p.m., eastern time. Dusk was settling in on the nation's capitol, but Nelson had much work to do. He'd been online with Michaud via laptop on the ride down and for once the genius of which Michaud was capable on occasion shone through at its brightest! Bud had shown the emailed idea to Fred and that had given foundation to a few other possible paths down which Fred and Dericksen could head.

"Freddy, this is my stop. You give my best to Gary and Sue and be really, really careful, okay?"

"You got it, Bud. You make sure you watch your back as well. I've been thinking that if this problem is inside the West Wing and if the steps that have been taken are as drastic as explained, then..."

"No need to finish that sentence, my friend. I've gotta go see a man about a mole. Call me when you get hooked up with the Admiral, okay?"

"Will do, Bud."

Bud had already grabbed his coat, briefcase, the sport bag that held the Shortcut digital recorder and the insulated bag containing the

President's shore dinner to-go. He thanked the Air Force sergeant who was holding the door open for him, went down the short stairs and jumped into the waiting car with Special Agent Tom Hannity at the wheel.

"Hey, Tom. How's the traffic tonight?"

"Not too bad, Mr. Nelson. We should be able to get you to the plant in about twenty minutes. That okay?"

"Should be good enough for government work, Tom. How's the boss doing?"

"He was in with Mr. Josten and a few people from NSA when I left. He asked me to get you back here as fast as possible. I would've thought if it was this important, he would have authorized the chopper?"

"Nope. Didn't want to cause any undo attention on the White House lawn this evening. Plus, it gives me a chance to get caught up with you. How's the wife and kiddies?"

"Just fine, Mr. N, just fine. Pip's working at Bethesda and the kids are all getting way too big. Driving lessons, college applications and the thrills of being teenagers."

Tom had been with the Secret Service for just over ten years. He'd come on board from ten years on the Baltimore Police force, but had shown some insight during a campaign stop by then-Presidential candidate Mike Dukakis. The Massachusetts Governor had come for a stop at Johns Hopkins, pushing his health-care reform platform. While on traffic detail at the hospital's campus, Officer Hannity had caught sight of a handgun sticking out from a woman's handbag on the front seat. He radioed in the make and model and a description of the woman. The Secret Service detail had asked that Hannity come to the rally point and identify the suspect. Tom had picked her out from among the hundreds of supporters and JH staffers gathered. A female agent worked her way into the crowd and was able to quietly escort the woman in question from the crowd. The gun was loaded and was intended for use on the Tank Driver. Her motive was never clear, but the Agent in Charge did give Tom a business card with the verbal instructions to call first thing in the morning. A quick drive to the District of Columbia, followed by an even shorter interview, gave Tom a one hundred percent increase in base pay and the job to which it seemed to all he was destined. He was assigned to the staff tasked with protecting Vice President Quayle in 1990, then, during the transitional period between the Bush and Griffen administrations, he'd impressed the incoming Chief of Staff enough to ask that Agent Hannity be assigned to protect the President.

"How was your trip? I hope it was good."

"It was Tom, thanks. Got caught up with some friends while taking care of a little business."

"Smells like you caught a little dinner, too? Is that a lobster in there?"

"Yep. The boss asked me to bring home a little local flavor, so here it is. That's the other reason to make some time. Don't want this to get too cold."

As the car rolled through the main gate at Andrews, Bud watched the G-IV climb up into the evening sky and make the turn south.

"Say, Tom. How familiar with South Carolina are you?"

"I've been through there a bunch of times. But I stayed a bit longer than General Sherman and don't believe I did as much damage. Our last trip down that way was the re-dedication of Patriot's Point. You ever hear of that? It's the floating Navy museum."

"As a matter of fact, Mr. Hannity, I drove by it every night while I was stationed in Charleston back in the Seventies. The Yorktown made for a nice centerpiece."

"Last time we were there, they'd increased the displays somewhat. There's the Yorktown and now they've got a sub, a destroyer and a few other ships. So why ask about South Carolina?"

"The President might have a special assignment for you, if you think it's workable with your schedule. I won't presume that he'd send you, but if you think you'd like a little time poking around Charleston for us, then I'll be more than willing to suggest you. You interested?"

"I'm not sure, Bud. You check with the boss and if he wants me to go, I'll go."

"Maybe when I get a chance to pick his brain and drop your name, he might be willing to give you a little something more to work with, as far as what's going to be involved."

"That sounds like a plan."

The traffic was lighter than expected. Hannity had gotten them to the gate by the West Wing in less than twenty minutes. The Marine guard waved them on through and Tom pulled the Ford up to the side entrance.

"Need a hand with that stuff?"

"Matter of fact, Tom, yeah. Could you run this bag down to the kitchen and tell them this is for the hot water they should have boiling. And tell them to melt up real butter."

"You got it, Mr. Nelson. Hot water, real butter. God, I love being a Secret Service agent!"

"Oh, just shut up and go do it!" Nelson laughed.

Tom held the door open for Bud and they went in their separate directions; Bud towards the Oval Office and Agent Hannity towards the kitchen.

When Bud arrived at the president's outer office, the president was standing in the hall talking with his chief of staff, Dan Josten.

"Bud! Nice to see you again. It's been, what? Eight hours? And where's my damn lobster?" asked the president.

"First question, yes. Second question, in a big pot of boiling water if you remembered to call down to the kitchen, sir."

"I remembered. And I remembered to tell them real butter."

"You're getting better in your old age, Mr. President. Danny, what's our status?"

Josten raised an eyebrow at Nelson, wondering about the required size of one's cajones to make an age crack at the President of the United States in front of another person.

"Bud, we've had the sweep team in there for about two hours now. They've checked everything and everywhere. Under the rugs, in the lining of the drapes. Hell, they even ripped the sofa apart. Neatly, of course. We had them pull all of the moldings and removed every electrical fixture and face plate. The personal items on and in the desk and on the shelves have all been individually x-rayed. There's nothing in there."

"I think we need to back up to this meeting you had. Who was there? Vice President Fulton, Terrio from CIA and Realto from NSA and you two. We checked the authorized audio and video equipment installed inside and there has been no tampering whatsoever. So that means, however your meeting was recorded, the device was brought in and taken out by one of you. It may not have been intentional, but the experts in that room," Dan gestured towards the Oval Office, "feel that this is the only way the unauthorized recording was made."

Nelson looked at the president and felt inside his suitcoat pocket. He'd taken to keeping notes on his personal p.c.. It was always with him and required a user password to even open the address book files. He pulled it out of his coat and looked at Josten.

"You know what? We've all been using these," Bud said, presenting the palm-top computer for inspection. "The size, the convenience and ability to assign our own personal security barriers to any and all files make the process of taking notes and kicking butt later that much simpler.

"Dan, take this into the boys in there. And if it's the culprit. Don't tell me. Just shoot me. Now."

Just then, Special Agent Hannity rounded the corner, wheeling a push-style serving cart. The large, covered serving dish was oozing steam and the aroma of boiled lobster, steamed clams and corn on the cob filled the hallway.

"No one is going to shoot anyone while I'm here, Mr. Nelson. Even if you're the target."

"Sorry about that, Tom. A bad expression used in one of the more inappropriate settings. I apologize."

"Besides, Mr. Josten is not authorized to shoot anyone in the White House. I, however, am. Mr. President, your gift from Maine and per the gentle prodding of yourself and Mr. Nelson, there's real melted butter in there, so they tell me."

"Thank you, Tom," said President Griffen. "You didn't have to bring this up here. That's the job of the kitchen staff. They get upset with me enough when I sneak down for a two am snack without asking them."

"Well, sir. Mr. Nelson had intimated that there might be something of import which we needed to discuss."

"Nelson?" asked the president.

"Yes, there is something which we need to discuss. Dan, we're going to head downstairs to the secure room. You take that thing in there and have them take it apart if they have to, okay? Then come down and tell me I am not the source of this Titanic-sized leak."

"Bud, that would be my distinct pleasure," Josten said, as he walked into the Oval Office with Nelson's personal p.c. in tow.

"Mr. President, shall we wheel your dinner down a few flights?" asked Hannity.

"Sure, Tom. Let's do that. I may be a mental mess right now, but I am still hungry."

The three walked down the hall to the elevator. Up would lead to the President's family living quarters. Down took them to the kitchen on the basement level. Using a lone key on a key fob embossed with the Official Seal of the United States, President Griffen inserted the key into the override slot. The elevator would now go several stories below ground level, to the secure National Security offices and communications area, made famous by Colonel Oliver North.

The elevator opened up onto a stainless steel lined hallway, with a lone Marine sentry seated at the desk at the end of the hall. The Marine corporal had been at attention when the enunciator had chimed the elevator's arrival. Seeing the president, the Marine snapped to attention and saluted sharply.

President Griffen returned the salute and said "Good Evening, Corporal Gooley."

"Good evening, sir," said the Marine in return.

"Mr. Nelson, Special Agent Hannity and I will be using conference room two for a while. My chief of staff, Mr. Josten, will be joining us shortly. Who's the duty officer inside this evening?"

"Sir, the NSA duty officer is Colonel Ailes, sir."

"Very well, Corporal. Take care and carry on."

"Aye, aye, sir!"

President Griffen saluted the Marine and stepped to the cipher lock. The security code punched in, the door unlocked with a loud click and opened outward. The President stepped back and stood still while the door finished its arc. The duty officer, Colonel Ailes, was at the desk within the entryway. The duty office was surrounded by several layers of bullet-proof glass, with an opening for an M-1 carbine, which was kept locked and loaded next to the desk at all times.

"Good evening, Colonel Ailes," said the president as he strolled into the command center.

"Good evening, sir," replied Ailes smartly.

"We'll be utilizing conference room two for a time. And my chief of staff, Mr. Josten, will be joining us shortly. I've informed Corporal Gooley to expect him."

Ailes looked past the president towards the cart being pushed by Hannity.

"That, colonel, is my supper. Flown in fresh from Maine and additional steaming courtesy of our own White House kitchen. And if I weren't so damned hungry, I'd pass around the steamers."

"Very well, sir," replied Colonel Ailes.

The door to the right of the duty desk buzzed and swung outward. Each of the separate rooms on this level were controlled by electronic access at the duty desk. The final door at the end of the hall was actually another elevator, this one with direct service to the National Security Crisis Center.

The three walked directly into the open portal and Hannity, after pulling the cart through, signaled to Colonel Ailes to close the door.

The door closed, the president sat down to enjoy his imported dinner and Bud started.

"You eat, Mr. President. I'll run some things by you. First, I'd like to send Mr. Hannity here down to help out Singletary and the Admiral. I feel a little authorized protection for those two would help, especially if they're going to be doing as much digging as I think they will. I haven't brought Tom up to speed with what's going on. Wanted to wait for your approval before filling him in. I did, however, give Fred the okay to update the Admiral."

The president had started working on his corn on the cob and grabbed a napkin to wipe the edge of his mouth.

"Briefing the Admiral is a good idea, Bud. And, while I get to work on this lobster, go ahead and bring Tom in on this. Tom, I trust you to take in all of the information and then do what you feel is appropriate. I will tell you both that I have arranged for Bud and I to get together with Chief Justice Quinlan first thing in the morning.

I am not going to leave this place without a fight, especially when I know I am not wrong.

"Additionally, I believe, wholeheartedly, in the Constitution and the system of checks and balances therein contained. I alone will take blame if all of this turns out to be a ruse. We all, however, will share in the good that comes of this should it be the unholy truth. Bud, we'll need to talk privately, so bring Tom up to speed."

The president grabbed the shell cracker and went to work on a claw, while Bud and Tom sat down at the far end of the conference table. Bud started with a story of a college professor in Charleston, South Carolina in 1976.

About fifteen minutes later, the president had finished the lobster and was savoring each little steamed clam. Tom sat back in the chair and let out a very heavy sigh.

"Tom, that's what we've got to this point," Nelson finished. "We'd appreciate your joining up with Mr. Singletary and Admiral Dericksen in Charleston. Keep an eye on them and an eye out for them. If they come close to crossing a line, legally, I'd appreciate it if you make the judgment call."

"You mean you want me to inform them that what they might be considering is illegal, should it come to that?"

"Yes. And then, I'd like you to get them coffee. Don't be there if they decide to cross that line. Your end of it is protection. Of the law. And of them. Fortunately, or unfortunately, however you view this, the alleged perpetrators of this operation did not have our American system of laws in mind when they began. When brought to trial, they'll be afforded every right guaranteed under the Constitution. I'm pretty sure that when they start kicking around the Hewes family plantation, that they will find some very strong evidence pointing towards the veracity of the facts as they've been presented to us."

"What of this operative you mentioned. The one who came forth and offered you this information?"

"Bud, I'll take this one," the president spoke. "Tom, I made a judgment call on allowing this man to leave. He gave us plenty of information on which to start to unravel this mess, but he promised complete details from his files, which he's assured us are safely stored in Moscow."

"Weren't all of the old KGB files destroyed or published after the deconstruction of the Soviet Union?" Tom asked.

"Yes. If this file had been found, we would have heard of it years ago," Bud responded. "The fact that Romanov is now into his second or third year as a revered, senior statesman after so many years in seclusion leads me to believe that the containment on this plan was, until we were told of it, very tight."

Nelson's cellphone rang.

"Speak to me, bud. Yes. Yes." Bud was nodding his head in agreement and making hasty notes. "Matter of fact, we're just finishing up a fairly big stratospheric meeting. Right. Perhaps you could call Mr. Goatman in the morning. He'd love it if you'd call while you're on the road, just to confirm things. Okay, bud. Take care, get some sleep, but make sure you make that call in the morning."

"Bud," President Griffen interjected. "Regarding Romanov. He's got a meeting with former President Carter scheduled for a few days from now. I know that Jimmy and I are supposed to get together at the E.U. Summit in Paris, then he was going to St. Petersburg for a "Habitat For Humanity" international gathering. Romanov was asked by Yevchenko to represent Russia and her interests in this worthy project. Romanov agreed and so they'll be on hand for the ground breaking ceremony on a new Habitat development. And if I know Mr. Carter, he'll hang around to throw a few nails and some shingles, too."

"Speaking of nails then, Mr. President, do you think we can work with President Carter to try and get Romanov over here?"

"Let's talk with Chief Justice Quinlan first and see where we stand, Bud. If the man is willing to listen to our story, ex parte, then we'll have a fighting chance. I've called in the White House counsel, the Attorney General and Senate Majority Leader Davis to be there as well. I want this all out, as we know it and then perhaps we can figure out in which direction the investigation should head. The more people we tell of this, the greater the risk of the word getting out. This is why it's imperative that we get as much confirmation as quickly as possible. Then, if we can get everything lined up neat and pretty, we'll proceed with a plan to grab Mr. Romanov."

"That phone call I just took, Mr. President, was that our confirmation is in the mail. Coming FedEx. It will, though", as was arranged, be coming in two parts. One is the detailed information, encoded, heading for a post office box in Virginia. The other is the decoding key, being sent to my cigar-loving friend in Maine. I wonder if we can get an intercept team to New York to get both packages? Or how about Heathrow? That's the European hub, isn't it?"

"New York shouldn't be a problem, but the London end might take some explaining. More than I care to let out at this point, Bud. We'll get the FBI to send a team out there for the early morning arrival. Then, they can personally get us the packages, both of them, in time for our meeting. How long do you think it'll take to decode his notes?"

"I'm not sure, Mr. President, but from what I've found out about this man, he's had enough and is looking to exact a bit of revenge. I would, however, suggest we get someone from NSA in on this. Realto, maybe? Wasn't he an old code guy?"

"He was, Bud. I'll call him before we get out of here," said the president, wiping the dripping butter from the corners of his mouth.

"Next item, sir. Can we at least start with the first phase of getting this thing cleared up? Go Team One is in place and awaiting the green light. Plus, we might be able to utilize the same team for a little moral support for our package-sending friend. Both steps are going to take your authorization."

"Let's do it and take it one step at a time. We'll round 'em up, one by one. But Bud, we've got to be really careful about this. If we do this, I'm taking full responsibility. And now, we've Mr. Hannity here as a witness."

"I can be a witness to your saying to do something, Mr. President and that you accept the responsibility. But I can't say what the action is that you just authorized. Do I want to know?" asked Hannity.

"No, Tom. You don't. But I ask that if this entire op goes down the toilet, that you emphasize that every aspect of this cluster-fuck was ad-libbed. We are literally making this up one step at a time.

We are doing what we feel is the right thing, but I feel that if we do not start to move on this thing now, we run the risk of watching these pricks either getting away, or getting away with it. Bud, make the call."

Nelson picked up the red secure phone and dialed the access code, then a direct number.

"Yo, it's a go for step one. That's an order from POTUS." Nelson paused and nodded while listening. "Yes, that's correct. Set him up and take him down. Quietly. And don't talk to the bastard until you hear from us. We'll handle things from this end to make sure it's not too much of an attention-getter, until we're ready for it to be. Once you've got him sealed up, there's another little matter we'll need your help with. Do you have a secure fax number?" Nelson made a note of the number. "Great. I'll call you before I send a cover page for you to confirm it's coming through. Then we can talk further if you've got questions. And Colonel, thanks again." Nelson hung up the phone.

"They'll be moving on it within the hour, Mr. President."

"How are they going to do it? I know we told them what we wanted, but I'm just curious?"

"They've got several scenarios mapped out and hopefully we'll catch a break. It's our turn, I do believe."

The president smiled. "Yes, Bud, we are long overdue for a break."

The black house phone on the desk rang and Nelson grabbed it.

"Nelson. Yes, Colonel, send him in."

The door to the conference room opened and Chief of Staff Dan Josten came in.

"Bud, your machine is clean," Dan said, passing Nelson his personal p.c. back. "But..."

"But what, Dan?"

"But, there's indication that the back panel on that thing was opened recently. Have you had to have it serviced? Or did you install any new hardware in the thing?"

"Nope. The hardware on this what was there when I got it. I have been looking at getting the modem adapter for it, but I haven't gotten around to that yet."

"Well, Bud, someone has been inside your machine and the scratch mark on the seam right... there," said Josten, pointing to a mark on the p.c.'s case, "looks to have been made recently. Last couple of days at most."

Bud sat for a moment and thought.

"Danny, I just don't know. I keep it in my suitcoat all day and usually leave it on the counter at my house with my wallet and keys. I can't even think of anyone who..." Bud let the sentence trail.

"Anyone who? Anyone who what?" asked Josten.

"Well, I guess I can think of someone who might have had the opportunity. But I'm gonna have to ask you to let me track this one down. Please."

"Bud, we've got no secrets here," said the president.

"Well, sir. There's a lady friend I've had occasion to spend time with, if you get my drift. The other night was spent at her house. She is the only one who could have had any time alone with this thing."

"And that would be?"

"Annie Fidrych, Mr. President. Vice President Fulton's Chief of Staff. We've known each other since Charlest...."

"Don't even finish that sentence, Bud. Looks like this fucking thing goes a bit deeper than we've imagined," said the president. "Gentlemen, care for a beer? If I wasn't going to see the Chief Justice in the morning, I'd suggest we just get good and shitfaced. But going into chambers with The Chief, two other sitting justices, the attorney general and the senate majority leader with a hangover just wouldn't be good form now, would it?"

Nelson's cellphone chirped again.

"Nelson. Talk to me, bud" Nelson had a brief exchange with Fred about food, Agent Hannity and phone numbers.

Nelson closed up the cellphone and set it on the table.

"That was Fred. He's settled in with Admiral Dericksen. They're grabbing a little southern cookin' for a late night meal and they'll be looking for Hannity in the morning."

"Men," President Griffen spoke, "I think we've done all we can for now. It's almost nine-thirty now and it's been a really long day.

Perhaps a good night's sleep and fresh brainpower in the morning will help us see this mess in a different light."

At that, the four men rose, gathered up their notes and departed the subterranean conference room. The president would simply head upstairs to his living quarters, while Nelson and Josten would head for their homes. Agent Hannity would head for his abode, pack a few things in a bag, offer a brief, non-satisfying explanation to Pip and grab a few hours sleep. Then, head for Andrews Air Force Base where he'd be flown to Charleston first thing in the morning.

twenty-five

Marvin Moore hung up the phone from his conversation with Speaker Hewes and grabbed his hotel key. It had been a busy day and being not yet nine p.m. and his body felt more like four p.m., he had time for a cold one.

Dimitri hated to leave Yevgeny flying solo. There had been occasions in the past, but this time was different. This time, they were no more than seven days away from pulling off the greatest coup in history. That's what it was, Dimitri knew, but it was more like a hostile takeover rather than a coup d'etat. The pieces had been in place for twenty-two years and the wheels had been turning on this for a bit longer. Dimitri knew his role coming in from that first meeting with Colonel Rostokovich in Murmansk. The role of baby-sitter to Yevgeny was initially tedious. By shaping and adding substance to the role of Marvin Moore, Dimitri was able to allow himself some diversion from the constant insecurities expressed by Yevgeny. And, Dimitri had obtained a level of confidence that bordered on insubordination. The initiating of the White House scandal without approval from Romanov or Rostokovich was an act of sheer brilliance. At least that was Moore's feeling. When the time was right, he'd inform President Romanov and maybe Colonel Rostokovich. Twenty-two years on the job had to allow for some initiative. The signals had been arriving that the time was drawing near and Hewes and Moore needed to be ready. The Cold War over, there was nothing like a little scandal to act as a huge diversion.

Which explains why most Americans had seemed preoccupied of late with the peccadilloes of President Griffen. The young lady and her allegations were easy enough to set up. She had been paid handsomely to learn her story, as had her supporting witnesses. The situation was set up for a late, working evening when it was known that the President was alone in the Oval Office.

The young lady was sent to the President bearing a large folder of papers from the State department that required his urgent attention. Just glancing over the thick sheaf of printed material would keep her waiting for further instruction a minimum of twenty minutes. An amount of time that would be noticed by the security detail as excessive for a simple delivery of information.

The senior secret service agent buzzed President Griffen after about five minutes had passed to check on him. The President, according to the statements of the Marine corporal sharing the sentry post, replied curtly that everything was under control.

The young lady emerged from the Oval Office, disheveled and upset. Her blouse was missing the three top buttons and her skirt was not completely pulled down in the back.

President Griffen had finished reviewing the papers, politely answering a few questions and when he initialed the cover page as having looked them over, he returned the folder to her. He graciously thanked her for bringing the information up and suggested that she call it a night. He returned his attention to the other work spread out on his desk and did not see it took her all of ten seconds to rip her blouse, muss her hair and fix her skirt to look askew before opening the outer door.

When asked by the security team what happened, she erupted in a fit of hysterics which brought President Griffen into the hallway. The president was aghast. One look and he knew what was going on.

Unfortunately for him, everyone else within sight at that moment, and those subsequently privy to the recall of events according to the woman, thought they knew what had transpired. The president's view and those of the others were not the same.

An American president charged with assault and attempted sexual assault. Griffen was completely dumbfounded. He maintained his innocence through the initial phase, which did include the pressing of charges and a hastily arranged private arraignment in front of a District of Columbia judge.

The media detail outside the White House had not completely folded for the night and the infamous photo of the woman in complete disarray was on the front page of the Washington Post by the time the early edition hit the streets at midnight. The photographer was unaware that his editor had received a tip on the phone that something big was going on at 1600 Pennsylvania Avenue. The photographer only knew that he was to wait a while longer before packing it in. He had one chance to get the shot when he'd heard the commotion near the entrance at the East Wing. His telephoto lens brought it all into focus just as she stepped through the door, being quickly escorted to a waiting Chevy Suburban, the big vehicle of choice of the Secret Service.

Mrs. Griffen, who had been on a national health care tour, heard about the incident on the Los Angeles eleven o'clock news. It was the first time she had heard of the woman, Pam Stark. But it was not the first time she had thought her husband capable of infidelity. The Griffen's marriage was considered in good shape, but the occasional late nights gave Anne Marie reason for pause.

That set-up had been Marvin's coup de grace. It was clean as a whistle and the money they'd paid Ms. Stark was money well spent. And Marvin even had his fifteen minutes of fame following the event, by appearing on the nightly newscasts as being shocked by the reported events and saddened that a young woman he worked with on a daily basis could be attacked in the supposed sanctity of the White House. But, he cautioned, we should all keep in mind that there is no presumption of guilt on the part of anyone in the United States. The presumption of innocence and an appropriate presentation of the facts was in order. Classic Moore, he'd thought upon reflection. Anyone who felt they knew the man from the early Seventies would think that, yes, that is Marvin Moore and he hasn't changed. Getting Moore "down to a T" was not an easy task, however.

The days Dimitri spent in Oslo following Yevgeny's reconstructive surgery were filled with hours upon hours of Dimitri's watching the final moments of Marvin Moore's life. Moore seemed like a nice enough fellow. Personable, smooth and extremely knowledgeable. Why the Directorate had not simply tried to recruit Moore for this project was a question Dimitri asked the Colonel once. Only once. Never again. Not after the ass chewing given by Rostokovich. Well, it might have been more of a stern warning to Dimitri to push that train of thought right out of his mind. Michail had warned him to especially never wonder that idea aloud in the presence of President Romanov. The litany of why's was lengthy. The primary one being that Americans, as a whole, are good for the short term and what might be considered small potato-sized information. But when talk turns to actually bringing down the entire country, then things had a tendency to change.

Moore had met a peaceful end. At least, peaceful as far as he was concerned. The actual murder was included on the tape. The preferred term was elimination. The man known as Dayle had gotten all of the useful information they would need from Moore. Most of it had been given freely. Some of it was extracted forcefully, with a few ugly moments when Mr. Dayle removed two of Moore's fingers. With garden shears. Then, when Mr. Dayle had found a touch of humanity and given Moore some Demerol for the pain. Once the pain had subsided, Moore was a bit more forthcoming with additional points, some of them salient. Then, when that avenue of opportunity had been taken to its end, Mr. Dayle broke out the sodium pentothal. The resulting answers to questions from Moore had been what had already been provided. The only sticking points had involved the whereabouts of the only known living family members, the aunt and the grandmother, both of whom died tragically in a fire at the grandmother's home. Once all the pertinent, possible information had been obtained, Mr. Dayle increased the intravenous drip of sodium pentothal to lethal. Mr. Marvin Moore, genius political consultant, yet virtual nobody, drifted off to sleep. Mr. Bello then performed his specialty that had endeared him to the community of the nefarious as "Lungboy." Using an eight inch hypodermic needle, he made a subtle injection of air into the chest cavity, through the back. The introduction of air into the pleural cavity outside of the lungs caused the lungs to collapse. The spasms Moore suffered and caught on video tape would probably have been very uncomfortable to a conscious person. Mr. Moore had been all but dead, but the body's natural reflex reaction indicated something excruciatingly painful. Lungboy's method had thus far proven successful and with the microscopic size of the hole made by the hypodermic needle, it had also, thus far, remained undetected by any one of a number of medical examiners in their post-mortem examinations of several victims of Mr. Bello's handiwork.

Once Yevgeny was healed and ready to begin his part of the briefing, Rostokovich had arrived back in Oslo. Three weeks had passed and the Colonel had moved up the time table to begin their part. They'd be leaving Oslo in just a few days, headed first to Montreal in Canada, then, via automobile to a border crossing in southern Ontario. They'd travel to Montreal under their Soviet Union passports as members of the diplomatic corps. Once in Montreal, Dimitri and Yevgeny would cease to exist. They would then travel into the United States as Marvin Moore and M.Bradford Hewes, with passports that had already been stamped for entry into Canada. They would both be accompanied by Mike Rosty.

For their final forty-eight hours in Oslo, Dimitri and Yevgeny were schooled and drilled by Colonel Rostokovich. Dimitri had Moore down cold. The facial mannerisms. The nondescript accent. Even the chortle-like laugh, which, Dimitri had assumed was Moore's way to acquiesce to whatever might have passed for humor from the politico du jour.

Yevgeny had his details down solid as well. The video tape Rostokovich had brought with him contained at least four solid hours of interviews he had personally conducted with Hewes. The setting was the study in the Hewes family manor house. Rostokovich had taken the lead as a campaign coordinator, doing all the background work on Hewes. The interview on video tape had been a natural. The Colonel had told Brad it was just a way to get him used to being in the media spotlight, having cameras record his every word and move. Fortunately for Yevgeny, Hewes was well spoken and easily understood, with just a touch of a drawl as an affectation on his speech. For the most part, he was a man at ease. Unlike Yevgeny. The physical aspects had also been caught on tape in the few instances when Hewes had gotten up and walked about the room, the camera following his every move. The slight stiffness of one knee, which the Colonel had picked up on and asked of, was explained away as the after-effects of an attempt at snow skiing during a long, Vermont weekend getaway a few years earlier.

The deeper emotions were brought out in the session just prior to the end of the life of M. Bradford Hewes. That being the occasion of the Romanov pep talk for Yevgeny.

Dimitri walked into the lobby of the Sheraton where they were staying and gave a cursory glance into the hotel's bar. A few businessmen nursing their drinks, a few expatriates enjoying some preseason baseball on ESPN off the satellite. Not much to his liking, Dimitri stepped outside into the cool Paris night air. The suitcoat was enough of a buffer to the elements. He nodded to the doorman, who promptly hailed a cab.

Dimitri settled into the backseat and asked, in flawless French, for any night-life suggestions. The cabby acknowledged the question with a nod and pulled the car out into traffic. A few hair-raising minutes later, the cab slowed drastically, cutting sharply from the flow of traffic and stopping abruptly at a curb. La Place de la Russe was the name of the establishment. Dimitri paid the cabby the fare and a modest tip and hopped out of the backseat. Ironic, he thought, that a random cab, with a random driver, asked a non-specific question about where to go, would drop him at a Russian-themed nightclub.

Smiling at the irony, Dimitri stepped out of the cab as the bouncer opened the club's door. Even at the relatively early hour of nine-thirty, the club was loud, crowded and definitely happening. He walked over to the bar, ordered a vodka, straight up and sat down on an open stool. The age range in this club was everywhere from eighteen to sixty, at least. The first drink went down smoothly, quickly. He ordered another, which disappeared rapidly, too. He decided that two was good for now and settled in with a cola to watch the nightclub's floor as it pulsed with the heavy rhythm of the music and rippled with the multitude of dancers. Around ten-thirty, he decided on another vodka. As he ordered his third, a woman, about thirty or so, approached him and asked him for a light for her cigarette. How cliché, Dimitri thought. He reached over to the container of matches on the bar and struck one, noticing her deep, blue eyes. She smiled and glanced at the empty stool next to him. He pulled the stool a bit closer and gently guided her to the seat.

She smiled and said "Je m'appelle ...."

Cutting her off, Dimitri replied "Pas des noms, s'il vous plaite. No names, please. Parles-tu Anglaise?"

"Oui. er, yes. I speak some English."

"Good. Will you dance with me?"

She nodded her approval and they worked their way through the crowd to the floor. They danced for what seemed like hours, to songs both fast and slow.

Dimitri thought to himself how time was indeed a cruel thief as they worked their way back to the bar. He ordered them each another drink. As they watched the crowd and the people around them, she leaned in.

"Come with me, please?" she asked. Not just a request, but almost a plea.

Dimitri finished his drink and she hers. They got up, he followed as she led. They walked out into the street and flagged down a passing cab. He opened the rear door for her and he got in after she was settled. She spoke softly to the driver, giving him the address. He was thinking how lucky he was at this moment. A beautiful woman, Paris in the early spring, the night still young. She leaned over and kissed him. Firmly. Strongly. Passionately. He returned her kiss. A glance in the mirror from the driver. A glance in return that spoke volumes from Dimitri helped to return the cabby's attention to the road. They kissed more. He felt her hand on the inside of his thigh. She felt his hand on the soft curve of her breasts. He was feeling the effects of the strong Russian vodka, but not to the point where he was unable to feel the effects of her fingers. The cab slowed down and turned onto a small street. A series of turns and then a stop. By now, she had her head in his lap, he exposed to only her lips. She came up with a sly smile on her face, he fixed the zipper on his pants. He paid the cab driver the fare and an equal amount for the tip. He held the door for her, she climbed out, her skirt showing more than a touch of thigh. He closed the door and gave a wave to the driver. The cab pulled away and he pulled her tightly to him. They kissed for what seemed like hours, she gently pulling away, guiding him to the door. Her apartment was dark, lit with a flick of a switch. A tastefully decorated living room, which passed him by on the left as she took him down the hall. A small watercloset on the right, offset by a tiny kitchen to the left. The bedroom, lit from the glow of the living room lights, was soft, inviting. Their clothes littered the floor, her soft moans filling the room. Dimitri was made to feel masterful. He could not remember ever evoking such a response from a woman. They cuddled for a bit and he laughed softly to himself. She asked why. He tried to explain the meaning of "being in the zone." She reached low below the sheets and once again, he felt like Bird and the thrill of a nothing-but-net three pointer. He caught a glimpse of the digital clock on the bedside nightstand, two-seventeen am. The night had gone quickly. He'd regret this when he met with Papparelli in the morning. It was the morning, he realized. In a few hours, then. In the meantime, he was a man enjoying the carnal company of a woman that he'd only ever been able to imagine. He was the one providing the soundtrack this time. Their first romp was heavy and unbridled. She flipped him easily as if she were a world class wrestler. He was unable to maintain a rhythm, finishing well before he wanted to and well before she was ready. She used her fingers to turn his frown to a smile and said not to worry. They were far from done. Working a magic he'd never before experienced, he was, surprisingly, ready again. This time, she was in total control. He'd never, ever experienced this. Oh, he'd been with his share of women. But this? Never! She'd slow him down, then speed him up, then, she'd demonstrate phenomenal muscle tone, keeping him still for an eternity, then relaxing enough to allow for more coordinated motion. By now, she was on top and he was in his own private world.

When at last she had probably lost count, she once again worked her magic on him. She tightened her hold on him and he pulled her closer, nearing his ultimate pleasure with a fury he'd never known. She folded herself to him, her chin over his shoulder. He massaged and gently scratched her back. Her breathing softened, then steadily, slowed. She was asleep. He noticed the time on the digital clock. Five-oh-six. He was soon, as she, also sleeping soundly, satisfied.

When he awoke, he was afraid of feeling hungover, the effects of multiple vodkas and an all-night love making session weighing heavily on his mind. But the heaviness was not on his mind. It was on his chest. His arms. His legs. He could not move, nor could he see. He was bound and blindfolded. And, he knew, he was definitely late for his meeting with Secretary of State Papparelli. And he was most certainly in a world of trouble from which he probably would be unable to easily extract himself.

twenty-six

Don had closed the door to Fred's office at the front of the radio station. The floor to ceiling sliding glass door was covered with tan colored horizontal louvered blinds. Don gently worked the metal chain which closed the blinds tightly. Dusk was just about to give way to dark and Don hated the idea of anyone just looking in from the outside, watching. The added feeling of paranoia included the knowledge of what was going on and the players involved. He checked the time. Four-forty-five. Sandra would be working hard at the Eye, finishing up her piece for the early network feeds, then editing the special version for use with Dan on the network broadcast. He picked up the phone and punched in the numbers. The connection sounded clean and the ringing stopped after one. It was her voice mail. Damn it, Don thought, as he waited for the greeting to stop and the tone so he could start.

"Sandy. It's Don. We need your help up here in Vacationland. There's a charity roast for the lovely Olivia, our senior Senator, planned for next month and we're looking for some various-stage footage of the Speaker. We all know just how well they don't get along... and we're thinking a little creative video work. Can you give me a call back at here at Fred's office number, area code two-oh-seven, seven-seven-five, four-three-two-one? I'd appreciate it. I'll be here for a bit. It's not quite five yet. Fred's kind of hot on this project and he's hoping we can make this work. Thanks, Sandy. I mean it."

Don hung up the phone. And waited. Too much waiting gave him time to think.

After the Navy, Don took his BA in journalism and his three years of navy experience to New York. He'd been told a great place to start was the network newsroom. And he'd been told that timing was everything. Friday was the best day to walk in, resume and writing portfolio in hand. Reason being that Friday was payday and the day that those newswriters who weren't cutting it would be given their paycheck, two weeks severance and the thanks of the network for giving it a try.

He walked into NBS headquarters and asked for the news director. He'd waited over two hours. Timing in this case was bad and good. Bad in that it was springtime, 1980. The Iranian hostage crisis was in full swing and the Presidential primaries were shifting into high gear. Good in that the news director had just given walking papers to a couple of writers who'd been spending too much time working on each other instead of getting the facts nailed down for a proper presentation by America's most trusted man and anchor. Don hadn't planned on it, but he went to work in the NBS newsroom that day, twenty minutes after meeting with the boss, Kevin Flannagan.

He was assigned a work station and shown where the AP and UPI wires came in, as well as how to access the network directory for contacting every NBS affiliate and foreign service bureau in the world. His first call was for a quick fact check on a allegation about a Three Mile Island technician and whether or not this man was seen holding court at a local watering hole prior to his shift the previous month. He nailed down the information, getting not only one additional confirming source, but three. He had names, addresses and invitations from two of them to send down whomever they pleased to interview them. The "fifteen minutes of fame" syndrome was running hand in hand with the "China syndrome." The American people had barely had time to digest the anti-nuclear sentiments of the Hollywood presentation of the most down side of nuclear energy, when reality reared its ugly head and imitated art, with the reactor core disaster at Three Mile Island. Don looked about and saw no one at first, then, he saw her. Another young writer frantically gesturing, yet speaking softly on the phone, attempting to persuade someone to confirm or deny or correct something. She was no more than twenty-two, by Don's guess. Light brown hair and fair skin. She turned, looking at no one in particular and Don saw the full face. She was a beauty. No doubt about it that someone in network saw this young lady and suggested a course of training, followed by years of high TVQ approval ratings. She hung up the phone, dejectedly. Don walked over and just as she was reaching for the phone to place another call, he cleared his throat.

"Er, hi. I'm Don Hough. New guy. Can you help me out on a quick question?"

"Hi, I'm Sandy," she smiled. "But only so long as it's really quick."

"I've just got three confirming sources on this Three Mile Island thing Flannagan tossed at me ten minutes after he hired me and I'm not sure who or where the managing editor is. Any clues? Directions? Maps?"

Sandy laughed and tossed her hair gently back off of her face. She pointed towards a closed, glass-fronted room towards the set entrance.

"That's Bob's office over there. Door's closed, he's in. And probably dealing with some prima-donna in the field over fees."

"Fees?"

"Yeah. The stars get a salary, then they get more money for live-shots, stand-ups, wraps, voice-overs. The union makes it pretty good for the performe...oops, excuse me. For the correspondents. When the weekly talent sheets come in, Bob spends more time re-watching all the network casts when he thinks one of them is trying to jam the network for a few extra alimony bucks. To be honest, if the correspondent in the field is okay, you know, not a major asshole to deal with, then he just signs off on their sheets. But the bigger the ego, the closer the scrutiny. It's his way of getting the bastards back down to earth."

"Gotcha. So, if the door opens, it's okay to go in?"

"Use your judgment. It's what, three-fifteen? So we're less than three hours to the first feed. And you've got three sources willing to confirm something for the Three Mile Island thing? Do they want to go on camera? The idiots upstairs love it when we get Mister or Missus America, live."

"Yes, two of them are willing to go any time. They even gave me addresses where they'll be for the rest of the day."

"Go knock and open the door. Now."

"I don't even know the guy," Don protested. "I just got here. For all I know, my car's been towed or stolen. I came in for an interview at eleven and by one forty-five, I'm fact-checking on this story."

"Timing *is* everything, isn't it, Don? Go in there now. Tell him what you've got. Then, when it sinks in and he asks you just who the hell you are, introduce yourself. Once the screaming stops, hand him the paper you've got in your hand and come back here. I'll get you a cup of coffee and you can work up the nerve to ask me out for dinner tonight. Say nine-thirty? I'll pick a place that's not too expensive and I'll treat. No, wait. I just paid my rent. You'll treat. I'll listen raptly to everything you say."

Dinner that night led to breakfast the next morning. Don didn't have to worry about finding a place to put his stuff. Sandy invited him to stay. She knew that workplace relationships were destined for failure, but Don was willing to try if she was. By the end of the first month, Don and Sandy were inseparable. By the end of the first year, both had been promoted to senior writers, sitting in on five o'clock script meetings with Cronkite. By the end of the second year, both were spending weekends on Long Island Sound with Cronkite. They both cried when "Uncle Walter" told them he'd be hanging it up and telling America that "That's the way it is..." for the last time. By the end of the third year, Bud had come into NBS News as the vice president of the broadcast news division. Bob kept his job, thanks in part to kind words from Don. But Bud had plans. Dan Rather was at the desk now and he'd noticed, as had far too many men, that Sandy was being under-utilized. Don held no preconceived notions that she would be his partner in the newsroom forever. By 1983, into their fourth year together, Sandy was in the London bureau, the primary European network mouthpiece and face.

Bud had seen, the minute he met Sandra Rose, that she was destined for greatness. She was not only beautiful, but she was highly intelligent and an extremely smooth communicator. Plus, as Bud had found out while spending lost weekends in New York at Sandy and Don's apartment, that Sandy was the equal of any man when it came to knocking back shots of Stoly and enjoying a good cigar. It was Sandy who'd pointed Bud in the right direction of the small tobacconist in the Village who, with the correct phrasing, could allow Bud to savor the highly rich, yet illegal, flavor of Castro's finest export, Cohiba.

Bud had wound up at the network through a stroke of luck and the aforementioned good timing. He'd been brought into the local Charleston NBS affiliate as an assistant operations manager, based on his Navy experience as the communications center's executive officer. He'd come highly recommended through his division officer and the base's commanding officer, Rear Admiral Mark Conlon. Conlon had gotten used to being called by Nelson at all hours, leaving him to wonder at what point Lieutenant (jg) Nelson took time for personal liberty. The base communications center was staffed twenty-four/ seven. It never closed and it seemed that whenever high priority or super-sensitive messages were received, Nelson was the one calling Admiral Conlon at home. Conlon's brother-in-law, Bob Scolan, was the general manager at the NBS affiliate and when it came time for Bud to separate from active duty, he'd walked into the job. He had been on the job for almost a year when Scolan moved Bud up to the operations manager position. Then, during his second winter at the helm of running the station's day-to-day operations, as well as doubling as news director, he'd received an invitation to play golf with Conlon, Scolan and the legendary William S. Paley. Paley was spending some vacation time at Hilton Head and had extended the invitation to Scolan and Conlon. The station's smooth, on-air presentation and slickly produced newscasts had caught the attention of Paley and he'd asked to meet the man responsible for making one of his fine affiliates look so good. Bud played the worst golf of his life, as did Conlon and Scolan. Paley left the course somewhat euphoric, having shot a respectable 85 and taken several dollars from each of the other three. Paley sprang for dinner and the conversation after lasted well into the wee hours of the morning. Nelson had excused himself during dinner to phone into the station, make notes on that evening's cast and passed along a few suggestions. Paley was duly impressed with Bud's dedication and taking advantage of a gut feeling, he asked Nelson how he'd feel about making a move to New York in the future. Bud had expressed interest, much to the chagrin of Scolan, who did not want to lose such a talented, versatile man. Bud got the call to come to New York a few short months later and walked into the NBS news division as its new vice president.

Don and Sandy were briefly reunited in London in October of 1983, as Bud wanted Don to base himself there in a new role as field correspondent. Don was invited to move in with Sandy, which he did gladly. Their brief long-distance relationship was taking its trans-Atlantic toll. Don, however, was in London for far too short a time. The bombing of the Marine barracks in Beirut was Don's first call to action. Filing on-scene reports while the rubble was being cleared and the victims were being recovered, Don distinguished himself as a find for the news division, one of many credited to Bud. But Don's ability to be the go-to guy for Bud and the network kept him away from London and Sandy. By 1987, Don was spending most of his time in the middle-east, covering everything from the hijackings of the TWA airliner and the Achille Lauro, to the Iraqi blasting of the Stark. Plus, the ongoing troubles in Lebanon, the West Bank and Gaza strip were creating enough daily interest that Hough soon became Bud's favorite desert rat. The kidnapping of Anglican envoy Terry Waite by radical factions had, in and of itself, created what would become a four year story. That in turn led to Operation Desert Shield which became Operation Desert Storm. Don had done one live stand-up during a missile raid and decided that he'd had enough. Had he hung in there for another one or two, he might've given The Scud Stud, Arthur Kent from NBC, a run for his money.

In March of 1991, just as Don was due to return to London, he'd gotten news from Sandy that she was getting married. Just not to Don. A call to the new news division chief changed the relocation of Don from London to the Washington bureau, where he spent time shuffling between the Pentagon and the White House. By 1992, he'd had enough. The lying and spinning that was put on everything, on top of the years of not being sure if he'd finish an assignment alive, led him to the hardest decision he'd thought he'd ever have to make. He submitted his resignation, with the only sure thing ahead of him being his destination, Maine. Even with the possibility of Bud coming to town with a new administration, which would have put Don in the most enviable of positions for political reporters, was not enough to sway his feelings about getting out. For now.

Bud had left the network in 1990 to venture into the world of politics. He bemoaned the fact that he'd missed the Desert Storm coverage. The high tech video capabilities from the actual field of fire alone had signaled a new era in news reporting and not being there for that had been Bud's one regret about leaving. The network hadn't been the same since Bill Paley stepped aside and he felt it was time for a new adventure. That was when the campaign of the incumbent Governor of New Hampshire had called and asked for his help. The re-election of John Griffen to the state house in Concord was struggling. Griffen had sent out feelers, asking for suggestions of who might be able to help. Bill Paley had been ill for some time and before his passing, had sent word to Governor Griffen that perhaps, Nelson might be the man to aid in pulling this one out of the fire.

Governor Griffen was re-elected, handily. And even amidst the post-victory celebrations, the network wags were talking of a potential Presidential candidacy in 1992. The 1992 primary was remarkable, in that Governor Griffen had received thirty-percent of the vote, as a last minute candidate. Nelson had carefully orchestrated the Governor's schedule so as not to interfere with the day to day running of the State and the media, as well as his opponents, had made note of this. In light of this astounding showing, based on minimal campaign appearances and letting none of the business of New Hampshire suffer, the dark-horse candidate ventured into Iowa. There, on the strength of only five pre-election rallies, he took the checkered flag. Subsequent caucuses and primary elections kept the Griffen for President machine rolling. That July, the delegates to the convention in New York unanimously nominated John Francis Griffen as candidate for President of the United States and the following day, Donald Robert Fulton, governor of South Carolina, accepted his role as Griffen's running mate. Once November had rolled around, the Griffen/Fulton ticket had won the general election and Bud's position on the inside had been secured.

About the same time, Fred Singletary had taken some profits from playing the market and bought a radio station in Portland, both as an investment and as something to do. Bud, Don and Chuck had made respectable careers in broadcasting and, with their insights and encouragement, he'd taken the leap. WCBR was a good little station and, by playing with the tax laws, he was carrying very little debt, avoiding the penalties that came with capital gains. When Don had told him of his decision to leave the network, Fred didn't blink twice before asking Don if he'd like to come and be the news director. Don jumped at the thought of being a simple newsman again. The network had gotten just too crazy. And, Don thought, by burying himself in Maine, he'd be less apt to ever cross paths with Sandy again.

The phone rang and Don brought himself out of his trip down memory lane. He threw a glance at the clock. Five-fifteen. "Hello?"

"Don? It's Sandy. How you doing?"

"I'm doing fine, Sandy. And you?"

"Just great." There was a noticeable pause on the line. "So, what's up with the video stuff? Is there a story in this for me?"

"Not much of a story, unless you want to hear a bunch of folks who say "ayuh" after every sentence extolling the virtues of Senator Olivia. We were just looking for some footage of the Speaker to put together a little montage to show how much he has aged and yet how Olivia has maintained that youthful look. They've both been in Washington since the late Seventies, so Fred was thinking that it'd be a funny bit. It's that Downeast humor, dontcha know."

Sandy laughed. And set off another flood of memories for Don.

"I think we can do that. How much time do we have? You, don't, like, need it tomorrow, do you?"

"Well, actually, Sandy, we do. I know it's asking a lot, but we're looking for no more than a ten second clip of the Speaker saying anything from say, maybe every five of the past twenty-two years. Looking for five, maybe six little bits at most. But the first one needs to be something from '76, preferably from the first campaign, if you've got any archived. Aren't there some tape hounds down there who can do this as a favor to you tonight?"

"Gee, Don. Put the pressure on a girl, why don't you. Are you going to be reachable this evening?"

"Yeah, I'll be at home. You have the number, right?"

"Yeah, I still have it. So how have *you* been?"

She was fishing, Don knew. She'd no doubt want to know if there was a new lady in his life. If he was over her and moving on. But Don knew he'd never be over her and had only taken baby-steps in any one of a number of short-lived relationships over the past eight years.

"I've been holding my own, Sandy. Fred's keeping me gainfully employed and I don't really miss the big leagues. It's nice to go into the supermarket and buy groceries without wearing sunglasses. I really got tired of the Scud-Stud comparisons. What about you? And Jonathon?"

"We're, um, trying to work though something right now. He's gone back to London to attempt to bring his feelings into perspective, or at least that's what he told me."

"Sandy, I'm sorry to hear that. Really. When did this happen?"

"About a month ago. I've been fortunate in that the gossips haven't gotten around to it yet. Jon's business ventures are all over there anyway, so it's not unusual for him to be gone for months at a time."

As soon as she'd said this, she wished it back, but it was too late.

"Oh," was all Don could muster in reply.

"Don, I'm so sorry. I shouldn't have said that. I know how it sounded and it was wrong of me to say it."

"It's alright, Sandy. Don't give it another thought."

"I do need to say this, though, while I've got the nerve. I am so sorry that we ended the way we did. And in seeing what a jerk Jonathon has turned out to be, well, I've been doing my own thinking. I was wrong to allow our physical distance become the chasm it did on the relationship level. If there was ever a time that I've needed your understanding, it would be now."

Don allowed what she'd said to sink in. She just admitted she was wrong for leaving him. Wrong for marrying Jon.

"Sandy, de nada. Why don't you plan on calling me later this evening when we're both at home. You can talk more and I'll listen. Okay? It's just been a really long day up here and I've got to get up in about nine hours to come back here and do it all over again."

"Okay, Don. Let me check on the video stuff and I'll call you. Is eight too late?"

"No, Sandy. Eight'll be great. I'll talk to you then. And thanks."

"Bye-bye, Don."

Don hung up the phone and was momentarily basking in the glow of a small victory. She'd admitted that the whole Jonathon thing was a mistake. Or, maybe a mistake. Don would take the maybe, regardless. Now, the question would be whether or not he should pursue this newly reopened avenue any further.

Sandy was on the verge of tears. She'd just opened herself up in a way that no woman should ever do. She'd admitted failure. She'd admitted ultimate bad judgment. And she'd realized that leaving Don hanging out to dry just when he was preparing to return to London was a cruel, cruel blow. Jonathon had, within their first two years of marriage, turned out to be a first-class bastard. His occasional physical outbursts were followed by endless hours of pleading and promises. She'd had to miss work for three days following one close encounter with his fist. The black eye would've shone through any number of layers of makeup. The final straw had come when one of his business ventures was losing money. Lots of money. He had taken his frustration out on her, leaving her to drive herself to the emergency room. If you could call it luck, she was driving with at least three broken ribs and the pain became too much for her to bear.

She lost consciousness and her car skidded into a brick retaining wall just south of Central Park. When she came around, she was in the back of a New York City Fire Department ambulance, on her way to the hospital. The doctors and there were several based on who she was, did a thorough check of her. She'd probably lost consciousness, they guessed, due to her being pregnant. It was not unheard of. The resulting crash, however, had left her with three broken ribs and suffering a miscarriage. When the doctor explained all of this to her, she'd cried. She hadn't known she was pregnant. And the belief that the broken ribs had occurred as a result of the accident would keep her from having to explain to the media how she could have put up with any type of physical abuse. Jonathon had come to the hospital the next morning. He'd found out where she was from a nurse who had called their house, out of courtesy. If the nurse had known that Sandy did not wish for this man to know, then that might have raised some eyebrows in suspicion. Sandy had looked at him and told him to be out of their house by dinner-time. She said that her lawyer was already working on the papers and they could make this as pleasant or as messy as *he* wanted. Jonathon was on the evening flight to London, with his possessions en route via UPS.

Sandy composed herself and picked up the phone to call the tape morgue. She'd told the guy in the tape room at the other end of the phone what they were looking for and why. The guy mentioned he liked Senator Olivia and would be honored to help out.

Sandy gave him the mailing address for Michaud Media in Maine, hung up the phone, checked her voice mail for any additional messages and left NBS for the evening. It would also be the last time she would ever set foot in the network's headquarters.

twenty-seven

Charleston, South Carolina Friday, April 3, 1998 8:30pm (local)

The Gulfstream touched down at the Charleston Air Force base at eight-thirty p.m.. The flight time from Washington was just a little more than an hour. Fred had told Gary to meet him around nine p.m., so Fred would have some time to kill. Of course, waiting on a military installation was not a lot of fun for a civilian. Especially a civilian who used to be in the military and knows how much the military enjoy keeping an eye on errant civilians. The feeling that Fred himself recalled passing on to unattended civilians while he was on board the Sierra, using mental-telepathy, was probably similar to that of a fine-collectibles shopkeeper to his or her customers: Look. But Heaven help you if you even *think* about touching.

But had the pilot realized it, or had Fred remembered, they could have just as easily taxied to the civilian side of the airfield and dropped Fred at the general aviation terminal. There, he would have been able to grab a quick beer or a bite while he killed time waiting for the Admiral to show.

Instead, Fred sat patiently in the Air Force duty office, watching the evening shift run through their paces. It was busier than a normal peace-time evening, however. The base had been a staging point for many of the flights heading overseas to help enforce the no-fly zones in Iraq, or to monitor the situations in Bosnia and Yugoslavia. The aircraft consisted mainly of the Stealth Bombers and conventional jet fighters. The troops being sent overseas were usually funneled through Pope Air Force base in North Carolina, due to its proximity to Fort Bragg in Fayetteville. The office afforded a view of the airfield and there were two of the larger, B-2 Stealth Bombers parked nearby on the tarmac, under armed guard.

He needed to make one phone call, though. But couldn't. Not here in the duty office. He most certainly didn't want to spend time trying to talk in circles to avoid mentioning any pertinent details in plain English. Not that the Air Force personnel on duty weren't cleared Top Secret or better, but there was still that "need to know" criteria that must be met before disclosing any sensitive information. He checked his watch. Dericksen should be arriving in about fifteen minutes. Gary was an okay guy, Fred thought. And he knew him to be a solid, stand-up kind as well.

While serving under Admiral Gary Dericksen, ComSubGru2, in Charleston on board the *Sierra* , they had become friends. It was unusual for an Ensign, not of the Academy, to befriend a flag-bearing line officer. Gary had enjoyed the education that Fred was able to provide in regards to investments and the stock market. On Fred's suggestion, Gary had bought stock in Digital and Disney. The Digital stock had a nice ride for almost seven years and Gary had reaped a five-digit profit. The Disney stock, bought for under thirty dollars a share, had grown to over two-hundred a share. Fred had taught Gary about when to sell, when to buy, when to hold and when to expect a split or a slip. By the time Gary was ready to put in his papers for retirement, after thirty years in the Navy, his stock portfolio was fast approaching seven figures. An Admiral had a bit more discretionary income than did an Ensign. Gary had enough invested to start up his own security consulting business. His Navy pension was three times as much as the salary paid to the lowliest Ensign. He and Sue were able to pay off their mortgage a year after hitting the beach. The business debt was cleared within five years, when it was no longer of advantage for their tax situation.

But within five years, the business had grown into one of the largest private enterprises in South Carolina. The advent of computers and the reliance on these beasts of technology by businesses, made for a bountiful harvest. Gary was on the cutting edge of helping his clients to prepare for and ward off, high-tech espionage. He'd been able to hire the experts as quickly as the Silicon Valley could produce them. These young guns would come east and have a background in the latest technology that couldn't be found in books. The manual had just enough of the basic information that a user could rely on for day-to-day. But the programmers had the know-how to make the collection of micro-chips and wires hum with the efficiency for which they were intended. Then, once a year or two had passed, the geniuses would head north or west, looking to hang out their own shingle on their own business. Gary would then grab the next kid heading out of The Valley with a full tank of gas and dreams of the east.

Gary and Sue had taken on Fred as their "little brother." Fred didn't mind the attention. It was nice. He had no family to speak of and there was no one at home to whom he would return at the end of each day. His getaways to Charleston were always welcome diversions. Nice weather, bad golf and great food. The money was nice, but he knew there was more in life to be had.

Fred didn't make his killing until the small company he'd heard of in 1976 went public. The shares in the Microsoft Corporation went ballistic. Fred's holdings of several thousand shares were enough to maintain a quality of life of which many can only dream. His net worth, based on his stock portfolio alone, enabled him to finance the purchase of WCBR. His actual worth, based on his many savings accounts, both in the States and in off-shore banks, enabled him to loan himself the money to buy the radio station. The high level of wealth he had achieved had become the only way of life which would keep Fred Singletary happy. He had financial independence and enjoyed the company of a beautiful, smart woman when the need arose. He still held a few beliefs that even those whom he held nearest and dearest would never fathom. It was his "dark side." They would, Fred knew, be first aghast, then repulsed, then angered.

Gary pulled up, still driving his now vintage 1973 MGB. Fred stood, gathered up his bag and gave a hearty salute to the Sergeant on duty at the desk. He stepped out of the door into the mild spring night. It was still as he remembered, Fred realized. Warm, a touch of humidity and the big, welcoming smile of Gary Dericksen, Admiral, United States Navy, retired.

"Hey, you old queer!' Fred yelled.

"Hey yourself, you floating fucking target!" Gary replied.

"At least I'm not the one who spent his time going down on things that are long, round, hard and full of seamen."

"Geez, Fred. Still using that one after all these years?"

"Still gets the occasional smile, so I'll keep rolling it out. How's the B running?"

"Just over two-hundred thousand miles and this little British piece o' shit will still hum very nicely at eighty. Last week, I had to pop in two new carbs and it took me three days to get 'em tweaked just right. Damn S/U's. They seem to do the job, but it's like the two batteries in the back here; the car won't run with just one of them, so why the hell did they bother?"

"Gotta ask yourself if it was simply a matter of revenge. You know, the Tea Party, the Revolution, the Declaration. Those Brits were pretty much put out with us, if I'm not mistaken. First the MG, then the Spice Girls. They're working on evening up the score, my friend, one decade at a time. The next big thing is the Teletubbies."

"Teletubbies? Do I want to know?"

"Not really. They might be just a bit advanced for a man of your age. Unless you've got grandkids kicking around. Then and only then, will you understand the warning I attempted to impart upon you. Speaking of which, any news?"

"What? Warnings? Or Grandkids?"

"The latter. Wasn't Brandi expecting? Due around now?"

"She is still expecting. Just running closer to past-due. Sue left today to fly out to San Diego to be there with her. My son-in-law is on day sixty of a ninety-day cruise. I tried to yank some strings to get him swapped over to the Blue crew, but the Gold c.o. is a son of a bitch and said no. Even a little friendly persuasion from my other sea-son, now ComSubGru1, Admiral Whithers, couldn't help. So, my grandchild will be spoiled rotten by the time Daddy gets off the boat. At least, that's my assessment of how Sue will leave things in California."

"Don't you need to be there, too?"

"I'd love to be there. But your call sounded important. Hop in and tell me what's up while we drive."

Fred ran him through the scenario as they understood it.

"It sounds to me like it's almost his word against theirs," said Gary. "Unless there's a boatload of documentation for evidence. What's Nelson want us to do?"

"He wants us to poke around the city and see if there's anyone who knew Hewes from college. Maybe knew him growing up. And although it's against the law, we probably will want to take a peek around the Hewes family plantation. See if there's any evidence of the murder, perhaps?"

"Twenty-two years is a long time to hope to find traces of a shallow grave or anything like that, Fred. Let's stop and get a bite to eat and then back to the Dericksen ranch. Grab a good night's sleep and then we'll start being private eyes in the morning. You feel like Tex-Mex? There's a great new place just up the road a bit."

"Sounds like a meal plan to me, Gary. What do we have for tunes in this thing?"

Gary popped a cassette into the deck and the unique guitar sound of Lee Roy Parnell flew out of the speakers.

"Thought this would be appropriate for us," said Gary as he reached over to the crank up the volume.

"On the road," Lee Roy was singing. *"Where the night is black. On the road, where you don't look back."*

Charleston was still pretty much the same as Fred remembered. The magnolias lining the road, with the palmettos sprinkled in with more frequency as they neared the water. It was a beautiful night. Warm. Not too humid. Gary was heading across the interstate now and the outline of the Cooper River Bridge loomed ahead. Fred looked right towards the downtown district. That, he realized, had changed. The late-night lights burning in the newer office buildings offset the brightly-lit Customs House. The new waterfront marketplace on the Cooper River side of the harbor was bustling. Fred imagined the sounds of live music filling the air around the walkways. Couples strolling, enjoying a perfect spring night in Charleston. As Gary's MG crested the high point of the bridge, the *U.S.S. Yorktown* came into full view. The spotlights tastefully lit the number "10" on the aircraft carrier's superstructure. Fred always enjoyed this part of his trips down here. Isle of Palms was a little bit of paradise right in the heart of a bustling city. Gary slowed at the lights at the entrance to Patriot's Point, the home of the *Yorktown*.

"The place I've got in mind for our late dinner is just about a half mile down the road here, Fred."

"Sounds good to me, Gary. I'm getting kind of hungry. Although, now I feel guilty about not bringing you some lobster or steamers. That's what we had for lunch."

"That's alright, Freddie. They would've been cold by the time you got them here anyway," Gary paused. "But just for the sake of satisfying my curiosity, where did you guys eat?"

"The Lobster Shack."

"Damn you, all. At least, from what I saw on the *Today Show* this morning, you guys had a respectable snowfall. This, Fred," Gary said with a sweeping gesture, "Is what spring should be. Notice the lack of snowblowers and sand trucks."

"I noticed, Gary. Believe you me, I noticed."

Gary slowed the MG down and pulled into the parking lot of the Tex-Mex place.

"*The Neon Goat*? You've got to be kidding me?" exclaimed Fred. "It sounds like a place Nelson would open."

"That's the exact thing that popped into my mind the first time I saw it, too. It's got "Bud" written all over it. And, the food is really excellent."

"I'll let you order," Fred said as he climbed out of the car. "I've got a phone call to make."

"Why don't you just use your cellphone?"

"Well, Mr. Security. You tell me."

"Okay, if it's a sensitive call, then you've got a point. There's a payphone right inside the door."

"I was thinking I'd use the old reliable phone booth over there," Fred said, pointing to the gas station across the street. "It'll give me a hair more privacy."

"Tell Bud I said hi. But don't tell him about this place. I want to surprise him with it the next time we get him down here for golf."

"Gotcha. Give me about five minutes, Gary. I'll be right there. And yes, you may order me a *Dos Equis*."

"See you inside, Fred."

Gary walked towards the front entrance, while Fred hustled across the street. It was close to nine p.m., he noticed as he dialed in the toll-free access number for his calling card.

"Bud, Fred. Got here just fine and I'm about to have a little late dinner with Gary."

"What kind of dinner? Grits and gravy and stuff I hope," Nelson drawled.

"Something different for a change this time, Bud. Tex-Mex."

"One of our regular haunts out there on beautiful Sullivan's Island?"

"No, it's not one of the usual places, but Gary says it has to be a surprise for you for the next time you come down here."

"So what is this place? Some dive with a donkey and a stripper?"

"Sorry, Bud. It's a secret that doesn't apply to what we're doing right now. Need to know and all that crap."

"Fine. Be that way. See if I sleep tonight. Hey, take some mental notes here. The president wants you two to have some official company. Secret Service Agent Tom Hannity is heading your way in the morning. He should be in around at eight at the Air Force base. Pick him up and be nice to him."

"Agent Hannity will be here in the morning. Around eight, you think? Great. We'll pick him up, although I for one am sorry we won't be using the MG. The weather down here is sure better than what it was up in Maine."

"You're at Gary's. Is he still at... ah, here it is." Bud read off the telephone number in his little directory.

"Yes, Bud. Yes, that's Gary number, still."

"Now you boys be careful and call me when you find anything. Notice I said when and not if. Got it?"

"Right. I'll call you tomorrow as soon as anything comes up. If not, I'll call you around five and give you a sitrep. I'll talk with you then, Bud. Bye."

Fred hung up the phone and hit the pound sign to make another call. This one was a bit shorter: One question. One answer. Not the definitive answer he wanted, but it would have to do.

Fred re-entered his calling card number and called Don at home. The phone rang twice and Don answered, somewhat sleepily.

"Don, Fred. Sorry if I woke you."

"No, that's okay, Fred. The phone was ringing anyway. What's up?"

"Got down here to Charleston about an hour ago and now I'm heading out for some Tex-Mex with Gary. Anything cooking up there?"

"Nope. Been a quiet day. Well... I think you know what I mean. I talked with Sandy. She's gonna get us those videos as quick as she can. Hopefully, Michaud will have them in the morning. You need me to fill in for you at the Chamber meeting tomorrow?"

"If you can make it, Don. And thanks. Call me at Gary's if you need me, or try the cellphone. But I think you'll have better luck calling Gary's. He's got the voicemail and we may be kicking around in places where we don't need a cellphone trilling to give us away."

"Got it, Fred. Take it easy and call me tomorrow when you get a chance. Good luck. And Fred, be careful."

"I will Don. And thanks. But don't worry. If something does happen to me, you'll be very well taken care of. Call you tomorrow. Bye."

"Bye, Fred. And goodnight."

Fred hung up the phone and walked across the street, back to *The Neon Goat*. He saw Gary sitting at a table near the back, which wasn't hard to do. For one, the place wasn't very crowded. And for the other, well, Gary stood about six foot five. He wasn't hard to miss in most settings.

"Bud says to say "hi." Hi."

"I'll make sure I tell him you said "hi" next time I speak with him," Gary laughed. "Here come our beers now."

The waitress brought the two *Dos Equis*, setting them on cardboard coasters on the table.

"Have you had a chance to look at the menu?" she asked?

"Not yet, Joannie. Give us a few minutes?" asked Gary.

"Sure, hon. I'll be over there if you need me," the waitress said and walked back towards her staging area.

"To lasting friendships," Gary said, raising his beer in a toast.

"To lasting friendships," Fred replied.

They both took a sip of beer and leaned back in their respective chairs. The chairs were high-backed wicker, with thick, comfortable pads.

Fred spoke, "Guy could get used to this."

"Yeah, it's a nice place, the food is good, prices are reasonable and it's still one of the best kept secrets in the South. So what's up with Bud?"

"I told him I arrived safely and that you have a surprise for him the next time he gets down here. And he has a surprise for us. Agent Tom Hannity from the President's Secret Service detail is coming down to keep an eye on us."

"A baby-sitter?"

"No. Well, yes. But, as Bud pointed out, the man is authorized to carry a gun and use it if needed."

"Okay. An armed baby-sitter. I guess if we're going to go snooping around the homestead of the Speaker of the House, then a little "authorized" support won't hurt."

"Our cover story, should we run into anyone, is that we're investigating one of the many threats on the Speaker's life. Bud says that threats are made on a daily basis against just about every ranking elected official in Washington and that the Secret Service investigates each and every one. We'll just be taking a quick look around the Hewes family home to make sure that "details" included in one of the latest nasty-grams aren't too on-the-money. Agent Hannity's shield and credentials will help us buy enough time to wrap-up whatever we need to and get the hell out of there."

"Ah, here comes Joannie. Hey Joannie?" called Gary.

Joannie came back over to where the two men were seated. "Yes, boys?"

"Joannie. My friend and I would love to have a healthy serving of the specialty of the house. Nice and spicy!"

"Are you sure you want the spiced-up version?" she asked.

"Yeah. Bring it on. Flaming!" laughed Gary.

"Uh, Gary?" asked Fred. "Am I going to like this?"

"Trust me, Fred. Trust me."

"Didn't I use the same phrase with you on a stock tip once?"

"Once? You're still a funny guy, Fred. Wait until you wrap your tongue around these fajitas. Chicken, steak and the combo. All with a secret seasoning that makes pan-blackened seem tame by comparison."

Joannie hurried out to the kitchen while the two men continued to nurse their first two beers. In less than ten minutes, she returned and set down two sizzling platters. She nodded towards their almost empty beers and Gary, in mid-sip, nodded in the affirmative and flashed two fingers.

Fred picked up his bottle and raised it in a toast. "To the new grandkid! May you live to see his or her grandchildren."

"Fred. You're a kind man. Thank God, though, that your sense of time is not at all shared by your financial intuitiveness. I was an old fart when you met me twenty some-odd years ago."

The two friends laughed and both thanked the waitress when the second round appeared. They enjoyed their meal and several more cold beers. By the time eleven-thirty had rolled around, they were both feeling the effects of the meal and the beer. After the usual friendly bickering over who would pay the tab, Gary put the meal on his company credit card and the two walked carefully out to the waiting MG.

"Damn, Gary. I was doing fine until we stood up."

"That's the way it usually works, Fred. Thankfully, it's a five minute drive that way to the house."

"Well, drive on, Deucey. And watch out for those damn palm trees. It's a bitch when they jump out into the middle of the street."

"Like my favorite bumper-sticker, buddy. Don't like the way I drive, stay the hell off the sidewalk."

Gary started the car up, eased it out of the parking spot and onto the roadway. Five uneventful minutes later, they pulled into Gary and Sue's beachfront home. The driveway lights were motion-sensitive and came on as soon as the MG swung into the carport. The two friends climbed out of the English sports car and while Gary punched in the code to de-activate the home alarm system, Fred opened the small trunk of the car and took out his overnight bag. Gary held the house's side door open while Fred came in and, being no stranger to the house, Fred flicked on the light switch.

"Wow! I like what you've done to the kitchen! Was this your idea? Or Sue's?"

"I have to admit, it was all Sue's idea. I like it, too. I just wish that this business of mine didn't require so much time on the road. Every time I go to a trade show or out of state to help set up things for a new client, Sue spends our money before we get it. You, on the other hand, have the kind of business I need. Get up in the morning, shave, shower, a cup of coffee and go tell Hough what to do. Count the money, go to the bank and enjoy the evening."

"I wish it was all as simple as that, Gary. You at least have Sue. Me, all I've got is Don."

"At least Don doesn't redecorate your house while you're out of town."

"True. Although I have seen him looking at office furniture catalogs from time to time."

"So how is Don doing? He tends to be a homebody of sorts, doesn't he?"

"I've tried to bring him down here with me for our little mid-winter golf excursions, but he's never seemed interested. He takes his vacation time and just flops around the 'Port. We'll have to work on him together."

"Speaking of working together, you know the way to "your" room. I'm done in and I'll be in mine. Do we have a wake-up time in mind?"

"Bud asked us to look for Agent Hannity at the Air Force terminal around eight or so."

"I'll set the alarm for six-thirty and hop in the shower. You want to get up then, too?"

"Sure. The guest bathroom still works, right?"

"Right as rain, Freddy. I'll throw something at you in about seven hours to wake you up. Just like the old days. You don't need the phone, do you? I'm going to call Sue real quick and get an update."

"No, I'm all set, Gary. Give my love to Sue and Brandi, okay?"

"Will do. Goodnight, buddy. See you before oh-seven hundred."

Fred walked down the hall into the guest room. Gary and Sue's house was actually three levels. The first level was built about ten feet up off the beach, on stilts, to help prevent the higher-than-normal tides that accompanied the notorious Atlantic storms from washing the houses out to sea. Gary had gotten permits to build up his front yard and side driveway to be level with the front and side entryways, as had most of the other homeowners directly on the water. The top floor was Gary and Sue's office space. Gary had a corporate headquarters in Charleston proper, but this area gave them the option of working from home when it suited their needs. The second floor was home to Gary and Sue's master bedroom suite, a family room and two smaller bedrooms for the girls whenever they came home for a visit. The first level of the house included the kitchen, a living room, dining room and what was originally a family room, which Gary and Sue had converted to a guest suite. This was what Gary referred to as "Fred's room." It had a king sized bed, a full dresser, as well as a private, full bath. Fred enjoyed it for its solitude, tucked into a back corner of the house that offered an unobstructed view of the ocean. Fred had helped Gary build the private deck that was set off the side of the room not directly on the beach. Shaded by a full thicket of palm trees, Fred had found he could just sit there for hours in the oversized wicker chair Sue had picked out especially for him. This option afforded Gary and Sue their privacy, even while Fred was visiting. There was even a time last year that Fred had come down for a visit and Gary must've forgotten what time he was due to arrive. Fred had seen neither of the Dericksen's cars when he pulled into the driveway, so he let himself in. He was in and settled out on the deck for an almost an hour, when Gary had come out onto the deck. Gary had been at home, but he was working up in the third floor office and hadn't realized Fred had arrived until noticing the rental car in the driveway.

Yes, Fred enjoyed his time here with Gary and Sue. And he hoped that they'd be able to do their investigating without incident. Gary was right. They were both getting on in years. Playing secret agent for Bud would probably have been fun twenty years ago. Now, with Fred closing in on forty-five and Gary fast approaching sixty five, they were both getting much too old for this stuff, Fred thought. He settled into the bed and, feeling the effects of a full day, topped off with a half dozen cold Dos Equis, he slipped into sleep easily. Seven am would come much too quickly. And the day ahead would prove interesting, to say the least.

twenty-eight

New York City   Friday, April 3, 1998   10:30pm (local)

At half past ten, Sandy Rose pulled up to the curb of her apartment building. Dominic, the evening doorman hustled out to the curb and opened the driver's door, allowing Sandy to slide out.

"Evening, Ms. Rose. Long day today?"

"You betcha, Dominic. How's things by you?"

"Just fine, Ms. Rose. Starting to smell a little like spring, don't you think?"

"That it is, Dominic. Better than what they got up in Maine, that's for sure."

"Maine. That place must be cold all of the time! Glad I'm here in the city, where winter knows when it's done and it gets the heck out of town."

"I'm with you on that score, Dominic. Where's Steve tonight?"

"He had a little family business to attend to, Ms. Rose. Told me to be extra careful parking his cars."

"I'm sure you will be, Dominic. Thanks."

"You have a good night, Ms. Rose. Oh, you looked great on the TV this evening, too!"

"You're too sweet, Dominic. Thanks again."

Sandy grabbed her valise from behind the front seat of her Miata and stepped around the front of the car. She was tired. And, after her conversation with Don, she was drained. Jorge, the uniformed security guard at the inside lobby desk buzzed her in and she waved hello on the way to the elevator. Her building was what might be considered an upscale, tony Park Avenue high rise. She'd found this location after returning from London, when the network security specialists suggested that, as a more-highly visible network reporter, she might want to look into something a little less accessible. Oh, she still had the loft apartment she'd shared with Don back in the eighties. She'd continued paying the rent while in London and was even renting it out to a couple of the girls from the technical side of the network operation and so far, they'd been absolutely fabulous tenants. She was able to purchase the building which contained the loft when she'd signed her last contract. It was more of a sentimental move than a financial one, but the long-term return on her investment would prove fruitful, so had said her accountant.

She pressed the number eleven for the quick ride to her upscale flat. The apartment was really a condo unit. In the city, they were still called apartments, even though most were not available for rent. One purchased one's apartment in this neighborhood. Again, another shrewd investment, with a touch of class. The living space was actually three former two-bedroom units. Once rent-control restrictions had been eased, many landlords took advantage of the financial boon of the eighties. The seventies had seen sky high interest rates, which created a glut of available properties. In the early eighties, interest rates were back down around twelve percent and the economy was making a healthy swing upwards. Landlords began the squeezing out of tenants by going co-op, giving them options to purchase their apartments. Most rent-paying customers, though, were unable to swing a mortgage payment. That led to interior renovations of some of the more desirable addresses, such as this building on Park Avenue.

The elevator doors opened at the eleventh floor and Sandy stepped into the hall. This floor had four total units, where there were once twelve, small apartments. Each unit had a large, spacious living room, which was settled into the corners of the building. There was also an oversized kitchen, a full dining room and three large bedrooms. Sandy enjoyed coming home to this place. In the summer, she'd get back from the network around eight or so each evening and that would give her time to kick off her shoes, settle in on the couch and just watch the sun go down over Central Park. She put her key in the door's lock and opened it. She stepped in, flicked on the light and stopped dead in her tracks. There, on the overstuffed couch, sat Jon.

She had to catch her breath. She had thought for sure the threat of her disclosing his propensity to take his frustrations out on his wife would have been enough to deter his ever setting foot back in this place, let alone the country.

"Hi, Sandy!" He said with an ear-to-ear smile, as if nothing had ever happened between them. It was just another night of him waiting for her to come home.

"Hello, Jonathon. What the hell are you doing here?" She was more than angry and well aware of what he did to her the last time anyone's temper flared while they occupied the same space.

"I had some unfinished business here in New York," was all he answered.

The room was still, punctuated only by the sound of Sandy's breathing. She still hadn't recovered. And with the silence, came the thought that she really should have opened the door and screamed. At least two of the other apartments on this floor had live-in help. Minimally, someone should have heard the scream to press the emergency call button.

Sensing her thoughts, Jon rose from the couch and with what seemed like no more than one giant step, he covered the distance from the couch to the door. He flipped the dead bolt and turning towards Sandy, he smiled. Then, he sent her reeling across the room with a solid right.

Sandy was dazed and when she pulled her hand away from her mouth, she felt the pieces of her teeth that accompanied the steady stream of blood that came forth. Jonathon stepped towards Sandy. She could not move, paralyzed with fear. He reached down and picked her up. She offered no resistance as he put an arm under her armpits and directed her towards the living room. As they approached the sofa, he suddenly, effortlessly, sent her flying over the couch, onto the chrome and glass coffee table. As her head smashed through the table's top, she had the strangest sensation of being absolutely calm. Her fear had left her and she actually had the funniest thought of how disappointed her mother would be that the table had gotten broken. Mom, after all, had given that to her, along with the rest of the living room suite. Sandy opened her eyes and all she could see was the beige rug.

"Sandy, Sandy, Sandy," Jonathon tsked. "You know, all you had to do was to do as I asked. In the hospital, didn't I simply ask you to forgive me? I even promised that it would never happen again. Hell, I had booked us a two-week romantic getaway to Saint Thomas. Little place on Bolongo Bay. Private beach. Stocked bar. Even a catamaran at our beck and call."

Sandy struggled to say something. Anything. She could hear Jon and was slowly realizing that she was in bad shape. Worse shape than before. Her head was pounding, the sense of serenity giving way to sharp, vicious pain.

Mercifully, as if there was a God above, Jonathon reached down to once again pick her up. He gently set her on one end of the couch and tenderly picked the glass shards out of her hair, forehead, cheeks. He left her for what seemed a moment and returned with a glass of water and a damp cloth. He tilted her head up and gingerly poured some of the water into her mouth. She nearly choked on the small amount of liquid, the subsequent reaction cleared more blood from her mouth, along with a few more large pieces of her teeth. She thought, not for the last time, that if there was a merciful God above, that she would die. Now. Jon continued to pick the glass from her hair and with the easiest of touches, pulled several long pieces from the left side of face. She felt each of the slivers sliding out of her skin. She wondered how long they must be. It felt like they were imbedded clear into her nasal cavity. As he pulled another from just below her eye, she was suddenly able to breath through her nose. Well, she thought, I wasn't wrong about that one being in as far as it could go. A gush of blood came from her nose and Jonathon eased one of the damp cloths to held stem the flow.

"Shhh, now, Sandy me sweet. Jon's here. I'll take care of you. Just relax."

He continued his meticulous clean-up and left several times to return with a fresh cloth.

"Now, you just settle in right there and we can talk. Remember how we used to do that? We could sit right here, on this couch and talk until we could see the shadows rising up over the park with the break of dawn."

She struggled to nod her head. Okay, she thought. I'm alive. I'm not ready for a box yet. Agree with him. Tell him what he wants to hear. And, damn it, make it believable.

"Oh, don't try to move. You took a nasty fall there. Would you like me to get you some ibuprofen? It might help to take the edge off of that pain?"

Again, she nodded her head and he left, returning moments later with a fresh glass of water and the bottle of pain reliever. She felt him place one on her tongue, followed by the edge of the drinking glass on her lips. She took a sip and with what felt like all of her strength, she managed to swallow the pill. A few seconds later, she felt him put a second pill in her mouth. Holding up a hand, she managed to open one of her eyes for a moment and seeing that the bottle of medicine was indeed the regular, over-the- counter ibuprofen from the bathroom's medicine cabinet, she allowed him to once again help her with a drink from the glass.

"That's two. Do you want to take three?"

Sandy thought for a moment. She'd taken three on occasion for those times when her cramps had been unbearable. Three had managed to take the edge off of those. This was worse.

"Yeth," she managed to mumble. Hearing her own voice dropped her spirits to a new low. The damage he'd done to her mouth must be extreme. So much for the years of orthodonture her parents had provided. Another thing of which Mom would be disappointed.

Jon placed a third pain killer on her tongue and this time, she was able to use her own hand to guide his hand with the glass to her lips. She slipped her fingers around the container, tightened her grip on the glass and felt his hold loosen. Finishing the drink herself, she lowered the glass, holding it out. He took it from her hand and passed her a cold, damp facecloth. The cold, she'd realized, was from the ice cubes he'd wrapped into the cloth. Hungrily, she accepted that and spent a few minutes moving the cold to her mouth and then up to the side of her face and back again.

"I hope you've missed me as much as I've missed you, love. I had been hoping we'd be able to get this thing worked out."

Sandy managed another nod of her head and opened her eyes once again to get a look at him. He was just sitting on the couch, smiling at her. The light, however, was blinding. Noticing her squinting, he walked over to the far end of the living room and turned on the small desk lamp. Then, returned to the switch on the wall and flicked off the overhead lights.

"That should be better, Sandy me sweet."

She attempted another eye-opening and found that the muted glow from the green-globed desk lamp was indeed easier on her eyes.

"I saw your piece last week on the new NATO agreements. ITN picked it up and used it on their evening broadcasts. You looked great. Even me mum thought you were fabulous. Hell, it helped me to close a deal. Bloody stubborn client was hemming and hawing. Then, the next morning, we were able to make some small talk about you and just like that, he signed. You know, it's really great to be back together again, Sandy m'sweet."

Sandy looked at Jon. He was just sitting there next to her, as if nothing had ever happened between them. She was in pain. She made a mental list as to the contributing factors as she knew them: broken teeth, multiple cuts, at least a broken nose, maybe a broken cheekbone and probably suffering the effects of a concussion as well. Got to stay awake, she thought. Got to try and stay awake. But all she wanted to do was go to sleep.

Jonathon stood up and reached over to the Shaker blanket holder. He pulled the hand-knitted afghan over Sandy, tucking it in gently under her chin and around her shoulders. Then, he took one of the oversized throw pillows from the end of the couch and placed it between the two of them. He tenderly guided her towards him, his hand on her shoulder, easing her down against the pillow.

"You look tired, me love. Try and get a little sleep. I'll make sure you're awake so we can watch the sunrise together."

Unsure. Afraid. Beaten. Sandy gave in to her body's urge to sleep. She'd lost all track of time, but at this point, could not care. Jon had promised her at least one more sunrise. She'd take that. Then and not for the last time, she prayed for any kind of help. If God was merciful, he'd help her get out of this mess. She could feel her breathing steady. Then, she drifted off.

Downstairs, Dominic checked his watch. It was about five am. The sun would be up in another hour and a half or so, then he'd be heading home. A white Chevy pulled to the curb and the passenger window rolled down.

"Did you do any damage to my cars?" The driver asked.

"Steve? What are you doing here? I thought you needed the night off?"

"I did have the night off. Took care of the family business and then, I couldn't sleep. So, I figured I'd come over here, take care of the morning rush and then give you a ride home. That okay?"

Dominic smiled. "That suits me just fine, Steve. Won't be much of a rush for Saturday, though."

"How's our Miss Rose doing? Did you do anything to that beautiful Miata of hers?"

"Not a scratch. Put it in her spot, head out, just like she likes it. She seemed a little tired when she got home, but I'm sure seeing the Mister when she got in would bring a smile to her face. He's been gone for a while now, hasn..."

"You mean Jonathon is up there? With her?" Steve jumped out of his car and was moving at top speed.

"What's the problem, Stevie-boy?" Dominic was baffled at this reaction.

"How long have they been up there? It's really important!"

"He arrived about seven last night, just after me and Jorge got on duty."

Opening the outer door, Steve ran into the lobby and grabbed the phone off of Jorge's desk.

"Police emergency? This is Steve Kelley. I'm the valet parking attendant at twenty-four-ninety-seven Park Avenue. We have a potential situation here that is probably going to require some police intervention. What situation? How about a well-known national television newswoman up in her apartment with her ex-husband who, last time he saw her, beat her senseless, causing her to lose their baby and breaking several of her ribs. This man is not even supposed to be in the country, let alone in her apartment. Please, send a unit over here right away. Thanks.

"Jorge, do you have a gun back there? If so, let's go. Dom, you stay here and watch the front. Let the cops in and send them right up!"

"Steve, you still haven't said what the hell is going on!" Dominic pleaded.

"Weren't you listening just then?" Steve was pressing frantically on the elevator's up button. "Last time that English prick was here, he was moving out. He beat her. Beat her bad enough that she tried to drive herself to the hospital. Crashed the car and lost her baby."

Dominic's face dropped at that.

"That's right, Dom. Remember when you said she had that glow about her? She was pregnant. This limey bastard put her in the hospital. Send the cops up when they get here."

The elevator doors opened and Jorge took out his service key, turning on the emergency run function. They pressed the button for the eleventh floor and were guaranteed an express ride. Not that the elevators were in that much demand at this time of day, but it would be just their bad luck that someone along the way would want to hitch a ride. Steve had taken the weapon from Jorge and was making sure it was loaded.

"Jorge, you ever have to fire one of these things?"

"Just at the training course, Steve. Hell, I hate to even hold the damn thing. But I do clean it, three times a week. What about You?"

"I'm not at all happy to be even holding this. Now the tough question. If you had to, do you think you could shoot someone?"

"Not sure, Steve. I am just not sure."

"At least you're being honest, buddy. I'll take the damn gun. You just be ready to pick it up if for some reason I lose it."

The elevator opened and the two building attendants walked softly towards Sandra's door.

Steve Kelley was as typical a New York Irishman as you'd ever meet. Lanky, standing just over six feet, he was solid as well. His bright red hair and freckles were very deceiving. His warm smile and bright green eyes were by no means a portent of what was within. Steve had served four years in the Marines and came home after his service to help care for his mother. He dated, but there was no one serious yet. His attitude was that he was still young. What's the hurry. Although the subtle hints from his mother were of the sort that occasionally got under his skin, he'd still reassure her that he would settle down, when the time was right.

He'd landed the job as the building's valet parking supervisor within a week of returning home. He'd been on the job for almost five years, now and had considered all of the building's residents as his responsibility. He'd even started an auto detailing business on the side, which was provided to the building's tenants, gratis. The word of mouth from the residents had grown the business to the point where, even though he was an employee of the management group who ran the building, he was an employer himself, overseeing five full-time employees.

Now, he was about to put all of the Marine training he'd gone through at Paris Island to good use.

Steve motioned to Jorge to stay back against the wall to the right of the door. Jorge was pushing fifty and had been a security guard for over twenty years. He had no desire to see any action, not at this late stage of the game. He knew, though, that this is what he was paid to do. He pressed himself back up against the wall so as to be out of sight of whoever opened the door. Steve reached out and knocked, taking a quick look at his watch.

He waited a moment and knocked a second time.

From behind the door, Steve heard the voice and unmistakable English accent of Jonathon. "Yes? What can I do for you?"

"Oh, uh, Jonathon. It's Steve? From the garage downstairs? Sandra had asked me to have her car out front at five this morning and, well, it's about a quarter past now. Just wanted to make sure everything's okay?"

Steve and Jorge stiffened as they heard the inside deadbolt click open, then the door opened a crack.

"Steve. Nice to see you. I didn't see you last night when I got in."

"My mom wasn't feeling too well, so I had to hang out with her for a bit. My sister was worried, so she came over to spend the night with us. I figured with her there, I could come over and take care of my cars for the morning rush. Sandra had asked me yesterday morning to have the car ready at five. She has an appointment at seven down in Philadelphia."

"Oooh. That could be a problem. As you can see," Jonathon opened the door a bit wider and Steve could see the top of Sandra's head on the end of the couch. He also caught a glimpse of the remnants of the shattered table. "She's still sleeping."

"Yeah, I can see that. Well, if she's not feeling well or something, you'll want to make sure somebody knows she won't be in Philly at seven. Nice to see you again, Jonathon," Steve said, offering his hand. Jonathon reached out to accept the handshake and, before he knew what had hit him, Steve had Jonathon out of the apartment and up against the opposite wall. Reaching behind to his waistband, Steve pulled out the thirty-eight caliber handgun and pressed it to the back of Jonathon's head.

"Jorge, get in there and check on Ms. Rose. Now!"

Jorge was almost a blur as he slid past Steve into the apartment and immediately muttered "Oh my God."

"Is it bad? Jorge? Answer me! Is it bad?"

"Steve, she's barely breathing. It looks like he put her through this table head-first."

"Jonathon. Don't move! Jonathon! I'm warning you. Don't move!

Jonathon wasn't moving at all. He was perfectly still. Steve pulled back the hammer on the weapon.

"Jesus Christ! Jorge! Come here quick, he's giving me a big problem. Jonathon, please, hold still! I can't warn you again!"

Jorge had started towards the hallway as he heard the shot. He reached the door and saw Steve standing there over Jonathon's lifeless body.

"Shit, Jorge. He was trying to get the gun out of my hand. I didn't have a choice."

"Why don't you go in and make sure they send an ambulance for Ms. Rose, Steve. I'll wait here for the cops."

"Good idea, Jorge." Steve's hands were shaking. He still had the gun in his right hand and Jorge gently reached out, guiding the weapon to point upwards. Clicking on the safety, he eased the weapon out of Steve's hand.

"I'll hold onto this for you, Steve. Go make the phone call. She's in really bad shape. God, I feel so fucking stupid."

Steve ran to the apartment and took a quick look around. He saw the cordless phone hanging on its charger on the kitchen wall. He grabbed it, dialed nine-one-one for the second time in five minutes and told the dispatcher to send an ambulance. No, make that two ambulances. He informed the dispatcher that there were two victims. One suffering serious wounds from a severe physical attack, female, still breathing. The second victim, male, was probably dead from a gunshot wound to the head. And could they please, please hurry.

He disconnected the call and dropped the phone on the floor next to the couch.

"Sandra? Sandra? Can you hear me, Sandra? It's Steve Kelley."

Sandra started to stir, moaning from what was obvious pain.

"Ohhh. Hurt. Really hurt," Sandra managed to say.

"I know, Sandra. I know you hurt. The ambulance is on the way. Hang in there for us, okay?"

Sandra's eyes opened with a start. "Jonason!"

"No, Sandra. He's not going to hurt you any more. Ever, ever again. Just hold still, now."

Steve picked up the damp cloth from the floor and placed it over Sandra's forehead. Jorge came in and took Steve by the shoulders, gently easing him up. Just then, the first two policemen arrived. One came in and checked Sandra's vital signs, taking her pulse and checking her breathing. The other was in the hall, giving a quick once over to the body of Jonathon.

"Officer? I'm Steve Kelley, the parking manager here for the building and I'm afraid I shot that man in the hallway."

"Sir, please don't say anything just yet, okay? Seeing what I'm seeing, it looks like to me that you two guys stumbled upon this assault in progress. And, you, security guard. What's your name?"

"Jorge Bonitas, officer."

"Right. You two guys come up here, catch a bit of what was going on in here and Steve? After this dead guy out here had knocked Jorge's gun to the floor, you picked it up and it went off, right?"

"As an ex-Marine, I'd be laughed out of the American Legion next time I go in for a beer if I owned up to that story, officer. But if it keeps things simple and keeps this lady alive?"

"It keeps it real simple, Steve."

"Then, damned if you haven't figured the whole thing out. Jorge? Give the man the weapon."

Jorge held out the handgun and Officer Dan Albertelli, using a pencil from his shirt pocket, inserted the pencil's tip into the gun's barrel and gently placed the weapon on the sideboard next to the front door. He then looked out into the hall where his partner was still checking the late wife-beater for life signs. The other officer just nodded his head that, no, the man was gone.

"Steve? Is this who I think it is?"

"Yes, officer. That's Sandra Rose, from NBS news. The bastard is her ex-husband. He put her in the hospital about five months ago. She had him all but deported as part of the divorce agreement. He came back here sometime yesterday, I guess. Showed up here without permission last night before she got home."

Looking at Jorge, Albertelli asked, "So how come you let him in? Was it your watch?"

"Yes, it was my watch. And damned if I don't feel like the lowest life form going for letting this son of a bitch in."

"Jorge. Don't," Steve interrupted. "Officer, Sandra had only told me about the divorce and what caused it when I came across her having a full-blown breakdown one day in the parking lot. She hadn't wanted anyone else to know and asked me not to tell a soul. As far as everyone here in this building knew, the dead guy was back in England doing business."

The elevator opened and the first of two stretchers rolled into the hallway. Officer Albertelli waved them into the apartment, where the paramedics immediately went to work on Sandra. They lifted her onto the gurney, covered her with a blanket, strapped her in and wheeled her out of the apartment.

Steve caught them at the elevator. "Sandra? Sandra? Is there anybody I can call for you?"

"Don Holf. Mumber in my phomeboof."

"Don Holf? And where's the phonebook?"

"Kiffen drawr. Faw wigh."

"Kitchen drawer, far right. Got it Sandra. I'll call him. Guys, take real good care of her, okay?"

The paramedics worked the stretcher into the elevator and the doors closed. Officer Albertelli had met with the first two detectives to arrive and the team was busy taking photographs of the late Jonathon, as well as doing a walkthrough on the apartment.

"Jorge. Thanks."

"Steve, I didn't do a thing. You did it all. Nice work."

Albertelli came over to Steve and Jorge standing by the elevator.

"Looks like we'll need to have you come down to the precinct, fill out a few statements for us and then we'll cut you lose. You guys probably saved her life. Judging from what I could see, she'd lost a ton of blood. She wasn't going to live much longer than an a few more hours. I'd say she's going to be a long time getting well, but she'll make it."

"Officer, she asked me to call someone for her. Can we go in the apartment and get her phonebook?"

"Sure. Let's go do it, then get you down to the house."

Albertelli escorted Steve into the kitchen. They opened the drawer on the far right hand side and took out Sandra's small phonebook, which was sitting right on top. Opening to the letter H page, there were several names, but only one Don. And the last name was Hough. Taking Sandra's mouth into consideration, that must've been the person she wanted them to call. There were two numbers. One home. One work. Steve walked back into the living room and picked up the phone off of the floor where he'd dropped it. He dialed the home number. The phone rang five times and an answering machine picked up. Steve looked at Albertelli and let the policeman listen. Shaking his head no, Steve disconnected the call and punched in the second number. The phone answered on the second ring.

"WCBR news, Don Hough speaking."

"Hi, er, Mr. Hough. My name is Steve Kelley. I'm calling on behalf of Sandra Rose."

"Yes, Mr. Kelley. What's up?"

"Sandra asked us to call you. It seems there's been an accident. She's on her way to the hospital, New York Presbyterian. She's in pretty tough shape, Mr. Hough. Do you think you can come to New York and be with her?

Don was silent. He'd talked with her just last evening. He'd waited up until midnight before falling off to sleep, waiting for her to call him back. Now, she'd asked for this guy to call him.

"Mr. Hough? Are you there?"

"Yes, Mr. Kelley. I'm sorry. Yes, I'll get on the next flight out of here and be there as soon as I can."

"Would you like for us to come and pick you up at the airport? It won't be any trouble."

"That would be, er, yeah. That would be great, thanks. Do you have a number where I can call you when I get my flight information?"

Steve looked at Officer Albertelli. "Do we have a number where Mr. Hough can call us to let us know what flight and what time so I can get him at the airport?"

Dan took out a business card with the phone number of the precinct on it.

"Mr. Hough? Here's the number."

Steve read the phone number and Don read it back.

"Thanks for the call, Mr. Kelley. I'll get you at this number in a little bit, okay? It might be an hour or so, but I promise I'll call you as soon as I'm on a flight."

"Gotcha Mr. Hough. Just so you know, they say she's going to be okay. Her ex-husband really worked her over good. You won't really recognize her when you see her, okay?"

"What do you mean?"

"Her ex-husband probably whacked her around a bit, then sent her head-first through a glass table. She's pretty gashed up."

"Aw shit."

"That's pretty much what I said when we found her."

"Do you have her parent's phone number there? I think I've got it here somewhere. Let me look for you."

Don was shuffling through the papers on his desk, trying to stay composed. This felt worse than when she told him she was getting married.

"Mr. Hough?"

"I'm here, Mr. Kelley. Here's the number. Her parents are Connor and Emily Rose. They live in Pennsylvania. Got a pencil?"

Steve reached over to Albertelli's shirt pocket and took out the pencil and wrote down the number.

"Got it, Mr. Hough. We'll call them, too. Call me at the number I gave you as soon as you get a flight number and arrival time."

"Will do, Mr. Kelley. And thanks again for calling."

Steve hung up the phone and walked towards the apartment door with Albertelli. They motioned to Jorge to join them, stepping over the yellow crime scene tape that now crossed the doorway and criss-crossed the hall. The elevator door opened, producing three more detectives who would be going over the scene and gathering evidence. Albertelli, Jorge and Steve all stepped onto the elevator and waited quietly while the elevator descended. Opening up to the lobby, the front of the building was blocked with at least five police vehicles. On the sidewalk, Dominic stood off to the side, in tears.

Stepping outside, Steve went straight to Dominic.

"She's gonna be fine, Dom. Just fine, okay?"

"This really sucks, Steve, you know?"

"I know, Dominic. You keep an eye on things for us for a bit longer, will ya? Jorge and I have to go down to the police station and fill out some forms."

At that, Officer Albertelli held open the rear door of a marked cruiser and motioned for Jorge and Steve to climb in. They did and the cruiser pulled away slowly, heading for the precinct house.

Steve glanced out the window of the police car, watching the brightening of the day. Now he wished he'd told some of the others about the Sandy situation. There were one or two other residents in the building who'd been in similar situations, but Sandra's was the one that had resulted in the most harm. And now this. Steve would have to check with the security company later on and see about making the building strictly coded access. The little keypads could be installed and networked easily throughout the building. This way, if a guy like Jon disappears for a time and shows up claiming to not have his key, he'd have to call the resident personally and get their code. If Jon had been forced to call Sandra, she would have been able to call the cops from work and have him removed from the premises.

Officer Albertelli spoke, breaking the silence.

"You did good back there, Mr. Kelley. Real good. That animal would have probably have come back to try it again, even after the justice system did with him what they could. Off the record, I'm personally glad you had to put a bullet into the back of his head."

Jorge looked at Steve. The impression was not one of admiration, nor was it one of condemnation. Jorge wasn't sure how to feel. He was in general repulsed at any situation that results in a life lost. But he didn't hold Steve in any sort of low regard. Ms. Rose had been a kind and sensitive resident of their building. She took the time to say hello. To ask about their families. To not adopt stuck-up airs in dealing with them. She was a good lady. And what that bastard of a husband, well, ex-husband, had done, was reprehensible.

Jorge was not aware, though, that his opinion of the situation would change, drastically, when agents of the United States' National Security Agency came calling, with agents from British intelligence in tow. He'd be more than surprised what he would learn about Jonathon. How he'd taken a simple London art gallery and turned it into a front for one of the largest black-market documents businesses in Europe. Documents that included passports and other identification papers produced for rogue elements still operating within many of the western European countries. Documents produced for clandestine operatives working for, as an example, the former Soviet Union's President Romanov. The same operatives currently cooling their heels in a duty office bunkroom at RAF Cheltenham who had been sent to Paris to abduct a United States' assistant Secretary of State. Yes, Jorge's opinion of Steve would turn to admiration. More so on the part of removing from Sandra Rose's life an animal hell-bent on making her existence miserable, if not shorter. But also on a level that he had been there when Steve took out a man who was currently a part of a larger plan to completely undermine and take down, his home; HIS United States of America.

twenty-nine

Moscow   Saturday, April 4, 1998   6:03am (local)

Michail rose early. Just past six am, he'd gotten maybe a little more than five hours sleep, total. Now, he had a full morning of driving ahead of him. He'd thought about taking a flight up north to Aleksandr's dacha on the lake, but he was not sure about what would await him upon his arrival. Too many questions and possibilities had arisen just from the Virginia-visit inquiry posed by Romanov. If they knew he was in Virginia just before returning to Moscow and they knew when he was in his apartment, there'd be no telling what they knew. Michail hadn't figured out how he would answer any question about his being at the White House, should it be posed. No, flying was not an option. The rented Ford Explorer was an option. He'd be able to muscle his way out of the wooded enclave that surrounded the new "provincial palace" of his brother-in-law, if need be.

He took a long, hot shower. He let the steam fill the bathroom, while he leaned in towards the wall, letting the water massage his neck and back. The process sometimes helped him to relax and put things in proper perspective. In this case, he worked through several possible escape plans in the event his ride wasn't able to make it to the lake, as well as how he could get into the dacha armed, without being detected. Aleksandr had retrofitted the house with a number of security systems, including built-in metal detectors at each entryway. Michail tried to remember every nuance about the dacha he could. The more he remembered, the better his chances for survival.

His concerns could also be for naught, he realized. What if Aleksandr suspected nothing. He could simply be extending this invitation as a normal matter of course. It had been done before, many times over the past few years, especially since Romanov the vanquished had become Romanov the revered.

Aleksandr had been brought into the new Russian order as the senior statesman. He'd represented Russia at a number of international functions, from weddings to funerals. He was a man whose council was now sought and heeded. He'd helped several younger up-and-comers in the right direction and these politikas were poised as the vanguard for the next generation of a new Russia. But if they only knew, if only all of them knew, that Aleksandr was willing to let them have their new Russia, they might regard him as progressive and even welcome him completely into their fold. His design was to simply resurrect the old Russia on the opposite side of the Atlantic. With Hewes in the White House and Aleksandr pulling the strings from the dacha, it would only be a matter of time. Within hours of Brad being sworn in as President, it would be constitutionally correct to implement a period of marshal law, to allow for a proper and timely transition of power. Once marshal law was imposed, Michail knew, Aleksandr would be able to bring the United States of America crumbling down in a matter of months.

Michail turned off the shower, grudgingly. For all he knew, this could be his last hot shower. His next encounter with water could be the icy depths of Lake Onega. He hoped that would not be the case. As he also hoped his risky conversation with Mr. Nelson this morning would bear fruit in the form of a little backup. He'd caught the man in, as Nelson put it, a very stratospheric-level meeting. The sat-phone had proven reliable and hopefully, secure. In a clear, non-encrypted mode, it was the best Michail could do and he apologized. Nelson did, at least, recommend perhaps a another check of things with Mr. Goatman, later in the day. Michail had understood. Once he was clear of Moscow and hopefully free of the baby-sitters, he'd call the phone number which Nelson had provided. Michail noticed it was a Virginia area code. Then, he'd be able to exchange and receive information a bit more freely, if he felt he was free of any possible triangulation tracing methods that could identify him based on the sat-phone's signal.

Toweling himself off, he thought of Anastasia. Madrid. What was she doing in Madrid? Damn the directorate, he thought. If they hadn't split us up, we'd be trying to figure out how to get our kids into a fine American or British university, instead of counting the days until we could start our lives together. Soon, Romanov had been saying of late, very soon, but you must exercise patience.

Michail dressed, but thought a moment and taped a sharpened, tapered piece of plexiglass to the inside of his leather belt. The piece was flexible enough to form itself to the natural curve of his back, yet firm enough to offer a level of protection. The belt had a small slot at one end into which he could insert the sharpened tip. The tape was a simple way to secure the blunt end that would serve as a handle. A metal detector, fixed or hand-held, would not pick up this item. It was just nice to know it was there if he needed it. He worked the belt through the loops and tucked in his shirt. No need for a tie today, he thought. No need for the suitcoat, either. He packed three pair of pants, three shirts and folded in a suitcoat just for good measure. If he left Aleksandr's in one piece, alive, he'd need some traveling clothes.

He grabbed his brown dress shoes and tossed those into the travel bag. Reaching under the bed for his hiking boots, the back of his hand brushed against one of the plastic corner pieces of the box spring. He felt one of the loose staples scratch the skin. He pulled the boots out and slid his feet into them. He reached to the nightstand for a tissue to wipe away the small streak of blood from the scrape. Then, he bent back down to check out the defect. He'd not noticed it before, at least not the last time he rotated the box spring and mattress. There was something in there. He tossed the mattress to the floor and lifted the box spring from the bed frame. There were several small, black computer floppy discs nestled inside the black cloth ticking. He took them out and noticed they were all unlabeled, but the little sliding safety switches were all up, indicating the disc was full, or not intended to be copied onto any further.

He pulled his laptop out of his carryall and hit the power switch. The only one he could imagine putting anything in the apartment was Anastasia. But she knew better than to keep things under the mattress, didn't she? While the machine was cycling through its startup mode, he held the discs tightly and walked to the kitchen. He had wanted to get on the road, but he'd be getting a later start than he'd planned. He ran the water for the coffee maker, filling it up about halfway. He had seven discs in all and figured that a quick perusal of each would take two, maybe three cups of coffee. He took a filter out of the cabinet and placed one into the coffee maker's basket. Opening the freezer, he took the can of ground coffee out. Keeps it fresher, he was told once, long ago, in a small city in the American south. He couldn't remember which city, just that the advice had been friendly and free. He scooped out three heaping measures of the ground coffee, slid the basket into the coffee maker and hit the brew switch. Then, he walked back into the living room where the laptop was ready and waiting.

He slid the first floppy into the laptop's slot and opened the computer's "a:\" drive. The window displayed several files, numbered sequentially, starting with number eleven. He pressed the small button next to the slot and ejected the disc, setting it to one side. He grabbed another disc and inserted it into the drive. He clicked on the open file button and watched as another series of folders appeared, also numbered. He'd gotten lucky and clicked on the first, numbered "one."

The folder was a series of notes starting with April, 1976. He scrolled down, reading and memorizing each startling detail. It was a diary, of sorts. An operational and personal diary. And it was Anastasia's. The first disc contained entries through 1981. The most interesting had been the first two and a half years. From the time when Donald R. Fulton, newly appointed manager of First South Bank and Trust, met his new marketing director in April of 1976, up to the gubernatorial inauguration of Fulton in Columbia, South Carolina in January of 1978. He read each file as quickly as he could, keeping in mind his schedule for the day. He had to hit the road and head for Lake Onega, but he'd have to find time along the way to lose any shadows and call Mr. Nelson.

Now, along with working out an escape plan and finalizing the arrangements for a little back up to make it possible in the event of trouble, he'd have to find a way to let Nelson know that there was more than one mouse in the White House cupboards. But he had to do it without bringing Anastasia into harm's way. From what he could make out from these notes, Fulton was a real deal American. He wasn't a double agent, nor was he a deep- cover operative. Just an American citizen who was more than a little pissed off at his country. But he was being steered by Romanov. The big question here was did Fulton know he was being controlled? Anastasia's notes contained detail, but lacked analysis or personal conjecture. There were strictly black and white facts.

Michail had copied all of Anastasia's discs onto a blank CD and once again, repeated the audio copying procedure he'd used for the Tajik goatherds tape. This time, he also included his own files onto the compact disc. He'd keep this new copy, complete with all of the files and have to find a way to send the extra copy of the first, with his Hewes files only, to Mr. Nelson, as a backup.

The other copy of the audio, with Michail's files enclosed, was a gift for Aleksandr. He knew his brother-in-law to be shrewd, smart and on top of his game. One thing former President Romanov was not, was technologically curious. Aleksandr could work his way around a word processing program and had the solitaire and chess games down fairly well. He hadn't shown any interested whatsoever in the newer capabilities of the latest computer designs and tools, hence the gift to Michail of the digital camera. The same digital camera used to copy Michail's files and the crude artwork of the original Tajik goatherd tape. The same device that enabled Michail to transform the hard copy files to computer files that he placed on the compact disc he would give to Aleksandr. Romanov might pop the CD into the player in the living room and give it a cursory listen. But Michail was confident his brother-in-law would never put the CD into the CD-ROM drive of the personal computer in the dacha, even though Michail had spent hours trying to teach his president how to listen to music on CD while surfing the Internet. Aleksandr just didn't grasp the concept of multi-tasking. That allowed Michail to be even more confident that Aleksandr would never put the disc into the CD-ROM and open the "d:\" drive to read the info on the disc. If he ever did, he'd see the dozen audio files, but he'd also see the beige folder icon which contained every bit of written information on "Operation No Corners." Michail grabbed his phone and called his brother-in-law.

"Sasha. It's Michail."

"Yes, Misha. You've not yet left?"

It was more a question than statement, Michail felt confident.

"Not yet, Sasha. I grabbed a few extra winks this morning and am just finishing up my third cup of coffee. I should be on the road in about twenty minutes or so."

He glanced at the clock and saw that it was almost eight am.

"If I get out of here in the next half hour, I should be up your way by, oh, two-thirty at the latest. It's not too late to drop a line in the lake, is it?"

"No, Misha my friend, the traffic should be light today, seeing as how it's a weekend and a cold one at that. There won't be too many other vehicles heading up this way, so you should be able to make good time. We'll have enough opportunity before dark to catch enough fish for an early dinner instead of a late lunch."

It was as strong a barb as Michail figured he'd receive. But, Michail reminded himself, Aleksandr was no longer the president. And if there was any justice left in this world, he'd soon be marking time in an American federal penitentiary. Or he'd be eye-to-eye with some of the bottom dwelling creatures of Lake Onega.

"Very well, then. I should see you not later than three."

"Good bye and travel safe, Michail."

Romanov hung up the phone and Michail breathed a slight sigh of relief. The audio tape had about another fifteen minutes to go. He took the seven floppy discs back into the bedroom and re-inserted them into the box spring. He repositioned the corner piece, bending in the sharp end of the staple that had given him the nasty scrape. He could save Anastasia a little discomfort in this regard. Hopefully, he'd be able to save her a lot of discomfort in the other.

He replaced the box spring and mattress and took the dirty sheets off the bed. He remade the bed with fresh linens, fluffed the pillows and then it occurred to him. The floppy discs must be the reason she'd made an effort to tell him not to worry about the bed. Well, Michail thought, this way she'd need to start her own guessing game about just who knows what. Perhaps it would keep her from repeating sloppy procedures, such as the one which resulted in him finding these discs.

Michail double-checked the obvious hiding places that most people utilized. Being trained as he was to know where the everyday spots for use in concealing items of value were, he himself had never thought to check his own apartment. But judging from the dates on the floppy discs, where the "properties" tab indicated the last date of modification to the floppy, some of these discs had been in existence for more than ten years. The most recent disc had a "last modified" date of February, 1998. If the discs, or perhaps previous incarnations of the information, had been so unprofessionally hidden, there might be additional stashes.

He checked the living room bookcase for noticeable differences in the accumulation of dust. Michail had intentionally not paid close housekeeping attention to certain areas of the apartment for just this reason. Sure enough, on the second shelf from the bottom, there was indication that a large encyclopedia volume had been moved. There was an ample dust accrual on the shelf area in front of the book, but it was less than that on the shelf's surface to the left and right. He gently lifted the volume and slid it forward. Being careful so as not to loosen anything that might have been slipped inside, he placed the book flat on the floor and, starting with the back, he meticulously fanned the pages of the book. About a quarter of the way into the pages from the back cover was a yellowed piece of paper. It was filled with Anastasia's flowing handwriting, in her perfect Cyrillic script. The missive was a letter, addressed to him.

My darling Misha. I hope that you will have found this letter only after feeling that you could no longer call this apartment "home" after learning of my failure. My failure, Misha, is what you must understand as my greatest gift to you. The mission to which I was tasked involved the aiding of one we now know as a coward, willing to sacrifice the lives of loving women and children. The coward had initially hoped to better our unified cause by means of beating our then-sworn enemy at their own game. Using Democracy as a cause to bring them down to our level, the effect.

I was, at the onset, a true-believer. Now, seeing the toll a single act of this coward has taken on you, my love, leaves me willing to sacrifice my own life.

My deepest hope is that my absence makes sense to you. That you will strive to ensure that the world we leave behind is better than the one we once tried to create, all in the name of our homeland.

My deepest desire, Misha, is that you will never need to read this letter. That together, we will pack the belongings of this space that we've shared separately, all these many years. That together, we will have the means and the opportunity to leave these dire surroundings and create our own Utopia, somewhere. That together, we will grow old and take small solace in the fact that those we truly loved suffered no more than they did.

If you have read this, you will know that I am gone. Gone to be with those we loved with a fervor very few will ever experience. Be strong, my darling. Do what must be done to prevent future acts such as those of the coward. Make it your gift to me. To my memory.

I love you. Always. Stasya.

The letter was dated about a month after the funerals for Elenya and the children. The placement of the letter was intentional. The one-volume encyclopedia was opened to the section on "Great Literary Works of The Twentieth Century." The page included a summary of Aldous Huxley's *"Brave New World."* Huxley wrote of a perfect world. Utopia. A utopian society was the once-common goal of those involved with "Operation No Corners."

Michail also understood, all too well, the references to the coward. The coward had left a woman and her two children to suffer and die at the hands of a mob. The coward had fled and lived, only to now be considered a great man in the new world order. Michail wondered what those who now hold this man in such high esteem will think when they learn the truth. That many innocent people have died as a direct result of the orders of a coward. A cowardly megalomaniac.

Michail placed the letter back into its place and gently closed the book. He carefully slid the bulky hard cover back into the slot, being cautious to leave no tell-tale in the dust.

He heard the tape player click off. The audio transfer was complete. He finished up the recording process on the compact disc and disconnected the various cables involved. He saved all the open files and shut the laptop down. Packing up all the gear in his carry-all and double checking his overnight bag for the basics and necessities, he took a last look around the apartment.

There was one more item he'd need to take. Everything else could be left. The things left behind were only things. Even the words written with the greatest love from a woman to a man that a man could ever read. He'd have the author for himself, always. She could speak the words to him herself. Or she could write for him another missive. Or she could just look into his eyes, saying more with a glance than could be held in ten hard-bound volumes. He took the tri-folded picture frame that contained photos, taken and chosen personally by him, of Elenya, Christina and Michail. The pictures were taken in the summer before their lives came to an end. Michail was home from university and was growing to be a handsome young man. He was not quite nineteen at the time. Christina was every bit as beautiful as her mother and at the tender age of sixteen. Looking as attractive as she did, it was indeed fortunate that she was the daughter of the president. Nary a Russian schoolboy would ever entertain the thought of attempting to allow his hands to wander, let alone give her even a glance of desire. Elenya had been caught in a moment of unguarded laughter, the expression of sheer happiness exploded from her face. Michail was unable to recall the moment that had caused this opportunity. He was, however, very much capable of always having this image of his sister and was ever thankful that his camera had film at that moment.

Michail opened the apartment door, setting down the Bean shoulder bag and his overnight bag. He walked back through the apartment, taking it in for the last time. It was the place he'd called home for more than twenty-five years. It could not be his home anymore. If he lived, he'd find Anastasia and together, they would find and make a new home of their own. He checked to make sure that he'd turned off all the lights and walked out into the hallway. He did not look at the door as it closed. He heard the click of the latch. He took out his deadbolt key and gave it a quick, securing turn.

Gathering his bags, he walked purposely towards the elevator. He had a fishing date with a coward. A coward who did not take kindly to being kept waiting.

But first, he had to drop another package off at FedEx. He did the math in his head. If he could get the package dropped at the airport directly, they might be able to get it on a flight by midday, provided they had weekend flights out. That would have it arriving in London by noon, then, stateside by noon, thanks to the time difference. Depending on the luck of schedules, it should be at its destination by suppertime, but Michail was simply hoping it could get out of Russia before he arrived at Lake Onega. Along the way, he would have to work in a very important phone call.

thirty

Paris. Saturday, April 4, 1998   4:47am (local)

Go Team One had lifted off from Cheltenham at 0300. The four men were briefed, prepped and ready. It was about an hour by air to the NATO airfield just outside of Paris where Colonel Menneally's frat brother, now Interpol agent, Greg Yearwood was awaiting their arrival. The plan was to arrive in Paris at least an hour before sunrise. This way, hopefully, they'd avoid any extra attention from passers-by. Their mission was to grab assistant Secretary of State Marvin Moore and bring him back to Cheltenham for safe keeping, awaiting further instructions from POTUS. The Blackhawk helicopter had performed flawlessly and was being given a once over by a U.S. Air Force ground crew. It was scheduled to be refueled and ready for lift-off for the return hop by 0600, keeping the team's Parisian incursion to less than two hours. That time frame was agreed upon by both Menneally and Yearwood, to keep any level of curiosity to a minimum. A cross-channel hop and back was not unheard of, especially for pilots who were supposed to be ready and sharp for any mission at a moments notice. And in this particular case, they had a tight time table to keep, with another, more complex sortie scheduled out of England around 0900.

Colonel Menneally and Go Team One were in a rented Chevrolet minivan on a side street not far from the club where Assistant Secretary of State Moore had been last seen. Interpol Agent Greg Yearwood was outside the van, talking fervently with a local contact. Yearwood had arranged for a high-priced call-girl to pick up Moore in the evening and keep him occupied until the team could come in to scoop him up for safe keeping in the wee hours of the morning. The lady had done as instructed, apparently. She followed him from his hotel to the nightclub and then proceeded to work her charms. Yearwood had gotten the name of the club from the doorman for a small fee. The contact with whom Greg was now talking was the woman's business manager. After what seemed an agonizingly long time, Yearwood shook the man's hand, handed him a roll of money and walked back towards the van.

Climbing in, he said, "She picked him up at *La Place de la Russe* last night. Her manager, the guy over there, says they went to her apartment. He was very reluctant to give me the address. I was, though, able to convince him that it was in his best interests to provide the information, or that we could arrange to put him out of business for a very long time. The tab, so far, Bob, is around seven hundred bucks American. It was five hundred for the lady, fifty for the doorman, fifty for the pimp there and the van rental is a hundred."

"You keep track of these expenses, Greg. I have assurances that we'll all be properly reimbursed for any and all expenses. *La Place de la Russe*, eh? Kind of ballsy, if you ask me. The guy is currently under suspicion of being a Soviet operative and he goes to a Russian nightclub."

"Well, M," Morris offered. "He can always blow off something like this with a nod to his position. Doing homework. Meeting with a member of the Russian delegation. Something along those lines."

"True, Hank, true. Greg? We've got the address?"

"Sure do, buddy. We're pointing in the right direction. It's about ten blocks that way," Yearwood said as he pointed straight ahead.

"Murph, follow this man's finger. And don't get us stopped. We should have some time, right Greg?"

"Yep. The five bills we paid are for the night. And her manager assures me she'll keep him busy 'til the sun comes up."

Murph put the van into gear and slowly pulled out into the flow of traffic. Ten minutes later, they stopped in front of a run-down building, across the street from a trendy looking apartment building, their destination. The hooker's apartment structure was very neatly appointed with flower boxes and a small trimmed lawn. The streetlights, however, revealed a couple of men lurking within the shadows of the building's side alley.

"Murph. We don't know who those two guys are. I need you and Greg to get into the hallway of this dump," Menneally said with a quick gesture to the building nearest them. "See if you can get in the front door quietly. We'll have to wait these guys out."

"What if they're in no hurry to leave?" Greg asked. "We're all on very thin ice here, Bob."

"If they won't leave, then we'll just have to proceed as if they're not here. And if they get in the way, we simply relocate them as well. We do not have a whole lot of time to spend on this. It's oh five hundred now. We've got to be back at Cheltenham in two hours.

"Go ahead, Murph. Let's hope the door is either unlocked, or very easy to open."

Yearwood and Murphy each got out of the minivan and walked across the sidewalk, chatting in soft voices that anyone within earshot would not hear them clearly. Yearwood stopped next to the door as Murphy gave the doorknob a turn. It was locked. Yearwood slapped Murphy on the back and let loose with a loud belly laugh. Using the laughter as a cover, Murph gave the doorknob a forceful shove and the latch gently gave way. They stepped into the hall and Yearwood reached over to flick off the light as Murphy closed the door.

Just as the two shut the door, Menneally saw the two in the alley venture towards the woman's front door.

"Colonel? What the hell is going on?" asked Zallonis. Normally very quiet and meticulous on a mission, any word from Z was a surprise.

"Swoop, I wish I knew. Hank, you getting this on film?"

"I'm on it, M. These guys look like pros. Yep, they're pros, all right. The lead one is picking the lock."

The van fell quiet as the door to the call-girl's apartment swung open and the two unknown men stepped inside.

The door across the street opened and Murphy and Yearwood returned to the minivan.

"What now, boss?" asked Morris.

"Shit, Hank. I'm as stumped about this as you. Greg, any ideas?"

"Maybe they're working with the pimp. You know, get the guy in a position of complacency, then go in and roll him. Take his cash, his watch. Something like that?"

"It's possible. Zallonis, you think you can get that minicam hooked up in a minute? Get us inside somewhere for a look-see?"

"Consider it done, Colonel."

Zallonis grabbed a handful of items from a small duffel bag in the back of the van and stepped out of the sliding side door. He worked his way over to the alley and disappeared around the corner. Menneally looked at his watch, keeping track of the seconds. He wouldn't allow Zallonis to be out of sight for more than a minute. They could not afford to be discovered operating in France for fear of creating a huge international incident. Just over thirty seconds after he left, Peter came back out of the alley, gave a quick look around and strolled back over to the minivan.

"All set, Colonel. You should have a nice clear picture of the bedroom right now."

Morris flicked on the small TV monitor sitting in the backseat. The black and white image showed the bedroom, softly lit by a light outside the room. Then, the five men watched incredulously as the two strangers from the alley strode into the room. One of the intruders took out a handgun with an elongated barrel. Without any time for consideration, the room was briefly lit by a flash from the weapon. The second man pulled something out of his coat pocket and placed it over what appeared to be the face of the bed's other occupant. After a brief struggle, the other person in the bed was still. One of the men flicked on the light on the nightstand, providing a clear picture of what was going on. The person closest to the nightstand and the bedroom's window through which the minicam had been inserted was Marvin Moore. The two men each grabbed an end of the listless assistant Secretary of State and pulled him from the bed. The image then offered a full facial view of the woman. Strikingly beautiful. And very much dead. A line of blood traced down the side of her face, emanating from the hole in the center of her forehead.

"I hope we got that on tape, Hank."

"Every fucking second, M. Every single one."

"Well, Mr. Yearwood. Having just witnessed a murder on your home turf, what do you suggest?"

"The actual murder in question would probably first fall under the jurisdiction of the local gendarmarie, if you want to get technical about it, Bob. But, seeing as it involves a ranking United States official, it most certainly does interest me. Let's see what these two mooks are up to."

"Mooks?" asked Menneally.

"An amazing thing, that satellite TV, Bob. We get all the networks over here and I just love *NYPD Blue*."

"Then I suppose we just hang tight and find opportune moment to pick up these two skels, right?"

"That would be the general idea, Bob. Your Sipowicz is pretty good."

"Thanks. We've had to watch most of the current TV stuff off tapes from AFRTS. It's hard to get a nice clear picture in Bosnia."

"Our TV viewing habits aside, Greg, I think I'm going to have to wake someone up about this. Just to make sure everyone involved is on the same page."

Menneally took out a small satellite phone and passed the antennae cord back to Morris. Hank in turn unfolded a small hand-held dish and took a quick bearing on his compass. The dish now positioned, Menneally dialed the number.

"Good morning, L. It's M. Sorry if I woke you, but something very much unexpected just occurred and we need to run a few ideas by you."

Three minutes later, Colonel Menneally ended the phone call and disconnected the satellite phone from the dish. Morris quickly folded the dish back up and placed it in the small pouch in which it was stored when not in use.

"We have permission to aid Mr. Yearwood in the apprehension of the two alleged murderers. And to rescue assistant Secretary of State Moore."

"We going to wait them out?" asked Morris. "Or are we going to get in there now before they do anything nasty to the man?"

"I'm on the side of getting in there now, Bob," said Yearwood.

"Then let's do it. I'm sure if they wanted to eliminate Mr. Moore, they would have done so by now. But we can't afford to take any gambles when it comes to the safety of a high-ranking American official, now can we?"

Menneally opened the sliding door to the minivan and removed his sidearm, flicking the safety off and chambering a round. Morris, Zallonis and Murphy all followed suit and all four of the Go Team members slid their headset communications gear into place. The whisper-sensitive microphones and hearing-aid styled earpieces were all active and working. Yearwood, feeling somewhat of a fifth wheel, checked his weapon, which was still secured in his belt holster and looked to Bob for instruction.

Zallonis went forward as the point man, with Murphy right behind. Morris, Menneally and Yearwood all took up positions on the alley side of the front door. The Colonel gave a nod and Zallonis gave the doorknob a gentle turn. It was still unlocked. Murphy reached up to the outside light fixture, removed the top of the housing and unscrewed the light bulb. Now, the front of the house was in darkness. He then backed up to the side of a car parked directly in front of the door and assumed a two-handed firing stance. The other three raised their weapons, barrels pointed upwards for safety, but fingers settled in on the trigger for easy firing. Z gave Menneally a nod, with a look towards the alley. The two officers motioned for Greg to stay with Murphy and Zallonis, then made their way down the narrow alleyway. They'd not had much time to worry about a rear-entrance or even the possibility of the man they were coming to pick-up trying to evade anyone. As far as Mr. Moore knew, he was picked up in a bar by a very beautiful woman and given a treat he would not soon forget. Bought and paid for, as a matter of fact, by the President of the United States, although, the president was not yet aware of the details of the accounting.

Menneally and Morris slid along the wall, just below the window sills, being careful to avoid any contact with stray lighting that might cast a shadow. The alley was dark enough to conceal their movement and there was no fence or barrier at the rear of the building they'd need to clear before gaining access to a rear entryway, if there was one.

Back out front, Yearwood still held close to the wall, just off to the side of the main entrance. Murphy was still in his ready stance, now having gone into a crouch position, keeping his line-of-fire angle high. Zallonis still held the doorknob tightly, with the latch fully released, ready to swing the door open on a signal from Morris.

There was a rear entrance. It was a simple door with no window and upon inspection, they saw it had a double-lock set. One for the doorknob and another which was for a deadbolt. There was a window just beyond the door, however and from the window, there was light. Morris stayed low, while Colonel Menneally used his six-foot, four-inch frame to its fullest, gently rising to see if there was a view to what lay inside the door.

The scene was somewhat surreal. The window afforded a full view into the kitchen where Menneally could see the two intruders sitting at the table, drinking beer. On the floor, just at the edge of the kitchen near a doorway which probably led to a small hall outside of the bedroom, lay the naked body of Marvin Moore. From this angle, the Colonel was unable to tell if the assistant Secretary of State was breathing. The upside was that Moore was at least a good ten feet from where the two interlopers were seated. Bob gently lowered himself to a stooped position and duckwalked back to Morris. Using hand signals, he indicated two men just inside the rear door, with a solitary, third man further away. Morris understood what was meant by the basic pantomime of two hands sandwiched together and set under the tilted head of his commanding officer. That was not a normal set of hand commands, but in this situation, it was the best that could be done to indicate that a third, solo target was removed from the line of fire and in this case, not in any sort of an active state. Judging where the rear door was in relationship to the front, Morris eased back to the edge of the building away from the door and relayed the position of the two targets to Z and Murph out front. Then Morris closed the communication with a simple "ten." Menneally heard them acknowledge and they all began their mental countdown. It took Morris all of two seconds to slide back over to the rear door, two more to firmly grip the doorknob and, another two to take a cleansing breath. He had four seconds to go before he would launch his huge body into the door. Four seconds to hope that the doorframe was as fragile inside as it appeared outside.

On the start of the countdown out front, Zallonis swung the door inward quietly, with Murphy right with him. Z's weapon was aimed high, Murph's was low. Yearwood stepped in directly behind Zallonis, offering another range of cover. Within five seconds, the three were in the hall, just a few feet from the entryway to the kitchen. They could see the limp body of Moore, naked, sticking into the hall. They could hear the voices of the two men in the kitchen softly speaking, but loud enough to cover any creaks or groans from the hardwood flooring of the apartment. By the time their silent count had reached three, the three team members inside were next to the kitchen doorway, Zallonis still standing, Murph in a crouch and Yearwood two steps in back, slightly stooped to offer a mid-level line of fire.

At the count of one, the sound of the rear door bursting in shook the entire apartment. Zallonis turned on his left leg, raising his right leg to allow Murphy to swing under and both had their weapons instantly locked on their targets. Menneally and Morris both had their weapons locked on as well, with Morris taking the lower angle and Bob the high.

Greg waltzed into the kitchen past Z and Murph and flashed his Interpol credentials at the two dazed thugs sitting at the table, each holding a beer can and each with mouths agape. Yearwood reached into the coat of the man nearest the doorway and removed the weapon. It's elongated barrel was actually a silencer attached to a standard 9 mm handgun. He clicked the safety on and tossed it to Morris. Hank caught the weapon effortlessly and clicked the safety off, training it on the other target. Murphy came in from his position in the doorway and held his weapon to the back of the first man's head. Yearwood then started around the table towards the second man, who at this point had five different weapons trained on his face. The man eased both of his arms up, extending them slowly straight out to either side. One hand held the beer, the other was empty.

"Smart move," said Yearwood as he stepped quickly around behind the second man and even more quickly handcuffed the man's hands behind the chair on which he was seated.

Yearwood checked the second man's coat and found a bottle and a rag.

"Chloroform. They still use this stuff?" he asked.

"Only some lesser developed third world countries where thuggery is still in its infancy," offered Morris.

"You got a name?" Yearwood asked the second man.

There was no response. Just the blank stares of two men totally flummoxed at what had just happened.

"Comment vous-appellez vous?" he asked.

Still no response.

"We could play this game all night, Greg. Or we could load all three of these guys up into the van and work on this later," Menneally said. "We still have another hop to run in a few hours and I can't take you with me on this one, pal. But we can go somewhere where you and our two friends here can be alone to get better acquainted. And we can get Mr. Moore here somewhere safer than these mean old streets of Paris."

"Okay, Bob. You're the boss," said Greg.

"Why don't you see how well that stuff works, Greg. It looked pretty effective when they used it on Mr. Moore," the colonel offered.

"Then we'll have to carry all three of them, but if you say so..."

Yearwood removed the cap from the metal bottle and held it away at arms length so as not to suck up too many of the fumes. He placed the rag over the open end and gave the bottle a little flip. Walking back around the table, he placed the rag over the mouth and nose of the first man, who was still sitting, hands-free, but with two weapons pointed to the back of his head. The man offered no resistance and took a deep breath. Instantly, he slumped onto the table. Then Greg returned to the second man, who put up a struggle, trying to fight the effects of the chemical. It took the second man a few seconds longer than the first to pass out, but he did so. Greg checked for a pulse and felt it beating faintly. Murphy checked the neck of the first man and gave a nod to the affirmative that all was well on that side of the table.

Menneally and Morris went over and picked up the naked body of Moore and carried him into the living room. Zallonis went into the bedroom, found what appeared to be all of Moore's clothing and shoes and brought them into the darkened front room.

"Let's not worry about the socks and skivvies, boys," Bob said. "We'll just get him decent enough to not attract any more attention than necessary."

At that, the three men wrestled the unconscious Marvin Moore into his Brooks Brothers pants and suitcoat. They slipped his shoes on his bare feet and stood him up. Morris held onto the limp form of the man, while Zallonis took out a length of self-securing plastic wire-tie. Z worked the heavy plastic piece around both of Moore's wrists and slipped the tip through the self-locking channel. Then, using two small cloth strips, Z worked one around Moore's eyes and another around his head and into his mouth to serve as a gag. Once Mr. Moore was "presentable," Morris lifted the man up and over his shoulder in a fireman-style carry and headed for the front door. Menneally opened the door, gave a look up and down the street and up towards the other darkened windows of the houses on the street for signs of life. Seeing none, he and Z stepped across the street to the minivan and opened the sliding side door. Morris quickly followed and the three worked to ease Moore into the rear seat of the vehicle.

Back in the kitchen, Murphy had performed a similar securing of the man without handcuffs, utilizing a blindfold, mouth gag and plastic wire-tie. Yearwood had taken care of the blindfold and gag for the handcuffed one. Zallonis opened the rear tailgate of the minivan and tapped Morris on the shoulder to stand watch this time. Z went back into the house, grabbed the handcuffed man and hoisted him effortlessly onto his shoulder, then carried him out, followed by Murphy with the other.

Colonel Menneally came back into the house and met Greg at the door to the bedroom.

"What do we do about the lady, Greg?" asked Bob.

"Well, we know she was murdered. We saw it. We have it on video tape. But we're removing the suspects, bound, gagged and knocked-out, from the crime scene. That's going to be a tough one to explain.

"Additionally, we can't just leave her here without someone knowing, though. Her *business manager* did give me the address to her house and that would put me at the top of any list. I have to make a call."

"How about if we leave you the video tape? You can say that the men were under your surveillance and are now in Interpol's custody pending interrogation. Make it an international drug thing."

"I do have a contact high up in the Paris police department. I'll have to call him direct. Let me see if I've got his number with me."

Greg pulled out a small, pocket-sized electronic organizer and flicked the "on" switch. "Great little gizmo. I'd be lost without it. It's got my phonebook and more, all in a convenient pocket size."

"Yeah, but they're way to easy to compromise in regards to security. Hell, you could slip a bug in one of those and wind up broadcasting everything you say to the world."

"That's true. I never thought of that." Greg held the device up to his mouth, "Testing. Testing one two three. Testing. Is this thing on? Just kidding, Bob. Here's the number for Jean D'entremont. He should be awake by now. It's about a quarter to six, so he's probably reading his paper and working on his second cup of coffee. He's a good man, Bob. You'd like him. Not at all snotty towards those of us not of French descent. Plus, he's a real good cop."

"Make the call then. We've got to get out of here before our sleeping friends wake up and start making noise." Menneally glanced at his watch. "Plus, the clock is ticking. We've got another flight to catch."

Yearwood took out his cellphone and called Chief D'entremont. After apologizing for calling so early on a weekend morning, he relayed the drug surveillance story and how they caught the murder on tape. He listened for a few seconds, promised to have the bad guys turned into the Paris police for questioning by Monday and thanked the chief for his understanding.

Disconnecting the call, Greg folded up his phone and placed it back into his coat pocket. "I think he bought the story, so we should get out of here, now."

"Consider us gone," Bob said as he wiped the rear doorknob clean with the rag used for the chloroform. The chemical-soaked cloth would help remove any fingerprint residue left by Hank. Menneally gently closed the door and the two men started through the house, giving it a quick double-check for any hint that Marvin Moore might have been there this evening. Yearwood stepped out the front door first, followed by the colonel. Once again, the doorknob was wiped clean. Starting towards the van, Murphy came over to his commanding officer and took the rag from his hands. A few seconds later, having replaced the lightbulb in the front fixture and having wiped down the bulb and the housing, Murph returned the rag to the colonel with a salute.

"Is that all?" asked Menneally.

"That should be it, sir," Murphy replied. "What do you say to getting the hell out of here?"

"I say that's an outstanding idea, Murph."

The two climbed into the minivan, Menneally in the middle seat next to Morris. Murphy climbed into the rear seat, keeping his weapon ready in case either of the two in back section awoke and to keep Mr. Moore company. Yearwood was driving and Zallonis had grabbed the shotgun seat. The minivan started without problem and pulled out into the still-quiet street. Twenty minutes later, the volume of traffic into Paris was increasing. Another day for the workers and citizens of France's capital, although there was at least one less living soul around to enjoy the days' beginning. The minivan pulled up to the gate at the NATO base, with Yearwood flashing his Interpol credentials and Zallonis presenting the official NATO i.d.'s all of the Go Team members possessed. The Belgian sentry on duty saluted the vehicle and opened the gate, allowing them through. The Blackhawk was already out on the tarmac with the engines running. Yearwood eased the van up alongside the helicopter and switched the vehicles engine off.

Climbing out of the side door, Menneally returned a salute to the ground crew chief and took his hand in a heartfelt handshake. Leaning in to the Air Force sergeant, he mentioned that they'd need some privacy in loading up a cargo. The crew chief nodded his acknowledgment and led his three team members back towards the hangar.

Menneally motioned to the remaining Go Team members to begin the offloading of Moore. Greg came around to the side of the Blackhawk and looked at Bob. "Do you think I should accompany you and our two other friends here back to Cheltenham?"

"That's probably not a great idea, Greg. We were not even supposed to be here, let alone bring back a few buddies. If base ops caught wind of that at the other end, there might be more of a shit-storm than I care to worry about right now. We've got that other hop to make in less than three hours now. We lost almost a full hour finding the hooker's apartment, then dealing with our two new friends. Why would you ask?"

"Considering that I never helped you here this morning because you were never here. That I am going to be the most popular person in Paris, at least in the eyes of the gendarmerie. And that I am supposed to have two drug smuggling murder suspects in my custody, both of whom were apprehended during a surveillance operation of which none of my superiors were ever apprised. I'm not sure what your thinking on this would be, but from my vantage point, to paraphrase W.C. Fields, I'd rather be in Cheltenham. Besides, aren't you the least bit curious why two guys with no i.d. would be busting into the Parisian home of a high-priced hooker, putting a bullet into her skull and taking the assistant Secretary of State, naked and knocked out, to God knows where? I know I am. But I would feel better finding out with a little sanctioned help, instead of having to explain how I came across this whole thing."

Menneally looked into the Blackhawk where Moore had been safely strapped into a rear jump seat. Murph and Zallonis were standing by the side door, while Hank was already strapped into the co-pilot's seat going over the pre-flight checklist. Bob motioned to the van with two fingers and pointed to the rear of the helicopter. Murphy and Z walked over to the minivan and opened the rear lift gate. They each grabbed a sleeping bad guy, hustled them over to the helicopter's passenger compartment and slid them in behind the seats. While the two team members used hold-down straps to secure the extra passengers, Bob looked at Greg.

"Better do something with that van. We're out of here in two minutes."

"Thanks, Bob. I feel better about doing it this way. It'll give me time to come up with a story. And maybe find out what these two assholes were up to."

Yearwood jumped into the van and pulled it over to the hangar. He waved the crew chief over and handed him a folder that contained the rental papers for the minivan.

"Sergeant, I'm going to be traveling with the colonel. Can you find a quiet place to park this until I return?"

"Can do, sir."

"These are the registration papers and rental agreement for this vehicle. Just keep them over the visor and if anyone asks, tell them the van is being used for official Interpol business. Here's one of my cards. Keep it with the papers. It's got my cellphone and pager number on it. The pager will work. I'm not sure about the cellphone, though. If you need me to call, use the pager and enter a 9 - 1 - 1 after your phone number. Thanks again, Sergeant."

Yearwood shook the crew chief's hand and hustled back over to the Blackhawk. Zallonis and Murphy were already inside and motioned for Yearwood to take the center seat. As soon as he climbed in and sat down, the helicopter's side door slammed shut while Menneally pulled back gently on the collective to begin his taxi for the runway.

Murphy handed Greg a headset and he heard the tower give Go Team One clearance for departure. The Blackhawk lifted up easily and, with Bob's firm grip on the throttle, the helicopter nosed down a hair while increasing its speed. Within a few minutes, they had leveled off at about one thousand feet, cruising at almost two hundred miles per hour. The French coast came into view, with a clear shot to the other side of the English Channel and the White Cliffs of Dover.

"So tell me, Greg," Menneally spoke. "What do you intend to do with our extra friends here?"

"I was kind of hoping your contact in Washington might have an idea or two."

"He just might at that, Greg. But if he doesn't, you're going to have to come up with some kind of way to get these two back to face charges. I can't guarantee a return trip. Although, if our Washington buddy can come through, then I'm sure there will be plenty of help in explaining most, if not all, of this mess away."

Yearwood just nodded and looked out the front of the cockpit. By six-forty am, the helicopter had made landfall on the English side of the channel. It was a beautiful Saturday morning in the British Isles. Hopefully, it would be a portent of the day yet to come.

The radio squawked a greeting from air control in Cheltenham and Menneally confirmed their flight level and speed. The tower cleared Go Team One, returning from a training hop, for landing on runway two-three, with winds out of the west at twelve knots, visibility unlimited. The colonel radioed his acknowledgment and were setting down at the Go Team One special operations center and hangar within minutes. Gunnery Sergeant Williston was standing by, being the senior team member present. He'd been manning the duty desk in case anything of import came through while the team was in Paris. Williston snapped a sharp salute as Colonel Menneally and Lieutenant Commander Morris alighted the Blackhawk. Both officers returned the salute, although Bob often found it uncomfortable to be returning the salute of a thirty year veteran Marine who had seen it all, including three tours in Vietnam, the last had involved a stint as a prisoner-of-war.

"Welcome back, sir," the gunny offered.

"Good to be back, Gunny. Anything happen while we were gone?"

"No, sir. All quiet for the past couple of hours. I see you brought some extra company back with you," Williston said, raising an eyebrow towards Yearwood and the three unconscious passengers currently being moved into the Go Team's operations center.

"One of them was supposed to come back. The others were a bit unplanned for. I've got to make a call now and wake someone up to find out where we should keep them. This may turn into an ugly, international incident. And we all know how much our hosts love seeing us at the center of attention."

Gunnery Sergeant Williston laughed at this comment. The British, who had rank and control over the airfield at Cheltenham, didn't mind the assets and abilities possessed by their American tenants. But, when it came to overstepping boundaries, the servants to the Crown were very much sticklers for propriety. Any time the Go Teams had come close to really going too far on an op, the kind that created headlines and international fallout, the return reception at the pub was chilly at best. It would take a few weeks for the British troops to come around to them again. Once the dust had settled and the cocky Americans had been properly chastised, then it would okay for all to be forgiven.

"Do we need to set up a guard rotation for these gentlemen?"

"That's a good idea, Gunny. Who's available? I know that the leave situation has left us pretty thin. And," looking at his watch, Menneally added, ."..we're back out and gone in about two hours and change."

"I think we can round up a couple of from Two. They're still on stand-down. Do you need me to come along on this one, sir?"

"Actually, Gunny, I need you and your persuasive powers of bullshit right here to help take care of the wagging tongues and their associated inquisitive minds."

As he finished that sentence, the two team members looked eastward as the huge, Air Force C-5 Galaxy roared in for a landing. Gunnery Sergeant Williston looked at the Colonel and Menneally nodded in the affirmative.

"That's going to be the big one to explain away, Gunny. Literally and figuratively. We're going in way over heads on this one and we've really only got about an hour and a half to make sure we've got all the I's dotted and T's crossed."

"The materials you requisitioned are palleted in the hangar, Colonel. The only thing left is for me to personally check your sidearms."

"Thanks, J.W. You are the man!" said Menneally with a smile, handing over his sidearm.

"It's my job, Bob. It's my job," said Williston in an unusual moment of candor. He released the weapons clip and un-chambered the round that had been readied in Paris. "Tsk, tsk, sir. You know better than that. Flying with a round chambered?"

"Sorry, Gunny. I got a little sidetracked during our return pre-flight."

"At least it's clean. You didn't fire it and now," Williston said as he took the extra bullet and replaced it in the clip, "you have a full clip to get you where you're going. Which, by the way, would be...?"

"Believe it or not, Gunny, I can't tell even you. Morris, Murph and Z don't even know yet. I hate working this way. The only thing I can do is give you a name. Nelson. Bud Nelson. White House communications director. He's the contact on this. And if shit really hits the fan, then you'll need to talk directly with *his* boss, Jay Griffen. We are cleared through the Joint Chiefs on this one, but the boys at 1600 want us to work through them, okay? What say we get our guests comfortable and then get the Blackhawk set. The Air Force will be loading her on the Galaxy in about thirty minutes. They like everything set at least an hour before take-off and we're not giving them much lead time here. Of course, flying a plane that size, I can't say as I blame them. Now, speaking of Nelson, I've got to make a phone call and wake someone up, again."

Menneally and Williston walked towards the Go Team's operations center. Inside, Greg had made himself at home at Bob's desk, while the three mystery guests were set up in the duty bunkroom: Mr. Moore on the bed, restrained and the other two on the floor tied to each other, back to back, legs, waists and shoulders. Moore was starting to stir.

"Looks like someone's waking up," said Yearwood, pointing into the room at the assistant Secretary of State.

Menneally held up a finger to his lips in a "shhh-ing" motion and walked over to the door. Reaching in, he turned a switch which turned on an old, metal rotating fan. The fan created enough of a breeze to keep the room's occupants comfortable and enough of a white-noise to allow anyone inside from being disturbed by the activity of the outer office. The bunkroom was used by the two person duty team, allowing one to grab a few hours shuteye, while the other kept watch over the business of the Go Team.

Closing the door quietly, Menneally gave Greg a look that inferred he should know better.

"I'd prefer, right now, that our primary guest have no idea where he is, or who has got him. If he is not who the White House thinks he is, we can just dump him off in a back alley in Paris and get on with our lives like this never happened, okay? The paperwork we had sent to his hotel indicates that we're just a local political faction unhappy about the impending switch to the E.U. So, just in case, we can not allow him to hear any voices other than the ones those in charge of this op determine he should hear. I'm betting that any questioning that is to be done will be done in French. It makes sense. So, Monsieur Yearwood, if one is to parle in front of our guests, then let's make sure the parle is en francais, okay?"

"Oui. D'accord, mon ami."

"I assume you didn't swear at me."

"You assume correctly, Bob," Greg laughed.

"Now, get out of my chair. I love you man, but you still can't have my Bud Light. Or my chair. I got a phone call to make.

Greg stood up and walked over to the bookcase on the far side of the room, admiring the photos and certificates of achievement that decorated the wall adjacent to the well-stocked bookcase.

"Er, buddy. I think I may need some privacy on this one."

"Um, Bob. You've got me in over my head on this. I'm staying right here. You're bugging out of here for God-knows-where in about two hours, while I have to hang here and figure out what the hell is going on? Nope. I'm right here. And you can work my predicament into your conversation while I am standing right here. I don't think it's a lot to ask."

"You're right, Greg. I'm sorry. The guy we're calling is President Griffen's communications director. The man should be his chief of staff, but I have a feeling that this guy gets more done hiding out in the press release office. His name is Nelson. L. Bud Nelson. He's a good man, Greg. I'm sure he'll have some options for us to exercise on your behalf. I just hate to call the guy again. We woke him up about an hour ago. And we're gonna do it again."

"He's probably half-expecting you to call again, Bob."

"Yeah, you're right. Let's do this now and get it out of the way."

Menneally dialed the phone and listened to the rings coming down the line.

thirty-one

Madrid, Spain   Saturday, April 4, 1998   5:45am (local)

Annie Fidrych rolled over in her hotel room bed and glanced at the digital clock on the nightstand. Five-forty-five. As good a time as any to get up and get this day over with. She had a seven am breakfast meeting with Vice President Fulton at the American embassy, then she'd be off for a final meeting with the other "junior" representatives working out the details for the senior heads of state Paris meeting two days from now. This Madrid trip had been seen as an opportunity for Fulton to show his mettle as a world leader and economic visionary. Although the election was two years away, Annie knew that this is what they had been working for since getting the state house in South Carolina twenty years ago. And both had their eyes on the big prize from the onset. That was, after all, their mission. Their original mission, that is.

When Aleksandr Romanov had proposed his little plan, Anastasia Fidoryvich had at first thought the operation destined to fail. The odds of placing an operative into the American government, unnoticed, were and still would be, astronomical. But placing an operative into the American society, who would then, by shear luck alone, rise through the ranks to achieve the presidency, seemed even more so mere folly. Immediately, she had brought up all of the "what ifs." The chances of being run over by a car in the United States were greater than being elected as its president. The American people had the opportunity to elect a new president every four years. And if the president was good at his job, then that time frame was increased to eight. The window of opportunity to gain the office, then put it to use for Romanov's purposes, was slim. Anastasia had even posed the question in regards to the chairman himself. What if he had a heart attack, was incapacitated, or even killed. Romanov had laughed it off with a tone that struck Anastasia as almost unbalanced. The plan, however, when laid out from beginning to end, had made sense. It was literally a case of beating them at their own game. So they had undertaken this mission, she and Fulton, with a quiet resolve.

Fulton had been a find on Romanov's part. His mother had given birth to him in a United States federal penitentiary in 1950. Both his mother and father had been convicted of espionage during the age of McCarthyism. His parents were Soviet-born scientists who had escaped Russia during the siege of Leningrad. Karolina and Pyotr Vashnovik found themselves working in post-war Los Alamos on the budding nuclear power programs. When word of leaks of technology to the now-Cold War enemies came to light, suspicion immediately turned to those who had come over from Europe and specifically, Russia. On hearsay alone, the Vashnoviks were convicted in a much-less publicized trial than that of the Rosenbergs and sentenced to life-terms in a Kansas Federal facility. Upon arrival at the prison, it was discovered that Karolina was three months pregnant. After much debate, the federal officials allowed her to continue with the pregnancy and also allowed Pyotr's involvement. During childbirth, Karolina's blood-pressure skyrocketed. Unable to counteract the rapid rise and subsequent fall in her blood-pressure, the attending doctor was able to deliver a healthy baby boy. They were unable to save Karolina. Pyotr was devastated to the point where, three hours after saying hello to his newborn son and goodbye to his dear wife, he took his own life by hanging himself with a bedsheet in his cell. The baby boy was placed, through an adoption agency, into the loving home of Donald and Marlena Fulton of Aiken, South Carolina.

They named the infant Donald Robert and raised as fine a son as any parents could hope. He was smart. No, he was actually brilliant. He excelled in elementary school and graduated first in his high school class. From there, he attended Yale on a full scholarship and went on to the exclusive Wharton School of Business. It was during his third year at Yale, though, that the search for his birth parents he had started during his freshman year yielded results. He had come across the proof needed to verify his true identity. Finding out the whole story had not been an easy task, nor, once he'd learned the facts, was it easy to bear.

At first, he was disillusioned. How could his real parents be spies against the country they had grown to love. A love indicated in the many writings left behind by Karolina and Pyotr. Each had kept a diary, with the entries of the final few months of their lives addressed directly to their darling, yet unborn, child. Donald had been granted access to the private effects of his parents, thanks to the efforts of the senior congressman from South Carolina. An additional grant received from the White House directly allowed him to keep their effects, along with an unofficial finding of innocence from the Justice department. Neither of these actions had ever been made public and were to remain off the record, not unlike a settlement in a lawsuit. Donald had accepted both graciously. But he had never shared this information with his mom and dad. He was unsure how they would react and his last intention was to hurt them in any way.

Once the reality of what had transpired hit home, Donald became angry. He became a man with a set purpose in mind. To bring down the system that would destroy the lives of two good people without providing an ounce of proof. The personal apology from President Nixon was appreciated. But the words of a man not involved directly with the case rang hollow. No, a mea culpa, delivered from straight from the bowels of hell, from the lips of President Truman, would satisfy. It was there that Donald assumed he would find the man in charge, the man ultimately responsible for what happened to two brilliant, loving individuals.

While in his senior year at Yale, he immersed himself in his studies, showing a level of mastery in a variety of subjects. He not only had the eyes of the professorial staff upon him, each vying for his talents as an undergraduate teaching assistant, but also those who wondered what his insights might do in aiding the completion of their own doctoral theses.

He had also caught the attention of several radical, underground student groups, most notably SDS, or Students for a Democratic Society. It was this group that had received interest in return from Don. Seeking change through radical, drastic measures, SDS and its intentions were well placed, but their methods left many not enamored of the tactics used. Peaceful displays in an attempt to right a perceived wrong or achieve change through gentle coercion, such as sit-ins or picket demonstrations, were considered to be acceptable forms of non-violent communications. The more radical factions took those basic tenets into a darker area, with violence as their only form of justification. It was from that darker area that Don made an ally who respected Don's desire to remain a brain behind the machine, anonymous yet influential. Those in the forefront gleaned funneled information from Don's acquaintance, information whose basis was founded in a number of plans Don crafted and authored. The friend was enigmatic. He was there. Then he was not. But when he appeared, he was able to divert attention from himself directly back to the cause and to the ideas brought forth.

It was this friend who had made contacts for Don to pursue in regards to exacting more than an ounce of revenge. It was this friend who, while the two were on a vacation to Germany, made an impromptu introduction of Don to an agent of the Soviet Union's intelligence organization. And then, the friend melded into the background and eventually out of sight. Once the way had been paved for Don to surreptitiously worm his way into the good graces of the infrastructure of the Soviet Union, Don was able to present his basic idea through channels.

On a subsequent trip to Europe during his second year at Wharton, he was properly introduced to a senior KGB agent in Berlin. It was through this agent that he explained his reasons and his plans, to bring the United States of America to its knees in repayment for what they had done to his parents.

In 1976, he was hired by First South Bank and Trust to run the Charleston, South Carolina office. With a masters degree in business administration and finance from Wharton, Donald Robert Fulton assumed control of one of the largest financial institutions on the Atlantic seaboard at the ripe old age of 26. It was then that he again heard from his Berlin acquaintance and within days, had welcomed Annie Fidrych on board as his director of marketing. Don knew that Annie Fidrych was really Anastasia Fidoryvich, special liaison to Soviet President and Party Chairman Aleksandr Romanov. He also knew that Romanov liked his plan. A lot. Romanov sent Annie to be his aide de camp in this campaign to bring America and her economy to a screeching, neck-breaking halt. One that would send the world's foremost economic power into a financial downspin that would make the Great Depression seem like a minor drop in the g.n.p. by comparison.

The relationship between Don and Annie was strictly business. Other than his mom and dad still living on the family homestead in Aiken, Don did not allow people to get close to him. Perhaps it was his desire to avoid having anyone harm, in any way, any individual with whom he might have developed a bond. He trusted Annie implicitly. Of that he constantly assured her. And of that, she was very much aware. If she were to fall suspect or victim through a lapse in security or blown cover, then he would fall with her. Donald knew Annie was smart. Annie knew Donald was brilliant. They were a lethal pair.

While at First South, the two had worked almost as one, fostering the right friendships and tossing aside those of little consequence. The underwriting of Charleston's historic waterfront restoration was the cornerstone to the gubernatorial election in 1978. The campaign was run on a single-planked platform. One of financial security and state profitability. Fulton had produced documentation that showed a balanced budget projected for the first fiscal year alone and a surplus which would allow for elimination of some taxes and the drastic reduction of others, by the end of the second fiscal year. With six years to take the state of South Carolina to a new position of leadership in the south, the voters overwhelmingly elected Donald Robert Fulton, a virtual political unknown, to the position of governor at the ripe old age of 28. Annie Fidrych came along for the ride, of course.

Subtle suggestions received through Annie from Romanov helped further shape the turnaround of South Carolina. Charleston alone became a showplace, even with the threat of military base closings looming. Governor Fulton had shown how to and, make possible, the further use and development of land long thought useless along the scenic waterways that surrounded Charleston's history Battery. Other actions followed which allowed for further voter confidence in South Carolina's new favorite son. His re-elections in 1984 and 1990 were landslides. His acceptance of the vice presidential nomination in 1992 was a moment of glory in which all of South Carolina basked.

Romanov had by now been forced from power, but urged Fulton and Fidrych to continue, reminding them that the long-term goal was now within reach. Annie had assured Aleksandr that they would indeed persevere. Romanov was aware that, publicly and, through channels, privately, President Griffen relied heavily on the insight and intellect of Vice President Fulton. Their first term brought about a booming economy, one of which the Republicans still laid claim to as the fruits of Presidents Bush and Reagan's work. The second term, however, saw the American economy take off like a rocket. The stock market was now measuring the success of its members in billions of dollars, as opposed to the now antiquated notion of millions. A million bucks? You could win that on a scratch ticket at the corner store. Or by pulling a lever in Las Vegas. But billions? Now that's a number hard won through shrewd business savvy and investment. Those now possessed of net worths in the billions had the direction and hard work of President Jay Griffen and Vice President Don Fulton to which to direct their thanks.

Then came the scandal. Annie had been floored, but like Don, saw the window of opportunity open wider than they had even anticipated or imagined. Yes, prior to the incident, they had played the "what if" game. Privately. Quietly. And not for any great length of time. Like all other American citizens, both Annie and Don truly liked Jay Griffen. The man was honest to a fault. He was a straight shooter. Played the game well when it needed to be played. But Jay preferred to not play. He always reminded those closest to him that this, the business of the United States of America, was not a game.

Annie had ample opportunity to speak directly with Aleksandr Romanov, by now living the good life as a "former head of state" and much-revered political icon in the new Russia. Numerous projects involving the highest levels of the United States government required face-to-face meetings, constantly. It was widely known that Annie Fidrych had majored in Russian languages while at college and was able to put her additional skills to work on a regular basis. She had become the de facto envoy in dealing with the new regime in the new Russia, as well as in the offshoot independent republics. What the Russians and Vice President Fulton did not know was that Annie had a new goal in mind. To not only prevent Romanov from having any input of significance to a possible Fulton administration, but to also make sure Fulton never sits behind the desk in the Oval office. And to make doubly-damn sure that Aleksandr Romanov is revealed for what he is. A coward. The American people would and will, respond sharply, swiftly, severely. Of that, Annie was sure. Romanov's fate would be determined in time. Of that, Annie could only hope, with all of her heart.

Annie had allowed one close friendship to develop beyond the casual. That was her bud, L. Bud Nelson. Everyone called him "Bud." She was one of the few allowed to call him Larry. He made her laugh. From the moment they first met at the gas station off of Interstate 26 when he pointed the way for her to find downtown Charleston, she liked Larry. He was capable of disarming charm and yet could retain a distance which kept him comfortable. His smile was infectious. Those who met him would be hard pressed to tell him no. One of his favorite characterizations of a person was calling them "Mr." or "Ms. Yes." No was a word seldom heard by Larry. Annie herself was unable to use the word no in first helping him to get the new car loan. Nor could she utter it when she accepted his invitation to pick-up the new car with him at the dealer and then go out for dinner the next evening.

They dated all during his time in Charleston while he was in the Navy and she was working with Fulton at First South. They used Larry's exclusive southern flair to work out the kinks in campaign speeches and literature during the first gubernatorial race. They also called on him to help during the subsequent re-election campaigns.

Romanov had been intrigued by the possibilities brought forth by Annie fostering a personal relationship with an active member of the United States Navy. Especially one of such importance, dealing in top secret communications at one of the busier submarine bases on the Atlantic. To that, Annie put her foot down. She'd explained that she would rather have a friend who was being utilized as an acquaintance for her cover than to possibly compromise him as an information source. Less than a year into this operation, Romanov had been taken aback, yet impressed with the guts it took for a lowly KGB operative to say no and take so strong a stand in this regard. He had told her that he'd allow her this one breach of protocol. This one crime against the state. But she would not be as lucky the next time. She assured him that there would be no next time, but putting Nelson at risk was not part of the plan.

When Larry was hired by the television station upon the end of his Navy obligation, they had been forced to cool their relationship, so as to not raise any questions of impropriety in regards to the station's coverage of the governor. They still managed to spend time together. Stolen weekends here and there. Even the occasional quickie in the Chief of Staff's office at the statehouse in Columbia. And yes, Larry still reviewed the written speeches and literature for Governor Fulton, even while running the NBS news division in New York and during his subsequent involvement with the New Hampshire campaigns of Governor Jay Griffen. That they had wound up together was no real accident. Once it had appeared a lock for Jay to grab the democratic nomination for president in 1992, Bud had dropped more than a passing reference to the sharp, astute, savvy and *southern* Don Fulton. The geographic factor was the deciding one which led to an unanimous acclamation for the completion of the ticket. The balance of north and south was important to the voters, even more than one hundred years after the Civil War's end. After the success of their first campaign together, Annie and Larry were able to pursue their mutual desires on a more open and more easily accessible, plane. Working day to day in Washington would provide enough distraction to allow them their own separate lives and yet keep them within arms reach when their physical or psychological needs arose. Annie cherished her time with Larry. She longed for her time with Michail.

The closest she came to telling herself that she truly cared for Larry was when she discovered the final conversation caught on the digital micro-recorder she'd planted in his personal p.c. Initially, she'd placed the device there at the suggestion of Vice President Fulton. As sharp as he was and as insightful and sure as he was, Don still had an occasional problem with confidence. Fulton was feeling neglected and was beginning to worry that he might not receive the total support of President Griffen in the 2000 election process. Try as she may, she'd been unable to impart upon him that the election was still over two years away and there would be time to get those on the way out to give a nod to those who would like to be on the way in.

Annie had passed along the personal computer to Larry as a gift, which came with a full written disclosure in accordance with the laws regarding gifts to government employees. They were spending enough nights together that she was able to insert the recording device into the miniature p.c. without him noticing. The device was voice activated, with a digital microchip capable of storing up to eight hours of sound. Since Larry always had the p.c. with him, either in his coat pocket or in plain view while it was in use, it would start with the first sound Larry would make. Then, after sensing ten seconds of silence, it would stop. The only conversations she and Fulton had heard that mentioned Fulton's name had all been extremely favorable towards the vice president. If anything, Fulton's chest grew with each passing minute of glowing praise they would hear.

Annie had taken the micro-recorder out of Larry's p.c. the night before she was due to depart for Madrid. That was the night following that day's high level meeting in which Larry detailed the plot by the KGB to usurp and destroy, the government of the United States.

The mention of Michail's name had made her heart stop. At first, she thought of simply destroying the device. Thinking it through further, she came to the realization that if she could bug a secret, Oval Office meeting, then anyone could. She loaded the conversation into her laptop computer using a simple sound program designed for the Windows operating systems. The program essentially turned a personal computer into a full-blown recording studio. Multiple track recording, cut and paste editing capabilities and even audio effects. She omitted the mention of Michail's name. She omitted the responses and questions of those in attendance. She merely kept the audio tracks of Larry outlining the plan as they knew it. When she'd heard the reference to assassinating Fulton, she had to stop and catch her breath. That, she thought, would eliminate one problem in giving Romanov his due. But her instincts were now to focus on protecting Michail. And Nelson.

Then, she remembered Don Hough. Don was Larry's friend, working with their other friend, Fred, up in Maine. She and Larry had slipped away to a small inn by the sea outside of Portland for an extended, snowy, five-day weekend the month before. She had wanted to call Larry's friends for a wild night like one they used enjoy in Charleston in the seventies. Larry wouldn't have it. This was just us this time, he had said. But he awoke early each morning to listen to the day's news on the small, bedside radio, artfully delivered by Don. Annie had asked Larry what time of day a person had to get to work to do as fine a job as that. Larry explained that to do the kind of news Don did, you had to be there at least two hours before your first newscast. Don was usually there at a minimum of an hour and a half early each day. It was just his way, Bud explained, that the more experience one had, the easier the preparation. Annie was somewhat incredulous that a person of Don's talent and caliber would still be at work not later than four am, when his first official duty wasn't until five-thirty. After all, wasn't he once a network news star? Yes, Larry had confirmed, he was and could do the news in circles around Rather, Brokaw and Jennings with two hands tied behind his back. So, for several lost March mornings, Larry and Annie listened to the entire morning programming in order to catch each and every newscast Don delivered.

Once she had remembered Don Hough and his routine, she knew what to do with the edited recording. Her flight left Andrews at seven the next morning. She'd simply get up early and drop the call to Hough before four am. The voice effects settings on the program were set for a "Darth Vader"-like sound. She and Larry had played with the program the first day she discovered it in her laptop. Larry had shown her how easy it was to use and how valuable it could be. Not to mention convenient. Engaging the effects settings, she previewed her edited work, then set her alarm for three-forty-five am. She'd make the call through her routing network, a series of numbers set up around the world to prevent any tracing. The audio itself was around a minute in length. A chance existed that she might be on the phone long enough to leave a trail, but in the more than twenty years she'd been doing this, no had tracked her down yet. Her hope was that, somehow, Don would recognize Larry's voice. That would give him a heads up to the fact that at least one more person knows about the plot than the White House would prefer.

She arose at three-forty-five that morning. Yesterday morning. She made some coffee and placed her call. On her first attempt, the routing was broken. The recording said that all circuits were busy. Please hang up and try the call again later. So she waited five minutes and tried again. This time, the phone rang. When Don answered, she pressed play. The auxiliary audio jack was wired directly from the computer into the phone's mouthpiece. Annie had accomplished this with a simple pair of alligator clips leads. When the audio finished, she disconnected the call, removed the clip leads from the phone and replaced the mouthpiece. She immediately called another number for the local weather and listened to the thirty second forecast. This would provide a record that she was on the phone at, what, nine past four in the morning. But she had merely called the weather. She erased the edited call from the studio software file. She then took the micro-recorder into her kitchen. Opening the sink cabinet door, she took out her trusty one-size-fixes-all tool, a hammer. She placed the micro-recorder on the solid wood cutting block and gave the device a good smash. That was the end of that, she thought, as she wrapped the minuscule remains a wad of toilet paper and flushed it down the toilet. Watching the water swirl and evacuate the bowl, she softly said "For you, Larry, I do this because I care. For you, Michail my love, I do this because I must."

She could have just as easily had told Bud that night, herself. That, though, would have led to more questions than she wanted to even consider answering. No, when and if Larry found out it she was a part of this ever-multiplying affair du Romanov, she'd rather be at least a thousand miles away.

Finishing her packing for the trip to Madrid, she was running the possibilities through her mind. She'd need to find a way to let Michail know that they were not only on the same original mission, but that they were now also on the same modified mission. Michail, she'd realized, had come forward with his details to prevent the ascension of Hewes upon what seemed to be the impending resignation of President Griffen. Her games of "what if" with Fulton had turned out to be for naught. According to Michail's plan, Fulton would be assassinated upon word of the president's resigning. On that score, she had mixed feelings. She'd come to actually like Don. He was witty, smart, insightful and, yes, sensitive. But, he was also a key player in Romanov's ultimate plan. Her hatred of Aleksandr overruled any feelings she had for Fulton. He was expendable. He had been put in that category the day she had learned of how Romanov allowed his family to perish.

Her next thoughts turned to Romanov. If he had been able to set up two, well thought out and executed operations along these lines, then there could be others. She supposed that if she and Michail combined forces, they'd be able to leave Romanov wallowing in a quagmire from which he would not easily extricate himself. Leaving him to suffer a long, painful death would better suit her current desires, but hanging him out to be pilloried by the world this time might bring a sweeter conclusion. From their island hideaway, wherever it might be, she and Michail could watch and savor the moment. And remember the lives of Elenya, Christina and little Michail.

Annie finished getting dressed, checking her look in the full-length mirror. Taking a deep breath, she reminded herself that this was almost over. That soon, she'd be able to put all of this crazed double life she'd been leading for more than twenty years behind her and enjoy a real existence with Michail Rostokovich. Perhaps, if they could begin soon enough, they could work at making a baby. Not one to take the place of Christina or little Michail, but one of their own, to proudly take his or her place in a world made a little better by her or his mommy and daddy. That would be a fitting tribute to the memories of those who had fallen victim to the whims of ego-driven world leaders like Romanov.

Glancing at her wristwatch, she grabbed her briefcase, double-checked the paperwork they need for this morning's meeting and stepped out of the hotel room. She closed the door behind her and as always, double-checked the lock. As she walked out of the hotel's lobby door, she saw secret service agent Dayle standing by the car. Good man, that Mr. Dayle, she thought as she climbed into the backseat. Dayle hopped into the front seat, put the car in gear and drove towards the American Embassy where Vice President Fulton was waiting.

thirty-two

Alexandria, Virginia   Saturday, April 4, 1998   5:50am (local)

Nelson was awake when the phone rang at five-fifty am. He'd been awake for most of the night.

The phone rang first about half past midnight when Colonel Menneally called to mention the unexpected arrival of two bad guys who appeared to be trying get *their* bad guy. The phone rang again a little later, just before two, when Menneally called to say they'd returned to Go Team One's headquarters, with assistant Secretary of State Moore in custody, as well as the other two, still unknown, intruders. After that call, Nelson had called the president, who in turn took down the information to forward to Central Intelligence Agency Director Terrio. Menneally and Terrio could exchange notes and fax numbers and email addresses and whatever the hell else they wanted. Nelson's concern was, at this point, the safety of Michail Rostokovich. Without him, anything and everything they could produce and provide would still most likely be treated as the desperate acts of a desperate man. President Griffen was seen as a desperate man in a perilous predicament. Too bad, Bud thought. Griffen was, if anything, desperate. Jay had resigned himself to the fact that, the truth notwithstanding, the American justice system would have its way with him, one way or the other. And President John Francis Griffen did not want it any other way.

"Good morning!" chirped Nelson.

"Bud? It's Don. How are you? And why are you so awake? I thought I was the only one who was supposed to be functional at this time of day?"

"Don, this little mess has allowed me about three hours sleep all night. Shit is happening fast and furious and given the time zones involved, it's going to be a long couple of days. And I hope it's only days. Whassup?" "Sandy's in the hospital. New York Presbyterian in New York City. She's in tough shape, so they tell me."

"What in the name of Frederick P. Goatman happened?" Bud was now enraged. "Did that fucking prick of an ex-husband come back?"

"Well, yes, he did apparently. Some guy called me at Sandy's request and gave me the scoop. The asshole apparently came back, whacked her around and put her headfirst through a glass coffee table."

"What? How the fuck did he get to her? Damn it! I personally arranged for a bodyguard to watch her until this prick was taken care of."

"Excuse me? First off, Bud, you knew she was divorced?"

"Yeah." Bud calmed down a bit at that. He'd known about the entire situation and at Sandy's request, had not mentioned any of it to Don. She had confided in Bud that she still cared deeply for Don, but was afraid of rejection. Nelson had assured her that Don would come a runnin' if she asked. Sandy, however, remained unsure.

"And you also mean to say that Jonathon had done something like this before? That's what I would assume based on your having arranged for a bodyguard to watch out for her. Man! How could you keep something like this from me, L? You know my world was rocked to the core the day she told me she was going to marry this guy."

"Don. Let me apologize. It may not mean anything right now, but I am sorry that I did not clue you in as to what was happening. Please understand that she told me the whole story, under duress, while she was recovering in a private hospital after her last accident. I arranged for the private care. She had been in that car accident and was in tough shape. Plus, she had lost the baby."

"The baby? That never made its way into the story."

"Here's the deal, in a nutshell. Jon used his fists on her. A lot. The last time, she was driving herself to the hospital. Jon had managed to break a few ribs. Jon did not know she was pregnant. She was in such pain that she lost control of the car and plowed into another car and a lightpole. When she came to in the hospital, not only had she lost the baby, but Jon was there by her side. She called me for help. I showed up with a few special agents from the FBI in tow and we helped Jonathon Earle pack up his shit and get back to London within the hour. Very quietly, at my request, a New York City judge annulled their marriage and NSA director Realto revoked his permanent-resident status. No longer married to a United States citizen, Jonathon Earle had no choice but to get the fuck out of my country. While we were at it, Realto dropped a couple of hints to his counterpart in Great Britain that it would be fun to watch this asshole squirm while a few agents of the crown crawled up his anus and took a good look around. The call was worth it. Jonathon Earle was not only a fairly successful art gallery owner, but the son of bitch was into some really naughty stuff. Last I heard, the intelligence community was very, very interested in his hobbies."

Nelson took a deep breath and could hear Don doing the same over the phone line.

"Don, I'm sorry I never told you. Please understand that it's how Sandy wanted it. What do we know about the bully?"

"Right now, nothing. This guy, Kelley, called me with the hospital info and a thumbnail of what happened to her."

"I hope Jonny-boy winds up in a jail cell with a few drunk Irishmen."

"I figured I'd let you know what I know, though. I know you and Sandy kept in touch with each other. Although not to the extent that I know now."

"You want me to find out more for you? I can do that now. I'm up, so it's time to get working anyway."

"That would be great, Bud. I'm calling over to the Jetport now to see if I can get on a flight to New York. Most of the commuter flights leave in about a half hour or so and seeing as how it's a weekend morning, there aren't as many flight scheduled, so I've got to get moving."

"What about the station?"

"I already called Dickie Johnson. He's coming in now to take over the morning drive shift. Should I call Fred? Or do you want to bring him up to speed?"

"You get your ass down to New York. I'll arrange to have someone pick you up, okay? Call me with the flight info. I'll call Fred right now and fill him in."

"The guy who called me, Kelley, has already offered to pick me up."

"No. Let me get you a real escort. At this point, I'm not sure who we can trust anymore. I'll ask for an FBI team to get you. They'll be very, very interested in seeing how this plays out ."

"I'll call you back as soon as I'm on a plane. Give me ten minutes."

"Okay, Don. I'll be here."

Nelson hung up the phone and grabbed his personal p.c., bringing up the phone directory with a touch and a click. He dialed the home number for NSA Director Realto.

After three rings, a sleepy voice answered.

"John? Sorry if I woke you. It's Bud Nelson."

"Hey, Bud. What time is it?"

"About six."

"Time to get up anyway. No problem. What's up?"

"Our friend, Jonathon Earle, got back into your country yesterday."

"Awww, FUCK! How the hell did that happen? Never mind, I'm supposed to be the one with that answer. Did he do anything?"

"Put Sandra Rose back into the hospital. Worse this time. I'm calling New York Presbyterian after I hang up with you to get an update. Find out what you can for me, will you? Like how this idiot got back here? What happened to the Brits' interest in this guy? And, more importantly, where he is now, okay?"

"I'm doing it now, Bud. And let me call the hospital for you. You at home?"

"Yep. Hanging here waiting for a few more calls before I head to the office."

"What's the latest on the other front?"

"You know we're not secure, John. We've got a coffee-klatch with Jay at eight. Bring you up to speed then. Find out what you can now, though, alright?"

"You got it, Bud. Give me about ten minutes."

"I'll be here waiting on your call, John. Bye."

Nelson hung up the call and dialed the home number for Admiral Gary Dericksen, USN, retired.

"Jeeeeezus, Bud!" Gary's voice came down the line after one ring. "It's not even oh-six hundred yet!"

"And a good morning to you as well, Admiral. How'd you know it was me?"

"Caller I.D., Bud. You heard of it? Amazing little invention now available through your local phone company for only three-ninety-five per month. Caller I.D. equipment extra."

"The only thing missing is James Earl Jones doing the disclaimer, Gary. Nice commercial."

"James Earl Jones?"

"Sorry, Gary. The man with Darth Vader's voice does the commercials up this way for Bell-Atlantic. Is Fred awake yet?"

"I'm gonna have to get up and go downstairs and see, Bud. We were up kind of late last night."

"Drinking heavily, I hope."

"There's no other way, Bud. At a place I'm saving as a surprise for you the next time you get down this way, as a matter of fact.

Bud could hear the admiral walking, making his way down the stairs. Then, he heard the knocking of a door down the phone line.

"Fred? Fred you awake? Nelson's on the phone!"

After a slight pause, Gary finished, "Here's Fred, Bud. Make sure you get your ass down here soon, okay? We've got some golf to play."

"Will do, Admiral. And say hey to Sue for me."

Dericksen passed the phone to Singletary.

"Yeah, Bud. What's up?" Fred asked a bit groggily.

"I hate to wake you like this, with bad news, but Sandy's back in the hospital in New York. The jerk came back to town and worked her over good. Don got the call this morning and he's on his way down there. He's got coverage for the station. I offered to call you so he could focus on getting out of Maine."

"When did this happen?"

"Sometime last night, I guess. Believe me when I say I am none too happy. I set up her security arrangements after the last time. Someone's got some real explaining to do."

"Keep me posted on this, will you Bud? She's a good lady. And you know how we all feel about Don. How did he find out about it? Was it on the wire?"

"No. Apparently Sandy had asked someone on scene to call Don."

"Well, let me know if anything else comes up."

"Absolutely, Fred. You're picking up Hannity in a few hours, right?"

"We'll be there, hungover and ready for action."

"Keep the action to a minimum, Fred. You guys are just there to take a look around."

"Got it, Bud. Roger, willco, over and out?"

"That's pretty much the drill, Freddie. Now get up and go find me some evidence to get rid of another bad guy, will you? Our boys did a little Parisian snatch 'n' grab this morning, so like Cool Hand Luke, we've got two in the bush, one in the box."

"That's good news so far. I'll have my cellphone on and Gary'll have his, too. You've got all of those numbers?"

Nelson scrolled through his phone directory on the p.c..

"Got them all, Fred. I'll call you when I get some more details on Sandy."

Nelson hung up the phone and reached for a cup of coffee. No sooner had he taken a sip from the cup, his phone rang again.

"Nelson."

"Mr. Nelson? I was looking for Mr. Goatman. Is he there? It's Mike Rosty."

Larry took a deep breath. "Yes, Mike, he's here. Let me get him for you.

Nelson put down the phone, walked loudly across the floor and returned to the receiver.

"Fred Goatman here, Mr. Rosty, How are you this fine morning?"

"I'm doing better than expected. It's actually a nice day here and I'm almost to my fishing date. I wanted to let you know that there is a little more to the project on which we are currently working. The components we've been discussing are as they were per the schematics. But one of the chips may be of a foreign nature and it could impact the overall performance of the unit. I've sent a few additional technical notes on the device to your attention. I think this will change your company's overall view of our product."

"I'll look for it, Mike. Anything else?"

"You have a major leak."

Nelson was struck silent. Instantly, his mind was reeling, trying to figure out, on a non-secure line, what Rostokovich meant.

"We've been working on those capacitors, Mike. We knew we had a small problem with those damn things holding the current."

"No, Mister Goatman. You have a major business leak. One of my professional friends is somewhat aware of our industriousness. Even though we had our last meeting at your company's headquarters, I had taken tremendous steps to ensure that my competition was not aware of our joint venture. You, of course, know how cut-throat our high-tech competitors can be. I have to admit I was somewhat dumb-struck when asked about the reason for my visit to your office.

Bud made sharp note of the emphasis put on the word "office."

"With all that in mind, though, I was wondering if you'd arranged with your friends to have my fishing supplies delivered?"

Nelson nodded to himself and to the phone, admiring how Michail was trying to talk in circles that would make no sense to anyone but them.

"Yes, Mike. I have talked with my buddy and you may rest assured that your fishing gear will be there. It may even be there now, as a matter of fact. Now, as to whether or not you catch the big one today, well, that's up to luck. Some people call it fishing. Others call it drinking beer. I'm pretty confident, though, that you'll at least be outfitted to the max."

"Thanks again, Mr. Goatman. Be sure to review both sets of schematics. And tell me what you think of the musical accompaniment. I found the recording and thought immediately of you."

"Thanks, Mike. Just to double check, what time are you going fishing?"

"We hope to have lines in the water around three, less than an hour from now. I'm looking forward to this. A lot."

"Enjoy it, Mike. And I look forward to hearing about the one that didn't get away this time."

Nelson hung up the phone and immediately his mind started reeling as to what was meant by a major leak. His thoughts turned to Annie. The Charleston connection was getting just a little too coincidental for comfort. If Annie had dropped the conversation to Don, she could have just as easily sent it back to Russia as well, assuming she was working with the Russians.

The fishing gear would be there by three, Russian-time. Actually, Bud thought, the gear should be getting there just about now, two p.m. in Russia, the original time requested. The authorization for delivery of "the gear," otherwise known as Go Team One, had been given the official go-ahead at about two am, eastern time. When Menneally had called after arriving back at Cheltenham, Bud had set up a quick conference call with President Griffen and Jay had given the orders for Go Team One to proceed, even with the hesitant blessing of the Joint Chiefs. Colonel Menneally, his pared-down team and their helicopter, would be air-lifted via an Air Force C-5 Galaxy to Finland. There, they'd join up, temporarily, with an on-going NATO exercise north of Helsinki. Once deployed, Go Team One would experience some communications and navigational gear difficulties and set down to do some repairs. Of course, they wouldn't set down. They'd be nose-down and heading north-northeast like a bat out of hell towards Lake Onega in Russia. They'd be doing it no more than fifty feet off the deck and hoping to God no one caught them crossing the border. They would have some protection by way of a secure link to the airborne AWACS on station to monitor the joint exercises below. Once the Blackhawk reached the northern tip of Lake Onega, they'd head due south along the water's edge to a point just north of the residence-in-exile of Aleksandr Romanov. From there, they'd hide the Blackhawk with brush and then deploy in a non-marked Zodiac-styled inflatable pontoon boat. When the boat was secured, the team was to avail itself to Colonel Michail Rostokovich in any and every possible manner. The Go Team's orders were to not only protect Michail, but return with Rostokovich, alive. Go Team One was to be dressed in black, having removed all Velcro-fastened insignia. They would, however, be allowed to re-attach the identifying patches if they were discovered prior to their return to Finland. The Blackhawk had been rigged with two additional external fuel tanks to increase its range. After all, they were going in and coming out. This was not a one-way hop. One of the tanks was also fitted with a detonation pack that could be triggered, remotely, by a dual-key activation transmitter. The two-tone signal would blow the Blackhawk sky-high in the event they were discovered by Russian ground troops. The Go Team would then be able to offer a semi-plausible explanation that the technical difficulties left them unable to land safely and that before they'd had the chance to land, they'd found themselves over Lake Onega in Russian territory. Forced to jump from their now out-of-control helo, they'd consider themselves lucky to be alive. Since Russia was now participating in NATO exercises, this breach of Russian sovereignty might be more easily forgiven or overlooked. The ultimate goal, however, was to keep Michail out of harm's way, at any cost.

Nelson looked at his watch. He picked up the phone and called Realto back.

"Hey John. It's Bud. Find anything out yet?"

"We did, Bud. Jonathon's dead. The building's valet parking guy took him out with the building security guard's gun. They found Sandy in really tough shape. The team working on her at New York Presbyterian reports she was almost gone when she got there. She'd suffered massive blood loss. She's stable now, though."

"Well, I'm glad. On both counts. Make sure we help out this parking guy in case the NYPD try to jam him up. He's got a friend in me for life, that's for certain. Do you have Hammett's phone number right there?"

"Keith Hammett's number? Yeah, hold on. Let me pull it up for you. Damn, I love this little p.c.. Great freakin' gizmo, Bud, you know? Got my phone book and a notepad all right here. Plus, I can even log onto the Internet and check the email with this thing. Here it is. Hammett. You want the home or cellphone?"

"Better give me both, John."

Realto read Nelson both phone numbers while Bud entered them into his own p.c.. Bud then made a mental note to let Realto know about the pitfalls associated with these little techno-marvels.

"Got 'em both, John. See you in the boss's office in about two hours."

"Catch you then, Bud."

Bud hung up the phone and stared at it. Then, he glanced at his watch. It was almost six-fifteen and he'd not yet gotten into the shower. He had one more call to come. Almost as if on cue, the phone rang.

"Is that you, Donny?"

"No, Bud. But now I'm jealous. I thought I was the only one who could call you at sunrise on Saturday."

"Chucker! Sorry, bud. I was expecting a call from Donny. Sandra Rose is in the hospital again."

"She wrack the car up again?"

"No. Her slimeball of an ex-husband violated several international laws and paid her an unauthorized and unexpected visit. Bashed her up pretty badly. Don's on his way down to the city to be with her."

"I guess they had a nice talk last night when he called about the video tape project. He was kind of blue when I talked with him after her call. She was having the tape morgue pull out the video footage you asked for. He had asked her to send it here to me."

"I almost forgot about that. And while I'm at it, I'm waiting to hear from an FBI team to see if they were able to intercept the FedEx package you were expecting from overseas. Figured we could use a little muscle to save an hour or two. If they weren't able to grab the package, let me know when and if you get anything. Also, there's another package possibly coming your way. My guess is it's a tape or something. Call me, but make sure you give it a good listen and once-over."

"Bud. You're almost terribly psychic. I've known all along you're terribly psychotic, but the tape thing brings us both to the same page. Remember, if you will, our little month together on the Isle of Palms. There you were, sitting on the floor of the beach house, going through your boxes of stuff. You had one box with college stuff. Notebooks, textbooks and cassettes of lectures you felt like saving?"

"Michaud! You are an absolute fucking genius! The goddamn tapes from Clemson. And I know at least one of them...."

."..was the original M. Bradford Hewes," Chuck had finished.

"Voiceprints! When the hell did this dawn on you?"

"About three this morning. Couldn't sleep. Did a lot of tossing and turning, then Sue gave me a whack on the back. Damn, I think I've got a bruise. Then, just as I was dozing off, it hit me like a ton of bricks. I was thinking that if there was no definitive proof of who Hewes *was*, then the Hewes that *is* is all we've got to work with. No fingerprints, as an example. Then it flashed! Voiceprints. Just as good as fingerprints when you ain't got fingerprints from which to work. There are couple of things to check on, though. First, make sure you grab all of his medical records, like, now. Make sure he's not had any surgery in his throat. Guys like Hewes who speak a lot during campaigns are more prone to vocal cord polyps than guys like us who know when it's time to shut up and protect our most valuable asset."

"You? Shut Up? Never in my lifetime."

"Very funny. True. But still funny, Bud. And make sure you still have those tapes, of course."

Bud thought for a moment. He'd made a lot of moves and accumulated a lot of stuff still living in boxes over the years.

"I'm going to have to check my stash, but I'm pretty sure I kept that stuff. You know, Chuck. I owe you at least a very large quantity of contraband cigars from an island nation to be named later and the opportunity to beat me at a round of golf."

"Regarding the cigars, so long as the island nation rhymes with Dooba, I'll be happy. Golf? I've never considered beating you as an opportunity, Bud. It's always been my pleasure."

"And fuck you very much."

"I'm up and dressed, Bud, so I'm going to call Don and drive him to the Jetport."

"That's a good idea," Nelson paused while the call waiting beeped. He was actually surprised that he'd gotten this much phone time with so many different people calling before the actual start to this morning. "Hold on a sec. Got a call coming in."

Nelson clicked the phone one time to grab the incoming call.

"Nelson."

"Bud? It's Don."

"Don. I've got Michaud holding on the other line. He's coming over right now to drive you to the gate. You got a flight?"

"Yep. Delta Express five-nineteen. Leaves here in about thirty minutes. Got a quick stop in Boston and should be at LaGuardia around eight-forty-five or so."

"Gotcha. And do me a favor, when Michaud tells you of his brainstorm, which we both know he will, give him a big, wet kiss for me. Chucker's on his way. I'll call you at the hospital later, okay?"

"Okay, Bud. And thanks."

"No problem, Donny. Have a safe flight."

Nelson clicked the phone back over to Michaud.

"Chucker. Don's flight leaves in thirty minutes."

"I'm on my way now, Bud. I'll call you later if I get any deliveries. They don't usually do Saturday drops, but maybe I can stop into their office while I'm at the Jetport and ask them to do me a huge favor. I'll talk to you later."

Michaud hung up the phone and Bud re-clicked his phone for a new dial tone. One more call and I can shower, he thought.

"Director Hammett? It's Bud Nelson from the president's office. How are you this morning?"

"Doing okay, Bud. What about you?"

"It's not even six-thirty yet and it's been one of the more interesting days so far in my life. I was wondering about a couple of things.

"Do you know if your agents had any luck checking the FedEx flights this morning in New York?"

"Just got off the phone with the agent-in-charge. They have both envelopes. One addressed to you in care of a Mike Rosty. The other addressed to a Fred Goatman in care of Michaud Media in Maine. Those are the ones you needed, right?"

"Those are the critters, Keith. Now the other thing. Have you heard about what happened in New York this morning?"

"My guys said there was something involving a network news lady and a shooting."

"The lady is a very dear friend of mine, Sandra Rose. Her ex returned, uninvited, from London and did a number on her. Building employee saved us all a lot of paperwork and time. One of my running mates is flying down to New York to be with her at New York Presbyterian. Is there any chance you could have an agent meet him at LaGuardia and get him to the hospital?"

"It's kind of an unusual request, Bud, don't you think?"

"Yes, Keith. It is. But, this friend is actually part of a major, ongoing investigation that I am not authorized to bring you up to speed on right now. I'm sure, though, that I can have President Griffen give you the details. It's just that too many funky things have been going down in regards to people working this case. I'm asking out of deep concern for the safety of all involved at this point."

Hammett paused for a moment then said, "All right, Bud. I'll have an agent meet him. Give me his name and flight number."

Nelson gave him the info, then added, "Are the packages on their way down here?"

"They left New York on our private jet about thirty minutes ago, with specific delivery instructions to President Griffen only. Special Agent Ned Talbot has possession of them."

"Keith, thanks again. I'll have the president call you, okay?"

"That would be nice, Bud. Since I'm sending my agents all over creation, it would be of benefit for me to know what's going on."

Hammett sounded somewhat put off, Bud noticed. The man had a right, though.

"I'll call the president right now, Keith. And thanks again. I owe you a beer."

Hammett lightened the mood a bit when he added, "No. You owe me two."

"My pleasure, Director Hammett. It'll be my pleasure."

Now six-thirty, Bud hung up the phone and made one last call. Then, he vowed, he'd really get into the shower.

"Good morning."

"Good morning, Mister President."

"Bud. You sound too awake for this time of the day."

"Sir, I've been on the phone off and on since midnight. Not much sleep, but all of the calls noteworthy."

"Run them down for me, Bud."

"First thing before I forget. Director Keith Hammett. We need to bring him up to speed. We're using his troops to dig through FedEx planes and now, at my request, they're going to be doing some baby-sitting and transporting for us."

"Baby-sitting?"

"I asked for an agent to pick up Don Hough at LaGuardia. Don's flying down to be with Sandra Rose. She's in the hospital, again. Thanks to her ex, now late, husband."

"Whoa there, Bud. Didn't we deport that man months ago? And take away his green card?"

"Yes, Jay. We did. He came back yesterday. Somehow, he gave British Intelligence the slip and got through customs here. The MI-5 boys had been watching him to try and take down his side-business of phony documents. Obviously, not close enough. He worked Sandy over but good this time. She's in New York Presbyterian. Don's coming down to be with her."

"Where's the guy now?"

"Dead. No longer a problem."

"Okay, I'll call Keith now. What else do we have before I see you in a little more than an hour?"

"We have a leak. Got a call from our fishing buddy this morning and his friend was aware of all of his movements in regards to his visits here. We'll need to flesh this one out and put some brain power together. Also, the pickup was made about midnight our time and there are the few unexpected passengers, which we discussed earlier. Another topic for the meeting. And the parcels from New York should be arriving at the office, your attention only, in about an hour. Let's wait until we have Terrio and Realto there before we dig into them."

"The chief justice and company will be here around eight, Bud. You know that doesn't give us much time."

"Time is no longer on our side, Jay. We've been up against the clock since the night you were arraigned. It's better if any and all discovery is made in full view of the people set to hold you in judgment. There's less of a chance they'll be able to say we made this whole thing up. Remember, you are still a defendant in a criminal case. That puts you on the defense. Additionally, you are the one who has insisted that this thing be put before a judge and jury next week. Get it out of the way for the good of the country and all."

"So the best defense is a good offense, right?"

"In this case, yes. So you call Hammett. Maybe we need to have him at the meeting this morning, too. It'll make him feel better to be in the loop."

"Bud, if this loop gets any bigger, we'll be able to put the people who don't know what's happening on a bus to Kansas."

"One other question. Have we heard from Secretary Paparelli? I'd hope that by now she'd have taken attendance."

"Nothing at this end yet, Bud. Did the announcement make it?"

"It was supposed to have been delivered to the hotel. I'm sure we'll hear something before the end of the day, though. When and if you get a call, make sure you ask if there's any kind of word. Maybe a note at the front desk or something."

"Okay. Bud. See you a bit."

Nelson hung up the phone and ran through a mental checklist of people who might be calling. It seems everyone had checked in. Next stop, the shower. He walked down the hall, into the bathroom and turned the shower on full. Thirty minutes later, he looked at his fingers. Wrinkled. He laughed to himself, remembering how wrinkled fingers were, to his mom, a bellwether of cleanliness after an hour in the tub.

He took a look, just on a chance, in the closet for the college box. He'd been good of late about labeling his random collections that marked the different stages of his life. Sure enough, towards the back of the closet in the spare room was the now-frayed cardboard container with the hastily-scribbled moniker of "college stuff." He pulled it out, opened the top and there, wrapped with a rubber band, was the stack of cassette tapes he had all those years ago deemed worthy of not being re-used. The tapes' labels were faded, the pencil markings no longer completely distinguishable. He'd need to bring them all and, then, one at a time, give each a quick listen. He knew he had one or two Hewes lectures in there. He took the tapes out to the kitchen table and placed them there next to his briefcase, then returned to the bedroom and got dressed.

As he came back out to gather up his briefcase, he gave a quick look towards the answering machine. He'd had at least one call while he was in the shower. The clock was working against him. Still, he walked over to the machine and pressed play.

The machine's computerized voice spoke the time stamp. "Message received today, seven-oh-nine am," followed by the tone and then the message. "Bud? Bud? You there? Pick up if you are?"

It was Annie. She was the last person he wanted to speak with right now. Which gave him an idea. He needed to find a way to have the president keep Fulton and his team in Madrid for another day or two. Keep them away until they could get his whole mess sorted out. And he still had to have some time to think and to get to the bottom of the Annie situation. If she was the leak, then he'd need to pass the handling of how to deal with her on to someone else. If she wasn't the leak, then he'd have to deal with himself in finding a way to apologize to her for doubting.

He pressed stop and left the message on the machine. He'd rather it appear he'd not gotten it. She was, like he, very ingenious when it came to technical stuff like checking an answering machine from away from home. Actually, he laughed out loud as he reminded himself that she might be even more technical than he. He patted his suitcoat pocket to make sure the personal p.c. was there, grabbed the briefcase and headed for the White House. It was sure to be a very busy day.

thirty-three

Madrid, April, 1998 1:25 p.m. (local)

Annie came back into the office area being used by Vice President Fulton. She'd just called back to Virginia in the hopes of catching Bud. She was surprised when she got the answering machine. Saturday was usually his day for coffee and casual phone calls. He was always on the phone for pleasure weekend mornings. She wanted to let him know that it was she who had dropped the bomb to Don in Maine. And, she'd hoped, that she could offer a brief explanation that would, if anything, help back up Michail's claims of who he was. Her letting Nelson know that she was in on the game as well, but from a different angle, would help give President Griffen easy access to all the remaining details. She also wanted to see how they would follow through on the cleanup of this operation and was willing to cooperate in any way possible to help them put all of the players away, save, of course, herself and Michail. She knew, though, that through this disclosure, she and Nelson would be no more. Yes, she cared for Bud. But her world was for Michail. Michail would be the one to suffer more if taken to task for his role in this.

She had started to map out an escape route. It was only a matter of time before the pieces all fell together. She was prepared, even right this very minute, to excuse herself from the upcoming meeting between the vice president and the French prime minister and board a flight for Algiers, with a connecting flight to Argentina, where she had already paid six months rent on a small, seaside villa to the north of Montevideo. She had mailed an envelope with instructions to a blind post office box in Munich, addressed to Michail.

The breakfast meeting had gone well. A quick rundown of the meetings to finish up with today and then back to Washington late this afternoon. They had met with the assistant finance ministers of Germany and Spain after breakfast. Next up was the one they had figured to be the tough nut to crack, French Prime Minister Jean-Pierre Moreau. France seemed to be a little unsure about losing its uniqueness by giving in to the impending switch to a common European currency. The goal of this meeting was to blow rosy little smoke rings up this guys rear end to make him and his country, think they were still the top banana in the eyes of the United States.

Annie knocked on the large door of the inner office and waited for Vice President Fulton to invite her to enter.

"Enter," came the voice from inside. Steeling herself so as not to indicate that anything was up, she opened the door swiftly and strode into the office confidently.

"Annie. Has Prime Minister Moreau arrived yet? I was hoping to get this meeting over with so we could get back home before midnight tonight."

"His office called and said he'd be along shortly. There's a problem across town involving anther car bombing."

"Would be nice if now that all of the individual nations over here seem to have worked out their problems, the people could just learn to get along in their own countries. Any group claiming responsibility?"

"Not yet, Don. The reports are leaning towards a similar bombing which an offshoot group of Basque separatists had taken the credit for. I'm all for getting home early tonight, though."

"Close the door."

Annie looked a bit puzzled, but turned and closed the heavy door.

"I need to ask you about that meeting I had with the boss the other day. Did you hear any of the details."

Annie instinctively played dumb. "No. What went down?"

"We are not alone."

"What do you mean by that?"

"It seems there is another team in place with exactly the same goal as ours. I would guess that our well-placed friend, to use a football analogy, sent everyone long and threw a "Hail Mary" pass. Just that now that we're near the end zone, it seems that there are two of us wide open."

Annie tried her best to look dumbfounded. Her initial shock had been registered and gotten over with two nights ago when she heard the entire conversation on the micro-recorder.

"Who's the other team? I assume they're on our side."

"The other team is Speaker Hewes. I would not, however, go so far as to saying they're on our side. They mean to kill me."

"Excuse me?"

"They're going to kill me and move on into 1600 Pennsylvania Ave. when President Griffen decides enough is enough and steps aside. Under the twenty-fifth amendment and the law of succession, Speaker Hewes would become president."

"Hewes? The man doesn't possess half the knowledge or confidence required to do the job he's got now?" Annie was somewhat incredulous. "What the hell was Aleks…, er, he thinking?"

"Beats me, Annie. Beats me. I just know we need to get a small defensive game plan going. I need you to bring Agent Dayle up to speed so that they'll be more on their toes. The way this thing was explained, I am to be taken out of the picture at the moment Griffen announces his resignation. Not before and not after. The law of succession was written for just such a scenario."

"How are you going to explain this to the Secret Service? I mean, are you just going to come out and say that there's a Russian plot to kill you?"

"No. But for my own safety, I'll let them know that there is a known threat against me and to be wary of even people with whom we work. For all we know, that nice little secretary of his could be a cold blooded assassin."

"You mean Robin? His girlfriend?"

"Yeah. The woman in his life that no one is supposed to know about. I have to admit, it's the best kept secret in Washington. The only ones who don't know are the two of them."

"So, do you have any other names? You mentioned "team" earlier."

"The other half of the team is apparently Moore. From State."

"You mean Paparelli's assistant?"

"That's the guy. Helped get Hewes elected to congress in seventy-six. Worked his magic in New Hampshire helping Griffen grab the statehouse. And Jay called him back to do his thing in ninety-two. That's what's puzzling about this team. I've done some checking in the past twenty-four hours. Moore's been around since the early seventies, doing exactly what he did for Hewes and Griffen, giving various campaigns much needed kickstarts. The guy's been all over the country, but no one knows him."

"Not even the cops? What about the social security office?"

"They had a record of him with a permanent California address up to about 1976. After that, his address, according to tax returns, shifted to a South Carolina post-office box. That's the one still on file with the IRS."

"You have been busy, Donald. Very busy indeed."

"Well, it's been my experience that when you find out that someone wants you dead, you try and find out what you can."

"What about Hewes?"

"He's a bigger mystery. Solid old south family. He still calls the plantation in Charleston home. He went to Clemson and taught there. Also, he started teaching at the College of Charleston just before the end of the '76 spring semester. That summer, he became really interested in politics. Apparently, he was a good enough student to get elected in November. Moore worked his campaign, so that puts them together from that point."

"Does Hewes or Moore have any kind of motive working for them? I mean, is there anything that indicates a big payoff for them if they're doing this for the same result as us?"

"Maybe the promise of a big payday. I don't know. Have you checked in lately? Might be a good idea. Bring the subject up. Directly. Please."

"I'll make a call before we leave this afternoon, okay?"

"That would be nice, Annie. Let this guy know that through a natural turn of events, we're set to do that which he asked. I didn't sign up for this to get this close and die."

The intercom on the desk buzzed and Annie reached over to answer it.

"Thanks," Annie said, hanging the phone back up.

"Is Jean-Pierre here?"

"No. You have a call from Jay waiting."

"What time is it?"

Checking her watch, Annie replied, "Just about one-forty-five here. Makes it not yet a quarter to eight there."

"They're up and at it early for a Saturday, aren't they?" Don said, raising an eyebrow at Annie. He reached across the desk and picked up the phone.

"Good morning, Mister President."

"Hey Don. How goes the battle over there?"

"Had good meetings this morning with the Germans and the Spaniards. Got the tough guy lined up to show up here any minute."

"That would be our friend Monsieur Moreau, non?"

"Oui, oui! Ton francais est bien, ce matin."

"You didn't just swear at me, right?"

"Jay, you know damn well if I were to swear at you, it would be in words that we'd both appreciate."

"Relax, Don. Relax. Listen. In regards to that little meeting the other morning, we've had a small meeting of the minds here this morning and we're thinking it might be a good idea for you to hang there until at least tomorrow."

"Jesus, Jay. Is it necessary? I mean, we're wrapping up here in about two hours."

"Just a thought, Don. Might be better if we keep you more than arms length away from the known players. Have you briefed your detail yet?"

"Just went over it with Annie. I also made Agent Dayle aware of it right after our meeting. I'd rather the rest of the team know about it before anything happens"

Jay let out a heavy sigh.

"What's the problem, boss?"

"I don't know how else to put this, but Annie might be a part of it. Don't say anything right now. I assume she's right there?"

"Yes."

"Well, Don. I'd make an effort to not let her be alone with you for too long. Just be careful."

"What leads you to your last assumption?"

"Well asked, Don. Not easy to do when you're talking about someone who is standing right there. The key word to what I said was "might." It's not definite, but we're trying to track down a few more details before we can say any more with confidence. Our assumption right now is based on a listening-device that might have been planted somewhere that managed to record our meeting the other day."

Don was nodding now, his brain working at full tilt.

"Thanks for the update, Jay. I appreciate it. I know you want me to hang tight here, but I'd rather get back for tonight, if we can. I've got Sunday school to teach in the morning."

Annie stood across from Don, putting on an exaggerated frown, as he hung up the phone.

"We've got to stay until tomorrow?"

"No. We're heading back today, but Jay thinks it best until they can work out some more of this little Hewes thing. He'd like to make sure we keep somewhat out of their reach. He also told me that you're playing dumb."

Annie was genuinely surprised at that.

"Now, don't give me that hooked-fish look of yours. You used the micro-recorder and heard the whole thing the other day. You just let me go through the whole plan and there you stood, taking it all in with rapt attention. Want to tell me why?"

"The operative is my significant other," Annie said without hesitation. "Michail Rostokovich and I have been together since the early seventies. I had no idea that he was a part of anything related to what we are doing. I got my orders directly from the top and have been going on this full-tilt ever since. He has apparently been working on his project just as long. But even when we've been able to spend time together, our discussions never, ever involve what we are doing. We don't discuss it for just this very reason. Now, he's compromised. Fortunately for you, I am not."

Annie was now fully animated and Don was attempting to get her to quiet her voice down somewhat, gesturing around him in a way that might indicated that the walls have ears.

"I'll keep my voice down, but at this point, it's anyone's guess as to who is really who. For all we know, Griffen may also be in on this and he beat us to the top floor."

"Doubtful about Jay, Annie. The American economy has never been stronger and the stock market now keeps track of the elite in billions of dollars. No, Jay is definitely not one of us."

"So what do we do? Why are you so calm knowing that there's someone out there with one job yet to do? That job is you, you know."

"Of that I am very much aware. I'll be honest, I haven't been able to pay much attention to anything else in the past forty-eight hours. Ironic, don't you think?"

"Please. The Alanis version was painful enough the eighty-fourth time through. Yes, we're talking O. Henry stuff now, Don. I wonder how Alek is treating all of this? Is he having a great laugh at our expense?"

"Let me just remind you of one thing, Miss Fidrych. For me, this is personal. I don't care about any motives that dwell in the deepest dark place of Alek's mind. And until we know what's driving Speaker Hewes for sure, I'm still moving forward. Just a bit more cautiously than before."

"You heard for yourself that Hewes is not really Hewes. He's an agent they put in as a replacement. Alek gave this man a job and the man has been doing it splendidly."

"If that is the case, what is the incentive for Hewes, for the lack of a better name, to keep pursuing his mission seven years plus down the road from the collapse of what used to be his employer? Where's the reward? There are no more "Heroes of the State" given out on

May Day, you know. Christ, the man actually in charge in Russia is a n'er do well drunk who keeps firing his cabinet when he wakes up without a drink."

Annie had to think about that for a moment. Donald had a point. A good point, as a matter of fact.

"Why not make a call to Mister Speaker and find out? We have our code word. Maybe his is similar."

"You expect me to call up the office of the speaker and tell the receptionist that 'Wolfman Jack rules?' You assume they've got similar reference points to use in normal conversation to allow the timely passage of messages without having to deal with encryption systems. Hell, we don't even know if Alek ever saw *American Graffiti*. I think if he had, my code name would be Toad."

"Still, you are the vice president. I'm sure a call from you would be put through."

"Right. Hewes is going to take a call from a guy scheduled for execution any day now? An execution of which he is perfectly aware and is actually partly responsible for the planning? Nope. We've seen this guy over the years, Annie. He's not that cool. The only thing missing from his coat most times is the hole where Moore should have had his hand. That Edgar Bergen - Charlie McCarthy thing, you know?"

Their conversation was interrupted by another buzz on the intercom. Annie grabbed the phone.

"Is he here yet?" She asked. "Oh, okay. I'll take it."

"Yes, Julie. How are things in Paris?" came the voice down the line. It was Secretary of State Paparelli.

"Going good so far, Annie. How's the Madrid confab working out?"

"We seem to have Herr Germany and Senior Spain in line. Now, we're just waiting for Monsieur le prime minister. He's been delayed thanks to another of those lovely car-bombs that so brighten any day here in Spain."

"Another one? Was it the Basques again? Don't they know those things cost around ten grand apiece? Sorry, bad joke in poor taste. No one hurt, I hope."

"The news broadcasts were talking injuries, not fatalities, Julie. What's up?"

"You guys, by chance, didn't hear from my trustworthy assistant Marvin Moore this morning, did you? He never made it to the morning meeting and there's been no luck in getting him to answer his hotel phone. I sent one of the service detail over to the Hyatt. His bed was never slept in and, according to the phone log, his last call was to Speaker Hewes. You know those two don't go to the bathroom without checking in with each other."

"No, Julie. Neither of us have heard anything from him. Actually, he had hinted before his flight over here that he'd give us a few of your crib notes on how to best deal with Jean-Pierre."

"Well, if you do hear from him, would you have the wandering Irishman give me a call? Just tell him I'm on the edge of forgetting about protocol. He'll get the message."

"If you do emasculate him and turn him into a gelding, you are certainly in the right place for him to find future employment. He could always star in La Cage aux Folles."

"Annie, you are wicked! I could never say that."

"No, but you are certainly capable of supporting the thought, right?"

"Yes, to that I will admit. Maybe you could help me out if it comes to that?"

"I would gladly do that, Julie. So, everything good in Gay Paris?"

"Things here are really nice. Spring came early this year and all of the blossoms are out along the Seine. Kind of like the Potomac two weeks ago. I wonder, is it still politically correct to call this wonderful city "Gay" anymore?"

They both shared a laugh, leaving Fulton looking at Annie with a quizzical look.

"Julie, we'll call if we hear anything, okay?"

"Great, Annie and thanks!"

Annie hung up the phone and looked at the vice president.

"This just got really interesting. Moore is missing in Paris."

"Are you shitting me? You don't just lose an assistant secretary of state before one of the biggest world economic conferences.

Someone said something to somebody. Let's call Alek and see what he knows," suggested Fulton.

"Do you think that's wise? I mean, calling him from here? We certainly can't leave right now. Jean-Pierre could be here any moment."

"What are they going to do? Kill me?"

thirty-four

Washington, DC   Saturday, April 4, 1998   7:40 am (local)

Nelson had made great time in getting from his condo to the White House. After five years, he'd learned what side streets to take that would circumvent most of the longer traffic light cycles and hit the ones that were usually in sync. It would take him about twenty minutes, on average, to make the trip. Today was almost a personal best. Eighteen minutes. Being a Saturday certainly helped. He had hustled into the White House, having slowed down at the various security checkpoints, allowing for the brief inspection of his person and briefcase. He walked towards the coat rack in the President's outer office as Joannie offered her usual, cheery good morning and she held out a cup of coffee for him on the way by. Bud stopped, bowed and placed his customary, friendly little peck of a kiss on her cheek. She blushed, as always and Bud greeted the Secret Service agent and the Marine Sergeant on duty outside of the door. The Marine snapped to attention, while Agent McGee opened the door for him.

"Thanks, Joe."

"No problem, Bud. They're waiting on you."

Bud came in and sat down, nodding his hellos to all seated around the coffee table and offered his hand to the FBI director, Keith Hammett.

"Bud. Just in time. First, I have to call Vice President Fulton. He needs to know everything we know, or," he said, looking at Bud, "suspect."

Chief of Staff Dan Josten passed the phone to Jay. The call had been placed. Jay related the story to Vice President Fulton in Madrid. Finishing the phone call, he passed the disconnected phone back to Josten and addressed the room.

"Gentlemen, as you've heard, I just had to clue the vice president in on the possibility that Annie might be in on this."

Bud felt like crawling under the sofa at that moment. He'd still felt more than betrayed at the thought that Annie Fidrych, his cohort in politics and bedroom antics for the past twenty-two years had been playing him like a fiddle. Then he cringed at the thought of himself thinking of such a tired cliché. The room was filled with those he knew best in this administration, NSA Director John Realto, CIA Director Bill Terrio and Chief of Staff Dan Josten. Also, he was very embarrassed at being unofficially introduced in this manner to FBI Director Keith Hammett, who had been invited into the loop, finally.

"Bud. You had no way of knowing. And for what it's worth, all of us gathered here and just about everyone else within the freakin' beltway, had actually been waiting for you two to just get married. You're both perfect for each other. Well, almost perfect for each other."

There was a burst of nervous laughter in the Oval Office. President Jay Griffen had actually just vocalized what so many had been waiting to hear since the final night of the 1992 Democratic Convention. The two of them actually made a very good team. They were good to each other and when together, everyone noticed that they were indeed good for each other. The others in the room could only imagine the level of devastation that L. Bud Nelson, the rock of this administration, was feeling right now. He had their sympathy. They now needed to reaffirm that he still had their respect.

"Bud," CIA Director Bill Terrio spoke. "Let's get down to work. You are now one of the focal points of this investigation at this point, in this room, so we really need you to keep your head in the game. Stay focused and stay with us. No one here doubts your veracity and your integrity is second to none, with all due respect to the Chief."

Jay smiled at that. "Sure, Bill. Let's measure the guy's integrity next to the 'first fondler'."

A natural round of chuckles and chortles filled the room which seemed to put everyone at ease.

Bud began. "Gentlemen, first, let me thank you for your confidence. Trust me when I say that for the first time in my life I was at a loss for words when Danny put the puzzle together about the bug and I provided the missing piece by accident. I'm still baffled as to how she's been this close for so long that nothing has come of it. If and I'm saying if here," he paused for emphasis. "If she is a part of this, then why hasn't she taken steps sooner? They could have easily have set something up by now. We've been here for over five years. You'd think that if their goal was this close, that they could have done something like this sooner, right?"

"I don't know, Bud. Let's look at this from the angle of Romanov." John Realto, the NSA director, was now working through his theory. "The guy spent our transition year still hiding out in the dacha on the lake as a man despised. The new Russian government was still trying to figure out which body part was the elbow and which was the ass. Once the Duma had started to point things in the right direction, expansion of industry began to happen publicly. This expansion had been slowly happening for years, controlled by the Politburo, but funded by American industrialists.

The room stilled for a brief moment, allowing the coincidence to sink in and Realto continued.

"A few of these American big business types had long been a friend of the Soviet Union, realizing the potential for the untapped labor market and the deep pockets of natural resources yet to be harvested. The overall situation in the USSR was ripe for the picking, so to speak. One of them was starting to make inroads, working as a public financier through the private levels of the Soviet's Politburo. After the death of the leading money man, the financing continued, but the factories were now being built in substandard fashion due to the number of people lining their pockets with the funds from alleged cost-overruns in the still-communal society. The number of those feeding at the trough became too large to keep hidden from the workers. The workers were still standing in breadlines while the privileged few were summering on the oceans. The average citizens knew there was a growing fragmentation of their society to a level of Orwellian proportions. Harkening back to the *Animal Farm* scenario where, at first, all animals are equal, then growing to the level that some are more equal than others. This awakening, so to speak, led to another people's revolt. The one that spawned the separation of the union and the sink or swim mentality that soon took over."

"So where does that put Romanov in this picture?" Bud asked. He felt he knew the answer, but was making sure his feelings were on the same track.

"Romanov fled the Kremlin, Bud, as we all know. He was reviled for allowing the Soviet Union to stray from its communal tenets to a more capitalistic slant for a select few. Strictly a case of the haves versus the will-never have-nots. Under Yeltsin, though, things did not improve overnight. But a freer and more open Russian society allowed for things like forgiveness. The liberal exchange of thoughts and ideas did not make things instantly better, but it improved the outlook of how life was viewed. The people came to understand that the grass was not necessarily greener in the other yard, but, by being able to express themselves, the people came to look back at what *was* with a bit more sentiment. With the sentiment came the sympathy for a man who was only doing his job and lost his wife and children in the process."

"This is what pushed him back into favor in the role of a senior statesman?" Chief of Staff Dan Josten asked. "It makes sense."

"It does make sense, Dan. It's just taken some getting used to on our part. The normal chain of events resulting from change in Russia did not lend itself to a "veteran's all-star team" of former heads of state. Usually, you were in office until you died."

President Griffen seemed somewhat impatient. "Gentlemen. I think we all understand the Romanov homeland situation. Now, my first question and it'll be the one the Chief Justice of the Supreme

Court will probably ask when he arrives in here in a little more than a half hour from right now, is how is Romanov expected to pull the strings over here to exact the changes alluded to, from over there? The man would need to be in constant contact with his puppet regime, don't you think? And what if his little master plan didn't work? What if instead of destabilizing our economy, the moves he ordered only helped to further strengthen it? I would think that if his plan was to put Hewes in here, then it would have to be a spoon-feeding situation. Hell, it would make more sense for a financial whiz like Vice President Fulton to be in this seat making moves to take us down."

"What's to keep that from happening, chief?" asked Realto.

"John, we all know that Fulton is a target and intended victim in this little plan. Why would Romanov sacrifice a player so well versed in the aspects of our economy? It doesn't add up."

"That's assuming that the plan you've stumbled upon can be confirmed as authentic."

As if on cue, there was a knock at the Oval Office door.

"Enter," said Jay.

The door opened and the secret service agent from the hall ushered in a well- dressed man.

"Mr. President. Special Agent Talbot, FBI. You were expecting these packages, sir?"

The agent was holding two FedEx envelopes.

"Yes, Agent Talbot. We were and your timing is perfect. Thanks much."

Jay offered his hand and the agent shook it, smiled and left. Once the door was again closed, Bud and Realto jumped for the envelopes.

"Easy boys, easy," Jay said.

"Can't, boss. We're playing beat the clock here, remember?"

"Why don't we spread this stuff out, Bud. Maybe a few minds working together will be able to put the puzzle together?"

"Actually, Mr. President, it would be easier if just Bud and I worked this through," Realto offered. "Bud has had the code key explained to him by his contact and I can work the decode side."

Bud had opened the envelopes and extracted several black and white photos, enlarged to eight by ten.

Jay whistled. "Boys. I think the cavalry has just arrived."

There was no doubt as to what the photos conveyed. One was a photo of a man strapped to a chair. It was no one they had ever seen before. The notes on the back were in Cyrillic script. Griffen held it out for Realto to examine.

"The notes say *Marvin Moore, New York, 1976*. And it looks like there's an address of some sort. A route number? No, wait, it's a rural route number. *Rural Route 38, Lake Placid*. Keith? Do you think you can a team up there to start poking around? Like, ten minutes ago?"

FBI Director Keith Hammett gave a nod towards the President's desk phone and Jay gave his permission with a wave of his hand. The FBI director moved his wheelchair over to the desk and began working the phone.

"John, what else do we have there?"

"This photo looks like it could be Hewes. Let me check the notes. Hmmm. Okay, this one is marked *Yevgeny Polnichy, Murmansk, March, 1976*. Certainly could be Hewes, though. No, wait, this one is marked *Hewes, Charleston, South Carolina, USA, April, 1976*. And there are some other notations here. They look like measurements. All in millimeters?" He passed the enlarged photos to the president for inspection.

Nelson was now glancing at the single sheet of paper in the envelope that was intended for delivery in Maine. "John, this sheet is in plain English. Our friend says here in paragraph four.... yeah, those are specific measurements that had to be taken for the plastic surgeon in Oslo. Measurements of the distance between the eyes and such. The rest is the explanation of the coding he used on the various documents. Looks like simple juxtaposition type stuff. But he varies each document by incremental steps."

Jay was glancing over Bud's shoulder and looking at the photos in his hands. "John, can we make a couple of copies of those photos, front and back and get them over to Admiral Lynch? I know he's just my personal physician, but he can track down someone to get this stuff into a computer and make the changes per the measurements."

President Griffen was now showing his famous knack for getting right down to the heart of the matter. His ability to instantly analyze and come up with an appropriate action kept those around him constantly in awe. Trying to keep so many things straight at one time would overwhelm the average person and even those slightly above average. Jay seemed to thrive on multi-tasking.

"And while you're at it, before you leave, why don't you and Bud decode this first page and leave it here. Then take the rest of this stuff over to your office. You've got a program to just pump this stuff in and get it back in English, right?"

"Yes, we do Jay. Bud, you want to write while I read?"

"It's a plan, Mister Realto. Let's go over here."

Nelson and Realto went over to the president's smaller writing desk at the far end of the office and began their task in earnest.

Director Hammett hung up the phone and returned to group assembled at the sofa, feeling much better about being in the loop.

"I've got four teams from the New York office on their way to Lake Placid, Mister President."

"Excellent, Keith. And, while we're here, like this," he said with a sweeping gesture that encompassed the room, "a bunch of us sitting around breaking the law while trying to save the country, just call me Jay, okay?"

"Yes sir, Jay.... er, breaking the law?"

"We'll be covering that when Attorney General Vernon gets here with the Supremes, the Senate Majority Leader and the House Majority Whip. Full disclosure. Better you not know anymore than you do right now. Trust me on this, Keith. By the way, what's the latest from the New York thing this morning?"

"I've got two teams devoted to that, working with the NYPD."

Realto piped up from the other table. "You're getting copies of that stuff to my boys, right Keith?"

"If you need it, John."

"We do. The dead guy was kicked out of the country by us about, what, three, four months ago, Bud?"

"That'd be right, John. Matter of fact, Keith, Jay signed the official order sending him back to London. Billy, have we heard from your buddy at MI about him, or that other stuff?"

"Talked with Sir Stephen this morning from home. He's e-mailing a bunch of photos that may or not may match up with what we sent. Should be in my computer by now. As far as the late Jonathon Earle, it seems we did more than send a bug up his ass. The Brits and Interpol were closing in on Jon for his ability to not only sell fine works of art, but also his talent for producing some of his own."

"His own artwork?" Jay asked.

"No, Jay. Seems he picked up a lot of the freelance forgery business when the Soviet-bloc countries got out of the business of producing their own travel packs for their own intelligence types."

"How long had he been into that?"

"He started dabbling in it in the late eighties and took off on a very lucrative tangent once the Union dissolved. He was probably doing very high six figures, American, each year since ninety-three, on the papers alone."

Jay was nodding, taking in all that Terrio had to say, while checking over the photos in his hands. The images were extremely disturbing. One sequence showed a man who was probably the younger, original Hewes. First, tied to a chair, with a set of hands holding his head, giving the impression that they were forcing Hewes to look at the camera. The next showed a gloved hand injecting a syringe into the left forearm. The additional photos were gruesome, including one which showed a hand holding a pair of garden shears, cutting into the fingers of Hewes' right hand. The final photo showed the slumped figure, arms secured to the chair and the right hand missing what looked like three fingers. He went through them once again and stopped at a close-up. The one with the two hands holding Hewes' head. Jay walked over to the bay window to get some better light and was better able to see that which had caught his eye.

"Bill? Take a look at this photo and tell me what you see."

The CIA director stood, walked over to the window where the president stood and took the photo.

"Well, for starters, I see what Mister Speaker must've looked like twenty years ago. I see two hands, one of which has a gold ring with a black stone on the right ring finger. And a scar on the right wrist, running down to just above the knuckles."

"Now, look beyond Hewes and the hands."

"Son of bitch! Nice pickup, Jay. There's definitely a face there, reflected in the mirror."

"You think the boys at Langley can pull that out and make some magic for us?"

"You bet your ass we can, sir."

"Why don't you get that over there now, Bill. And check your e-mail while you're there. Then, please, get back here for the pow-wow. I need some talent on my side to help explain this mess. They'll be hearing it as the desperate words of a cornered man."

"Aye aye, sir. I'll get back here as quickly as possible."

Terrio straightened up his tie, put the photo into a large, manila envelope and waved goodbye to the assembled team with his trademark hello and farewell. "Hibbly he. Hibbly ho!"

"Hib," responded all but Hammett. He had not yet been indoctrinated into the little unofficial klatch.

"Hib?" Keith asked.

"It's a long story, better understood after many potent drinks," explained the president. "Many, many potent drinks."

Bud looked up from his paperwork. "Yeah, Keith. Between "Hibbly" and the story of how it was he, Bill, who wrote the oft performed mic test you hear before every live concert performance. You know, "check one. one two. check. check. two. two. two." He will, after about the fourth beer confess that it was not really written by him, but, he certainly was on the mark when he said he should have copyrighted the damn thing and registered it with the music license organizations. And you know? He'd probably have made millions by now."

"I, er, see," said Keith. He thought that maybe during one of those marathon sessions, he could teach them his decadent-days party theme song, as performed by Ian Dury and the Blockheads, *Boogie Til You Puke.*

"Just remember to say "hib" when he finishes his one-size-fits-all greeting and farewell. It's kind of like *Aloha.* It makes him feel warm and fuzzy all over."

"Okay, Bud. I'll try."

"Nelson, how we doing over there? It's closing in on eight. The Chief Justice, is, if anything, prompt."

"Just about finished with the first page, boss. Shouldn't be but another minute."

One of the several phones on the president's desk began ringing. Jay noticed it was the private, secure line for use by only those to whom he'd provided the number.

"Bud, any idea who this might be? Dan?"

Dan shrugged his shoulders, but Bud's eyes began to brighten.

"It's about five 'til eight here, boss. That makes it almost four pm over there."

The president answered the phone on the fifth ring.

"Jay here."

"Colonel Menneally here, sir." The voice was somewhat distorted and the noise in the background was definitely that of a helicopter.

"Bob? It's tough to hear you. Are you airborne?"

"Airborne, if you can call it that. We're about fifty feet off the surface of Lake Onega and rippin' back for Finland at about a buck-thirty."

"I know you need to concentrate, so give it to me in a nutshell."

"The short version, sir, is that we've got your friend."

"Excellent."

"And his boss."

thirty-five

Lake Onega, Russia   Saturday, April 4, 1998   2:43pm (local)

Michail pulled off the main roadway and onto the pathway that led to Aleksandr's dacha. The woods were still sprinkled with leftover snow patches and yet along the clear sides of the road where the sun did touch, the early season crocuses were already beginning their springtime stretch, awakening from their long slumber. He slowed as the Explorer began to bounce between the ruts created by somewhat heavier vehicles that had made this trek throughout the winter and the early spring thaws. He smiled as he watched his shadows try to keep pace in their standard, mid-sized sedan, their front end occasionally airborne from the bouncing.

His ride north from Moscow had started about six and a half hours ago. He had left the apartment complex with his two shadows. He had lost them in short order during the morning rush hour traffic, or what passed as such on a weekend. That allowed him the time necessary to head for the airport and drop the package directly at the regional FedEx terminal. He had been told that it would be on the next flight out, heading for Heathrow. From there, it should make the connecting flight to the United States. That, by his reckoning, would put the package in Maine before the five p.m. traditional close of business, although he had been told that there were not scheduled deliveries on the weekends.

Once the drop-off had been made, he wound his way back towards the north and was not surprised to see his baby-sitters at a roadside phonebooth. He was in a steady stream of traffic and they did not seem to notice him. Or, trying to be nonchalant about their predicament, they chose not to acknowledge him. The further away from Moscow proper his driving took him, the lighter the flow of traffic. Once he was about two hours north of the city, he was able to relax. There was no one in front of him, nor was there anyone within view behind. He reached into his Bean carryall and pulled out a cassette.

"She couldn't keep from crying, when she told me goodbye.
I knew, lord, it was breaking her heart and she was breaking mine."

David Lee Murphy was singing about looking for his *Party Crowd* and Michail was singing along. American country music was the sort of music that did cross international boundaries. It had for generations and would continue to do so. Although, with country music, there was an underlying mystique that most Europeans associated with cowboys, horses and six-guns. Michail had learned that it wasn't all riding on the open range. There was a lot to be said about riding around in a pickup truck with a pretty girl by your side. That's the feeling Michail got from David Lee's music, for sure. He wondered what it would be like to get Anastasia in a tight pair of blue jeans and then head out for a night at the honky tonk. Some line dancing and cold beer. Might be fun. Of course, being somewhat of a realist, Michail did not know if he would even see her again, let alone get the chance to take his best girl out for a wild Friday night.

Around noontime, he pulled off the highway and found a place to get gas and a bite to eat. He grabbed a quick sandwich and what passed for a soda. He also made a quick pitstop in the men's room before paying the attendant for the gas. He got back on the road, with at least another hundred-fifty miles to go. Still no sign of the trailing team, though. He wondered if they were still back at the phonebooth, waiting for him to drive by. He cranked up the volume a bit on another David Lee tape.

"Another time. And in another place.
He might have rode with Jesse James.
And though he rides, he can't outrun his fate.
'Cause he was born one hundred years too late."

Well, Michail thought. I may not be able to outrun my fate, but I'm sure going to be riding with Jesse James. At least he hoped the man in black would be well represented by the time he arrived at Aleksandr's. He made a mental note to make sure that he tried to see Mister Murphy perform live sometime. Just another incentive to make sure he did nothing stupid. Nothing to give Aleksandr even the hint of an advantage. His mind was racing with all of the possibilities surrounding the past days' events. Most notably, who was the leak? Who was providing the information to Romanov? Who was aware of what was going on? It was obvious that there was another agent in the loop. There was at least one other person with a direct pipeline to Aleksandr. Someone who was intent on seeing this mission through to a successful conclusion, unlike Anastasia and Michail. Michail had plenty of time to think the scenario through and kept coming up blank. There was obviously someone close to President Griffen who had Romanov's ear. If anything, Michail had to admire the sheer audacity of Aleksandr. The man had possessed the foresight to make his plan so redundant that, even given the long-shot odds of one of the operatives making it to the finish line, Romanov now seemed to have his choice of who would be the one to live. And who would be expendable.

The remaining hundred or so miles was on a fairly deserted stretch of road. Michail set the cruise control to one-hundred-twenty kilometers per hour, or, roughly seventy-five miles per hour. This would get him to Aleksandr's in about an hour and a half. He popped in yet another David Lee Murphy tape and powered the windows down while he turned up the volume.

"'Cause in my mind you're in my arms.
I hear your voice and all my dreams come true.
And girl, it's almost like being there.
And all my dreams come true."

Michail pulled himself out of his little Anastasia-driven daydream in time to notice the train station off to the right. The train station would have a payphone and being too early for the tourist season, the station would most likely be all but deserted. It would be his chance to make the phone call to Nelson. He made a note of the time on the vehicle's dashboard clock. Just about a quarter past two. He still had about another thirty miles or so to go. That would put him at the dacha around three. He had to call Nelson and tell him of the leak. He'd have to find a way to drop the not-so-subtle hint that the leak was going directly to Romanov. He'd pulled into the train station and waved hello to the sole person in the train's office.

"No train today," the attendant said from behind the glass.

"I know that, friend," Michail replied. "I'm here to use your phone. Is it working?"

Appearing somewhat put out by Michail's question, the attendant pointed towards the payphone. "You'll have to use the public phone."

Michail laughed, immediately grasping the interpretation of the working-phone request. "That's what I meant, comrade. That phone is working?"

The man's ice-cold visage melted into an almost detectable smile and he nodded yes.

Michail gave the man a friendly wave, walked over to the payphone and called Nelson. He'd made sure to remember to ask for Mister Goatman and could hear Nelson softly swearing to himself for answering the phone with his name instead of a generic hello. Little did Michail know that all kinds of things were at that moment demanding Nelson's attention. Once the method of discussion had been set, the conversation shifted from production to fishing. Knowing his gear would be there, Michail finished the phone call and went back to the Explorer.

The vehicle started right up and he pulled back out towards the highway. Wheeling the big sports utility vehicle hard to the right, he continued north, hitting his cruising speed with very little effort. The road was still deserted as far as he could see. The only other traffic he'd seen had been a handful of big logging trucks heading south towards the mills outside of Moscow. It was pretty country up this way, Michail thought. The tall pine trees swayed in the gentle April afternoon breeze. The wind was still out of the north, which added a chilly touch to the already cooler temperatures. Michail had to remind himself that he was a full four hundred plus miles further north than where he'd been in the morning. He'd always been amazed at the early spring differences just between American cities up and down the Atlantic seaboard. In Washington, the Japanese cherry trees would be full of their bright, pink blossoms along the Potomac, while up in Boston, not more than four hundred miles in a straight line to the northeast, most of the trees would yet to even have the little green buds indicating their readiness for another season.

Looking intently now, Michail began to search the woods on his left. The road that led to Alek's dacha was fairly well hidden from approaching traffic. If one knew where to look, one would find it with very little effort. Michail hated driving by it. It made him feel like a city boy who couldn't find his way around the country. There! He picked the road out of the clump of trees about a half mile ahead. The muddy tracks that led from the woods helped to better point the way. Michail slowed as he approached the entrance. He tooted a friendly beep on the horn to his two pals from Moscow. It seems they'd made the drive without him. At least now, they'd be able to follow him into the lakeside homestead and save a little face. Michail decided that he'd save them the embarrassment by making mention of their dogged determination to Aleksandr. It was the least he figured he could do. Too bad, thought Michail, that the future of Russian intelligence was in the hands of guys like these. Who knows? With a little direction, they might stand a chance in the real world.

Michail was still smiling at the beating the two behind him were taking on the trough- infested road when the dacha came into view. He'd give Aleksandr the suggestion to upgrade the utility vehicles the boys use. The house was bigger than he'd remembered. And it had been recently painted. The parking area in front of the house held only two other vehicles. One was Aleksandr's favorite western toy, a bright blue Jeep. The other was a Dodge pickup truck. Both vehicles lent themselves better to the terrain up in this part of the country than did the sedan of the two poor men behind.

He pulled the Explorer up next to the Jeep and waited a moment. The two agents pulled their vehicle in head-first along side of the pickup truck. Michail then backed his vehicle up and did a three-point turn. He backed his vehicle up so that it blocked the other vehicles. Climbing down from the oversized s.u.v., he smiled at the two agents and walked quickly past them, directly to the stairs leading up to the main floor of the dacha.

The house itself was a huge A-frame style chalet, adopted from a Swiss version Aleksandr had seen during one of his many visits abroad while on his official duties as President of the Soviet Union. The main levels were all glass on the front and back, while the house's roof literally came straight down into the ground on either side, A huge, stone chimney marked the living room's main fireplace to the left of the main entrance. Two, smaller chimneys to the right emanated from the second floor's master bedroom suite and the children's suite. Each suite had ample room, closet space galore and it's own private bath.

Aleksandr had redecorated the children's room around the time that little Michail had gone off to the university, removing the oversize twin beds and the teddy bear wallpaper. The room was now tastefully decorated in a natural wood paneling, with a pair of king-size beds, as well as a fold-out sofa. The second suite was now used for visiting foreign dignitaries, the ones who could stomach being around Aleksandr. It was the one used by several heads of state who had come for a weekend of fishing and boating. Even President Griffen had stayed here during a visit. They had exchanged frank talk about strategic arms reduction and compared notes on their speedboats. It was also the room where Michail stayed whenever he came here. He had convinced Aleksandr to keep a few of the children's favorite stuffed animals on the window seats. It made it feel homey, he'd explained to his brother-in-law. Romanov had actually shown a level of pain when considering this request.

Michail had noticed that Aleksandr had purged the dacha of many of the reminders of his family. There were still the framed group photos on the mantel and even one or two now-faded pieces of school art on the refrigerator. The children had laughed at Michail when he had first demonstrated how a magnet could become a masterpiece holder and they had shown the faux pain that only a teenager can exhibit whenever they'd attempt to get their parents to finally retire the family treasures to a less obvious place. Each of the rooms still had at least one watercolor painted by Elenya. She had dabbled with painting since she was a teenager. The most startling of her artworks was the oversized landscape she had painted of the lake from the waterfront deck. It had caught the evening sun going down over the western mountains on the far side of Lake Onega. This one was hung in the entryway of the dacha. Aleksandr was not totally heartless about the loss of his wife and children. It was just the method in which they lost their lives that Michail held in contempt.

The construction of the home itself had brought about some minor cries from the proletariat, its sheer size was alone enough to raise eyebrows. The governing body, though, had managed to allay the protests from the vocal few who knew of its existence by authorizing construction of additional chalets up and down the same stretch of lakefront. Labor leaders and mid-level managers were offered time at the additional units for summer family getaways. The use of the chalets was eventually extended to the above-average worker who, in the eyes of the party representatives and managers, exemplified the true Soviet way of life. Be a good party person and a strong, happy worker and there was the promise of a week's stay on the lake. Elenya had actually gotten Aleksandr to host Saturday cookouts for the families finishing up their weeks. This had created a security nightmare for the elite troops tasked with guarding the family Romanov, but Elenya had persisted and Aleksandr had acquiesced. He'd actually had fun in the occasional field-day type activities they'd been able to host and had once won the three-legged race he ran with little Michail. Plus, many a vacationing worker was skilled at fishing and it was not unusual for President Romanov to pull his speedboat up to a lakeside dock and join the vacationers in dropping a line. Elenya had managed to humanize Aleksandr and the word-of-mouth tales a returning laborer would bring back to the factory or university gave many incentive to work harder with the hope of a vacation on the lake.

Michail gave a cursory look around the home site and out towards the lake. The waters were tipped with gentle whitecaps, whipped up by the stiffening late afternoon breeze. The sky was filled with puffy, fair weather clouds, somewhat darkened by shadows from the encroaching sunset. Dusk would be upon them in a little more than two hours, Michail noted. Hopefully, the twilight would provide cover for a hasty retreat should one be needed. Not only for him, but for his guardian angels, whom he optimistically thought were already around. His perusal of the surrounding area gave no clue as to whether or not the team being sent by the Americans was there. He steeled himself, took a deep breath and knocked on the sliding glass door that was the main entrance to the house.

"Good afternoon, Colonel Rostokovich," said Yuri Romanov.

"Good afternoon to you too, Yuri," Michail smiled, warmly embracing the younger brother of Aleksandr Romanov.

Yuri was a good ten years younger than Aleksandr and had been but a schoolboy when his big brother had ascended to power. Aleksandr had made sure Yuri worked hard at the university and when time came for him to enter the military for his required term of service, Yuri was assigned to his brother's security team. Yuri had grieved with Michail over the loss of Elenya and the children. He too loved being uncle to little Christina and Michail the younger, but Yuri was completely loyal to his big brother. He worshipped the ground on which Romanov stood and, like any little brother, would do whatever was requested, without question or hesitation.

"It's been a few months, Misha. How have you been?"

"Busy, to say the least, Yuri Fedorovich. But overall? I have been well. At least I've got my health."

"And a large amount of frequent flier miles, no?"

Michail smiled politely, now on his guard. Yuri never mentioned business. They talked of many things, especially American sports.

Yuri had joined a fantasy league on the Internet and often e-mailed Michail with insights to players who might make good additions to his teams.

"Let's just say that I could fly us all to Nepal and back and still have enough left over to spend many weekends in Paris."

"You look well, Michail Ivanovich. Come. My brother is growing somewhat impatient. The coals are already hot and he's two trout up on you."

"It figures he'd get a head start on me. I drove as fast as I could, but it was a fun ride." Michail gestured out towards the parking area where the two trailing agents were stretching from their version of the drive from Moscow.

"Who else is here today? It looks like a ghost town."

"Aleksandr gave the rest of the crew the day off, so they've gone in search of female companionship. Right now it's just me, Feliks and the bobsey-twins there. Later on, there's a party at the upper cabin, if you care to join us."

"How late? I've been going non-stop for two days, but a chance to cut loose might be fun."

"It depends on how lucky the others get. They said they should be back by eleven or so. There's a baseball game on satellite tonight. Spring training, of course, a nothing game. But a game is a game and if we sit close enough to the television, we can almost feel the warmth from Florida."

"So who are those two?" Michail asked with a nod towards the trailing team.

"Stephan and Pavel. They're new."

"No kidding, Yurochka. I left them a couple of beers last night and they didn't even say thanks."

"They're upset that you felt the need to remove yourself from their watchful eyes. It's given Aleksandr cause for pause, if you catch my drift."

"I catch your drift. I just think I'm a little old for a baby-sitter, that's all. I do have my pride, too. Since we all became mere businessmen, the thrill of the chase is one of life's little pleasures that occurs much too infrequently. I can't let myself get stale, now can I?"

Michail felt the irony of the statement as he made it. He had been followed, apparently. Now, the method of how it happened remained to be disclosed by his waiting fishing buddy.

"Let's go catch some dinner, Misha. It's getting colder outside by the second," Yuri said plainly with an "after you" gesture.

Walking through the chalet, Michail felt the warmth from the roaring fire blazing in the huge fireplace in the great room. He went for the stairway leading towards the upper level, but Yuri gently took his arm, guiding him towards the lake side of the house.

"Can't I just drop off my bags in my room?"

"I'll take those for you, Michail. The boss really wanted to see you as soon as you arrived." Yuri reached for the Bean carryall.

"On second thought, Yuri, I'd better keep this with me. There are some things I need to go over with Aleksandr and most of it is in my laptop," he said, patting the side of the well-packed bag.

Having taken the overnight bag full of clothing from Michail, Yuri approached the sliding glass door and gave it a firm tug to the left. The door opened onto the sprawling back deck and the force of the winds from the water hit Michail full in the face. He reached into his overcoat pocket and pulled out his favorite leather gloves. The gloves had been a gift from Anastasia. They had become well-worn with age, yet served their purpose over the past twenty some-odd years. At the motion of reaching into the coat pocket, Yuri tensed and drew his weapon.

"Relax, Yuri. I'm just getting out my gloves. It's cold out there."

"Sorry, Michail. You know the drill. Which reminds me."

Yuri took Michail's other bag from him, set it on the deck and proceeded to frisk Michail for any sign of a weapon. Finding none, he opened the bag and offered a cursory inspection. He did pull out the compact disc case and examined it.

"A gift for your brother. It's a little something I was given on my last trip to Tajikistan. I have my own copy, so I made one for Aleksandr as well."

"Do you really think he'll like goat songs?"

"Yuri. Open your mind! It's a big world we live in. Besides, it's funny as hell after a couple of drinks."

Michail straightened his gloves, picked up his bag and walked ahead of Yuri towards the stairway. At the top of the stairs, a well bundled up Feliks waved his hello to Michail. Michail walked over to the man and gave him a friendly hug in return. Feliks had been one of Michail's first trainees and was a part of Aleksandr's security team based on Michail's recommendation. Feliks swung his 9mm assault weapon to the side and returned his mentor's gesture.

"You look well, Colonel."

"And you, also, Feliks Eduardovich."

The silence between them spoke volumes, Michail realized. There was no way this fishing trip would end with left-over trout bones and hot coffee in front of a roaring fire.

As Michail pulled the second glove over his chilled fingers, he made note of the time. Almost three. The team he'd hoped would be in position would surely be getting cold. If they had arrived per the original schedule, they would have been in place for over an hour by now. He himself knew that reflexes required to pull off any kind of an offensive would be diminished greatly due to prolonged exposure to elemental extremes.

Yuri took Michail by the elbow and walked him down the stairs towards the beach. The lower level of the chalet was a fully furnished bunker-like facility, also wall-to-wall glass like the other levels of the house. The drop in height of the terrain from the front of the house to the rear allowed for a daylight basement set-up. It was here that the security team on duty would bunk. It was fully equipped for communication and operations. From the latest in satellite radio technology to both high and low level radar gear, Aleksandr had been able to ensure his continual safety while here at the lake. There were also four, fully furnished bedrooms, a living area and a full kitchen. This level served not only as the quarters for the duty staff, but also where the security teams for any visiting dignitary could be housed. Michail gave a glance to the near corner window and saw that the other two agents had made their way inside already. The glass was glazed to prevent prying eyes from seeing inside, but Stephan and Pavel had forgotten that when illuminated from inside by white light, the one-way function was negated. Both men were busily consuming cups of coffee and, as Michail noted, had hung up their coats and their sidearms.

Yuri and Michail crossed the beach quickly and stepped out onto the dock which extended a good sixty feet out into the lake. Aleksandr's boat was tied about midway out the length of the dock and there were two folding chairs set up at the very end. Michail saw Aleksandr reeling in yet another good sized lake trout and smiled as his brother-in-law worked feverishly to unhook his catch, attempting to get it safely into the large bucket positioned between the chairs. Along with the chairs and fish bucket, there was a cooler and another small box. As they got closer, the glow from the box-like object was steady and red. A space heater.

"Nice to see you know how to really rough it, Aleksi."

"Misha! It's about damn time you got here. How was your drive up?"

"Uneventful, Aleksi. It's easy to get lost among the trees and the blue sky up this way. It's still beautiful."

"Yes, it is. But it's still cold."

"Nice heater. Propane?"

"Da. Actually got it from the L.L.Bean catalog," Aleksandr replied, giving a nod to the Bean emblazoned shoulder bag Michail was carrying.

"You'd like Maine, Aleksi. It's just like this place."

"This cold, too?"

"Pretty much. Yuri would never make it through an early season baseball game there. At least the evening ones."

"Speaking of which. Yuri? I need you to leave us. Michail and I have much to discuss. And a few more fish to catch."

Yuri nodded his understanding and turned to walk back towards the dacha.

"Sit, Misha. Grab your rod and help me get some supper," commanded Aleksandr. "The coals are ready for cooking now, but we have time to catch up and to catch a few more of those," he said with a nod to the fish bucket on the dock.

Michail took the second fishing rod and saw that the hook was already set and equipped with a fly. He set his carryall down on the dock, then reached back and sent his hook flying well out into the lake.

"Did you tie these flies yourself, Aleksi? They look great."

"Yes, Michail Ivanovich. It gives me something to do in my quiet time. The fish seem to like them."

"So I noticed. Yuri tells me you got a head start. I'm sorry it took me a little longer getting here than I had planned."

Aleksandr reeled his fly in and gently cast it out from his side again. The two of them could grow old doing this, Michail thought, if only circumstances had been different.

"Tell me, Michail. How is President Griffen?"

Michail paused for only a moment. "You take no time getting right down to the heart of the matter, do you Aleksi?"

"I have no time to dally about, Misha. We have reached a point where we must act. And act decisively. The Americans are now riding a wave of financial security which they've not enjoyed in years. If our plan is to succeed, now would be the perfect moment in time to make it happen. So tell me of your meeting with President Griffen."

"He was a nice man. A gentle man. Actually, the kind of man you would not mind having for a friend. He is honest. Not from what he says, but for how he says it. You can see it in his eyes, Aleksi."

"I have seen it in his eyes, Misha. He's been right here, sitting where you are now. We have fished and shared stories. You've still not answered my question, Michail Ivanovich. Why did you tell the American president of our operation? Have I not been good to you all these years? Have I not seen to your every need and comfort? Why is it you would turn on me this way? I know full well that you offered the Americans every detail of your assignment. They know of Yevgeny. They know and actually have in custody, Dimitri. They are aware of the murders. And, they are aware of the plan to assassinate Vice President Fulton."

Michail reeled his in his line and sent the fly back out for another swim.

"Aleksandr. If you know of all this, why are we out here fishing? It would seem that you have your facts and are merely going through the paces in asking me about this. Are you expecting me to deny that a meeting with Griffen took place?"

"I was hoping that you would have tried to offer an explanation, Michail. Your lack of remorse on this is troubling."

"My lack of remorse? Do you think I take pleasure in being forced to do what I did, Aleksi? I am and have been, very much a proud professional. I am the best at what I do. For over twenty years, I have personally run the Hewes operation, at your direction, flawlessly."

"Not completely, Michail. The running of certain parts of the operation have not been in your control. The Stark woman? She was Dimitri's doing. He paid her, handsomely. She performed fabulously. And she still stands ready to testify, driving the final nail home in Griffen's political coffin. Dimitri had seen to every aspect of her performance. And Dimitri reported directly to me on this matter. Yes, his vanity has become somewhat of a hindrance to our overall plan. I feel that he has his own designs on how to best utilize Yevgeny as president. Excuse me, I should have said *had* his own designs. Now that he is in custody of the Americans, his talents will be truly tested. I suppose you are wondering how I know of Dimitri's being in custody?

Michail gave his brother-in-law a soft nod to the affirmative.

"I had actually sent two agents to pick him up for me. This morning, as a matter of fact. Dimitri had gotten sloppy and the fact that he had been exposed left me in grave danger. Accusations from a drowning man could set me back months. I merely wanted to make sure we understood each other. That he was still working for me. And that I could leave him hanging in the wind should he find himself at risk. Now, he is at risk. As am I. The Americans have not only Dimitri, but also my two agents. They pose no threat to me right now. Should they reveal any link back to here, which I doubt they would, I will be able to dismiss as preposterous. Who am I, Michail? I am but a former head of a country that no longer exists? What possible power could I wield? None. But, just the inference will lead to investigations. And those investigations might expose the other operatives in place."

"Such as Anastasia."

"Yes, such as Anastasia. You might know her better as Annie Fidrych. She and the vice president have been quite a team. Actually, until the Stark thing unfolded, I had every intention of simply letting Fulton run and be elected. From there, we could have modified our plan."

"So Fulton is part of a team? Not just someone who Anastasia was assigned to?"

Aleksandr felt a tug on his line and began the process of gently bringing in his latest catch.

"Fulton was a spectacular find. Brilliant. Savvy. Possessed of a great political mind. And hell-bent on bringing down the country he holds responsible for his parents' deaths."

Michail was taken aback by this. "His parents are still alive in South Carolina, Aleksi. They're on the news at least once a week saying how proud they are of him."

"His adopted parents, Misha. His real parents were Russian."

While he landed a healthy-sized trout, Aleksandr recounted the tale of Fulton's birth parents. As he reset his fly on the end of the now-empty line, he finished the story.

"So you see, Michail. We lucked out. Not only did we wind up with a successful staging on your end of this, we were doubly lucky with Anastasia's end. I have still been of the mind, though, that if I were able to get one of our own into the Oval Office, it would better suit our needs. Fulton could always have a change of heart. You know how sentimental Americans can be."

"You mention luck, Aleksi. Were there others with whom you were not so lucky?"

"Yes, Michail. There were a handful of others. Some of whom had risen to a level not unlike your operation. One was an assistant cabinet member, who was, unfortunately, found out while touring Croatia. He was one of the victims of the 1996 plane crash that killed a sizable number of American businessmen, as well as the Secretary of Commerce. He had performed as expected. He knew he was exposed. So he did what needed to be done to protect the entire plan."

"Are you saying that plane crash was a result of an agent doing the honorable thing?"

"There are those who still feel that incident is rife with conspiracy, Michail. Our agent's action was of a noble nature. It served to protect us all.

"There were several others who had started out about the same time as you. A few of them were similar operations on the west coast. One agent assumed the role of an up and coming young woman. Got her elected to the California assembly, then into the House of Representatives. She was killed in an automobile accident in the early eighties. Another young man got very sloppy after being caught up in the decadent lifestyle associated with Hollywood and he died of a drug overdose. Cocaine. The other was a financial analyst who was killed in a senseless street mugging in New York City about ten years ago as he was poised for nomination to the American Federal Reserve board. We've since replaced him. And then of course there is your own brother."

"Konstantin? You're telling me Konstantin is a part of this?"

"Yes, Michail Ivanovich. Your brother Konstantin has been in our service since before you graduated from the university. Surely you must have had some idea? His first assignment was to help the rabble-rousers at the American universities and colleges. He had great ideas. Planted the seed. Then moved on. He is the one who directed Fulton our way. Along the way, he developed quite an understanding of the American stock market. He made us millions, Misha. Who do you think was responsible for the continued, limitless funding you and the others enjoyed? Did you think that the government's coffers here remained open to me for my every whim? All of the operations, including yours, have been constantly funded by the sheer financial acumen of your big brother. Without Konstantin, none of this would have been possible. We gave him approximately fifty thousand U.S. dollars in 1973. He invested it shrewdly in the stock market. By the time your operation was ready to roll in 1976, he'd increased the portfolio to more than seven figures. The interest alone was taking care of the daily expenses of all of our operatives. He has been my direct source since day one. He's still there, keeping me posted on everything."

Michail was stunned beyond belief. His own brother? They'd kept in touch and occasionally managed visits while both were passing through Europe. He worshipped Konstantin, as any younger brother did of his older sibling.

Trying to look less stressed about this bit of news, Michail opened the cooler and took out a bottle of beer. He offered one to Aleksandr, who politely declined. Opening the bottle, he savored the taste as it washed down the back of his throat. After a minute's silence, Aleksandr continued.

"Tell me, Michail. How is it you know of Anastasia's involvement? I would hate to think that you've been comparing notes. You know that goes against everything you've both been taught."

"I didn't know of her involvement for sure until you just told me, Aleksi. I had my suspicions over the last few days, but as of three minutes ago, I honestly did not know what she was working on."

"You mean to tell me that as close as you two are, as in love as you two are, that you have never discussed either of your assignments? And you never once crossed paths in South Carolina or Washington? She was on the news enough, offering opinions and campaign strategies. Annie Fidrych. One of the most powerful women in American politics and you never placed her? I find that hard to believe, Michail Ivanovich."

"As you yourself just said, it goes against our training. Against everything we have been taught and put into practice. We both know that being uninformed can never work against us. There is no chance of exposing each other, even accidentally, if we didn't know the situation. It's a matter of survival for those of us whom you send out into the field. Besides, this Fidyrch woman of whom you speak? She's a red head. Anastasia is a blonde, with much shorter hair."

Aleksandr laughed heartily. "Wigs, Misha. You've never heard of wigs?"

Less than fifty yards away, Go Team One's commander Colonel Bob Menneally and Master Sergeant Peter Zallonis were gently shifting in their perch halfway up a sixty foot pine tree, just north of the dock. Both had their communications headsets on and were listening to the exchange from the two fishermen. Both also were using the high-powered scopes affixed to their long-range rifles to view the exchange.

Approximately thirty yards to the south of the chalet, also settled up in two different trees, Lieutenant Commander Hank Morris and Senior Chief Mike Murphy were struggling to maintain their positions. They were the ones operating the video camera and the sound equipment. Murphy was holding a sensitive, long-range microphone attached to the small, hand-held video camcorder being used by Morris. The microphone's cord was stretched to the limit of its twenty-five foot length, allowing Hank and Murph little room for movement.

They had been in these positions since fourteen hundred hours. After an hour of maintaining their positions, the cold and the winds were beginning to take their toll on the soldier's extremities.

The audio was being fed into the team's wireless comm system and each member was listening to the exchange between Michail and Romanov intently.

"Hank?" whispered Menneally. "Please tell me we're getting all of this."

"It's a five by signal, M. So far, we've gotten it all."

"Now all we need to do is get Mister Rosty the hell out of there."

"I'm all for that, sir. It's starting to get chilly up here."

"Just be ready, boys. Let's get back to maintaining silence."

Back on the dock, Aleksandr was taking in all that Michail had to say. Michail felt a tug on his line and started to reel his catch in, bringing a smile to Aleksandr's face.

"See, Misha. Patience. It what I've been telling you for years. Just wait and let them take the bait."

Michail worked his line easily towards the dock and, while reaching for his catch, the trout squirmed vigorously and slipped back into the water.

"Well, Aleksi. Sometimes they get away."

"That is not to be the case today, I'm afraid. My other source tells me you've told all. As a matter of fact, he should be getting ready to cover some tracks for us at the other end about now. But, from what he has told me, sadly, I have no option than to terminate our partnership. Before we sever our ties, though, Misha. I must know why."

Michail was struck with an anger he'd not felt in years.

"Why? You have to sit there and ask me why? You old hypocrite. Here you sit, designing to control the world with a wave of your hand, while my sister and her children lie in a Moscow cemetery. And you need to ask why? Well, there is your answer. You are nothing but a bully. That now goes with your title of coward."

"Michail. My love for your sister, my wife, was immense. She had opened my eyes to the joys that life could hold. And of my children, my heart aches each and every day. I was prepared to shuffle them out of my existence, relegating them to the occasional fond memory. You, Misha, helped me to appreciate them even more after their passing. I owe you a thanks for that. But branding me a coward? I am deeply hurt, Michail Ivanovich. Big words for a man who just skulked his way into the lair of the enemy and told all."

"Aleksandr. My skulking is my repayment in kind. When you could have returned to your home and saved your family, you did not. You came up here, leaving them to fend for themselves."

"At that moment, Michail, there was no immediate danger."

"Exactly my point, Aleksandr. You did what was prudent for you and chose to save, to borrow an American expression, your own sorry ass. You left them there, when they could have been brought to a safer place. Surely you must have realized that there would be personal ramifications from your removal from office. For years, you had allowed the police forces of our country to detain, torment and torture thousands upon thousands of citizens. Did you not think as a result that there would be a price to pay?"

"Michail. I feel our discussion on this matter is over. Finish your beer. It's the least I can do."

Michail turned around in time to see Yuri and Feliks approaching, each with their weapons trained on him.

"So I gather that there's not a fish-fry for me this afternoon?"

Aleksandr smiled and stood. He reached over and gave his former friend a pat on the shoulder, then turned towards the two approaching men.

Michail stood, suddenly aware that he was very much alone. If he had been a religious man, he was sure that this is where the praying would begin. Instead, he held up his beer bottle in one hand, while the other had extracted his little flexible blade from the back of his belt.

"Aleksandr. Wait one moment."

Romanov stopped and turned towards Rostokovich.

"Please, Aleksi. Surely there is some way we can work this out."

"No, Michail Ivanovich. I'm afraid the time for working things out has long passed. Yuri. Feliks. You know what must be done."

Michail estimated the distance between himself and Aleksandr at about three meters. Three big steps and he could be on the man without offering the two guards a clear shot. In a flash, he covered the distance, while smoothly bringing the pointed end of the Plexiglas shiv up to the neck of Romanov.

"Yuri. Feliks. Put the guns in the water. Now," commanded Rostokovich.

Neither man moved, each with their weapons trained high, presumably sighted in on Michail's head.

"Boys," Aleksandr said. "Do what you must."

The gunshots echoed off the chalet and across the lake. Michail and Aleksandr were both frozen, as they watched the lifeless bodies of Yuri and Feliks tumble into the icy waters of Lake Onega. Michail tightened his grip on Aleksandr, his mind working furiously to figure out what had just happened. Michail suddenly felt a sharp pain in his right shoulder, then heard the report of a gunshot. He knew he'd been shot. But where did it come from? The house! The two agents in the basement control center. Michail tried to focus in on the area around the bottom of the stairs on the beach. The pain was searing and his eyes were unable to focus. He thought he saw movement, but could not be certain. Then, within seconds, the sound of two more gunshots echoed out across the waters of Lake Onega.

Out of the woods, just to the right of the beach came the silhouetted figures of at least two men, Michail noted. They were joined by maybe two more from the left hand side. Aleksandr was dumbstruck. Michail had tightened his grip on his brother-in-law, the point of the blade working it's way into Romanov's neck a little bit deeper. Michail's pain was now blinding, his eyes filled with large white spots that obstructed his vision. He was starting to get dizzy and was on the verge of passing out. Two of the darkened figures came out onto the dock at a furious clip. Michail saw that both had weapons raised and ready.

"Mister Rosty? Are you okay, sir?"

The Americans! "Yes, I am. Thank you."

"Mister Romanov?" the voice asked respectfully. "Sir, I need you to put both of your hands in the air and step away from Mister Rosty, please."

"American soldiers? You have no authority here. You'll stand before the World Court for this, this," Romanov was now stuttering, angered to a point of exasperation. "This is a violation of international law. You've just invaded sovereign Russian territory. Have you any idea of what the consequences will be?"

"With all due respect, Mister Romanov, we are aware of the consequences. And whereas we have absolutely nothing left to lose, I will ask you once again to raise your hands and move away from Mister Rosty." This time, the request was followed by the sound of both weapons being switched off of their safety mode.

Michail saw his chance at revenge slipping away, as was his ability to think clearly. His shoulder wound was bad and he could feel his consciousness dwindling with each passing second. He put further pressure on the blade now digging deeply into Aleksandr's neck. He could feel a warm trickle of blood start to make its way over his fingers. Just one good push and Michail could send Aleksandr the coward to a cold, dark place forever.

"Mister Rosty? Please, sir. Release your hold on Mister Romanov. Killing him here and now will not serve anyone to the good. We have his confession on video tape, Mister Rosty. Can you hear me, sir?"

Michail nodded his acknowledgment and slowly removed the blade from Romanov's throat.

One of the men stepped forward and separated the two brothers-in-law, removing the blade from Michail's hand at the same time. Michail then collapsed on the dock and felt himself spinning, falling, out of control.

When the intent of the two armed guards on the dock was clear, Menneally had given the order to find a target and take the shot. He had Yuri scoped and locked. Zallonis had Feliks zeroed in on his weapons laser sighting system. Morris and Murphy had to first set down their recording equipment and then had to allow their eyes to adjust. They had both been able to see the two agents in the lower level of the chalet with their naked eyes. The interior lights aided by the growing, late day shadows offered a clear, unobstructed view into the room where the two had been. Once Yuri and Feliks had made their way out onto the dock, the other two agents had come outside to watch from under the deck, just behind the stairs.

When Menneally and Z saw their two marks raise their weapons, Bob and Peter each squeezed their triggers and watched their targets fall.

"Two down," said Bob.

"Two to go," replied Hank.

The muzzle flash from a weapon being fired from under stairs afforded Murph and Morris clear shots. They could have both zeroed in on the shadow from whence the flash originated, but Morris had shifted his sights slightly higher and picked up the second man who appeared to be readying himself for a shot. Not quite in tandem, Hank and Murphy each acquired their targets and dropped them effortlessly.

"Two down under the stairs," said Hank.

"Roger," replied Colonel Menneally. "Let's get down there, now."

Zallonis had already dropped to the ground and was running full tilt towards the two figures on the ground under the stairs. Menneally made a bee-line for the dock. He was joined there by Morris, while Murphy split off towards the chalet to help Zallonis.

"Both bad guys dead here, skipper," said Murphy.

"Copy that, Murph," responded Menneally. "Check around the chalet and make sure there's no one else."

"Doing it now," replied Murphy.

Menneally and Morris made their way directly towards Romanov and Rosty. Once they'd had a chance to identify themselves and to let Mister Rosty know that there was no point, right now, in killing Romanov, they were able to move in. Rosty collapsed and Morris checked him over quickly.

"Bob? He's got a real bad shoulder wound here. He's losing lots of blood."

"Let's get him back to the bird, now," said Menneally. Turning to Romanov, he inquired "Is this thing ready to roll, Mister Romanov?," gesturing towards the boat.

Romanov was brazen, offering nothing in the form of a reply, simply a look that was lethal.

"I'll take that as a yes. Hank, get Rosty on board. I'll drive."

Morris eased Rosty up and over his beefy shoulder and stepped towards the speedboat. Menneally had Romanov at gunpoint and directed the former president to step into the boat. Bob climbed in with Aleksandr, not once lowering his weapon. Menneally directed Romanov to sit in the rear seat and then helped Morris onto the boat with Rosty.

"Z? Murph? This is M. We're taking the speedboat here to the bird. Are you secure?"

"Yes, sir," Zallonis replied. "We're all secure in the house. We'll grab the zodiac and meet you in a couple of minutes."

"That's a rog. Clean up the beach and dock before you boogie. See if they float and make it quick."

Menneally started the boat, while Morris made sure Rosty was settled in the front passenger seat. Hank then stepped back, weapon held tight into Romanov's ribs.

The trip from the dock to the where the helicopter was hidden took less than ten minutes. The Go Team Blackhawk had set down in a small deserted clearing at the edge of the lake, about a mile north of the dacha.

On the way in, Go Team One had received direction based on satellite imagery which had picked out three possible landing sites. The three clearings had been chosen based on their proximity to the water. The distances between the possible landing zones had been spread out to give the team room to operate depending on the wind direction. The wind would carry the sound of the approaching helicopter, so they had to pick their landing spot based on the winds' direction. They had flown low, hard and fast from the NATO operation area and slipped down below radar level about three miles from the Finland/Russian border. Once they'd crossed the border, the American AWACS that was tasked as the NATO eyes and ears for the ongoing joint exercise, quietly assumed control for the Go Team intrusion. The airborne AWACS crew had directed the Blackhawk to a flight path that was slightly above tree top level, running the length of a small mountain range that made up the northern border of Lake Onega.

Staying just below the southern rim of the mountains, the Blackhawk had traversed virtually uninhabited country. In a few months, when the summer visitors had made their treks to their family vacation retreats, the entire area, though remote, would have been full of curious eyes and ears. A last-minute satellite pass had produced a heat-resonance imaging of a five mile radius of the chalet. The only detectable heat signatures came from the actual dacha site, what the techs at Langley had correctly perceived as radiated heat from in-use chimneys at the Romanov compound. To the north, there were no observable heat-emitting readings. There were, however, several SAM sites of which they had to be careful. The AWACS could pick up any active radar targeting system and that had been one of their primary tasks in an effort to ensure the helicopter didn't pick up any unnecessary attention.

The Blackhawk was heading due east, flying low over the water. As they approached a promontory of land towards the northeastern corner of Lake Onega, the AWACS had given them the latest wind conditions as steady, from the west, at about twelve knots, with gusts to twenty. Go Team One was cleared to target the southernmost of the three sites, the one less than a mile to the north of the dacha. Once they had landed and off-loaded the Zodiac, they took a few moments to cover the Blackhawk with a large, camouflage netting and added a few large pine boughs for local texture.

Romanov's boat was approaching the landing zone and Bob eased the boat's throttle forward, slowing it down. The late afternoon shadows began to grow and the clouds took on a darker, storm-like appearance. Menneally beached Romanov's boat, the rocks grinding the hull noisily as the Colonel offered the former president a sheepish grin.

"Sorry about that, sir."

Menneally climbed out first and then, once Romanov was on the shore, took out a length of wire and secured the prisoner's hands behind his back. He sat Romanov down on the ground and helped Morris to offload Rosty. Hank made short work of removing the brush and scrub which had concealed the Blackhawk, while Menneally had begun the pre-flight powering up of the aircraft's systems. Morris then directed Romanov to climb into the back of the helicopter and sat the man down into one of the rear seats. He secured Aleksandr with the shoulder harness, then took out the litter from the aft compartment. Having set up the stretcher for Rosty, Morris lifted the wounded man from the ground and gently placed him on it. As he was securing the litter to the aircraft's floor utilizing the recessed tie-down d-rings, the zodiac pulled up onto the beach. Murph and Zallonis quickly popped the seals on the inflated pontoons, removed the engine from the mount and slid the entire assembly into a rear compartment.

"Z? Any problems ridding the beach of litter? You know we always leave our campsites cleaner than we found them."

"Yes, Colonel. We cleaned the beach and the waters adjacent to the dock."

"How far out did you pull them before you dumped 'em?"

"At least a half-mile, sir. They were already sinking before we cut 'em loose."

"Very well. Gentlemen? Are we ready to get the hell out of here?" asked the Colonel.

"Yes, sir," came the reply from the other team members.

"Hank? Got the camera?"

"Right here, Bob. Let's get home for supper. I'm getting hungry."

Menneally throttled up on the collective and the Blackhawk lifted up effortlessly. Within minutes, they were on a direct course for Finland, traveling at more than a hundred and thirty knots, no more than sixty feet off of the surface of Lake Onega. Bob had wanted to be feet-dry before the sun finished setting. It was hard enough to fly at tree-top level during the early evening hours, but over water, the murky darkness made it almost impossible. Fortunately, there was enough daylight left and the winds were still whipping up the whitecaps. The remains of the day combined with the small, breaking waves gave Menneally enough visibility to maneuver and plenty of reference points to his horizon as well as the surface below.

When Michail regained consciousness, he was at first struck by the pain in his shoulder. As his senses returned, his ears were filled with the loud noise of an engine. He opened his eyes, slowly. Looking up, he saw the smiling face of a man wearing a black uniform and a helmet. He turned his head to the right and was able to make out his surroundings a bit more clearly. Helicopter. The noise was a helicopter and they were, as he could now see, flying. He moved his head to the other direction and saw another man with a helmet, dressed in black, holding a weapon on Aleksandr. The look on Romanov's face was a combination of fury and hopelessness. Michail smiled to himself as he closed his eyes again, allowing the constant bumping motion of the helicopter to lull him back to sleep. The pain he was experiencing right now must be minuscule compared to what Aleksandr must be feeling at this moment. Good, Michail thought. Let the bastard suffer.

thirty-six

Don Hough stepped off his Delta Express flight at LaGuardia, welcoming the warmer weather. He'd left the radio station in Maine with the temperature still a very chilly forty-two degrees. Although the Portland forecast had predicted seasonable highs around fifty-five or so, the heavy snow cover kept the surface air that much cooler. He had rushed to catch the six-thirty commuter flight and had lucked out, thanks in no small part to Michaud's lead foot. The plane leaving Portland was full of New York bound passengers, many on their way to catch a Broadway play, so the need to stop in Boston was negated. The airline would simply stick another plane into service at Logan and keep the Boston to New York leg moving.

Don knew his way around the city better than most of the passengers alighting into the always-busy airport. He could have easily gotten to the hospital on his own, but Nelson was insistent upon providing transportation and protection.

"Christ. They let anybody into this city, don't they?"

Don looked around to see if someone was talking to him.

"Over here! Yoo hoo! And you call yourself a newsman? You wouldn't know a story if it was standing right beside you."

Don turned and was torn between smacking the wiseguy, or hugging him. Opting for the latter, he embraced the solid, well-dressed young man and stepped back.

"Jimmy Fahey? Good lord! How long has it been? Five years?"

"At least, Don. At least. Damn, you look great."

"It's all that time I spend in makeup every morning."

"Right. The infamous radio makeup routine. Let's see if I remember it correctly. Wake up. Put on a clean T-shirt. Brush teeth. Wet down the bed hair. Grab Dunkin Donuts coffee mug. Drive to the double D, get coffee. Drink coffee. Find radio station. Do show. And leave."

"Ah, Jimmy. You can take the boy out of radio, but you can't take the radio out of the boy. Glad to see you remembered everything I taught you."

"Boy? I'm all growed up now, Don," laughed Jim with a feigned affectation. "Did you know I've got twins and another on the way?"

"No, I hadn't heard. Congratulations. I think."

"The girls are just about sleeping through the night. They just turned a year old last month. Dawn's about four months along now with number three."

"Three? Or three and four? You know, Jimmy, they've figured out what causes that baby thing."

"Yeah, the doctor clued us in at the ultrasound. Now they tell me."

"So how'd you grab me for an assignment?"

"Let's head out to the car. I'll tell you on the way."

Jimmy Fahey had started out in radio at WCBR in high school, working part- time on weekends. After high school, he opted to pursue radio full-time, moving to Florida for a year before returning home. While working at the small Biddeford radio station, he'd become a phone-friend with Don who was working in the NBS newsroom. Since Reagan's election, then-Vice President Bush put Maine's York county on the map by spending much of his time at his family's compound in Kennebunkport. Being the V.P. was mostly ceremonial, but with his statesman's background, Bush was more than comfortable hosting world leaders, which helped ease America's dealing with foreign nations. If the vice president had returned, Jimmy would often scoot down to Walker's Point, gather enough material to file a story with the wire services and, when called, to Don. It was an easy way to make extra money and when one is employed at an entry level station such as the one in Biddeford, Maine, every little bit helped. The wire services usually paid twenty-five bucks a story. Don had seen to it that Jimmy got a standard union-scale filing fee of two-hundred fifty dollars per story. Yes, NBS had their own network correspondents covering the national news, but Don relied on Jimmy to get the local flavor of the story. It was kind of a Maine thing, but it always showed in the news copy Don would produce based on Jim's reports.

Whenever Don would come home to Maine to visit, he'd make it a point to take Jimmy out to lunch. Of course, lunch would start at eleven am and finish around the time the last-call lights came on at J.R.Flannagan's in Saco.

Shortly after Don left the network newsroom to become an in-the-field reporter, Jimmy had decided to pursue law enforcement. Upon his completion of training at the police academy, he was hired by the South Portland Police Department. He was more than surprised to flip on WCBR one morning and hear Don Hough as the new morning anchor. Jimmy had still kept his finger in the broadcasting business, mostly as a free-lance voice over talent and doing the occasional weekend radio show at his old stomping ground, WCBR. They were able to renew their friendship and spent, by their own reckoning, way too much time buying drinks for Billy Joel at the singer's favorite port of call on Portland's Commercial Street.

In late 1992, Jimmy's boyish good looks helped steer him towards an undercover assignment with the Cumberland County Drug Task Force, overseen by both the Drug Enforcement Agency and the FBI After six months of flawless work and a one-hundred percent conviction rate, owed purely to his detailed police work, Jim was offered and accepted, a position as a special agent with the Federal Bureau of Investigation. His one regret about the new assignment was having to leave Maine, bound for the busy New York City field office.

Now working on his sixth year with the bureau, Jim had still been able to maintain his genial nature, working smoothly with his law enforcement brethren from both the federal and local ranks. There wasn't a desk sergeant in New York City afraid to call Jim for advice or to offer a lead. Jim was also not above returning the favor, sending witnesses and tips to the local precincts' duty desks.

Jim had first heard about the attack on Sandy from the nightwatch desk sergeant at the city's central precinct. His pager beeped just about 5:40 am while he was on an assignment early that morning, working with Agent Ned Talbot at Kennedy International. He'd answered the page and was informed by one of the friendlier desk sergeants about the attack on Ms. Rose and that there was a shooting involving a foreigner. Anytime there was a crime involving a high-profile victim or perp, Jim liked to be in the loop. It made it easier for him in the event he was called in to help on the case. Not that the FBI was called in on every case, but when they were and if Fahey was the agent assigned to investigate, then he simply liked to be prepared. It made the suits at the higher levels happier to have quick answers when being pressed from even higher levels. A network newswoman as a victim in this case was going to have some powerful people calling in favors to get some fast answers. Plus, with his personal connection on this case, his thoughts turned to Don. He'd made a mental note to make sure to call him when he finished at the airport.

Small world, Jim had thought as he and Ned rummaged through several piles of incoming FedEx packages. Picking through a pile of mail was not a routine assignment for the FBI, but the field office had been requested by Washington to do this. And, once they'd found what they were tasked with locating, one of them would have to personally deliver the parcels to the White House. The fact that one of the packages he was trying to locate was addressed to Michaud Media in Scarborough, Maine made him laugh.

Jim had spent a large amount of time doing freelance commercial voice work at Chuck's, whose sessions usually consisted of an hour of conversation and several cups of coffee, or several beers. Then, fifteen minutes in the studio, followed by another thirty minutes of listening to Michaud pontificate on the issues of the day. Jim hadn't been home to Maine since the New Year's holiday and now, during the course of one assignment, he'd been reminded twice over that he needed to make the short trip more often. Talbot had located the Rosty package with the Virginia post office box address and Jim had picked out the Goatman/Michaud address. With the unfolding Sandra Rose investigation at the top of his mind, Jim offered Ned the opportunity to meet the president. He had some things to check into before he'd call Don at the radio station in Maine, assuming Don was doing the Saturday morning thing.

Fahey arrived at the Rose crime scene around six-thirty as the coroner was wheeling out the body of Sandy's purported attacker. Jim flashed his federal credentials, introduced himself as merely a friend of Ms. Rose and informed the lead detective that he was not, at present, on official business. The detective was more than accommodating, now that he understood the Feds were not about to take the lead on what was instantly a high-profile case. The locals hated it when federal-level officials got involved. In most cases, the locals wound up being pushed aside, with the government troops gleaning already- acquired evidence and leads, then winding up with all the glory. Jim was allowed a quick look at the fatal wound. He made a mental note of the powder burns on the hair. The gun was obviously fired at point blank range. He was allowed by the detective in charge to look at the personal effects, which had all been bagged and tagged. Slipping on a pair of latex gloves, he examined the passport. The name was noticeably different than the one told him by the precinct sergeant. Jim didn't immediately recall the name the sarge had given him, but he certainly knew that the name and address on this passport did not belong to the stiff currently being loaded into the coroner's van. Fahey motioned to the lead detective to come over for a moment. Handing the detective the passport, Jim used his cellphone to call his buddy at the precinct.

"Hey, Sarge. Jim Fahey here. Listen, I'm at the Sandra Rose apartment building with Detective Gordon. What did you say the name of the dead guy was again? That's what I thought you said. British fellow? It's not what his passport says. Uh-huh. Yeah, Ms. Rose is the very dear friend of one of my very dear friends back home in Maine and I was going to call him shortly to fill him in on this. I say was, but I may have to hold off on that right now. Right. Yes, Sarge, the passport is bogus. Uh-huh. How did I come to this conclusion? The name on the passport happens to be the name of the guy I was going to call. Yep, the guy in Maine belongs to the name and address on this passport. The one with the dead guy's picture in it. I'll let Detective Gordon know. Thanks again."

"Gordon, remember how I said I was only here as a concerned friend?

"Yeah." The tone of disappointment rang through loud and clear in one simple word.

"It looks like this case is going to draw some interest from one of the offices here in the city who get their paychecks from the home office in Washington."

"Phony passport?"

"As you no doubt heard. See the name in that little green book right there in your hands."

"Yeah."

Taking a small phone book out his suitcoat pocket, Jimmy opened it to the "H" page. "See this name and address here?" he asked, pointing to the entry for Don Hough.

"Yeah," replied Gordon.

"As you can see, the resemblance between the information you have in that passport and the information I have here in my very own personal phone directory, is very remarkable. And since I know the gentleman in question, the name not the stiff, I can assure you that the gentleman with the oozing bullet hole in his head is not my friend.

"Additionally, the sarge just said that the building employees here who rescued Ms. Rose have all said the now-deceased wife-beater is a British guy named Jonathon Earle. They know, er, knew the guy on sight."

"Shit," was all Detective Gordon could muster for a reply.

"Did the deceased have any other documents? A drivers license or anything like that? Or what about money?"

"Just the passport and a gold card," said Gordon, holding up the evidence bag.

"Lemme take a peek at that card?"

Jim held the bag up to the light and saw the raised lettering on the American Express Corporate card.

The detective stood there, silent. Fahey made note of the corporate name, AFR Enterprises, Inc. The card issued to Donald Hough.

"Listen, buddy. I'm not trying to bust chops here. I'm just trying to help make both of our jobs easier, okay? Make a note in your little book there right now that you noticed the difference in the names. It makes us both look good, right?"

Gordon nodded his agreement and took out his pen and small notebook, making a quick notation.

"What now, Agent Fahey?" asked Gordon.

"Can we go up and take a look at the apartment?"

"Sure."

Fifteen minutes later, Fahey and Gordon returned to the lobby. The apartment had been thoroughly inspected, dusted and detailed. The inventory was lengthy and the photographers had just been finishing up their job. The hallway had been fully documented and photographed, giving the building's management a chance to get things back to normal shortly. The apartment would be cleared for cleaning by the afternoon.

"So, how'd we do?" Detective Gordon inquired curtly.

"Aw, c'mon. Cut me a little slack, okay? I'm not here to steal your case. You caught this one and it's yours. There are parts of it, though, that just aren't NYPD jurisdiction."

"Sorry, Fahey. Just, it's tough when you catch one and then the next level of the food chain comes along and scarfs it up. You wouldn't understand."

"Actually, Gordon, up until five years ago, I was driving my unit around one little section of a small city in Maine. I'm only hefting this badge now because of my ability to pass for eighteen."

Detective Gordon cast a wary eye at that comment.

"Okay, so I'm starting to look my age now. But five years ago, I'd get carded buying a six pack. The DEA took advantage of that. The FBI agent with whom I worked sent a copy of my packet to Washington. So here I am, still a street cop at heart, okay?"

"Sorry about any attitude, Fahey. Anything else we need to do?"

"You guys continue to do your job. Here's my card. It's got my cellphone, my pager, my work phone and home phone. Even my e-mail address. Need me for anything, or if you find out any other items of federal interest, let me know. And thanks."

Fahey and Gordon shook hands and Jim went back to his car. He had his cellphone in his hand, ready to dial Don Hough's radio station number when the phone began to trill. He checked the caller i.d.: It was Director Keith Hammett.

"Good morning, Director Hammett."

"Good morning, Agent Fahey. Were you on your way to bed? I know you've been up for a while."

"No sir, just made a quick stop here on Park Avenue. Agent Talbot is en route to Washington with the packages. Left about six or so."

"Nice job on that, Jim. Made the bureau look real good. Listen, I've got a bit of a baby-sitting detail for you. Might preclude you getting to bed until a little later today, but this is another direct request from President Griffen."

"Shoot, chief."

"Need you to meet a man coming in from Portland, Maine and get him over to New York Presbyterian. He's coming down to be with Sandra Rose, the NBS newswoman. You've heard of her?"

"Boss, you'll never believe this. I'm outside her apartment right now. I got a heads-up from the nightwatch Sergeant at New York Central. He figured since Ms. Rose was high-profile, the bureau would probably get a call about it. He tipped me, so here I am. Who's the guy? Don Hough?"

"Well, yes. How did you know?"

"Didn't know, Director Hammett. Just a hunch. Actually, I was just about to call him and tell him about the situation. I know Don from back home. We worked and hung out together."

"Worked together?"

"Yeah. While I was covering a beat from my patrol car overnights, I also did some part-time radio work. This guy Hough is a former NBS network newsman and he's been back home in Maine doing radio for about seven or eight years now. We worked at the same station."

"A little odd, isn't it? Moving from a network career to a backwater like Portland?"

"Don't let Chief Mike Chitwood hear you call Portland a backwater, boss. No, Don just got tired of the bullets and lies. He went from Riyadh to Washington. Said to hell with it and went to work with a buddy of his. The buddy owns the radio station."

"So you can pick him up? He should be getting into the city in about an hour or so. His flight was leaving Portland around six-thirty. Delta Express."

"It'll be my pleasure, Director Hammett. Oh, by the way? This ex-husband?"

"The deceased? Yes. What about him?"

"He had a passport. Phony. His picture. Wrong name."

"How do you know the name is wrong?"

"The name and address on the passport is Don Hough. Kennebunkport, Maine."

"You're kidding me, right?"

"Serious as a heart attack, sir."

"The man was a British national, if I'm not mistaken, correct?"

"The guy stole the girl from Don while Don was on assignment. She sent him a "Dear Don" letter. That and a waiting assignment in DC is what put him back up in God's country."

"Was there anything else besides the passport?"

"Yeah. A corporate gold card. American Express. AFR Enterprises, Incorporated. Also in the name of Donald Hough. Can we check the company out?"

"That'll be done by lunch, Jim. Thanks for doing the escort thing. I know it's grunt work, but the president is still the boss, no matter what we all think of him right now."

"Innocent until proven, sir, correct?"

"Point taken and noted, Fahey. Thanks again."

"Uh, sir? Before you go? Can you ask someone to message me on what you turn up on this corporation? Just really curious."

"I'll make a note of that, Jim. If you don't hear anything, call me later."

"Will do, sir."

"Goodbye for now, Fahey."

Finishing up the story, Jim was pulling into the parking lot at New York Presbyterian in midtown, having made great time by taking advantage of the grill and rear-deck mounted blues.

"That's what we've got so far, Don. The government is going to be very interested as to how this guy came up with that passport with your name on it."

"Well, it kind of explains one thing. This morning, my American Express corporate card got shot down. I haven't needed to use it in, God, must be a year now. I was able to use my own, personal card though. Damn plastic and computers."

"Your corporate card? You got it on you?"

"Yeah, right here," Don said, reaching around for his wallet. He pulled out the credit card and passed it to Jim.

"Wicked Good Radio? That's the company name? I never knew that."

"Fred has so many holdings from his stock successes, that he's incorporated in several countries. WCBR Radio, Incorporated is a wholly-owned subsidiary of Wicked Good Radio, Incorporated, which is a wholly-owned subsidiary of American Financial Resources, Incorporated. You were never full-time, so you never got the chance to get in on the stock options and 401k plans. The monthly statements include all that information."

"American Financial Resources? AFR? That's the corporate name on the card in your name the late Mister Earle was carrying.

Jimmy gave this a moments thought and continued, "My guess would be that Mister Earle somehow tapped into one of Fred's offshore accounts and gathered up some useful information. I wouldn't be surprised if the rest of the full-time WCBR staff were gallivanting around the world, running up a huge bill for Fred to pay come the end of the month."

"They'll have to spend a ton of money before he notices it, but maybe I should give him a call."

"No, better let the Bureau do that, Don. No need in having him get all excited before he really needs to, eh?"

"Just make sure someone calls him today? I know he'll want to check into it himself and he'd kill me if he knew I didn't pass on what we've found out."

"I promise. We'll call him today."

"Here's his cellphone number. He's in South Carolina for a few days, but he's very reachable."

Don handed Fahey one of Fred's cards. Jim pocketed the card and opened the driver's door while Don did the same on his side. They walked towards the main entrance of the hospital. Don's mind was really racing. How had so much happened in just twenty-four hours? Life was not normally this exciting. Or complicated. The two men stopped at the main information desk and were directed to a set of elevators that would take them up to the intensive care unit. At the ICU nursing station, Jim presented his FBI credentials and introduced Don as the person requested by Ms. Rose. They were escorted to the glass- enclosed critical care unit.

Inside on the hospital bed, Sandy was propped up gently, several intravenous lines emerging from her left forearm. She was surrounded by several monitors, only one of which appeared to be doing anything of import, measuring her heart rate and respiration. Her face was a tapestry of bandages and dressings. Both of her eyes were covered with protective gauze padding. Her right arm was above the blankets, now encased in a cast from her shoulder to her wrist. The nurse briefly explained the nature of Sandy's extensive injuries. Her eyes had required some opthomolic surgery to remove slivers of glass. Prognosis on that area was an expected full recovery and that they'd hopefully be able to remove at least one of the bandages by later in the afternoon. Her arm was broken in three places. The forearm fracture had been severe, requiring the insertion of a metal pin to hold the bones together, allowing them to heal properly. The other two fractures, one at the elbow, the other at the shoulder, were clean breaks. The facial lacerations had required too many stitches to count. A reconstructive surgeon had been present when Sandy was brought in to the emergency room. They felt that any scarring would be minimal, at worst. Sandy also was going to be a long time in just taking it easy while her seven broken ribs were mending. She had been fortunate, the nurse explained, that she did not suffer a fatal injury as the result of the body blows. Two of her ribs had actually splintered, the resulting sharp-edged bones just missing both lungs and an artery.

Don took a deep breath, exhaling long and slow. Damn good thing Jonathon was dead, he thought. Then he made a mental note to take that nice Mister Steve Kelley out for a couple of beers later.

The cellphone on Jimmy's belt began to vibrate as it was in the silent pager mode. Stepping out past the nursing station, Fahey checked the number and walked to the bank of payphones just around the corner, as hospital policy here included a request to refrain from using cellular phones within the building. He punched in the number, followed by his company calling card number. The phone picked up on the second ring.

"Hammett."

"Director? You paged? It's Fahey."

"Jimmy. Are you with your buddy Mister Hough?"

"Yeah. He's in the ICU with Miss Rose right now."

"How's she doing?"

"She's in really tough shape, sir. They're being cautiously optimistic. Some of her internal injuries were borderline fatal. I'm with Don on seconding his sentiments that these two guys from her building did the right thing. Big time."

"I'll call NYPD and make sure they get a pat on the back and a ride home."

"That'd be great, Director Hammett. What else is up?"

"We got a couple of good hits on that American Express card. Hough's was reported canceled about five weeks ago and the new version was placed into service the same day. It's been used a couple of times in the last two days. Three in England, including the plane ticket. Two there in New York. One for the cab ride. The other was at a pawn shop in mid-town."

"Got the address of the pawn shop?"

"As usual, Jim, you're a half-step ahead. Makes my job easier. Here you go."

Fahey made note of the address and bade the director a good day. He walked back to the ICU and pulled Don aside.

"The bureau's already started on finding out about your card and passport. Your card was canceled a few weeks back, replaced by the new one I told you about. The guy used it to buy his plane ticket, pay for a cab ride and a purchase at a pawn shop."

"Pawn shop?"

"Hopefully, the guy just picked up a bauble or two to try and impress his former wife. The downside is that it was probably used for a weapon purchase. Or worse."

"Worse? As in something more dangerous than a gun?"

"Yep. Anyone can buy just about anything in New York City with enough money. I'm hoping this whack-job didn't leave something in her apartment for us to remember him by, if you catch my drift."

"What now?"

"You need to call Fred and bring him up to speed on the credit card thing. Surely someone at some level of his bookkeeping department, or departments, must've gotten a call or some paperwork to authorize the change in the credit card."

"I'll do that. What time is it?"

"Just about nine-fifteen. We are in the same time zone as Maine, you know," Jim said, pointing at Don's wrist.

Don returned the sheepish-grin and shrugged.

"Cut me some slack, will you? I woke up yesterday morning to a half a foot of snow and the weekend has gone downhill ever since."

"Just go ahead and call the Fred-meister. And tell him I said hi. I'm sure he'll rest easier knowing we're on the job. I'm heading over to check out that pawn shop. Promise me you'll stay here until I get back. I am your shadow, per the director of the FBI, who got his marching orders from the President of the United States, okay? They want us to keep a very close eye on you and Sandy until we can sort this mess out."

"I'll be right here, Jim. Be careful."

Agent Fahey stopped and whispered some instructions to the uniformed New York City Police officer outside of the intensive care unit, then hustled for the elevator.

thirty-seven

Gary and Fred were standing outside of the base operations building, sipping on a cup of coffee as they watched the Air Force G-IV make its landing. It rolled right up to the building's rear entrance. A moment later, the two saw a man casually dressed come to the main desk inside the building. He was dressed in a pair of casual slacks, a golf shirt and a lightweight blazer.

"If that's our guy," Dericksen said. "At least we know he's on the ball as far as clothing goes."

"I always thought those secret service types had to wear their heavy, dark suits and sunglasses all the time."

"Well, looks like he got permission to dress down for this assignment. Which is good for us."

"How so?" Fred asked.

"He won't stand out and look so much like a cop."

"Even so, he's still overdressed compared to us, slobs that we are."

"Not slobs, Fred. Let's just consider ourselves meteorologically enhanced."

360

"Ooh. A new nineties term! Are you the one responsible for making all of those up?"

"My favorite, for which I never accepted a dime, is follically challenged," Gary replied, running his hand across Fred's ever-growing forehead.

Inside, Secret Service special agent Tom Hannity was waiting at the counter. The duty officer, a young lieutenant, stepped towards him with a gray, plastic message pouch.

"Agent Hannity? I'll need to check your official i.d., please."

Tom removed his wallet from the inside coat pocket, opening it up to reveal his official shield and photo identification.

"Please sign here, sir," she requested, presenting a hard-bound ledger. Inside the official looking green book, the white lined pages were filled with notations of dates, names and then, on the far right of each line, a signature. She pointed with her pen to the last line, indicating where Tom should sign his name for receipt of the envelope.

"Is that all, Lieutenant?"

"That's all we've got for you, sir," she replied.

"Thanks again. Have a great day. Hey, Colonel?" Tom spoke to the G-IV's pilot filing some paperwork across the office. "Thanks again! Maybe catch you on the return leg."

"My pleasure, Mister Hannity," the colonel replied with a wave.

Tom stepped outside and saw the two men working on their coffee.

The taller of the two spoke first. "Mister Hannity?"

"Yes, sir," Tom said as he extended his hand.

"I'm Gary Dericksen. This balding little man here is Fred Singletary. Nice to meet you."

"Same here," replied Tom, shaking Fred's hand.

"Whatcha got in the little pouch?" Gary asked.

"Just something to keep us out of hot water. Search warrant. Signed by the Attorney General and a federal judge."

"That certainly makes this fishing expedition easier. Shall we go?"

"Let's do it."

The three climbed into Gary's Lincoln and the car slowly pulled out of the parking lot onto the base's perimeter road. A brief wave to the sentry at the main gate sent them on their way towards the Hewes plantation.

Fifteen minutes later, the car pulled to a stop at the end of a long, well-paved and landscaped driveway. The property was fronted by a long, handsome white square-railed fence, which allowed the front lawn area to serve as a large horse pasture. Two horses were standing out in the middle of the right-side pasture, gently grazing, oblivious to any activity around them. The driveway was gated, with two hand-formed stone stanchions on either side. The one to their left, which would be the driver's side of a car on approach, had a small electronic call box. The pasture area to the left of the driveway was a mirror-image of that to the right, with the long, railed fence stretching back towards the rear of the property, out of sight.

"We can either be bold and brazen about this and waltz in the front door," Gary opined. "Or, we could be quiet about this and see if there's a road that runs parallel to that fence over there."

Hannity concurred with Gary. Fred was still looking out the passenger side window.

"I don't see any sign of life down there," offered Fred. "Let's just head in the easy way. We've got papers, right?"

"Fred, let's think this through. Yes, the Speaker is in Washington. But, you don't suppose that he's going to leave things like those two beautiful horses to fend for themselves, do you?"

"Gary's got a point, Mister Singletary."

"Please, Tom, call me Fred." Fred paused. "I'd still feel better if we just announced ourselves. You've got that search warrant, right Tom?"

"True. But, Fred, by announcing ourselves, we run the risk of getting stonewalled until whatever caretaker has a chance to get a hold of Hewes' lawyer or something. I'm sure they're under strict instructions to allow no one in without someone of authority present. And, knowing how shrewd a man the Speaker has become, he's no doubt got a local lawyer on retainer for any kind of official work to be done on his behalf in absentia."

"Like a power of attorney?" asked Dericksen.

"Yes, Gary. Something like that. Probably very limited in what he or she is allowed to do or authorize, but certainly very specific in regards to his interests here in South Carolina during his absence. I say we check to see if there's a back way into this place."

Fred sat back in the front passenger seat and shrugged his shoulders. Gary put the car back into gear and eased away from the front gate area. Less than a quarter of a mile down the road, just beyond the far end corner section of the plantation's fencing, there was indeed a small path. Still somewhat muddy and rutted, it was narrow as well. Gary pulled the big car into the bushes and eased the front end through the overgrown bushes that all but hid the path. Gary was only able to drive the car down the path about one hundred yards or so. Ahead, trees turned the road to a footpath, the roots and trunks narrowing the opening from more than fifteen feet to less than two feet. Gary backed the car up to a small clearing about thirty feet behind them. He worked the wheel on the oversized vehicle easily, doing more than a three point turn, but successfully pointing the car head-first back towards the street.

"Would've been easier in the MG," Gary said as he shut the car off. "But then Tom would've been riding on top of the batteries, stuffed into the little rear deck."

"Never would've happened, Gary," Fred added smiling, giving a look over his shoulder at the six-foot-three secret service agent.

"Well, gentlemen, looks like we hoof it from here," Gary said, getting out of the car.

The other two got out as well, closing the car's doors behind them. The three men began their walk towards the narrow section of the pathway, the white fencing visible through the trees and low bushes serving as a guide. The fence turned to the right, away from the small opening where they now stood. The path still continued through the woods and just as they were about to make their way towards the fence to head in the direction of the barn now visible in back of the main house, Tom caught a glimmer of sunlight off something set back into the tree line.

"Hey guys? What's that over there?" Tom asked, pointing to small grove of trees less than a hundred yards from where they stood.

"What do you see, Tom?" asked Gary.

"I'm not sure. There was a flash, like the sun off some glass or something. Some kind of a reflection."

Hannity led the way, as the other two followed. Fifty yards closer, they were able to see what had caught Tom's eye. It was a small, stone cottage, apparently a part of the plantation. The stonework allowed the small outbuilding to blend in with the trees, the tans and browns of the tree bark masking the like-colored stones. The same stonework made up the rear portion of the main house. From their current vantage point, the three could see a full side-view of the large plantation home. The main house was fronted with a traditional southern-style portico, supported by four large, white columns. The main body of the building was a combination of brickwork, woodwork and, at the rear of the building, stone, exactly the same as this small cottage. They increased their pace down the path. Once they were parallel with the smaller building, they left the path, heading for the secluded structure.

There were two doors to this outbuilding. One in the front off of a small porch that they'd not been able to pick out from the heavy growth that shielded this house. The other was on the side, towards the rear, directly in their line of approach. Hannity was the first to reach the side entrance. He made a quick check of the doorframe looking for any kind of security system contact switches. He scanned the surrounding wall surface. Seeing no wiring other than the main electrical line and phone line that entered the dwelling at the front corner, just up from where he now stood, he tried the doorknob. It was locked. There was a small window just around the back corner. Tom stepped around the edge of the house and gave a look inside. Again, the window appeared to be free, inside and out, of any contact switches that might be linked to a security system. From this point, Tom could see that the outer side door was the second of two doors. The area inside of this window was a small hallway. He could see the interior door that would lead into the main body of this house. He could also see a deadbolt on the outer door. It was just a sliding bolt, easily unlocked from inside. Not accessible from this point, though. Plus, even though their getting inside would be easier from the rear, Hannity would rather see if they could gain entrance without leaving any sign that they were there. Getting in from here would require smashing a window. Hannity also noted that both doorframes were free of any motion-detection devices.

Moving along the outside of the back wall, the three picked their way through some low brush. As they neared the next corner, Tom stopped and signaled for the other two to stop. Peering around the edge of the house, he saw someone moving around by the barn. Although they were a good hundred yards or more from the back of the barn, he hadn't wanted to take any additional chances than needed. From this distance, it appeared to be an older woman. She moved well, Tom could see, but had that slightly stooped posture that seems to come with age. She closed the barn door and started back towards the main house. Once she was around the front of the barn and no longer in view, Tom made his way towards the front of the house.

The porch and the front entrance were totally blocked from any view of the main house or barn area. They stepped gently onto the old, wooden porch. There were no railings or steps. It was more of a platform, no more than eight or nine inches off the ground. There was a wooden screen door in front of a six-light door. Tom was cautious, looking at each board where he stepped. The shaded area and the dampness of the ground would no doubt do a number on the wood's ability to resist rot. He reached the screen door and eased it open. It offered barely a creak, which was surprising, given the rust-encrusted hinges. The door had no spring or closing mechanism attached, so it opened without any resistance. Hannity had taken a look through one of the side windows on their way around. There were no telltale plastic and metal plate assemblies that might be linked to a security system to be seen on any of the windows, or around the inside of the front door. Tom grabbed hold of the front door's knob, taking a deep breath and thinking a quick, silent prayer. The doorknob turned. He gave the door a soft shove. It was completely unlocked and the door swung inward silently. Tom motioned for Gary and Fred to hold their position on the edge of the porch and pointed towards the main house. Gary nodded his understanding of Tom's desire for them to keep an eye open for anyone coming this way.

Hannity stepped into the small house. It was dim, but not completely dark, lit by the filtered sunlight that found its way through the dense foliage. It was, by appearance, a study or a library of sorts. As his eyes adjusted, Tom saw books. Hundreds and hundreds of books lined all four walls. Gauging by the distance they'd come from the back of the house, this room was all there was to this building. A large oak desk centered the oval, braided rug that filled the middle of the room. Tom did not see a doorway in the rear corner of the room. He didn't see anything along the back wall save the overly full bookshelves. He made a mental note to check for a hidden panel. His had now fully adapted to the low light of the library. The desk had a small, green-globed table lamp, a simple desktop telephone, a pen holder and a few picture frames. In the middle of the desk, in a place of honor, sat a deskplate, gold plaque on dark wood, inscribed *The Honorable M. Bradford Hewes, Speaker of the United States House of Representatives*. To Tom's right, there was a small typing table with an old fashioned manual typewriter. Behind the desk was a traditional high-backed leather swivel chair. The furniture in this room, Tom guessed, was at least seventy years old. Perhaps older. The room was surpisingly dust-free. Even with the dampness of the surroundings and given the speaker's Washington schedule, Tom would have thought there would be some accumulation. Maybe the old woman was some sort of caretaker or housekeeper. She probably had a schedule for her duties which included the regular dusting and cleaning of this building.

Tom now stooped low, looking for any kind of security system telltales or motion-sensitive devices that might have been placed. His natural radar had been beeping full-tilt since the discovery of the open door. Odd, he thought, that a man they were investigating for murder and espionage would leave his fortress of solitude unattended. Then again, Tom reminded himself, this wasn't the city. This was an area where everyone knew everyone and probably knew where the cream and sugar were when they let themselves in for tea or coffee. Still, he got low to the floor, working his away around the outer walls of the room on his hands and knees. As he neared the right rear corner of the room, he noticed a larger than usual spacing in the floorboards. He traced one of these spaces under the edge of the braided rug. He gently lifted up the rug and saw the small, recessed metal handle. A trap door? He hadn't seen much more than a six inch space under the front porch. The dampness of the ground did not lend itself to a basement. Many of the homes down here in the south were built at, or even below, sea level. The groundwater levels were too high to even bother. The moisture would erode whatever served as a foundation in very little time. Tom finished his crawl around the room and paused at the left rear corner of the room. He examined the floor at the base of the bookcase. There was a slight scratch in the floor which originated at the edge of one of the sections and traced out into the room in a sweeping arc. That would be the door to the rear hallway. Now, to figure out how that opened from inside.

Hannity finished his inspection of the last side wall and worked his way back to the front door. He stood up, brushing his pants off as he did. He realized that it wasn't necessary, doing it more out of reflex than requirement. He stuck his hand out through the front door and motioned for the others to come inside. As they stepped in, Hannity closed both the screen door and the interior door and pulled the small, sheer curtain back to the side. This afforded them a view at a glance of the barn and the main house. They could not see the rear entrance of the big house, but would be able to see anyone, particularly the older woman, coming their way.

"Okay, boys, here's what we've got," Tom began. "A big room full of lots of books. If there is any kind of a paper trail, it's either hidden in those books, or behind them. Let's do the quick look first. Gary, you start over at that corner and make your way to the back. Fred, you take the front wall here. Start in the same corner as Gary and work your way across. This way, you can keep an eye out for anyone who might be wandering out in our direction. I'm going to start in the back right corner. That's where the panel for the back door is. Let's do this quickly and quietly. Oh yeah, be real careful. If this guy is a Soviet spy, there actually may be a tripwire for some kind of booby-trap. Make sure you look at the books as you slide them out. I've already checked the floor. Questions?"

"Sounds like a plan to me, Tom," said Gary.

Fred just nodded his agreement and started for his assigned corner.

"Hey Fred? Everything okay? You seem a little off right now?" Gary asked.

"Oh, I'm fine, Gary. Just trying to stay focused while we do a little b and e on the Speaker of the House's house, that's all."

"Tom's got a warrant, Freddie. Don't worry. We're just helping to put to rest a nasty rumor. Doing our patriotic duty and all. Besides, where's your sense of adventure?"

"With all due respect, Admiral, I left my adventure in the Navy, remember?" Fred said with a smile.

"I should smack you one, you know that?"

"Yeah, yeah, yeah."

While Gary was getting Fred back onto a lighter tack, Tom was busily checking the left rear corner of the bookshelf. His first priority was to get access to the rear door, in case they had to beat a hasty retreat. He traced the seam of the bookcase up from the floor where the scratch originated. It stopped just about six feet off the floor. Now that he had a starting point, he worked his way down along the outline, just to the non-moving side of the unit. About three shelves down, he removed an encyclopedia volume and felt a small pin sticking out, just beyond the wood's surface. His bulky fingers managed to get it to spin, then, he gently slid it out. As soon as the pin was free, the bookcase actually swung inward on its own weight. He reinserted the pin into its hole and ducked through the opening into the back hallway. The deadbolt was very much wedged into place, probably from lack of use and the now-swollen wooden door. He grabbed the raised end of the sliding latch and gave a hearty pull. It snapped loudly as it slid to the open position. At the sound, both Gary and Fred stepped towards the windows, certain that someone must've heard that. Tom was shaking his hand as he slipped back into the room, raising his pinkie finger to his lips.

"Damn thing bit me," said the president's protector.

"It was loud enough, wasn't it?" asked Fred, still peering out the window.

"Loud, yes. Enough? I don't think so. Remember, we're pretty well surrounded by sound-deadening trees and brush. It was loud in here and maybe right outside that door. But beyond the porch? I don't think it would've registered with a horse."

"Let's hope the speaker doesn't have a dog," said Gary with a wink.

"You guys find anything of interest?" Tom asked.

"Nope. Lots of first editions, though. Most of the ones along this wall so far are from the late eighteen-hundreds. Ran across a couple published up in Boston in the early eighteen hundreds," Fred commented.

"Keep checking the front there, Fred. I'm going to take a quick peek in his desk. Gary? Would you witness this for me? I'd rather be safe in the event we find any national-security type stuff stashed in here. Knowing the kind of ego Hewes swings around, I wouldn't doubt that he has his own copies of a few operational secrets."

Tom walked behind the desk and moved the chair out of the way. He looked under the desk calendar. There was a key. He picked it up, slid it into the middle drawer and turned. The long, slender drawer opened and the room filled with the aroma of fine tobacco.

"Damn! That's a Monte Christo, isn't it?" exclaimed Fred from the other side of the room.

Tom picked the cardboard box out of the now-open drawer. Lifting the lid, he examined the label.

"Fred? You got a nose for things that cost money, don't you?"

"Tom, I've got a nose for things that come from Cuba that cost money. It's a talent I learned from a certain retired Navy flag officer who shall remain nameless right now, as anything I say might incriminate Gary, er, him."

"Thanks, Fred. Your ability to keep a secret is surpassed only by your talent for hanging me out to dry. Here," said Gary, reaching into the cigar box. He tossed a cigar to Fred. "Consider it a gift from the government."

"Uh, gentlemen? I don't know if that's covered by the warrant."

"Tom?" Fred asked. "Do you really think Mister Speaker will report the theft of a few, illegal cigars?"

"He's got a point, Tom. Want one?" asked Gary he held out the box.

"Naw, not right now. Maybe if we find something, then I'll feel better about helping myself to some of his stash."

Tom opened the left hand top drawer. In here, he found only standard office desk fare. Stapler, tape dispenser, a ruler and a pocket calculator. The middle drawer on the left had a couple of old issues of *The Washington Post*, dated from March. The bottom left drawer had a half-dozen hanging file folders, each tabbed and titled. Tom pulled out the first one, titled Amerifunds. Tom made a quick pass through this file, which was merely a collection of a few financial statements. Probably one of the many retirement funds scattered about in the name of M. Bradford Hewes, the agent thought. The other folders were constituent correspondence, each sorted in five-letter sections by the author's last names.

"Gary? Can you hold these for me for a minute?"

Hannity gave Gary the folders and then reached down, extracting the drawer completely from the desk. He flipped the drawer upside down, examining the bottom. Then, he got down on the floor and stuck his head inside of the opening where the bottom drawer was.

"Sometimes, Gary, you get lucky," said Tom as stood up, holding a brass skeleton key.

"What's that go to?" Gary asked.

"I don't know for sure, Admiral. But I do have a hunch. Help me finish checking this desk out and then we'll see what this opens."

The other drawers were removed from the desk, checked in and out, yielding no further finds or documents of note. Tom did pocket the flashlight that was kept in the otherwise empty right hand bottom drawer.

Fred was still making his way towards the back corner along the left side of the room, having discovered nothing remarkable along the front wall.

"Gary. You've got a fan over here."

"What do you mean, Fred?"

"To paraphrase George C. Scott as Patton, if I may.... Dericksen, you magnificent bastard! He read your book!"

Hannity laughed at the more than passable imitation and Gary blushed.

Tom asked. "What book?"

"Tom, you didn't know we're in the presence of a noted military scholar and author? Admiral Gary Dericksen's finest military tome,

The Art of Submerged Navigation, written in his last year of active naval service. Hey Gary? You signed this one to Hewes?"

"He came to a book-signing night a few months after I published it. The local news made a big deal about it. Lots of photos. Sold a few hundred additional books. I'm not dumb, you know."

Tom had walked over to the edge of the braided rug and lifted it up.

"Fred? Why don't you mark your spot there. I need you both with me over here."

Gary and Fred walked to the right rear corner of the room where Tom was inserting the skeleton key into the opening on the trap door.

"How'd you find that?" Gary asked.

"When I did my little scouting mission on my hands and knees earlier. I hadn't seen the keyhole until just now. I saw the handle, though. Knew this door had to go somewhere. Let's see what we can see."

Hannity flicked on the flashlight and cast the beam down the opening. There was a steep set of stairs, all made from the same types of stone as the building itself. The drop to the floor was more than ten feet. It was most certainly a full basement, as opposed to a crawl space. The musty smell escaped with the introduction of fresh air flow. Tom went down first, with Gary right behind, while Fred stayed at the top of the stairway, holding the trap door and constantly glancing out the windows.

Tom shone the flashlight across the overhead. There was a single, bare bulb in a pull-string fixture. He gave the string a tug and the room was lit by the seventy-five-watt bulb. He motioned to Gary to hold steady on the bottom step. Still using the flashlight, he checked the walls behind the stairs, then made a few passes through the shadows on the walls beside them. In front of them was a stone wall also.

"Not much down here, Tom?" asked Gary.

"Looks that way, Gary. But, as we've found out so far, things in this little house aren't as they always appear."

Tom stepped to his left and saw a series of rings mounted on the wall. He flipped one up and let it drop. The rings appeared to be set in pairs, roughly thirty-six inches apart. The lower sets were no more than six inches off the floor. The upper sets were approximately six feet off the floor.

"What do you make of these, Admiral?"

"I'd almost say they look like some kind of restraint system, Tom. You think the slave masters of old sent some of their more uncooperative help down here for some quiet time?"

"That'd be my guess, Gary. Your basic dungeon."

Tom gave one of a the rings a solid yank and the wall moved.

"Practicing for the FBI annual picnic there, Tom? What do you do, circus strongman?"

"Come on down here and give me a hand."

Gary stepped onto the rotted boards that made up the basement floor. The click was deafening.

"Oh shit."

"Don't move, Gary. Don't move one freaking inch."

Tom moved along the wall and got to within two feet of the stairs, looking below them. He saw the wire. The wire ran below the floorboards and up the wall behind the stairs. Nestled into the overhead floorboards was a small packet. The wire ran into this packet, or, did. Hannity could see one end of a metal pin protruding from the packet. The now-free end of the wire was still nestled into the top metal eyelet through which it had been threaded. The end of the wire held a small, metal ring. Tom came under the stairs and got a closer look with the flashlight. The broken pin assembly had rusted, thanks in no small part to the amount of dampness down here, plus, he assumed, age. The pin that was still in the package had not fully deployed. The package, wrapped in frayed plastic, appeared to be a small amount of plastic explosive. The detonator had become exposed due to the aging plastic wrapping having decayed. This exposure had most certainly saved their lives.

"Okay, Gary. We dodged a bullet on this one. The detonator pin snapped, instead of pulling out. The wire was set to pull the pin when you stepped on that board. Take a deep breath. Now, exhale and be happy we're alive."

Gary took the breath and exhaled. He still didn't move.

"I'm sorry I didn't see that, Admiral. I suppose you'd feel better if I give another look around the room?"

"The thought had crossed my mind, Tom. Thanks. I'll just step back up here on the stairs."

"No, just to be safe, stand there."

Tom moved rapidly around the room, using his hands to feel the walls this time, as well as his eyes.

"Got another one here, buddy. It's not where you are, though."

Tom bent down and turned the six-inch wide plank back towards himself, exposing the anchored end of the wire. The board itself was placed over a small trench that had been dug out for the length of the board only, with enough of a small dirt lip at either end to support the board. Stepping on the board would lower the wood enough to put pulling pressure on the wire, which in turn would free the pin on the second small package of explosives. Certainly enough, Tom thought, to pretty much ruin Mrs. Hannity's and Mrs. Dericksen's day, given the tight quarters they currently occupied. He worked the board up the wall gently, allowing the line to slacken. Once the wire was hanging loose, he gave the small eyelet on the board a turn. The rotted wood gave way on the first twist, releasing the eyelet and trigger wire.

"Any more over there, Tom? Seems like whoever put this stuff here didn't want anyone snooping around."

"That would be an understatement, Admiral. Let me make sure we got them all."

Tom finished circling the room, leading with the flashlight and his hands. Other than the series of wall-mounted rings, his searched produced no further traces.

"Let's see what's behind door number two, Gary."

"If you say so, Tom."

The two men stepped towards the section of the wall that had swung inward. In relation to the building, this would be the front section, facing the barn and the main house. The two grabbed a metal ring and pulled with everything they had. The door, though sluggish and heavy, opened inward. It was a wooden framed door. The stones on the front were not complete, just fragments that had been chipped and attached with mortar to a wooden surface. Tom and Gary noted that the facade was enough to fool them on the first pass. Behind the door, there was a dark tunnel. Tom shone the flashlight down the passageway and saw that the tunnel split about twenty yards in.

"Hey Fred?" Tom spoke up the stairs. "Come on down here."

Fred stepped gingerly down the stairs and saw the other two standing beside the open door. At the bottom step, he stopped.

"Come on, Freddie," Gary chimed. "We're going spelunking!"

"Fred, we need you to stay down here. Keep an ear open and give us a yell if you hear anything out of the ordinary."

"Out of the ordinary defined as what, Tom?"

"Oh, maybe somebody coming who isn't us?"

"Gotcha. I catch on quick, you know. Just ask the admiral." Fred smiled at Gary.

Tom and Gary made their way into the passageway. It was hard-packed dirt, damp and musty. The walls were stone, covered with moss, The passageway was no more than five feet by five feet, forcing both to stoop. Tom was using his hand to feel the wall ahead on right, while Gary did the same on the left, the flashlight's narrow beam sweeping across the floor for more trip wires. They got to where the tunnel forked and stopped.

"What do you think, Tom"

"I'd say this one to the left heads towards the barn and the main house. I have no idea where this one on the right might go. Let's go right and see how far we get."

"Sounds like a plan to me."

Moving into the passageway to the right, they were soon enveloped by the darkness, the solitary overhead bulb back in the main basement room no longer offering any light or shadows. The flashlight's sweeping arc stopped on a wooden door just ahead. Tom stepped forward and reached for the rusted metal handle. The door opened sluggishly, releasing an odor that was more stench than musty. Tom grabbed one side of his shirt and brought it up over his mouth and nose. Gary had done likewise, fighting back a gag. The beam of light stopped on a mass in the far corner of this tiny room, a white footbone protruding from the edge. Tom focused the flashlight on the lump. As his eyes adjusted, he could see that the lump was a rug of some sort. He swung the beam of light around the room quickly and stopped it on a metal box. He stepped to the box, grabbed the rust-encrusted handle on the top and picked it up. Stepping back out of the room and into the tunnel, he heard Gary retching. He set the box down on the dirt floor and closed the door with a rapid shove. He grabbed a hold of the box and took the three steps needed to reach the admiral.

"Sorry about that, Tom. That was very unlike me. I'm not normally that quick on the gag reflex."

"It's pretty bad, Admiral. Let's get back to the main basement and get some fresh air. You take the light. I've got a little parting gift for us here."

"What's that?" asked Gary, shining the light on the metal box.

"Looks like a strongbox. Although, judging from the rust on this thing, I don't think strength is one of its future, lasting qualities."

The two men made their way back to the intersection of the two tunnels and swung to their left. The main passageway was now lit up by the bulb from the entry room just ahead. They stepped into the room, waving to Fred who had been sitting at the top of the stairs. Tom led Gary to the stairs, passing him the strongbox. The agent then turned and re-closed the hidden door. Gary was now passing the metal container up to Fred and was nearing the top step. Tom pulled the small string on the overhead light and turned it off. By the time he was at the top step, Fred was at the front window, looking out, while Gary was sitting in the swivel chair, using a small handkerchief to wipe his face, the metal box at his feet.

"Are we still clear, Fred?" asked Hannity.

"Yep, we are."

Tom took out his cellphone and powered it up.

"Gotta phone this in, boys. We're now officially no longer unofficially being nosy."

"What was in there, Tom?" Gary asked.

"By my best, un-medically educated guess, Admiral? I'd say it was definitely a body, or what was left of one. The cool, damp conditions there have certainly prolonged the decaying process. I'm going to make sure there's a full forensics team here to check the rest of this little maze out."

"What's with the tunnels?" asked Fred.

"Probably a part of the underground railroad, Freddie me boy," responded Gary. "I've done a lot of reading up on this lovely little area of Charleston and there were a good deal more plantation owners who were sympathetic to the plight of their slaves than believed. The tunnels were a place to hide any runaway slaves who might have been making their way north. These moleholes were also a good place for the plantation owners to hide valuables when the Union troops came through. The false wall in the cellar had the restraining rings. It gave the resident master a chance to show either a bounty hunter or a Union army officer that he knew how to keep darkie in line. The bounty hunter, of course, would be impressed, especially if the overseer had one or two unruly slaves tied up for a lesson. The Union army officer would most likely have been unimpressed and more inclined to give the proud southerner a smack upside the head. Still, the shackles on the wall were camouflage enough to end any additional curiosity, leaving the contents of the tunnel unmolested and safe to see another day."

"Mister Nelson? Hannity here. We're now officially investigating a crime scene. That's correct. We're in a small cottage on the Hewes property and along with a couple of packets of plastic explosives, there's what's left of a body. That's correct. Paperwork? We're just about to look. Want to hold for a second? Sure, it's a 703 area code. Right, 637-5289. Yes, I'll be here and ready."

"Perfect," Tom sighed as he disconnected the call. "Griffen is about forty-five minutes into his telling of this tale with an assembled group lacking only the Queen of England. Nelson's calling me back and wants me to do a recitation on the speaker phone for all there to hear. I hope this relic doesn't blow up on us."

Hannity bent over and flipped the decayed latch on the metal box open. He lifted the box's hinged top, reached in and extracted a handful of sealed plastic bags. Each bag contained a folder with numbers, the first in red magic marker reading 1976. Tom walked over to the desk, opened the middle left drawer and took out a pair of scissors. He unsealed the bag and, using the sharp end of the scissors as a handle, opened them to slide the rounded handgrips over the folder. He laid the bag on the table and, pulling gently, the scissors' finger holes now securely pinching the folder, slid the folder out onto the desk's surface. He opened the folder and put the phone back to his ear.

Tom's cellphone began it's electronic ring and Tom answered it before the first ring finished.

"Bud? Oh, yes, I understand. Good morning Mister President, Mister Chief Justice and all the rest. I'll read this and hope you can all hear me clearly.

"This doesn't look good for Mister Speaker. The box has a bunch of folders, all marked by year. First one here is from seventy-six. Top page is long hand, Cyrillic. That's right. It's all in Russian.

Flipping the top page over, he continued.

"Next page is photocopy of an i.d. card of some sort. Photo is of a person who could be a much younger Hewes, but I can't be sure. There is an official seal though. Yes, sir. It is the old USSR one. Next page is another i.d. card. Yeah, that's definitely our Mister Moore. Better get a team from the bureau down here. Right. We're going to go wait in the car on the road and hang tight until the team arrives. Then we can make an official entrance. Yes, I've got the warrant right here," Tom said, patting the sealed message pouch that was tucked into the front waistband of his pants, under his shirt.

"Tell Nelson I said hi," Fred said from the front of the room.

"Tell him I said thanks a lot for dragging me into this," added Gary.

"Your friends send their regards, Bud," Tom laughed. "Yes, I know they didn't word it with quite the same level of civility, but we're out of this now. I will, Bud. Thanks and we'll see you at the office later. Good luck, Mister President. Yes sir, I am being very careful. No, Admiral Dericksen is not trying to get me to crash on the rocks. Yes, sir. Goodbye."

Hannity disconnected the call and slipped the phone back into his suitcoat pocket.

"Bud said to make sure you guys take me out for a nice lunch. He mentioned something about a place you won't tell him about, but that you guys swear is great and he'd love?"

"The Neon Goat," said Gary.

"It's a great little Tex-Mex place out on Sullivan's Island, Tom," Fred said. "It's on the way to Gary's house. I'm game if you are, Admiral."

"I want to clean up first, Fred. Plus, I need to give my tummy a minute or two to regain its senses."

"Fine by me. Gary? What's with the rocks reference?" asked Tom.

"Then-Governor Griffen came through here on a campaign swing just after the book was published. Same book place, I think, where I signed the one for Hewes. The president actually read the damn thing. I hope. I had no idea he remembered me."

"That's what makes him a remarkable president. And I'm not just saying that because I work to keep him safe. I see him do stuff like that ten times a day. The look on the faces of the people he remembers is just like the expression you're wearing now, Admiral. We need to hang out for a few, though. The bureau has a field office in Charleston and another down Savannah way. The local boys should be here in about fifteen minutes. Once they get here and I give them a walk-through, we'll be gone." Tom replaced the folder into the plastic envelope and put the envelopes back into the metal box, closing it and securing the rusted latch.

Gary was feeling a bit better, now giving himself a little spinning ride in the swivel chair. Fred was watching his friend go 'round and 'round. Gary stopped and pushed himself on the rolling chair towards the rear bookcase.

"I still can't over this book collection. It's got to be worth a fortune. I can't believe that Hewes would keep it out here in this dampness. Look at this one," Gary said, reaching for a thick, leather-bound edition.

"Which one is that?" asked Tom.

"It's a beauty. Leather cover. Tolstoy. *War and Peace.*"

Gary pulled the book from the shelf just as Fred dove across the desk towards the Admiral.

"No!" screamed Fred.

What Tom and Gary had missed in the basement was the wire leading up from the second explosive pack they had thought they had disarmed when they removed the wire from the basement's floorboard. Nestled in the overhead, the wire was connected to a second detonator on the plastic explosive, one that was on top of the package, not visible unless the package had been removed. The other end of the wire was connected to the leather bound, first edition of *War and Peace*.

The three were tossed away from the backwall bookshelf like dried autumn leaves in a stiff November breeze. The roar from the explosion was deafening. The floorboards lifted up and from the resulting hole, a fireball erupted, passing through the room and out through the roof of the building. The entire room was ablaze, the years and years of collected books belying the assumed dampness of the cottage.

Tom had been fortunate in that the force of the detonation had sent him out through the side window. His ears were ringing. His extremities numb. His vision blurred. Dazed, he picked himself up from the brush that had broken his fall. In front of him, the outbuilding was completely engulfed in flames. It took him a moment to regain a small amount of his wits. Trying to shake off the effects of the blast on his ears, he remembered the other two. His first attempt at walking was unsuccessful, falling flat on his face into the mud along side the burning building. He stood again, this time using the lower edge of the house for support. He crawled up onto the porch, the heat from the raging flames searing his exposed skin. He took off his coat, emptied the pockets and put the contents on the ground, off to the same side from which he'd just come. He removed the gold Bulova watch Pip had given him on their tenth anniversary. The crystal was cracked and it was stopped at 9:12. He removed his service pistol from its shoulder holster and put that with the other items on the ground. Wrapping the coat around his right hand, he crawled to the front door, pushed the screen door open and gave a shove to the solid wooden door. As the door swung inward, a stream of fire rolled out of the top of the doorway. Tom dropped low on the porch and pulled himself to the edge of the entrance. Peering inside, he could see the limp bodies of Fred and Gary. Gary was closest to the doorway, with Fred laying on the floor next to the remnants of the speaker's desk.

Tom crawled towards the admiral who was lying still, lifeless, in the middle of the room. Reaching for Gary's neck, Tom did not detect a pulse. He peered over Gary's body and could see Fred moving. The flames were tracing a line across the shattered floorboards towards Fred, his feet already obscured by the rising wall of red. Tom got on his hands and knees and crawled to Fred, wasting no time in grabbing the man by the left arm. Pulling as hard and fast as he could, Tom rolled Fred out onto the porch and off the nine-inch drop to the ground, falling off himself as well. Using his coat, the secret service agent smothered the flames which had enveloped Fred's running shoes. He placed a finger under Fred's nose and determined he was breathing.

Hannity then stood, now feeling a bit more steady on his feet and made the leap back onto the porch and into the raging inferno that was once one of America's best book collections. He reached the unconscious admiral, got a hand hold under the man's armpits and dragged him outside. Once they were clear of the porch, Tom began performing cardiopulmonary resuscitation on Dericksen. The heat from the burning building was becoming more intense, yet Tom persisted. The ringing in his ears was still the only thing he could hear as he did the repetitious chest compressions followed by mouth-to-mouth breathing. The admiral's chest was rising with each breath. After the seventh set of compressions, Tom felt Gary's body begin to spasm. If he could hear, Tom would have heard the struggled cough. Instead, the small stream of vomit that came from Gary's mouth was the indicator that this procedure was working. Tom rolled the admiral up onto his side and gave him a firm pat on the back. This freed another small stream of liquid from Gary's mouth. Tom felt for a pulse again and this time, there was one. Steady. Strong. He looked down at Gary's chest and took small comfort in the steady rise and fall of the man's chest.

Tom crawled back over to Fred and began removing the vinyl and cloth running shoes. The left slipped off easily and Tom removed the sock as well. The right shoe had fused to Fred's skin. Better to leave that for the hospital, Tom thought. He saw a large piece of what had been one of the window frames laying on the ground less than ten feet away. Scrambling over to it, Tom grabbed it and gave it a few good slams into the ground. It freed the remaining glass from the grooves of the wood, leaving a not-quite complete rectangle. He rushed back to Fred, straightened the man out from his somewhat curled position and buried the two shorter ends of the window into the ground. He then took Fred's feet and placed them gently across the longer section, giving the injured man's lower extremities about twelve inches of elevation.

As he walked back to Gary, Tom saw the old woman coming at them, quickly. He turned back towards the porch and made it to his pile of belongings when he stopped short. Something had hit him square in the middle of back. Turning, he found himself looking at the woman and at the business end of what looked like a twelve-gauge shotgun. He raised his hands and nodded towards the pile, which was topped with his service revolver. She stepped around him, keeping the gun pointed directly at his midsection. Stooping low, she picked up the secret service issue nine-millimeter Glock and motioned for him to step away. Tom persisted in motioning to the other materials on the ground and she used the handgun to give him permission to allow him access to his remaining items. He pocketed the cellphone and gently stood, arms extended to the side, with his right hand holding open his wallet. The star-shaped badge glowed orange from the reflected flames of the fire raging beside them. The woman lowered her shotgun and extended her arm to return the handgun to Hannity. She was saying something, but Tom could still only hear the constant ringing in his ears. He nodded towards the two men on the ground and she turned first to walk in their direction.

Gary was still coughing, his eyes slowly opening when Tom got back to where he'd left him. Tom looked at him and made the universal hand gesture with thumb and forefinger for okay. Gary nodded and Tom patted him on the shoulder. Gary pointed to his ears and Tom returned the affirmative head motion, pointing to own ears and shaking his head side-to-side to indicate a negative.

Meanwhile, the old woman was tending to Fred, stroking his hair and saying something. Tom moved the four feet to where Fred was and, in the woman's face, Tom saw compassion, something akin genuine affection. She took off the apron she had been wearing and wrapped it gently around Singletary's right arm, which was bleeding as a result of a large fragment of wood still protruding from his forearm.

Before he could make anything further out of this, Tom looked up and saw the first of two white sedans speeding across the back pasture, heading straight for them. The blue lights mounted in the front grill were offset by the wig-wag of the vehicle's headlights. Thank God, Tom thought. The cavalry had arrived. The woman was now next to him, softly touching his back, up near the left shoulder. Tom looked back to see what it was she was doing, but couldn't turn his head more than a few degrees backward. The pain he felt between his shoulder blades was excruciating. The woman came around to his front and picked up a piece of fragmented glass from the ground. She used her right hand to reach over her own left shoulder and made a slow, stabbing motion. Then, she looked at him with an expression that asked if he understood. Tom nodded yes. He motioned for her to pull out whatever was in his back. She tapped him on his right shoulder to get him to stoop down. Tom went straight to his knees as the woman went behind him and pulled. He felt her hand pressing where the pain had been worse. She used her free hand to reach around to in front of him and there he saw a dagger-shaped chunk of glass at least twelve inches long. The blood stain was evident on about six inches of the fragment. Going to take a few stitches to close that one up, he thought, noticing for the first time the numbness overtaking the pain.

The first of the men from the newly arrived vehicles came rushing to them. Tom flashed his badge while the lead man did the same. FBI, Tom saw. The agent's mouth was moving, but Tom could still hear only the incessant ringing. He spoke what he hoped were words.

"I can't hear a thing. Explosion. Ringing," he said, pointing to his ears.

The agent nodded and held out his credentials for Tom to examine. Tom did the same.

"Sorry if I'm yelling, Agent Daniels. These two men are with me. We have a warrant," Tom said as he slid the message pouch out of the waistband of his pants. "Better get an ambulance out here as soon as possible. Do you have a piece of paper?"

Agent Carlos Daniels took out his notebook and offered it, as well as a pen, to Tom. Hannity scribbled a few words and showed them to the agent. The agent nodded, which gave Tom the confidence that he needed. Confidence that the other agent would be able to read the chicken-scratch, as Pip like to call it, that Tom called handwriting. Tom made hasty notes on what they had found, on the metal box and on the explosion. He managed to jot down the number for the White House secret service detail, along with Nelson's name. Then, Tom saw the building begin to waver, the flames looking more like a rolling river than a steady wall. Agent Daniels caught Hannity, eased him to the ground and took over the scene.

thirty-eight

"What? You've got Romanov with you?"

"It was that or kill him, sir. I had no problem taking out his little friends. There are four bad guys currently enjoying an early spring dip in the lake. But as much as I wanted to let Mister Rosty get something off his chest, I thought, for the big picture, you needed the man."

President Griffen had to think. And fast. Before Go Team One left Russian airspace. Before the act of kidnapping a now-respected senior statesman of one of the world's superpowers became a world of shit from which none of them would be able to escape. Before the Chief Justice of the Supreme Court, the Attorney General, two other sitting justices and the senior members of the house and senate walked into his office.

"Bob? You're sure we need to have this man in custody? You sure we couldn't have looked the other way while something might have happened to him, accidentally?"

"Skipper, when you see the video and hear the soundtrack, you'll be glad you have the star of the show in the house, so to speak."

"Bob? Give me updates. Call me when you clear the airspace. Call me when you're back at your Finland staging point. Call me when you're airborne for Cheltenham. Call me when you get Mister Moore and Mister Romanov face to face. And be sure to call me at any point if you run into a problem, with anyone. Especially the NATO generals in charge in Finland."

"We developed nav and comm gear trouble about, oh, three hours ago. We'll pop up where they lost us and give them the old fashioned fake radio static when we're close enough for them to see us."

"Aren't your comms digital, Bob?"

"That's the beauty of this, Jay. We've got the old fashioned radio gear on board, too. Amazing how useless a digital communication unit is when one of the chips is not properly slotted."

"Bob, I'll trust your judgment. But get the hell out of Russian airspace, now. Remember, call me when you clear the airspace."

"Yes, sir. That should be in another hour and a half or so. Bob out."

Menneally ended the call and Jay stood there looking somewhat dumbfounded at the phone in his hand.

"Jay? Did they do what it sounded like they did?"

"Yep. They saved Michail's ass and took his brother-in-law along for the ride. Had to splash four bad guys. But he says they felt Romanov was a must-have based on the video they got. Must be one hell of a story."

"Um, Jay?" Keith asked somewhat sheepishly.

"Yeah, Keith?"

"If you're building up a stockpile of high-profile perps in England, don't you think you need someone who's a bit more well versed in asking questions and getting information over there?"

"Who'd you have in mind?"

"Er, Hibbly hee. Hibbly ho?"

In unison, the other four in the Oval Office responded. "Hib!"

Jay grabbed the phone off the desk, checked the pull-out phone directory and hit the speed dial for Terrio's cellphone.

"Bill. When was the last time you went across the Atlantic at mach three?"

"Well, Jay. Never. Why?"

"Looks like there's a first time for everything. Get that photo to your lab boys, then get to Andrews. I'll make a call now to COMNAVAIRLANT and get you in the backseat of the next really fast bird heading for Cheltenham."

"Cheltenham? England, sir?"

"Yep. It'll give you a chance to compare some notes with Sir Stephen at British Intelligence. Have some tea with the man. Oh and interview Sasha for me while you're there."

"Go Team took Romanov, right?"

"You, Billy, are a man possessed of an extremely analytical mind. That's why you get the big bucks. Yes. How much longer until you get to your office at Langley?"

"Just getting on the beltway now, Jay. About another twenty."

"I'll call you with the name of the pilot. He'll be expecting you. Go. And catch a little nap on the way over."

"Yes, sir. Hibbly he. Hibbly ho."

"Hib," said Jay as he hung up the phone.

"Lab work!" Bud said somewhat loudly. "I knew I had forgotten something. Christ. Keith? How good are your boys and girls with voiceprints?"

"Voiceprints?" Jay asked.

"They've got it down to a science now, Bud," said Keith.

Bud got up and picked up his briefcase. He reached in and pulled out two cassette tapes.

"These tapes were made while I was in my senior year at Clemson. Had a poli-sci class which was handled on a few occasions by the professor's sharp teaching assistant."

"Bud? We've got about five minutes before our jury arrives and you're flashing back to college?"

"Jay, work with me on this, okay? Keith, these tapes are old. I listened to one on the way here this morning. It's a bit fuzzy, given the age of the tape and the relative crudeness of the tape recorder, circa ninety-seventy-two. My folks had given it to me during my sophomore year. All of that notwithstanding, the teaching assistant was M. Bradford Hewes."

"Our M. Bradford Hewes?" Jay asked. He was actually smiling. "How the hell did that ever happen?"

"Jay. You owe our good friend and audio production wizard Chuck Michaud several well-aged bottles of scotch and some fine, hand-rolled tobacco products from that place to the south of Florida. It was his epiphany slash flashback that came up with these. And you know what? It ain't the first time he's woken up in the middle of the night with similar solutions. Keith, along with this tape, our friends at NBS were forwarding a compilation video of Hewes highlights to Mister Michaud in Maine. We'd told them the tape was for part of a roast for Senator Olivia. The bits will date back to his first campaign. A provable non-match will place the impostor with the murder timeline we just received. We also thought that maybe we could check the hangers-on to see if there were any common, familiar faces. People who might have been with Hewes all along but slipped to other ventures, such as Moore."

"We might be able to access some recent footage, too, Bud. Just to get some comparisons rolling."

"Keith, let's get cracking on this right now. I'd appreciate it if you'd see to this personally, okay?" requested the President.

"Do you want me here for your meeting?"

"Jay," Bud said. "It might be good for credibility if he's here with Gayle. A solid law enforcement presence won't hurt."

"All right then, Bud. Good point. Keith, hand pick someone to start working these up."

Keith thought for a moment. "I have just the guy in mind to start on cleaning these up. It's so easy now that we've got gadgets that can eliminate hiss and hums. Wish I had them to set up my home stereo."

"Go. Now. And then get back here. And Keith? Thanks."

"My pleasure, sir."

As Keith left, Joannie knocked and entered the office.

"Mister President? They're here."

"Thanks, Joannie. Can you ask Gayle to come in first? Alone?"

"Yes sir, I will."

Bud shot the president a quick look.

"Bud, get Paparelli on the phone, now."

"Yes sir," replied Nelson.

"Danny? I need you to buy me at least five minutes. Go out and brief the Chief Justice on our unexpected delay. That we'll be right with him. And that I am truly sorry."

"Will do, Jay."

Josten was opening the door as Attorney General Vernon came into the Oval Office.

"Gayle. Great to see you and your timing is perfect," said the president. "Remember that warrant we had drawn up and faxed to England? I need another one faxed to the same number, like, now. And how quickly can you draw up an extradition agreement?"

"An extradition request? That could take some time, Jay."

"Gayle, time is one thing we don't have. The warrant and extradition paperwork are for Aleksandr Romanov."

"Is this for show?"

"No show. No bullshit. Our team has Romanov. The mission commander assured me it was that or kill the bastard. He's promised that we will be glad we have him."

"Can't they just take him back? The Russians will never agree to extradite."

"I know that. That's why we're going to fax the extradition form to Julie in Paris within the next fifteen minutes."

"Fifteen minutes! Jay, you can't be serious. I have to draw it up, with specific charges and get it signed off by a federal judge."

"Jay? Got Julie on the line," Bud interjected.

"Gayle. Use my computer. It's on. Start writing this thing up."

The president took the phone from Nelson.

"Julie? Jay here. Listen, have you had your meeting with the Russian prime minister yet? No? What time are they due in?"

Jay nodded his head, making quick notes.

"Listen carefully. We've got one chance to do something here and it goes against everything you've worked for as our Secretary of State. But I need you to trust me and make it happen."

Jay outlined his plan to Secretary of State Paparelli. He then gave her the only option available. The optional plan explained the on-going KGB operation, as they knew it and as it applied right at this moment. It also explained that the United States would be on a mission to keep the Russians out of the European Economic Union.

The hard-ball approach was a fallback. The initial plan was to slip the extradition document into a stack of papers which both Julie and her Russian counterpart would need to initial. The prime minister would be a ranking-enough official to sanction the extradition of a Russian citizen. Not that the Russians and the Americans had any reciprocal extradition agreements in place, but a signed document was as good as gold. Three minutes later, having run through the abbreviated version of events and his ideas, the President finished and listened.

"Yes, Julie," Griffen responded to her question. The remainder of the answer filled in the missing body of the query. "Yes. We have Marvin in custody. No, that's all I want to tell you right now, but I think it can help you stay focused on what we need to accomplish right now. As far as you know, he's still missing. You call me if there are any problems. Gayle will be faxing the document to you within the next ten minutes. Please, stay next to your fax machine, call me when you have it and then we'll all start praying."

President Griffen addressed his attorney general.

"Gayle, are we making some headway on that thing?"

"Yes sir. Still, before we fax it, it's going to need a federal judge's signature."

"Bud? Dial Judge Noga for me, please?"

Nelson was getting a workout, handing the phone to the president once again.

Jay listened to the ringing on the line. "Jimmy? Jay here. Yes, *that* Jay. I need you here on official business in the next fifteen minutes. Can you do it? Need a sign-off on an extradition request. Trust me, you won't regret having your scribble on this one. I promise. Not right now, but I can have Attorney General Vernon fill you in when you get here. You'll be here in ten minutes? Jimmy, as they say, you rock! I'll see you then."

Griffen handed the phone back to Nelson. "Gayle? Judge Noga will be here in about ten minutes. Bud? Can you call the gate and have them bring him up here as soon as he arrives?"

The attorney general and the president's communications director both acknowledged the president with vigorous nods of their heads.

President Griffen walked towards the Oval Office door and opened it, stepping out into the reception area.

"Mister Chief Justice? I'm so sorry for the half-hour delay. I appreciate your being able to come here this morning. Please, come on in. We have some interesting things to discuss."

As the assembled group took seats around the Oval Office, President Griffen took a moment to make sure all those present knew who the others were. Especially in the case of the three sitting Supreme Court justices. Chief Justice Terrance Quinlan and the Associate Justices, James Jalbert and Margaret Charnoff, had come in rare civilian attire. They were not easily recognized for the most part when not wearing robes. Also present were Senator Davis Wilson, the senior republican senator from Texas, currently entrusted with the role of Senate Majority Leader and democratic House Minority Leader Kevin Billingsly of Minnesota. All were dressed casually, as requested by Dan Josten when the invitations went out. No need to call extra attention to who is coming and going at the White House on a Saturday morning.

"Before we get started on what I feel is of major importance to the United States of America, I will offer up an apology for any and all interruptions that may occur. I assure you, though, that these intrusions on your valuable time have everything to do with why I asked you here. It is my desire that you do not feel slighted in any momentary distraction which will occur. Currently, Attorney General Gayle Vernon is drafting an order to extradite a foreign national. We have one chance within in the next twenty minutes to get this signed and agreed to, or else you will be meeting next to decide on how best to rid our government of a major embarrassment. Namely, me.

"Additionally, I have asked several ranking members of the administration to handle some matters personally, in the interest of keeping what you are about to be told strictly contained. These people, notably National Security Advisor Realto and FBI Director Hammett will be coming in here with what I hope is further evidence to support what you will hear. I know this is sounding somewhat like an opening argument. In a way, it is. I am here to ask your help in how best to keep this nightmare with which I am currently attempting to prove, or debunk, from becoming the undermining force I believe it truly capable of being. I want you to know, up front, that I hope to God that I have made a shambles of the civil rights of a handful of very good people. Unfortunately, I am discovering, minute by minute, that I am doing the right thing. That distresses me more."

One hour later, having run through the entire chain of events, the President sat back in his armchair. There had indeed been a number of interruptions.

First, the appearance of federal judge Jimmy Noga who put his signature on the order to extradite Aleksandr Romanov. That was followed about fifteen minutes later by NSA Director Realto returning with the fully translated file from Rostokovich.

The biggest smile was owned by FBI Director Hammett, who came in to the meeting almost on cue, approximately forty-five minutes into the president's monologue. He whispered the findings of his task to President Griffen, who, sadly, did not share Keith's enthusiasm. The voice-prints were most definitely from two different people. The Bureau had been able to compare the Nelson-made tapes with a recording of the previous weeks Republican response to the president's weekly radio address. They had a full five minutes of the current Speaker Hewes with which to work on the week-old tape and had managed to clean up at least the first ten minutes of audio from the college lecture that had been taped some twenty-four years previous. The pencil marking on Nelson's tape was faded, but careful analysis proved that the type of graphite used was more than twenty years old. The bureau had run this test to verify the time frame of the recording, just in case there were any challenges raised. The FBI had also made short work of calling Clemson and asking for a syllabus for the course Nelson attending during that specific semester. Not only was the professor's outline available, but the earnest teaching assistant of record, M. Bradford Hewes, had actually provided the records department with a full transcript of his lectures. The tape and the transcript were word-for-word. The president patted Keith on the back and bade him to take a spot for the remainder of the meeting. Hammett deftly turned his custom-fitted wheelchair and swung over next to where John Realto was seated.

At about a quarter to ten, Nelson excused himself to take a phone call. That call was the icing on the cake. Bud came back into the Oval Office and informed President Griffen of what he had just been told. The president then invited the others to move a little closer to his desk, where Nelson was now dialing a number on the speaker phone and they all proceeded to listen to Agent Hannity explaining what had been discovered in Charleston. Attorney General Gayle Vernon was making frantic notes, while President Griffen was noticeably worried. His slumped shoulders and the lack of sparkle in his eyes were all of the indicators needed to convince the others in the room of his true feelings on what had been revealed. Bud finished the call with a few cordial remarks and disconnected the speaker phone.

The president asked to be excused and motioned to Chief of Staff Josten to step to one side of the room.

"Danny. That Charleston stuff they've found confirms way too much of this. I'd feel better if Fulton were back here, now. Make sure they're getting ready to get out of Madrid, okay?"

"Will do, Jay."

Dan excused himself from the meeting and stepped out of the Oval Office while President Griffen opened the floor to questions.

"I appreciate your including me and the other two justices here," said Chief Justice Terrance Quinlan. "But why are we here? Is it not possible that we are dealing with a simple case of mistaken identity?" he asked, with the emphasis on we.

"Well, Mister Chief Justice, let me answer your second question first. To be honest? I wasn't sure at first. Now, I feel certain that it's more of a case of taken identity. No mistake about it. As to why you are here, we," said the president gesturing to those of his staff present. "My team of advisors, my attorney general and some of my cabinet have walked through this mess. I realized that our country could, in all actuality, have been facing the first true test of the succession laws. We've had sitting vice presidents step into the role of president on a number of occasions. And we've had an opportunity to see how a vice president is appointed instead of elected. In one case, we had an appointed vice president assume the presidency. The constitutional issues on this current situation remain to be seen. If I were to resign, which, by the way, I will gladly do if the outcome of my upcoming federal court date is anything short of complete exoneration and if the other variables I have outlined for you are true to course, then it will interesting to see how the combined house and senate view the ascending of the Speaker of the House to this office."

"The law of succession has been passed and twice modified, most recently as 1979, I believe," spoke the Chief Justice. "The actual testing of this law at the federal level or higher, remains to be seen. The way we have set up our system of checks and balances and our judicial system, all are designed to bring a true and fair hearing to the validity of that which has been passed and accepted as the law of the land. For us to sit here, now and debate the possibility strikes me as a waste of time."

"With all due respect, Justice Quinlan, it was neither my intent or aim to waste yours or anyone's time. I stand right now, before you and these other highly respected members of our government, as a man humbled by an accusation of felony assault and also as a man burdened by what I absolutely believe to be the truth. I have heard the details of this plan for myself, from the man who claims to be the local level control for this. I have also received documentation from this source which, at least in black and white and in plain Russian, supports everything we've been told. And we also have the full version, as you've heard, in the handwriting of the man currently believed to be Brad Hewes. Were I to present this to a federal grand jury, impaneled by Ms. Vernon, I would get a true bill. Of that I am now absolutely certain. I asked you here because the timeline on this is running out of room. Draw a point starting in 1976. Now see where it ends, next week. I am using this end point as a starting position from which you may inevitably need work your way back. We have a start. We have an idea of the ending. It's just the final course of events that have yet to be determined. I wanted you to know, in the event you are called in to adjudicate this matter in any form, so that you would be able to make the most timely, informed decision you've ever passed down. You need this head start. Regardless of my outcome in the former matter that puts me in front of a federal judge next week, my conduct of now, involving international border and treaty violations, will be of concern for you and the other learned members of our government, those of you who will be tasked with deciding whether or not these actions I have authorized were indeed in the best interest of America. I care not if Vice President Fulton assumes office next week. He is extremely well qualified to run this office. It is why I am openly encouraging him to seek this office, through the normal election process, come November of 2000. He is knowledgeable beyond compare in the area of large budgets. He cares about people. He understands how this country has gotten to where it is today better than any other person I know. He can also spell."

Those gathered offered polite chuckles, save Senator Wilson.

"I'm sorry, Davis. I was going for the cheap laugh there and I should not have done that at this point."

"Accepted, Mister President."

"Thank you, Senator. Back to Don Fulton. I do care if he lives to get his chance in the voting booth. From what we've been told. From what we've been shown. And from what I now feel that we will prove beyond any and all doubt, I am afraid that he will not get that chance."

"Mister President?" Justice James Jalbert asked. "The involvement of the Go Team. You did receive clearance from the Joint Chiefs of Staff?"

"Yes, Justice Jalbert, I briefed General Edwards and the Secretary of Defense prior to authorizing the Go Team intrusion into Paris. They in turn briefed the Joint Chiefs who all concurred with the use of the Go Team in this situation. Minimally, we took a valued assistant secretary of state into protective custody. As it turned out, we probably saved his life."

"And did Colonel Menneally raise any doubts about performing this mission?"

"Good and fair question, Justice Jalbert. I did, on the record, remind him that he could, without fear of recourse, refuse to do what we were asking. It was an unlawful order. I asked the man to violate the terms and conditions of several treaties in force with one of our allies, France. He understood that he could tell me to go take a flying leap..."

"Which no doubt would have been spelled with a capital F, Mister President."

"I'm sorry?"

"I went to college with Colonel Menneally. And with the Interpol agent you mentioned, Yearwood. We spent many a long weekend mired down in the combination of doing good work with our fraternity and enjoying a few cold ones while discussing situations not unlike this one. We were all in the ROTC program and almost this exact scenario was brought up in one of our military protocols classes. Given the knowns versus the unknowns, if I remember correctly, Cadet Menneally did respond with a correct refusal to obey an unlawful order. You must have made your case to him convincingly."

"I made it to him truthfully, Justice Jalbert."

"Mister President, if I may?" asked Senator Wilson, the senior senator from Texas and second in Republican party stature only to the speaker of the house.

"Yes, Davis."

"Looking over the documents and photographs you've presented here and the story that you've told us, I'm trying really hard to believe that this is not a partisan politics issue. You yourself have said that you believe the woman problem was a set up. I'm just attempting to keep my thoughts clear as to whom you are referring in regards to the set up."

"I am referring to the Russians, Davis. I wouldn't be going through all of this," the president said, sweeping arm gesture encompassing the room. "If I thought it was party issue."

There was light knock at the door and Joannie stuck her head into the office.

"Excuse me, but Mister Nelson has a phone call. It's important."

"Better go see what's up, Bud," said the President.

"Yes, sir. Please excuse me, Mister Chief Justice."

"Go do what you have to do, Bud."

The room filled with a light laughter as a result of the Chief's light-hearted candor, as well as the familiarity afforded Nelson. Not many within earshot of the long-sitting Supreme Court leader were ever called by their first name, let alone nickname.

Nelson returned in a moment, bearing a look that spoke volumes of the world of shit that had just come down upon them all.

"Bud? What's wrong?" asked the president.

"Which do you want first? The fact that two of my best friends have been severely injured by an exploding cottage? Or that Go Team One is currently taking fire from Russian ground-based missiles?"

thirty-nine

En route to the Finland/Russia border Saturday, April 4, 1998 5:09pm (local)

"Mother Hen, this is Rooster, over."

"Rooster, this is Mother."

"Mother Hen, requesting a quick check of conditions to the western horizon, over."

"Rooster, Mother. Clean and green. Winds from the southwest at fifteen. Gusts to twenty-five."

"Roger, Mother Hen. Anything else I need to know? Over."

"Rooster, Mother. Recommend you maintain current flight level. We detected an artist with a brush earlier, fifteen klicks north. Recommend you hug the other side of the ridge, over."

"Mother Hen, Rooster. Hugging now and thanks. Are you receiving our sat sig, over?"

"Roger, Rooster. Mother has your sat sig five by five. Please let us know when you need to send, over."

"Will do, Mother. Rooster out."

Go Team One was a little more than an hour into their return leg, not quite at the halfway point. Colonel Menneally and Lieutenant Commander Morris were alternating at the controls, with Bob doing the bulk of the flying. The high speed and low level maneuvering took its toll on the senses. A normal flight path in a helicopter was tough enough on one's bottom. Zallonis was helping Murphy hook the video camcorder up to the hand-held digital satellite radio. They wanted to send a backup copy of the lakefront conversation to the circling AWACS via a secure, encrypted satellite link. The radio had been tested and according to the AWACS, Mother Hen, the signal was being captured as strong as could be.

Inside the circling AWACS, the flight crew had been busy on-station all day, monitoring the joint NATO exercises on the ground. The aircraft had been refueled twice and was getting ready to take on one more load of AvGas to allow them to return safely to the airbase in Finland. Once there, the information being retrieved and stored in a wide array of computers could be analyzed by the NATO commanders. The plane's commander, Navy Captain Jim Donahue, had taken a secure call from The Chief of Naval Operations, Admiral Jack Joseph Wright shortly after noon. Donahue had been instructed to stay on station until Rooster had resolved its technical problems. The technical problems, of course, were non-existent. Admiral Wright requested hourly updates personally and Captain Donahue had complied.

Senior Chief Vinny Pilato, a Navy cryptologic technician, had been exclusively assigned to oversee the operation and comms. Pilato had been giving Rooster wind and atmospherics every five minutes, as well as keeping track of what prying eyes were opened on the ground. Onboard the AWACS, several radar technicians were glued to their monitors, keeping an eye on all airborne craft within a five hundred mile radius. One technician, Petty Officer second class Dave Fantasini, was dutifully reporting to Senior Chief Pilato of any radar signals emanating from ground-based positions across the Russian border. He did not know why he was tasked with this, he merely did it. If it made the senior chief happy, then everyone on board was happy. He had picked up the radar signature from a ground based station about seventy miles west of Lake Onega and reported it immediately to Pilato. The AWACS had a number of computers to help identify just about every object on the ground and in the air, as well as what type of electronic signature came from what type of radar system. The detected sweep was from a soviet-made SAM site and the Go Team Helicopter was just beyond the outer circle of the radar. Although the Blackhawk was flying low, less than seventy feet above the trees, the adjustments in speed and altitude required by simply following the contour of the terrain could leave them momentarily high enough to be detected. Pilato had alerted Rooster to the presence of an artist using a broad brush. The term "painting" was associated with a radar system locking onto and identifying a solid object.

"Colonel? We're ready to transmit this up to Mother Hen. Are we good to go?" asked Murphy from the back compartment. Zallonis had finished wiring the connectors from the camcorders digital data output jack to the hand-held satellite radio's auxiliary digital input. The radio was designed for both voice and data, allowing commanders in the field to speak via a secure satellite connection, or to transmit any kind of digital data by way of the separate line input. The digital imaging from the camcorder can be viewed conventionally on any television monitor and can also be played back as a digital stream for viewing on a full-sized computer monitor or even on a laptop screen.

Menneally checked his heads-up display. Their navigation gear was showing them on course, but they were approaching the area where the AWACS had detected the SAM site radar. "Give me two minutes to clear the other side of this ridge, Z. Once we're there, you should have a direct line of sight to send them the package."

"Roger, Colonel. Standing by."

Menneally started to bring the Blackhawk up near the top of the ridge, staying just above the treetops. They'd gone feet dry about ten minutes back and were now hoping to follow this little mountain range straight west, back to Finland.

"Mother Hen, Rooster."

"Rooster, Mother here."

"Looking to slip over the tip here. Anything I need to know, over?"

"Still picking up the paintbrush to your south, Rooster. Haven't seen anything of note, over."

"Rooster's checking the other side of this fence."

"Roger Rooster. Got some extra eyes helping out now."

Menneally and Morris were working as a team now, with Bob doing the flying and Hank ready at the stick while keeping one eye on the Blackhawk's altimeter and one out the window, just in case one of those hundreds-of-years old Russian pine trees were taller than they looked. The Blackhawk was now no more than twenty feet above the treetops, having slowed to one hundred knots. Bob wanted to crest the ridge as low as possible and the slower speed would allow him to drop his altitude to a bare minimum. He could have had the helicopter's rungs brushing the tips of the trees, but it was his first time flying in this particular area. He laughed to himself, finding the thought he was currently entertaining funny.

"What's so funny, M?" asked Hank.

"Just thinking that next time we're here, I'll be able to knock the buds off the top of those pines with confidence."

"Next time? You are a sick man, M. That's why we love you so."

"Mother Hen, Rooster," said Menneally.

"Go ahead, Rooster."

"Heading over the top."

"Good to go here, Rooster," came the reply from the AWACS.

Bob continued his ascent and brought the Blackhawk to the top of the ridge. Just as they did, several of the Blackhawk's electronic alarms began to squeal. The flashing red light indicating they had been targeted by a fire-control radar.

"Rooster, Hen! You've been painted."

"Shit, Bob. They got us," Hank said calmly.

"Mother this is Rooster. Where the hell did that come from?"

"Verifying right now, Rooster. The sweep is from directly below you. Must've got you on a visual. They were not, repeat, not active."

"Going back to the dark side, Mother."

"They'll get you there as well, Rooster."

"Gotta hide from this one first, Mother."

"That's a roger, Rooster."

Onboard the AWACS, Petty Officer Fantasini was frantically fine tuning his scope to make sure the Blackhawk didn't fly directly into anything else.

"Senior Chief! Rooster's been lit up."

"How the hell did that happen, Dave?" asked Pilato.

"They were topping the ridge to avoid the one we knew about to the south and they must've gone right over a mobile site. I guess it was a visual at first, then they painted 'em up."

"What do we have for overhead recon? Anywhere for them to hide?"

"The last pass was just over an hour ago. I've been asking the home office for a look-see, but haven't gotten anything yet."

Senior Chief Pilato put on a headset.

"Cap'n? Vinny here."

"Yo, Vinny. What's up?" asked Donahue from the cockpit.

"Bad news. Bad guys popped Rooster. Lit 'em up like a Christmas tree. We need the latest overhead view of this area to see if there's anyplace they might drop down into for a moment or two."

"Did we ask for a copy?"

"Yes, sir. The home office is either on a coffee break or they don't know how badly we need that photo."

"How much time do they have?"

"Not much, sir. They flew right over one SAM site while trying to avoid a different one just ahead of them. They're about to get whacked, sir."

"Comms," Donahue said addressing his communications post.

"Comms, aye, skipper."

"Comms, I need CNO secure now."

"Roger, Cap'n."

There was a long, fifteen second wait.

"Cap'n, comms. CNO on line, sir."

"Thanks, comms. Admiral? Donahue here. Rooster was shifting course to avoid a hot SAM site we picked up and flew right over another. They managed to shift back to their original position, but they'll be heading straight for the one we know is there. Langley is taking their damn sweet time about getting us the last pass pics, sir. We need what they've got to give these guys a place to hide."

"You'll have the photo in sixty seconds, Captain. Keep this line open."

"Aye, aye, sir. Donahue standing by."

Flicking the headset comm switch, Donahue was back on the aircraft's intercom system.

"Senior Chief? CNO says we'll have the image in sixty seconds. Advise Rooster."

"Aye, aye, sir. Standing by." Pilato keyed his external comms. "Rooster, Mother Hen."

Menneally replied. "Go ahead, Mother. Give me some good news."

"We're getting a new look at the property right now, Rooster. Trying to see if there's someplace close where a rooster could make like a fox."

"I'll gladly crawl into a fox hole right now, Mother."

"Stay low and slow. We're watching both sides right now. The guy behind you is looking like crazy. The one in front of you is showing a bit more interest. We have all of your transferred material, by the way."

"Roger the material, Mother. Eyes only at the direction of POTUS."

"Say again, Rooster?"

"Eyes only per POTUS, Mother. Got any questions, call him yourself."

"Roger, Rooster."

Hank was smiling at that last exchange. "That certainly messed with his mind, you know. Not many people get to drop a name like that."

"Hank, we're just practicing the golden rule. C.Y.A. Now, find me a hole to drop into if we need it. I can't wait for Langley to decide to help us out."

Hank grabbed a set of binoculars and began scanning the lower edges of the ridge, looking for a clearing or a tunnel that might accommodate the Blackhawk. Bob was tempted to activate his own fire control system and radar. Once they did, the ground sites would have no problem locking in on the electronic trail from the equipment. Go Team One would only do that in the event they needed to activate their counter-measures, both physical and electronic. The electronic counter-measures, ECM, were designed to help make the helicopter look bigger than it actually was, as well as occasionally throw a wide enough sideband to make them appear a little bit more to the left or right on the radar screen of the firing system that might be tracking them. That gave them the chance of evading a missile that might be locked on and looking to take them down.

"Colonel? I think I've got something. Two o'clock, low."

"Take the stick, Hank. Let me take a look."

Menneally took the binoculars and zoomed in on the spot Hank had seen. It looked like a small hunting camp of some sort. Just a cabin, with a good sized clearing to the side. That'd be a big enough spot to put the Blackhawk down.

"What do you think, Bob?"

"Looks big enough to set down and hide for a few. Let's see what Mother thinks. Mother Hen, Rooster."

"Go Rooster."

"We see a small cabin and clearing about four klicks west. Anything from the home office yet?"

"Just receiving the image now, Rooster. Recommend you head directly for that spot in the meantime. It'll get you closer to where you want to be. We're checking the overhead view now."

"Roger, Mother. Keep me posted. My ETA to the clearing is two minutes."

On board the AWACS, Senior Chief Pilato and Petty Officer Fantasini were checking the high resolution photo taken from the overhead reconnaissance satellite. They now could see the SAM site nestled into the top of the ridge, the one the Blackhawk had accidentally overflown. The SAM site to the southwest was also visible, four missiles were out and on the rails, pointing east. Suddenly, Fantasini's scope started flashing with several warning lights, accompanied by an audible beeping.

"Aw, shit, senior chief. They've launched."

Pilato pressed the button on his headset.

"Rooster, Mother. You've got company. We mark one bird free, repeat, one bird free, coming from ten o'clock. The southern site must've marked you. Recommend you hit the ground and pray."

"Mother, Rooster. Appreciate the recommendation, but I'm not getting blown up sitting on the ground. We're going to see if we can slip over the tip of the ridge. Can you find out why they're firing on a NATO IFF? And have you got any good spots on the other side, over?"

Senior Chief Pilato was scanning the photograph. "Rooster, Mother. We see a highway tunnel on the other side of the ridge, about seven klicks north-northwest. You want to try that?"

"Going to have to try something other than nothing, Mother. We're going active on our gear."

"Roger, Rooster. Understand you're lighting up. We're talking with their ground control now, by the way. Some young officer got a little itchy, but they're following their SOP. We've got two guys on the comm link with them doing their best to get them to not blow you out of the sky. Good luck."

Menneally flipped the switches to the onboard radar systems and activated the electronic countermeasures. The Blackhawk increased speed, still hugging the treetops. The missile-warning klaxon was now sounding, the yellow warning lights adding to the attention-getting distraction. The onboard radar scope showed the inbound missile at ten miles and closing fast. They had no more than fifteen seconds to clear the ridge and hope that there was enough room to hide on the other side.

"Murph? Z? Secure our passengers and get ready to hang on. We've been locked onto, plus we've got an incoming. It's going to get real bumpy in here in a minute. Hank? Are we set to deploy the chaff dispensers?"

"Ready to roll, skipper. Let's get over to the other side and see what happens."

Menneally took the Blackhawk up to one hundred seventy knots and got as low to the treetops as he dared. The scope showed the missile less than five seconds away. Looking to his left as he cleared the mountain, he could see the SAM closing in on them, the white of the missile's body standing stark against the deep green of the tall Russian pine trees.

"Hank, deploy counter-measures," ordered Bob.

"Chaff one and two deployed."

The missile had been at first targeted to the electronic image on the ground control's targeting radar. The electronic countermeasures from the Blackhawk had been designed to keep the missile guessing just where dead center was. The fluctuating electronic pulses being emitted by the helicopter's ECM gear gave the impression that there were multiple aircraft where there was only the one containing Go Team One. The shifting signals made it appear that there might be as many as three, then just two, then three again, then only one. The ground control operator might try to interpret these images and launch multiple missiles, but fortunately for the Blackhawk, the visual had confirmed only one missile launched. The missile would have been initially launched, with its targeting systems locked to the center of the radar images. Once it got within ten miles, the missile would then be switched to target a heat source, in this case, the Blackhawk's engine. The manual chaff dispensing countermeasures released from the helicopter would create both an intense, momentary heat signature, as well as a sky full of metal shrapnel. The missile should instantly track onto the larger heat signature from the exploding canisters and the resulting shrapnel should do some damage to the missile itself. At least that's how it was designed on paper. Once in the air, the missile did not always do as the airborne target might have wished. Menneally was often quoting Murphy's law, which made it more ironic for Go Team One since Murphy was usually riding along in the back of the helicopter. Murphy, however, was just as quick to point out that missiles don't read books and that in turn made it harder for any device to perform as they, the targets, desired.

Murphy and Zallonis both had their eyes peered behind to see if the metal-filled containers did their job. The two small white flashes of light indicated that the canisters exploded as expected. The large flash of light that followed showed that the missile fell for the ruse.

"Hang on, Colonel. Here comes the blast wave," said Murphy from the back.

Menneally and Morris each had a hand on the helicopter's control stick, Bob flying, Hank ready to help steady the craft. The wave from the exploding SAM caught up to the Blackhawk and shook it violently, sending it downward momentarily. Menneally used his rudder-pedals and increased the backward pull on the stick in his attempt to get a little higher above the ground. The helicopter continued to shudder, but smoothed out as the aircraft got over more open air, once they'd cleared the topmost portion of the ridge.

"Rooster, Mother Hen," said Pilato from the AWACS.

"Mother, Rooster, go," Menneally replied.

"Rooster, be advised that your NATO IFF is squawking the proper code and that they fired on you anyway. The Russian ground station is attempting to raise you on the NATO frequency of the day. We've been advising them that your comms are out, per your report earlier in the day. Suggest you head down real low, due west, as fast as you can. We'll try to buy you some time, over."

"Mother, Rooster. We'd appreciate not getting any more missiles fired up our butts. Please keep me advised, over."

"Rooster, we'll be right here. Both sites have you targeted. Suggest you keep your ECM's active, but power down your radar now."

"Radar powered down now, Mother. Request immediate advisory to turn it back on if needed, over."

"Roger, Rooster. Hit the gas and go like hell. We've got all eyes up here looking your way."

"Thanks, Mother."

Menneally increased his airspeed to almost one hundred seventy five knots, with an above-ground altitude of seventy-five feet. That put him no more than thirty feet off of the treetops. The missile-warning lights continued to flash, but the sound had been muted. The ground radar systems still had the Blackhawk targeted from both known locations. For all they knew, Go Team One could be targeted from four or five different sites.

"Mother, Rooster."

"Roger, Rooster. What's up?"

"You got a distance for me to the border, over?"

"We show you approaching one hundred klicks, Rooster. Recon shows the SAM sites off of your six and nine o'clock still with missile-lock on you. Be advised that POTUS is involved with keeping you airborne right now. Recommend you keep it low, but put that pedal to the metal. The more distance you close between where you are and where you want to be, the better off you'll be."

"Roger, Mother. Keep me posted. Update every twenty klicks, please."

"Roger, Rooster. Will mark your progress every twenty. Will give you immediate missile-launch notification as well."

"Would prefer not hearing of any more missile-launches, Mother. But thanks for keeping us in your thoughts," Bob managed to convey the tense smile plastered on his face.

Menneally turned to Morris and asked "When was the last time we went to church, Hank?"

"Didn't we go one Sunday morning back in Bosnia?"

"I hope that mass came with a six-month warranty. Z? How are our passengers doing?"

Zallonis responded. "The big guy is just sitting still. He's a little pasty from the blast wave. I think he understands that his own guys are trying to bring him down. Mister Rostokovich is still unconscious, though. His bleeding has slowed, but his respiration and pulse are both good. The guy's in pretty good shape, Colonel."

"Mike? What do we have for weapons if we need 'em?"

"Enough to knock off a convenience store back home, Colonel. We've got a thousand rounds boxed and clipped and we've got one shoulder launcher with two missiles. The MD60 is locked and loaded. We've got more than ten thousand rounds in reserve for that. Plus the 8 Hellfire's ready to rock and roll, sir."

"How many countermeasures do we have left? Two?"

"Roger that, sir. We used two and have two left."

"Bob?" asked Hank. "What say we transfer fuel from the externals to the main and then we'll have those tanks to pop-off if we need to come up with a little extra speed or a back-up countermeasure."

"Good idea, Hank. Murph? You think we could hit those externals with the 60 if we were to pop them off and get them to go boom?"

"Like shooting moose in Maine, Colonel. You thinkin' we drop the externals and light 'em up if we need an extra countermeasure or two?"

"You read my mind, Mike. You read my mind."

"Rooster, Mother Hen."

"Go ahead, Mother."

"You're eighty klicks, repeat eight-zero klicks from the border. Still being targeted from the hilltop singers off your six. The guy on the other side of the mountain seems to have lost you. They're looking everywhere, but we don't think they have you. The ridge is going to turn southwest in less than twenty klicks. That should help you hide from the guy off your six. There is another missile site to your north, however. They've just started their sweeps, but I think you're too low and a hair too far south for them to get you. Maintain flight level and speed. We'll keep you posted."

"Roger, Mother. Thanks."

Murphy had put on a life line and harness to man the MD 60 machine gun. If they had to, they could deploy the external tank with the push of a button from the cockpit. Murphy was a damn good shot. Deadly with a sidearm, long rifle or big ass gun such as the 60. He was more than sure he'd put a hundred rounds on the mark to make the cast-off auxiliary fuel tank blow. The flash and metal shrapnel would be as effective as an onboard countermeasure. Once the tank was ejected, Murph would use a few tracers to find his range, allowing the Blackhawk to put another few seconds between itself and the resulting explosion. The remaining gas from inside the tank would create more than enough of a heat signature to draw the attention of any incoming SAM.

"Colonel? We're harnessed and ready back here. Has the fuel been transferred?"

Hank replied. "Yeah, boys. We're empty on the outside and we've got that nice full-belly on the inside."

"Rooster, Mother Hen," Pilato called from the AWACS.

"Mother, Rooster. Go," Bob responded.

"Sixty klicks, repeat, six-zero klicks to the border. We've been able to get the ground sites to listen to reason. Be advised that you are still locked on your six. The site to your north is close to acquiring you. You're still just out of range. The mountains are starting that southwestern turn right about now. We'll keep you posted."

"Roger, Mother Hen. How did you get them to listen, over?"

"We told them you have a cellphone and that we are in contact with you. There's some general on the ground though who's not that impressed. Be advised that there are high level negotiations going on right now to keep you from becoming scrap metal, over."

"Roger, understand all, Mother. We're starting the southwestern turn, flight level still seven-five, airspeed one seven five, over."

"Roger, Rooster. Will advise at forty klicks, over."

"Thanks, Mother."

The Blackhawk's ECM gear was doing its magic, keeping the Russian ground radar guessing as to how many aircraft there were and just where the targets actually were. The external tanks were wired and prepared for jettisoning if needed. The NATO IFF transponder was still functioning and the missile-warning lights were still flashing.

"Bob? Do you think we're going to make it?" asked Morris.

"I can't be sure, Hank. I just can't be sure. Let's hope the diplomats can do some magic."

"Colonel?" yelled Zallonis. "There's another flash from down there."

"Where, Z?"

"Coming up fast off your side. Nine o'clock and moving like a sonofabitch. Shit! It must've been a hand-held."

"Mother, Rooster," Bob called while twisting his head to get a view.

"Rooster, Mother. We see it."

"Mother, Rooster. Deploying port side countermeasure."

"Roger, Rooster."

Hank hit the button to deploy the remaining port side countermeasure while Bob leaned forward onto the stick and nosed the Blackhawk down. As the Blackhawk increased in speed, the missile reached the top of it's arc and began to nose over after them. The crew of Go Team One said a silent prayer as Menneally took the helicopter down to a flight level of forty feet off the ground, the missile still following them, the countermeasure ready to do its thing.

forty

Paris, France   Saturday, April 4, 1998   2:25pm (local)

Secretary of State Julie Paparelli had been at the diplomatic game for over twenty years. Having started as a college intern in the state department after her junior year at Harvard, she quickly showed an above average aptitude in dealing with delicate issues. She had been offered and accepted, a staff position before she finished her senior year studies. She further showed an amazing ability to help turn a seemingly-dire situation into a workable one. Sitting in on her first staff meeting, she made two suggestions that were at first taken lightly by some regarding the ongoing roundtable discussions on the Middle East, but were noted and acted upon by the then-Secretary of State. Two months later, she was elevated to an assistant secretary of state and was invited to be present at the signing of the Camp David accords.

In early 1979, she left Washington at the request of the of the secretary to become interim ambassador to Columbia. Six months later, she was asked to step into the role of ambassador to China, again temporarily. Once the Reagan administration had settled in, she returned to Washington and her role as an assistant secretary of state. During this period, she had become a master of that in which she had previously been superb: The art of negotiating. Being able to turn a negative into a positive was a talent that very few people possessed. Having witnessed her adeptness at putting out fires, then-Governor Jay Griffen made copious notes on Julie. The New England coastal states were embroiled in a battle over fishing rights and limits with the Canadians. Paparelli had come up with a compromise plan in short order that kept tempers from flaring and kept both country's fishing industries working. Two weeks after the election, President-elect Griffen had asked Julie if she was ready to take over as Secretary of State. Three weeks after the inauguration, Julie was confirmed easily by both the house and senate.

Now, just over seven years into her tenure, she was faced with a dilemma that left her feeling uncertain for the first time in her professional career. Her orders from President Griffen had been to first try to slip the damn piece of paper into the pile and hope it was initialed without notice. She was morally and ethically split on how to best proceed. Morally, if the Hewes-Moore story was true as told, then the Russians be damned. Ethically, however, she felt honor-bound to explain the situation and simply play hardball on the matter. If the Russians wished to continue receiving large amounts of money from the International Monetary Fund and if they wished to become a part of the new, European regional economic community, then Prime Minister Bakunin would have to sign off on this little deal-breaker.

Julie pulled the document off of her fax machine and studied it carefully. It was a simple agreement to allow the United States government to take into custody one Aleskandr Romanov for crimes against the people of the United States, specifically murder in the first degree. It was signed by both Attorney General Vernon and Federal Judge James Noga of the U.S. District Court in Washington, DC.

She turned to open the door to head into her meeting with Prime Minister Bakunin when she was somewhat startled by a knock on the door.

Opening the door, she saw her personal secretary, Stacy Downs, visibly upset and holding a document of some sort.

"Stacy? What's the matter?"

Sobbing, Stacy handed the paper to Judy. "Th-This."

The secretary of state took the document and read it carefully.

"So, I guess we know what happened to Marvin, don't we," Julie said with a bit of a stage-sigh. "When will these groups learn that they can accomplish more at their own voting booths than by kidnapping foreign nationals? I'm sorry to say that there will nothing we can do right now about this, Stacy. Our first priority is to get Russia onboard for this economic package. Then and only then, can we spend some time seeing what we can do. I'll call this into Washington. You go and calm down a bit, okay? I'm sure he'll be all right, but I'm going to need you now, more than ever."

"Yes, ma'am. I will," Stacy sniffed.

"Is Bakunin here yet?"

"Not yet. Hi-his embassy called and said he'd be here in about five minutes. Poor Mister Moore."

"Stacy. Please, get back in the game here, girlfriend. He knew that he ran the risks of being a target every time he stepped onto the soil of a nation not controlled by the United States, just like the rest of us. It was his own lapse in good judgment that sent him out carousing last night. He's a big boy and he'll have to fend for himself until we work something out with this group, *Faction du l'argent*. Go get a cup of tea or a soda or something and then make sure we're all set for the Russian delegation."

Julie walked past Stacy and offered a pat on the shoulder in an attempt to comfort her. Then, she went down to the embassy's communications center where she would call the White House and inform them that she had indeed received the document.

At about a quarter to three, Secretary of State Paparelli and Prime Minister Vladimir Bakunin sat down to finish going over the documents that would pave the way for the Russians to join the remainder of Europe. The proposed economic union was designed to help struggling nations keep even with the stronger, more developed ones. The common currency that would be adopted, the EU, would make trans-border business transactions more equitable, making the weaker nation's money worth more as opposed to regular currency exchange rates. It made sense for Europe, currently home to existing industrial and political powerhouses such as Germany and Great Britain, as well as emerging new democracies, such as Russia and her former Soviet Union siblings. There had been one or two sticking points that Julie had managed to remove or modify to the liking of Vladimir, yet retained the intent of the overall agreement. Small concessions went a long way, Paparelli knew. Let the other guy think they're getting something and everyone's happy.

"Now that we've put that behind us, Vladimir, there's one, not so small item to be addressed."

"Julie? I thought we'd worked out everything already. Didn't we just sign-off on all of that? Russia is more than willing and ready, to... how do you say it? Jump in with both feet?"

"That's the correct expression, Mister Prime Minister. It's just that there is something that has come up, only recently, as a matter of fact. It seems that certain people of your country have been up to some very nasty things in my country. Things of which my president is now aware and is currently undertaking steps to set them right. Allow me to walk you through a scenario and then I'd like you to tell me how you and Russia might respond. Would that be all right?"

Now very interested, Vladimir responded simply. "Yes."

"Let's assume that a foreign nation which had been at odds, ideologically, with your country for years, devised an ingenious plan to crumble your government from the inside."

"That would be implausible, if not impossible, Julie."

"Uh-uh. No interruptions just yet, Vladimir. Again, assuming what I said happened actually transpired. And that along the way, this foreign nation directed some of her assets to commit major crimes."

Julie paused a moment to take a sip from a bottle of water, allowing Vladimir to digest this scenario in small bits. His English was good. Certainly better than her Russian. She needed to formulate her thoughts into simple words and sentences to avoid any idiomatic confusion.

"Let's also assume that these major crimes were actually committed on your sovereign soil, against your sovereign citizens."

"Julie, if I may ask. What type of major crime is included in this fable you wish for me to, er, understand."

413

"Murder."

The pause was intentional. The silence was overpowering. The look on Vladimir's face was what Julie had needed to see. The message was no longer being dismissed.

"Murder? Are you suggesting that you have knowledge of this crime being carried out on Russian soil against Russian people?" Vladimir was almost outraged at the thought that the American secretary of state would know of this without telling him sooner.

"No, Vladimir. We have knowledge of this crime being committed against the United States. In the United States. The crime of murder has been committed against at least two known citizens of the United States. By agents of your country."

"When were these crimes committed, Secretary Paparelli. You know that the current government does not officially sanction human assets doing simple information gathering anymore, let alone to bring matters such as these to a physical level. Most of our information is gleaned in the same manner as your country now obtains theirs, electronically. You know what a twelve year old can do with a computer now."

Julie smiled at that. She had a twelve year old at home, actually upstairs here in the embassy. A very precocious twelve year old at that. "Yes, Vladimir. I know all too well. However, these events are now only coming to light as the main objective of this mission is close at hand for the agents of the KGB who have been involved."

"The KGB? Julie, you can't be serious? The KGB was disbanded and even the files made public, as a show of good faith by the new regime. You yourself were there. You toured the headquarters. The dungeons. You saw the grieving families of those who perished there. You even hugged one woman. Why would we even possibly think to sanction anything by the KGB?"

"The crimes of murder were committed over twenty years ago, Vladimir. We are in no way thinking that President Yevchenko or any current member of his cabinet have anything to do with that. Do you understand?"

"Da. Continue, please," Vladimir was looking a little stressed at this point.

"The crimes were committed by assassins from the KGB, directly under orders of Aleksandr Romanov."

Again, a moment for this to register and Julie sipped while Vladimir nodded.

"Romanov has been running and funding these operatives in my country since 1976. Some of these operatives have actually reached notable positions of standing in my country. In my country's government."

Vladimir's eyes widened at that.

"One of these operatives was even one of my assistants. These agents were good. Very good. And very, very patient. Unfortunately, for them, the details are known and the players are being very quietly rounded up."

"I assume then, that the matter will be handled privately?"

"No, Vladimir. That is not the way my country operates. Not yesterday. Not today. Not tomorrow. The matter will be handled quietly. If our press corps gets wind of it, then the details will be released for mass distribution. For now, we would prefer that, although it will be public knowledge, the public not know. Not just yet, at least. Just as you would no doubt want to try to do, we will try to analyze exactly how all of this came to transpire and then set up procedures to prevent this from happening in the future. No need in giving anyone, yourself included, any bright ideas. You do understand that, I hope."

"Yes, Julie. I do," Vladimir said, sitting back in his chair, fingers to his temples, thinking. "So what's in it for us?"

"Before I go there, Vladimir, I need to know how receptive you are to letting us have Romanov. I'm showing nothing until I sense a willingness. I'll let you know for starters that you will not have to deal with the wrath of the world for allowing this attack on the American governmental to happen. If you insist on dealing before giving, then we will disclose all and you and your country will find yourself back behind your own iron curtain, vilified in the eyes of the democratic societies you which to join. Now, with that said, I hope you understand from where I am approaching this. I know where you are, so I don't feel that's a problem. You have what I desire. I have the ability to help you get what you need. That willingness to provide you with what your country requires hinges solely on your signature on this document, right now."

"Julie. I am going to hand over a national treasure in the form of Aleksandr Romanov before you even consider making this worth my while?"

"Vimka, I care for you and enjoy working with you. The clock has started. We have three minutes for me to call my boss and inform him of your decision."

Julie sat back in her chair and reached for her water bottle, glancing at her watch. A dangerous game of poker had begun. It was a game that Secretary of State Paparelli never lost. Never.

Vladimir closed his eyes in thought. One minute passed and still he'd shown no sign of reaching a conclusion. No facial expression to give any indication in which direction he might be leaning. Julie was glad his eyes were closed. She was unsure of herself in how long she could hold her game face, a steel gaze with her steel-blue eyes. She gently sipped her water, checking her watch. Two minutes. Vladimir took a deep breath, eyes still closed, fingers massaging the sides of his head. Julie stood, the sound of her chair moving bringing Bakunin back to reality, his eyes locking in on her as she walked to the desk where a telephone sat. She sat on the edge of the desk, her mid-length skirt showing just enough of a well-toned calf to catch his interest.

"Thirty seconds, Vimka. I have to make this call. We have things in motion already and we are also aware that Mister Romanov may be leaving your country as we speak. Yes, we've been watching him, but because of his high level assets, we can do nothing without your signature on that paper. Ten seconds, Vladimir. Do what's right. You will not be sorry."

Julie picked up the phone, dangling the receiver from her right hand, left forefinger extended over the phone's keypad.

Vladimir took out his pen and slid the document closer to him on the room's coffee table. He re-read it and set the pen to paper.

"We have a deal?" he asked.

"We have a deal in that I will not send you and your country back to the dark ages, financially and socially, if that's what you mean," responded Julie. "And we have now a mutual understanding that will help motivate me to help you stay in the good graces with the IMF."

Just as Vladimir was about to sign the document, the knock at the door was followed by the door opening and Stacy stuck her head inside.

"Prime Minister Bakunin? You have an urgent phone call. Line two there on the desk, sir."

Vladimir signed the document and walked to the desk. Julie passed him the phone and offered him a warm embrace before she depressed the button for the holding call.

Vladimir answered his call, asking several questions in Russian before placing the call on hold. Looking at Julie, he asked. "Are you already in possession of Comrade Romanov?"

"No, my country is not in possession of Romanov." Julie knew this to be basically true. She had been made aware that persons who may or may not be American are in the company of Romanov, but she was not certain that her country was in possession of the man. At the least, he was still leaving Russia, bound for England. "This document is the instrument we need to accomplish that, Vladimir. Why do you ask?"

"This is my army's Chief General Yuri Kashinkoff on the phone. One of his ground-based commands is currently tracking an outbound helicopter, presumed American."

"What of the IFF codes? Surely all aircraft in and around Europe are now equipped with the transponders?"

"It's squawking a NATO code, but the aircraft is, upon a visual sighting, not carrying any markings whatsoever. If it is yours, I can tell them to let it pass. But, if it is yours, we will have much to discuss, Secretary Paparelli. Our troops have already launched one surface-to-air missile at it. The helicopter was lucky. It will not be so lucky against a full-battery of missiles."

Julie had to think and do so quickly. Vladimir never addressed her as Secretary Paparelli. Always Julie. Or when being somewhat formal, Madam Secretary. He was not a happy man. If she said yes, the United States would have much to pay for the use of the Russian airspace. If she said no, the helicopter would be knocked from the sky without so much as a second thought. The former presented a volatile situation from which the United States would be unable to extract itself cleanly. They would be considered worse than the old Soviet Union for overtly violating treaties and boundaries, for kidnapping and unlawful search and seizure. The latter would result in the loss of life of some fine American servicemen. And one Russian son of a bitch.

"I told you Romanov had friends in high American places and that we believed he was planning on leaving Russia. I could guess that Romanov is on board that helicopter, but it would only be a guess, Vimka. And the helicopter could be American. If I am not mistaken, our country, yours and the others are involved in a large NATO exercise in Finland. If this helicopter is part of that military exercise, it could also be one of yours, could it not? But I can not say for certain without checking back at my end."

Vladimir spoke into the phone and put the line on hold.

"You have exactly three minutes, Julie."

Julie picked up the phone on the coffee table and dialed the president's direct number.

"President Griffen's office, Mrs. Blackstone speaking."

"Joannie? It's Julie Paparelli. It's urgent I speak directly with the president, please."

"Just a moment, Madam Secretary."

Julie heard the line go on hold. Moments later, the president picked up.

"President Griffen here. What's up, Julie?"

"Mister President, we have a possible sticky situation here. Can we confirm or deny an American helicopter currently in Russian airspace? We have two minutes to provide an answer to Prime Minister Bakunin. If it is ours, it puts us in a tenable position. If it is not ours, then the Russians will take it down."

"Does he know we have Romanov?"

"No, sir."

"Do they know where Romanov is?"

"Not for certain right now, sir."

"I know time is short, Julie and that Vladimir is right there with you. Just keep looking positive as I'm sure you are. What do they know?"

"What Prime Minister Bakunin has been told is that it's a non-marked helicopter using a NATO IFF code."

"Tell him that one of the NATO helos developed navigation and communication gear problems three hours ago and that the full NATO exercise has been looking for them. Now that the sun is nearing the horizon there, it's possible for them to use the sun as a guide to head back west where they belong. It's the one chance we have to let them clear Russian airspace. We have heard from them and they are under fire. They also say they need another fifteen minutes to cross the Finland border."

"Vladimir? President Griffen has informed me that there was a NATO helicopter involved in a joint NATO exercise in Finland that developed navigation and communication gear problems about three hours ago. It is possible that it might be American, but with the extent of the electronic failures, it is not possible to verify that at this time. The president has asked me to ask you to allow it to finish its transit. Now that the sun is nearing the horizon, the pilots can better navigate west, back to Finland."

"You have two minutes, Secretary Paparelli. I will consult my with my general."

Julie went back to her phone conversation with the president while Bakunin, at the office's large desk, consulted with his army's General Kashinkoff.

"Julie? What's going on?" asked President Griffen.

Julie turned her back to Vladimir and spoke at a barely audible whisper. "Well, sir, Prime Minister Bakunin is consulting with General Kashinkoff about whether or not to allow them to finish their crossing."

"What did we have to tell them, Julie? This could put us in a world of hurt, you know."

"Mister President, I told him what was required to get our message across and to get the order signed. Pen was on the paper as Vladimir got the call from Russia. They know that Romanov is wanted by us for murder and more. They know that we can make their life in the E.U. more comfortable. They know that we can try and keep their link to the IMF open as well. They know of no specifics at our end, other than the fact that Russian persons are masquerading as

Americans of note. We also played hardball. I promised to make their recovery from the embarrassment with which they'd be dealing a living hell that would make the Stalin years seem like a day at EuroDisney. On a bright note, the paper is signed."

"Can you get that faxed out of there?"

"Not while he's standing right here, Mister President."

"Offer to help bust up the stateside version of their Russian Mafia. If we clean up our end, then they won't lose so much of the international money to the bad guys."

"That is, or should I say, was, going to be my thank-you gift to them for the signing. I offered only to keep them from reverting to a Stalin-like existence."

"You got the paper signed without giving up anything?"

"Nothing more than a little information, Mister President. I was hoping to really make them feel good by helping to clean up the money trail."

Vladimir cleared his throat, getting Julie's attention. "We have less than sixty seconds, Julie."

"Excuse me, Mister President," Julie covered the phone's mouthpiece, her shoulders shrugged with a somewhat pleading look on her face. "Vimka, my president is doing what he can right now to find out whose helicopter it is. What of your end?"

"General Kashinkoff informs me that there are two missile batteries tracking this helicopter. The helicopter is now less than fifty miles from the border. We need an answer from you. Our airspace is being violated and your country would react in no lesser fashion."

Julie removed her hand from the mouthpiece and spoke once again to the president. "President Griffen? Have we found anything yet?"

"There is an AWACS that is command-control for the NATO op-ex. Tell the prime minister that the NATO aircraft has been tracking them for over an hour now. And, one second, Julie. Aw, shit. They've fired another missile at them. It's probably from a shoulder-launcher. They'll never get out, Julie."

"Vladimir? President Griffen has said that the NATO exercise is being monitored from above by an AWACS aircraft and that they believe it is the craft which reported technical problems several hours ago. They were thought to be landing on the Finland side of the border to avoid just such an issue, but apparently, they were mistaken and strayed into your airspace."

"Are we at least saying that this is a NATO aircraft?"

"We are saying that we firmly believe this to be the NATO helicopter that developed problems. The AWACS confirms the IFF signal as authentic. The AWACS now also confirms another missile launch. They're guessing it's from a portable launching device."

Vladimir spoke to General Kashinkoff and hung up the phone.

"Julie, my friend. General Kashinkoff wishes no ill to come to a NATO aircraft, especially since we've only recently, er, how would I say this? Recently been invited to the dance?"

Julie nodded, in agreement and relief. "Yes, Vimka. And we're glad you are picking up the steps so easily and so expertly. Allow me one moment?"

Vladimir nodded as Julie went back to the phone and President Griffen.

"They're backing off, sir. General Kashinkoff accepts the IFF code verification as acceptable and authentic. Thank God for the AWACS was on station for the exercise. Did the second missile miss?"

"AWACS reports that the Blackhawk's countermeasures worked again. The last missile is no longer an issue. Tell Vladimir I offer my heartfelt thanks."

"Why not tell him yourself, sir? Would help to make the rest of this easier."

"Put him on, Julie."

Julie held out the phone to Bakunin. "President Griffen would like a word with you, Vladimir. Will you?"

Vladimir strolled over to the coffee table where Julie stood and took the phone. "Yes, President Griffen?"

"Prime Minister Bakunin. I can not express my thanks at your handling what could have been an uncomfortable situation for both of our sides. The last missile has been destroyed by the defensive countermeasures from the helicopter. I'm not sure if the crew on board that helicopter is American, British or even Russian, but I do know that there will be several families spared the agony of grieving over the loss of loved ones. You have my thanks, Vladimir. I will see you in a few days to thank you personally, right?"

"You are welcome, Mister President. And yes, I look forward to seeing you as well."

"Do you still enjoy a good cigar?"

"Da. Perhaps we can share a smoke and a few stories?"

"You can count on it, Mister Prime Minister. Thank you again, for your help and your understanding."

"Do svidaniya, President Griffen."

Vladimir hung up the phone and slid back onto the sofa, crossing his legs and tossing his arm along the top edge of the sofa. Julie came and sat next to him. "Vimka, thank you."

"I am not stupid, Julie. You know more than you wish to tell. That is how we do what we do. So," he said raising an eyebrow. "What's in it for me?"

Julie slapped his leg and laughed. "You're still a wicked man when it comes to being a man, Vladimir. But seriously? Please listen to this and let me know what you think. It will involve a large amount of trust on both of our sides."

Julie stood, the signed order to extradite Aleksandr Romanov in her hands.

"First, though, if you'll excuse me for just a moment, I need to get this to the proper authorities. I'll only be a minute," Julie said.

Vladimir offered his permission with a friendly wave of his hand. Julie opened the door and handed the document to Stacy, the White House fax number on a yellow sticky-note attached to the form. Julie came back inside and grabbed a legal pad from the desk, along with her pen.

"Thank you, Vimka. Now, we need to get some of your money back to you."

"Money? My money?"

"Yes. We know that the reason so much of your country's economic recovery has been slowed to almost a stop is due to the theft of funds by organized crime. Most of the pilfered cash winds up in our banks. We have been working for over a year, tracing much of the money by way of international wire transfers to the American bank accounts used by what we call the Russian Mafia. We have seized control of an amount of money which will no doubt be a welcome sum to you and your people. The people who most need it."

"How much money?"

"At last tally, it's just over a billion dollars, American."

Vladimir smiled and sat forward, hands folded across his knees. "That's a lot of money, Julie. What do you need?"

"Two things. One, the secure bank account numbers for us to transfer the money back to you. Secure, Vladimir. Not controlled by your treasury. They are the leak. You will need to deal with them. But in the meantime, we can put this money into an account accessed only by you and President Yevchenko, where it will earn millions in interest while you do some housekeeping."

"We can do that, Julie. What is the other?"

"This is kind of a condition. Please understand it is no way a penalty, but merely as a safeguard for the investment made by the members of the International Monetary Fund who initially signed off on this money the first time around. The IMF has requested that you allow an international team of accountants to help you square away your business departments, including your treasury. This team is capable of everything from security background checks of prospective employees to training your new hires on how to best safeguard against any future abuses. This is a deal-breaker, Vladimir. Before the money can be returned, you must agree to this. The team of advisors will be there to advise and help. They will initially have control on how the disbursement of funds is handled. Once they feel that you have taken the proper steps to making sure that the money is used for your country's infra-structure, instead of providing luxurious lifestyles for common criminals, then you will be on your own. You will be able to provide your people the one thing they truly need to build a stronger Russia, money and guidance."

Vladimir considered this for a moment and nodded his agreement.

"This is acceptable, Julie. The organized crime factions have been a thorn in our side for far too long. If you can indeed take them out of the equation from your side of the ocean, then we can take the steps needed to clean up our end. Do we have time to go for a late lunch? It's almost three-thirty."

"Yes, I think we do have the time, Vladimir. Let's go."

forty-one

New York   Saturday, April 4, 1998   10:20am   (local)

Agent Fahey got to his office after a quick, thankfully uneventful stop at the pawn shop. Jonathon Earle had indeed made a purchase of a handgun using the credit card issued in the name of Don Hough. The clerk made a positive identification of Earle from the passport photo. Fahey thanked the clerk for his cooperation and assured the man his cooperation would be duly noted in the subsequent investigation that would be resulting from the selling of the gun in violation of the Brady law. The initial probable cause search of the store revealed only the usual items one might find in a New York City pawn shop, such as watches, rings, televisions, video tape machines and an assortment of handguns and rifles, some of them automatic. The records for the materials all seemed to be in surprisingly good order. Each item had the names and addresses of the persons who had brought them in. Of course, any follow-up on the names and addresses would no doubt show that a majority were made up.

Jimmy was more intent on getting to the bottom of the AFR Enterprises quandary. He turned on his computer's Internet connection and began his search.

The first web page that was listed on the search result was the AFR Enterprises corporate home page. Jimmy clicked on the hyperlink and waited for the graphics to load. He took out his notebook and reviewed the information he'd written down thus far. The AFR Enterprises corporate home page was a simple index to the many, independent holdings of AFR. Jim made more notes of some of the companies listed, such as the Earle Import Galleries of London and Wicked Good Radio, Incorporated. There was a link labeled "About AFR Enterprises" and Jim clicked on it. The page opened up and Fahey read the narrative.

American Financial Resources Enterprises was established in 1973 to help small businesses incorporate and grow through financial investment strategies. Since our inception, we have provided the needed capital to aid newly-incorporated entrepreneurial ventures in making the transition from market newcomer to market leader. Our diverse holdings now extend beyond the American market to include numerous overseas holdings. With careful planning and shrewd investment, American Financial Resources stands poised to be a leader in venture capitol into the next millennium.

As Fahey read this, his thoughts turned to Fred. He'd known Fred only as an employer and more recently, as someone he could say hello to in passing. He'd guessed Singletary to be about forty-five or so. If AFR was Fred's business, then he would have had to start this thing up when he was all of twenty, probably still in college, if Jim remembered Don's Navy stories correctly.

He picked up the phone and dialed the customer service number for American Express. The customer service representative forwarded his call to an on-duty supervisor. Agent Fahey identified himself and asked for as much information as could be provided about the account without a warrant. The supervisor was hesitant to provide any information, so Jim asked questions and hoped for yes or no responses. Yes, the account was registered to AFR. Yes, the card had been issued in the past three months. No, the account was not a domestic account. Yes, it was an international account. No, they would not provide any information about how the account was paid. Jim thanked the supervisor and hung up.

He went back on line and brought up the American Express International page. He typed in the account number. The account access page then asked for a password. He tried typing "Fred." No luck. Next he tried "WCBR" and again, no luck. Just on a whim, he typed in "1973." The page changed and he began to make notes of what he was seeing as quickly as he could.

The new web page was a statement of the past thirty days activity. It outlined charges to cellphone companies, airlines, restaurants, gas stations, hotels and more. He was very careful in transcribing the payment notation. It had been an electronic payment, as opposed to a written check. The payment line included a wire-transfer coding. He pulled a thin manual out of his desk and looked up the first three digits of the wire transfer code. It was from a bank in the Grand Cayman Islands. Nice place to hang on the beach, Jim thought and a great place to keep your money your own business. The remaining digits of the transfer code would be the account number and authorization sequence. This way, whoever was responsible for paying the bill would be able to do so via phone or computer. The top of the statement showed only the corporate name and a post office box number in Portland, Maine.

Jim closed out the American Express web site and typed in a request for a web search of the bank in the Grand Caymans. The search yielded one exact match, so he once again utilized the blue hyperlink.

The web page that materialized was for *Firstbanc GCI*. It had the usual bank hyperbole about safety and security, investment teams and such. Jim clicked the computer's mouse on the *Accounts* icon and watched as the secure page opened up. The page was secure, Jim knew, from the small yellow padlock icon that appeared in the lower right hand corner of the web browser. There was a blank data box for the account number and for a password. Jim entered the account number and then entered the previous "1973" password. This time, he was denied.

"Damn!" he said to himself. He then tried his other guesses for passwords, but to no avail.

The chiming sound from the computer brought him up for air for a moment. His buddy Tim from Maine was online and trying to reach him through one of the on-line personal chatting features.

Jim clicked on the "accept" portion of the separate dialogue box that had appeared.

"Hey jimmy, whatcha doin'?"

Jim typed in response. *"Not much, Timbo. But your timing is perfect. I need you to do something illegal for me."*

"Excuse me, but aren't you Mister FBI guy and stuff like that?"

"Yeah, Tim. But I'm running out of time here to find out some stuff. If i send you a web address and an account number, can you hack the password for me?"

"Illegal search? for the FBI? must be big...?"

"It is big, Tim-ster. but if anyone can sneak in, it'd be you."

"Give me the url and the account number and we'll work this together."

"Let's hope it works, buddy."

Jim sent the web page address and account number, as well as the passwords he'd already tried. There was slight pause while Jim imagined Tim working things from his end up in Maine. Jim watched the personal message dialogue box as Tim finally responded.

"Jimmy. I'm in. It was a combination of the year and the name. Here it is for you: 1 F 9 R 7 E 3 D."

Jim typed back *"Thanks, Timmy. as usual, you are the man!"*

"What's this all about?"

"Fair question, Tim. Can't get into it now, but will over a burger and a beer in your backyard next time i'm up your way? be sure to lose and forget what we just did, okay?"

"Consider it gone, buddy. Dawn and the babies doing good?"

"Everybody's doing great down here, Tim. I gotta get working on this, though. I'll catch up with ya later. promise."

"C U later," typed Tim.

Jim closed the personal dialogue box and logged back into the Firstbanc GCI account page. The master account list for AFR Enterprises loaded. It read like an international phone directory. Jim clicked on the master account icon box and read it very carefully. In the past month alone, the master account had registered over two hundred million dollars in deposits and roughly thirty million in transfers out. Jim made note of the half-dozen or so active accounts that had been the destinations of the outward bound transfers and returned to the main page. Selecting each of the named accounts that had received monies from the master account, he scanned the transaction records of each, carefully. On one account, something clicked that he couldn't quite put his finger on, but re-read it several times. The account was for *M&M, Incorporated*. There was a deposit amount of six million dollars registered on the first of April and a like amount for the first of March. Jim scrolled through the past twelve months and saw that the amount had not changed, but the deposit was made as an electronic transfer from the master account on the first of each month. There was a large amount that was transferred out of this account on the twentieth of March, though. The ledger indicated a two million dollar transfer to a different account. Jim made note of the transfer routing codes and account number. The transfer was made to a different bank. Jim pulled out his bank code manual once again and looked up the numerical identifier. It was to a bank in the Bahamas, Jim saw and he was going to make that his next stop on the web once he finished making notes on the AFR holdings. There were additional transfers out, all with amounts varying between seventy-five hundred and ninety four hundred dollars. The routing codes for these he knew to be American banks and the dollar amounts made sense. Anything under ten thousand dollars did not have to be reported to the Federal banking authorities, so the various amounts, under the legal reporting limit, would raise no eyebrows. He then opened up the *Earle Import Galleries* account and saw a number of deposit transfers, as well as cheques issued in like amounts. Fahey made more hastily scribbled notes on these routing numbers and found that the country of origin was Great Britain. The cheques would take some physical on-site digging, he knew. He glanced over two other account folders that had shown recent activity. One was for *TDSecurity, Incorporated.* The other was for *BLBB Enterprises.* Both accounts had transfers from the master AFR account inbound and the outbound records had various dollar amounts heading for the same bank in, Jim opened up his routing code manual quickly, Virginia. He double-checked the stateside destination codes from the *M&M* account and saw that it was the same bank. Well, he thought, this should be easy enough to investigate at this end. One stop banking. That made him laugh out loud as he returned to the master account list. There were some other transfers out of the primary account and the routing code was to a bank in Russia. The amounts were all six figures or more and that, combined with the Russian bank destination, made him pick up the phone and call Director Hammett.

While dialing the phone, he put in a blank floppy disc into his computer and saved each of the web pages that he'd visited onto the disc. He could print this stuff out later.

"Director Hammett speaking."

"Director? Agent Fahey from New York."

"Yes, Jimmy, what's up?"

"Couple of things. To update, I safely picked up and escorted Mister Hough to the hospital. He's with Ms. Rose right now and they're both under the watchful eye of an NYPD uniformed detail. I know you asked me to watch them personally, but there was a pawn shop charge on the credit card that the late Mister Earle was carrying. I checked it out. Just a handgun purchase, nothing else. We've shut the shop down pending the Brady violation. I've been here at the office for about an hour now, doing some on-line research."

"What did you come up with?"

"Lots of real interesting stuff. Let me start with something we need to check out down your way. Here's the name of a bank in Alexandria. There are three accounts that are related to this whole mess."

Jim gave the director the account names and numbers and waited while Hammett put him on hold in order to dispatch a team to the Virginia bank.

"Okay, Jim. I'm back. Now, tell me why we're digging into these accounts."

"The credit card Jonathon Earle was carrying was issued in the name of Don Hough within the past three months by American Express International. The authorization for the card was made through the London office, as requested by the parent holding company, AFR Enterprises, Incorporated. AFR has two corporate headquarters, but are financially held through a three-name trust in a bank on Grand Cayman Island. Do we have a connection to find out what three names are on the master account?"

"Let me call over to Treasury real quick. You got the account number?"

Jim read him the master account number and went over his notes while the director put him on hold again. After a three minute wait, Director Hammett came back onto the line.

"I'm back, Fahey. Treasury has a guy who knows a guy at that GCI bank. We should have the names in a few minutes. Tell me more."

Jim outlined the various transactions from the associated accounts and Keith let out a low whistle.

"That's a lot of money flowing around, Jim. The Earle connection is very intriguing. You say this guy Singletary is a self-made man?"

"Yes. He apparently goes back with Hough and Bud Nelson to their Navy days. I worked at the radio station he owns up in Maine. I had no idea of the multi-national aspect of his holding company. The Russian bank numbers cause me concern, especially the transfers to Earle's company account. You have some figures and names and arrows in front of you now, Director Hammett. Have you come up with anything yet?"

"I'm thinking this Russia connection is probably related to the fake passport. Mister Earle has been under scrutiny by the British for maybe providing phony paperwork for use in international travel. The credit card is probably an offshoot of that. I've spent the morning with Nelson and knowing how he feels about this Singletary guy, my guess would be is that Mister Singletary would never put someone like Hough or a friend in a bad position. Besides, right now Mister Singletary is in a Charleston hospital awaiting transfer to an Air

Force med evac. He, a retired Navy Admiral and a secret service agent were all injured in an explosion this morning in Charleston."

"When did this happen?"

"Around nine-thirty or so. They were checking into some matters of national security at a Charleston area plantation when the building they were inspecting blew sky high. Some kind of booby-trap."

"You let a civilian do an investigation, sir?"

"No, Fahey. I did not allow a civilian to conduct an investigation. Mister Nelson asked the admiral and Singletary to take a look around. Just be a couple of curious tourists. The secret service agent, Tom Hannity, was sent by President Griffen to personally make sure that nothing bad happened. They even had a warrant. I did tell them that sending two civilians in on an official investigation was wrong, wrong, wrong. They claimed it was informal and wanted the matter strictly contained."

"What the hell could be so important that they trusted a couple of non-law enforcement types to go nosing around?"

"Singletary found out about what was going on by accident. Hannity is part of the president's detail, so he's been pretty much within earshot. The admiral was asked to go along because of his familiarity of the area. This matter, Jim, is enough to shake the government down to it's foundation, hard enough to create possible panic in the public at large. I'm not in a position to say more, but the information you've obtained is probably going to be the icing on the cake. I'm especially curious about the two million dollar transfer on the twentieth. That's the day after the alleged attack by President Griffen on the young lady. I'm willing to bet two, no, three cups of coffee that the account in the Bahamas will be in the name of Pam Stark. She was just a little too believable, in my opinion. I've just spent the morning in the Oval Office and I now know Jay Griffen better than I thought I ever did. He did not do that of which he's preparing to stand trial. Not in this lifetime, anyway."

"So where do we go from here, sir?"

"You head back to the hospital and bring your friend, Hough, up to speed. He may need to call back up to Maine to make some short-term arrangements in the handling of Singletary's business affairs. Make sure you've got your phone on in case we have any more questions. Let NYPD know that the assault case on Ms. Rose looks closed to us. Perp is dead, justifiable under a good Samaritan clause. But let them also know that the credit card and passport are now ours. We'll have to spend a great deal of time tracking this stuff down, on both sides of the Atlantic. Thanks for the great work, Fahey. You've done the bureau proud today."

"My pleasure and duty, Director Hammett."

"Oh, Jim? Before you go, do I want to ask you if I want to know how you got this information?"

"No, sir. I don't think that's a question you would want to ask, officially."

"Off the record, give me the short version."

"I got into the credit card account web page with a lucky guess on the password. The GCI bank required a little outside help from a computer whiz I know from back home. Again, the lucky guesses made it all too easy."

"Short enough for me, Jim. Thanks again."

"Good day, Director Hammett. Call me if you need anything else."

forty-two

Agent Thomas Dayle the United States Secret Service stepped out into the bright, Spanish afternoon sun. He reached into his suitcoat pocket and pulled out a pack of cigarettes. Shuffling one out of the pack, he retrieved his well-worn Zippo lighter. Out of habit, he ran his fingers over the etched initials. *M.M.* Oh well, he thought. Mister Marvin Moore should have known that smoking wasn't good for his health. Well, to give the long-since dead man some credit, he had kicked the habit, just hung onto the lighter. Dayle flipped the hinged top back and worked the thumb wheel. The scent of lighter fluid was replaced by the burning tobacco of the cigarette. He took a couple of deep drags, then, swapping the Zippo for his cellphone, he pressed the power switch and checked the signal meter. Good, he thought, there's a nice strong cell tower somewhere nearby. Selecting the memory function on the phone, he hit the number 1. The phone dialed automatically as he held it up to his ear, waiting for the connection to complete. The phone rang three times and still no answer. Odd, he thought. Usually this line is answered on the first ring. On the fifth ring, the connection was

433

completed. He listened. The voice on the line had informed him that since no one was present to take his call, he should proceed to the next call number on his assigned list and be prepared to follow through.

Dayle disconnected the call and took another deep drag on the cigarette. He was walking around the parking lot when another member of the Secret Service detail, Agent Brian Bello came out into the parking lot.

"Tommy? Tom!"

Dayle waved him over and pressed memory number 2. As Agent Bello came trotting over, Agent Dayle was listening intently to the recording.

"Tommy. Change in plans. We gotta saddle up and head back to Dodge. The plane's warming up and the boss says we're out of here in ten minutes. You packed?"

"Yeah," said Tom, folding up his cellphone and slipping it back into his pocket. "I am. Are you?"

"Yes. Packed and have my bag right over there waiting for the van that'll take us the hell out of here."

"No, Brian. I mean are you *packed?*

"Are you serious?"

"Listen carefully. I called the base number per the instructions we got the other day. Call every day and confirm orders. Every day. I called just now and got a machine, Brian. The machine tells me to call the next number on the assigned call list. Punched in number two. Another machine. This time, the message says to proceed without prejudice. So, if you're packed, we're on the short road out of this thing, BB. It's time to rock and roll."

"Any suggestions?"

"Remember *Fantasy Island*, Bri? Let me paraphrase. Da plane. Da plane."

"On the plane? Now?"

"Yes. Now. Where's the nice lady?"

"She's taking all of their paperwork to Paris. The boss asked her to hand-deliver it to Secretary Paparelli."

"So she's not going with us?"

"That's right, Tommy boy. We're going west and she's heading north."

"That will make our job a bit easier. She does have a tendency to hover."

"You think the man will want to catch his customary trans-Atlantic snooze? If today's the day, then we won't have a better opportunity."

"I would guess that him grabbing a little nap would make the whole thing that much more explainable. Sounds like a plan to me."

"You better go pack your stuff, Tom. I'll keep the watch out here until we're ready to roll."

"You know, we've gotten pretty good at this Secret Service gig."

"Nice benefits, the money's not bad and the travel has been great."

"It's a shame we won't be working the same duty when it's time to hail in a new chief a few years from now. We would've finally gotten to the big house."

"Well, if all goes according to plan, Agent Dayle, we will be in the big house very, very soon."

Dayle hustled back into the hotel while Bello took up a position just outside of the hotel's main entrance. At the elevator, Tom saw Annie Fidrych heading for the front desk, briefcase and overnight bag in hand.

"Heading for Paris, Miss Fidrych? It's beautiful there this time of year."

"Yes, Tom. It is. You take care of the boss on the way home, all right?"

"We'll get him there in one piece, ma'am. That's our job."

"Thanks again, Tom. We'll see you at the office day after tomorrow."

"Good day, Miss Fidrych. Have a safe trip."

Dayle got onto the elevator and watched Annie walk to the hotel's front desk. He remarked to himself and not for the first time, that she was a very good looking woman and that damn presidential lackey, Bud Nelson, was a very lucky man. The elevator doors closed on Dayle's fantasy and began its upward travel to the tenth floor. He got off the elevator and walked down the hall to his room. Once inside, he grabbed his suits and shoes and laid them out in the hanging travel garment bag. The rest of his clothing was set on the end of the bed, bundled up nice and clean from the hotel's laundry. He took the wrapped package and slid it into his suitcase, while sliding out an extra clip of ammunition for his service weapon. The travel routine required them to have a full clip locked and loaded, with two additional full clips on their person, especially when traveling overseas. The kidnapping game had gotten very nasty over the past few years in Europe and losing a head of state, such as Vice President Fulton, was not something Agent Dayle wanted on his permanent record. Well, at least losing the vice president to some rebel with a cause, anyway. He suppressed a laugh at that thought. He was, after all, a rebel with a cause himself. He sat down on the bed for a moment to gather his thoughts.

This entire mission had started out just after he left the university in Moscow and enlisted in the army. Tomas Doyestka's knack for picking things up quickly never came across well in the classroom, hence the hasty retreat from academia. He was able, though, to demonstrate his quick uptake while undergoing his basic training. His class had just finished a segment on basic first aid. As they had stood to depart the classroom, en mass, the instructor grasped his own chest and fell to the floor. Dumbfounded, the new recruits stood still, silent. Tomas had rushed to the front of the room, screaming for someone to go and get some help. One recruit came forward to assist. Tomas looked the young man in the eye and knew instantly they were on the same tack. Tomas started doing the mouth-to-mouth breathing technique they had just been taught, while the other young man held the instructor's limp neck up a bit and level. The breathing was helping but the young man stopped Tom for a moment and began pressing on the still-lifeless chest of the instructor. After a few moments of this, the young man nodded to Tomas to begin the mouth-to-mouth breathing again. This time, the instructor coughed himself back to life. By the time the ambulance had arrived, the instructor was sitting up, breathing and thanking the two young recruits. The instructor was lifted onto the stretcher and patted both of his young students as he was carried past them and out the door. A senior sergeant came into the room and motioned for the two young men to accompany him. Two days later, Tomas Doyestka and Boris Billovina were attending advanced medical training, on their way to bigger and better things than those were awaiting their fellow infantry trainees.

During their stay at the medical school, a senior KGB recruiter had come to visit them and given them a series of aptitude tests. Both had scored off the charts, surprising even themselves. Their proficiency at languages, most notably English, had put them on a fast track to doing their military service in places far more than exotic than an outpost in the Ukraine. Once they had completed their medical courses, they were whisked away to East Berlin, where they were initially tasked with running a mini-hospital for taking care of the needs of operatives in the field. That assignment lasted only a year and they wound up in the office of the directorate in Moscow, being given their instructions by none other than President Aleksandr Romanov.

It was a fairly simple assignment. Go to America and await further instructions from Comrade Konstantin. They'd enjoyed a three month vacation in the United States, spending the last few weeks of fall on the ski slopes of Aspen, Colorado and then eight weeks on the beaches of Sunny Florida.

By the end of January, Tom Dayle and Brian Bello had completed training at a coastal Florida criminal justice academy and were fully credentialed to apply for jobs at any law enforcement agency in the country. Of course, if they wanted to go for specialized training, such as the FBI or the customs service, then they would have required additional training at one of those service's schools.

In February, they were contacted by Comrade Konstantin, who gave them a photo and background on a political consultant, Marvin Moore, currently teaching school in upstate New York. They'd gone to an area just outside of Lake Placid and rented a small, deserted farm house. It was a six month lease, but the money wasn't coming out of their pockets. They went to a local department store and bought a few household necessities, such as curtains, a few chairs, a few folding tables, a couple of rollaway cots, bedding and the like.

They took a day or two to set up house and in between, followed Moore to see if he had a routine. Like clockwork, Moore retired to a local watering hole each evening. It was on the third night that they made their introductory move.

Tomas remembered hearing Boris tell of how he suffered from a series of collapsed lungs as a young boy and during the time spent in hospitals, Boris had first expressed an interest in things medical. The doctors had explained what caused a pneumothorax and that knowledge had stuck with him. He told of how he had exacted a bit of revenge on a schoolyard bully, using an empty syringe to cause a collapsed lung in the thug. It was easy, Boris had remarked.

"Just tell the guy there was a bee on his back, then slip the needle right into his back, about midway down, under the right shoulder. Then you tell the guy to hold still and you'd help the jerk get the stinger out. Hit the plunger, pull out the needle and rub his back on the needle mark. Next thing you know, the big jerk can't breathe and you're back playing with the other kids in the schoolyard."

And yes, Boris finished the story, that was how he got the nickname of *Lungboy*.

By the end of the week, their task was completed. Moore was buried in an empty well under the storage shed out in back of the farmhouse and the two were on a plane to Munich with files in hand. From Munich, they'd rented a car and drove to a KGB safe-house in the Bavarian woods, not far from the border of Soviet controlled Czechoslovakia. It was there that they first met and impressed, Colonel Michail Rostokovich. They had thought him young for a KGB colonel, but the family link probably had something to do with it. Still, Tomas and Boris were instantly comfortable with the man. There was one thing that might have prevented a problem in their dealings with the Colonel. Comrade Konstantin. When they had gotten their orders on what to do with the information they obtained from Moore, they were told to never mention the name of Konstantin to any agent to whom they might be assigned. An order was an order and as such, they followed it as was their duty.

The Moore assignment was followed by the Hewes assignment. That one had required a bit more time and some less than gentle persuasion from Tomas involving garden shears and the removal of fingers. The final session with Mister Hewes had been uncomfortable. Tomas had found he almost, no, did enjoy inflicting the pain upon Hewes. It got the desired results as far as obtaining information vital to the future of the operation and it was then that he pretty much put the Hippocratic Oath out of his mind. They'd helped finish briefing the two incoming replacements for Moore and Hewes who had come in from Oslo, Norway.

Once the Hewes for Congress campaign started, Mister Dayle and Mister Bello had used their criminal justice academy training to become licensed bodyguards for the fledgling Congressional candidate. After the election, they were recommended to and accepted by, the training academy at Quantico for the intensive course required of candidates for the United States special law enforcement agencies. Upon completion of their training, now members of the U.S. Secret Service, they were at first split up, with each being assigned to the field offices located around the United States. Agent Tom Dayle had been sent to Boston, while Agent Brian Bello was placed in Houston. For the next two years, they served quietly and proficiently, each being recognized for outstanding work in the field. Additional postings to Sacramento and Chicago rounded out their next three years.

On the occasion of their fifth anniversary in the Secret Service, each had finally been granted the request to serve together. They arrived in Washington in 1984, just after the November election. They were posted to the Secret Service Headquarters, where they served in a variety of functions, from investigative work to routine protection duties. Each thoroughly enjoyed the investigative work. It got them away from the strict settings of the home office and allowed them to work out the occasional frustration on a less-than-stable person who may have actually been intent on following through on a threat. The threat inquiries were numerous; sometimes droll and harmless, other times the real deal.

After eight years on the Washington assignment, the change of scenery they'd anticipated came to fruition when they were assigned to the protective detail of the Secretary of State. This assignment allowed them to travel the world and once again work with Marvin Moore, the new Moore, that was. Marvin's help in getting President

Griffen elected was rewarded with a position on the secretary's staff as an assistant. The two agents saw much of the world, especially some of their favorite haunts in Europe. The overseas trips brought with them a risk of being inadvertently recognized by an old colleague from Russia. The stock-issue dark sunglasses helped to cut down on that risk and they did, for what it was worth, do their jobs well.

They had the discussion at one time about whether or not one of them would take a bullet while on the job. It was, after all, what the Secret Service was designed to do. Not to go out and get shot, but to do everything within their power to prevent anything happening to the person whom they were to protect. Sometimes, that might mean stepping between their charge and the attacker with a weapon. They were filled with professional admiration for the work of Agent Timothy McCarthy when he threw himself in front of President Reagan during the 1981 attempt *to impress an actress*. On the contrary side of that particular discussion was the fact that they were actually serving two masters, one of whom wanted them to expressly stay alive to perform future functions.

The 1996 attempt on the life of Secretary of State Paparelli was every Secret Service agent's nightmare from the beginning and it was an attempt on Paparelli, not on Moore as *he* would have had anyone believe. A crowded reception on foreign soil in a hotel which they were not able to be granted complete control. Dayle and Bello were close by the secretary. Then, suddenly, out of nowhere, a piercing feedback forced all of the agents to rip the earpieces for their two-way communications systems out of their ears. As quickly as that happened, Moore was returning with drinks for both he and Ms. Paparelli. Dayle saw the glint of a silver-coated handgun come out from a suitcoat in the crowd, not ten feet away. Tom stepped toward the gun's barrel, not taking his eyes from it and had not yet identified the face. Moore stepped through a couple who were chatting next to the secretary and Dayle timed his arrival just as the gun fired. The bullet hit him in the mid-section. He reached for the hand holding the gun, but came away with only the weapon. Unable to communicate with the agents in and around the exits, Dayle could not have them intercept the assailant. Bello came running and quickly bundled Secretary Paparelli and Moore out through the service entrance, as was their plan from earlier preparations. The assembled guests had reacted as expected to the gunshot. In a dignified panic, if it could be viewed that way, they quickly crowded the exits and filled the streets outside. Dayle was helped from the ballroom to the main entrance, where a local police officer escorted the wounded man to a waiting patrol car, then hurried him to the nearest hospital. Fortunately for Dayle, the wound was not serious, although it certainly did bleed plenty and the doctor on duty at the small hospital was competent. The bullet removed, the wound sutured, Dayle was then taken to a waiting Air Force plane, the official transportation for Paparelli on this trip. Since the reception was the closing to a successful negotiation session, the delegation all hurriedly packed their bags and headed for home. Bello came on board and checked on his friend. Moore came by and offered his sincerest gratitude. Tom was suspicious, but said nothing until Moore left. Bello looked at Dayle and they both nodded their agreement in thinking that Moore had set this up for future personal gains. Secretary Paparelli was more than gracious in offering her thanks and instructed Moore to make sure that Agent Dayle was well taken care of at home. The on-plane review of the incident by the agents in the detail came to a consensus conclusion that whoever was behind the attempt had to know the frequency of the communications system in order to cause the feedback. The shooter no doubt had been watching for the agents to remove the earpieces before acting. That Tom had been shot was deemed the only reason why the shooter got away from him. That the communications system had been temporarily disabled was deemed the reason that the shooter got away from them all.

Moore did make sure that Tom was well taken care of at home. A commendation from President Griffen was accompanied by reassignment to the office of Vice President Fulton, made at the suggestion of Secretary Paparelli.

What Tom did not know was that Moore had nothing to do with the assassination attempt. The gunman was a person with a beef with the government of the United States and decided to make his own forum for expression by using the U.S. Secretary of State for target practice. Tom had acted instinctively, an act he would be chastised for, personally, by Romanov. The actual reassignment, though, was suggested to Moore and to Fulton, by Konstantin. Separately, of course. Moore's suggestion was funneled through Paparelli. That suggestion was seconded as a request from Fulton. A general agreement that Agent Dayle would best utilized with protecting the vice president was reached and done.

Now, four years into his assignment with Fulton, here he sat, ready to finish what he started in 1976. The instructions from forty-eight hours ago were explicit. Call the lake. If all was well, have a nice, polite conversation and move on. If all was not well, as the answering machine seemed to have indicated, call the second number. The second number was the pager built into the cellphone. The person with the cellphone would have it on vibrate and return the call within sixty minutes. The second call was made, but was instead answered by a voice mail with instructions to proceed with the primary assignment. Odd, he thought, but he'd re-dialed the number just to be sure, with the same result. Tom double-checked his watch and did the math on the time zones. The second number was supposed to be in the eastern time zone, six hours earlier than it was here in Madrid. That would make it a little past ten in the morning. Oh well, he mused to himself, orders is orders. He gathered his bags, left a twenty dollar bill on the bathroom vanity for the housekeeping crew and went downstairs.

Outside, he found Bello pacing, watching, doing his job.

"You ready to fly, Bri?"

"You bet your ass, Tommy-boy. We got the posse all rounded up?"

Tom glanced towards the white Suburban that was serving as their duty vehicle. It had been provided by the embassy, where the vice president was staying.

"We've you and me, two in the van and two at the embassy, right?" Tom asked.

"Yep. The only other one was Miss Fidrych and she's on her way to Paris."

"That's a trip I'd like to make today, Mister Bello."

"Now, now, Tom. One, you're married. Two, she's with Nelson. He's a nice guy and you're still married."

"Oh, thanks for reminding me. Sheila will love that you've been keeping me in line."

"Now me, Mister Dayle, I'm separated. I should be joining her on the trip to Paris."

"Two, she's with Nelson."

"You're right. Bud's an okay guy. No sense in causing him any grief."

"Let's get home, Brian. We have a funeral to attend."

The two agents walked towards the oversized wagon, tossed their bags into the open rear window and settled into the big, rear seat. From here, they'd go to the embassy and meet up with Vice President Fulton. Two of them would ride with him in the embassy's limousine, while a police escort, front and rear, with the Suburban directly between the limo and the rear escort, would lead the way to the airport where Air Force Two was running and waiting for them.

forty-three

The president and the distinguished entourage sat quietly in the large conference room in the subterranean National Crisis Management Center. Director Realto switched off the television feed, while the Chief of Naval Operations, Admiral Jack Joseph Wright was thanking the AWACS commander, Captain Jim Donahue and his crew for a job well done; for both getting Go Team One successfully back to the NATO airbase and for the most interesting television program that would never see the light of a cathode ray tube on any conventional broadcast.

The assembled power-crew had just finished viewing the digital satellite feed of the video taken by Go Team One at Lake Onega. The image quality was excellent. The sound quality had some wind interference, but was otherwise clearly audible. The gaping holes that were at first the tightly-clamped lips of those seated in the conference room had grown to chasm-like proportions when Romanov had started his laundry list of who used to be who in American politics. Or at least American politics in the eyes of Aleksandr Romanov. The room lights had been dimmed for better viewing of the feed from the AWACS and were programmed to come back up to normal level lighting once the projection screen was deactivated. Now that the room was better illuminated, all eyes turned to President Griffen.

"Ladies, Gentlemen. I took a chance. I took a huge chance. With the country's best interest in mind, I took chances that less than thirty minutes ago were probably seen and rightfully so, as selfish by most, if not all, of you."

Jay used his arms in a sweeping gesture to motion to the witnesses seated around the NCMC conference room table.

"Let me assure you that I wish, truly, that I were wrong on this whole thing. That all of the allegations of which we have become aware in the past forty-eight hours were baseless. And that I would simply be facing a federal judge on what far too many viewed as a no-win situation come next week."

"President Griffen? If I may?"

"Yes, Gayle?"

"I know I speak for many here and maybe all, that we had hoped the charges involving the Stark woman would be proven false. I for one am truly relieved that they have been, based on what we have seen and heard for ourselves right here."

"Thanks for the confidence, Gayle. Coming from you, that means the world to me. I also must applaud you for vigorously doing your job. You were faced with the task of bringing a sitting American president in front of a federal judge to face federal charges of assault. I'd take a moment and look up the precedent, but we can probably say with confidence that I'd be hard pressed to find one. Thank you for doing your job, Gayle. The American people have no idea what a fine, fine person they have doing their bidding and upholding the laws of our land."

There was a small round of applause, including the Supreme Court Justices.

"I don't intend this to be a victory speech, gang," continued the president. "We have two large questions yet to answer now that we have most of the key players in this intriguing tale rounded up or accounted for. The first question is two-fold. What do we do with the collection of people we have? And how much do we tell the general public? The second question is going to involve the full

House and Senate, as well as further review and testing right up to the top," said President Griffen, nodding in the direction of the three Supreme Court Justices. "How will we prevent this, or anything like this, from ever, ever happening again?"

"Mister President," spoke Chief Justice Quinlan. "Of course, any proceedings that are conducted under United States Law must be public. Let me just offer you the notion that you needn't necessarily make the information about the proceedings public. There is a slim chance that any actual courtroom appearances would go unnoticed. Perhaps on a remarkable day in an unremarkable courthouse, a few people might be brought to stand in front of an unremarkable judge and allowed to plead guilty to charges, allowing the unremarkable disposition to be filed away for another day. Someday, someone will no doubt stumble upon the complete public record of the proceedings and may or may not make anything of the names of those who stood and faced adjudication of their cases."

"What do you suggest, sir?"

"Next, when is it, Wednesday? When you yourself stand in front of the federal judge here in Washington to defend yourself against charges, those people who need to face a judge of the United States federal court system could possibly do so in say, Charleston, South Carolina or even in Virginia or Maine."

President Griffen's eyes sparkled with the recognition of what the Chief Justice had suggested.

"Very, very nice idea, your honor. While everyone in the world will be watching me and listening for each and every little salacious detail, we allow these people to experience due course as afforded them under the law. Brilliant, Mister Chief Justice. Brilliant!"

"I thought you'd like that, Mister President. Even though you would rather not be run through the wringer and subject the American people to each little nuance, it will allow you to know the outcome of your trial before it actually happens. If we were to allow Attorney General Vernon to, rightfully, recommend dismissal of all charges and the complete expurgation of your still-spotless record, something she could do ten minutes from now, that would put everything else back on an everyday track."

Attorney General Vernon rose to speak. "Mister Chief Justice? I tend to agree with you on this, inasmuch as I would now prefer to not have the president suffer the indignity of even stepping near a federal courthouse, I am concerned about the eventual fallout from this matter, the assault charge, which will leave a taint on the legacy that this fine man," she said pointing to the president. "President Griffen, will leave for future generations to review. He has done absolutely nothing wrong, as we all now know. But even with a finding from a federal judge, there will be those whose ability to be vocal will cry "foul," echoing the sure-to-be thought sentiments that it was fixed, somehow. Will we be able to positively ascertain a positive finding that will remove all doubt from the people that justice has indeed been served?"

"Gayle, your point is well made," replied Chief Justice Quinlan. "Regardless of any outcome in this matter, as I'm sure you're aware, there would be those who will say it was a foregone conclusion. A guilty finding would have the president's supporters screaming conspiracy. A finding of not-guilty would have his detractors screaming conspiracy. On this point, under our First Amendment, the good man is in a no-win situation. The best I feel we can hope for is a convincing, public recantation from the alleged victim."

All eyes locked in on the Chief Justice at his use of the word alleged. Meeting their gaze, he nodded his head and added, "She is still an alleged victim in this case, in very much the same way our president is an alleged perpetrator. The word allegation will apply until the moment the federal judge tasked with the adjudication of this delicate, nasty matter drops the gavel and proclaims his court adjourned."

"Well said, Chief Justice Quinlan. Thank you for your eloquence and insight," said Gayle.

"I see that it is coming up on eleven-thirty now and my fellow justices and I have some other matters of import that do require our attention. If we may take leave at this time, Mister President?"

"Allow me to walk you out, Mister Chief Justice."

As the three Supreme Court justices rose, the president walked to the door of the conference room, opened it and nodded to the duty officer at the desk. The lieutenant colonel on duty in turn motioned to the uniformed sentry to summon the elevator. The justices and the president walked toward the elevator, when Justice Jalbert turned to President Griffen.

"Mister President? Are you going to be able to do anything about recognizing the efforts of all of those fine people in the field?"

Stepping into the elevator, Griffen said, "Trust me when I say that you might feel free to call your friend Bobby "The Texaco Man" from now on."

"As in *you can trust your car to the man who wears the star?*"

"If you remember that old advertising ditty, Justice Jalbert, then I think we're on the same wavelength."

"Pretty much my line of thinking, sir. When it's time to anoint him, would you consider inviting me? I'd love to be there, Mister President."

"I would be honored if you would be there, Justice Jalbert. He'd probably like it as well."

The elevator opened up to the hallway that led back to the Oval Office and the West Wing entrance. President Griffen escorted the justices to the doorway near the portico and shook the hands of all three.

"Mister Chief Justice, Justice Jalbert, Justice Charnoff, thank you again. For your understanding, your patience and your wisdom."

"You're welcome, Mister President," responded Justice Charnoff, not waiting for an opening. "Since I didn't really have much to add to my learned colleagues observations and interpretations, allow me to thank you for inviting us in as witnesses to this event. Whatever plan is formulated in an attempt to prevent this from ever happening again will no doubt be put to the test and will most certainly wind up before us. I think I speak for the Court when I say that our having been there," she said, gesturing with her arm to the Oval Office. "Will aid us in considering this matter carefully when it does come before the Court for interpretation."

President Griffen shook the hands of the three again and watched them exit to the carport and into their waiting vehicle.

As he walked past Joannie's desk, he smiled at her as she was setting the phone down on the cradle, her face an ashen gray.

"Joannie? What's wrong?"

"There's a call for you, Mister President. I think you need to take it in private."

Jay hustled through the door of the Oval Office and stepped to his desk. He picked up the phone. "President Griffen speaking."

"Mister President? It's Bill Terrio, sir."

"Billy. Where the hell are you? You sound like you're in a car wash."

"If you remember, sir, you asked me when the last time I sat in the backseat of an F-14 was. Well, it would be me in the backseat, sir, now."

"So I'm assuming there's something really, really wrong for you to be calling me between stomach-retrievals?"

"If it wasn't so wrong, sir, that stomach line would be really, really funny. We came up with a face on the photo."

"The photo? Bill, I'm sorry, but refresh me as to which photo?"

"The one from the Hewes file, sir. The reflection in the window?"

Recognition sparked in Jay's voice. "Yes. Okay, Bill. How wrong is this?"

"The face is Dayle's, sir. As in Secret Service Agent Tom Dayle, currently assigned to Vice President Fulton's detail."

"Must be some mistake, Billy. That's the guy who took a bullet for Moo.. "

"Bingo, sir. I'm sending Al Dowd over right now with the hard copy prints for you to examine."

"Bill, thanks for the great work. Call me when you land at Cheltenham. Just to give you the short version of things right now, we have a video of Romanov confessing. The whole thing. I need to figure how to handle this Dayle thing, though."

"Handle Dayle, sir? Just stop the bastard. He's a sick, sick man. And he no doubt has at least one more job to do."

"Here's where this gets a little ironic, Billy. Fulton is one of Romanov's pupils, too."

The rush of the F-14 traveling at close to mach-two over the Atlantic was loud and clear as President Griffen tried to imagine the look on his CIA director's face.

"Hibbly-freakin'-ho."

"That about sums up how we're feeling here, Billy. Call me when you land. Hib."

President Griffen put the phone down and patted Joannie on the shoulder on the way by. Obviously, Joannie had screened the call, as that is one of her duties and managed to get a summary of what the CIA director had needed to tell the president. Terrio had certainly made his impression very clear.

"Joannie? Come in the office for a moment."

Jay stepped back inside the open Oval Office door and Joannie quickly came inside the door. Leaving the door open, he leaned down to her and spoke softly.

"Joannie. I need you to be my rock. You're one of the very few people who have given me your full support through all of this. I will tell you that there is a big, big problem within our government right now and it has nothing to do with that stupid little girl. We have the proof to clear me, completely. We now know that certain people in very sensitive positions are not what and even who, they appear to be. Did Bill tell you about the photo?"

"Yes, sir. He most surely got my attention on that."

"So you know that Agent Dayle is now a suspect in a murder. Vice President Fulton is in danger. And right now, the two of them are on-board Air Force Two over the Atlantic coming back from Madrid. Give me a few minutes to work on this, but you must know that as good a man as Don Fulton is, at least as we know him to be, he is also not completely who he appears to be. That's all I can tell you for now, but trust me, we'll figure this whole mess out."

Joannie nodded and Jay once again offered her a reassuring pat on the shoulder. They both stepped out of the Oval Office and she returned to her desk, while he walked back to the elevator for the return trip down to the NCMC. On the brief ride down, he thought to himself that this little sub-sub-basement set-up was aptly named.

He walked off the elevator and returned to the conference room which had returned to a somewhat frenzied hub of activity. There were senior administration level people making phone calls and comparing notes.

"Mister President?" asked Hammett.

"Yes, Keith. What do we have?"

"One of our agents in New York did some amazingly fast work. In the past hour, starting with the credit card that the late Mister Earle was carrying, he's uncovered a trove of offshore accounts, loaded to the gills with money. Nothing necessarily illegal about that in itself, but given what we saw on the video feed, this is starting to make a ton of sense. We've got a master account in a Grand Cayman Islands bank and a couple of related accounts here, in Virginia."

"Tell me what we need to do, Hammett."

"We need a warrant to peek at the names listed as the account holders of these accounts in Virginia."

"Gayle? Can you start on a couple of more warrants right now? We'll see if we can get Judge Noga to sign off on them."

Attorney General Vernon came over and sat next to the FBI director and began making the appropriate notes.

"What else is there, Keith?"

"Who do we have who can get a couple of names from the Grand Cayman bank?"

"What names do we need?"

"Just the signature cards. If we can get those, we might be able to find out who this Konstantin is. The money guy to whom Romanov referred."

"Maybe Treasury Secretary Sorrentino can get that for us. Danny?"

"Yeah, boss," replied the chief of staff, eager to be put to work.

"Get Chipp on the phone and give him this information. Tell him we need to have a copy of the account signature card on this account."

"Let me see that, sir? Okay. Is this AFR Enterprises, Keith?" Josten passed the notepad back to the FBI director.

"Yep, that's my chicken scratching."

At the mention of AFR Enterprises, Nelson put down the decoded and translated Rostokovich files the NSA had brought over, stood and just about ripped the notepad from Hammett's hands.

"Excuse me, Bud?" questioned Hammett, more than taken aback.

"Sorry, Keith. AFR is Fred Singletary's company. What's this got to do with anything?"

"The paper trail from Jonathon Earle starts in the Grand Cayman Islands. Offshore account for AFR Enterprises. A series of transactions in the past month include transfers to banks in the Bahamas, Virginia, Maine and Moscow," explained Keith.

Now it was Nelson's turn. "Excuse me?"

"Either someone is using your pal for a dupe, or he's been running a pretty good scam on you for a long time, Bud. There's a lot of money associated with this AFR Enterprises."

"How much money?" asked the president.

"A rough guess? Our wonderkid in New York, Jimmy Fahey, hacked these accounts fairly easily and saw a couple of numbers in excess of ten digits."

"Billions? With a B?"

"Yes, Mister President. With a capital B. Bud, I'm not jumping to any conclusions until we see the account cards on these. This one here, Mister President, the Bahamas bank? There was a transfer of two million dollars from one of the Virginia accounts to this one in the Bahamas. See the date?"

"March twentieth," remarked Jay.

Bud's ears perked up once again. "Day of the arraignment. What's the name on the Virginia account?"

"Let me double check that, Bud. It's *M&M, Incorporated*," Hammett replied.

"M could be for Marvin Moore. Or Marvin and M. Bradford. Smells like a payoff to me, sir," Nelson commented.

"Yes, Bud. It does. Just another document the defense can have ready for trial next week," Jay said.

A knock on the conference room door gave Nelson a momentary distraction as he got up and hustled over to open it.

"Al Dowd! Nice to see you, bud. Come on in! We're having a helluva party and it just wouldn't be the same without you."

Al Dowd, the CIA's Deputy Director for Intelligence gave Nelson a puzzled look and entered the room.

"Good morning, Mister President. Director Terrio said you'd want to see these."

"These? I thought we just had the enhanced photo from the Hewes file?"

"Well, there were a few e-mailed image files from the British he said you'd want to look at also, sir."

Opening the first of two large, brown envelopes, President Griffen pulled out the enlarged and computer enhanced photo from the Hewes file.

"Man. That is Agent Dayle. No doubt about it. The years have been kind to him. Only wish he'd been nicer to others. As a Secret Service agent, he's good. Real good. Too bad he's probably going down for murder. We need to get a call into Air Force Two. They're about an hour and a half out of Madrid, over the Atlantic. Who's onboard other than Dayle we might be able to trust, Bud? Any ideas?"

"I know that Dayle always works with the quiet one. What's his name again? Bello?"

Dan Josten piped in. "Yeah, Bud. Brian Bello. Good guy. Our kids are in daycare together. I know he usually works with Dayle, but I can't say that I've ever seen them together outside of work."

"Your call, Danny," said the president. "Do you think we can trust Bello to keep Dayle away from Fulton until they land?"

"I don't know any of the agents assigned to the V.P.'s detail personally, sir. I'd say it's worth a try."

"Make the call, Dan. Have the call routed through the cockpit and tell Colonel Porter to make up some excuse to get him to take the call up front. But make sure you tell the colonel to have one of the crewmen keep an eye on everybody."

"Yes, sir. I'm on it now," replied the Chief of Staff, picking up the phone.

"What else do we have there, Al?" asked Griffen.

"There were a number of matches from the old photo files from MI-6, sir."

"A number?"

"Here they are, sir. The new, current photos are paper clipped to the matches that came out their computer data base. The matches have at least one, if not more, photos and an intel brief on who these people were believed to be."

"Let's see who came up a winner, then, shall we?"

The president opened the second envelope and pulled out the photo of Rostokovich that was taken by the NSA staff before he was allowed to leave. The paperclipped document underneath had a rather lengthy write-up on the subject, but only one photo. The image was of a face through the glass of an automobile. No doubt on that one, Griffen thought. It was Rostokovich, in a photograph dated from 1976. The notation made at the time that the subject might be Michail was only an assumption. The notes went on to explain that there was no known positive photo of the KGB operative. Jay scanned the rest of the analysis and handed the document pack to Realto.

"Next, sir, is a guesstimated match on the Speaker of the House. I remind you that the computers did the scanning and matching. The top photo is the one from his press kit, the attached image pages contain shots of a known KGB agent, Yevgeny Polnichy."

The president checked these photos, including a full contact-sheet of nearly three dozen photographs, all black and white, of a man who certainly could have been Hewes. Three of the shots were of the man getting out of a car, with the notation of Oslo, April 76 underneath. The next dozen or so were daylight photos, also noted as Oslo, April 76. This time, the subject was sitting on a bench outside of a building, his face bandaged. The remaining shots were of the man, face no longer bandaged, but most definitely bruised. The notes under this strip were Montreal, April 76.

The president took the remaining paper-clipped packets from Dowd and gave them a quick once over. There was a positive subject match on the photo of Marvin Moore's State department identification file and a multi-image contact sheet with photos from Berlin, Oslo and Montreal.

The fourth bundle of photos were images that returned no results from the foreign agents files in the British intelligence computers. These included Nelson, Terrio and even Griffen himself.

"Nice to know that I'm not a secret agent, Al. At this point, I think I needed the reassurance."

Those gathered around the table laughed at the remark, enjoying an albeit brief moment of levity.

The fifth packet contained a few more contemporary photographs, attached to a single British analysis page.

"Bud? You're going to want to see this one."

forty-four

Paris   Saturday, April 4, 1998   6:30pm (local)

The flight from Madrid was quick and easy. Annie Fidrych made her way through Orly airport on her way to a waiting car for the ride to the American Embassy. She had to bring the documents that had been finalized in Vice President Fulton's meetings with the various ministers in Madrid to Secretary of State Julie Paparelli. This little errand had been designed, no doubt, to keep her away from Fulton for the time being. After all, as Annie had found out, the White House believed Annie to be a part of the Hewes coup and that they knew of a standing threat against the vice president. Vice President Fulton had left Madrid about three hours ago against the better wishes of President Griffen and would be more than halfway back to the United States. This was fine by her, she thought. It would keep her away from whatever was coming down and if she were in Europe, there's no way she could be tied into anything that happens from this point on. It also, though, gave her the opening she'd been seeking. She now had a way out. And after her meeting with Julie and maybe a brief girl's night out, she was gone.

She had her ticket to Munich purchased and set aside in a locker at the airport. Her United States government passport would get her through customs in Germany, where, she decided, Annie Fidrych would perish in an automobile accident. Before she dropped off the face of the earth, though, she'd call Nelson. As of now, the White House was only suspicious of her. They were not assured that it was Annie acting in concert with the spies. They would be pleasantly relieved to know that she had used the recording device at the behest of an insecure vice president who had hoped the reigning powers-that-be would be openly supporting his bid to be next in line for the throne.

Additionally, Annie thought with some comfort, the White House was no doubt somewhat leery of her motives, but still comfortable enough to entrust her with being a diplomatic-pouch errand girl. She did have some very important documents in her possession, plus her own personal analysis of the meetings to offer Secretary Paparelli. That alone left enough breathing room for her to escape with the benefit of the doubt. Fulton had promised to come clean to President Griffen that the bug was his idea and that the accidental discovery of the conversation was just that, an unintended accident. He'd take a few lumps for that, but that would get any wandering, wondering eyes away from the two of them. That would be Annie's chance to get the hell out of this once and for all.

Stepping out of the arrivals terminal, she saw the diplomatic vehicle bearing consulate plates with the small American flags. The black Mercedes was idling, with the driver, a young Marine in civilian attire, standing sharp outside of the passenger door. She waved her hello and he acknowledged her with a polite nod, followed by the opening of the rear door.

"Good evening, Marine."

"Good evening, ma'am. You would be Ms. Annie Fidrych?"

"That I would, kind sir. And you would be?"

"Lance Corporal Michael McGee, ma'am."

"Pleasure to meet you, Corporal McGee. I assume Secretary Paparelli is waiting on me?"

"Yes, ma'am. She asked me to get you to the embassy as soon as possible."

"Then let's not waste any more time, Corporal McGee."

The Marine closed the passenger door, walked around the vehicle and slipped into the driver's seat. The traffic was heavy, as usual, leaving the airport. Once they slipped out into the steady stream of cars heading for Paris proper, the car settled into a steady line. Thirty minutes later, the Mercedes pulled to a stop at the wrought iron gate that marked the entrance to the American embassy compound off the Champs Elysees. The gatehouse sentry saluted the arriving vehicle as the gate swung inward and the pneumatic concrete pylons recessed into the ground. The additional security features had been added to all of the embassy compounds in Europe and the Middle East after the Beirut Marine barracks bombing in 1983. Over the past fifteen years, the sites that were prone to regular, heavy traffic, had been equipped with portable, yet solid barriers. The retractable pylons had been an innovation in the past three years or so. Annie remarked at the simplicity of the design, yet the sheer formidability of this type of barrier. The concrete-wrapped solid steel pylons stood forty-eight inches off the ground when raised, yet dropped into their holding chambers in less than thirty seconds to be a barely-perceptible speed bump.

The black sedan drove past the small, well landscaped lawn on either side and began its counterclockwise turn into the circular driveway at the front of the building. A uniformed sentry stepped smartly to the rear passenger door and opened it, allowing Annie to slide out. She caught the young soldier giving her a once over with a look that was not designed with security in mind. She smiled at him, flattered, although he'd most likely interpret it as politeness. Annie was, after all, a seasoned political insider who could easily have an enlisted military man sent to points not yet placed on a map for an action as harmless as trying to catch a view to a thrill. She slid the diplomatic pouch under her arm as she reached back inside the car to retrieve her shoulder bag. She turned around and stopped short, somewhat surprised to be face to face with Secretary of State Paparelli.

"Go-good evening, Secretary Paparelli," Annie stammered.

"Good evening, Ms. Fidrych," responded the secretary. The icy tone of the voice was nothing compared to the steel-blue eyes.

458

"I take it you've spoken with Washington."

"Very good assumption on your part."

"Do you have three minutes for the short version of the number two side of the two-sides-to-every-story thing?"

"Inside. But I have to warn you, my mind is not very open."

"Of that, I am quite sure, Secretary Paparelli."

Julie turned and walked briskly back into the embassy, Annie right behind. As they entered the main hallway, two young children dressed in pajamas ran to Julie. She warmed, her body language softening as she bent down to hug the two kids.

"You two are ready for bed early tonight. What gives?"

"We have the field trip tomorrow morning, remember?" asked the older of the two, a boy.

The other, a girl, maybe a year younger, offered. "The bus leaves at seven. Do you know if you can still be a chaperone?"

"Oh, honey. I completely forgot. Let me check my desk schedule real quick and see if I'm free. Tomorrow's what? Sunday? I think we wrapped up everything here today and Miss Fidrych just flew in tonight from Spain to give me the other things I need to make sure everything is set for next week."

"Is the president still coming?" asked the boy.

"Yes, Joe, he is still coming. Why don't you two head up to bed and I'll be up in about a half an hour to tuck you guys in, okay?"

"Okay, Mom," they replied in unison.

She bent over and gave each a hug and a kiss and watched them run up the stairs.

"Beautiful children, Julie."

The icy stare returned. "Thank you," came the curt reply. "This way, Annie. We can get the paperwork out of the way and then you may leave under armed escort."

"Excuse me?"

"The Marine detail, Annie. They're under orders to take you into custody pending a full stateside investigation. Don't play dumb. The whole scenario has been laid out to me and you, unfortunately, are no longer trustworthy in the eyes of our president. Excuse me, *my* president."

"You're talking about the recording of the meeting that I, yes Julie, I obtained and made sure that Bud Nelson, my closest, yes *closest*, friend knew had been inadvertently made public?"

"Want to run that by me again?"

"Fulton had me bug Bud's pocket PC. Donny-boy was concerned that the big boys were not as behind him as he would like. As you've no doubt noticed, the front office has been grooming number two to take over in two years. It seems that the only one who hadn't noticed was number two himself. Don had somehow worked himself into a lather about whether or not the president was truly supporting him, or merely shining him on. It wouldn't be the first time that a lame-duck president offered token lip service to the candidacy of the V.P.. The recording of that meeting was purely accidental. The way Nelson found out about it was by way of a phone call from the three people on earth who know him better than he knows himself. I dropped the recording on one of the three at a radio station in Maine. The other two listened to this recording and came up with Bud. Had Bud been a bit cooler of head, he could have laughed it off as no doubt his friends were prepared to do: A very interesting practical joke, shared amongst four completely different, yet totally compatible, friends. Instead, Bud reacted as he should in his position. He reacted with the assumption that there was a White House breach of security and that a shape-taking investigation was now out in the open. The recording and the leaking of it to Nelson's friends was my way to let him know that Fulton was insecure, curious and willing to stoop to any level to be sure of their approval. If I had come right out and told him, he would never had believed me. This way, I got his attention, but was unable to straighten him out. Now, you and the rest think, what? That I'm a spy? That I'm part of this rogue KGB plan? If that were the case, would I be dragging my ass up here to bring you paperwork when I could be on a plane to Argentina or someplace? I was actually hoping that after the hellacious day we've both had that maybe we could sneak out and get drunk and have a little fun. A girl's night out is how I was looking at this side trip. That's my story and damn it, I'm sticking to it."

"Are you quite done?"

"Yeah, I am. Thanks for letting me vent. Here are the Madrid papers."

Julie's steel visage relaxed, allowing the natural sparkle to return to her eyes. "Have a seat, Annie. Tell me about Jean-Pierre's meeting."

The two sat, sipped on coffee, while Annie went over each of the day's Madrid meetings as she had viewed them.

"So Jean-Pierre was receptive to our proposals?"

"At least the way Vice President Fulton was able to present them, yes. I was expecting J.P. to be a real s.o.b."

"He must just be one of those Neanderthal European males. You know the kind, right? They prefer to deal with the man, not with the woman. That's all right, though. We accomplished what we needed to do. I even got the Russians in line for this economic deal."

"Good for you, Julie! That made the trip worthwhile." Annie looked at the desk clock on the office's desk. "Don't you have a couple of kids to tuck in?"

"Oh! Thanks, Annie. Can you wait here for a few minutes? Or would you like to come upstairs and freshen up? One of the guest rooms is vacant. The ambassador has been extremely understanding about our, my family, moving in. I just couldn't pass up the chance for the children to spend a couple of weeks in France. The American school has temporary programs for kids like mine. They actually check with the schools back in the States to make sure the youngsters don't miss any of their regular schoolwork. Plus, the kids get to experience life in a new country with other children their own age." Julie had returned to her normal, vivacious self, much to Annie's relief.

"Maybe I'll take you up on the offer to freshen up, Julie."

"Right this way, Annie."

The two women walked up the wide, spiral staircase to the second level of the embassy. The walls were tastefully decorated with a variety of portraits, a succession of images of Presidents and Ambassadors, past and present. The deep maroon rug was plush and created a an eye-pleasing contrast to the natural, high-gloss woodwork of the banister and baseboards. The wallpaper was a simple line-pattern cloth type, the soft rose colors helping to further brighten up the hall.

The main entry was illuminated by an ornate chandelier which had been dimmed for the evening now that the official business of the day had been concluded. The soft wall-mounted sconce lights took over the chores of allowing those still inside to see where they were headed. At the top of the staircase, the landing allowed passage to the second floor rooms or to the next stairway which went up to the ambassador's living quarters on the third level. Julie directed Annie down the hall to their left. The Presidential Suite, as evidenced by the Great Seal of the United States on the door, was where Julie was spending her three weeks with her family here in Paris. Julie opened the door across the hall from the suite and led Annie inside.

"Here's the spare room, Annie. If you want, go in, wash up, whatever. I'll be back in a few minutes. There's a television remote control in the nightstand drawer, if you want to catch up on the news. The building has a satellite service with CNN, MSNBC and a few local channels."

"Thanks, Julie. I'll be right here."

Julie closed the door and Annie checked out the room. There was a queen-size bed as the centerpiece, with two big armoires on the wall opposite the foot of the bed. A large, overstuffed reading chair with a floor lamp was in the near corner to her right. The nightstand was between that chair and the bed. She walked over, opened the drawer and removed the television remote control. The armoire directly at the foot of the bed opened to reveal the television and a stereo system. She flicked the power switch and sat on the edge of the bed, watching the latest news on CNN. There was a live report on about a fire in South Carolina, as indicated by the graphic across the bottom of the screen. Annie turned up the sound to hear the report and began walking to the bathroom. She stopped short when she heard the on-scene reporter mention the name of M. Bradford Hewes, Speaker of the House. She crawled quickly over the bed to get ahold of the remote and turned the volume up a bit more. The reporter was nearing the end of his report.

"For now, this is being handled by the federal authorities, with neither any further comment available on the condition of the three men reported

injured, nor on what may be considered the cause of this explosion. Live from Charleston, Dick Gosselin, CNN."

Annie was dumbstruck. What the hell was going on? And what three people were hurt by an explosion? She picked up the phone in the room and pressed "O." The embassy was staffed with a twenty-four hour a day communications staff and they would be able to put her call through to the White House communications office directly through the government's long-distance system.

"Yes, this is Vice President Fulton's chief of staff, Annie Fidrych. I'm here in the embassy on business with Secretary Paparelli. Would you put me through to Bud Nelson's office in Washington, please. Yes, thank you."

Annie listened while the satellite connection was made and Bud picked up his phone on the first ring.

"Nelson."

"Bud? It's Annie."

Silence came down the line, offset only by a heavy sigh.

"Yeah, Annie. What's up?"

"I need to explain this whole situation to you. Can you give me sixty seconds?"

"I'm starting the clock right now."

"Before you start the clock, what's this about an explosion at the Hewes home in Charleston? It said three people were hurt."

"Yeah, three would be right."

"Is it anyone we know?"

"No one really important. Just Agent Hannity."

"From the president's detail? Oh my God. Bud, who else?"

Nelson was silent for a moment and the breath he took before speaking told Annie volumes.

"Gary Dericksen." Bud paused again and Annie heard a distinct sniff. "And Fred."

"No," Annie said, losing control of emotions. "How in the world did that ever happen?"

"You probably know better than I, Annie. Why don't you check your little bug to see if there was anything else you missed. The clock is now ticking. You have sixty seconds."

"Bud. The bug was Fulton's idea. He was insecure about the support he might expect from you guys. He wanted to be sure that if you were talking about him in private, that it was all good. And you did. He was satisfied. I took the bug out of your p.c. before leaving for Madrid. I should have just destroyed the damn thing then, but I listened to it. Then, I destroyed it. I needed you to know what we had done. The easiest way I could think of was how I did it."

"Oh? So listening to a twenty minute meeting, re-recording it, editing out everyone's voice but mine, working it through a little voice-enhancing harmonizer program and dropping it down a phone line at four in the morning was the easiest way? How about if you just told me, face to face?"

"Bud, I, I'm so, so sorry."

"What in hell possessed you to call Don Hough up in Maine and take something that was supposed to be dealt with quietly, public? You've been around this game long enough to understand the meaning of security and compartmentalization."

"I was hoping that when, not if, Don called you on it, that you could laugh it off as a belated April Fool's joke."

There was a short silence. "Don, Fred and Chuck did give me the chance. I had the opportunity to blow it off and didn't."

"See, I didn't mean any real harm."

"Well, you certainly did when you got to Charleston."

"Excuse me?"

"I had the privilege of watching an exclusive video interview with Alexandr Romanov a little while ago. Your name came up. As did Fulton's. As a matter of fact, the son of a bitch was very forthcoming. But I'm sure he would not have been as vocal if he'd been aware that he was being videotaped by a special forces unit. Additionally, I'm sure he would not have been as open if he'd not planned to kill Michail Rostokovich. As it stands right now, Rostokovich is on his way to a hospital in England for treatment of a gunshot wound. He's in serious condition, but is expected to make a full recovery."

Annie was beginning to lose her composure. Years of training and working and practicing, all giving way to as many years of pent up emotion.

"Who shot Michail?"

"One of Romanov's goons."

"Why?"

"Somehow, *Annie*, Romanov got wind of the unveiling party at the White House. The only one I know of who has, well, *had* a pipeline to Romanov was you. The recording you heard had all of the details. Rostokovich had practically the whole Bud version given back to him, verbatim, by his brother- in-law."

"Are you saying that I would give up Michail to that, that, coward?" Annie stammered. "How dare you? I care for you, Bud. Deeply. More than I think you will ever, ever realize. You got me through the past twenty years. But my love is for Michail. We have had this discussion, Larry. You've just never heard his name from my lips before. Had you been ready for marriage at any point in the past two decades, I would have married you. You, though, were not ready. That made it easier for me to continue carrying the torch, as the saying goes, for Michail. It turns out, by the way, that he and I were on the same wavelength. Since learning of the full truth behind the story of how Romanov did nothing to help Elenya and the children, we have both grieved and desired to avenge that most cowardly act. What's that saying about great minds thinking alike? That's us. Although, I'd like you to know that until I heard the recording of the meeting, I had no idea that he felt the same way. And, I'm sure that as of right now, he has no idea that I also desire nothing else but to see Romanov suffer the consequences. Our brief moments together in the past twenty-two years have never once included discussions about what we were doing. We were simply on assignments, both of us, that we had started and intended to finish. I had no idea he was working in America and I'm sure he did not have a clue as to my whereabouts. Amazing, though, that we never once crossed paths in the United States."

"Not once? Not once in more than twenty years?"

"That's correct, Bud. If we had, then all of this would have been taken care of seven or eight years ago, minimum. I would have dimed out Fulton in a heartbeat if I'd known Michail was working with Hewes."

"You mean Yevgeny?"

"I never knew the man before I met him campaigning in South Carolina. He's only been Hewes to me. Although, rest his soul, the real Hewes is long since dead."

"How long have you known about the Michail-Hewes thing?"

"First I heard of it was the other night listening to the recording of the meeting. Other than that? I had no idea. Honest."

"Honest is not a word you may bandy about lightly, Miss Fidrych."

"Fidoryvich. Anastasia Fidoryvich. Stasya, to you if you'd like, Bud."

"Bud-ski, if you wish, Annie."

"Ooooh. A touch of humor. I'm still in deep shit, but there's a glimmer of hope."

"Just a glimmer, Annie. Yes, you are still in it deep, but you have been extremely forthcoming."

"So how bad are the three of them hurt? And how the hell did that happen?"

"Last question first, Annie. Booby-trap. They went into a detached building on the Hewes property and discovered a neat little hiding place. Seems Yevgeny liked to keep annual scrapbooks, diaries and such. Oh and he forgot to really bury the body we assume was the original Mister Hewes. He kept his treasure trove in a small room in a tunnel under this little cottage and in the same room, all that is left of whom we assume is Hewes."

"Sick, sick, sick. Bud, I had no idea."

"It's your line of work, Miss Fidry, er, Fidoryvich. You must've been used to it?"

"I never, ever killed anyone, Bud. Never. The most I did was play footsie in public with Michail while we transferred information from trashcans next to the Berlin Wall. I was, repeat, was a deadly shot with a handgun. But I haven't touched a weapon in more than twenty years. So what of Fred and Gary and Hannity? What were Fred and Gary doing there?"

"Fred's familiarity with the case, Gary's knowledge of the Charleston area and Tom, Agent Hannity, was an afterthought, sent with warrant in hand. We never expected anything even remotely like this happening. Tom will probably never have more than limited movement in his left arm again. His days as a Secret Service agent are over. He was blown out of a window and wound up with a twelve inch shard of glass right through his left shoulder. Tom managed, though, to crawl in and pull Freddie out of the flames, put out the fire on his feet and legs, then went back in for the admiral. Gary was pulled from the building, basically dead. Tom brought him back."

Annie was silent, stunned, crying. "Oh, Bud. I'm so sorry. What's the prognosis?"

"Tom I told you about. Gary's touch and go right now from the smoke inhalation. Fred is probably going to lose one of his feet, possibly some of the leg. The doctors are trying to stabilize him and the president has ordered all three transferred to Bethesda once they're fit for moving, which will hopefully be within an hour or two."

There was a noticeable pause, then Annie asked, "So where do we go from here, Bud?"

"To be truthful, Annie? Ten minutes ago you were on your way back here under armed guard to face some serious charges. Right now, I'm not sure. I'm not really sure."

forty-five

Cheltenham, England Saturday, April 4, 1998 6:39pm (local)

Colonel Menneally and Lieutenant Commander Morris were first off the black lear jet with the United States flag emblazoned on the tail. They were met on the tarmac by Gunnery Sergeant John Williston and two men in Brooks Brothers suits.

"Colonel, welcome back, sir."

"Thanks, Gunny. Who're your friends?"

"I'm Bill Terrio, CIA. Nice to meet you, Colonel. And this is Sir Stephen Jennings, British Intelligence."

"Yeah, nice to meet you, too. Gunny? We need an ambulance. Got one guy with a bullet hole and he's been hurting for about, oh, five hours now."

"The transport is right over there, Colonel," said Williston. "We've got an American doctor waiting to treat him back at the base hospital."

"Do we have a...."

"Set of greens? Yes, sir. The change of clothes is in the back of the transport. Got the name Michaels stenciled on the pocket. Think that'll be okay?"

"Gunny, you are always a step ahead of me when I need it most. You, CIA," said Bob addressing Terrio. "What brings you and the gentleman from MI here?"

"Colonel, if I may?" Williston softly interrupted.

"What, Gunny?"

"Mister Terrio here is the *director* of the CIA, not just some spook in a suit they dug up to hang around here for a look-see. Sir Stephen is the British Director for Intelligence, sir."

"Thanks for the proper introduction, Gunny," said Bob, beginning to turn a slight shade of crimson from the faux pas.

"I tried, sir. I really did," the sergeant said with a slight shrug of his shoulders.

Terrio spoke up. "Not to worry, Colonel. I know you've had a long day. Started out, what? About nineteen hours ago? Paris. Helsinki. An afternoon at the lake. Then a stress-free tour of the Russian countryside. I understand the black flies are murder this time of year?"

"Sorry about my lack of class, Mister Terrio. Sir Stephen. Can I try this again? I'm Colonel Bob Menneally." He extended his hand which was welcomed warmly.

"Bill Terrio, Bob. Nice to meet you. You did some fine, fine work. I understand there's another passenger in there?"

Bill pointed to the lear jet as Michail was being taken off on a stretcher.

"Yes, sir," Bob responded while shaking hands with Jennings as well. "We do have someone of note in there. I assume that's why you're here?"

"It's the only reason we're here, Colonel."

"Then, sir, let's help him into the duty vehicle here."

The three men walked to the small ladder at the side of the lear jet. Gunnery Sergeant Williston was already there, while Zallonis and Murphy were inside the plane standing at the open door. A light rain had started to fall as the tired face of Aleksandr Romanov came into view. Terrio stepped onto the bottom rung of the ladder-cum-stairway and offered the man his hand.

"Thank you," said Romanov, with a slight hint of recognition in his eyes. "You're Terrio, aren't you?"

"Yes, Mister President. Bill Terrio. CIA. We met several years ago in Moscow."

"Da," said Romanov, a touch of a smile creeping across his face. "We drank some vodka that night. Too much, perhaps?"

"Yes. Definitely too much. You look well, sir."

"I don't feel well, William Davidovich. I am sure that I am not here as a welcome guest."

"That's not a totally correct assumption, Mister President. We do, however, have much to talk about. Actually, you have much to talk about, we have much to learn. I believe you know Sir Stephen Jennings, also?

"Da. Stephen Eduardovich. It is nice to see you again. How is your lovely wife? It's Anne, is it not?"

"That's correct, Mister President. She is well, thank you for asking."

Terrio took Romanov's arm. "Could you come with me, please? Thank you."

Romanov ducked his head under and through the small airplane door and stepped down onto the tarmac. Terrio waved off Williston and escorted Romanov to the waiting duty vehicle. While Terrio and Jennings helped Romanov into the rear seat, Gunnery Sergeant Williston hopped into the driver's seat and started the car. Menneally finished checking on the ambulance crew loading up Rostokovich and directed Morris to ride along with the injured man. The Colonel then ran the fifty yards across the airfield's runway and climbed into the front passenger seat with Williston.

"J.W.? I think we're ready to roll."

"What about Z and Murph, sir?"

"They're going to double-check the floor and the seat cushions for anything that might have fallen out of the pockets of our passengers. They'll be along shortly."

"Yes, sir. You wouldn't mind if I come back and pick them up, would you sir?"

"Not at all, Gunny. Not at all. How are our guests back at the duty office?"

"Somewhat restless, sir. But they'll get over it."

Menneally turned to the back seat and addressed Romanov. "We have a couple of people with whom you are probably familiar back at our office, sir. No doubt, you'll want the chance to say hello. But that, I'm afraid, is all you'll get."

Romanov looked from Menneally to Terrio to Jennings.

Bill then said, "We have Dimitri and two of your more-quiet types in custody, Mister President."

Romanov's face drooped, showing a level of age Terrio hadn't seen moments before.

"We can be civil about this, William, no?" asked Aleksandr.

"Unfortunately, Mister President, the time for civility has long since passed. You'll be treated fairly, in accordance with our laws. I can assure you, though, that you will not be greeted with open arms upon our arrival back in the States."

"The United States? As it is, William Davidovich, you've violated several international laws in taking me from my home and through another country, no less. I'm sure the Ambassador to Finland would have something to say about this? What of the British, Sir Stephen. Surely there is some kind of protection offered to someone like me here in Great Britain? I was taken against my will from my own home fifteen hundred miles and five countries away."

"Not to worry about that, President Romanov. Prime Minister Bakunin signed an authorization to extradite earlier today in a meeting with Secretary of State Paparelli. They have a suspicion that you were on the helicopter leaving Russian airspace. They allowed your trip here to continue, even though one or two of the young, eager soldiers on the ground tried to blow you out of the sky. No, the only thing people will have to say about you is maybe what a nice man you were, or something like that," said Sir Stephen.

Terrio added, "The discovery of the link between you and an international organized crime syndicate will lead to much speculation as to what became of you. As far as the Russian government is concerned, you are gone and they will work their way through an appropriate period of hand-wringing with a billion dollars or so of recovered Russian funds."

"You are blunt, William Davidovich. You seem angry as well."

"Let me think about this for a moment, Aleksi." Bill looked the man in the eyes for a solid minute as the car pulled up to the Go Team One building. "Yes, I am being blunt. Perhaps almost borderline rude. Maybe more than I should be with you. Angry? I don't think so, Mister President. I am hurt that you, a man to whom many of my country's leaders over the past twenty-five years looked upon as a friend, as an ally, would do that which you've done."

"What have I done, William Davidovich. Do you have proof of anything? Or is this entire episode a result of baseless accusations?"

"You know, Mister President, your English has gotten extremely better over the past few years," Bill managed a polite smile. "So much so that when you held your little meeting with Colonel Rostokovich on the lake earlier today, our friends here were able to hear every word you said, nice and clear."

"Again, accusations."

"No, Mister President, videotape with crystal clear audio."

Menneally turned around in the front seat of the car and held up the digital camcorder. The whiteness that was already the base color of Romanov's face slid from the pasty pale to an unhealthy looking ashen gray.

"Are you all right, Mister President?" asked Terrio, winking at Menneally. "Come. Let's go inside and get you a drink of water. And maybe a dime so you can call a lawyer."

The inside of the duty office was beginning to get somewhat gamey from the closeness of quarters and the three individuals who'd been tied up inside the duty bunkroom all day. Colonel Menneally ushered Terrio and Romanov into his office.

"Uhmm, Greg?" said the colonel to his friend still seated at the office desk.

With feet propped up on the desk and chin nestled into his chest, Yearwood was dozing in the colonel's chair. Bob walked around the desk and gently shook the Interpol agent's shoulder. Greg slowly opened an eye and looked up at Menneally.

"Hey, Bob! Nice of you to drop in. You know, this chair is pretty comfortable. I could get a lot of investigative work done sitting here."

"Yeah, Greg. So long as the crime-scene clues were tattooed to the back of your eyelids. Now, if you wouldn't mind?"

"Oh, you want your chair? Okay. I can take a hint." Greg put his feet on the floor and looked up, the sight of other people in the room catching his eye. "Jesus, Bob! You didn't tell me we had compa... holy shit."

Menneally was smiling as he made a somewhat informal introduction. "Aleksandr Romanov, Bill Terrio, Sir Stephen Jennings, I'd like you to meet one of the finest American expatriates working for Interpol, Greg Yearwood."

Greg sheepishly came around the desk and shook hands with the former Russian president, then two intelligence men.

"Hey, Greg. I'm Bill Terrio. Nice to meet you."

"As in CIA Director Bill Terrio?"

"Yeah, it rhymes with stereo. Easier to say than to spell."

Bob was trying his best to not laugh out loud at the position in which he'd placed his friend.

"Agent Yearwood, I'm Sir Stephen Jennings," offered the British intelligence chief.

"Sir Stephen, a pleasure. Your reputation precedes you, sir.

Greg stepped back towards Menneally and leaned in to whisper in his ear.

"Bob? You. Me. No gloves, buddy. We'll get one of those Texas cages and only one of us, read that me, will come out."

"Greg, please. I didn't intentionally set you up like this. You're the one who decided it was time to catch a few winks."

"Fine, then. You live. For now." Greg's whisper had grown to a stage whisper and he returned his voice to a regular speaking volume as he addressed the entire room. "I suppose there's a reason for you all being here, so I'll step outside and get some fresh air. If you'll excuse me, I'll just go lay down in front a large aircraft that's approaching take-off speed and put an end to my embarrassment. Mister President. Mister Director. Sir Stephen. Colonel."

Greg made his way past Terrio and Romanov, then stopped at the door. "Oh, by the way? Our two friends there had left some paperwork in their rental car. The one back in Paris?"

Bob nodded in recognition of the two assassins they'd picked up earlier that morning.

"They're both traveling on American passports," Greg continued. "Bogus, of course. But we're checking them out for a source. My guess, based solely on the conversation we, me and the Gunny, overheard is that they're Russian. And that Mister Moore guy we saved? His Russian's pretty good, too."

"Thanks for tip, Greg. Now if you will excuse us?"

"Sure, Bob. No problem. I can take a hint." Greg stepped through the door and pulled it gently shut behind him.

Colonel Menneally waited for the door latch to click before speaking. "Mister Terrio? We'll need to give those two other guys back to Interpol. Greg Yearwood was with us when we picked up Mister Moore and his two, would-be executioners slash kidnappers. They killed a high-priced call-girl and were going to either take Moore or kill him, we're not sure which. We do have the murder on tape, though. Cold blooded. One shot. Right about here," Menneally said as he pointed to his forehead.

"Let's see if they want to say hello to Mister Romanov here. If so, we'll let them exchange pleasantries and send them on their way with Agent Yearwood. First, though, we need to call the home office," said Bill with a point to the desk's telephone.

Menneally offered the phone to Terrio, sliding it to the front edge of the desk. While Bill dialed, Bob opened the small refrigerator tucked into one of the corners of his office, took out a three bottles of water and offered one each to the three others. Each accepted theirs graciously, Romanov voraciously sucking his down, draining it in seconds. Bob offered the as-yet-unopened bottle he still had in his hand to Romanov. Again, the Russian took the bottle, but this time sipped it slowly. Bob reached down and took out a bottle for himself and savored the first cool rush as it relieved the parchedness of his mouth. Bill was finishing up his very brief conversation with Washington when he handed the phone to Bob, mouthpiece muted by hand.

"It's the president, Colonel."

Taking another sip of water, Menneally took the phone. "Yes, Mister President."

"Bob? Helluva job, sir. One helluva job. Are you guys all okay?"

"Tired, but doing fine, sir. Mister Rosty's on his way to the base hospital."

"How's he doing?"

"He was in and out all the way back. Out for most of the trip, sir. He lost a lot of blood. I wouldn't venture a guess right now, sir. I'll check with the base hospital in a bit, though."

"Do that, Bob. And thanks again."

"My pleasure, Mister President."

"Oh, by the way. Did you save any receipts?"

"Actually, sir, I do have a line-by-line accounting. There's one item that'll be listed as entertainment."

"Is that the hooker, Bob?"

"Yes, sir. That would be the late lady of the evening, now deceased."

"Make sure we get the name of her family from your Interpol friend. We'll see if we can't slide some kind of compensation their way. I feel badly that we were there and didn't do anything, but we had no way of knowing."

"That's correct, sir. It happened too quickly for us to have even sneezed. I'll make sure Yearwood gets us the next-of-kin information. Other than that, sir, there was just a lot of gas."

"Munitions?"

"Nothing we wouldn't have used in the NATO op anyway, sir."

"Good. That'll help keep the GAO people off my behind for a while. They pay close attention to lame duck presidents like me, you know."

"I didn't know, sir. But now I do."

"Oh, Bob? Before I let you go, I was asked to tell you to make sure you check the brakes? I assume you know what that's all about?"

"That would be Justice Jalbert's way of telling me hello, sir, I would guess."

"Yes on the source. You can fill in the blanks on the story for me next week, when we get this whole thing cleared up and set aside."

"Will do, sir. Are you all set with us for now?"

"Yes, Bob. I told Terrio to get Moore and Romanov back here as soon as possible. I'm also authorizing you to release the two men you picked up in Paris back to Interpol. Let Interpol and the French deal with the murderers in their own fashion. You mentioned earlier that there was a video of that?"

"Yes, sir. There is."

"Good. Edit out Moore, if he is at all visible and then give Interpol the tape. That should help them earn some cooperative points with the local Paris police."

"We might need some authorization for transportation for the three back to France, sir. And maybe a couple of escorts?"

"I'll have it taken care of immediately, Colonel. Once again, just outstanding work. Thanks ever so much."

"My pleasure, Mister President. Do you need to speak with Director Terrio again?"

"Nope. I'm all set with him. There's a 737 on it's way into Cheltenham right now, coming down from Mildenhall. They'll be getting on that and getting out of your hair in the morning. We'll talk again soon. Goodbye, Bob."

"Goodbye, Mister President."

Menneally hung up the phone, looking at Sir Stephen and Terrio.

"There's a plane on it's way here, Director Terrio. Until it gets here, may I offer you the use of my office?"

"That would be great, Colonel. I know you're tired, hungry and well, kind of ready for a hot shower."

"I won't take any offense at that crack, sir."

"None intended, Bob. Go have a cold one with your troops for me, first, okay?"

"Is that an order?"

"Consider it straight from the lips of POTUS."

"Very well, sir. We'll be just down the road at the base watering hole. If you have time, why don't you stop in for a quick one?"

"I just might, Colonel. Is it okay if I bring Sir Stephen?"

"The more the merrier, sir."

"We'll try and pop in, Bob. Thanks again," Bill said offering his hand.

Hearty handshakes all around, Menneally stopped and addressed Romanov.

"I wish you well, sir, however this turns out."

Bob shook the man's hand and walked out of the office. Before the door closed, Terrio stepped to the doorway and asked for an extra chair. Menneally pulled one of the outer office desk chairs from its place and gave it a gentle push towards Bill. The chairs having been set up around Menneally's desk in the office, Terrio, Jennings and Romanov all took seats. Sir Stephen had been offered the bigger chair behind Bob's desk.

"Aleksandr," Terrio began. "I will call you that from this point forward. I apologize for any perceived informalities that take place from this point on, but you, sir, are a criminal, plain and simple. The more forthcoming you are with information, the easier it will be for us to dispense of your legal case. I can only urge you to be completely candid in your answers to us. From the American side of things, we have absolutely every available resource standing by to check out each and every missing detail you will provide to us. I'm sure that it won't take but ten minutes for Sir Stephen to get things fired up on this side of the Atlantic."

"I am not sure what you think you have, William and I am not sure what it is you seek from me. Ask away," Romanov said somewhat flippantly.

"Aleksandr, let me remind you that we have a full confession, from you and from one of your operatives. There is no court in the world that will not allow justice, in this case especially, to be served. Let me start with the big question and we can take it from there." Bill sat forward on his seat, resting his forearms on the edge of the desk.

"What was your general plan for the future of the United States?"

"As it was when I was in office, William Davidovich. To make the USSR the world dominant power. This plan to which you refer was merely a means to a goal."

"What was the ultimate goal, Aleksi? What was going to happen to put you in the driver's seat for your desired super superpower?"

"Simply? We were going to destabilize the American economy. The people of your country would wake up one morning and find that all they thought they possessed was gone. A devalued American dollar would lead to chaos in your streets. The president of your country would be forced to declare martial law. From there, the restructuring of your government would be a simple task, with the eventual controlling of business being handled by Washington. Funnel all the profits to one central point, then dole out whatever is necessary to provide for the basics for the American people. Food, medicine, education. All would be of an acceptable quality, available on a more equitable level. That's it in a nutshell. The same philosophy we practiced in our own country."

"I won't get into questioning the philosophy of holding your people in a lifetime of indentured servitude without the ability to speak freely, Aleksi. We'll leave that to the brain-trust that will eventually learn of this and wish to probe deeper. Next question concerns the number of active operatives. We know about Rostokovich, Fidrych and, for lack of easier names, Hewes and Moore. Where does Fulton fit into all of this?"

"Fulton is an American citizen. The answers to any questions about him are in a set of sealed adoption records in New Mexico. The short version?" Romanov paused to take a sip from his water. "The short version is that his birth parents were both Soviet, convicted and jailed under false pretenses. Fulton was born in prison, William, and both of his real parents died in prison. He researched his adoption process and upon learning the truth, was directed our way with his hopes to exact revenge on a country he truly believed heartless. He came to me. We did not recruit him. He was merely directed to us."

"Directed by who? This Konstantin we've heard about? Rostokovich's brother, if I understood you properly from the tape at the lake?"

"Da. Konstantin is Michail's older brother. Konstantin, unlike his younger sibling, is faithful and loyal. He was enrolled in college in America when he met Fulton. Yes, he suggested a meeting with my country's representatives. Konstantin, however, has done nothing illegal in your country. Unless you count making more than twenty-five years of investments pay off. He has a very, very sharp business mind. Oh and there were those years he spent in your military. He did, perhaps, provide information from time to time that did not pertain to the ongoing process."

"So this Konstantin Rostokovich? He's still active in doing your dirty work in America?"

"You call it dirty work, William. I call it being professional. Yes, he is still there as we speak."

"What of his role in the events that have transpired, Aleksandr? Has he played a part in the murders of the real Messers Moore and Hewes?"

"No. He knew of them. He helped provide information to the persons responsible, including me. But did he aid in the planning or execution or disposition? No."

"So what does he do when not doing your bidding?"

"That's a sensitive question, William Davidovich. He's basically doing that which I asked him to continue to do. Be a solid member of the American society and provide support to the active participants as needed."

"Support? Do you mean money?"

"Money, yes. And also information. As a matter of fact, since I am no longer available for contact, he now speaks for me. If there are things in motion, those tasked with following through on their assignments will get their instructions to proceed or abort from him."

"Such as the Fulton scenario?"

"Fulton scenario? What do you mean by that?"

"Your plan was to get Griffen to resign and eliminate Fulton to allow Hewes to move into the White House, was it not?"

"Yes. That was before Fulton was able to be fully trusted by those who seek the same goals."

"You're saying that Fulton is no longer a target?"

"I find him more than acceptable as a president, now. He's a fine man doing an excellent job."

"Then why would you allow an assassin to be responsible for his security?"

"What is that they say, William? Keep those you trust, close. Keep those you don't, closer? I simply have made it possible to keep all of my options open."

"Are there any other operatives, Aleksi? Any other deep seeds you planted and are now waiting to bloom?"

"There were others, yes. Sadly, most of them have died."

"Died? Or eliminated?"

"The end result is the same, William. It's all the same in the end."

Terrio sat back in the small office chair, took a deep breath and leaned back onto the desk.

"Let me ask you one more time, Aleksandr. Who is Konstantin now?"

"This one point gives me a position of advantage, does it not? I need some kind of assurance from you in return."

"The only assurance you'll receive from me at this point is that, right now, I won't wrap my hands around your neck and choke you until you cease to live. Other than that, you are in the giving position of this negotiation. You've already used up all of your taking points."

"Konstantin is someone known to your president and many of his aides, maybe even yourself."

The knock on the door broke the uneasy silence that followed. Terrio got up and opened it. Menneally was standing there. "Mister Terrio? I think you're going to want to see this."

"Bob? I thought you were going out for a beer?"

"I was, sir, until my other two men came back from the Learjet. I sent them in for a last minute clean-up. They found a compact disc of some kind of goat music and it's got more than music on it."

"Goat music?" asked Bill, stepping out of the office for a moment.

"Well, goatherds singing. It's a thing from Tajikistan."

"How do we know it's got more than singing Tajiki goatherds on it?"

"The Gunny likes to listen to his Dixie Chicks CD's on the computer. Saves space here in the office," explained Menneally. "We popped it in to see what it sounded like and when we opened the "d" drive, it had the music tracks and some hard files."

Bill stepped by the Colonel and sat down at the chair. He guided the mouse cursor to the first of the yellow computer folder icons and clicked on it. He scrolled down through the document and then looked at Menneally.

"How much of this did you see, Bob?"

"Enough to know that even though I don't speak Russian or read Cyrillic, you've got one scheming son of a bitch in that room and that you should probably call President Griffen right now."

forty-six

New York City   Saturday, April 4, 1998   2:47pm (local)

Special Agent Jim Fahey parked his car in an *Official Vehicles Only* spot outside of the New York Presbyterian hospital's Weill Cornell Center. Flipping his visor down to reveal his official FBI vehicle credential, he hopped out of the vehicle and stepped onto the sidewalk leading to the main entrance. Camped outside of the main entrance were a slew of reporters. Slipping through the assembled crowd, he overhead one of them mention Sandra Rose by name. Good news travels fast, he thought. Just not fast enough, or they would have been here before the ambulance arrived. Well, he thought, it was a weekend. Some of these poor slobs had probably gotten called back in from a weekend in the Hamptons. He made a quick look at the group and saw one or two recognizable logos, including Entertainment Tonight, NBC, ABC and CNN. Noticeably absent was NBS. He was pleased to think that Sandy's own employer would have the decency to allow her some level of detachment from the media circus that usually evolves from tragic events such as this. He made his way through the halls easily, returning to the Intensive Care Unit where he'd left Don Hough only a few hours ago. He waved hello to the nurses at the unit's central station and knocked gently on the glass door to the unit in which Sandra Rose had been recovering from her savage beating at the hands of her now deceased ex-husband. The light blue curtain was pulled back a bit to allow Don to take a peek out. The door opened and Don stepped out into the busy yet quiet hallway.

"Hey, Jimmy. What's up?"

"We found out more than I think we wanted to, Don. There's a lot of gray area surrounding Fred's businesses. The fish stinks from the head, as they say, buddy. For starters, it looks like Jonathon was working for Fred."

"Excuse me?"

"Probably one of the most heard phrases making the rounds today, I'm sure, Don. Jonathon's money trail leads to and from AFR Enterprises."

"Surely it's just some kind of an international name thing, Jim. I've known Fred for over twenty years now. We went through Officer's Candidate School in the Navy for Christ's sake. Are you suggesting that he was into some sort of international crime thing?"

"The paper trail leads in that direction, Don. I know you're preoccupied with Sandy right now, but can you give me a ten minute thumbnail on Fred?"

"Yeah, I can, Jim. And I'm certain you'll find that there's really no basis for traveling down the road on which you're heading."

"Let's go over to one of those little conference rooms, buddy. Did you have lunch yet?"

Smiling, Don shook his head. "No. Actually haven't had anything to eat since The Drummer gave me a hot muffin on my way out this morning."

"The Drummer? Is he still writing for the papers back home? I always loved his stuff. Made me laugh out loud most of the time, especially his cat columns. Of course, we have two kitties at home ourselves now, but don't ever tell him, okay? The last thing I need is to be a subject of one of his pieces. Let me call out for a sandwich for us. While we're waiting for the food to show up, we can do the quick version of Freddie."

Jim stopped at the nurse's station, flashed his i.d.. and asked if there was good deli nearby that delivered. The smiling nurse pulled a dog-eared photocopy of a take-out menu from the small corkboard behind her chair and passed it to Fahey, along with the phone. Jim dialed the number, ordered two sandwiches, some chips and drinks. Nodding his yes while saying the words, he told them, yes, it was an order to go and that, yes, he'd like it delivered. He provided his location, hung up and, thanked the nurse as he returned the phone.

"Could you do me one more little favor, Nurse," he paused to make sure he had the name on her nametag correctly. "Madsen?"

"What's that Agent Fahey?"

"I'm impressed. You remembered my name from a simple flash of my i.d. card? And here I am cheating reading your nametag."

She simply smiled at him and asked, "So what's the favor?"

"When the deli guy or gal comes up, could you send them into us over there?" he asked, pointing towards the now vacant room.

"Certainly. We'll also let you know if there's any development with your friend," she replied, gesturing towards the now-closed and curtained unit that currently housed Sandy.

"Thanks again."

Jim placed his hand on the back of Don's shoulder and guided him to the conference room. Once inside, they sat down in the comfortable, plush chairs, placed, no doubt, for easing the pain of what families often heard from caring physicians in this room. It also served as a quiet place for a patient's loved ones to sit and gather their thoughts and wits. Jim had shut the door and taken out his notebook and pen.

"I just need the brief version, Donny. Enough to figure out where this Earle guy comes into play with Fred and his company."

"Here's the Fred I know, Jim. He was born and raised in Illinois. Waukegan, as a matter of fact. He said his dad retired out of the Navy up there and landed a job as a government worker at the boot camp. His mom died before he went off to college. His dad died before Fred finished his first year of college."

"Where did he go to college?"

"He started at Marquette University, up in Milwaukee. It was close enough for him to commute and save on the room and board, plus they had a really good business program. That was back in 1968. After his dad died, he took some time off and then, in 1971, he enrolled at Yale. He had the chance to live a wild, rebellious existence, even in the Ivy league halls of Yale. He told us he dabbled in some activities with the various student groups. At the time, Jim, there were some changes comin' down in America."

"That's an age crack, isn't it, Don?"

"Even with your obvious lack of chronological advancement, you show a wisdom beyond your years."

"That's why I'm a government investigator, old man."

Laughing it off, Don continued. "He hung out with the SDS most of the time. He often said they had the right idea, just the wrong way of going about it. They were on-campus at Yale, but most definitely not a welcome presence. Fred even mentioned he was an underclassman when the vice president was a senior."

"Vice President Fulton?"

"Yeah, the present V.P., Jim. Fred said that Fulton was a smart, impressive man even then. Always applied himself and even helped pass on some study tips for working through the more difficult professors' classes."

"What did Fulton get out of this friendship?"

"How about an uncanny knack for picking winners in the stock market? Fulton turned the knowledge Fred had shared into a full-scholarship to the Wharton School of Business, which had him, at something like twenty-five or twenty-six, running one of the largest banks in the South. Fred was paying cash for his tuition by the end of his second year at Yale. His dad had left a tidy sum that Fred used in a very unlike-a-nineteen-year-old fashion. He invested it in several blue chip stocks, such as IBM and AT&T and Boeing. Eighteen months later, he had diversified his portfolio and was soon the most self-supporting second year Eli in New Haven."

"Fred actually told you all of this?"

"Yeah. Fred, Bud Nelson, Michaud and I are more like brothers than friends. We shared so many things, that between us, we've all said several novenas in hopes that the statutes of limitations have expired on most of them. Want me to continue?"

"Sure, Don. Go ahead."

"Now, for the adventure of it, so he said, Fred signed on the dotted line, with a bachelor's degree in business from Yale in hand and joined the Navy. That's where we all got introduced, Jimmy, at O.C.S. in Newport, Rhode Island. Fred and I got orders to the staff of the Commander of Submarine Group Two in Charleston. He was the admiral's administrative guy, I was the communications officer. At the end of our three year obligation, I resigned my commission and wound up putting my journalism degree from Holy Cross to work in the NBS newsroom here in New York. Fred decided to stay on, saying he was really having a good time. He and the admiral, Gary Dericksen, were quite a team. When Dericksen got shifted from Charleston to the Pentagon, he took Freddie with him. For the next two years, the two of them basically ran the U.S. Navy's submarine fleet. Then, when Dericksen decided to put in his papers to retire, Fred resigned his commission."

"When was that, Don?"

"That would be early 1982 or so."

"So what happened with Fred then?"

Don nodded to the window of the conference room and saw Nurse Madsen approaching with a young, casually dressed man holding two brown bags.

"We'll pick it up after we have some food, okay?"

"Sounds good to me, Donny. My treat this time, though. Put your wallet away."

"Not a problem with me, Jim. Make sure you get a receipt to expense this lunch. All part of your investigation and stuff like that. I'll vouch for you."

Jim stood and opened the door and turned to Don. "Thanks for the offer, Donny. In case the Bureau's bean-counters call me on this, I'll give them your number."

Jim took a twenty out of his wallet, took the bags and nodded to the delivery boy to keep the change. The kid smiled and bounced away, while Jim used his foot to close the door behind him.

"That's a nice thing you just did there, Jimmy. Glad I taught you well."

"You betcha, Don. Tip 'em good and they'll remember you next time, right?"

"Never failed us at Flannagan's in Saco, if I remember correctly."

"You do remember correctly, buddy. Remember Cindy?"

"Downright Bubbly. D.B. Yeah, I do have more than a passing recollection of her, too."

As they sorted out their lunches, Don went on with the story of Fred.

"So in 1982, Fred went out to California. He said it was to find himself. I'm pretty sure it was to check into which Silicon Valley companies were going to be worthwhile investments."

"What made you think that?"

"Oh, little hints, like the company he bought and ran for five years, then sold off at an ungodly profit."

"Computer company?"

"Actually, just one that made microchips. They were on the verge of a breakthrough in development when he purchased it. He had a tidy little portfolio and pumped the needed funds into the project. The chips went into production six months after he took over and within three years, became the most sought after product on the market. He hung out through two years of obscene offers of even more obscene money for the company and finally, when the amount got to eight digits, he took the cash. That would have been the spring of 1987. He reinvested the money into a small business that was ready for an infusion of capitol to take it to the next level. Cutting edge security firm called Periscope. This was an idea that Admiral Dericksen had been kicking around and started up shortly after his retirement from the Navy. Dealt with addressing corporate security issues, such as computer networks and keeping the files safe from prying eyes. The home office was literally that, an office in Dericksen's house in Charleston. Within six months, Fred had not only infused the venture with money, but had added his administrative expertise to send Periscope up in a big way. By early 1988, Gary and Fred held a grand opening at the new corporate headquarters in downtown Charleston. They even paid my way down for a long weekend. I wound up writing the copy for a Dan Rather piece that ran on the Evening News.

"All that aside, Fred spent the next two years traveling the world, coming back every couple of months to check in on Gary and on us. In 1991, Freddie bought WCBR and the waterfront condo next to DiMillo's in Portland. When I got back from the Persian Gulf assignment, Sandy had written me off in favor of Jon and I was on my way to Washington to be the White House correspondent. The network had figured that since I was tight with Nelson, who was now on his way to DC with the Griffen administration, that I'd get more than the occasional inside scoop. What the network hadn't figured was that I was ready to let my brain go into neutral and veg out for a while. That's when Freddie came to the rescue. He not only made me the offer to be his news director, but he also made me a V.P. of Wicked Good Radio. I was and still am, getting an obscene salary as well as a piece of the action. Other than running the station, which he does every day, he travels occasionally to check on some of his other investment properties."

"Where are the other properties, Don? Are there any in England?"

"England. France. Germany. South America. Japan. From what I know and I've not made it a point to pry up to now, he's got a knack for picking the next *big thing* and riding it to the winner's circle."

"You've given me more than enough to work with Donny," said Jim, finishing his sandwich.

A knock on the door was followed by Nurse Madsen poking her head into the room. "Miss Rose is awake, Mister Hough. I thought you'd like to know."

"Thanks, Gina. I'll be right there," he said, glancing at Jim.

"Go, Don. I'll be there in a moment. Let me call the boss."

Don got up from the table and followed Nurse Madsen to Sandy's unit. Gina opened the door for him and he slid around the blue curtain.

"Hi there," Don said.

Sandy was awake, her eyes were bandaged as a result of the surgery, but she was able to see out of her left eye. Lifting the dressing up and peeking out from behind the bandage she said, "Hey, Don. Fanks for coming. I couldn' fink of anyone elf to call."

"Well, Sandy, I'm glad you did. I haven't called your folks, yet. I wanted to make sure you wanted them to know before I did."

"'at alone is worf a hug and I could really use one right now."

"How about a soft one, though, kiddo. You're in pretty tough shape."

Don stepped to the bed and gingerly put his arms around her. The memories came back with a rush and a roar, overloading his senses and filling his eyes with tears. He heard her sobbing softly into his shoulder.

"It's okay, Sandy. I'm here. And I'll be here. For as long as you need me. It's all right, now."

Sandy continued to sob, the heaving of her body increasing in intensity. Don tightened his grip, ever so gently, being mindful of the multiple wounds she had suffered at the hands of that bastard, Jonathon. Reminding himself that he shouldn't think ill of the dead, he shook off the proprietary tenet of good upbringing instilled in him by his mother and promptly returned to his vision of Jonathon Earle beginning a very lengthy stay in the fiery pits of hell.

"That's what Don was able to tell me, Director Hammett. Anything else come up down that way?"

"Yes, Fahey. Too much. None of it looking very good. Not good at all. Also, there are a few things that have come down just in the past half-hour that will be of concern to Mister Hough, but I'd prefer we let Mister Nelson handle the news."

"Bad, sir?"

"Really bad, Fahey. Just absolutely bad. It's almost four in the afternoon and you must be overdue for sleep by now. Why not head for home and grab some sleep. I'd like you down here in the morning for a briefing. It'll be a fairly high-level thing, so wear your best suit."

"Bad news and a get-really-dressed-up high-level briefing? Can you give me a thumbnail, at least?"

Jim listened as the FBI director ran through the rough outline. Five minutes later, Fahey let out a heavy sigh.

"Holy shit."

"What was that, Fahey?"

"I said "holy shit," Director Hammett. Sorry if that offends."

"No offense at all, Jim. Matter of fact, I heard President Griffen use those very words not ten minutes ago."

forty-seven

President Griffen stood on the tarmac of Andrews Air Force Base, alone, in a gentle spring rain that had just begun. He wore a windbreaker over his white shirt, long since free of its tie which was shed at lunch. His black wing-tips had been exchanged for a pair of white athletic shoes. He was tired of looking important today. Now was not a time for formality. There would be plenty of that in the coming days. His tall, solid frame was somewhat stooped from the combination of mental fatigue and the deep feeling of loss he was experiencing at that moment. He'd lost his wife, although, she'd be back. Of that he was sure and he would welcome her with open arms. He'd admitted to himself when this Stark thing had happened that he'd have reacted the same way as those he thought should have known better. Now, a good man he'd sent to do what might have been, what should have been, a fool's errand, was coming to Washington for the final time.

With two more hours to go before landing at Andrews, Agent Brian Bello went forward in Air Force Two for a cup of coffee. The

490

stewards had cleared the inflight dinner-slash-lunch trays an hour before, about one pm Washington time and had stowed the serving carts in preparation for landing. The atmosphere on board was, for the most part, informal. The members of the press corps, as well as the vice president's staff were well acquainted with each other. It was not unusual to see a senior political reporter engaged in a high-stakes game of cards with one of Fulton's junior staff members. It always brought smiles from the press corps whenever Fulton would pull up a seat and asked to be dealt in, then team up with the reporters to chase the younger staffer from the game. Fulton always, privately, slipped his charge enough money to cover the loss, adding the gentle reminder about a fool and his money.

"Hey, Jonesy? Can I get a cup of coffee?" Bello asked the steward.

"Certainly, Mister Bello," said the Air Force airman, rising from his jump seat.

"Don't get up, buddy. I can get it, if that's okay?"

"It's fine by me, sir."

"Thanks."

Bello poured himself a fresh cup and continued his walk forward. Just aft of the cockpit, there was a small conference room. He knocked on the door and stepped back. The plane's Sergeant-At-Arms opened the door. Brian gestured with a hand and a shrug of his shoulders that asked if he could step inside. The Sergeant opened the door and allowed Bello to enter. He walked into the room and nodded to the Air Force Captain sitting near the door.

"Permission to speak with Agent Dayle, sir?"

"Granted," came the official response.

Brian walked to the far end of the table and looked at Tom. "So have we found out the reason you're under arrest?"

"Maybe it was those deductions on my tax return. That'll teach me to file early. I don't really know, B. They either don't know themselves, or they're just not talking."

"I'm sure we can get whatever this is straightened out when we get back to the office, buddy. Can I get you anything?"

"No, I'm all set. Captain Radler there has been most kind. Like I said, I think they're just as in the dark about this as I am. Just doing their jobs. Can't hold that against them."

"Hang in there, Tommy. We'll be on the ground in a bit."

Brian patted his friend on the shoulder and left the room. Sipping his coffee, he checked on the other Secret Service agents seated in the duty area. He pulled back the curtain that kept this area somewhat private. Three of them were sound asleep, catching a few winks to ward off the jet lag. The fourth, Agent Beal, was reading a paperback.

Bello nodded and whispered to Beal, "Hey? Whatcha reading?"

Beal held up the book's cover. "One of those straight-to-paperback Clancy books. They're really good for a trip like this."

"Let me read it when you're done?"

"Sure, B.B. I'll pass it on when I'm finished."

Bello closed the curtain that served as a privacy partition. At least as much privacy as one might hope to find on this flying fortress. He continued back through the passenger area. Most of the press corps had returned home on commercial flights earlier in the day, so there were not that many of their number on board. The remaining few staffers were all sound asleep, enjoying the rare pleasure of putting their seats all the way back and stretching out over a couple chairs.

Bello approached the vice president's private cabin, where Fulton had been since just after take-off. This trip had been tiring in that they had accomplished much in just a few days and Fulton was looking forward to spending a few days with his family once they got back. Too bad, thought Bello. His family was certainly going to be disappointed. He gave a gentle knock on the door. There was no response from inside. Brian opened the door and slipped inside. Fulton was asleep, rolled up onto his side, facing towards the outside of the airplane, back exposed. This would be too easy, thought Bello as he removed the six inch syringe from his coat pocket. He pulled back on the plunger, ensuring it was full of air and gently guided it into the vice president's back, just to the left of the man's spine. The needle went in effortlessly, with barely a perceptible motion from the sleeping Fulton. Bello eased the plunger in and quickly removed the needle, slipping the cover back over the exposed tip and sliding the package back into his suitcoat's inside pocket. The vice president began to cough. Softly at first, then more vigorously. His snoring stopped as his breathing became louder, more labored. The breathing turned to gasping as Don was unable to take and hold a breath. He rolled over onto his back, now face up, clawing at his chest, mouth wide open in anguish. He was frantic at first, then, slowly, his motions ceased. His eyes were open, but not focused on anything. Brian stepped back towards the small bed. He moistened his finger and placed it under the vice president's nose. There was no air coming out of either the nasal passages or the mouth. The visual of Fulton's chest indicated no movement. Bello then gently placed the back of his hand on Don's neck, verifying that there was no pulse. Too bad, thought Mister Bello. Fulton was really an all right kind of guy. But Fulton was in the way of Hewes on the road to the Oval Office and orders were orders.

Agent Bello eased the door open to make sure there was no one nearby and slipped out, quietly closing the door behind him. He used the designer handkerchief that was neatly folded in his front coat pocket to wipe the door handle clean of fingerprints, just in case. It was a moot point, as his would be the next hand on the door when it came time to wake the vice president up prior to landing. Of course, he'd have at least one witness to their horrible discovery that Donald R. Fulton, Vice President of the United States, had passed away.

The autopsy would reveal the cause of death as a severe myocardial event. The abnormal arrhythmia indicated on the last EKG in the vice president's medical file would be the leading indicator that something had been wrong prior to what they would wrongly assume was the result of some sort of an aneurysm. This misguided finding would be reached as a result of the discovery of the fragmented mass that would occupy the space in chest cavity where once Fulton's heart had beat. Instead of using his favorite means to an end, the injection of air into the victim's pleural cavity which caused a painful, sometimes fatal collapsed lung, Mister Bello had injected a syringe full of air directly into the vice president's heart, causing it to explode, as well as inducing a pneumothorax.

Agent Bello took a seat in the last row and reached for one of the magazines stored in the seat-pouch in front of him. He opened to an article in the middle and waved hello to one of the groggy press members making their way to the plane's aft restrooms. Bello turned to watch the man go into the lavatory and went back to reading his magazine. He made a mental note of the time, 2:23pm eastern, having set his watch for the home zone as they took off from Madrid. Another two hours or so and they'd be back at Andrews, wringing hands and comforting each other in their moment of loss and sorrow.

✳ ✳ ✳

The medical flight from Charleston had taken off at 2:25pm with the badly injured trio on board, stabilized and ready to receive more intensive care at Bethesda Naval Hospital on orders from President Griffen.

Admiral Gary Dericksen, USN, retired, was currently breathing with the aid of a ventilator, the cumbersome tubing snaked down through his tracheal airway to make his lungs take in much needed oxygen. His smoke inhalation had not been all that severe, but he'd managed to scorch the tender matter that made up his lungs by breathing in the heat blast from the explosion. Along with the cautious concern for his lungs, the team of medical professionals were paying close attention to his cardiac condition. Although his EKG had been showing a steady, consistent rhythm since he was revived, his age combined with the fact that his heart had stopped gave them reason to be especially vigilant.

Fred Singletary was in serious but stable condition. He was breathing on his own, as well as semi-conscious. The burns on the lower part of his legs were second and third degree, with the most serious being his feet. He'd probably lose one of his feet at least. Fred was aware of this and had nodded resignedly when asked by the trauma team who had worked on him in Charleston if he understood. He was able, through the pain, to reply that, yes, it would suck, but it beat the alternative.

That kind of attitude always made it easier for the doctors and nurses and therapists working on a trauma victim to do their jobs efficiently and without reservation. The patient's attitude in this particular case was that he wanted to live, regardless of the cost. A doctor trying to save a patient can make less judicious decisions in regard to a part in order to once again make healthy the whole. Fred was being provided pain medication, antibiotics and much needed fluids intravenously and, was for the most part as comfortable as he could be. The emergency room staff had all but given him up for gone when he was brought into Charleston General. Once they'd done an initial débride of the burns, wrapping his feet and legs in the specially treated bandages designed to promote faster healing and skin-regeneration, as well as a generous application of topical antibiotics, he awoke, still shocky and disoriented. He was given a small dose of pain killer that brought him a little bit back somewhat closer to reality and from there, he was able to direct the doctor as to when he was no longer feeling the pain. Being able to talk to the doctor made it easier for all concerned, especially Fred. He wanted to live. He needed to make sure Gary would be okay.

Agent Tom Hannity had regained consciousness on the way to the hospital, but was feeling funny on his left side. Funny was the only word he was able to use to describe to the doctor what he was experiencing. The doctor examined his wound and had ordered a series of x-rays as well as three units of blood to help replace that which had been lost. Tom's hearing was still off, the ringing had somewhat subsided in the forty minutes or so that had passed from the time of the explosion until they had been brought into the emergency room. The doctor assured him that the ringing would most likely go away, in time. He might be left with tinnitus, which, though aggravating and distracting at first, would become less and less noticeable in time. The x-ray results were not quite so promising. The hospital's plastic surgeon was working on suturing the multiple facial lacerations Tom had suffered, while the orthopedic surgeon was delivering the not-so-good news about the funny feeling on his left side. The glass shard, Tom was told, had severed a half-dozen ligaments, as well as the muscles that control his left arm. The nerve damage was significant, but he should consider himself lucky that it was the muscles and ligaments that suffered the wrath of the glass and not his heart and lungs. The glass dagger had stopped just short of puncturing his left lung and had it been a few inches further to the right, it would have taken out his heart.

Now, on board the Air Force medical transport, the three were lined up along the same side of the aircraft, each with a team of doctors and nurses on hand to attend to their needs specifically. Tom had waved one of the officers over to him so he could inquire, softly, about the two men with whom he'd been tasked with protecting. About, he felt, the two men he'd failed to protect. The Air Force nurse, Lieutenant Jan Speary, had informed him that they were both resting comfortably and that he should also try and rest. He asked how much longer until they landed at Washington and he was told no more than another half-hour. Tom gently closed his eyes, the hum of the aircraft slowly filling his head with enough vibrations to override the ringing in his ears.

He was abruptly brought back to reality by a steadier ringing sound. Shaking his head, he looked above him to see the monitors to which he was connected. His heart rate and breathing rate appeared consistent and none of the lights on the display were flashing. He lifted his head a few inches off the pillow and could see a flurry of activity a little further down inside the aircraft. He did not know who was where in the order of the gurneys that were parked in a row on this one side of the airplane, but whoever was furthest down the line was in deep trouble. The ringing subsided enough to give him the opportunity to focus his hearing on the activity twenty feet away.

"Charge to two hundred. Clear," he heard someone say.

"Not working, sir."

"Damn it! Charge to two-fifty. Clear."

"Still nothing, sir."

The group had grown to include the other physicians on board, with Tom and his immediate neighbor being gently distracted by their respective nurses. Tom's nurse got up and walked down to the edge of the activity and pulled the dividing curtain closed, leaving Tom to wonder who was in that much trouble. Leaving Tom to feel that much worse than he already did for having failed at his duty.

* * *

Having blown out of Washington for the weekend, M. Bradford Hewes and Robin were settling in at a table, having been seated by the window overlooking Chesapeake Bay by a very impressed host. It was a small restaurant, neither flashy nor trashy, a short drive from the bed and breakfast where the two had decided to make camp, away from the madness that is Washington. It was a simple, plain restaurant, with nice linens on the table and a well-rounded menu.

Brad and Robin often sneaked away to the small, out-of-the-way eateries and hotels to enjoy each other's company away from the prying eyes of the Washington paparazzi. Sometimes they'd come out this way for a meal. Other times, they'd make it a day, or several, such as this particular weekend getaway.

They'd left the capital last night at separate times in separate cars, having met in the parking lot by the MCI Center. They'd taken Robin's car, free of the official license plates that designated the vehicle as the one issued to The Speaker of the House, as well as the official driver that came with the license plate. Brad dismissed his driver in his usual, courteous fashion, bidding him a good night and to enjoy the weekend. After a brief stop at small diner on the way east, Brad and Robin had checked into the quiet, private little bed and breakfast that appreciated their business and respected their privacy. They'd spent the night in bed, as well as the morning and afternoon. There was neither television nor radio in the room, as was Brad's request. Here, they could escape the world and just be themselves, free of concern.

Now, at the restaurant where they watched the gentle rain moving across Chesapeake Bay, heading for the Delmarva Peninsula, she wondered if he would ever make the step to just fire her, then marry her. He wondered if he could keep on living this lie, being with this woman for whom he cared deeply, without letting on to what he, no, who he, really was. The waitress brought their menus and asked if they cared for a drink before dinner. Yes, they had said. Brad ordered his usual Stoly on the rocks, while Robin asked for a strawberry daiquiri. The waitress returned with their drinks and leaned into the table while setting the beverages in front of the two.

"Mister Speaker, I'm so sorry to hear about your house. That was just awful."

"Excuse me?" asked the puzzled Hewes.

"Your house. In South Carolina? It's been on the news all day. You didn't know?"

Brad was up from the table before the sound of the waitress's question had a chance to resonate off the rain-splattered windows. Robin was sitting, just watching as Brad bounded out of the dining area towards the entrance. At the front desk, he asked the hostess if there was a television in the building. Yes, he was told and was escorted into the small room that served as the office and employee lounge. Brad flipped the set on and handed the remote control to the hostess, asking for her to turn on CNN. The image came onto the screen and Brad felt his heart sink, his stomach drop and his blood run cold. The graphics across the bottom of the screen indicated the feed was "Live from Charleston. 4:33pm," with the bold banner proclaiming this story "Breaking News." Brad turned up the volume as he saw the reporter standing in front of what was left of the Hewes Family Library and Study, built in 1803, now destroyed in 1998.

The CNN reporter was saying. .".. *Officials believe the three men injured here earlier have all been transported to other hospitals, out of the Charleston area. Damage to this historic building on the Hewes Family plantation is extensive, most likely a total loss. The cause of the explosion, which was heard for miles around, is still unknown and under investigation...*"

Hewes reached for the telephone on the manager's desk and without hesitation, dialed a long-distance number. Waiting through the third and fourth rings, he began to feel sick to his stomach. On the fifth ring, the phone was answered.

"Hello?" he heard the voice coming from the other end.

"Mother? Are you all right? I just saw the news."

"I am fine, Yoshi. Just fine."

"Can you tell me what happened? I mean, are you there alone right now?"

"Yes, I am alone. There were three men here. One of them a policeman of some sort. He showed me his badge. One of them was Kostya. The other one I didn't know."

"I need you to pack a bag with some clothes. Enough for a few days. Do you understand, Mother?"

"Yes, Yoshi. I do. We are going somewhere?"

"I'm afraid we'll have to, at least for a short while."

"Do you feel there is danger from what happened here today?"

"There's a long story that goes with this, Mother. I have to ask you to trust me and just be ready to go when I get there."

"All right, Yoshi. I'll see you when you arrive. I love you."

"I love you too, Mother. See you very soon."

Hewes hung up the phone, looking down at the desk. The CNN newscast had moved onto another story. He picked up the remote control and powered the television set off. How could this have happened? Then he remembered. The explosive devices. He was always careful with the one at the bottom of the cellar stairs. Perhaps they were in the basement, these three men. If so, then they probably didn't get as far as the tunnel. He could take care of that leftover task as soon as he got to South Carolina. He felt confident they couldn't have made it to the tunnel and so, at least from the Hewes end of things, there was no reason for concern, other than the well-being of the three injured men. Especially Kostya. What in the name of all that was holy was Kostya doing there? The voice from the doorway pulled him out of his trance-like thought process.

"Sir? I'll need you to come with me, please."

Hewes turned around to see the flash of the shield of a federal officer, held by a man he did not recognize. Next to the officer was a person with whom he was very familiar.

"You heard the officer, Mister Speaker. Or is it Yevgeny? We have that to figure out and we have much more to discuss, sir," said the other.

Dejectedly, Yevgeny's shoulders slumped as he stared into the cold, dark eyes of one very, very unhappy lawyer.

"What of my mother?" Yevgeny/Brad asked.

"One of many questions to which we will hopefully find the answers, Yevgeny. Now, if you would, please, come with us."

Yevgeny steeled himself. He could try and run from this place, taking the bullets that would no doubt fly in the attempt to stop his flight. It might be better for all concerned, though, if he simply went quietly. Then, he could have a chance to discuss this with Dimitri. Yes, Dimitri would have a solution to get him out of this mess.

"Very well," he said to the person he recognized. "Ms. Vernon, I'll come."

Stepping out of the room into the restaurant's lobby, there was one other law enforcement officer. And Robin. The look on her face was a combination of anger, pain and puzzlement. The two officers walked out of the front door first, followed by Yevgeny and then the attorney general. Before the door had closed, Robin called out.

"Excuse me? Ms. Vernon?"

"Yes, Robin." The attorney general knew Robin well enough, but was, as of now, very unsure of the woman who had done the speaker's bidding for these many years.

"Can I ask what's going on?" Robin pleaded.

"Look me in the eyes when you answer my question first, then I'll decide if I can answer your question." Gayle paused while locking her eyes to Robin's. "How well do you know this man you've been working for and with whom you've had a relationship for all these many years?"

"I know Brad very well, Ms. Vernon. He's a good man. A good Christian man."

Gayle detected no sign of misdirection, a trait often utilized in Washington and now, for her at least, very easily detectable.

"What do you know of his life before the House of Representatives."

Robin responded with the textbook version of the Brad Hewes biography. Gayle then dropped the bomb.

"Are you aware that Brad is not really Brad but a Soviet agent sent here more than twenty years ago to be Brad?" Gayle asked softly.

The look on Robin's face, the utter shock of what was just said, cleared her of any and all suspicion in the attorney general's mind.

"Th-that ca-can't b-bu-be!" stammered Robin, the tears instantly flowing down her face. "Nu-no-not Brad?"

"Have you ever been to his home in South Carolina?"

"Yes, m-many times. Wa-wha-why?"

"What of the old woman? The one with the accent?"

"That's Varinka, sh-she's the housekeeper."

"No, Robin, she's Yevgeny's mother. That's his name, by the way. Yevgeny Polnichy. I wasn't one hundred percent sure until I overheard his conversation with his mother just now. Up until now, I was about ninety-nine percent sure."

Robin stood in the middle of the small entryway, sobbing uncontrollably. "What d-do I do nu-now?"

"I suggest you go back to your room or wherever you're staying and spend another night. Then, once you've pulled yourself together, go to work on Monday. The offices will be closed for the next few days, anyway."

"Just the speaker's offices?"

"No, Robin. The government will be shut down in order to properly honor the memory and the life of the late Donald R. Fulton, Vice President of the United States."

Robin's gaping mouth could not have opened any wider without requiring reconstructive surgery. Gayle nodded to the stunned woman, turned and walked out of the restaurant.

✳ ✳ ✳

Back on the rain-soaked tarmac of Andrews Air Force Base, President Griffen stood, silently, looking at the reflections of the runway lights in the puddles that surrounded him. His chief of staff, Dan Josten, came from the hangar where the rest of the official party had repaired for the arrival of the two flights. Four ambulances sat idling just outside of the hangar, the crews having gone inside the hangar also for a hot cup of coffee. A MedFlight helicopter was also at the ready. Dan popped open the black umbrella.

"Jay? You okay, buddy?"

"Yeah, Danny. I'm as good as I can be right now, considering."

"I thought I'd better come out here and keep you from being totally soaked to the bone and wind up, well, dead from pneumonia. That'd be a kicker right now, wouldn't it."

"It would certainly send Romanov into an apoplectic fit."

"Speaking of which, do you want to arrange to have them brought here in the morning?"

"That would be good, Dan. I spoke with Bill and told him their plane would be at Cheltenham this evening. Better to let them all catch a little sleep. We can give the two no-names to Interpol and let the French deal with them. Make sure our offices over there keep an eye on the two of them, though, in case some liberal French judge gives them a slap on the wrist for taking out a prostitute."

"We can do that, Jay. What about the others? Want to have them come in through Brunswick? We can keep them there for a day or two and then bring them down here when we need them."

"As usual, buddy, you read my mind. Have them go to Brunswick. Stick 'em out on Little Birch. We'll figure out what to do with them later. Maybe bring them down here during the funeral? Have the Marines fix up a couple of the cabins at Camp David for extra security. If we tell them now, they'll have a heads up and a head start. How many total are we going to have again? Five? We can get this Dayle character out to the camp tonight, though," Jay said.

"Five'd be right, Jay. I checked with Cheltenham about five minutes ago. Michail is going to be okay. They said he'd be fine to fly in the morning. Annie just arrived at the hospital there. I figured you wouldn't mind."

"I don't mind that at all. Just don't talk about this to Nelson, okay? He's kind of rattled, a state in which I have never seen him." Jay paused to gather his thoughts for a moment. "Knowing what we know, I'm torn, Danny. Really not sure which way to go with those two, Annie and Rostokovich. They came here with one thing in mind. Fate intervened and helped to change their course of thinking."

"Michail's case is a bit different than Annie's, Jay. He was a party to two murders and ran the scenario. Annie was given the same ultimate goal, but she never, that I know of, did anything wrong."

"Legally, we don't have a case against her then, do we? It's all pretty much hearsay evidence. Now, we don't even have Don to corroborate their plan. As far as I can see, we have a situation where she falsely represented her true identity, but like a lot of guys and gals who come to our country illegally, she's led an exemplary life. If more actual Americans had dedication to their jobs like her, we'd be a lot better off."

"I think we could have Lindsey file motions to have any charges against Annie filed away and probably work out some sort of plea deal for the others."

"Romanov is going to be our guest for the rest of his days, Danny. No doubt about that. And that little prick Moore? I want him to be the most popular guy on date night."

"What about Hewes? From what we've read, he appears to be an almost reluctant party to what has transpired. He's done a great job representing South Carolina and he actually has been a very fair speaker."

"Putting the past four weeks aside, yeah, he's been fair. But he was there, Danny. He was in the room when they put the real Hewes to sleep. He was there when that sadistic son of a bitch Dayle used a pair of garden shears to take off three of the man's fingers. Christ, Dan. Just the fact that he kept his little year-by-year journal in the same room with what is probably all that's left of the real Hewes is enough to give me the creeps. Give me a suggestion."

"Let him publicly resign as being a party to the Stark thing. We'll hang Moore out to dry in court. Moore, if you remember, is missing in France right now. We'll allow Brad to comment on the case after court is dismissed and he can publicly apologize and announce his decision to step down."

"I'm not up for letting him publicly say anything right now, Dan."

"We have his mother, Jay."

"So the rest of your thoughts?"

"He resigns. Let's have someone else make his statement. We can come up with a reason. He retires, in shame, to Charleston. We'll find something productive for him and mom to do for us. We can do the house-arrest thing."

"Living somewhat large, don't you think?"

"Living large? Perhaps, but with a price. He's actually very knowledgeable, you know, even if we don't see eye-to-eye on political issues. Keeping him out to pasture but just within view of the public eye, though... I think that's the key to keeping this mess quiet. His political legacy is the stuff of legend. Just look at the health care package he pushed through yesterday."

"I have, Dan. That's why I opposed it. How the hell will the country ever fund that thing? It's a better health package than we offer our own military."

"How about the AFR accounts? There are billions in there, Jay. Billions! We apply the benefits to the lowest level income Americans first. Full coverage. When their situations change, as a result of getting a better job that has a decent health plan, then their benefits spread out, maybe up to the next tier. A trickle-up kind of plan."

"Speaking of AFR, though, what about Nelson's friend? Any ideas on this one? The man has done some nice things and been a party, apparently, to some very bad stuff as well."

"Let's see how he makes out with his injuries for starters, Jay. He's in pretty tough shape. As far as grabbing the funds, though, we should be able to quietly arrange that."

"Using the AFR money for health care? Pretty ingenious, Danny-boy. When did you come up with that?"

"Right after I heard the figures of the nest-egg that was grown with Romanov's seed money. I like the Hewes health plan, Jay. Have from the start. The funding is there right now, if we simply scale back in some excessive spots."

"What spots? Military? Education? Transportation?"

"No, Jay. I was thinking more along the lines of force reductions. Fulton's plan to scale-down the governmental workforce was right on the money. Why does an employee who actually performs the work need four or five supervisors? Why does it take seven people to approve a purchase order for a box of paper and three dozen pens? We have tried to keep you on the track of worrying solely about your job. These issues are what concern our fellow citizens most, Jay. They take jobs for five, maybe six bucks an hour. Hell, that's as much as your dad paid us when we were in high school for cleaning up the truck bays."

Jay Griffen and Danny Josten were boyhood pals. In Jaffrey, New Hampshire, the small town setting made for a community where everyone knows everyone and living next door to each other in the shadows of Mount Monadnock, the two were at first de facto friends as a result of their moms being friends. Their fathers worked together. Jay's dad was the founder of Griffen Trucking, whose biggest client was the local match company. Dan's father was the trucking company's attorney-at-law. Jay and Dan grew up together, went to school together, played hockey and baseball together, went off to Dartmouth together. After college, Jay went to work for the family business, becoming his father's operations manager. Dan continued on to Harvard Law, then after graduation, he returned to Jaffrey, hanging out his shingle to begin a budding law practice, side by side with his father. Within a few years of Dan's return to Jaffrey, Griffen Trucking expanded their routes, growing their fleet and doing more business than they could have ever imagined. Jay's father decided the time was right to retire and pass the business on to his son. At the same time, Dan's law practice was struggling, his father having passed away as the result of a heart attack. Jay saw the company's liability issues growing with each additional mile driven. It was a win-win situation when Jay asked Dan to join him as the company's in-house legal counsel. The partnership continued on the road to Concord and the State House, then to Washington.

The two were as close as could be and at this time, when it was most needed, Dan was able to answer the questions before they were asked. Jay would need that, for at least another week. The rain began to pick up in intensity and Dan made sure the umbrella covered them both as they watched the flashing lights of the approaching airplane reflecting off the once-again growing puddles on the runway.

forty-eight

Cheltenham, England Saturday, April 4, 1998 9:37pm (local)

Anastasia Fidoryvich stepped off the small, United States Air Force Learjet onto the runway and into the cool, damp English night air. The Marine guards at the bottom of the small stairway directed her to the black military staff car waiting fifty yards away. She walked towards the car, flanked by the two armed escorts and was somewhat relieved when she saw the familiar face of Bill Terrio ease out of the rear door.

"Bill. Nice to see you. I'd say it's nice to see a friendly face, but I understand how you probably feel right now."

"You can consider me friendly, Annie. Or would you rather me call you Anastasia?"

"Annie's fine, Bill. Thanks. So why am I here?"

"Getting right to point, as usual, Annie. You're here because we have some people with whom you are acquainted in custody and, specifically, Michail is in the base hospital. He's going to be okay, but we thought we could do the decent thing and let you visit with him."

"What happened?" Annie asked, a small tear coming from the corner of her eye.

Bill placed a friendly hand on her shoulder. "We can talk about that on the way to the hospital, Annie. Come on. Let's get in the car."

He held open the rear door for her and, once she'd settled in, he closed it and walked around to get in the other side. As he got in, he nodded to the driver and the car slipped into gear.

Annie looked at Bill, taking a tissue out of her bag and dabbed it softly on her eyes.

"What happened to Michail, Bill?"

"The short version is that he was at Romanov's place at the lake today and Romanov had intended to kill him. Fortunately for Michail, he took a bullet in his left shoulder. It missed the heart and the important stuff. He lost a lot of blood, but he's resting comfortably now."

"What's the long version?"

"You know most of it by now, I'm sure, Annie. Answer me one question. Would you have allowed Fulton to become president?"

Without any hesitation, she answered firmly. "No."

"Any reason why?"

"Fulton as president would have given Romanov what he wanted. Romanov is a cowardly son of a bitch who allowed his wife and children to be murdered. He then turned their loss into his gain by way of pity from the people of Russia who felt bad for him. Fulton had his own agenda. He's a smart man, Bill. And if he weren't hell-bent on revenge, he'd make a fantastic president. Instead, his goal and Romanov's were one and the same. No, I would have sent my files to someone like you and beat feet out of town."

"Maybe you can help us with something. What do you know of Dayle?"

"A nice, considerate man. Very diligent in his duties. He's always sharp and on top of things. Why?"

"Turns out Dayle is *also* a KGB graduate. We noticed his face in a photo that Michail had in his files. The photo was taken when the original Marvin Moore was killed."

"You have Michail's files?"

"Michail sent them to us from Moscow, before he went to the lake."

"I have files in Moscow, too, Bill. If that will help."

"We have them already, Annie."

"You what?"

"Apparently, Michail found your files and transferred them to a compact disc. I have it right here in my pocket." Bill slid the disc out of his coat and passed it to her.

"Tajiki goatherd songs? What the hell is this? It sounds like something Bud would love."

"That's almost a long story, Annie, but suffice it to say that the goat thing is a running thing between Bud and Michail."

"The goat thing is a running thing between Bud and everyone, Bill."

"True. Before I bring you into see Michail, Annie, I need you to join me in a visit with somebody else."

The car pulled to a stop at small barracks-type building. The outside door was flanked by two armed, uniformed soldiers. The four corners of the building were also guarded by armed men. The driver, an Army lieutenant, got out of the vehicle and came around to open Terrio's door. Annie slid across the seat and followed Bill out of the car. The armed men at the door snapped to attention as Bill opened the building's outer door. The inside of the building was basic military white walls and green doors. There was a guard at either end of the hall and one seated at a table in the middle of the passageway. Bill nodded to the captain on duty as they opened the center door on the left side of the hall.

"Aleksi? I brought somebody to see you," Bill announced.

Annie stopped dead in her tracks in the hall at hearing the name.

"Bill? Can you come out here for a moment?" Annie asked.

"No, Annie. It's okay. Come in," Bill replied.

She stepped through the open doorway and looked at the man whom she despised above all others.

"Stasya? How nice of you to come and join us. Come. Sit down. Tell me of your travels," Romanov said cockily.

"Bill, I have nothing to say to this man. I've put up with his crap and done his bidding for far too long. Can we please go?"

"Annie, this will only take a minute. It's an official thing, to be done by the book. Orders from the boss, okay? Miss Anastasia Fidoryvich? Can you positively identify this man here," Bill requested.

Annie took a breath and said, "This man is Aleksandr Romanov, former president of the USSR"

"And can you tell me of your relationship to him?" Terrio inquired.

"Mister Terrio, since 1973, I have been an agent of the Soviet secret service, better known to you as the KGB. Since 1976, I have been on assignment in the United States, placed there at the direction of this man, Romanov," she said, pointing to her former employer.

"What is your assignment?" Bill asked.

"Up until three hours ago, I was to aid Donald Robert Fulton in becoming President of the United States. From there, Fulton would be acting in consort with Romanov to first destabilize the financial structure of America, then, by declaring martial law, Romanov would be able to direct the daily business of the United States through Fulton. If that is what you needed to hear, Mister Terrio, I'd prefer not to stand here and breath the same air as this coward."

Bill looked from Annie to Aleksi. "Good evening, Mister Romanov. If you'll excuse us?"

Aleksandr Romanov stood still, straight, attempting to keep a defiant, strong face. He nodded to Bill and simply looked at Annie. She turned and walked back into the hallway and waited out of sight until Bill came back out of the room, closing the door behind him.

"Can you take me to Michail now, Bill?"

"Sure, Annie. I had to do that. I'm sorry, but if we are to prosecute Romanov for what he's done, we need to do it by the book."

"How did you get him?"

"We arranged for some transportation for Michail today. Aleksandr just happened to be there. Taking him was not our intention, but it turns out to have been for the best. Prime Minister Bakunin granted us permission to take him into custody."

"And what did you have to give him in return? Bakunin does nothing without compensation."

"Oh?"

"Bakunin's been dying to become president himself. Romanov has been gloating for years that he hand-picked Bakunin and anointed him successor. Romanov was the key for Bakunin to get elected as president before he got fired as prime minister. You know how the current president likes to clean house whenever it suits his needs. So Bakunin must've been given something in return."

"There are a billion somethings in return, Annie. We tracked down a bunch of Russian Mafia money and will be sending it back to Russia. Bakunin looks like a hero for working with the Americans in getting this money returned and allowing for productive use of the funds."

They exited the barracks and got back into the staff car. Five minutes later, they pulled up in front of the hospital. They walked inside and were directed down a hallway to an elevator. The ride up to the third floor was quick and quiet. Bill allowed Annie to gather her thoughts. The United States government had all the information it needed to close this dark chapter in her history. Annie and Michail had provided all of the confirmation the government required. Bill guided her to an open door and Annie paused at the opening. Michail looked good. His eyes were closed and the steady rise and fall of his chest showed that he was breathing on his own. Annie tapped on the open door and watched as the light from the hallway cast a glow on his face as he turned towards the sound. His eyes opened slowly, squinting.

"Stasya? Is that you?"

"Yes, Misha. Can I come in?"

He patted the top sheets that covered him, the invitation made. She stepped quickly to the bed and sat down gently, her hand reaching out to stroke his hair.

"What are you doing here? I thought you were in Madrid?"

"I was, Misha. Apparently they found out that I was not really Annie Fidrych and sent me to Paris on an official errand. From there, they brought me here."

"They know we are both on their side, I hope?"

"Yes, they do. I know they're trying to decide what to do with us, but I don't care anymore, so long as we can be together."

"The Americans don't usually put their male and female prisoners together, Stasya my love."

"Actually, they did at least once that I know of, Misha. But you rest for now, okay? I'll be right here, if they'll allow it."

Michail brought his right hand up to cover hers as she continued to warm the side of his face. He closed his eyes and returned to his sleep. Annie looked at Bill standing in the doorway. Her eyes asked the question and his nodding head responded. He waved while reaching for the handle on the door, pulling it softly shut behind him. Annie stood and pulled the green padded chair across the floor, placing it next to the head of the bed. She sat down, still lovingly stroking Michail's face. She closed her eyes and slipped into a sleep of her own, laced with dreams of she and Michail living out their lives free of secrets and secret missions. A short time later, a nurse had come in to check on Michail and had taken a blanket and pillow from the room's closet, slipping the latter behind Annie's head, covering her with the former.

Down the road from the hospital, the men of Go Team One were enjoying a steak dinner and several pints of fine English ale. Sir Stephen Jennings was seated at the table with the men, watching them unwind and living vicariously through their tales. His had been an existence short-lived in the field and twenty-times longer in the offices of British Military Intelligence. Now, at the ripe old age of sixty-four, he felt very much alive and yet at the same time, felt left behind for having missed the adventures now being shared by these fine young men. Bill Terrio came in and took a seat at the table next to Sir Stephen. A half-yard was slid in front of the CIA director and, raising the glass in silent toast, he readily allowed it to flow down his throat.

"Nice of you to join us, Mister T," said Menneally.

"And nice of you to invite me, Bob. Since I'm here drinking with you, I'd appreciate being called Bill. As in, "Bill? Will you get the next round?" Yes, I will!"

The small group laughed and looked at Terrio.

"What? What did I do?" Bill asked with feigned surprise.

Hank spoke up. "Did you not just offer to get the next round?"

"Yes, I did. I'll be right back." Bill made a quick head count and stepped up to the bar. The young barmaid came over and he indicated with his empty glass that he'd need seven more just like it. He pulled out his wallet and noticed all he had was U.S. currency.

"Excuse me? Do you accept American dollars?"

"Yes, love. Dollars. Fives. Tens. Twenties. Whatever you've got, we can take it."

Bill smiled back at the woman, thinking that if he were twenty years younger, he'd probably make an idiot of himself while making a play for her. She, of course, was no doubt used to the attention that came from working on a military base predominately staffed by males.

"That'll be twenty-one dollars, sir."

Bill gave her a twenty and a ten, then thanked her as he gingerly picked up the tray containing the seven beers. He made it back to the table without spilling. Not bad for a guy on the wrong side of fifty, he thought. The beers disappeared from the tray as Bill took his seat once again next to Sir Stephen.

The MI chief leaned in towards Bill, asking softly, "Is everything taken care of now, Bill?"

Bill responded quietly as well. "Yes, Sir Stephen. The two no-names are on their way back to Paris with Yearwood from Interpol. The looks on their faces and the return gape from Aleksi was worth it. That gives Interpol a starting point in tracing these guys' steps and actions. Rostokovich is resting comfortably in the hospital and Miss Fidrych is with him. Excuse me, Fidoryvich. Moore and Aleksi are cooling their heels in the barracks."

"Do you have any idea yet on how you're going to deal with these blokes?"

"The details are being worked out as we speak, Sir Stephen. I'm sure that once we handle the disposition of their cases in chief, then we should be able to make them available to you and your office."

"That's what I was hoping to hear, Bill. Thanks. If they'd managed to penetrate your government the way they did, then I shudder to think of who's guarding the Crown Jewels right now."

"Let's enjoy the beer while we can, Sir Stephen. Have I missed a bunch of good war stories?"

"Be glad you did. I'm suddenly feeling very old," Sir Stephen chuckled.

"You are, Sir Stephen. But you're in fine company." Bill offered his glass in toast which Sir Stephen returned. The two of them sipped and returned their attention to the recountings going on around the table. Bill's cellphone softly chirped from within his coat pocket. He took it out, nodded his understanding of what he was told and placed it back in his coat.

He looked at Sir Stephen. "Looks like we're taking our guests home in the morning."

"Well then, Bill old boy, there's no time like the present to eat, drink and be merry."

"Merry within reason, Steve. I needn't return to work hungover. Wouldn't be, as you say over here, good form."

"No, that it wouldn't. Even so, you all should be proud of what you've managed to accomplish in, what? Forty-eight hours?"

"Two days is a pretty good turnaround, but the fact that it took more than twenty years and one pissed off agent to bring it to light gives us more reason to pause than celebrate. We've got a bunch of work to do in regards to cleaning up our house so that this won't ever happen again."

"You'll never be able to say ever, Bill. But I'm sure you'll make it pretty damn hard for anyone to even think about it," Jennings commented.

"Pass me some of those buffalo wings, will you please? The chicken stuff."

Sir Stephen reached across the table and grabbed the serving dish from the middle of the table. Bill unfolded his napkin and took one of the spicy chicken pieces. As he took his first bite, he realized he never had lunch. Not the first time that had happened, he thought and not the last time it would happen, he knew.

forty-nine

Washington, DC   Saturday, April 4, 1998   4:39pm (local)

The flurry of activity that now surrounded the recently landed Air Force Two was a stark contrast to the rain-soaked solitude President Griffen had experience not five minutes before. The first ambulance had pulled up to the rear door where the airport's service lift had been positioned. The emergency team had scurried up the mobile stairway that was placed at the forward hatch. The word had come in almost two hours before that the vice president was dead. The official White House physicians wanted to put their talents to the test to see if they had any miracles left in their little black bags. While the EMT's did their thing, the second flight for which the president and medical crews had been waiting made its approach and touched down smoothly, taxing to the same area as Air Force Two. The three passengers on board this plane were still in a position to appreciate the efforts of the high-profile medical team that had been summoned.

The president's personal physician, Admiral David Lynch, came out of the forward entry of Air Force Two and descended the stairs.

"Dave? Anything?" Griffen asked solemnly.

"No, Mister President. He's gone. We'll know more when we get him to pathology. He appears to have gone quickly. The level of rigor is consistent with having passed within the last couple of hours. We're taking blood samples right now and will have some results on those in about twenty minutes."

"We're checking his blood for...?"

"Toxins. Poisons. Drugs. You did say there was a chance that this may have been more than an unnatural event."

"Yes, Dave. Thanks for everything on this. Remember, we're keeping this quiet for now. I'll make a statement tonight once you've gotten some preliminary findings. I already spoke with Peg and she agreed to the autopsy."

"How'd she take it?"

"As well as could be expected. She's a strong woman. A good woman. I asked Anne Marie to go and be with her and the kids. The next couple of days are going to be really tough."

"Is this the next round of patients coming in now?"

"Yes, Admiral. Please do whatever you can to help them. And take really good care of Hannity for me, please."

"I'll make sure we give the three of them our all, sir."

Admiral Lynch offered a salute to the President and walked behind the now-rolling stairway that was on its way to the Charleston med flight. He waved to the other waiting ambulances to have them come over and line up, then he made it onto the stairway before it stopped moving and was on the top step while the aircraft's front hatch was being opened. He scooted inside and came back out immediately, waving frantically for one of the ground transport teams to come quickly. President Griffen started to jog over to the stairway when he was stopped by Dan.

"Wait here, Jay. The plane radioed us a few minutes ago to let us know there's a big problem with one of the patients. Let them get him off, then you can go in and check on the other two."

"Which one has the problem?"

"Bud's friend, Fred. His heart stopped fifteen minutes ago. They were able to get him going again, but they're not optimistic about saving him."

The two lifelong friends looked up and watched as a team of six gowned people worked the stretcher carrying Fred out of the front door and down the stairs. The waiting ambulance had its strobe lights flashing and was rolling as soon as the rear doors were closed. The team waved the ambulance away and it drove straight for the MedFlight helicopter, overhead rotor blades now spinning.

"Where's Bud?" asked Jay.

"He's in the hangar, making some calls."

"Does he know?"

"Yeah. We told him as soon as we knew there was a problem. He's torn between ignoring him and being with him."

"Go tell him I said to go to Bethesda right now. Bud's only known Fred. He had no idea who Konstantin is or was. Help Bud out on this, Danny. He's a good man and he needs us right now."

"Nelson has had a bad day, hasn't he?"

"This morning, my world was a bucket of shit. Now, I'm off the hook all the way around and exactly half of Nelson's closest friends are not whom everyone believed. Find out if he needs us to help him get his other two buddies down here. We can do that, Danny. Let him know."

"I'll do that, Jay."

The president's chief of staff hustled back through the rain towards the hangar where Bud Nelson now sat alone on the bumper of the president's limousine.

Nelson had been on the phone non-stop since just after midnight, or so it felt. So much had happened in the past month, each event leading to another revelation that Bud had been sure could not be topped. This latest, he thought, could only get worse if he were to find that Don and Chuck were also working with Fred. He'd known all three since OCS in 1976. They'd bonded quickly and had maintained that closeness to this day. Now, Nelson was, for the first time in memory, rattled beyond comprehension. The allegations against President Griffen were at first, laughable. For a time, they were believable, as the Stark woman had made a convincing victim. Bud never, ever let on to Jay that he entertained the thought. Of that, it was the one comfort he had at this very moment. Had he been counted among Griffen's detractors, he'd no doubt be trying to put the fragments that were his life back together.

"Chucker? Bud," Nelson spoke into the phone.

"Nelson! I've been trying to get you all day! Please tell me that what I think happened in South Carolina, didn't," Michaud pleaded down the phone line from Maine.

"I can't, Chuck. It did. And it's worse than it would appear."

"You're telling me three people get blown up, one of them being an individual to whom I would gladly give one of my kidneys and half of my liver and it's worse?"

"You sitting down?"

"Yeah, I am."

"Fred is not Fred Singletary. He has been Fred for almost thirty years, while also being a guy named Konstantin Rostokovich."

"Fred is a Russian spy? Jesus, Bud. You had me going there for a minute. That serious tone in your voice got me, you bastard," Chuck laughed nervously.

Nelson screamed into the phone. "Will you just fucking be real with me this one time?? Chucker, the guy we've known as Fred is right now on his way to Bethesda Naval Hospital with second and third degree burns over the bottom half of his body. He technically died about twenty minutes ago, but they brought him back. The helicopter you hear in the background has him inside, departing Andrews Air Force base, right now. The man in that helo is not the person born as Fred Singletary. The real Fred Singletary is believed to have died in a car wreck in Illinois in 1969. There were no family or friends around to confirm it was or wasn't the real Fred. Our Fred assumed the identity of this young man. I'm not saying our buddy had anything to do with the car crash that claimed a life. I am saying that our buddy did make use of the name and history of that young man. The man we know as Freddie is the real life brother of that Russian colonel I told you about."

There was a silence on the line. Michaud was processing what Nelson was saying.

"So what? Has our Freddie done anything that would be against the law? The man we've known and gotten drunk with and hung with and gone to weddings and funerals with is a good man. A good man with a huge, caring heart, Bud. The Navy gave him a top secret clearance, for God's sake."

"There's instance number two of crimes. He was feeding intel to the Soviets while he was working for Dericksen. Remember, he spent a couple of years in the freakin' Pentagon's submarine command center."

"There's just no way, Bud. No way at all."

"Chucker. Denial is a powerful thing."

"Yep. And a really big river in Egypt."

Bud exhaled loudly, trying to maintain what little composure he had left. "I've been doing the same thing all day, Chucker. Telling myself and anyone who will listen that there's been a really, really big mistake made here. Here's where it gets difficult. Are you ready?"

"Ready for what? You've already told me that you now believe Fred is a spy. Maybe even a murderer. What's next, Nelson?"

"A couple of photos of Fred with Fulton. One of them taken in Berlin. There's also a bank account with Fred's name on it."

"Fred has a couple of bank accounts, Bud. With lots of money in them."

"Yep. Just that the really big one is joint."

"Joint? As in two names on the account?"

"As in two other names on the account. Fred Singletary, Konstantin Rostokovich and Aleksandr Romanov."

"Wow! You guys are grasping at straws, aren't you? Have you lost all of your dignity playing with the big boys in the beltway, Bud?"

"Listen, Chucker. You'll believe what you want to believe. I have to look at this from the reality side of the story."

"What's the reality side?"

"Listen to what I'm going to tell you, all right? Then, when you get down here, I can show you the indisputable evidence. I hate using the word evidence, Chuck. I am hating this day more as each minute passes. Trust me, please, when I tell you that in the dictionary of life, under the word sucks, is the date April 4, 1998."

"What else is there that makes this so bad, Bud? What? Have you been sleeping with the enemy, too?"

"As usual, Michaud, you are right on the money. Annie is really Anastasia Fidoryvich. I'll get into that little nugget in a moment."

"So when do you accuse me and Donny? Is that tomorrow's little thing? Just completely destroy everyone and anyone around you?"

Bud took the hit without a grimace. He knew Michaud was more than upset. It had taken more than three hours to work up the courage to call the man.

"Here's the short Fred tale, Chucker. 1970. Twenty-two year old Konstantin Rostokovich, fresh faced and wide-eyed out of the university system in Moscow. KGB trainee based on his financial acumen and high intelligence. His initial assignment was to come to America and help the student radicals stir things up. He wasn't a front man. He gave them the idea and occasionally some money, to go throw a few bricks. The Soviet government staked him fifty thousand dollars to complete his mission. He turned the fifty k into seven figures in less than a year through the stock market. Then, he finds a kindred spirit at Yale in the person of Donny Fulton. Fulton's the adopted son of a loving couple in South Carolina. Birth parents were a pair of Soviet-defectors who came to work on the budding nuclear program in the late forties. Accused and convicted of spying, she gives birth in their jail cell and dies from a blood pressure thing. The father is distraught and hangs himself. Konstantin helps Don research his birth story and then helps to stoke the blaze that has combusted. A few random ideas and a formal introduction later, Fulton is now on the job twenty-four-seven, thanks to Konstantin. Romanov is thrilled that this wonder kid, Rostovich the elder, is on his side and makes him the U.S. point man for everything that is about to happen. While Romanov sends a whole bunch of people over here to try and topple the American government from the inside, Freddie's doing double-duty on Dericksen's staff, plus he continues to work the stock market. Did you know that Fred had a portfolio in the high eight figures by the time he got out of the Navy?"

"Keep talking, Bud. You asked me to listen, remember?" Chuck said sternly.

"Fred gets out of the Navy and, by now, he's bankrolling not only the United States operation, but he's also letting Romanov live off the interest from the investments. Now that Fred's out of the military, he starts to wander the country. We see and know the guy whose shrewd intuition steers him towards purchases of small companies that turn around with a ten-fold return in a year or less. Remember the early 80's? When he jumped in with both feet to the microchip revolution?"

"Yeah, I remember it well, Bud."

"At the same time, he was gently guiding a few elected officials through the maze that is American politics. There were three, maybe more, West coast plants. All the same as the story we heard about Hewes. People taken out, identities taken over."

"So in this fable, Bud, what happened to the Westies?"

"Fate has a nasty way of intervening, Chucker. Auto accidents, natural physical infirmities, changes of heart, drug overdoses. Konstantin has done what he can and comes back East. He's getting tired of the mobile game and buys the radio station. The condo on the Portland waterfront. He's now available for coffee and cigars at Michaud Media, a growing business in Maine. Even you begin to benefit from his closeness, Chuck. The cutting edge technologies wind up in your studio. You think it's because of your fabulous ability to bullshit... that's a compliment, by the way."

"Thank you."

"You're most welcome. Actually, Fred has a controlling interest in these up-and-comers. You're getting the beta gear as a result of a directive from the top. The stock tips you got were technically illegal. Insider trading is a no-no, as you well know. Those little newspapers with the occasional pen marks next to a stock that closed at eight bucks yesterday were never, ever accidental. I even found a few of those on occasion. And, yes, I did. I'm not stupid, so don't ask the question."

"I was going to ask, you know. Keep going," Chuck replied.

"A suggestion from Konstantin to the Griffen campaign consultant, Moore, had me answering the phone at NBS one day and working in New Hampshire the next. That was no accident, Chucker. Fred has helped steer us every step of the way. He didn't control us, but he certainly had a hand in what we have achieved. So now, here I am telling you that one of the four has a secret and it's not that he's a girl."

"Good. I hated *"The Crying Game."* Bad movie. What do you want me to do now?"

"What do you want to do, Chuck? I'm on the fence about going to the hospital. Do I go and be with the man we know? Or do I let the fact that he's been lying to us get in the way of that? Hell, bud, he's even used me to a point where if he wasn't in a hospital, I'd help put him in one."

"How's that?"

"Everything we talked about at lunch yesterday? I heard it played back, word for word, in a videotape of Romanov. That bastard knew everything we knew. The link to that is now clear, unfortunately. That's where I am conflicted."

"How about if I come down and we help you figure out which end is up?"

"That's what I was hoping to hear, Chucker. And thank you for hearing me out. I hope you have an idea of the kind of crap I've been trying to sort through all freakin' day."

"Back to the beginning of this call, Bud. Fred's in tough shape. What happened to the admiral?"

"He's been touch and go, too. I feel like a total shit for not mentioning that sooner, Chuck. He is a good man. Griffen is ready to resign just on the basis that he asked Gary to go on that little exploration and now, the man is fighting for his life. And there's the secret service guy, Hannity. He's done as an agent. Left side took a chunk of glass that cut some muscles and took out the nerves."

"What about Don?"

"Fulton? He's dead, Chucker."

"Excuse me? I meant Hough, but since you brought this up?" Chuck inquired eagerly.

"Vice President Fulton apparently suffered some kind of a major heart thing on the way back from Madrid. He was found dead in his bed on Air Force Two about two hours ago."

"You guys will be checking for bad guys, right?"

"Inside and out, Chucker. The Fulton thing is very ironic. I told you he was one of Romanov's pupils. If this was murder, it's pretty weird that not all of the bad guys were on the same page, after unknowingly working together for all this time. We had one bad guy in custody on Air Force Two, another in custody in England. Hell, we let Annie cool her heels in Paris. Now she's in England."

"Well, it's now later," Chuck said refering to Bud's offer of the story of Annie. "What's this crap about Annie?"

"Anastasia Fidoryvich. KGB agent, United States, class of '76. Her job is to work with Fulton. She's hired as his assistant in Charleston and the rest is history."

"That's all there is?"

"On her? That's all we've got for now. More later, film at eleven and all that shit."

"And Donny? Hough, that is."

"Regarding Mister Hough, he's still in New York keeping an eye on Sandy. I'm going to call him when I get a sitrep on Fred from the hospital. He'll probably want to come down here, too. I'm not giving him the shock-treatment on this one, though. I think if you're here and have a chance to look at the hard copies of this nightmare, you can help talk me through it. By the way, Sandy's ex-husband?"

"Yeah?"

"His art gallery is one of Fred's corporate holdings."

"Are you shitting me?"

"Not one iota. Anyway, how about you get down here as quick as you can. I know you'd like a chance, at least, to check on Fred."

"If that's really his name."

"It is to us, Chucker. Other than putting my words into Romanov's ears, he's never been anything but a good friend and a kind man to me. And to you, since it turns out he's been your patron saint."

"I'm on my way to the Jetport right now. Oh, Bud?"

"Yeah?"

"Do you want me to bring this CD I got for Mister Goatman? It's got goatherds singing and stuff like that. You'll love it!"

"Goatherds?"

"Yessiree, Bud. Real, live Tajiki goatherds. And some lovely file attachments that you can't hear, but you can certainly read."

"Are these files in Russian?"

"Yes. And there are some interesting photographs, too."

"Definitely bring that down here. That's the backup copy and I would rather have it here than in your building, unattended, thank you."

"I'll call when I get there?"

"Just come straight to Bethesda Naval Hospital. I'll have a car waiting. Let me know which airport and airline."

"Bud? If it doesn't look like he's gonna pull through, will you tell him I said to have a scotch and a cigar waiting on the other side?"

"I will, Chucker. We'll see you at the hospital."

Bud folded the cellphone and slipped it back into his pocket. He saw Dan Josten walking towards him through the rain and the encroaching darkness.

"Danny? Where are the service boys?" Bud asked.

"They're on a perimeter set-up, Bud. They've got the usual sharpies on the roof, two watching each exit from the planes and one with each ambulance." Dan was pointing them out while explaining their whereabouts. Bud nodded and noted each.

"What about Dayle?"

"He's in cuffs on his way out now. He's been Miranda'd and knows something's up, but he's not sure what. The FBI's going to keep him in the dark until they make sure they've got everyone we know about," Dan paused and stroked the five o'clock shadow that was evident on just about every member of the inner circle at this point.

"The boss asked me to ask you to reconsider and go to the hospital to be with your buddy Fred."

"I'm going, Danny. I'm going right now. Thanks for the extra effort. And for keeping my head in the game."

"You have had a shitty day, Nelson."

"As I just told my friend in Maine, it'll be in the new dictionaries come next year as the definitive definition."

Nelson's cellphone chirped. He smiled at Dan as he said, "You know what I'm doing tomorrow?"

"What's that, Bud?"

"I, L. Bud Nelson, am going to see how far across the Potomac I can toss this. I hope it's not much more than halfway." He pushed the button and answered the incoming call. "Nelson. Yes, operator, I'll accept. Thanks."

Dan shuffled his feet while Bud talked with his friend Don Hough. Trying not to listen, he heard things get tense when the discussion turned to Singletary. The conversation ended and Bud held up a single finger to indicate he'd be just one more minute. He made a call to the White House transportation office which was short and sweet, the arrangements to have Hough flown to Washington took less than thirty seconds. The two men started to walk from the hangar and out into the rain which was now falling with a renewed intensity.

At the same time, they saw FBI Director Hammett lowering himself on his wheelchair lift from the conversion van that served as his official vehicle. President Griffen stood at the intersection of where those deplaning from the Charleston flight and Air Force Two had to pass. He was shaking hands with some, hugging and consoling others. Jay had bent down to spend a private moment with the body of Vice President Fulton before it was placed into the ambulance. The MedFlight with Fred as its passenger had departed almost ten minutes ago. Now, it seemed that too much was going on much too quickly.

The president's chief of staff and communications director both watched as the FBI director worked his wheelchair at a furious pace, heading straight for the president. The two men heard Keith's shouts and both put all of their energy to run to where Griffen now stood. The secret service agents were now alert, yet not moving, although one agent was nearing the president. His movements gave no one reason for concern as the man was busy looking under the aircraft and the stairways and casually checking each deplaning passenger.

Over by the medical transport plane's nose gear, two secret service agents stood keeping a vigilant watch on everything that was going on around them. It had gone from nothing to very, very busy, plus dark and rainy, in an extremely short amount of time. Sunset wasn't for another hour or so, but the dark clouds had put an early end to daylight as they knew it. The two saw one of their own walking to their position.

"Yo? B.B.? Is that you?"

"Yeah. Hey, Smitty. Downsy. How you guys doing?" asked the agent, offering his hand.

The first, Smitty, returned the shake and replied. "Probably doing better than you? What the hell happened?"

"Number two had a heart attack in his rack. He was catching a little prevent snooze and apparently went just like that," responded the newly arrived secret service agent with a snap of his fingers.

Agent Downs offered his hand in consolation and brotherhood as well. "That really sucks, B. What's this shit about Dayle being under arrest?"

"Downsy, on that one, you know what I know. One minute, we're just finishing up with the inflight meal, the next thing, Dayle's asked to head to the forward conference room. I go to check on him and he's under armed guard, under arrest pending investigation. I tried to get something out of the Air Force sergeant, but he wasn't talking if he knew."

"That's really weird, B."

"Weird is an understatement, boys. I'm gonna go pay my respects to the boss before things get into hyperdrive. See ya."

"Catch you around the office, B," said Smitty.

"Hang tight, Brian," offered Downs.

Agent Bello simply waved as he casually strolled to where the President of the United States stood in the rain. From his angle of approach, he hadn't seen the FBI director arrive. Bello had merely dismissed the metal glint near the president's legs as a piece of aircraft or ambulance apparatus.

"President Griffen," huffed Director Hammett.

"Yes, Keith. What's up?"

"We got the bank cards on those Virginia accounts. The manager there was being a real prick about it, telling us what we could do with our warrants. After a phone call to the attorney general and the casual mention of ten years for federal obstruction charges, we got the info," Keith said, pulling out a small notebook. "The M&M account is a joint thing for Moore and Hewes."

"We have both of them in custody, Keith.

The FBI director nodded and continued. "The TD Security is an account for Agent Dayle."

"Whom we now have in custody, Keith," said the president, gesturing towards Air Force Two. "We had him placed under house-arrest while they were airborne."

"The last account, the one for BLBB. That is an account for Brian Bello, also part of Fulton's detail."

"Agent Bello? He's the quiet, skinny kid, right?"

"Skinny? Yes. Kid? Not this week, sir. He's as old as we are, sir. Fifty if he's a day."

As he spoke, Hammett caught sight of a dark figure casually approaching the president from behind. Keith gently gave the president a tug down to be closer.

"Jay?" Keith whispered. "Don't do anything until I tell you. When I say now, I want you to dive to my left, your right. Understand?"

"Yeah, Keith. But why?"

"No time, sir."

The figure closed the distance and was now no more than six feet behind the president.

"Now!" said the FBI director, calmly.

President John F. Griffen launched himself forward and to the left of Hammett's wheelchair. The FBI director caught the brief flash of something metallic in the hand of the shadowed interloper. The face of the approaching man was one of a person who had been truly surprised. Hammett's lightweight, nine millimeter weapon had been at the ready, pointing down, safety off. The FBI director squeezed off four quick shots before the weight of the oncoming, now lifeless, man fell on top of him and toppled the wheelchair. Keith used his well-toned arms to move the dead body off him and looked to where the President lay, spread out in a puddle.

"Are you okay, sir?"

"I am wet, but unharmed, Hammett. Or should I say, Hammer. Now I know where you got that name."

Jay was getting to his feet and watched as Keith effortlessly righted his wheelchair and climbed back onto the seat. Hammett still held his weapon at arm's length, trained on the now slumped form in front of the two of them. Four suit-coated agents arrived within seconds, immediately forming a wall around the Commander in Chief. One other agent came running, trailed by Dan Josten and Bud Nelson.

"What the hell was that?" asked Nelson in his deep, distinct southern drawl.

"That, Bud, was our FBI director proving to me why he has the job," said Jay, stepping out of the human bubble.

They all watched as the fifth agent on scene turned over the shadowed intruder and saw the boyish face of agent Brian Bello. The shot cluster had all been heart-shots. The right hand still held the empty syringe, plunger fully extended.

"What do you think he was trying to do?" asked Josten.

"I believe, Dan, that he was going to stab the president with that syringe," Keith offered. "All I saw was the metal flashing. It could have been a knife, for all I know. I didn't have time to do otherwise."

"And from what I remember from our reading material, the notes were tough to translate in some of the terms, but I do recall one of the subjects being made to suffer a collapsed lung," offered Bud.

"Actually, Nelson. I believe there were notes on both cases to that effect," said Josten.

"Danny. Make sure we call Bethesda and tell them to investigate this possibility in their post-mortem of Fulton," said Griffen.

"I'm on it now, sir. Are you okay?"

"Dan, I may be old and tired, but I ain't dead yet."

"Amen to that, sir. Amen."

The president, his chief of staff, his communications director and his FBI director all stood around, watching as the Secret Service detail swung into crime-scene mode; making note of the weapon, the body, the position and the situation. There would be an official report. But there would not be a public report. This would be handled internally and used as the starting point to a complete overhaul of how trainees were selected and screened at Quantico.

Having seen enough, the president motioned to his team so they could give the investigative team room to work. They walked to the rear of the Charleston transport and waited as the stretcher carrying Admiral Dericksen was lowered. Griffen watched the admiral being moved into the ambulance and the president motioned to the attendant in the back. Jay stepped in through a side door of the truck-sized unit and sat down on one of the jump seats along the wall. Dericksen was awake, but had a tube down his throat to help him breathe. The sound of the ventilator's mechanical functions kept a steady beat and kept Griffen temporarily from maintaining control of his emotions.

Wiping a tear from his eye, Jay said, "I am so, so sorry, Admiral. I never in my wildest dreams thought that something like this would happen. They tell me you'll be okay?"

Dericksen nodded his agreement.

"Good," continued the president. "I know this is not the most opportune of times, but how open are you to another request? There's this situation with a dear friend of mine who might be in need of something constructive to do with his time. And I have a need for someone to also do something constructive with his time. Interested?"

The admiral again nodded as the president then lowered his head and whispered his proposition into the ears of the intubated patient. Dericksen closed his eyes for a moment upon hearing the president out, then simply indicated his approval with a thumbs up from his free, right hand. Jay gently took Gary's right hand, shook it and patted the admiral on his shoulder.

"Thanks, Gary. Again, I am so sorry. But I hope that we can somehow work to make sure that something, or anything, like this never occurs again."

Jay slipped out of the side door and waved to the driver in the front seat. The driver lowered the passenger side window.

"Take real good care of this man, driver. And thank you," Griffen said.

"My pleasure, Mister President."

The window powered back up as the driver put the vehicle in gear, pulling away from the motorized lift that was now being lowered with the stretcher carrying Tom Hannity. Again, the president repeated the wait and watch routine before climbing into the side door of the next transport. This time, he stuck his head out of the door and motioned for Dan to come over.

"Yeah, Jay?" Josten asked.

"Danny, I'm going to ride to the hospital with Tom. Have my car meet me there. I need to talk with this man for more than a minute, okay?"

"Sure, Jay. Did you ask the admiral?"

"Yeah. I think we'll be able to do some real good, Danny. Gary's a fine man."

"Do you want me to come to the hospital with the car? Or shall we all meet back at the office?"

"Why don't you take Bud out for a quick bite to eat. No, better yet, take him by Bethesda. We can all head to the office from there. I'll have them bring us all some food from the kitchen when we get back to sixteen hundred. Let Downs and Smith know what we're doing. I know they're going to want to play 'follow the leader'."

"That's what we pay them for, Jay. See you back at the office."

President Griffen strapped himself into the jump seat next to Tom's stretcher. Secret Service agent Downs hopped into the vacant front passenger seat, explaining to the driver that they now had two very special passengers. Smith came in the side door and stood out of the way, but no more than an arm's length away from "Bunsie." "Bunsie" was Griffen's code name, as suggested by Chief of Staff Josten. It was an inside joke and one that had been kept inside for almost six years. Josten had explained it was a high school nickname that had landed as the result of a passing compliment from an admiring schoolgirl.

The doctor and nurse from the Air Force MedFlight also squeezed into the back to attend to Hannity and motioned to the EMT in the back with them that they were all set to roll.

"Mister President?" asked Tom as he looked up groggily.

"Tom. Glad you could join us," said the president. The comment brought chuckles from all in the back, even Agent Smith.

"What's up? Is everything okay?" Hannity inquired.

"As fine as can be, Tom. First, I need to apologize to you for what happened. I can't believe that I sent you there and this, this tragedy happened. I am so very sorry."

"It's in my job description, sir. Don't worry."

"No, Tom. Your job is to keep an eye on me. Not to do my dirty work. I need to ask you a few things. Are you awake enough to listen and give them some thought?"

Tom nodded his head as President Griffen leaned in and, not unlike his private conversation with Admiral Dericksen, whispered his questions and proposals. The others in the back took their cues to focus on something else for a few moments. Agent Smith kept watch out the side window as the multiple-vehicle escorts did their thing, the blue flashing lights of the Maryland State Police running roadblock for the motorcade that included this ambulance. It would take only a few minutes at this pace to reach Bethesda Naval Hospital. That was all President Griffen would need to present his proposition to a good man left maimed by the afterthoughts of a sick, demented man.

fifty

Fahey had just gotten off the phone with Director Hammett. The news about Singletary's health was not good at all and Hammett had asked Jimmy to pass the word to Don Hough.

There was also the matter of the master account for AFR Enterprises. The director had told his field agent that the handwriting analysis of the master account card revealed that Fred Singletary and Konstantin Rostokovich were one and the same. A photographic identification pulled from the bank's master files confirmed the dual identity. The individual photo i.d. cards had been produced on two separate occasions, with two separate bank representatives. So long as the person presenting himself as a named individual had the requisite three forms of identification, then the bank's personnel could proceed with their duty. Singletary had opened the off-shore account in 1975 and had made arrangements for the other account signatories to come to the Grand Cayman Islands at their leisure to complete their paperwork. The dates on the bank's records indicated the processing of the Rostokovich paperwork late in the fall of 1975 and the Romanov documentation was handled by notarized proxy

531

in the summer of 1976. The subsequent diversification of the AFR financial structure made it almost impossible to track the distribution of funds. Fahey had gotten lucky. Also, the Virginia bank accounts had turned up one unexpected surprise plus the confirmations that they'd hoped to find.

Now, while Director Hammett was on his way to Andrews Air Force base to brief the president about the Virginia bank accounts, Fahey had the unenviable task of letting Don know that his boss and buddy, Fred, was both dying and spying. That Fred was apparently an agent of the old Soviet Union was a puzzle indeed. Here's a man who has achieved the American dream in a fashion larger than Fahey could ever imagine and the paradox is that he is a communal member of a socialist society. That Fred would put all he has earned alone on the table and allow those around him to help themselves was beyond the FBI agent's comprehension.

Jim was about to head back to the hospital where Don continued his bedside vigil with Sandy when his desk phone began to buzz.

"Fahey," he said answering the phone.

"Agent Fahey? I'm Special Agent Carlos Daniels from the Charleston office."

"Carlos. Please call me Jim. What's up?"

"We've been working this Hewes blow-up down here today and we found the vehicle that brought the secret service agent here. It's a nice Lincoln Towncar. Belongs to a Dericksen, Gary. I understand he's one of the people injured. In the car, I found a cellphone, one of those multi-purpose units."

"Pager. Voice mail. Phone. That type?"

"Yeah. It's registered to this Fred Singletary. So we turn it on and there are a couple of messages waiting. One call is from a Washington, DC number. We traced that to the White House. It stops there."

"The White House? Probably Nelson, the president's communications director. What else?"

"There was a pager message to call a Virginia cellphone. We traced that number through the GSA. It's a secret service communications center phone, issued to an Agent Dayle, with the vice president's detail. The GSA did a routing check on the call to this Singletary phone and it looks like the Dayle call originated in Madrid, Spain."

"This is creating more questions than it's answering," said Fahey.

"Yeah, it's got me guessing, too, Jim. I'm trying to figure out how these three got tangled up? You got a DC agent, a retired Navy Admiral and a radio station owner? Kind of a weird trio."

"The matching up of these guys will make sense when this gets a little closer to wrapping up, Carlos. Thanks for the info on that cellphone."

"The boys in Washington asked me to fill you in on anything concerning this Singletary guy."

"Give me your number down there, Carlos. I'll call when I get the okay from the top to bring you up to speed and fill in the blanks." Fahey opened his desktop card file to the D section and filled out a card with the agent's name and office number. "Thanks again, Carlos."

Fahey hung up the phone and slipped his suitcoat back on. Straightening his tie, he slipped his weapon into its spot on his belt and walked out of his office, heading back to New York Presbyterian's Cornell Center hospital.

In Sandy's glass-enclosed room in the ICU, Don sat on the small chair to her right. Sandy had been awake for almost thirty minutes and they were now awaiting the attending physician to arrive. Nurse Gina Madsen finished removing the gauze covering from the less-badly injured eye and had suggested that Sandy might be more comfortable out of the Intensive Care Unit. Sandy wholeheartedly agreed. She was allowing Don to spoon a small amount of smoothed ice onto her tongue. The inside of her mouth was stitched up and she'd be a week or two before she could be fitted with some sort of dental prosthesis. The nurses had combined a small amount of fruit juice and ice and then blended them thoroughly. It was a simple pleasure for someone in Sandy's position who had suffered a severe internal mouth injury but was no doubt parched beyond compare. Once the small chips had been smoothed, removing the naturally sharp edges, the mixture could be placed onto the tongue, away from the injured portions of the gums.

Sandy had held up her good hand to indicate she'd had enough of the ice. The attending physician had given the go-ahead to remove the bandage from her better eye, but he had insisted on leaving the other eye-patch where it was for at least a few days until she could be checked out. She was using a pad and paper to communicate with Don and had just written, for the third time, her question. It saved her from trying to speak and aggravating the sutures on her gums.

Don read the note. "All right, Sandy. The doctor asked me not to get into this with you. But, here goes. Jon had been let into your apartment and you walked right into him and his demented version of reality."

Sandy used the pen to vigorously tap on the paper.

Don nodded. "Jonathon's dead, Sandy. He will never, ever be able to hurt you again."

Sandy's look pleaded with Don to tell more, but he merely shook his head no. She wrote the word "how?" on the paper.

"Jon was shot while resisting arrest. That's all you need to know. He's gone. He can never again do to you or anyone else what he did to you."

She looked reflectively down at her notepad. She then wrote the word "Fred."

"Why would Fred need to know?" asked Don.

She flipped the page and scribbled out her response. Don looked at the page. A sudden realization hit him like a ton of bricks. "Yeah. I had heard their businesses might be related. I didn't realize that Fred owned Jon's import business."

Don paused while Sandy wrote more and placed it in front of Don for him to see.

Reading it slowly, his shoulders slumped momentarily. He straightened himself out and then answered. "No, I didn't know that Fred had introduced the two of you. He never told me. Nor did you." Don was trying to maintain a level temper. She was, for whatever reason, pushing his buttons, or so he thought. Sandy wrote a little bit more on the notepad. Showing it to Don, he could take no more.

"Sandy? Do you know what that sadistic son of a bitch of an ex-husband of yours did for a living?"

He waited while she wrote out her response.

"No, Sandy. He did not sell fine works of art to people with too much money." He looked at her vigorously shaking her head "yes."

"Sandy. Jonathon was in this country on a passport with my name and address on it. He was using a company credit card with my name on it. My card had been canceled for whatever reason. I didn't know that until I went to purchase my ticket to get down here this morning. The FBI is very interested in Jon's little expedition here. So is the National Security Agency, Interpol, British Intelligence and the President of the United States. Do you now understand that you were unfortunately suckered in by an international criminal who apparently made his sideline much more profitable than his chosen field and that he hated to take the word no for an answer?"

This was now Sandy's turn to look dejectedly at her hands, folded softly in front of her. The soft, pink blanket that covered her was smooth and wrinkle-free, save the outline of her legs underneath. She had been nervously straightening the top of the white sheet poking out from under the blanket, working the edges in order to give her hand something to do when not writing. She was also allowing her thoughts to gather while working herself through what Don was saying. She put the pen to paper once again. Don read it.

"No, Sandy. The government does not believe that you are in any way involved with Jonathon's illegal activities. You are merely a victim in a marital dispute. That is what you are, right?"

The portion of Sandy's face visible through the bandages and clear adhesive tape turned a crimson. She nodded her head yes. She then wrote out another two lines and passed the notebook to Hough.

Don looked it over and felt somewhat hurt again. "I'm sure you were hoping that you two might be able to work it out. Didn't last night remove all doubt?"

She once again nodded her head in the affirmative. Then she jotted two quick words.

"Yes. Your mom and dad should be here in a few minutes. The FBI is involved in this Jonathon thing now, Sandy. They've sent for a car to get your folks. I called them and brought them up to speed. They don't need to know about the counterfeiting aspects. It would be better if you just tell them that he came back to New York and went ballistic on you. Simple as that. He was a man who didn't like the word no. You were made to suffer for that. That's what I've told them, so that's what they know."

Sandy made a gesture as if to call attention to her current physical look.

"Yeah. I told them you were pretty badly beat up and that they should be prepared for lots of bandages and stuff. I'm hoping your doctor will get you out of here before they arrive. It would be less traumatic for them if you weren't in the ICU.

Sandy looked at Don, puzzled.

"Oh yeah, babe. You are in the Intensive Care Unit, under protective guard from both the FBI and the NYPD. You had lost a lot of blood and were actually touch and go when they brought you in. You were unconscious for almost twelve hours. I told you that Jon really worked you over good."

Sandy made reference to one of their favorite songs.

"Like a Waring blender. That's for sure, Sandy babe. Big time."

Nurse Madsen came into the unit, followed by two orderlies.

"Miss Rose? We're going to get you out of here and up to a private room. Something with a view, hopefully. You ready to move?"

Sandy nodded her head as Don stood to step back out of the way. The uniformed policeman held the door as Don stepped out, followed by the rolling bed that held Sandy. A few looks from the people lingering in the ICU's central area made Sandy feel uncomfortable, Don picking up the glint of recognition in their eyes. The elevator was waiting, another uniformed policeman holding the door. Sandy was quickly wheeled into the lift and the doors closed, the elevator beginning its ascent. The elevator stopped at the sixth floor and the entourage began their short journey to a private room just down the hall, towards a corner past the central nursing station for this section of the hospital.

The room was large enough to hold two patients, but the hospital had cleared out the second bed in order to make Sandy feel that much more comfortable. It had its own private bath and shower, as well as several closets and a good sized television mounted on an overhead bracket.

The move had taken no more than three minutes, but already Sandy felt better. She pointed to the window and Don stepped to the curtains, pulling them back to reveal the outside world. She could see the sky, cloud filled as it was, announcing the arrival of the April showers yet to come. There was a knock at the still-opened door and Agent Fahey stepped in, carrying a small, black nylon overnight bag.

"Hey Don!" he said. Looking at Sandy, he continued. "You must be Sandy? I'm Jim Fahey, FBI, New York field office. I stopped by your apartment and grabbed a few things. I hope you don't mind terribly." He passed the bag to Sandy. She opened the bag and pulled out the soft, pink bathrobe that was folded onto the top of the contents. She looked through the rest and nodded her thanks to the agent. She motioned to Nurse Madsen to come over and jotted a quick note.

"Gentlemen? Could you two step out for just a moment, please?" asked the nurse.

Don and Jim left the room, Fahey closing the door gently behind.

"Hey, buddy. We found out some more very interesting stuff. None of it looks very promising for Fred's business ventures. Also, the Charleston field office has Freddie's cellphone. They traced an incoming message to his pager and it was from a Secret Service agent in Madrid."

"So? Fred's got lots of friends of in high places, Jimmy."

"No. This Secret Service agent is currently being taken into custody at Andrews Air Force base. He's been implicated in at least two murders committed over twenty years ago. Murders nobody knew about. Fred's apparently tied into some kind of a spy ring that's been at work since the 70's, Don."

"Fred's a spy? That would make me Mata Hari."

"No, I'm sorry. You just don't have the legs for that role, Mister Hough. But there's something else."

"What?"

"Fred's in serious condition. There was an explosion in South Carolina this morning. A house on a plantation was rigged with some type of plastique. Fred, his buddy the admiral and a different Secret Service agent were all badly hurt."

"The Hewes place was rigged? How bad is Freddie, Jim?"

"They're not sure if he's going to make it. He suffered some real bad burns over the lower part of his body. My director didn't want me to tell you. He wanted Nelson to let you know what was going on."

"Well, Nelson hasn't called me once all day."

"He knows where you've been. He thought that your taking care of Sandy was a more productive use of your time. Fred's being moved to Bethesda Naval Hospital. He's probably there already. I'm sure Nelson's just waiting until there's some kind of good news for you. Or bad."

"Let me go call Bud, please. Can you go in and sit with Sandy? Her parents should be here any minute, right?"

Jim took a glance at his watch. "Yes. They're probably just getting into midtown now."

Don walked down the hallway to the small waiting area where there were a couple of payphones. Jim leaned against the wall and waited for Sandy's parents to arrive.

Hough punched in the phone number for Nelson from the official White House business card. Then, he punched his calling card number. He listened while the recorded voice told him his calling card number was invalid and to re-enter a valid calling card number. He punched the 0 and waited for the operator to respond.

"Yes, operator. I'd like to make this call collect from Don Hough. Yes, thank you, operator."

Don played the third party, listening to the phone call make its connection and then listened while the operator asked Nelson if he'd accept the call.

"Bud? What the hell is going on?"

"Don. I was going to call you. Really. But I figured you'd be of better use to Sandy than you would to Fred."

"I wish you would have let me make that decision, Nelson. Fred has basically been all the family I have left in the world, man. At least you could have touched base with me and given me some details."

"Here's what we know, Donny. Fred's on his way to Bethesda right now. It doesn't look good. Do you want to come down here? I can have you here in an hour."

Don thought for a moment. "Is this crap about Fred being involved with all kinds of spy stuff true?"

"Yeah. Fred Singletary is really a Soviet agent named Konstantin Rostokovich."

"As in your other spy? Rostokovich? Romanov's brother-in-law? You're absolutely positive?"

"That's affirmative, Don. Fred, also known as Konstantin, is Michail's older brother. Michail had no knowledge of his brother's involvement. The confirmation came from British Intelligence. They had a couple of old photos of Fred and Fulton together in Europe in the early seventies. Before we knew him."

"Fulton? The vice president?"

"Yep. Just keeps getting better, doesn't it, Don? Remember our trip to the Lobster Shack yesterday and that conversation we had? You suggested it first and Fred even filled in the doubt-filled blanks for us."

"Which part was that, Bud? The part about there being more than one?"

"Bingo! There were, as far as we know, as many as five. We're waiting to ask Romanov a few questions to get the final head count."

"How long will that take? If what you've said is true, then Romanov is not going to make himself readily available for questioning, Bud."

"Oh, he's plenty available, Don. That's all you need to know on that score for now." Bud listened while Don exhaled heavily, trying to digest all of the new information.

"Do you think I should come down to Washington?"

"If you want to, Donny. I'll have a plane waiting for you in five minutes. It's your call."

"Get the plane ready, Bud. I'd at least like the opportunity to say goodbye, if he's in as tough a situation as you say."

"He is, Donny. I'll get the transportation set up for you. See you at Bethesda."

"Okay, Bud. See you in a bit."

Don hung up the phone and walked back towards Sandy's room. Fahey was standing in the hall, just outside of the door to her room. He glanced down the longer hallway to his right and saw the older couple getting off the elevator, looking around as if they were lost. Don waved to Jim, pointed down in the direction of the older couple and took a couple of quick jogging steps to them.

"Emily? Connor? It's Don. Don Hough."

"Oh, Don. You look great, dear," said Emily Rose, Sandy's mother.

"Don. Nice to see you again. Just wish it weren't under these circumstances." offered Sandy's dad, Connor.

"She was in rough shape for a time, but she's doing better now. Come this way. I'll take you to her," Don said.

The three turned in the direction of Sandy's room and met with Fahey outside the door. After brief introductions, Jim opened the door and allowed the three to enter. Sandy had changed into one of her own nightgowns, brought in the overnight bag by Fahey. With some help from Nurse Madsen, she'd had a chance to brush her hair to at least make herself look somewhat presentable to any visitors. Don walked in first and whispered to her that he'd be leaving for a bit. She nodded her understanding and he kissed her gently on the top of her head. Sandy's mother became visibly emotional and Connor tenderly guided his daughter's mother to the bed. Don made his apologies to Sandy's parents and grabbed Fahey's arm, motioning to him to step outside of the room.

As the FBI agent closed the door behind them, allowing the family their privacy, Don spoke.

"Jim. I need a ride to the airport. Nelson's going to have a plane waiting for me to get me to Washington so I can see Freddie."

"We're there, Don. Let me make arrangements with the uniforms to make sure they keep a close eye on things here."

Don walked to the elevators and pushed the down button. Fahey finished his instructions to the policemen and walked quickly to join Don. Three minutes later, they were in the main lobby. The media throng was still positioned outside, though not as numerous as earlier in the day. The white spotlights were blazing into the lobby from the other side of the large windows. The time was right for the five-thirty newscasts to be going to their reporters for the latest live update. Jimmy escorted Don out through the revolving door and onto the sidewalk. A senior reporter was just finishing his report as the two walked past.

"Don? Don Hough? Donny! Wait a second!"

Don looked to see Terry Roberts moving toward him.

"Just a second, Jim," said Don.

"I'll get the car, Don. We've got to hustle if we're going to get you to DC," Jim replied.

"I'll only be a minute." Don turned to the reporter. "Terry. How've you been?"

"Good, Don. Real good, thanks. What, er, brings you here?"

"Just visiting a friend, Terry. No story to tell."

"The friend wouldn't be Sandra Rose, would it?"

"Yeah. It's Sandy. She's doing just fine. Why don't you guys just pack it up and go home. Let the lady get some rest. Maybe recover her dignity at the same time."

"Don, you know the drill. Got a story to cover, you cover it. Sandy's the story today. That's the way it is."

"Well, Terry. The story is a non-story as far as she's concerned. You guys have your semi-juicy tidbits to work with, so just go ahead and keep all consideration of the facts and people's feelings out of it. It's what you do best."

"Hey, c'mon, man. You know we're just doing our jobs."

"That's right, Terry. You're just doing your job. Take care and say hi to Mary for me."

"Mary? We got divorced about six years ago, Don. I know you've been out of the loop for a while. You're working, where, up near Canada or something like that?"

"Yeah, Terry. Up with the polar bears and Eskimos. Catch you later."

Don left the senior network reporter standing on the sidewalk and climbed into the official government vehicle. Fahey put the car in gear, heading for the airport. Don watched the raindrops begin to spittle across the windshield and cover the side window of the car as it made its way through the now-heavy Saturday evening Manhattan traffic. Just a lovely finish to a perfectly screwed-up day, he thought. Just lovely.

fifty-one

In the vast expanse that was the Rotunda situated in the United States Capitol building, the air was still. The only sounds came from the steady shuffling of feet and the occasional soft or muted cry. The flagged-draped casket that held the body of Donald Robert Fulton, Vice President of the United States of America, lay in state. The coffin was open, allowing those filing by to gaze one last time upon the face of a man they knew to be a good American. A man who had done much good work and had yet much more to accomplish. A man who had died much too young.

The state funeral with full-honors was unhesitatingly decided upon by President Griffen. He'd felt that what they knew and what they thought they knew were two different things. The things they knew that were yet to happen were now and forever only speculation. Jay had pointed out that medical science had not yet perfected the ability to steal the thoughts from a dead man's brain. Up to this moment in time, Don Fulton had done nothing untoward in regards to his country or his duty. He may have done things that, eventually, might or might not have contributed to what he hoped to achieve when and if he got to team with Romanov. The mights and the ifs were the keys, Griffen had maintained. The issue regarding Fulton and his involvement with this nightmare would be kept low key. There were plenty of bigger, breathing fish to fry.

Now, on a bright spring morning, Don Fulton lay forever still, the sun's early morning rays creeping across the wide open floor to where he now rested. There would be another day of lying in state, then, the funeral would be held Wednesday morning. The heads of the countries who had gathered in Paris for the economic conference postponed their official meetings for forty-eight hours and were due to begin arriving late this afternoon. President Griffen had stated his desire to join them in Paris, as scheduled and had outlined a rescheduled calendar for their approval. All had agreed to the changes, yet wondered privately whether or not the American president would be able to be in Paris for the final approval of the revolutionary realignment of Europe's economy.

Jay stood silently and slightly in back of Don's widow, Peg and their two children, Jason and Caitlin. They were flanked by Don's parents, Don and Marlena. Don's brothers and sister had come as well, with their respective spouses and offspring. Jay had been given the opportunity to spend a quiet moment with Peg and the kids, as well as with Don's parents. For that, the president was truly grateful. Don's ulterior motives notwithstanding, Don's family were indeed fine people, far removed from the darker desires of their now-deceased husband, father, son.

In the line of mourners, a securely yet clandestinely guarded Anastasia Fidoryvich made her way past, being allowed to pause briefly. She was granted the request to step forward into the V.I.P. line and address Peg and the rest of Don's family. A tearful hug covered the gap for which none of them could find the words to fill. Annie hugged the children and stooped to offer the only words of condolence she could find for Don's seated parents. She stood, nodded to the president, as well as acknowledging the new vice president with a warm embrace and resumed her journey with the rest of the American people filing by, paying their last respects to a good man taken too early.

※ ※ ※

Saturday evening, after he had escorted Tom to the hospital and looked in on the others, President Griffen returned to the White House at six-fifteen. There, he met with his full cabinet, Senate Majority Leader Davis Wilson and the two ranking house members, majority whip Albert Roulo of North Carolina and minority leader Arthur Francis of Massachusetts.

The president's briefing was short, yet blunt. For those not aware of the actual events of the past forty-eight hours, Griffen gave them more than an earful. He also included the details of the recently discovered evidence regarding the Stark woman and her accusations. On this matter, he was aided by Attorney General Vernon who revealed some additional items unearthed within the past few hours.

Once all had been updated, the president bluntly took control of the meeting and laid out his suggestions as to how the various matters would be handled.

Regarding Speaker Hewes, his resignation, effective immediately, was based on the appearance of impropriety in his relationship with Marvin Moore, as well as for his own future safety, given the results of an investigation into the explosion at his home. That investigation had revealed that certain, still-unknown radical elements had been responsible for the potential attack on his life by the planting of explosive devices in and around the Hewes homestead. Fortunately, Hewes would go on to elaborate, the devices were apparently faulty and detonated at a time when there was no one present.

Regarding the known reports of three persons injured at the Hewes homestead, that issued had been clarified. Yes, there were three persons transported from the site of the explosion, but their injuries were not as a direct result of the incident. Admiral Gary Dericksen, United States Navy, retired, was driving a vehicle which also included as passengers, Fred Singletary, a long-time personal friend and Secret Service Agent Thomas Hannity. The three were on a routine advance mission on behalf of the president's detail, going over site plans and locations for an upcoming presidential visit to the scenic Charleston area. At the time of the explosion, they were driving down the road which the Hewes estate fronts. Distracted by the explosion, the admiral lost momentary control of his vehicle, but it was long enough for the car to leave the road, careening into a tree. Airbags and seatbelts notwithstanding, the injuries to the three were severe, including the subsequent death of Fred Singletary.

This day of note in American history was capped by the news of the passing of one of the United States' brightest lights, Vice President Donald Robert Fulton. A preliminary autopsy confirmed the initial findings that the vice president had a slight heart defect in the form of an undetected aortic aneurysm. The wall of the aorta had suddenly and without warning, let go, causing an instantaneous death. Mercifully, the president would be allowed to add, the vice president passed in his sleep.

At the conclusion of his outline of events, there were many questions. Jay addressed each one. By six-thirty-eight p.m., the bulk of the questions had been answered. Each question posed was regarding the spin being put on each individual story. Jay had to ask each of the posers to answer the question themselves with one thing in mind. The confidence of the American people and how would that confidence stay intact if the people were presented with the actual facts. Once the esteemed gathering had satisfactorily been briefed, they adjourned to allow the president the opportunity to grab some dinner and a shower before his televised event.

The address to the nation was timed for eight p.m.. Being a Saturday night, the audience would not be as large as a prime-time address during a weeknight. A large majority of Americans would learn the details upon opening their Sunday papers in the morning. The word had gone out to the networks on very short notice, immediately after President Griffen had concluded his briefing to the assembled national leaders. The networks scrambled to track down their anchors and have them available for air at five minutes to eight. The only thing the networks had been told was that the president needed to address the American people regarding a major change in the administration as well as one in Congress. This had the networks salivating at the thought that President Griffen might have decided enough was enough and was going to throw in the towel. The word of this rumble had made its way back to Nelson's office less than five minutes after the networks had been informed. Nelson, Josten and the president shared a knowing smile at the rumor-return, in regards to both the speed and the inaccuracy with which the tale had been spun and brought back to the point of origin. None of them took any pleasure at the real reasons for this assumption being completely wrong.

In general, Fulton and Hewes had both served America admirably. But the direction of an America under their leadership was a question that, as of now, was best unanswered. The president's speech had been written earlier that evening and was prepared for the TelePrompTer before the meeting with the cabinet and congressional leaders. Nelson had outlined this speech while they all waited at Andrews for the airplanes to arrive and had finished it just before the meeting was convened. Nelson had an hour before the president took to the air, so he excused himself to meet with Hough and Michaud who were arriving at Bethesda at that moment.

Fred had not survived. He was on life-support for the benefit of the two friends to come and say goodbye. Then, Fred, also known as Konstantin, would be allowed to die with dignity, his usable organs and tissues harvested to continue the good work that Fred had started. Only the good, Bud had told himself. The hospital visit had been emotional and yet Nelson had finished his good-byes and returned to the White House.

At exactly seven-fifty-five p.m., the networks had managed to round up their first stringers and all were reading hastily prepared introductions from their various TelePrompTers. Two of the anchors went so far as to assume the basis for this address was the expected resignation of the president.

At exactly eight p.m., a chorus of "The President of the United States" resounded from television sets all over the world, each network anchor introducing President John F. Griffen.

"My fellow Americans. I thank you for allowing me into your homes this evening. I come here with sorrowful news for us all. Today, at approximately two-forty-five p.m., eastern standard time, while en route from Madrid, Spain onboard Air Force Two, Vice President Donald Robert Fulton died as the result of a major coronary event..."

Down in the White House communications center, Nelson and Josten watched the networks' off-air pre-feeds, cameras not currently on-air, but live and focused on the anchors sitting at their respective desks.

"Holy shit! Did you see that?" laughed Josten.

"The mouthful of coffee? Yep. We are rolling video tape on these clowns, right?"

"Bud, you better believe it. I feel guilty about laughing while the boss is breaking the news, but the humor is in watching these guys who had it all figured out."

"I'm sure if Fulton were here, he'd be enjoying this as well."

."... I had the unenviable task of informing Peggy and her children of Don's passing. She wishes to pass along the thanks of her family to you for your prayers, kind thoughts and kind words during this, their most distressing time. Vice President Fulton will lay in state on Monday and Tuesday, with a state funeral from the Cathedral of the Immaculate Conception Wednesday morning. Burial with full honors will take place at Arlington National Cemetery. We have declared the nation to be in an official state of mourning for the next thirty days and I have directed all United States flags to be flown at half-staff for this period in recognition of the life a fine man who served our country with distinction..."

"Okay, Bud. You are the master."

"Shhh, Danny. I want to hear how he delivers this one."

."... In regards to a successor, I have asked and have had my offer accepted by, Peg Fulton to serve in her husband's place on an interim basis, until such time as both the House and Senate have had the opportunity to conduct official confirmation hearings on a permanent replacement. Mrs. Fulton has been sworn in by the honorable Terrance Quinlan, Chief Justice of the United States. I have submitted to the leaders of the House and Senate the name of Admiral Gary Dericksen, United States Navy, retired, of South Carolina, as my choice for a permanent vice president for the remainder of my term as your president. Admiral Dericksen served our country with distinction for more than thirty years and has gained a national reputation as a highly-respected and trusted businessman in

his new-found field as an operation security expert. His ventures extend beyond our borders as well, which makes him not unfamiliar in dealings with our foreign allies. I have asked the Congress to schedule their confirmation hearings to begin one week from Monday and I trust that our elected leaders will agree that Admiral Dericksen is the kind of person of whom we will all be proud..."

"That went well, don't you think, Dan?"

"It went very well, Bud. Wow! Look at them scurry back there in New York."

"Yep. I can hear it now. "Who the hell is this Dericksen and why don't I have his bio in front of me? NOW!." Glad I got the hell out of there, or otherwise, that'd be me saying what I figure they're saying."

"Man, Nelson. I had an English teacher who'd give you twenty bucks to diagram that last sentence."

"Dan? Shut up."

.".. *There is one other piece of national business I must address. This evening, I received word from Congressman M. Bradford Hewes that he was resigning from the office of Speaker of the House, as well as relinquishing his seat in the House, terminating his representation of his district and the good people of South Carolina. I have spoken with Governor Hunsucker and informed him of the speaker's decision. The governor is convening his council this evening and hopes to have a consensus nominee ready to assume office once the government returns to its full-time duties Thursday morning..."*

"Those poor bastards don't know what hit them."

"Dan, I've been those poor bastards. It couldn't happen to a nicer bunch. Well, except maybe him," Bud said pointing to one of the monitors. "And her, over here in Atlanta? She's a real nice lady."

"I've always had a thing for the glasses. I love when she wears the glasses."

"That's why I tried to hire her. She looks okay when she's wearing the contacts, but the glasses are the real deal."

"Okay, here comes the big finish."

"We are going to take some serious shit in about sixty seconds, aren't we?"

"Yep, Bud. YOU are going to be getting it from at least five different directions."

"Bailing out on me?"

"Hey, I've got a funeral to plan," Dan said as he stood to take his leave of Nelson.

.".. I'd like to address one final item that is still very much in the minds of you, the citizens of this great country. The business of our government runs twenty-four hours a day, seven days a week. The day-to-day routines will indeed be halted while we pay our respects to Vice President Fulton. Thursday, the offices of the Federal government will return to full, normal operation. That includes our Federal courts. My defense team has requested that my appearance in U.S. Federal Court here in Washington be rescheduled from Wednesday morning to Thursday morning. The attorney general, who, as prosecutor of this case, has agreed and Judge O'Reilly has approved. I assure you that there will be a full and public airing of the charges of which I stand accused. You, the American people, will have the opportunity to see that even I, as president, am not above the law..."

"I'm putting my five bucks on MSNBC," Dan opined from the doorway.

"MSNBC? You really think Brian can top the big boys tonight?"

"Five bucks, Bud. Put up or shut up."

"Okay, Dan. I'll take your money. I'd rather go with my other Danny-boy," Nelson said, the emphasis on "rather." "He's easily going to have a half-dozen within ten minutes."

"Last time we had something this big, Williams had eight, spread out over six cities, within fifteen minutes."

"Dan. Count with me. One, this is a weekend night, not a weeknight. Most of the talking heads are out of town. At least an hour or more away. And two? We've never had anything this big."

"Okay, Bud. I'm still going with Williams. He can round up more talking heads in a pinch than the others, that's why I'm putting my fiver on him."

"It's a bet, Josten. Start the clock and let's start the count."

."..In closing, I wish to once again pass along our gratitude and deepest condolences to the family of my friend, Don Fulton. And my thanks to Peg for being willing, even in this time of unspeakable grief, to step forward and help to continue the good work of her husband. Let us all take a moment during the next few days and remember a man who was a devoted husband, an outstanding father, a loving son and most of all, was a good man. Thank you. God bless you all and good night."

"Dan? You're on the honor system now. I'm off to answer my phone."

"How do you know it's ringing?"

Nelson just looked at Dan, patted him on the shoulder and pointed to the two fives sitting on the edge of the counter in the monitoring room.

✳ ✳ ✳

At the same time as Annie Fidrych was making her last public appearance in Washington on a Monday morning, a small graveside service was being conducted at a small cemetery in Woodbridge, Virginia. Present were a minister, a grieving widow, her two small children and one White House Chief of Staff. Brian Bello was being buried quietly, out of the limelight and without the fanfare one might expect for a fallen agent of the United States Secret Service.

Bello's widow was not told of the secret life her husband had lived. There had been much discussion as to whether it would make what had happened any easier for her to understand. The story had been presented that he and Agent Dayle were, for whatever reason, embroiled in a conspiracy to assassinate the president, that Brian had been stopped with lethal force only inches away from inflicting a mortal wound upon President Griffen.

The White House was not unsympathetic to Mrs. Bello's plight. They were arranging for an educational trust fund to be set up for the children and that she would receive her husband's government life insurance policy funds, as well as a pro-rated payoff from his retirement benefit account. President Griffen had even extended an olive branch of sorts with a generous offer to have her come to work for the government. There were plenty of good jobs, with flexible hours and at more than respectable wages. She was considering that offer strongly. This area was her home now. It was the only home her children had known.

Dan Josten was in attendance at the funeral for her and the children and in his own small way, he was there to remember the good man that Bello was publicly. Brian was first to volunteer to be a T-ball coach. He was right in the thick of the latest day care fund-raiser. Bello had even paid for the lumber for the day care center's playground and led the beer-filled Saturday that resulted in an almost-perfect playscape constructed by a dozen caring daddies. Even as they were currently separated, Brian continued to provide for his wife's and the children's needs beyond a level of expectation. She understood why his colleagues did not, could not, come to the service. The children were too young to really understand that their daddy was not coming home from work this time. She could tell them of their father in years to come and as would be her right, she'd be able to tell them only of the good things that their daddy did. The minister finished his reading and commended unto the heavenly Father the soul of Brian Bello.

❊ ❊ ❊

At a quarter to ten Monday morning, while Anastasia Fidoryvich was being ushered back into the line of mourners snaking through the Capitol Rotunda and the small gathering in Virginia was burying a man without honor, a luxury fishing boat had reached its mark some three miles out into the Atlantic, having left an hour and a half before from its berth at the United States Naval Academy in Annapolis. The trip down through Chesapeake Bay had been quiet, thoughtful. At the helm of the boat, Admiral Darrell Bullinger, United States Navy, retired, dropped the throttle to neutral, allowing the craft to bob gently in the bright, April sun.

It was a nice day on the blue waters of the Atlantic, the warm air aided more so by the warm waters of the Gulf Stream. The passengers on board this morning were seated about the boat separately, each with their own thoughts. Not a word had been spoken since the cordial hellos offered to Bullinger by each as they boarded. Now, it was time for the group to say goodbye to man they called friend, considered brother. For one of the men, the word brother held a deeper meaning.

"Boys? It's time we did that which we've all no doubt dreaded since Newport. Nobody wants to bury a shipmate, but we now get to do just that," said Don.

"I for one, Don, am struck by the irony here," drawled Nelson.

"What irony is that?" asked Chuck

"It's one that Michail would not be able to appreciate without the benefit of a sea story," said Bud.

He reached into his coat pocket and extracted a handful of beige plastic cylinders. He passed one to Chuck, Don, Admiral Bullinger, Michail and Admiral-slash-Vice President Dericksen. Gary had been released from the hospital on Sunday with a clean bill of health and with the admonishment to go a little easier on himself next time around.

All six removed the tops of the containers and allowed the rich, hand-rolled Cuban cigars to slide out into their palms. Each went about his own unique pre-smoke ritual. One sniffed the sun-dried leaf. Another slid each end into his mouth to savor the flavor. One simply used his teeth to clip an end, while Chuck, ever the boy scout, pulled out his chrome clipper and trimmed his to his liking. Chuck and Bud passed around their monogrammed Zippo lighters, gifts that they had each bestowed upon the other many Christmases ago, the same year. Once the air was filled with a haze, Bud sat back and nodded to Chuck.

"I feel it only fitting that a favorite Fred story be told by the master of the telling. Chucker, would you do the honors?"

"I'd love to Bud. Can you point me in the correct direction?"

"It starts and ends with our host, the admiral."

"Oh! The foibles of youthful indiscretion. You know it was nothing personal, Admiral, right?"

"Just so long as history does not dare to repeat itself, ensign," laughed Bullinger.

Chuck began the story of the borrowed, neigh, hijacked boat from the Commandant's pier at Naval Station Newport, Rhode Island. The cigars were good and the story long. Long enough for each man to enjoy a smile, a tear and the beginning of life-long friendships. By the time each man had gotten through about half of his cigar, Michaud had gotten around to the story's end.

"So imagine, if you will, kind sirs, Fred denying Don and Bud and me the privilege of painting the admiral's yacht and yes, we fell for it. Next thing you know, Fred's in his usual position, supervising from on high, while we three were having a blast working the paint brushes. Fred decides he's hot and thirsty and repairs to the admiral's liquor cabinet. Freddie's now stretched out comfortably in the admiral's captain chair. Is that a proper term, Admirals?" asked Chuck, getting smiles from the two retired flag officers. "So, assuming it is, Fred's so busy riding us while we work the seaward side, that he fails to see Admiral Bullinger approaching from the parking lot. Bullinger's standing right behind him, while we keep painting and trying not to laugh."

Michaud continued on with the story of how the admiral and the ensign not only wound up sharing drinks, but how Fred got the admiral to properly demonstrate how to paint a boat. Michail listened intently as he realized these men had known his brother in a way he himself never had. Michail held the tightly folded piece of paper, fingering it nervously as he listened and reflected.

The note in Michail's hands had been delivered by an attorney from a large Portland law firm. The envelope had been addressed to Michail, with the notation "On the event of my death." Michail had read and re-read the letter from beyond many times in the hours since he received it yesterday afternoon in Maine. Don Hough, one of the men sitting with him right now, had been contacted by his brother's law firm as the person Fred Singletary had designated to handle the affairs of Fred's estate. The packet Hough had received contained specific instructions on all of Fred's concerns, including the delivery of the five envelopes, one addressed to each of the people Fred considered close. Don had read his and had brought Michail's as the first to be delivered. Hough and he had boarded a flight from the Brunswick Naval Air Station late yesterday afternoon for the trip down here. The other envelopes, for Nelson, Michaud and Dericksen, were hand-delivered last night upon the flight's arrival at Andrews Air Force Base. All had spent a few quiet moments with Fred's body as it lay in a viewing room at a Virginia funeral home. Michail had been allowed to spend his time with Konstantin separately, alone.

Michail silently read the letter his brother had written. It spoke of lost opportunities, of lost memories. Konstantin had become "Fred," so the letter said. He had been the friend and confidant of the men with whom Michail now sat on this boat.

...These are good men, Misha. Very good, very honest men. They cared for me and I for them, in a way that I wish you and I could have done also, to have been more like brothers than strangers. I am so very sorry about our missed life together. You made me proud with the way you handled yourself. I was never more proud than when I saw how you were able to expose that miserable bastard for the fraud that he was. Yes, Misha. I, too, grieved for Elenya, for Michail, for Christina. But I was too afraid to defend them to the extent with which you did. Yes, Misha, I knew of your plan to bring Romanov down. I acted too slowly in helping you. I tried, as these men will come to see, to expose Romanov as well, to expose that which you had expertly told them. That you are reading this means my life has come to an end. But with the end of my existence, please accept my apologies, my love and my wishes for a long, happy life for you and Anastasia.

The letter had been dated April 3, 1998. Just one day before his death. What Michail did not know was that there had been other versions of this letter. A different one drafted at the beginning of each month since 1976, when Konstantin realized that he and Michail would never be allowed to be brothers in the way each had desired. Konstantin had no way of knowing that he'd not come back alive from his trip to Charleston. The letter was just something the man had come to do as a matter of course. Michail would no doubt have preferred to hear these words as opposed to reading them. Konstantin would rather have been able to speak them instead of writing them. Both men, both brothers, knew that not coming back was always a possibility when employed in the silent, secret service of their country. Now, Michail knew, that if there was a place where we go when we die, that Konstantin would be there to look after

Elenya and the children and to hold a spot for him until it was his turn to go.

Michaud's story had finished and the laughter mixed with tears. Nelson had come over and sat next to Michail.

"Colonel? Do you wish to add your thoughts on your brother?"

"Yes, Mister Nelson. I would."

Michail rose and opened the letter. "Gentlemen? If I may, I'd like to read you my letter from Konstantin." He cleared his throat and read. When he finished, he paused a moment.

"My brother, Konstantin, was, to me, a hero. I think that any boy with an older brother looks upon him as a hero. Konstantin, though, left me much too soon. He was off to the university and off into the world before I became a teenager. It was that part of growing up that I feel I will forever miss, of having an older brother around to impart upon me his wisdom on girls and cars and sports, the things which older brothers know so well, so much better than the younger. I hope that to you he was the type of older brother I know he would have been to me."

"He was, Michail," said Chuck, standing up and placing a hand on Michail's shoulder.

"I know none of us want to, but it is time to say goodbye," intoned Nelson. "Michail? Would you do the honors? He'd kill us if he ever found out we threw him overboard."

The chuckles were met by a smile from Michail. The younger brother stood up and took the lid off of the small, ceramic container. He checked the wind direction and gently poured the earthly remains of Konstantin Rostokovich, also known as Fred Singletary, over the side of the boat, into the blue waters of the Atlantic Ocean.

"Men? You know what Fred would do in a situation such as this?" asked Michaud.

"Other than make you go in there and pull him out?" asked Hough.

The laughter brightened the moment instantly and it got brighter when the cold beer appeared out of a cooler under the seat in which Gary Dericksen, Vice Presidential nominee sat. The cold drinks were passed to all on board, including the hesitant secret service agent, now very much a part of Gary's life.

"Agent Leonardo? I think for this occasion it'll be okay. You don't even have to drink the whole thing if you don't want," opined Gary as he passed the beer to the young man.

"To Fred," said Gary. "Fair winds and a following sea."

The assembled group raised their cans in toast and drank to Fred, to Konstantin.

fifty-two

The small jet taxied down the runway after a long, slow approach over Casco Bay and up into Merrymeeting Bay. The bright afternoon sun had given the small whitecaps on the water below an extra level of brightness in contrast to the deep, blue ocean. The small islands dotted the coastline like summer freckles on a young, red-headed child. One of the islands was the location of the secure housing where they were being kept. Michail and Anastasia had been allowed to share one of the small, waterfront cottages, while Romanov and Moore were being held in separate quarters in the center of the island. Now, the long-separated couple were together, their ultimate fate not yet decided. What they did know, however, was that they were free from Romanov. They were willing suffer whatever penalty might be imposed for their roles in that which had transpired and conspired to usurp the United States' governmental power structure, in order to be rid of the bondage in which they'd been kept by Aleksandr.

Michail and Anastasia had been allowed to travel to Washington. She to pay her respects to the late vice president, he to say goodbye to his brother. They were also given the opportunity to stop at their respective DC area apartments and pack clothing. Their belongings would be inspected, thoroughly, then shipped to a holding area while a final destination was determined. They'd been brought here to Maine from England only yesterday morning. That flight had been interesting enough. Although today's was more somber, the flight from Cheltenham had gotten down right raucous.

* * *

The Air Force transport was a modified Boeing 727, with a small passenger compartment, as well as a private conference area and a couple of small bunkrooms. The guests had been escorted to the airplane at the airfield in Cheltenham early Sunday morning. Michail was feeling well enough to walk, but the doctor attending him had asked to be humored and to please allow them to carry him onboard and get him settled in one of the beds. The wound to his shoulder had been severe, the blood loss great. Fortunately, Michail had kept himself in fairly good shape. The doctor had told him that his physical condition is what saved his life, no doubt about it. Romanov and Moore had been brought on board in handcuffs, under armed guard. Anastasia had been allowed to walk on under her own power.

She and the CIA director, Terrio, had taken seats adjacent to the bunkroom in which Michail had been settled. The open door allowed them to converse. Romanov and Moore had been seated in different rows, on separate sides of the forward compartment. Unfortunately, they were not seated far enough away from Terrio, Anastasia and Michail's location. The two who had the most to lose at this point were within hearing distance. Annie had used this to her advantage and Terrio had done nothing to discourage her from speaking up, loudly and clearly. The conversation, until it got out of control, concerned Annie's dealings with Romanov and how she interpreted events in relationship to Moore and Hewes. Michail did all he could to keep from laughing aloud at her intentional fabrications. Her goal was to goad the other two into perhaps offering additional clarifications that might not only put a little more distance between she and they, but to get Bill a little more with which he could work.

She hit the nail on the head with one far-fetched suggestion and when Aleksandr responded, she watched Bill's eyebrows go up and his pen go down, right onto the blank page of the notebook that was sitting on the tray table in front of him. She glanced down at his notes and he used his hand to make a small twirling motion, as if to get her to try for an elaboration. She threw out a name and Romanov, by now livid, dropped a correction, followed by very loud rants about the true evil empire and just who was going to take it up the rear end when this was all said and done. Bill made one last note and unbuckled his seatbelt. He walked to the rear of the cabin where the conference room was. There was also a secure phone he could us to make the call that needed to made. He returned ten minutes later and saw Annie in the open cabin with Michail. He was asleep, she softly stroking his hair. Bill gave her a thumbs up and a nod and walked forward to sit with Romanov and Moore, allowing her some private time.

The Air Force transport landed at the Naval Air Station in Brunswick, Maine, just about forty minutes north of Portland. Nestled in the tall pines that gave the state its nickname, the air base had been saved on a few occasions from suffering the ultimate fate at the hands of the Congressional base closure committees. In the very intense era of submarine warfare in the Seventies that carried into the Eighties, the P-3 Orion aircraft squadrons that called this idyllic spot their home port spent many hours in the air, monitoring the movements of the Soviet submarine fleet. The six squadrons from Brunswick rotated through overseas deployments to locations such as Keflavic in Iceland, Lajes in the Azores, as well as to Rota, Spain and Sigonella on Sicily.

The P-3's were lined up on the runways as the plane eased gently to the ground in a landing that all on board had barely noticed. The aircraft rolled to a spot near the control tower and its adjacent building, the closest thing the base had to a terminal. A Marine security team was waiting on the concrete tarmac and there were several vehicles waiting to transport those of the passengers who were staying. A quick stop at the base customs inspector resulted in a very uncomfortable body-cavity search for Moore, while the others were smart enough to answer the few questions promptly and honestly.

Of course, Romanov had nothing to declare. He had a small brown grocery store bag in which he carried the now-laundered clothes he had on his back when he left Russia. The tan jumpsuit he had been given at Cheltenham made up his current ensemble. Anastasia and Michail each presented their shoulder carry-all's for inspection. This had been done once already by the Go Team's security chief in England, but both knew they no longer had anything to hide and everything possible to lose.

Once they had cleared inspection, the CIA director offered a semi-formal, almost respectful goodbye to Romanov with the promise that they'd be meeting again, very soon. Bill ignored Moore completely and came to Michail and Anastasia.

"I can't make any promises, but I assure you that I will do whatever I can to make your situation less stressful. Can you both live with that?"

The two had nodded their agreement and understanding.

"Good. Because it's the best I can do right now. Annie, at least you were not involved in anyone's death that we know of, right?"

"That's correct, Bill."

"Michail, though," Bill paused for a moment. "Your's will be a tougher case to blow off. You have put yourself, through your own journals and notes, at the scene of the Charleston murder. In the United States, we do not have any statute of limitations on the big one. That is the biggest of our concerns and again, all I can do is put in a good word with the boss and we'll take it from there."

"Mister Terrio, it's more than I should be allowed to ask. Thank you."

Terrio had left instructions with the Marine captain heading this special detail to transport the prisoners in two vehicles on the initial leg of their short trip.

The first part was by way of the white Chevy Suburban vans with the black-tinted windows. The small motorcade made its way down the base's access road that led to a lesser-known entrance to the base, away from the busy shopping center known as Cook's Corner situated just outside of the air station's main gate. This small road traveled along the base's perimeter and then turned into a smaller road before stopping for clearance from the Navy SEAL chief petty officer controlling the heavy, automatic gate. Normally, a CPO would not be on gate duty, but today's transport and security was being handled exclusively by the hand-picked Marine detail and overseen by the UDT detachment on the base. The small road led to a smaller path that was actually reserved for the grounds crew responsible for maintaining the base golf course. This method of access was one of the little known secrets on the base, utilized by officers and the occasional enlisted man or woman who might live off-base on this, the southeast side of Brunswick, or out in Harpswell on the neck, which is where this small convoy was headed. The vehicles exited the golf course's main gate and swung left out onto the Harpswell Road. The trip out Route 123 was a short, scenic fifteen minutes, where the cars pulled onto a small, unpaved road. The road went over a small rise and dropped down to the water's edge in a small, sheltered cove.

At the end of a small, wooden dock, an idling lobster boat waited, manned by other members of the UDT detachment. The passengers were off-loaded from the vans and escorted onto the boat. Romanov and Moore had been taken below into the tight crew's quarters, while Anastasia and Michail were allowed to remain in the pilot house, Michail having been given a deck chair on which to rest. The boat's crew cast off the lines as the sturdy vessel eased out into the waters that fed Potts Harbor. The surface offered up only small swells, which made Michail's somewhat not-quite-steady stomach feel not as queasy.

The lobster boat's trip was over in less than twenty minutes, although it could have been shorter had the crew not stopped to pull a few of their own lobster traps. The crew secured the boat to the net-and-trap covered pier on Little Birch Island and the passengers were escorted to one of the three central cottages on the island. The center building was actually more of an expanded Cape Cod style house and this, as Michail and Anastasia learned, was the off-base headquarters for the Navy's UDT detachment.

The two also learned that this UDT detachment was primarily responsible for the training of prospective Navy pilots in the skills of survival, evasion, resistance and escape. The program, known as SERE, was mythical in its methods and legendary because of the myths. It was the possibility that these highly-trained men and women were authorized, in the course of their duties, to break bones and cause severe medical discomfort to those with whom The Team had been entrusted, that kept those under their tutelage alert. And obedient. The military sent their pilots and other potential at-risk troops to SERE school to be instructed in the ways that any U.S. military officer or senior enlisted were expected to behave if they found themselves in a world of shit, also known as being a potential prisoner of war. Michail smiled when Moore attempted to impress them with the knowledge of who he was. The lack of insignia on the four men in whose presence the Russians now stood was interesting to the three who knew better, but obviously not of any concern to Dimitri. Romanov looked at his brazen protégé with disgust as the now-crumpled man attempted to stand and regain his breath. He'd not even seen the single punch to his border-line paunchy gut coming.

As Dimitri regained his balance, the four took turns reciting what was acceptable on this facility. The list of acceptable was very short. It included doing what you are asked when you are asked. And doing nothing until you are asked. The four identified themselves as Alpha, Bravo, Charlie and Delta and instructed the four guests to refer to them only by those names. Use of the word "sir" was unacceptable and therefore no longer a need for further discussion. Michail had guessed that this was the way they trained the pilots. It left no room for interpretation of rank as well as removing one of the basic advantages any fighting man or woman had, that one should know thine enemy.

Romanov was escorted up the stairs to one of the rooms, while Dimitri was informed that he was not to claim the name of Marvin Moore while a guest on this island. Dimitri nodded his understanding and the man who had taken him down put a friendly arm around his shoulder and escorted him out the front door to one of the other nearby buildings.

The man who identified himself as Bravo nodded to Anastasia and Michail to follow him. They walked through the small dining room and out a side door which led to a deck. The two followed Bravo down the small stairway and onto a small path. When they'd gotten fifty feet from the house, Bravo motioned for them to catch up.

"Hi. I'm Commander Alec Brindle, the commanding officer of this UDT detachment. Please, though, if we are in the company of the other two, call me Bravo, okay?"

Michail and Anastasia shook their heads yes and listened while Brindle continued.

"I have been asked to see to your safety, personally, by the Secretary of the Navy. I intend to do that. SecNav has also asked me to see to your comfort while you are here." They stopped walking and peered down from the top of the small hill where they now stood. There was a single, white clapboard cottage with weathered-red shutters all around. A small plume of smoke rose from the chimney. "That's the Presidential Suite here on Little Birch Island. President and Mrs. Griffen were up here for a long weekend just this past fall. This," he said with a sweeping gesture. "Is one of the best kept secrets in the United States. One of the other best kept secrets will be your being here. You two are free to walk the island and to come and go as you please. I would request that you not go outside of the house at night, though. You may make use of the porch at night, but please, just make sure you don't step down onto the rocks. The night air and moisture here combine to make them really slick when it's dark. If you fall onto those things, it'll make your shoulder wound look like a paper cut." Michail nodded his comprehension. "Come on, I'll show you to your home for the next few weeks."

They finished the walk down the path and followed Commander Brindle through the back door. The kitchen's woodstove was plenty warm against the cool April Maine air. The small wooden table in the middle of the kitchen was set for two, with traditional red-and- white checked placemats and neatly rolled napkins in solid red rings.

"As you can see, it's got all the comforts of home. Dishwasher, microwave oven and a fully-stocked refrigerator. The living room has a nice big television with a satellite service, all connected. The den over there is just a quiet room with a lot of books and magazines. There's also a computer, Internet-ready. I will warn you, though, that we had to install monitoring software for the duration of your stay. You're welcome to access your own personal accounts, but make sure if you do that there's nothing there you'd rather not let the government, or me, to see. Upstairs, there are three bedrooms and a full bath. That's the nicest part of the house, folks. The bathroom has a shower and a nice Jacuzzi. I'm sure it'll feel good to just climb in and soak, Colonel. I know you must be still hurting."

"You've been briefed on who I am?" Michail asked.

"Who you both are, yes. Miss Fidoryvich? May I call you Annie?"

"Yes, that'd be fine, Commander," she replied.

"Thank you, ma'am. Is there anything you need before I leave you two alone?"

"What do you know that we don't?" asked Annie.

"I'm afraid I know more than the higher-ups want you to know right now. I will suggest that you grab a nice hot shower or tub and maybe take a nap. I have orders to escort you two back to Brunswick for a flight to Washington tonight."

"Do you know why?" she inquired.

"Yes, Annie. I do."

"But you can't say."

"Yes, ma'am, that is correct. I'm sorry about that. Again, mi casa est su casa. Enjoy. I'll call you on the in-house phone at about sixteen hundred, okay? That should give you a good seven hours or so to get some rest."

"Thank you, Commander Brindle," said Michail, offering his hand.

"No offense, Colonel Rostokovich, but, as naturally hospitable as I am, I'm not inclined to shake your hand. Remember, I have been briefed, as have my men. Good day."

Brindle turned and left through the kitchen door, closing it behind him. Annie stood silently with Michail and tenderly placed her head on his good shoulder as his embrace pulled her close. They walked through the house to the front and opened the door, stepping onto the porch. The water was close enough to touch, although they could see that the high water mark was a good twenty feet below where they stood. There were a number of small islands all around, but enough distance separated each to make the dwellings on them all but invisible. The two went back inside the house and walked up the stairs. Michail stepped into the larger of the bedrooms and laid down on the king sized bed.

Anastasia had gone into the bathroom and started the Jacuzzi's motor. The SEALs had filled it with fresh, hot water before they had arrived and it had been seasoned with some very pleasant smelling bath salts. She helped Michail up from the bed and led him to the bathroom. In helping him to undress, she eased his shirt off of the wounded shoulder. He crawled into the tub and she joined him. They were unsure at how they should proceed. Was the room monitored? If they became intimate, would they be putting on a show for their hosts? She gently washed his back, being careful to not allow any of the treated water to touch the wound. They kissed. Tenderly, tentatively, at first. Then, swept away by passion, they made love, slowly, easily. Michail was on the form-fitted seat in the tub and he used his good arm to keep her steady on top of him. Her movements were gentle, deliberate. He met her with just as much cautious purpose. They finished together. Then, softly, she toweled him off and guided him into the bed. He was asleep before his head hit the pillows that she'd arranged to accommodate his healing shoulder. She tucked the blankets in around him tightly, to help minimize any movement that might aggravate his upper body.

Anastasia returned to the bathroom and finished drying herself. She sat on the small bench that was placed in front of the vanity and explored the drawers. Finding an electric hair dryer, she plugged it in and worked her fingers through her hair, now and forever allowed to remain its natural blonde color. Unless, she thought playfully, Michail would like the auburn wig every now and then, hopefully assuming that their being together was at all possible. She looked behind the bathroom door and found two very soft, white, terrycloth robes. She slipped one on and returned to the bedroom where Michail had begun to snore softly. She placed the other robe at the foot of the bed so he'd have something to put on himself when he awoke. Checking the digital clock that had been placed on one of the room's bedside tables, she figured she'd have time to work in a quick nap. First, though, she went downstairs and decided to check her e-mail.

Flipping the single switch on the power strip, she sat on the padded office chair that had been positioned in front of the small computer table and watched while the machine whirred and started up the computer's operating system. In less than a minute, she was logged onto her Internet account and smiled at the jokes she'd been forwarded by her Washington friends. Once she got through the incoming messages prior to Saturday, she saw at least a half dozen waiting to be read, the subject lines all asking the same question. *Is it true?*

She read the first, from one of the young assistants to Vice President Fulton. She started to type her response, that yes, it was true. No, she would not be returning to work. She added she was sorry if her moonlighting job caused anyone discomfort. Before she clicked on the *send* button, she stopped. No, she thought. She can't respond to these. Anything she did from this moment on can and would be held against her in a court of law. Additionally, anything she sent out over the Internet would become fair game to anyone with an axe to grind and a good computer hacking program. By admitting to this, she'd be making public that which was probably best left quiet. She was going to Washington this evening, so she'd been told. She'd check with Bud to see what the official story would be and how she should react or respond to any and all inquiries. She knew now that she should take a firm stand of deny everything and confirm nothing. In the direct handling of the matters, she would make sure they were taken care of properly, but very quietly. She deleted the response and deleted the other waiting messages. No need in leaving explosive questions like those hanging around. Had she read the subsequent messages, she might have learned the terrible truth moments sooner.

She returned to her home page and clicked on the blue *News* link. She stopped and cried out loud at the lead story. Weeping uncontrollably, she scrolled the copy, her eyes fighting through the tears to read the words. Don Fulton was dead. Nobody had told her. Not even Terrio.

"Son of a bitch!" she screamed. "You sons of bitches couldn't even tell me?"

The house was still. Her screams had fallen on deaf ears. She closed down the computer and walked back upstairs, suddenly cognizant of the result her outburst might have brought. She tiptoed into the bedroom where Michail lay soundly sleeping. She went to the bathroom and splashed her face with some warm water. Taking a few deep breaths, she returned to the bed and crawled in under the covers, being careful to keep some room between she and he. Anastasia used one of the extra pillows on her side to slip between herself and Michail as a buffer. Another check of the clock indicated she'd get about four hours of sleep, if she could fall asleep.

Back at the island's operation center, Commander Brindle picked up the phone and made a brief call.

"She went online. Checked her e-mail."

"Did she do anything with the stuff that wasn't jokes?"

"Deleted it all," said Brindle.

"Good girl. What else?"

"She went to the news site. Completely lost it."

"Your assessment, Commander?"

"She had no fucking idea, Director Realto. None whatsoever."

"What are they doing now?"

"I'm going to assume they're sleeping or whatever, upstairs."

"You don't have any way of telling?"

"Other than going over there and peeping in the windows? No, sir, we don't. My best guess is that she got him settled in for some more sleep, took a shower or a bath and came downstairs to use the computer."

"Commander? It's Bud Nelson, the President's communications director. What's her status?"

"Now, she's back upstairs and we've got to get them up in about four hours or so for the trip back to the base, per instructions."

"That's correct, Commander. We're bringing them down here for the evening. They each have a function which I'm sure they'll want to attend first thing in the morning. Then, we'll be putting them back on a plane to come back up your way late tomorrow."

"Aye, aye, Mister Nelson."

"Commander? Thanks for the sitrep. Take care of them for us, okay? I know you probably think they're just a couple of commie bastards. They are. But they're also a couple of people who at least are making an attempt at doing the right thing and were both more than prepared to keep the wrong thing from happening."

"Understood, Mister Nelson. Goodbye."

"Thanks again, Commander Brindle and good night."

* * *

Now that they'd been to Washington and back, she and Michail got off the plane and were greeted on the Naval Air Station tarmac by the SEAL known only as Charlie. There were no armed Marines present or within sight. Only Charlie and the waiting Chevy Suburban. His only form of greeting was to open the rear door. He aided Michail, gently helping him to steady his upper body while he swung his legs inside. He walked around the other side of the vehicle and held the door for Anastasia while she settled herself next to Michail.

Getting into his driver's seat, he checked the mirror, put the vehicle into gear and started the slow drive around the outer perimeter road that disappeared into the woods on the far side of the runway. The trip through the golf course took less time than it took for Charlie to get out of the vehicle, activate the mechanical gate, pull through, close the gate and return the control box to its secure ready-position. The drive out the Harpswell Road was uneventful and they arrived at the secluded cove for boarding the lobster boat. As they got out of the vehicle, Charlie once again was at the ready, helping to steady Michail as he got out of the car.

"Thank you, Charlie."

"Not a problem, Mike. Been there, done that. It's a bitch, so I know how it feels."

"Where and when?" Michail asked.

"Took one right about in the same spot as you," Charlie said pointing to his shoulder. "In Kuwait. That whole op was a mess. We hit the beach, found ourselves up shit creek and wound up having to pull back on an abort order. Me? I was glad we had to go back. I probably would've bled to death right there and then if the OIC didn't call the no-go. That man even carried me across the beach and into the water, then swam me out to the waiting rafts. Morris is the guy's name. Big guy. I know he did the SEALS proud that day."

"This Morris? About six foot three, sandy brown hair, big smile?"

"That's him sir! Or it could be."

"That's him, alright, Charlie. We have more in common than you realize. I'll tell you my story later on the island."

"Look forward to it, Mike. Here we go," said Charlie stepping onto the lobster boat and reaching across for Michail's hand. "Now you, ma'am," he said as Annie grabbed the man's hand, stepping gingerly across the small space between the gunwale and the dock.

Sitting in the pilot house seat, Michail looked to the cove's opening and the dark water beyond. Sunset was occurring just then and the colors from the sky created a reflective sheen of reds and oranges across the smooth surface of the inlet. Charlie fired up the boat, backing it slowly away from the dock, then coming about to head back to Little Birch Island.

After the brief trip across Potts Harbor, they were met by Alpha, Bravo and Delta. Charlie worked at shutting down the boat, while Alpha and Bravo helped Michail up from the boat onto the island's dock. The tide was low and it created a five foot step up to the dock. The two men then each gracefully helped to guide Annie up to the wooden surface. She had caught a glimpse of their approving eyes as her legs cleared their line of sight. They each gallantly and quickly looked down, not wanting to appear to be gawking. Too late, she thought with a sly smile.

The walk back to the Presidential Suite was an escorted one, as Commander Brindle walked with them, he having shouldered the duffle bags each had filled with clothing and offered them both a small condolence on their loss while lighting the pathway with the powerful flashlight. He left them at the door to the cottage and asked if they had any particular time they wanted to be up in the morning. They looked at each other, fully expecting to have to get up early or whenever they were told.

"No, you may be in custody, but this is not prison. The cold, bare room with only a small metal cot where Dimitri is? That's a prison cell. The room with all of the amenities but none of the freedom, plus a constant audio and video surveillance that Romanov is currently calling home? That's a prison. You two are free to relax and get caught up."

"In that case, Commander, I don't think we need a wake-up call in the morning," said Annie.

"Good night then."

Brindle waited for them to turn on the kitchen light, then turned and walked back to his headquarters.

Michail and Annie went into the cottage and retired to the living room. They caught the coverage of the events in Washington regarding Fulton's death, wake and upcoming funeral and the Hewes resignation. Michail fell asleep on the couch. Annie got up and covered him with a small, knitted blanket from the Shaker-styled holder in the corner. He had experienced a very tough day, she thought. His brother! Konstantin. She'd met him on a few occasions in Moscow, during the happier days, but never, not once, had she made the connection with him being Fred. Although, she reminded herself, that those happier days were also hippier days and Konstantin was both bearded and long-hair shaggy. She was ashamed of herself for having been unable to place him. When she was with Bud and the boys, Fred had always made her feel comfortable. What a waste.

She turned the volume down a bit and channel surfed through the satellite. Pulling the second afghan off of the rack, Anastasia made herself comfortable in one of the reclining chairs in the living room. She found an old Jimmy Stewart movie, the one where he sets Washington on its ear and watched it until she fell asleep herself.

fifty-three

"Let me see if I understand this correctly, Nelson..." Chuck was holding court in Bud's living room. Don sat nursing his second beer, after a really nice dinner, in one of Bud's overstuffed chairs, while Bud sat in The Chair, always and forever reserved for Bud.

Not even company got The Chair, although many had valiantly tried and failed. Bud's chair was broken in just perfectly, in all the right places, plus, his armchair organizer was set up for sightless remote control operation. He didn't even need to remove the battery-operated device to make it function flawlessly. The organizer, he recalled as he sat listening to Chuck prattle on, had been a gift from Annie back in the early Eighties in New York. She'd picked it out at a novelty store, using that innate sense of fashion to purchase just the right one. It was perfect. The accessory's material and color were identical to the fabric that covered The Chair and it had served him well all these many years.

"Hewes, otherwise known as KGB Agent Polnichy, has done what for our country?" Michaud paused for the dramatic, but expected no response, as Don and Bud well knew the correct answer to any question was forthcoming. "I'll tell you what. Just look at the health care package he pushed through the other day. It's designed to cost us, the taxpayer, nothing extra and will provide more than minimum care for the thirty percent of the population that does not currently have sufficient, if any, health care insurance. Where's the bad in that?"

Don looked at Bud as if to say *I'll take that*. "Chuck? He didn't draft the bill. He simply lined up the votes and was even earnestly working on the Senate, one member at a time. He had an ultimate goal, you know."

"What? To make sure that the lowest level of wage and non-wage earners in America could go to a doctor or to the emergency room without fear of being turned away because they could not pay?"

"Wow! That even rhymed, Chucker. I'm impressed," said Bud, taking another sip of his drink. "If I may?"

Chuck sat back on the couch and nodded his approval.

Don chimed in, "The man from Maine yields to the Bud from Biloxi, Mistah Speakah."

Chuck smiled at that and listened. For a change.

"Donny? I thought y'all had lost that New England thang," Bud drawled intentionally. "Chucker. As a congressman, Yevgeny Polnichy in the role of Brad Hewes was good. Remember, though. That was his job. To be good, as Brad Hewes. I'm not saying that the man didn't learn how to get things done. If anything, he, meaning Hewes, is a role model for every incoming member of Congress. Those in the know right now have already checked their playbooks to make sure they have the notes on Hewes in the correct order. For a spy. For a murderer. For a man who sought to spearhead the charge to make us merely a new location for the Communists R Us headquarters, Hewes was good, but he was still on the wrong side."

Michaud was chomping to pipe in with more of his sage political wisdom. Bud held him off with a raised hand.

"I'm not discounting all of the good and there has been a lot, that the man was able to accomplish," Bud added. "He knew how to get that *one* point across. The point that would make someone, even a person such as yourself, rethink his or her position on the matter at hand. President Griffen knows that. We intend to use Yevgeny as

Hewes on a daily basis. That will be his sentence. Political Machinery one-oh-one."

At this, Chuck sat forward, as did Don. Both were more than interested in hearing how this one played out.

"That's right, boys. Hewes started out as a professor and will once again be a professor. We will be working with him in, first, rebuilding the Hewes family library. It will be in there that Yevgeny will test and if necessary, teach, our incoming elected and appointed officials in the fine art of compromise and persuasion. Son-of-a-bitchin' accessory to murder that he is, he is also one of the best communicators this country has ever seen. The man's training in the Soviet University system was able to help him refine a quality that we all possess, the ability to instantly analyze and adapt. Yevgeny could sit down with any one of us, right now and wind up taking any single idea that we put forward, work his magic on it and have convinced you that the finished product was yours from the start. The finished piece might be no where near where you began. It might be changed only slightly. On the rare occasion, your idea might be a solid suggestion from the get-go and not need his refinement at all."

"It's a sound theory on paper, Bud. But what's to stop him from molding someone in his own image?" asked Don.

"Good question, Don. Each novice will be fully briefed about the man with whom they are dealing and of what he stands convicted. They will be monitored by a video link that will be staffed by the NSA whenever school is in session."

"Excuse me, Bud. You did say 'convicted?' Did I miss something?"

"Hewes went before a federal judge this morning and pleaded guilty to accessory to murder, espionage, as well as several counts of sedition and high treason. Not to mention the litany of charges involved with unauthorized possession by taking regarding everything that had been Hewes' prior to the murder. He will be confined for the rest of his life. His sentence is one of the secrets that will kept in perpetuity. Oh, there's is a public record of a conviction of Yevgeny Polnichy filed in the records at the federal courthouse in Petersburg, Virginia. The public charge to which a guilty plea has been entered is accessory to murder, with confinement to an undisclosed federal penitentiary."

"When the hell did all of this come down?" asked Don, the newsman's nose twitching.

"This morning, while we were cruising down Chesapeake Bay and while thousands of Americans took the time to pay their respects to Vice President Fulton."

"Very nicely done, Bud. Very nice, indeed," added Michaud. "So what other players are in the fold?"

"We have Annie, Michail and Dimitri, also known as Marvin Moore from the Department of State. Plus the Secret Service Agent formerly known as Dayle."

"What happens to them?" asked Don.

"Michail will be pleading guilty to accessory to murder, along with the same charges as Yevgeny. Annie will be pleading guilty to espionage and sedition. The federal penalty for these charges is life in prison. The attorney general has recommended expulsion from the United States, with the knowledge that if either of them ever again set foot on American soil, they will be arrested and sent to the nearest federal pen for the remainder of their days."

"Dimitri, the obnoxious little prick, is going to be some big, ugly son of a bitch's bum chum. He's going to do life at a maximum security federal prison."

"Dayle, whose real name is Tomas Doyetska, is going to have to undergo a full-fledged trial in a federal court. That court, however, is situated in the United States territory of Guam. His is an open and shut case. He'll wind up doing time in the maximum security section of a federal prison, also. That is if he doesn't get the death penalty. It's in his best interest to enter a guilty plea and beg for mercy."

"How is it open and shut?" asked Chuck. "Presumption of innocence until proven? Or has that been pitched out the window?"

"There are several hours of videotape that he had egotistically preserved in a safe deposit box at a bank here in Virginia. I don't know what it is that makes these people who had literally gotten away with murder for more than twenty years want to keep any trace of what they'd done laying around."

"The tape must be in pretty poor shape, Bud," said Chuck.

"The outer layers were pretty dried out, but the environmental system in this bank has been well ahead of its time since the early Eighties. This is the old, reel-type video tape, Chuck."

"I'd say "duh," Bud, but I am above that. The video cassette didn't make it's arrival until the early Eighties. Until then, you bought and used video tape just like we did with reel-to-reel audio tape. This guy Dayle? He did the actual murders?"

"He and his now-deceased and buried partner took out the real Hewes, Moore and possibly Moore's aunt and grandmother. Those last two are being investigated right now. We're also waiting to confirm the identities, real or otherwise, of the West coast cadre."

"West coast cadre? You mean there were more?" asked Don.

"According to Romanov, he had a small crew working out of the western states, also. We're hoping to get firm details from him, personally, in exchange for his future health and well being. We've got two choices for his incarceration. And Dayle and Dimitri may wind up with him for one of them. Right now, Romanov's a guest on an island off the coast of Harpswell and the details are being worked out to see if that's not a potential permanent home for him."

"Harpswell's a pretty close-knit fishing community, Bud. There's no such thing as a permanent guest about whom the locals wouldn't eventually get around to meeting," Don said. "How in the world would that happen? Keeping him there permanently and quietly?"

"The island is an outpost of sorts. An off-base home-away-from-home for the SEAL detachment at Brunswick. The boss has even used it for a quiet getaway with the little woman. At least when she was talking to him."

"What happens with the president now? This one should be good. Griffen must be more than a touch cracked up here," Chuck said, pointing to his head. "To follow through with this thing so soon after Fulton's death."

"That's a game plan I'm not tipping. Jay will go before the judge Thursday morning. He will be represented by his personal counsel, Lindsey Dean."

"Dean? A White House lawyer named Dean? Doesn't your boss and our fearless leader read the papers? The history books?" asked Don. "I'm not the superstitious type, but those who ignore the past..."

"I know, Don. Are condemned to repeat it. No, this guy Lindsey is a good lawyer. Oxymoronic, I know. But still, he's on the ball. Plus, I will tell you that the resulting investigations have turned up some interesting evidence, not previously available during discovery."

"Not being a lawyer, Bud, but having played the voice of one on the radio, won't this set back the timetable? Obviously, the government will object and request a one or two day recess to review the new information, won't they?" inquired Chuck.

"Here's the beauty of this one, boys. The government is the side responsible for the discovery and is therefore not going to object. We had played with the idea of allowing Moore to testify, but we don't have to now with the paper trail we have. Besides, Moore is currently missing in France, having been kidnapped by some radical faction the other night."

"Have you thought of informing the judge as to the true identity of Mister Moore?" asked Don.

"That's a real gray area that's being discussed at some very high levels right now. It's not really national security, but national peace of mind we're seeking to maintain. The security aspects have been shot to hell. Thank God that the people don't know that. And we're praying they never will."

"Is that where Gary comes in?" asked Chuck. "Operational security is his, and Periscope's, bailiwick."

"Wow, Chucker. That's the first time I've ever heard you use bailiwick in a sentence. I'm impressed," said Don.

"Thank you, Mister Lexicon."

"You're welcome, kind sir," Hough smiled in return.

"If you two will drop the mutual admiration society for a moment?" Bud interrupted. "Yes, this is where Gary comes into the picture. Very ironic, though, as to how Periscope achieved such a level of respect in the field. Fred," said Larry, getting up with his empty drink glass. He looked to the other two to see if they'd like another. Both shook their empty beer cans and Bud took the hint. He continued with this portion of the story while walking to the kitchen.

"Fred was the one who helped Dericksen fine-tune the more intricate aspects of how people get where they shouldn't be and find things they shouldn't. Just like in the car the other day, Fred, er, Konstantin, was feeding us. He was doing it all along, actually. I'm sure if we all think back to situations and conversations we had with him, he was trying to tell us what was going on."

"Are you warming up a bit there, Bud? You called him Fred twice," Don said. "It's okay by me. He's only been Fred to us and from what we just heard, he wasn't a real bad guy, after all. What did your letter say? I'll tell you what mine said. It said he was sorry to have had a past of which there were only portions he was proud. The fact that he did nothing when he could have to help avenge the loss of his sister was his biggest shame. That he would consider it a personal favor if we were to help clear the perception held by Michail of him. And that he would further appreciate it if we were to somehow let Michail know that Romanov knew of the level to which the brothers held him in contempt. Romanov was using Michail's life as an incentive to keep Fred from trying anything. Fred wrote that he had lost one sibling as a result of Aleksandr's despicable lack of action and that he'd not allow a single bad thing to happen to his baby brother."

"Mine was of a similar nature, Don. Was yours written in January?" asked Bud.

"Yeah. Just before the Superbowl if I got my dates right."

"As was mine. My copy included a list of all the bad guys. People to whom we should dig deeply in regards to their past. The roll-call includes everyone we've got and one more we don't."

Don and Chuck both looked at Bud with their full, undivided attention.

"That's all I can say for now, boys, other than the fact that this week's leak back to Romanov wasn't Fred slash Konstantin. Sorry," Bud said. "Hey, look what's on! It's *Mister Smith Goes to Washington*! I love Jimmy Stewart."

Bud sat back in his chair, thumbed the volume on the remote and simply shrugged his shoulders at his friends, both sitting with mouths agape waiting for a deeper explanation. Realizing that one was not forthcoming, they settled in to enjoy the classic film about doing the right thing for America.

fifty-four

Peter O'Reilly had, for the past two years, put himself, heart and soul, into his work. Even this morning, while the federal government paused in its travails to honor the memory of the late Vice President Fulton, Peter was here at his desk, having taken a quick moment this morning to pay his respects at the Rotunda. He'd not been quite his old self since the tragic accident that claimed the life of his bride, Sarah.

They'd been on their honeymoon in the Bavarian Alps for skiing and, well, things that young couples do on their wedding getaways. He and Sarah had put off getting married until they were both certain that it would be the right thing for them and for their careers.

Peter was on the fast track in the financial world. His acumen for developing the perfect plan to save struggling banks was the stuff of legend. He'd been on the short list of candidates for a choice assignment in 1994. Having been passed over, he took little solace in the encouraging words from his peers to persevere, that the next term was only two years away.

In the fall of 1995, he'd been given a confidential memo which had his name on the list of nominees for the two-year term that would begin in February. With that knowledge safely tucked away, he suggested to Sarah that the time was now. She agreed and they'd had a small ceremony for family and close friends on Thanksgiving weekend. The trip to Europe was a wedding present from both sets of their parents and they'd been able to clear enough time to spend the entire month traveling the continent. Skiing in Switzerland and Germany was to have led to subsequent stops at the French Riviera for a little fun in the sun, then on to Rome, Paris and London for the Christmas holidays through New Year's day.

Heading back to their hotel from a day on the slopes, the rental car had been struck from behind, sending it spinning into the trees. The crash had killed Sarah instantly. Peter was pulled from wreckage, lifeless as well. His mother and father rushed from America to be with him in Germany during his lengthy recovery. His injuries were extensive, especially around his head. The impact had deployed the airbags, as designed. Unfortunately, his head slammed sideways through the driver's door window. Facial lacerations and broken facial bones notwithstanding, he'd apparently suffered some memory-loss. The doctors had tried to assure his parents that he should regain his ability to recall just who they were. For now, Peter knew his name was Peter and that he'd been in accident.

He was also able to demonstrate that he was fully capable in his area of expertise, finance. The medical teams that assembled to work with him at a large, private hospital in Munich were astonished at the fact this portion of his memory had not been disturbed. Peter had been able to recite, chapter and verse, his Doctoral dissertation on the effects of market fluctuations on an economy on the rebound. Yet, he was not able to recognize anyone to whom he'd been close before the accident. Using photographs, he was able to pick out certain individuals of renown from the world's financial circles, such as the current leaders of monetary concerns in New York, Chicago and Washington, DC.

He was deemed fit to be released from the hospital in February of 1996, but not in time to claim his place as promised. A new chairman had assumed the head position of the venerable committee to which he'd aspired and took the time to meet privately with Peter upon his return to the States. A gentle assurance that he would indeed be on top of the list for the next term gave Peter the motivation he needed. He buried himself at work and asked friends and family to forgive him this, but it was something he needed to do to try and get his life back and maybe regain his memory at the same time. The American doctors to whom he'd been referred all agreed that Peter's nose-to-the-grindstone approach might be the impetus required to jog his memory back into place. Peter was grateful for the support from the doctors. It gave him a chance to keep some space between himself and the strangers who insisted they were indeed best of friends.

Peter's mother was the one who was most respectful of his wishes. She bade him to come for a meal, when he felt like it. Peter appreciated her hands-off approach and he did come. Often. She would allow him to visit in silence, although they would make polite conversation. She'd not subjected him to the bombardment of stimuli that the others had. There were no photographs being constantly shoved under his nose, no cassette tapes of favorite songs they'd sung together, no bar napkins or swizzle sticks from places they'd frequented together. She used her time with him to relearn his face. A mother knows many things and foremost among them is her baby's face, now and forever. Peter's face had been heavily bandaged when she'd arrived at the first hospital in Germany and the nurse had taken the time to tell her she might not recognize him. When those bandages were finally removed, the changes were astounding, but at least in the eyes, his eyes, she believed he was Peter. That gave her the courage to help him move forward.

Having demonstrated to those around him that he'd not lost the knack for reading the economy and offering the proper suggestions for moving things in a positive direction, he had gotten the call which he'd been awaiting. His second meeting with the chairman led to a subsequent sit-down with the President of the United States. The initial reaction from those in the know was disbelief. How could Peter now be given more than a courtesy interview? His accident had made headlines on the pages of the world's financial journals. But President Griffen had made special time to not only publicly announce Peter's nomination, but also to remind those detractors that America under his leadership was an equal opportunity employer and he'd even cited his choice five years prior of the wheelchair-bound Keith Hammett to become the director of the FBI. Peter's name was forwarded without prejudice to the House and Senate banking committees, where he breezed through the confirmation process and proudly, finally, took his seat on the board of the Federal Reserve in February of 1998.

This appointment had set in motion events which were accelerating at a rapid pace. The reasoning behind this escalation was that the time was now. If it were to happen, it had to happen now. Peter was not only appointed for a two-year term as a member of the Governor's board, but was also being groomed to ascend to the hot seat in the year 2000. With Fulton or Hewes in the White House and Peter O'Reilly as Chairman of the Federal Reserve Board, the dream would come to fruition more easily than was imagined.

Of course Peter's mother did not recognize her son back in that hospital in Germany once the bandages came off. As much as she had wanted to believe that this man was her son, there was one extenuating circumstance that would forever prevent her desires to be fulfilled. That's because Viktor Milochnev was not her son, but as far as the world was concerned, Viktor was now Peter.

Peter O'Reilly *had* died in the crash in the Bavarian mountains. And it was not an accident. It was an opportunity. The planning had been brief and had been done strictly by assets in Europe, assigned personally by Aleksandr Romanov. That Peter was in the headlines constantly as a leading choice for the upcoming Federal Reserve Board term presented a challenge to Romanov. Aleksandr had known that if he really wanted to destabilize the American economy, then he'd need a way to get someone on the seven member panel who was on his side. Combine a seat on the Fed with a seat in the Oval Office, then it wouldn't have taken much time at all to help it all come crumbling down. The position of power Aleksandr would achieve as this plan's mastermind would come from the rebuilding process. Only the United States would be rebuilt to his specifications. Romanov had come close once before to getting someone on the board, but sadly, that person had been killed in a senseless street mugging in New York City.

Having a truck with a hand-picked team following the young honeymooners was not tough. Nor was it difficult for the truck to pick up enough speed to hit the rental car from behind and send it spinning into the thick, Bavarian forest. The truck was used to cart away the automobile's wreckage, as well as transporting the victims to a hospital of the Russians' own design. That had been the most difficult.

The abandoned building was in reasonably good shape and it took a team of painters and carpenters less than a week to transform the single-story warehouse into an acceptable medical facility. The "hospital" had told the family that only Peter's parents should come and that when he was well enough to be moved to a larger facility in Munich it would be a better time for other family members or friends to come. The Germany team had even arranged to transport Sarah's body home for a proper burial and had received letters of thanks from her family for their caring and compassion. Peter's parents had been picked up at the airport in Munich by a private vehicle and brought to the "hospital." There had even been a private suite set up for them to stay right there in the building. They'd made the trip with Peter in a rented ambulance hired to do the transport. The ambulance crew had been selected, for a price, from a medical employment agency who had provided a doctor and nurse to care for the patient during transit. The Russian team then watched as the ambulance carrying Peter headed down the road for the private hospital in Munich, with Peter's parents, the hired health care professionals and complete, detailed medical records from a hospital that, three hours later, no longer existed.

The soft tapping at the door was followed by the door's opening. Peter O'Reilly, somewhat perturbed at this breach of his domain, set his pen down and removed his eyeglasses, looking at the person who'd possessed the audacity to disturb him.

"Peter. Nice to see you hard at work, but then, you're always hard at work."

"Good morning, sir. Do I know you?"

"No, Peter. We've not yet met. I'm Terrio. Bill Terrio, CIA. And this man with me here is John Realto, NSA."

"Well, I'd say nice to meet you, but as you can see, I'm actually trying to use the quiet time here today to get some additional figures ready for the president's pitch to the economic conference."

"Oh, that won't be necessary, Peter," said Bill, smiling.

John stepped towards the desk where O'Reilly was sitting, stunned by the sheer rudeness of these two.

Realto reached down and grabbed hold of Peter's arm. "You'll need to come with us, Peter."

"Excuse me? Just who in the hell do you think you are?"

"Like my friend said, I'm John Realto. NSA. Director. Need some additional explanation? My friend there, Terrio. First name William. CIA. Wanna guess his job? No? Okay, I'll tell you. He's the director."

"John, while we're playing guessing games, let's play I've got a secret," Terrio said.

"Bill, I love that game. What about you, Peter?"

Peter was beginning to lose the color from his face, the red-flushed cheeks standing stark against a pale, white background.

"John, I don't think Viktor wants to... Oh, damn. Now I just ruined the game again, didn't I?"

"Bill, you never were very good at that one," John said through badly stifled guffaws. "Viktor Milochnev, also known as Peter Paul O'Reilly, I'd love to tell you that you have the right to remain silent and stuff like that, but we reserve those rights for real-live American citizens. You might consider how you'd like to handle your situation. We'll give you a few days to gather your thoughts. Quietly. After all, the government is shut down until Thursday morning, at which time, we'll make arrangements for you to contact an attorney of your choosing."

"That is, provided you know a good attorney in Germany," Bill added.

"That's right, Bill! Tell him what else he's won!" John bellowed.

"He's won an all-expense paid trip to Deutchland. He'll be traveling in fabulous first class seating on a United States Air Force personnel transport flight. You'll depart in, oh, a mere twenty minutes for lovely Wiesbaden! We hope you will have a tremendous time on your vacation for life. Johnny, do we have a nifty parting gift for Viktor?"

"As a matter of fact, Bill, we do. It's a pair of sterling silver tennis bracelets," said the NSA director, putting Viktor's hands behind his back and applying the handcuffs.

Two plainclothes Secret Service agents came into the room, trying not to laugh out loud at the two senior officials, the smiles spread wide across the agents' faces.

"Oh? You two liked our little show?" asked John.

"Yes, sir, Mister Realto. It was pretty funny," said the first agent.

"Too bad you'll never be able to tell even your grandkids about this one. Capice?" John offered with a raised eyebrow.

"Yes, sir," they both replied in unison as they escorted Viktor from the room.

"Bill, I got to hand it to you. This one might've slipped by if you hadn't gotten Romanov to slip his name out on the flight back from England."

"Actually, John, Annie was the one who did the baiting. I just reeled it in. Plus, Bud's friend, Fred or Konstantin or whoever he was, left the same info in a note to Bud that was to be opened in the event of Fred's death."

"What would have happened if we hadn't stepped into this one and this Fred guy didn't die?" Realto asked.

"Bud's note was fairly explicit in that this whole thing wouldn't have gotten to the finish line. Fred was prepared to drop a dime on the whole mess before it was too late."

"Too late for who? Look at Fulton. And this guy Viktor was dropping his own dimes all week. We'll need to remind the Cabinet members about what should be mentioned and what should be kept quiet."

"Granted, Fulton was a good man, as far as we knew. Whether or not he would have followed through on his vendetta? We'll never know. I'd prefer to leave that one alone. The Cabinet stuff. Yeah, that's one the resident will have to address behind closed doors. I'm just glad I'm not the Secretary of the Treasury today." Bill sighed. "Let's go report in to the chief that this is wrapped."

"Bill, for all of our sakes, I hope to God it is done."

"I'm pretty sure it is. Now, we need to get the boss through the next forty-eight hours. The trial should be a lot more fun than anyone anticipated."

fifty-five

The assembled crowd of media and a few select onlookers had stopped their chatter as the president entered the room. No one was sure as to how protocol should be followed in this situation. The man was in this room as a defendant, but he was still the President of the United States. Tentatively, the senior White House reporters stood, out of habit and deference, followed by the remainder of those assembled.

Griffen nodded to his attorney general as he took his seat next to his personal counsel, Lindsey Dean. The two went over some brief notes as the sound-level in the room once again reached a more than discreet level. The court's bailiff called for quiet and that brought the voices back to a softer volume.

"All rise," spoke the bailiff with authority. "The honorable Dennis Wentworth presiding."

All in the room had risen and watched as Judge Wentworth took his seat.

"Be seated," said Wentworth. "Bailiff? Please call the first case."

"The United States of America versus John Francis Griffen, your honor."

"Very well. Would counsel please rise and be recognized?"

The two lawyers stood and identified themselves for the court.

"Gayle Vernon for the people, your honor."

"Lindsey Dean for the defense, your honor."

"Very well, please be seated. The defendant has waived his right to a trial by jury, for the sake of expedience, is that correct?"

Lindsey rose and said, "Yes, honor, that is correct."

"Very well, so noted. As I will be the sole arbiter and my attention to all that is said and done being required to properly and judiciously weigh the evidence presented, here are the ground rules for the expected decorum in this court. This proceeding will not become a circus. With that in mind, here are the three commandments. First and foremost, I have allowed the use of the pool cameras in this room. For the benefit of those watching these proceedings on live television, this is how you will see these proceedings. I have determined where the technical equipment is allowed and where it is not. If it is not where I have deigned it to be, it will be removed. Is that clear to the technicians? Good. Second. There will be an immediate clearing of this courtroom in the event of any, I repeat, any outburst. No sighs, no groans, no cries, no laughs. I do hope that is clear. Finally, in deference to the defendant, he will be addressed as Mister President, or Sir, in my courtroom. The court also recognizes the presence of the Attorney General of the United States as representing the interests of the people of the United States. Ms. Vernon, with your permission, I'd request that the court be allowed to address you as Ms. Vernon. Is that acceptable?"

"It is, your honor," Gayle said as she stood and just as quickly, retook her seat.

"Very well. Are the people ready to proceed?"

"The people are ready, your honor."

"Mr. Dean? Is the defense ready?"

"We are, your honor."

"Very well. Bailiff, please read the official warrant specifying the charges that bring the defendant before the bench of this court today."

The bailiff rose and read the document that detailed the charges lodged against the President of the United States.

"The defense has previously entered a plea of not guilty on all counts. Is it your intent to maintain that plea this day, Mister President?"

Jay rose and looked the judge in the eye. "It is, your honor."

"Then we are set to proceed. The court would like to inform, for the record, that all documents submitted to this court as evidence have been presented for verification and have been reviewed and accepted by both sides under the terms of disclosure set forth in pre-trial motions. The people may proceed. Ms. Vernon?"

Gayle stood and walked before the bench. She had a game face that was both pleasant and disarming while at the same time held the fury of a person seeking to right a million wrongs.

"Your honor. It is our intention, as representatives of the people of the United States, which, by the way, includes you, to put forth evidence that will support a finding of guilty on the specified charges that have been filed against that man, the defendant, the President of the United States. We will present testimony from the victim who will testify, for the record and the country, that on the evening in question, during the simple performance of her assignment as an intern for the State Department, in this particular situation, delivering documents to the defendant, that she was physically attacked and touched in a most unwelcome manner. That the defendant did willfully attempt to force himself upon this young lady in a sexual manner. That the defendant did willfully ignore her pleadings to stop. That the defendant did willfully violate not only her personal being, but violated the trust with which he'd been bestowed to keep honorable the office of President of the United States of America."

Gayle turned and took her seat, opening her yellow legal pad and had pen at the ready to take notes.

"Mr. Dean? Would the defense care to make an opening statement now? Or do you prefer to deliver your opening address after the people have rested their case in chief?"

"Your honor? If it please the court, the defense would like to reserve an opening statement until after the people have rested."

"So noted and granted. Ms. Vernon? Are the people prepared to call witnesses?"

"We are your honor."

"Very well. Please call your first witness."

"The people call Pamela Jean Stark."

The door at the rear of the courtroom opened and in walked Pamela Stark, escorted by two armed court security personnel. She was dressed somewhat demurely in a simple blue skirt and matching jacket, with a plain white shirt, the top button only undone. The skirt was midlength, but was tight enough to be eyebrow raising. Gayle stifled a groan, but allowed those in the courtroom to notice her displeasure at the show this woman was currently putting on for a national audience.

The bailiff had sworn in Pam and asked her to state her name for the record.

"Pamela Jean Stark."

Judge Wentworth addressed her with a terse "Very well, be seated."

Pam sat down, smoothing the front of her skirt with her hands and straightened her posture on the large wooden chair, her hands now folded on her lap.

"Good morning, Ms. Stark. For starters, in your own words, would you please tell the court what happened on the night of March nineteenth of this year?"

Pamela began her story in the office at the State Department. She told of how she was looking forward to meeting friends in a Georgetown nightspot after work. She told of her disappointment when asked by her supervisor to hang around for an extra thirty minutes as there were some documents that needed to be delivered. She then spoke of her excitement when informed to whom she was to personally deliver these sensitive papers.

"Ms. Stark. You mention your supervisor. For the record, who was your supervisor at the State Department."

"Marvin Moore, assistant Secretary of State," Pam said, leaning into the microphone.

"And to whom were you to deliver these documents?"

"President Griffen. Personally," she replied.

"Thank you, Ms. Stark. Please continue. And if at any time you need to take a break, for water or to gather your thoughts, please do so."

Pam needed no break. No water. No gathering of thoughts. At the point where she was describing the president pawing at her breasts, she began to sob. When she attempted to detail how the president lifted her skirt and attempted to digitally penetrate her, she lost control. Having been given a moment to steady herself, Pam nodded and Gayle resumed her questioning.

"At that point, Ms. Stark, can you tell the court what happened?"

"I screamed and opened the door. In the outer office, I was met by a Secret Service agent who was able to come between the president and me. I was a mess. I mean, my clothes were all, like, coming off and stuff," she said as the first signs of her youth slipped through, just as the attorney general had suggested in their pre-trial conferences.

From there, Pam described how she was escorted to a waiting vehicle which took her to the nearest police station for photographs and statements.

"The people have no further questions, your honor," Gayle said before taking her seat.

"Mr. Dean?" asked Judge Wentworth. "Do you wish to cross-examine?"

"I do, your honor."

Lindsey stood and straightened his suitcoat. His six-foot frame was lean, almost lanky. His black hair had more than a few touches of gray mixed in, but was neatly styled and combed. The dark eyes were off-set by slightly grayed eyebrows, adding a touch of distinction to his handsome face. He checked his notepad and took a sip of water before taking the few steps to the witness stand.

"Good morning, Ms. Stark."

"Good morning," she replied.

"You've testified, under oath, that you were sent to the White House by your supervisor, assistant Secretary of State Marvin Moore. Is that correct?"

"It is."

"How long had you worked for Mister Moore?"

Gayle rose. "Objection, your honor. Relevance?"

"Your honor, we request a little latitude here. We are merely trying to establish the working conditions and experience of the witness."

"Overruled. The witness may answer the question," said the judge, looking down at the young woman.

"I've worked, er, I worked at the State Department and with Mister Moore for four months," Ms. Stark explained.

"What was your starting pay grade?" Lindsey inquired.

"G.S. four."

"Not that it's a big secret, but how much was the weekly salary of a G.S. four?"

"About six hundred fifty dollars a week. But we got paid twice a month."

"So you grossed roughly thirteen hundred dollars every two weeks?"

"About that, yes."

"And what was your pay grade when you left the State Department?"

"G.S. five."

"So you'd received a promotion in under four months?"

"Yes."

"And what was the bi-monthly salary rate of a G.S. five?"

"Roughly fifteen hundred dollars."

"Before you were hired at State, had you known your supervisor, Mister Moore?"

"No."

"I'd like to ask the court to allow the witness to take a moment and perhaps rethink her answer, your honor."

"Objection, your honor. The witness was asked the question and it was answered," said Gayle.

"Mister Dean? Do you have somewhere you're going with this?" asked Judge Wentworth.

"We do, your honor. Permission to approach?" Lindsey requested.

"Granted."

Lindsey walked back to the defense table and gave the president a wink. All over the country and around the world, millions of viewers caught this seemingly innocent action. Picking up several pieces of paper, Dean strode back to the bench where the attorney general was waiting.

"Your honor," Lindsey began. "The defense recently came into possession of the following documents that link the complainant to her supervisor at the State Department. These are bank statements from a bank in Virginia," Lindsey said as he handed the documents to the judge for review and continued. "And these are statements from a bank in the Bahamas. The Virginia account is in the name of Marvin Moore. The Bahamian account is in the name of Pamela Jean Stark. You'll see that the account was opened in November of last year, prior to Ms. Stark being hired at State. The amount listed as the opening balance coincides with the electronic transfer on that same date from Moore's account. The transfer codes on both documents, as you can see, contain like digits on each ledger. That would indicate the money was electronically transferred by Moore to the Stark account. The deposit code on this initial statement contains the routing code from the Virginia bank."

"Your honor? The people were not presented these documents during discovery. I'll have to object to them being allowed," Gayle protested.

"Noted, Ms. Vernon. Mr. Dean? Before I rule, do you have anything else?"

"Yes, your honor. The defense only came to have possession of these certified copies yesterday. I did send copies to the office of the attorney general."

Lindsey sheepishly looked at Gayle. Her face was solid and unemotional.

"Ms. Vernon?" the judge asked.

"Your honor? May I have a five minute recess to check with my office about this?" Gayle inquired.

"Granted." The judge waved the two lawyers to step back. "The court stands in recess for five minutes. The witness will remain seated. Five minutes."

The gavel banged down, Judge Wentworth stood and departed the courtroom before anyone had a chance to even attempt to get out of their chairs.

The talking heads on the various networks were given a chance to do that which they do best, which is to second guess what was actually going on in the courtroom. In this particular case, they were doing it very, very badly.

Attorney General Gayle Vernon came back into the courtroom three minutes later and took her seat. The bailiff saw her return and opened the door which led to the judge's chambers. Judge Wentworth came out in a flash, his black robes flowing. All in the courtroom made a vain attempt once again at standing and had not even gotten up before the judge had banged the gavel and bade them to once again be seated.

"Approach," the judge ordered the lawyers.

The two attorneys returned to the bench and Wentworth looked at Gayle.

"Your honor," Gayle began. "The people are embarrassed. My office was in receipt of these documents, along with a written invitation to go over them with the defense. The people will stipulate to these documents."

"Very well. Go back to your places," Wentworth ordered.

Vernon returned to her seat and made notes, holding her copies of the bank records. Lindsey stepped to the witness box and repeated his earlier question.

"Ms. Stark, once again and remember, please, you are under oath, did you know your supervisor at the State Department, Marvin Moore, prior to your being hired at the State Department?"

"Er, uh. No," she stammered, looking to Gayle for help. The attorney general could only shrug her shoulders as a sign of helplessness.

"Ms. Stark. Would you identify these documents for the court?" Lindsey asked as he slid the copies of her bank statements into her hands.

Softly, she responded. "These appear to be copies of my bank statements."

"A little louder, please, Ms. Stark?"

"These appear to be copies of my bank statements."

"Thank you. They are copies of your bank statements. They are certified copies and are affixed with the signature of the president of the bank that originated and still maintains this account. There's also the signature of the Bahamian attorney general on them as well to attest to their validity.

"Now, can you tell the court and you may use the statements to help refresh your memory, when this account was opened?"

Looking at the damning piece of paper in her hands, she read the date. "November eighth, nineteen-ninety-seven."

"And can you tell us the amount of money that appears as the opening balance?"

"Fifty thousand dollars."

"And now, if you would, Ms. Stark, please look at the most recent statement. The one from March. Would you read the date of the last deposit?"

Shuffling the papers in her hands, she squinted at the fine print. "March twentieth, nineteen-ninety-eight."

"And the amount of that deposit?"

Pam started to shake, her eyes welling up with tears.

"Ms. Stark? Can you answer the question?" asked Judge Wentworth.

She nodded her head yes and took a sip of water. Setting the glass down on the edge of the witness box, she looked back at Lindsey.

"The amount of the last deposit was two million dollars."

You could have heard long-distance telephone rates drop in the silence that followed. Apparently, all present had taken the judge's warning to heart. Right now, none of them had any intention of going anywhere.

"Two million dollars. Did you win a lottery?" Lindsey asked.

"No."

"Did you go to Atlantic City and hit it big on a slot machine?"

"No."

"Did you write a screenplay?"

"No."

"Can you tell the court how you came to have possession of this much money?"

"The money was a payment."

"A payment? Please, Ms. Stark, tell the court what kind of payment."

"It was a payment for services rendered."

"Are you suggesting that you are a high-priced professional of some sorts?"

"Some sorts, yes."

"Your honor? I request that the court direct the witness to answer the question clearly. We could be here all day with these non-specific responses," Dean requested.

"Ms. Vernon? Objections?" asked the judge.

"None, your honor," Gayle replied softly.

"Very well. Ms. Stark, you will answer Mr. Dean's questions with exact detail, please. Proceed, Mister Dean," Wentworth said as he sat back to hear the rest of this himself.

"Ms. Stark, will you tell the court from whom you received this money?" Lindsey asked. "A name, please."

"I, I can't," she sobbed.

"Why?"

"He said he'd have my mother killed if I did."

"He? So we know it's a male. Ms. Stark, your mother is right here in this courtroom. This building is surrounded by armed personnel from more federal agencies than you or I ever even knew existed. I'll ask you again. Who is this man?"

Breaking down completely, she wept and hit her thighs with her fists. "It's Marvin Moore, okay? He paid me to make it look like the president tried to rape me."

The world stood still at the open court revelation, broadcast via satellite to anyone with a television or a radio.

❋ ❋ ❋

At that same moment of revelation from Ms. Stark, the gavel came down in the federal courthouse in Portland, Maine. Dimitri Brishev had entered a plea of guilty as an accessory to murder, as well as to charges of espionage, sedition and the federal charge of misrepresenting his identity while in the service of the government of the United States. The judge sentenced him to life in a federal penitentiary without any chance at parole. He was told he was lucky he did not get the death penalty. Dimitri was taken into custody immediately by the U.S. Marshals in attendance. Other than the

U.S. attorney for Portland and a retired United States Senator still licensed to practice before the bar, the marshals and Aleksandr, were the only ones present.

Aleksandr was led to the defense table and the quick procedure was repeated. The defendant had entered a plea of guilty on all counts, of which there were three charges of murder that had been openly admitted to in court. The other charges against Aleksandr Romanov ran the gamut from accessory to murder almost down to jaywalking. The plea agreement had been reached prior to their appearance here this morning and once again, the gavel rang down. The judge sentenced Romanov to life in a federal prison as well. The U.S. Marshals took Romanov immediately out of the courtroom and down the stairs to the waiting tour bus. Romanov was escorted to the rear of the bus and hand-cuffed to the seat's arm rests. Dimitri had already been brought to the vehicle after his finding and was secured in a like manner a little closer to the front.

Back in the courtroom, the two lawyers stood next to the bench while the judge affixed his signature to the official documents that were the only written records of the cases against Romanov and Brishev. The disposition pages had been initialed by all present and placed into a large, leather valise, then secured with a heavy padlock. The U.S. attorney took possession of the bag, shook hands with the judge and the retired senator and walked down the stairs in time to see the flashy tour bus with the bright logos painted all around pulling out of the secure parking area located within the walls of the courthouse. He stepped into a waiting black limousine and took the short ride to the General Aviation terminal at the Portland Jetport for his flight back to Washington.

The tour bus was on its way to Montana, a wide open state with plenty of room to raise cattle and to hide federal prisoners of world-wide renown. The destination of the two, who would soon be joined by Tomas Doyestka, was a ranch up near the Canadian border. The land, some five thousand acres, was wooded and pristine. The dwellings on this land were yet to be built and for the time being, the residents would be housed in mobile homes. The plans called for a large, bunkhouse-style building to be constructed. The outside was to be of a traditional, multi-story home design, with log cabin type walls and rustic porches and balconies. The inside of the upper level would be reinforced concrete, with steel-doors to provide constant security for those who would call this place home for the rest of their life. The lower level of the main building would provide more of a home-setting for the permanent guard detail. It would feature the best in creature comforts for those tasked with keeping the facility secure. The other dwellings would be located closer to the outer, southern edges of the land. These would include a new medical facility and schools for the native Americans who call this land home. The funds for all of this were already transferred from some of the off-shore accounts of AFR Enterprises, Incorporated. It had been Hough's idea to put the money to good use. It was a great idea. And it was only the beginning.

* * *

At the moment Ms. Stark had a startling case of total recall, a scene exactly like the one played out in Portland was occuring in another courtroom on the other side of the world. The U.S. attorney for the territory of Guam was waiting for the federal judge to sign-off on the paperwork allowing the people of the world and the United States, to never again live in fear of the man who lived as Tom Dayle. Doyestka stood silent in the courtroom, realizing that to do otherwise was foolish. Had he attempted to make a scene of any sort, he knew that he could very easily become the victim of a horrible, over-ocean accident. He knew well that airplane doors can and do pop open without reason and that unsecured persons in the vicinity of such an event experience the sensation of flight, momentarily, at least. It was midnight in Guam, the new day was just beginning on this side of the international date line.

* * *

Back in Washington, Judge Worthington had asked for objections to the defense's motion to dismiss all charges. The attorney general had stood and cited no objections whatsoever in light of the circumstances. The president was offered the chance to make a statement, which he graciously declined. Griffen knew that whatever he might have wished to say was said loud and clear by Pam Stark, now on her way to facing federal charges of her own. This was one aspect of this case that would not be kept quiet. Moore had been kidnapped in France by a radical faction and was still being held by his captors. He'd be unable to testify for or against Ms. Stark. By her own admission, she'd lied, in both her original complaint and again on the stand. Lindsey had even offered her a chance to correct that misstatement.

Judge Worthington then ruled, officially, all charges against John Francis Griffen, President of the United States were dismissed. He stood and slammed down his gavel. "God Bless the United States of America. This court stands adjourned."

fifty-six

The true smells of spring assailed his senses as he stepped down from the stairs of Air Force One and hustled over to the waiting Marine helicopter. President Griffen had returned from an abbreviated stay at the European Economic Summit in Paris and was now ready to get on with taking care of the matters that were of concern for his people, the good people of the United States.

* * *

The day before the trial, Wednesday, the State funeral for Don Fulton had been magnificent in scope and simple in its message. They had gathered to say goodbye to a man who had served his country well. A man who aspired himself to be the president. Jay had given a brief, touching eulogy, written by Bud and edited by Jay and Dan together. The closing comments were vague enough to be interpreted by future scholars that perhaps Griffen had indeed made reference to the scandal of which the present generation, at least, would hopefully never hear.

.*"...As we say goodbye to Don, I hope that we will carry with us this thought. That the events which brought us here to this point will have a profound effect on those things yet to come. Who knows how far America could have gone, in which direction she would go, under the direction of Don Fulton. I have my vision of what might have transpired, but only our Heavenly Father can know for sure. ..."*

At the reception Tuesday evening before the funeral, President Griffen had personal conversations with Russian Prime Minister Bakunin and German Chancellor Kroll.

His tête-à-tête with Bakunin was warm and cordial, with a brief outline of how the new-found monies would be returned to Russia, as well as a repayment plan, utilizing the interest earned from the large sum, to allow the Russians to improve their standing with the International Monetary Fund. Bakunin told Griffen of a sad discovery at Lake Onega. The boat belonging to Aleksandr Romanov, the former president of the Soviet Union, had been found, crashed upon the rocks. The bodies of four of Romanov's protective force had been found floating in the waters of the lake. The results of an official investigation, which would soon be made public, were that the boat must have gotten caught in a squall of bad weather. The body of Romanov, sadly, had not been recovered. Perhaps, Bakunin added, that someday the murky depths of one of Russia's largest inland bodies of water would someday return the body of Romanov for proper burial. He'd would be long remembered as a man of vision. Bakunin was asked about his familiarity of a few people from Russia who had recently come to the attention of American intelligence. Of the names mentioned, the names of the Rostokovich brothers had indeed brought a spark of recognition to Bakunin's eyes. President Griffen and Prime Minister Bakunin ended their meeting with one final document being signed, that which allowed the Russians to take control of the AFR assets currently on deposit at the Central Bank of Moscow. These assets, Griffen had requested, should be used to improve schools and medical facilities in Russia's most needy areas. Being as it was found money which would make him look even better in the eyes of the people and there was the possibility of an election coming up, Bakunin agreed to the terms and signed off on the document.

In his meeting with the German Chancellor Kroll, President Griffen outlined the known details involving the tragic accident in the Bavarian Alps that had claimed the life of Sarah and Peter O'Reilly. The chancellor had made a brief phone call from the Oval Office to the head of the German Intelligence Unit, explaining that they should take into custody a man currently being held at the American airbase at Wiesbaden. There was a detailed outline of the actions that had been taken, as provided by Viktor Milochnev. The Russian had not been totally stupid, especially when told that Romanov was no longer around to save his sorry ass.

After the reception had ended, Peg Fulton came into the Oval Office looking understandably weary and drained. Jay informed her that she would be at the helm for a day or two, starting immediately after the trial. Her look of shock was quickly replaced by relief when he'd informed her that the business of the country was pretty much on auto-pilot. Were there a true crisis, the president's Cabinet and the Congressional leaders stood ready to govern by consensus. If, and only if, Peg were called upon to act as Commander in Chief, the one responsibility she would have would be to sign the executive order. Jay had asked Peg to trust her instincts first, if such a situation did arise, but to also keep in mind that some of these men and women from whom she'd be receiving advice and counsel had been in the business of keeping America on course long before he or Don had hit their stride. The confirmation hearings on Admiral Gary Dericksen were to begin Monday morning, as the second order of business for the House of Representatives. The first order was to elect a new Speaker of the House.

* * *

The Thursday economic summit in Paris was brief and was followed by a Friday signing ceremony and reception which doubled as a victory party for President Griffen. Many a world leader had expressed their apologies for not having been possessed of true faith in a good man in regards to the Stark matter. Jay accepted each set of kind words graciously, accompanied by a warm hug or handshake. He'd had one private meeting outside of the reception, in his vehicle on the way to United States Embassy where a warm bed and a contrite Anne Marie Griffen were waiting.

Inside the vehicle, the French president expressed concern and regret the inability to recover Marvin Moore from the extremists claiming responsibility for his kidnapping. Jay listened intently, looking appropriately appreciative of the efforts being put forth by the gendarmerie. President Griffen offered his and his country's thanks. He'd told President Difficille that this incident would in no way reflect upon the relationship of their countries.

Inside the embassy, the kitchen staff had made pizza for Jay, his favorite evening snack. The ambassador had put a case of beer on ice, set up American-style in a large, plastic cooler. Jay was joined in the kitchen by Anne Marie. The staff began to take their leave from the room and Jay bade them all to stay.

"No need to go anywhere. Anne and I will be just fine. She reacted in the same way I would have if the situation had been reversed. Hell, guys are even worse when it comes to jealousy. She's got nothing to be sorry for, okay? Let's have some pizza. And somebody get me a nice, cold one, please?"

* * *

Now that he was back on his home turf, with the nightmare behind, it was time to begin anew with getting the job done for America. They'd now have a chance to do some extra good works thanks to the generous funding of a new foundation from AFR Enterprises. As the helicopter touched down on the south lawn of the White House, he saw a few men in military uniforms waiting on the edge of the grass. Shit! He thought. He and the country were long overdue for a nice, quiet weekend. Then he remembered why there'd be a contingent of America's protectors waiting.

"Colonel Menneally, reporting as ordered, sir," said Bob, sharply saluting his Commander in Chief.

Jay returned the salute sharply and the introductions continued. The small group walked in through the portico and towards the Oval Office. In the waiting area outside of the president's office, two other men were seated and rose when Griffen arrived. The honorable James Jalbert, Associate Justice of the Supreme Court, took a moment to introduce Greg Yearwood, the Interpol agent who'd aided Go Team One in Paris. Jay took a moment to thank each for their help and in turn, introduced them to the NSA Director John Realto and of course, they knew CIA Director Terrio. The Joint Chiefs of Staff and the Secretary of Defense were also present.

Once the informal formalities were completed, Jay stopped to whisper something to Anne Marie, kissed her tenderly and told her she could go up to the living quarters or join them for this ceremony. She opted to come along and watched proudly as her husband, the President of the United States, pinned a single star on the uniform collar of the U.S. Army's newest Brigadier General, Robert Menneally. The star was accompanied by a meritorious unit commendation medal, as well as the official Congressional proclamation affirming the official presidential field promotion. Menneally would not have been on the list for selection for consideration for this promotion for another two years, at least.

Jay repeated the pinning of insignia which resulted in the promotion of Henry Morris to the rank of U.S. Navy Commander and the elevation of Staff Sergeants Peter Zallonis and Michael Murphy from non-commissioned officers to fully-commissioned officers. Z was now First Lieutenant Zallonis and Murph was now Ensign Michael Murphy. These promotions were also accompanied by meritorious unit commendation medals and the appropriate documentation for field promotion.

The ceremony was brief and heartfelt and Jay asked Annie if he could have a few private minutes with these fine men. The meeting took only a few minutes, as the president outlined to Brigadier General Menneally his newest assignment, if he wanted it. The Go Team operations had been successful to the point where the Joint Chiefs of Staff, along with the Secretary of Defense, wished to expand the number and placement of Go Teams. It took Menneally a millisecond to respond with a hearty *"Hell yes!,"* provided he could keep his second in command with him. President Griffen informed Bob and Hank it had already been done. Zallonis and Murphy were to aid in the setting up of the new teams and would then join their individual teams as executive officers.

"Gentlemen, may I offer you a celebratory cold beverage?"

"Yes, sir!" said the four in unison, the way they'd been trained to respond. To both a question from the Commander in Chief and to the offer of a cold one.

"Danny? Are we stocked in there?" asked the president.

"Yes, sir. Come on in!" replied his chief of staff from the presidential study.

"Gentlemen, I'd prefer to crack a cold one right here, but protocol and my chief of staff, insist we keep this room as a business area. My study, though, is a different critter. Come on, the Sox are playing."

fifty-seven

The steam was rising from the large, black pots that had been set upon the propane burners, the aroma of lobster and clams filling the air around where the group of friends had gathered. The weather Gods had been kind and saw fit to bless this day with a balmy, unlike-Maine-spring high temperature of almost sixty-five. The blue skies were dotted by puffy, fair weather clouds. The breeze, mercifully, was out of the west, keeping the coolness of the ocean's water out at sea, where it belonged on a day such as this. The evergreens were swaying gently in the easy breezes and a few of the faithful had actually shed their lightly-lined jackets, although the outer coverings would be needed in an hour or so once the westerly winds subsided, allowing the cooler air to flow in from the ocean.

Don and Sandy were playing the gracious hosts, glad to have these people as their closest friends. Since getting out of the hospital two weeks ago, Sandy had cut all contact with co-workers from the network, with the exception of the girls from technical who were still renting the apartment in Greenwich Village. She'd gone home with her parents for a few days, then had decided to take Don up

605

on his offer to come and recuperate in his home at Turbat's Creek. She'd not be going back to the network. The litany of surgeries that had been outlined by the reconstructive specialists had sounded more than overwhelming. The doctors who had taken care of her at the Cornell Weil Center had done a fabulous job. The specialists had said a number of additional steps could be taken and that she would perhaps wind up with the same, stunning facial features. The lack of a one-hundred percent guarantee had been enough to help her decide against any further hospitalizations. Don had assured her that he did care for her the way she was, now and forever. She'd sighed loudly on more than one occasion at the thought of the years lost for the two of them. Yet Don had been the one to remind her that they were only in their mid-forties and that plenty of people their age were starting families.

"Was that a proposal?" she asked.

"It was if you want to consider it. No rush," he smiled.

His intent was to make sure they did not rush this prospect. There was time and she'd need time to heal, mentally as well as physically. She had said there was no time like the present, which had brought them to this day. They'd had a quiet, civil service on the rocks at one o'clock, attended by those present here.

Sandy got up, laughing at the camaraderie that was in evidence. She knew Don, Bud and Chuck, although it seemed as if it was from a long time ago. Time had been kind to these men, she realized. They still had and shared a special bond that enabled them to simply pick up wherever they had left off, as if months or years had not passed since they were last able to be together.

Gary was a bit older than she remembered. She'd met him on one or two brief occasions in New York City when he'd come north with Fred and Bud for some big city excitement. Now, here he was, complete with men in dark windbreakers and dark sunglasses spread all over this rocky promontory on the Maine coast. After all, Gary was now the Vice President of the United States and he required round-the-clock protection. He'd been sworn in on Wednesday the fifteenth, just three days ago and President Griffen had given him this weekend off. Gary was busy showing off photos of his first grandchild, not yet three weeks old! The little bundle swaddled in pink was blessed with a perfect little nose, round face and big, brown eyes. His wife, Sue, was present in the delivery room in California two weeks ago when the baby was born, early on a Saturday morning and had gotten the shock of a lifetime when it took her a dozen phone calls to finally track down her husband that evening at Bethesda Naval Hospital. Sue had given her husband permission to come here, so long as there would no machismo or exploding buildings. Having been assured that there would even be women present, she warned him to behave and allowed him to come. She, being the doting grandma, flew back to California to be with her daughter and her daughter's daughter.

Tom was a nice man. He was quiet and his wife, Pip, was a gem. They were a special couple, she could see. Tom had been injured in the Charleston explosion that wound up killing Freddie and he was now unable to use his left arm as a result of the severed nerves and tendons he'd suffered. While he was also still recovering, Pip had come with him to help him as he learned to re-master simple, everyday tasks. His days as a Secret Service agent were over, but his new life as the head of a multi-million dollar security company were just beginning. Gary's company, Periscope Security International, was now in need of a chief operating officer. The duties of Vice President of the United States had Gary once again obligated to serve his country for the next two years, until the end of the Griffen administration. Tom had been first asked to consider the possibility as he was being transported to Bethesda Naval Hospital. President Griffen had accompanied him on the short trip and had suggested that Tom give the idea some serious thought, especially since Dericksen had already, unequivocally, said yes to the idea. Tom had spoken with Gary about the idea while the two were in Bethesda and Gary had assured him it was just like being a policeman, only with more money and electronic toys. Gary would be able to continue to contribute his expertise, but the handling of the business aspects were to fall on Tom.

"Are you boys almost ready to eat?" asked Sandy.

"Sandy, we were ready about ten minutes after breakfast," replied Chuck. "You've got an especially hungry man, right here. Yeah, when you go out to the golf course and play the sport of kings, it's a wonderful thing. But when you kick the ass of the Vice President of the United States, well, that's just orgasmic."

"Gary, you'll never, ever live this down," said Don.

"Donny, it's okay. He's got something to tell his grandchildren, now. Up until today, what did he have? The story of the hooker and the donkey?" Gary said wryly.

"Gary, that was you," interjected Bud. "Remember? You're the one who thinks he vaguely remembers a lost, margarita-induced hazy night in Tijuana after a Pacific tour. Chuck never made it to TJ."

"Good thing that didn't come up on the floor of the Senate last week, huh?" offered Gary, sheepishly.

The gathering burst into laughter at the comment and the men shared knowing smiles.

"Gary? What's it like being number two?" asked Don. "Oh, sorry, I didn't mean it that way."

"What way? Number two being the V.P.? Or the other number two?"

"However you'd like to interpret that one is fine by me," Chuck smiled.

"Michaud, I'm going to get you down to Charleston and I promise, I'll teach you how to play golf. And I'll have to do it soon. Otherwise, I'm condemned to live with this indignity forever."

The group shared yet another laugh, something none of them had been sure they'd be able to do collectively again.

"Oh, by the way," added Gary. "I can't believe I have to do this, but here goes. Michaud?"

"Yes, Mister Vice President?" he answered without a trace of sarcasm.

"Wow! Sincerity. I could get used to this gig," Gary said, flashing his winning smile. "Chucker, I need you to head over to the rocks near where Agent Leonardo is."

"Which one of the personality boys is that?"

"He's the one with the blue windbreaker and dark glasses, Chuck. Do I have to explain everything?"

Chuck flipped Gary a single-fingered salute and headed over across the rocks to near where the Secret Service agent was pointing. He bent down and picked up a clear, plastic wrapped package. The seams of the package had some seaweed stuffed into them and Chuck returned, plucking the ocean-growth from the parcel and proceed to unwrap it.

"Chucker. I was asked to make sure you understood that the package you hold in your hands washed up on the rocks. Like a gift from on high. Or, maybe like a gift from the south," the vice president explained.

Chuck removed the tattered, heavy-duty plastic and his mouth fell agape.

"Camera? Anybody? He's got nothing to say," laughed Bud.

"Son of a bitch," was all Chuck could muster. "Are these real?"

"Real as they get, shippy. The skipper sends his regards. And his thanks," replied Gary.

"Boys, I say we eat now so we can enjoy an after dinner smoke. Better yet, let's enjoy a before dinner smoke and an after dinner smoke!" Chuck said, cradling the two boxes of hand-rolled Cuban cigars. "Don? I have to get down here more often. I never knew stuff like this washed up on the rocks," Chuck added with a wink to Gary and Bud.

Inside the house, Sandy's parents, Connor and Emily were relaxing in the living room that now belonged to Don and their daughter. Sandy had come in to check on them and they assured her they were fine. She told them she'd return in a few minutes with a couple of plates of food and they simply smiled. They were pleased that their little girl seemed to have found happiness. Sandy had a look about her that wasn't visible at her wedding to Jonathon, they'd commented to each other.

Outside in the front yard, the sound of children playing rose to a frenzied level, the joyful noise filling the space in between the pines as the Hannity kids and the youngest of the Michaud children were engaged in "doing the Dopey." Sandy had spent the better part of a week in the hospital recuperating and hours of channel surfing had landed her on MTV on more than one occasion. "The Dopey" was a new dance being fueled by a video of the song of the same name. A fresh, new singer with the single moniker of Erin was part of the up and coming class of dueling teen-queens and boy-bands. The kids were wildly performing the dance, while the eldest of the Michaud children, Jennifer, was attempting to teach them the right way to do it. The music was poppy, the lyrics catchy.

"Now jump up and come down, touch the ground and turn around.
Make your legs do three kicks, that's the Dopey 04106!
When you're blue and want some fun, it's dance that can be done.
Shimmy up, shimmy down, touch the ground and turn around.
Feel the music and the mix, that's the Dopey 04106!"

Well, she admitted. Catchy the first time around. Maybe even the second. She was able to see where the disdain for hearing these dance songs originated after the fifteenth or sixteenth time. The dance did look like fun. Maybe she'd give it a try, she thought, once her ribs had stopped hurting and her arm was out of the cast.

Sandy took a moment to calm them down, with a little help from Jennifer. After a quick check to see who was hungry, or thirsty, or had to use the bathroom, the frivolity commenced once again. Sandy noted to herself that this was the right thing to do, at the right time and definitely the right place. This would be a fine place to have a baby and add to their world.

Out in back, Don had gotten up to check on the boiling seafood and he was joined by Bud.

"Donny, how's it coming? I'm getting kind of hungry."

"They'll be ready in about ten minutes, Bud. I really appreciate you standing up for me today."

"It was my pleasure, Mr. Hough. I know Freddie would've been your first choice and I am honored that you thought to ask me."

"Is Chuck pissed at me?"

"Naw. He even said that after the month I've had, it'd probably be the closest I ever got to the altar."

"Some blessing," Don chuckled.

"Yeah, I slapped him upside the head and we both laughed. You going to be okay running things at the station?"

"I'm finding it very easy to do. The place is debt-free and there's a great sales staff to keep the money coming. The programming staff is thrilled with the semi-autonomous collective we've set up. It's not programming by committee, but there is latitude with what the show's hosts would like to do. They simply need to get an outline to the program director and he'll either say yes, or offer a few suggestions."

"What about you?"

"I'm not getting up at three in the morning anymore, that's for damn sure. Well, okay, I should qualify that. I have told Dickie that I'll be available from time to time, when I get an itch to get on the air. I am doing some things in the newsroom during the day, covering the phones for lunch, recording wraps they can use in the afternoon, stuff like that. Fred left the station's business accounts with enough cash to run the place for the next hundred years. Hell, the interest alone will run the place forever."

Don needn't have mentioned that Fred had left him, Bud, Chuck and Gary over fifty million dollars each. Those funds were clean, all as a result of Fred's numerous AFR ventures in the United States. The government had decided that Don's decision to turn the remainder of the liquid assets of the estate back to the government for funding social programs was more than they would have, or even legally could have, hoped. The will was now in probate and there was no family left to contest. Michail was already well taken care of, financially and otherwise.

"Sounds like the dream job. I'm jealous."

"It's yours if you want it, Bud. You'll be looking for work in another two years, right?"

"I don't know about that, Don. Gary's looking pretty comfortable around the halls of the big house. Shit, he trained half of the Navy staff currently serving in the higher, executive positions. The rest of the people in the beltway have a huge amount of respect for the man just based on his thirty years in the Navy and there's a small number of highly placed individuals who know the story about how this old timer got his ass blown sky-high and lived to tell the tale. I got a feeling that when it comes time to turn the keys to the front door over to someone new, it's not going to be someone too new."

"Have you talked about it? You know? You being with him for the long haul if that's what he wants?"

"Does a goat shit in the Tajikistan mountains? You better believe it."

"What did he say?"

"Off the record, Mister Newsman? He said he wouldn't have it any other way." Bud took a sip of beer and peeked in the lid of the lobster pot.

"What's up with Annie and Michail?" Don asked.

"They're on their way to Montevideo, down in Argentina, with our blessing."

"Montevideo? Nice little place."

"Not their final destination, though. We took care of spinning one of the larger, separate accounts from AFR into a South Pacific real estate purchase."

"Didn't Annie always say..."

."..That'd she'd love to someday buy an island in the South Pacific and just live out the rest of her days? Yeah. She did and now she will."

"Are you okay with that?"

"I had my chance, Don. I had my own agenda and when I made that clear at the time, she just nodded and set her sights on her own agenda."

"Did you have a chance to talk with Rostokovich? Like why the hell didn't he tell us about Dayle and Bello?"

"He said that at the time, he'd not included their names in the reports because of the ongoing "forward" operation. They were in there, just referred to as "Mister D" and "Mister B." He said that he'd hadn't realized we didn't have their actual names. Hey, the guy gave us what he did and for that we can be truly thankful. So how did you know we didn't know about Dayle and Bello? I don't recall talking about that."

"The night of Freddie's service? Remember? We did kind of put a few away."

"I guess I must've. I do recall the next morning, though. What other state secrets did I reveal?"

"Other than the nuclear launch codes and that the Secretary of the Interior used to be a guy? None."

"How cold is that ocean this time of year, Don?"

"Major shrinkage, Bud. Hey, these things are done. Let's eat."

Bud and Don each grabbed a pot holder and a handle, moving the containers closer to the picnic table where Don had put a couple of saw horses with a few pieces of heavy lumber to act as a serving table. The children had come around back just in time and the feasting had begun. While Sandy, Pip and Sue worked to get the children's plates filled and set, the men took care of the drinks and napkins, helping the younger ones with the process of cracking the shells and getting at the white lobster meat inside.

The kids were taken care of and it was now time for the adults to enjoy their own repast. Don and Sandy each filled a couple of plates with the steaming lobster and clams and corn on the cob. Sandy tried to handle the two she had prepared for her parents and was intercepted by Sue Michaud.

"I've got two good hands working here, Sandy. Come on. You lead, I'll follow."

"Thanks, Sue," she replied, glancing at the painful reminder of Jonathon.

Don, meanwhile, walked through the house and down the path to the Williamson house. He walked up to the steps, doing his best to juggle the plates while avoiding the family's dogs. They were playful and were no slouches when it came to mooching food. Using his foot to rap on the door, Don lifted the plates high while trying to order the two canines down. Bill opened the door and bid Don to come in.

"What have we here?" asked Williamson.

"Some lobster and steamers for my favorite neighbors, neighbor."

"Thanks. You didn't have to do this, though."

"Just wanted to. It is supper time, you know."

"Ayuh, it is, Don. Congratulations again, by the way. It was a lovely ceremony."

"I wished you two had stuck around. It's been a fun afternoon," said Don.

"We were honored you asked us to come over for the ceremony, Don. Sandy's a wonderful lady."

"I think so as well, Bill."

A beep from a car's horn out on the edge of Bill's driveway led the two men back to the front door. Peering out from behind the window curtain, Bill asked. "Anyone you know or were expecting?"

"Nope. They're too dressed up for my house, Bill. I smell reporters."

"Yeah, me too. You know what they say about taking one to know one."

"And since we are members of the sacred brotherhood, we should know one if we see one. Would you do the honors?"

Bill smiled and nodded to Don, opened the door and stepped across the porch over to the edge of the driveway.

"Hello, there! Can I help you?" asked Bill.

"Hi. We're from *The Inside Scoop*, the television program?"

"Oh, television. I've heard of that. Heard of your show, too. What is it you need?"

"We received a tip that the former NBS News reporter, Sandy Rose, was now living up this way. Can you tell me if we're in the right neighborhood?"

"Sandy Rose? Oh, you mean that really beautiful woman who spent some time a while back in one of those foreign countries? England or some such place, wasn't it?"

The reporter in the driver's seat looked at her camera person seated in the passenger's seat and made an exaggerated face as if to say they'd hit the motherlode on Rube City. "Yes, that would be her. Here. I have a photograph of her."

Bill stepped closer to the car and gave the photo an intentionally long look. Standing up, he added to the theatrics, hitching up his blue jeans.

"Oh, ayuh! I know her. Gosh, she is a wicked pretty lady, by gum!"

"Then Sandra Rose does live around here?"

"Oh, no. Gory, I know I'd remember it if there was a pretty lady lookin' like that going by the name Sandy Rose. It's not your average, everyday kind of name like those of the folks 'round here," Bill said, exaggerating the "here" with the New England affectation of two syllables and the dropped r, making is sound more like "he-ah."

"So you're saying that this is not where we might find Sandy Rose?"

"Well, not exactly in that form of a sentence, ma'am, but you are correct. There is no Sandy Rose living in this neighborhood."

"You were just putting me on, weren't you?"

"As far as the dumb hick thing goes, yes. Bill Williamson," he said offering his hand. "I write for the local daily papers around the state. I do opinion pieces. When I'm not doing that, I'm busy shining-on the flatlanders, giving them the little Maine show they were hoping to find. By the way, these are my dogs and no, they don't bite. But honestly, there is no Sandy Rose around here, okay?"

The reporter laughed and thanked Bill as she backed her car out of the driveway and headed back in the direction of downtown Kennebunkport.

Bill came back into the house and found Don doubled-over.

"Are you okay, Don?"

Don came up smiling, tears running down his face. Through his laughter, he managed a reply. "That, Drummer, was a column in itself. How the hell did you lie to her like that with such a straight face?"

"Don, I didn't lie."

"You did, Bill. You looked them straight in the eye and told them there was no one named Sandy Rose here, did you not?"

"I did, Don. But it wasn't a lie. Sandy's last name, as of four hours ago, is Hough. Sandy Hough lives here. Your wife, remember?"

"You, Drummer, are one in million. Now eat your supper before it gets cold."

Bill gave Don a friendly pat on the back as he walked out the door and towards the path that led back to his house.

Don enjoyed the waning moments of sun and warm breezes on his trip through the woods, back to his and Sandy's house, on this, another extraordinary day.

Printed in the United States
88080LV00001B/49-300/A